THE NETWORK

Book Guild Publishing
Sussex, England

First published in Great Britain in 2006 by
The Book Guild Ltd
25 High Street
Lewes, East Sussex
BN7 2LU

All characters in this publication are fictitious and any resemblance to real people, alive or dead, is purely coincidental.

Typesetting in Baskerville by
Keyboard Services, Luton, Bedfordshire

Printed in Great Britain by
Antony Rowe Ltd, Chippenham, Wiltshire

A catalogue record for this book is
available from the British Library

ISBN 1 84624 002 6

'Know your enemy better than yourself and understand his battlefield.'

Sun Tzu, *The Art of War*

'War is not merely an act of policy, but a true political instrument … the political objective is the goal, war is the means of reaching it, and means can never be considered in isolation from their purpose.'

Karl von Clausewitz, *On War*

For my family, Diana, Portia, Rosie and Hester,
with love and admiration

Author's Note

In an effort to avoid liability many authors cover themselves with disclaimers and create fictional places or entities rather than research real ones. I am no different. Certainly, I would rather do almost anything than verify the details enclosed in this book. Fiction is a readily accessible shield to an author, and it is very easy to hide behind. But I believe that such is the contemporary relevance of the scenario portrayed in this book that it would have been wrong for me to entirely fictionalise it. I have attempted to be accurate where at all possible and have ventured as close to the truth, or probable truth, as I dare. No official secrets are contained in this book, and should a reader consider otherwise then it will be because I have simply stumbled upon what can be deduced.

The inner workings of the Secret Intelligence Service, or MI6, and the Secret Service, or MI5, remain a mystery and rightly so. So, too, does their autonomy from Government, for none of us, I hope, would like to see a unified, single-track national intelligence structure with a political head in Cabinet. That way tyranny lies, as the Soviet Union found to its cost with its Ministry of State Security, the KGB. Any resemblance between the intelligence services portrayed in this book and those of which we are rightly proud are purely coincidental.

Although I have striven to make this book as realistic as possible, I have been fully prepared to move streets and buildings when necessary to help the story along. Nothing has hindered my path. If a suitable street did not exist then I invented it; if I could not find a suitable building then I constructed one in my mind and committed it to paper. I have been lucky enough to visit most locations portrayed in this book, and have had a great time doing it, but I would guess that only ninety per cent of the places are described correctly. The remainder either do not exist or have been modified or relocated to such an extent that no one would ever find them. What I am attempting to convey is that readers looking for answers in the war against terror are wasting their time.

The story was dependent on advice and ideas from military and intelligence community friends and to them, one in particular, I owe a huge debt. Members of my mother's book club painstakingly read and commented on an early draft. They didn't reject it off-hand but provided many constructive and timely criticisms that helped me achieve publication. The professionals decimated later drafts, but they encouraged and persuaded me to rewrite it and produce a much more enjoyable book. I owe a debt of gratitude to everyone at Book Guild Publishing for believing in me, for making all this possible, and for bringing out the best in me.

So many valued friends have helped me as I wrote this book, and in so many different ways. It would be wrong of me to name some, but not others, because there are several who must remain anonymous. But they all know that I cherish their energetic support and boundless encouragement.

There are no words that can adequately thank my wife, Diana, and my three children, Portia, Rosie, and Hester. Without them I would never have finished this book.

It remains for me to hope that you, the reader, will enjoy the product. We all know that any mistakes are entirely mine.

PROLOGUE

November 14th, Lailatul Qadr, Z – 169 Days
Pamir Mountains, Tajikistan

Frustrated, Malik ground his spent cigarette underfoot as he observed the incoming Hip helicopter that had been scheduled to arrive some twenty minutes earlier at midnight. The weather could not be blamed for the late arrival of the last flight for, despite ten thousand feet of clouds blocking the light from the moon and stars and the extreme cold, there was no wind, snowfall or lashing rain. After months of detailed planning, there was only a four-hour window in which the most powerful terrorist leaders in the world could travel and meet, yet remain entirely undetected from the ground, air and, especially, space. The Hip's twenty-minute delay meant that only sixty-five minutes were available for the Gathering. There would be little time for consideration of the nation-shattering proposals put forward by the world's most wanted terrorist, Osama bin Laden of al-Qa'eda.

The Gathering of the Powerful was taking place on Islam's Lailatul Qadr, the 'Night of Power'. It was one of the most symbolic nights in the Islamic calendar because it was during Ramadan on the Night of Power that the Qur'an was first revealed to the Prophet Muhammad. The religious significance of the time of the clandestine mountain gathering was not lost on the leaders of world terror. Soon, neither would its operational significance.

Mid November in the snow-capped Pamir mountain range of south eastern Tajikistan presented one of the most inhospitable places on the planet and a secure and convenient location for the Gathering. The site was less than forty kilometres from the ill-defined borders of China, Pakistan and Afghanistan, and at this time of the year it could only be accessed by air. Earlier this summer, Malik had paid a local warlord handsomely for the identification and provision of a suitable meeting place, and for a ground protection force comprising forty heavily equipped mercenaries. The warlord had chosen the location well for the terrain was easy to defend against an enemy but not inaccessible to welcome visitors. Given the desperate poverty of some sixty per cent of the population of Tajikistan, its crumbling infrastructure and general level of lawlessness, Malik guessed that raising this number of mercenaries had not proved difficult. The mercenaries were mostly ex-Taliban soldiers who had fled from their homeland of Afghanistan as refugees when the US-led coalition had invaded in late 2001.

Malik had dealt personally with the Tajikistan authorities. It had cost little in bribes for the local police and border guards to be identified and paid to look the other way and certainly intimidation had never been necessary. More challenging had been his need to deal with aerial surveillance. With the help of desperate Russian experts, he had been able to predict the movements of hostile overhead satellites and high altitude surveillance aircraft. This information had determined a four-hour window during which unwelcome onlookers would be blind, but Malik knew that the absence of satellites and cloud cover could not guarantee invisibility from the skies. His handpicked team of ten Kashmiri Mujahidin, all of whom had received basic training from the US in the 1990s as Afghan freedom fighters, operated ground radar equipment that kept a dutiful eye on the skies. As an offensive measure, his team were also trained and equipped with six hand-held, Russian-made SA-16 Gimlet surface-to-air missile launchers each with three heat-seeking 9M313 missiles. Also to Malik's advantage, the skies above the Pamirs were accustomed to sporadic military air activity intended to provide a presence over disputed borders. Should anyone care to take notice, tonight's pattern of air traffic on one of the few winter nights fit for flying would not be considered unusual.

The Algerian terrorist group, the GIA, were the last to arrive, having been collected from a rendezvous inside China. The deafening civil variant of the Russian-made MI-17 Hip multi-purpose helicopter, ideal for high altitudes and low temperatures, landed momentarily on the small flat outcrop of rock that was the landing zone. Although the passengers had been thoroughly identified by the crew before boarding and the aircraft challenged by his team via radio during its approach, Malik took the added precaution of personally identifying each visitor as they alighted. The Hip, adorned with false Chinese Air Force military insignia, noisily departed immediately after the passengers disembarked, in order to maintain its deception plan and pretence of a routine reconnaissance mission along the borders of China, Pakistan, Afghanistan and Tajikistan.

Each of the seven visiting terrorist organisations had been allowed no more than three representatives each armed with just one personal weapon, whatever the type. Typically, variants of the AK-47 Kalashnikov proved most common, though Malik had noticed many visitors clinging doggedly to their ancestral daggers.

Content with the final identifications, Malik ushered the late-arrivals into a small, vertical fissure in the rock that was no more than thirty metres from the landing zone. This entrance was an illusion for it opened into a vast cavern of cathedral-like proportions that in the more accessible summer months was an illicit drugs processing lab that produced heroin for the European market. As he entered into the flickering yellow light of ancient oil lamps and fires, Malik noted the increasing joviality and excitement from the swollen numbers of occupants. He also caught the familiar scent of alcohol and burning opium.

The Gathering was made up of the leading Islamic extremist terrorist organisations, all of whom were signatories of bin Laden's recent fatwa that had called for worldwide attacks against US and Western interests. Leaders represented groups from across the world and included the Egyptian Islamic Jihad known as the EIJ; the Islamic Movement of Uzbekistan, the IMU; the Kashmiri independence group the Harakat ul-Mujahidin, or HM, previously known as the Harakat ul-Ansar of which Malik was a valued member; the Palestinian Hamas Izz al-Din al-Qassem Brigade; the Iraqi militant Shi'ite Mahdi Army; the Algerian Groupe Islamique Armée, or GIA; Chechen Islamists; the radical Islamic group Jemaah Islamiyah and bin Laden's own al-Qa'eda council.

As Malik stood by the only exit and watched as the proceedings began he reflected on how much the West would like to destroy the Gathering which represented many of the allied Islamic terror groups known internally as the Network. For a brief moment he considered what this information might be worth to the West and the considerable power it represented.

Ayman al-Zawahiri, bin Laden's second-in-command, received a nod from Malik, leant over and whispered in bin Laden's ear. Bin Laden, frail from years of evasion and hiding in Sudan, slowly arched his arms above his head and the Gathering abruptly descended into a reverent silence. In a style befitting that of a cleric preaching in a mosque and with surprising energy, he launched into a noisy prayer to Allah that bestowed the virtues of encouraging and supporting the participation in jihad, or holy war, against Americans, the British and all infidels across the world who wished to corrupt Islam, whether they resided in Arab states or in their own homelands.

'...and we will destroy godless Arab regimes corrupted by selfish and greedy Western culture and return our people to the purity of the Qur'an. It is the will of Allah.'

'Praise be to Allah, the Lord of the Universe' was the immediate and unified response before bin Laden continued with examples of their recent successes. While privately accepting credit for supporting the 9/11 attacks on the US, he extolled the virtues of publicly blaming the attacks on a Jewish plot in order to incite confusion and distrust among the infidels. He also claimed the Challenger space shuttle disaster was a punishment from Allah, before adding further anti-Western sentiment and the advocacy of violence as a means to the ultimate end – the establishment of Muslim states run by Shari'a law. In particular, he castigated the US and UK, but then surprised his audience by focusing his fury on the latter country for providing the US with international support and recognition for their war against Islam. He held the British responsible for providing the Americans with credibility and declared that it was the British who held the key to isolating the Americans. Removing the British, he claimed, would quicken the downfall of the most powerful nation on Earth and provide ultimate victory in the jihad. He declared that previous attacks on London had revealed the true path and Allah's will. Finally bin Laden announced his plan to isolate the US by destroying the city of London in one cataclysmic blow, a blow that would inevitably cause the infidels to turn against each other. As his rhetoric drew to a close a loud cheer and lengthy applause resonated throughout the cavern. Thankfully, thought Malik, no one thought to fire off their rifles.

Malik considered himself a mercenary, not a militant and certainly not a fundamentalist or idealist. His name had been forwarded by one of bin Laden's top lieutenants, Abu Zubaydah Saudi, the only Palestinian in bin Laden's inner circle. Nicknamed 'Mailman', Abu Zubaydah coordinated al-Qa'eda's substantial support to other terror groups as well as its own operations, and he also assisted with the organisation of recruits for training at an elite al-Qa'eda camp in Iran. Unaffected by the rhetoric, Malik studied the Gathering for dissenters but there were none. The Network, it appeared, were hungry for a plan of such devastating scale. It seemed to Malik that the burning opium, which was being generously distributed and replenished by three aged veterans from the Arab Mujahidin, was creating the soporific effect bin Laden desired.

Once calm was restored al-Zawahiri called for the leaders to come forward and sit with bin Laden in a terrorist cabal. As soon as they were settled out of earshot from the lieutenants and bodyguards, al-Zawahiri called upon Abu Zubaydah Saudi to address the leaders. Abu Zubaydah began by summarising the West's war against Islam and their response. He reviewed the jihad as it had unfolded since 9/11, focusing on the US-led invasion of Afghanistan followed by Iraq, at the heart of the Islamic world, and the latter's ensuing insurgency led by the recently formed Mahdi Army who had honoured the Gathering with their attendance. He captivated his audience and left them hungry for revenge and victory.

Bin Laden spoke again, this time calmly and with great deliberation. After praising Allah and the Holy Prophet Muhammad for their guidance, he remonstrated about the need for strength through unity and then outlined his plan for the most terrifying single terrorist act of premeditated and sustained fear ever to be enacted against one city and nation.

After a passionate and sometimes heated discussion over financial support, bin Laden finalised the agreement by securing the sworn agreement of all leaders to his plan. There were no dissentions; in fact there was an air of perverse excitement, a thrill underpinned by the now dense smog of opium. He concluded his part in the Gathering by giving thanks to his assembled brothers and prayers to Allah the Almighty and the Holy Prophet Muhammad.

Abu Zubaydah handed to each of the terrorist leaders a single sheet of paper. On each was the same date and time, the address of a bank and a series of numbers preceded by a letter that represented a bank account. He spoke of a number of other simple coordinating instructions before ending the cabal by simply and reverently reminding everyone of the need for security. The leaders were proud and any greater emphasis on security would have insulted them. No one expected to meet again to discuss the mission, for their utmost loyalty and commitment to fulfil their promises to Allah was not in question. Each of the visiting leaders rose and left to rejoin their groups, knowing that they were part of a cataclysmic attack in the West on the Prophet's Birthday, although none of them enjoyed detailed knowledge of the plan. Though curious, no one expected otherwise.

Though Malik remained out of earshot he knew the operation intimately for much of the planning was his own. In fact, although the concept and outline plan had been explained by bin Laden to those sitting in the cabal, only he and his partner, a Kashmiri freedom fighter called Dalia, knew the details. He felt a shudder of unease as he studied the body language of each fanatical leader in turn as they returned in the flickering firelight to their groups. He was to command this shocking mission and as a reward he would enjoy enormous wealth for the remainder of his life.

A fit, intelligent and attractive man of Western appearance, Malik had been a rising star in Pakistan's Special Forces until his resignation a year ago. Eighteen months previously Pakistan's army had successfully completed the last government's unpopular directive and enforced the withdrawal of the loyalist Mujahidin forces from the Indian province of Kashmir. Soon afterwards Malik had lost his sense of purpose when his wife and three of his four children were murdered by a car bomb, driven into their home as they slept. Although the suicide bomber was never identified and no group ever came forward to claim responsibility, it was widely believed the bombing was an indiscriminate warning to the army from those opposed to the Pakistani Government's unexpected U-turn. Paradoxically, the strength of Malik's own sympathies towards the resulting formation of the hardline

Kashmiri Independence Group known as the Harakat ul-Mujahidin and his outspoken criticism of Western countries for, he believed, manipulating this impoverished and underdeveloped region for their own ends, had ultimately led to the unsolicited approach for his help from the leaders of the HM. That was where he met Dalia, and where they had both come to the attention of Abu Zubaydah Saudi.

Many of the Kashmiri Mujahidin had fought for the Arab Mujahidin against the Soviet Union's invasion of Afghanistan. Looking for a new cause to fight, win and possibly die for, they were fully prepared to fight the Indian Army for a fully integrated Kashmir as a province of Pakistan. It was these ruthless warriors, sickened by Pakistan's failure to maintain their promise of military and financial support for their winning invasion, who were now at the core of the new demand for independence. After the failed invasion, the Mujahidin allied themselves to the goals of Islamist extremism and sought the financial support of their old leader, bin Laden, to replace that lost from the Pakistan Government.

Although too late for the HM, and for that matter Malik's family, discontent had grown among many of Pakistan's senior military officers who felt as Malik did about the Government's role in the failed invasion of Indian Kashmir. Only three months after Malik had resigned his post for the sake of his remaining daughter, General Pervez Musharraf successfully assumed the presidency following a military coup.

Al-Qa'eda were confident that, for Malik, it was not simply ideology but the lure of ten million US dollars that would transform what was left of his and his young daughter's lives. It was certainly enough to buy Malik and his daughter, who currently lived with his wife's widowed sister at Gilgit in northern Pakistan, a new life wherever they wished. Malik's fee, which had already been paid in full after a circuitous and untraceable journey, now lay in a personal offshore bank account at Global Financial Services Limited in the Cayman Islands.

Immediately after the Gathering concluded its business, Malik ordered one of his men to contact the Hip for it to return to the landing zone and begin the recovery of passengers to their chosen rendezvous points, all within a fifty-kilometre radius of the Gathering. All drop-off points were inside the borders of any one of the five countries of Afghanistan, China, Pakistan, Tajikistan or Uzbekistan. Transit and security arrangements beyond the rendezvous points were the responsibility of each group of travellers and did not trouble Malik. At 3:50 a.m. the last flight left the windswept outcrop with Malik and his team. On departure he gave a single wave of gratitude to the local warlord who had played his part efficiently and who was left two hundred thousand US dollars richer.

On the short but uncomfortable flight back to a makeshift al-Qa'eda encampment hidden among two million displaced Afghan refugees camped on the foothills of the Hindu Kush mountains of northern Pakistan, Malik reflected on his Arabic nom de guerre proposed by Zawahiri, 'Malik' meaning, 'The Master'. Not for the first time he also pondered on why Dalia and he had been singled out to lead this apocalyptic terrorist operation. He surmised that al-Qa'eda's belief in his hatred of the West, his military experience and his controlled ruthlessness, fitness and intelligence - and also his availability - were all factors. Perhaps the Network considered that a potentially hot-headed idealist or someone ill-educated in the ways of the West could not be trusted to successfully conduct such a costly and devastatingly appalling act, against such a complicated target and over such a long period of time. More likely, perhaps, he and Dalia were selected because of their Western education and appearance, and because the Network believed that they could be bought at the right price.

NEW AL-QA'EDA

Chapter 1

November 28th, Z – 155 Days
Chertsey, Surrey, England

'Hi Tally, you're looking very nice today,' greeted Harry as he walked passed his PA's desk in his outer office, his black Labrador, Max, trotting happily by his side. It was 8:15 a.m. 'I hope you had a good weekend.'

'Great, thanks – quiet though,' answered Tally haughtily as Harry disappeared through the inner door to his office. The door sported a brightly polished brass plaque that pronounced Harry Winchester as the Managing Director of Mercury, a privately owned private investigation firm that had accepted Harry just one year ago on his resignation from MI6, the British Secret Intelligence Service. Harry had taken charge from his father who was also 'ex-Six' and who had established Mercury some thirty years before.

Tally was a single, 35-year-old, attractive brunette who loved horses. She was highly regarded by all the staff and after sixteen years she had become the heart of the firm. Tally was normally the first to arrive each morning and was meticulous in her work. Harry often boasted to his visitors that when it came to coffee, she made the best cappuccino in England from the grand and multi-faceted chrome coffee percolator that appeared to him to dominate the outer office. Tally had insisted on the purchase and, he had to admit, the machine made great coffee as well as entertainment.

The office building was in fact an old Tudor manor situated on the outskirts of Chertsey in Surrey, England. Still owned by Harry's father, the manor retained thirty acres of grass and woodland, the once vast estate having been sold off under a compulsory purchase order for the Government's Defence Research Agency. Harry lived alone in a smaller, three-bedroomed converted barn that nestled close to the manor, his father having moved from the estate on retirement to live with his partner, Joyce, in a mews cottage in Kensington, London. The double garage and stables were exclusively Harry's, and it was within these that clues to his hobbies could be found, including a cream-and-brown coloured 1936 MG PB sports car aptly named Cream Cracker, of which only twelve were made, and a more recent 1968 MG BGT that had not been strangled by American environmental and safety legislation or by British Leyland's penny-pinching. In the stables were three ponies that represented half a string of polo ponies; the other three were owned and cared for elsewhere by a close friend. Remaining outhouses were given over to the firm for storage.

Having made coffee for them both, Tally picked up the two mugs in one hand, grabbed her legal pad from her desk with the other, and joined Harry in his office. Harry's office was situated along with the other directors' offices on the first floor, with his in the centre above the main entrance, from where he had a clear view of the driveway.

As usual Tally began as soon as she entered. 'You have prayers with the heads of sheds at nine, and you're due at the Hilton, Park Lane, for a late-lunch meeting at 2 p.m. with your father, Jarrad, Lawrence and Victoria. I guess that will be you for the day.'

Lawrence and Victoria were the firm's City-based accountant and lawyer respectively, neither of whom was averse to a long lunch courtesy of their client. Harry was not looking forward to it as nowadays every discussion with his father came around to his single status, and Victoria was a natural predator. Until this point in his life Harry had spent much time travelling and he had had few close female friends, all of them in his line of work. Casual pick-ups were out of the question. Harry avoided one-night stands on the theory that intimacy equalled vulnerability; that it didn't make sense to let down his guard with someone he knew nothing about.

'My father is keen to switch all his remaining assets in the firm into my name to avoid inheritance tax. I guess he'll continue to matchmake between Victoria and me too.' Harry laughed uncertainly. At forty-one and thirty-eight respectively, Harry and Victoria were both single and ideally suited in all respects except one – Harry simply could not feel any attraction towards her despite her beauty. Secretly he thought that Tally was more his type, though he was unsure how he should proceed, as he didn't want to endanger their professional relationship should any personal one go wrong.

With no other immediate business, Tally returned reluctantly to her desk.

Harry was a hands-on MD who focused on the operational aspects of the firm, leaving the administration to others. In MI6 he had been renowned as an outstanding field operative and an expert in counterterrorism. Since his retirement a year ago the Director General MI6, who had been Harry's line manager on three separate occasions in their parallel careers, had approached Mercury for advice and support and to take on specific missions. These unclassified missions had been handled impeccably despite their mundane and insignificant nature, and Harry was hoping to widen Mercury's market share. It was sometimes the case that MI6, or more precisely the Government, did not want direct involvement in a mission and the use of Mercury could spare scarce resources or potential embarrassment. To Mercury's benefit, the receipt of outsourced work from a shrinking MI6, who faced an increasing need to demonstrate efficiency to the Treasury, was on the increase. This source of work known in the firm as 'Government Ops' was managed directly by Harry with the assistance of his Operations Director, Pat Bronson.

Harry disliked administration and was fortunate enough to be able to leave the daily running of Mercury to his highly capable Finance Director, Jarrad, and, of course, Tally. Jarrad and his father had much in common, and Jarrad would, as usual, make lunch more tolerable and provide a buffer between Harry and Victoria.

Harry easily pushed the afternoon appointment to one side and focused on his pending 'daily prayers' meeting. At 9 a.m. promptly, Tally opened the door and the 'A team' comprising the Finance Director, the Operations Director, the Training and Support Director, who was also lovingly known as 'Q' for Quartermaster in the military as well as for his James Bond manner, and the Intelligence Director walked in, along with Tally, taking up their regular seats around the small conference table. Daily prayers only covered new ground, was unceremonious and very precise. It did not circumvent the need for monthly conferences and if anyone wanted coffee they came with their own. If they forgot, a mug from Tally would cost them dearly. Prayers rarely lasted more than ten minutes and Harry accepted that if members of the A team could not make it then so be it, though they always sent an understudy instead.

Jarrad began as usual. 'Apart from a new clerk, Susie, starting today in the registry, there's nothing new. We're still short of help with updating the firm's Health and Safety instructions, a corporate governance and ISO 9001 requirement, but the team assure me it will be completed on time.'

'Tally, is Susie booked in for a welcome?' asked Harry.

'Yes, tomorrow at ten-thirty.'

'Thanks.'

Pat continued, 'We currently have nineteen security surveys, three close protection tasks, six security tasks, ten courier tasks one of which is to Hawaii, twelve missing person investigations, including an absent employee believed to have disappeared from a privately run waste disposal site, three possession recovery tasks, twelve insurance fraud investigations including six fires, seven financial or debt recoveries and twenty-two lifestyle surveillances ongoing. Here's the daily situation report.' Sam handed everyone a single-page summary sheet as he did every working day which provided a short update on every investigation or task the firm was conducting. In the main, 'lifestyle' was the buzzword that included extramarital affairs.

'Thanks, Pat. Shane, anything new from Training and Support?'

Shane answered in his soft Irish voice. 'We received four new US-made Exon KXR-320 Infrared Ground Scanners for body detection yesterday, the best gear on the market. Pat's team will be using them at the waste disposal site this afternoon. We also received six new Garrett MD3 hand-held weapons scanners, four new Inceptor 3000 hand-held bug detectors and six of the threeway mains adaptors complete with UHF transmitters, although Pat has bagged all of those already. The first batch of our body armour was returned to the manufacturer yesterday for a recall that will take two weeks' turnaround and we have no reserve. Other than that, we're in good shape.'

'Romeo?' Harry enquired of the affable and street-wise black Londoner.

'Nothing shattering,' he replied casually. 'We're at full stretch, as you know, in support of ops. I've received ten complimentary tickets for the annual European Military and Emergency Services Equipment Exhibition in Paris next month and I'd like to recommend that we all go along with several of my team. All the latest gear and ideas will be on show and it presents a great opportunity to broaden our knowledge of the markets and evaluate our current equipment and methods.'

'Great idea, Romeo; please fix it,' responded Harry, thinking of the rare opportunity for socialising. 'As for me, there are no government ops ongoing, although I understand that we may be asked to track down some missing persons on behalf of the interdepartmental board that is inquiring into the death of the junior minister several weeks ago. The board is being led by the Met's Deputy Chief Constable and is to be supported by Five and Six as necessary. Anyone got anything else to add?'

Harry paused and looked around the table but no one answered.

'I'll wander about downstairs before lunch and visit anyone who happens to be around. Incidentally, I did notice people working through this weekend again. I hope that we can all maintain some quality of life. If anyone can pinpoint where new full-time staff can relieve the burden and reduce casual staff, then please, let's identify, specify the job, and recruit. I would much prefer full-time staff, they are far more effective. Tally, diary check, please.'

After the diary check which looked two weeks ahead, everyone filed out of Harry's office, all contented that nothing had materialised to disrupt his or her already busy schedules.

As Tally returned to her desk she felt the familiar tightness in her chest as her fondness for Harry grew. She found it difficult to drop impious thoughts of Victoria.

Chapter 2

November 28th, Z – 155 Days
Larnaca, Cyprus

As he stepped onto the cool tarmac of Larnaca International Airport, Malik mentally praised the efficiency of the Pakistan International Airways flight from Islamabad to Athens and the Cyprus Airways connecting flight to Larnaca. It was vital that there were no serious delays on this journey for by 2 p.m. local time Malik must have spoken with the manager of the Premier National Bank of Cyprus located in downtown Larnaca. At ease travelling with a new identity as a Pakistani businessman named Muhammad Afzal Saudi there was no need to waste valuable time with additional personal security precautions. Malik's doppelgänger, a Pakistani who had lived a wretched life in Rawalpindi, had been paid handsomely for his identity. With nothing more than hand luggage Malik casually passed through immigration control before catching a waiting taxi.

'Caleta Hotel, please, as quickly as you can,' Malik said confidently in English.

'No one can get there quicker than me,' the Greek Cypriot taxi driver replied in equally good English.

Caleta Hotel stood directly on the sandy beach of Larnaca Bay and was ideally suited for a short taxi trip to the airport or a short walk to the city centre. Malik's executive room enjoyed a seaside view overlooking the azure waters of the Mediterranean Sea and was exotically decorated and furnished with the usual modern-day refinements including Internet access. Despite his desire to order room service and eat something substantial, Malik sat at the small desk then plugged in and switched on his laptop computer. As it booted he removed a sheet of paper from his wallet that listed various names, personal details and account numbers. Accessing the World Wide Web he logged onto his private offshore bank account at Global Financial Services Limited, Cayman Islands. He could not help but smile at the balance that flickered back at him – over ten million US dollars. Online he left instructions for the full balance less closing charges to be immediately transferred to a private Swiss bank account that he had already opened at the BAE Export Bank SA, Geneva in the name of Jamil Rahman, an Egyptian entrepreneur. Jamil Rahman, once an Arab Mujahidin freedom fighter, had been shot dead in Afghanistan several years ago though few people knew it. After clicking on the 'Send' button a 'Status: Pending' window opened. Another minute and a 'Status: Approved' window appeared, followed swiftly by 'Status: Paid'. On confirmation that the transaction was concluded, Malik closed the laptop and walked down to the hotel foyer where he found a pay phone.

'BAE Export bank,' a female voice answered in Swiss German. 'How can I help you?'

'Hello,' Malik replied in English. 'My name is Jamil Rahman and I wish to confirm that a recent wire transfer in US dollars has arrived in my account please.'

'Just a moment, please,' the woman answered, effortlessly switching to English. 'May I have your account number?'

Malik read the details from the sheet.

'And please will you give me your date of birth, memorable date and seventh and ninth letters of your password?'

Malik provided these from memory. He could hear the tapping of keys as she typed the information.

'Now, that's fine ... an incoming transfer ... yes, I have it here,' she said calmly. 'There was an incoming transfer from the Cayman Islands for over ten million US dollars. It arrived several minutes ago at eleven-thirty this morning, sir. The precise amount was ...'

'That will not be necessary, thank you.'

'Is there anything else I can help you with, Herr Rahman?'

'No, thank you for your help. Have a nice day. Goodbye.' Malik returned the handset to its cradle and as he walked out of the hotel he considered moving most of his money into bearer bonds, and for their safe keeping, into another bank. He would have plenty of time in several months when he visited the European mainland. Tipping the hotel doorman on his way out, Malik walked the short journey to the Premier National Bank. On arrival at 1 p.m., he asked a receptionist if the manager could be notified of his arrival.

'Ah, good afternoon, Muhammad, it's so good to meet you,' exclaimed Christos flamboyantly as he stepped down a narrow marble staircase to the bank's small but beautiful marbled foyer. Shaking hands, Christos added, 'Would you like some refreshments?'

Malik followed Christos up the staircase and agreed to some coffee. On entering the room Malik was offered a large Havana cigar, which he accepted, and then Christos rang for his secretary.

Once his cigar was lit, Malik began. 'As you know, I recently requested that you open a new business account on behalf of a number of people, some of whom are already clients of this bank. It's their wish that this new account is managed exclusively by me and my partner on their behalf. You will by now have received letters of introduction and authority from each of the syndicate members.'

'I've received the letters which are quite satisfactory. I can confirm that a private account has been opened in joint names.' Clearing his throat, Christos continued politely. 'There's the small matter of confirming your identity and activating the account by choosing an eight digit password, then you may provide me with any instructions that you may have.'

Malik drew the necessary documents from his small case. Christos beamed with apology and after inspecting them, he handed them to his young secretary and ordered her to copy them.

'One can never be too careful you understand. Your account number and my contact details are written on this bank card,' said Christos as he handed it to Malik. He ushered Malik toward the computer terminal at his desk, and invited Malik to enable his account.

'Also, I understand that four or more of the syndicate can override your authority,' continued Christos as Malik completed his registration at the terminal.

Malik merely nodded, and just as he finished, his documents were returned.

'So, what can I do for you?' asked Christos eagerly.

'You will receive eight equal payments totalling eighty million US dollars deposited into the account by 3 p.m. this afternoon.'

Christos whistled.

First, I would like ten million dollars to be paid to a Durriya Abdullah at the Bank of International Settlements, Montenegro, account number M362869134.'

Christos scribbled fast.

'Second, fifty million US dollars is to be transferred to CWI Shipping at the Bank of Credit and Commerce, Switzerland, account number S698635427. That will leave twenty million dollars in this account from which you will withdraw your fee.'

At this point refreshments arrived. Malik and Christos drew on their cigars and after the secretary had withdrawn, Christos checked his notes with Malik and then served the thick black liquid.

'Everything you have requested will be completed, Muhammad. Perhaps you wish to stay ...?'

'That will not be necessary. My clients and I demand the usual discretion and security.'

'Some of your clients are my best customers. It's the most important rule of my bank. Without it I would have few clients.'

'My partner or I will contact you, no one else.'

'That is perfectly satisfactory, Muhammad.'

After another twenty minutes discussing the world's bond markets, Malik left the bank and spent an hour shopping in the city centre for clothes before returning to the hotel. Back in his room he changed into newly acquired jogging gear then once again accessed the World Wide Web on his laptop. After logging onto the CWI Shipping account in Switzerland, he arranged for the transfer the following morning of fifty million US dollars to another offshore bank account, this time in the name of REM Exports at the Global Bank, Panama. Although the necessity of opening offshore bank accounts and the wiring of money across continents were tedious, the combination of the differing privacy, information sharing and security laws among the different banks and countries provided additional financial security and anonymity.

After a refreshing run, Malik enjoyed a swim then sauna in the hotel's fitness suite. It was while he was in the pool that his mind wandered from his daughter to his beautiful partner, Dalia, and her sea shipment of auto tyres destined for Buenos Aires from the port of Karachi. Restricting themselves to contact through brief and infrequent electronic mail messages, Malik longed for more.

Chapter 3

December 9th, Z – 144 Days
Phagwara, Punjab State, India

It was the middle of a cold, blustery night in the Punjab State of northern India. A group of twenty-one lightly equipped Harakat ul-Mujahidin terrorists lay in wait in the darker shadows of the edge of a wood that began just metres from the railroad tracks. In the distance, the sound of a whistle announced that the overdue train was on its way.

'Switch on the light,' ordered Dalia. On her immediate right, Darwish, who had previously rewired the railroad signal, pressed the button in front of him and the universally recognised stop signal changed from green to red.

Intelligent, courageous and well honed, Dalia was a formidable opponent. She had quickly gained the respect of every terrorist in her group as her reputation spread. They knew that she had become a warrior at an early age and had served with distinction in the Pakistan Army before joining the Harakat ul-Ansar, a group dedicated to the unification of Muslim and Indian Kashmir with Pakistan. Two years ago she had crossed the border into the disputed region of Indian Kashmir with the HUA comprising over four thousand Kashmiri Mujahidin and seized military positions. For six months she had fought bravely alongside her comrades against the twenty thousand Indian troops sent to expel them and only the Pakistan Government's inexplicable U-turn and their forced withdrawal had prevented final victory. On one mission during the occupation of the Indian province she had been captured by Indian soldiers, brutally raped then tortured before being left for dead on the foothills of Pir Panjal Range near Tisa on the disputed border. Rescued by her Mujahidin comrades, now she enjoyed the rank and privileges of a senior Kashmiri Mujahidin freedom fighter and was the most senior female terrorist leader in the recently formed Harakat ul-Mujahidin. Sold-out by the Pakistan Government, after the withdrawal the group had reorganised itself, changed its name, and altered its goal to establishing Muslim and Indian Kashmir as an independent Islamic republican state.

Like most terrorists worldwide, no one in Dalia's group carried any item upon their person that could identify them, much less identify them as Mujahidin or members of the HM. Their assault rifles were the ubiquitous Russian AK-47s, some over thirty years old but still entirely dependable and deadly. Just as useful on this mission, each terrorist also carried at least one knife. In any event, Dalia had reasoned to herself, an attack such as the one that she was about to conduct was likely to be blamed on anything but terrorists; the Indian Government would not want the world to know that it could not safeguard its own nuclear arsenal. The objects of this attack, two wooden crates each no more than the size of a large suitcase, were in themselves believed by the HM to be the beginning of a clandestine and potentially cataclysmic Indian operation against Muslim Kashmir.

During this mission, like so many others before it, no person could risk being identified dead or alive. If there was a risk of capture a quick suicide by knife or gun was expected, death being the merciful alternative. One of your colleagues, invited or otherwise, was expected to complete the task.

Next to Dalia lay Arjan Singh, a Sikh of around forty who had worked on the railroads of the Punjab and Haryana regions north-west of Delhi for twenty years. With a dependent family of fourteen, Singh had readily accepted a very generous offer from the Network to provide Dalia with vital information.

'There it is,' Dalia said. 'See the light over there?' Abbas and Singh nodded their agreement. Along the wood line, the other terrorists passed the word and prepared themselves for the silent and swift attack.

The whistle shrilled again, this time much louder. As the train came into view it slowly drew to an unscheduled and alarmingly loud halt as the screams of protesting metal rose from the wheels of the locomotive and each railroad truck in turn. With the exception of the locomotive and a nondescript boxcar immediately behind it, the train comprised a long fleet of liquefied gas or petroleum railroad tanker trucks. The boxcar had originated from the Bhabha Atomic Research Centre, the centrepiece of India's prolific nuclear weapons programme near Mumbai on the east coast of India, and was destined for Jammu on the northern Pakistan border.

The terrorists advanced out of the shadows towards the slowing train, some climbing aboard before it halted. Dalia and a handpicked team of nine that included Singh made for the boxcar. Meanwhile another team was securing the locomotive while the remainder were already busy laying magnetic explosives around the tankers before activating preset timers.

Opening the outer bolts to the boxcar door, Singh called out authoritatively to the guards inside. 'Come out for a while. We'll be stopping here for twenty minutes.'

If the guards chose to remain inside then minor charges had been prepared to blow the door in. But as Dalia had suspected the guards did not hesitate and the boxcar door rolled open and four dishevelled Indian soldiers in field artillery uniforms gratefully emerged, climbing down to the trackside. As soon as the fourth guard reached the ground, terrorists emerged from the darkness and the four men were killed quickly and quietly where they stood. As Abbas checked the dead, Dalia and four men climbed into the boxcar and surveyed the cargo of four wooden crates each lashed down across the centre of the boxcar with rope. The only other cargo was the scattered personal belongings of the four dead men.

'Take two crates,' Dalia whispered, unnecessarily as the men had practised the attack on the boxcar many times. Once the five intruders had left with their plunder, another man jumped up and fixed preprepared explosives to the remaining two crates before following the other terrorists who were already withdrawing to rendezvous with the transport some two hundred metres away.

As the group withdrew, one of the terrorists detonated a small plastic explosive charge wrapped around the trunk of an old, tall tree. As it fell, it brought the adjacent power lines down, directly onto the train.

Four minutes later a huge explosion was heard and seen from as far away as Amritsar, two hundred kilometres to the northwest. Just five kilometres from the epicentre, near the town of Phagwara, night turned into day for the departing terrorist convoy and they, along with thousands of others, experienced the shock wave and intense heat from the resulting massive fireball. As the seconds passed and darkness returned, the convoy sped away unharmed from the huge cloud of dust and smoke that was developing over the area.

In the midst of the desolate mountains of the Pir Panjal Range, somewhere close to where Dalia had once escaped death, the terrorist convoy stopped for a short break. Singh would not resume the journey but was left alive on Dalia's orders, standing on the roadside. Dalia had considered with good reason that the man could never tell of his treachery and that he may once again prove useful.

En route to the border crossing point, Dalia reflected on the mission that had been a complete success, not only for the snatching of two pure fission, weapon-grade plutonium bombs each with a yield of twelve kilotons but also for the conventional destruction of two similar bombs that were destined, it appeared, to be targeted at Pakistan or Muslim Kashmir. Dalia offered a prayer to Allah and thanked him for her safety.

The Indian Government reported through the world's media that an explosion in the Punjab had killed over one thousand people and injured another six thousand. They added that the explosion occurred on the outskirts of the town of Phagwara when a train carrying petroleum and other hazardous materials had touched power lines that had been felled in a storm. Over one thousand buildings, including many homes, had been destroyed in the incident and another two thousand badly damaged. Apparently the train had been carrying much-needed fuel to the energy-starved Kashmir and dynamite for open-cast mining.

Later, an MI6 report into the disaster was to conclude that the devastation caused on the outskirts of Phagwara was comparable to the aftermath of a nuclear explosion with a yield of one kiloton. Its summation did not rule out some form of subnuclear or radiological explosion due to several unconfirmed reports of increases in levels of radiation in the vicinity and it concluded that the railroad catastrophe was unlikely to be the responsibility of terrorists or mobsters but was likely caused by a freak incident such as the one put forward by the Indian Government.

It was one of the worst train disasters ever, outweighing the 1981 accident in India that had killed more than eight hundred people, and it attracted millions of dollars of world aid.

Chapter 4

December 9th, Z – 144 Days
San Carlos de Bariloche, Río Negro, Argentina

It was early evening in the suburbs of San Carlos de Bariloche, when Dr Sultan Hussain Baloch heard the front door bell ring. He was already enjoying his third Jack Daniels since returning home from the office an hour ago. Rising stiffly from his old, threadbare couch he shuffled over to the front door and pulled it open. Before him on his porch stood an urbane man who was unfamiliar to him, though by appearance the stranger looked Argentinian. Behind the man, Baloch saw a late-model Toyota Land Cruiser on the sandy drive complete with an Alamo rental sticker on the windscreen. He felt a familiar warning sign of tightness in his chest, and considered whether this man was here to hurt or worse, kill him.

The man standing before him smiled warmly then spoke in Punjabi. 'Dr Baloch, I have a proposition for you from some old friends that you will want to hear and will not wish to refuse. May I enter?' The bedraggled and drowsy doctor of science who rarely had visitors was sufficiently intrigued and with little to lose he moved aside and beckoned the stranger in.

Baloch was once heralded as one of Pakistan's leading nuclear engineers. He was a key part of the team that first developed the country's very own arsenal of atom bombs, an act for which the entire team was decorated for services to their country. According to many people, he was also a little flaky. For several years this loose nuclear cannon had been travelling in and out of the Taliban stronghold of Kandahar where he had helped them construct a complex of buildings he later described to the world's media as flour mills. It was for this reason that the Islamic Republic of Pakistan eventually detained Baloch and two of his colleagues to determine if the three scientists may have been passing nuclear expertise, raw materials or, worse, functioning weaponry on to the Taliban. Because there was no evidence that the men had been trafficking in secrets, and because they were national heroes, they were released. International pressure for his re-arrest, however, caused Baloch to flee to a new life in Argentina, a country that had acceded to the terms of the Non-Proliferation Treaty as a non-nuclear weapon state some six years previously.

It was the kind of tenacity expected of the Network that also sparked the three arrests in Pakistan. Baloch, the best known of the detained scientists was a vocal supporter of the Taliban, calling its members 'upholders of a ... movement of renaissance of Islam'. He compared the journey of the soul from life through death and thereafter to an electric current passing through a wire, and said the energy of the spirits known as *jinn* could be harnessed to solve the energy crisis in Pakistan. Such seemingly loose-screw ideas coming from a man with so much knowledge of the Pakistan nuclear arsenal always troubled Islamabad, Washington and London. When Baloch retired from government employment in 1999 and began travelling in and out of Afghanistan to establish what he said was a 'relief organisation', antennae went up.

Once American military action began against the Taliban, Baloch's flour mills were razed to the ground. At about the same time, the three engineers were detained for questioning. Later, the US Secretary of State for Defence was to admit publicly that the three were high up on the CIA's 'worry list' and the ensuing publicity killed off Baloch's chances of working legitimately in the region.

Without difficulty, Baloch secured himself a job in Argentina as a nuclear scientist with Investigación Aplicada, a State-owned company that developed custom design technology in a number of areas. INVAP had started thirty years earlier as a supplier in the nuclear field, and it was in this division, with its headquarters in San Carlos de Bariloche in the province of Río Negro, where Baloch now worked. He held a mid-league position in a design team for several uranium enrichment plants commissioned by the National Commission of Nuclear Energy.

Despite this job that he had found through contacts in the global nuclear marketplace, life had not met Baloch's expectations.

He was not well paid, and his run-down timber-framed bungalow near his office that he originally purchased as a temporary consideration now appeared permanent as he forwarded as much money to his family as he could. Originally he had hoped that his estranged wife and four children would be able to join him, but that dream had almost disappeared, just as his hopes of a dramatic rise through promotion or through lucrative job offers also proved elusive. Nuclear research and development in Argentina truly was not cutting-edge, it was dull, under funded and unproductive.

Baloch watched nervously as the fit, well-dressed man with a military-style haircut entered the house. 'I only have Jack Daniels,' he offered, sticking to his native Punjabi.

'Thank you, yes,' replied Malik politely, as he continued his tactful examination of the environment. The man before him was short, overweight and perspiring. His dishevelled suit, flushed cheeks and poor pallor betrayed a man that drank excessively, ate poorly and took little exercise. His raspy voice was that born from many years of heavy smoking. The filthy, foul-smelling lodgings came as no surprise. 'And how is your family?' Malik enquired sympathetically, hiding his disgust.

Baloch faltered, needing to know how much this messenger from home knew of him and whether the mention of his family was some kind of veiled threat. Carefully choosing to ignore the enquiry, he asked tentatively, 'Why I should listen to you? Who exactly are you, and how did you find me?'

Malik was expecting this and without touching on the purpose of the visit, he divulged inside knowledge of the Network that was known exclusively to Baloch and very few others. It was to Baloch's credit that he had not divulged this information to anyone else, particularly with the huge international bounties on offer. Soon Baloch was satisfied and waving at Malik to continue as he eagerly gulped at his drink.

'My name is Malik and I represent the Network. Collectively they would like to make you an offer that will involve no more than three weeks' work, all of it in Buenos Aires.'

'When you work with man-made weapons of mass destruction you begin to understand the true value of pure Islam as an alternative to annihilation,' Baloch interrupted, somewhat unconvincingly. 'I have retired from all of that. Not least of all

I have come to Argentina, a nuclear weapons free country, to demonstrate that I have no wish to work on nuclear bombs. I'm in the industry for the good of mankind, to construct not destruct.'

Malik ignored the ideology and continued unabated. 'The work is very easy for a man of your knowledge and experience. Absolute discretion and secrecy is demanded. Do you really think that the rest of the world believes Argentina has freed herself from nuclear weapons? Their weapons programmes have been supported by a number of Western nations in the past including the Soviet Union, Canada, Germany and even Switzerland. Back home people are convinced that you have simply changed employers but your job is the same.' Malik saw Baloch looked frightened and understanding the fruitlessness of this tack he continued. 'Regardless of your current work, it will make no difference to the proposal.'

'I've been here for several years and have no reason to believe Argentina is even close to producing and delivering a nuclear bomb,' Baloch persisted. 'So, what does the great bin Laden want of me now?'

Malik stared into Baloch's deep set eyes. Sensing the lie and a clever effort to feign interest, possibly in an attempt to manoeuvre into a bargaining position, he appeared doubtful. 'Although I do not question your discretion, you will appreciate that if any of what I am about to say should ever be repeated to anyone other than me, mistakenly or not, the consequences will be permanent. Do you understand, my friend?'

'I have never let down my colleagues before,' replied Baloch desperately.

Malik knew this was true, otherwise Baloch would be dead or at the very least he would not have been located and recommended by Ayman al-Zawahiri.

'In two weeks a shipment will arrive in Buenos Aires that we wish you to examine and prepare for further transit out of Argentina. The work will involve checking and preparing two twelve-kiloton nuclear bombs, advising upon and preparing timers, and preparing suitable concealment devices. You may need to provide some specialist equipment too; that is your decision as long as the task is completed. That is all. You will conduct the work at a secret location in Buenos Aires. I am here to secure your services for a maximum of three weeks, hopefully less, and to ensure your loyalty for the Network. In the future there may be other opportunities. Who knows? I need to discuss any specific requirements with you, but I cannot do this until you agree.'

Despite the enormity of what was being asked, Baloch could not help chuckling; it was obvious that his reward would be substantial. He found himself not caring about the nuclear effects of two twelve-kiloton blasts and was quite content to know as little as possible about the terrorists' plans. He also realised that if he did not agree this man would kill him. His face turned sallow

'That is enough yield to destroy any two cities in the world. What may I expect in return?' asked Baloch, coughing as he spoke.

'Cash or wire transfer, it's up to you. You may name your price?' replied Malik, grimly amused.

Baloch stared at Malik in amazement. He had never negotiated his payment before, even in Afghanistan, and this sounded like a well-funded operation. But what to suggest? This time he took a deliberate sip of his drink and seriously considered his position. He knew that the bombs must be on their way so the Network was committed. On the other hand, Malik would probably kill him if he refused, though it would be hard to find a replacement, someone as qualified and trustworthy, and available. One thing was for sure, no one would find his body for days lying in this shack in the cheaper suburbs of San Carlos de Bariloche - he had only colleagues and no friends, and his colleagues were used to him flitting between divisions and construction sites for weeks on end. He decided to demand one million US dollars.

Baloch's eyes shone with an eerie lustre. 'You understand there is no other person in the world that is available to you and has the expertise you require? I am an expert in detonators, the nuclear core zone, and the mathematics and geometry of a fission explosion.'

Malik remained tight-lipped, not wanting to either pamper or hurt the scientist's ego. The money was not the issue.

'One million US dollars and I will provide the vital equipment I will need,' Baloch said mechanically, expecting a full rebuttal.

'Agreed,' said Malik without hesitation. 'Now, let's get on with the planning.'

Baloch was dumbfounded. He felt he was hallucinating. His heart pounding, he immediately wished he had demanded more.

Without any thought he grabbed the open bottle from the low grubby coffee table and refilled his glass.

Malik rejected an invitation for more whiskey and continued the discussion. 'We have two pure fission, weapons grade plutonium nuclear bombs. Each was manufactured in Russia in about 1987 for use as suitcase bombs on special operations. They were sold as part of a batch of twelve to India in 1997. Both appear to have been well maintained since. It is even probable that they have both been refurbished recently. In its case, each bomb measures about sixty by forty by twenty centimetres.'

Still quivering, Baloch was stupefied and said nothing.

Malik continued patiently, keen to conclude the business and leave before Baloch lost his senses. 'We would like one bomb to be rearranged and secreted in a large drum of cooking oil and the other to be packed inside a ship's fender. The bombs are self-contained and, as you probably know, originate from a particularly potent Russian bomb. Each bomb was designed to destroy the deployed area of a NATO tank division and comes with the complete and modernised physics package of neutron generators, arming mechanisms and the other essentials of a medium-sized atomic bomb. We may have to purchase suitable batteries that can outlast the timer.'

Dr Baloch was impressed with Malik's knowledge and was beginning to wonder why he was required when Malik continued. 'Each is essentially a plutonium-fuelled atomic bomb with a yield of twelve kilotons.'

'What nature of border controls must they breach?' asked Baloch doubtfully.

'Maximum reduction in radiation emission is required. You may be able to improve on our basic ideas to fool officials, though the methods of entry are fixed.'

'What about arming requirements?'

'Each bomb is to be preset to detonate at midday on 2nd May next year.'

Baloch thought for a moment. With remarkable lucidity he explained, 'There is only one self-powered timer I would trust over that period of time, a Zeon Tech 3000. They are used on small satellites and unmanned spacecraft because of their robustness, accuracy and two-hundred-year life. You can buy them on the Internet from the United States. It would be even more reliable to use the same timer to detonate them as radiological weapons, that is, as dirty bombs.' Conventional explosive packed with radioactive debris or nuclear bombs detonated conventionally were known worldwide as 'dirty bombs'.

'No, our friends desire nuclear-fission explosions. Their goal is to spread fear and they wish to do this with the greatest possible effect.'

'I see,' replied Baloch, his eyebrows creased together. 'The Russians used tritium to boost fission and allow for a reduction in the size of the bombs. Clever bastards. A true multi-stage thermonuclear device using tritium provides a large yield from such a small bomb. Despite its size, one of these twelve-kiloton bombs will destroy everything within a radius of ten kilometres and cause massive damage up to thirty kilometres. Boosted fission increases their efficiency and yield you understand. I assume that the tritium triggers needed to ignite our bombs are sufficiently active? Tritium decays over six years or so.'

'This is something we require you to check, though as I said, they have been well maintained and, we believe, recently refurbished.' Malik was relieved. The Doctor clearly knew his trade, and was still lucid.

'I have access to equipment that can do that,' Baloch replied, rubbing his fleshy jaw.

Malik knew the Doctor was hooked. Work like this was a drug to people like Baloch. 'And what sort of location would you require for your work Doctor Baloch? Whatever your requirements, it must be located in Buenos Aires.'

Baloch looked puzzled. 'Let me consider that for a moment. I should not need any additional staff apart from you,' he added, anxious not to share his windfall. 'It would be wise to find a sufficiently large lead-lined container to work inside. In the early days it was what we used in Karachi. Walk-in cold rooms or refrigerators are commonly used as covert storage locations in numerous Third World countries. I suggest you look for a disused meat-processing factory. Argentina, particularly Buenos Aires, has many of them as the entire industry has been downsizing for years.'

'I will deal with that. We'll live and work at the same location. You can expect to be living there throughout the period, starting two weeks from today.'

'I will need to organise some holiday.' Baloch's pulse was racing now. 'One last question, when do I get paid?'

'Half now, half on completion,' said Malik dryly, 'I hope American dollars are acceptable?'

Baloch, whose legs were like jelly, followed Malik to the car and stood watching from the front door. He glimpsed the bags that Malik left behind and felt sickened, wishing he had demanded far more.

Cell phone coverage in Argentina remained limited, but Malik had received strong signals in Buenos Aires and at Baloch's home in the suburbs of San Carlos de Bariloche. Malik tried calling his own hotel in Buenos Aires using his cell phone and was successful. Removing another cell phone and charger from the car, Malik switched it on, checked it, and then handed it to Baloch who until now had never possessed his own.

The two men spent another hour discussing detailed equipment requirements, travel and accommodation arrangements and methods of communication. Malik spent some time impressing on Baloch the need for security, and the need to cover his tracks, particularly at work and home.

Soon after Malik left, Baloch fell asleep lying on his threadbare couch, dreaming of a new life with his family.

Chapter 5

December 10th, Z – 143 Days
West of Riasi, Jammu and Kashmir Province, India

The wind had turned bitter though the night remained dry. On the foothills of the Pir Panjal mountain range there were no towns or villages, only isolated farmhouses whose lights illuminated the dark night like distant stars. Overhead the sky was filled with dense rain clouds that prevented starlight from reaching the earth.

Two vehicles drove along a pitted asphalt track, a white Mercedes transit van followed by a two-axle Bedford truck with a cargo compartment enclosed by canvas. Their headlights were extinguished and a partially dimmed flashlight carried by hand in front of each vehicle was the only sign of life in the sinister night. Beside the road was a large border fence of woven wire topped with three strands of barbed wire. Occasionally, large rusted metal signs were attached to the fence, their lettering all but illegible but their meaning clear. This fence represented the demarcation line along the Indian side of the contested inner Kashmir border with Muslim Kashmir, known internationally as the Line of Control.

Dalia was very familiar with the area and after several minutes she recognised the sharp left turn taken by the fence line. Walking ahead to inspect the ground, she removed a strand of red tape from her path that marked the forward edge of a minefield then signalled with her flashlight. This directed the van and truck to turn off the asphalt onto the barely distinguishable, and supposedly mined, track that continued to follow the fence down into a dark valley. Dalia knew that the border guards would not depart from the asphalt for fear of the mines. After twenty minutes of slow progress, the convoy reached the valley bottom and came to a stop. A lone man known as Farooq approached Dalia out of the shadows and whispered instructions. Dalia returned to the van and beckoned for two of its occupants to assist Farooq at the fence.

The three men rapidly reopened a break in the fence wide enough for the two vehicles. Farooq waved the vehicles through and they carefully closed the gap. This section of the fence line had taken many hours of painstaking reconnaissance to find, situated as it was in 'dead' ground protected from observation by the higher ground surrounding it. The gateway had proved invaluable to the terrorists since its discovery and inauguration at the end of the last conflict in Kashmir eighteen months before. The fortuitous discovery of landmines in the vicinity by an Indian border patrol had helped maintain the secret.

Farooq and Dalia proceeded to walk in front of the slow-moving vehicles until they rejoined a forsaken asphalt road in the middle of no man's land that was out of sight of both the Indian and Pakistan border posts. On joining the road, the van and truck illuminated their headlights before topping a rise. Farooq, now sitting with Dalia and the driver in the front of the van, spotted the familiar light in the distance. As they drew closer, they could see it was a naked bulb swung high over a gate. Beside the gate was a guard shack. Four armed soldiers, all of them smoking, lounged near the gate looking over the borderland as if expecting someone on this ghostly night. Two were seated and two leant against the gate itself, a red and white metal pole that blocked their passage.

Farooq jumped out from the passenger seat of the van and approached the guard shack. He spoke to one of the guards. In a moment a sergeant came out of the wooden shack. He nonchalantly shined a flashlight into the front seat of the van and gestured at the rear doors. The driver went around to the rear and opened the doors, allowing the sergeant to take a look inside with the flashlight. Five men holding assault rifles were sitting on the floor, one nodded and the sergeant nodded back. He saw several sacks that might have contained food and a variety of water containers and cooking utensils. During his cursory inspection of the dark interior he failed to spot the large black canvas shroud at the back of the cargo bay, immediately behind the driver. Grunting, the sergeant moved towards the truck and once again he inspected the vehicle. Nodding briefly to the two men in the cab, he walked to the rear. On lifting up the tailgate canvas, he used his flashlight again and picked out a larger group of men casually sitting with assault rifles slung over their laps as if their presence was entirely natural. At the back of the cargo area the flashlight happened upon some unremarkable stores and he merely grunted his satisfaction.

Content that what he found was as Farooq had explained, the sergeant wandered back to the shack to conclude business. Inside, Farooq paid the sergeant the second instalment of three million Pakistani rupees, approximately fifty thousand US dollars. Both men stepped to the door of the building and the sergeant motioned to the expectant soldiers. They opened the gate and waved at each driver to pass.

The two vehicles left the ghostly guard shack and its bare light behind. The road wound up a gentle ridge out of the valley, topped the crest and continued towards Jhelum that lay on the Lahore-to-Rawalpindi carriageway. At the junction the van turned south to Lahore and the truck north to Rawalpindi.

Chapter 6

December 10th, Z – 143 Days
Karachi, Pakistan

Zaffar Khan sat in his tastefully furnished apartment in the smart Clifton suburbs of Karachi watching satellite television, a drained tequila bottle and today's *Dawn* newspaper strewn across the floor. In his early forties, Zaffar had the calm self-assurance of a skilled artisan, a mason or a carpenter, or perhaps a tradesman who was good with his hands. He was known and feared for those giant hands and his sweet, clear voice. Zaffar was a muscle-bound mountain of a man and a hit man who killed with those sledgehammer hands as ruthlessly as he wooed women with his voice and charm. But now, Zaffar was frustrated, for he was suffering a severe losing streak on the horses. Nowadays Zaffar subcontracted much of his work out to a stable of killers, dozens of younger men who prefer a handgun to Zaffar's more intimate way of death by close embrace. He pulled hard on his cigarette.

Murder was depressingly familiar in Karachi. There were six hundred cases last year, the most of any city in Pakistan. Zaffar's rates were five hundred thousand rupees a hit, unless it involved a prominent figure, which upped the fee to a million rupees, the equivalent of less than seventeen thousand US dollars. His thugs also had a profitable sideline in intimidation. An electric drill applied to the kneecap had a wonderful way of loosening tongues and wallets.

Karachi, a port city of fourteen million on the Pakistani coast, where the Pab Hills and the Sind Desert gathered into a brick- and dust-hued urban sprawl before tumbling into the Arabian Sea, was the battlefield in which an assassin like Zaffar thrived. In Karachi there were ethnic feuds. Gangs of Indian migrants fought against the Pathans, Baluchis and Sindhis. There were extremists from rival Sunni and Shi'ite sects battling each other, and there were the supporters of radical Islamic groups that sheltered terrorists and fugitives. According to Karachi counterterrorist police officers these supporters were terrorists themselves, helping fugitives from outlawed groups such as al-Qa'eda and the Egyptian Islamic Jihad to plan their next terrorist strikes. One senior officer had expressed concern over circumstantial evidence that suggested bin Laden and al-Zawahiri were known by senior members of the Islamic Republic's government to be hiding out in Karachi but he had since been assassinated.

Karachi faced endemic and systemic corruption on a daily basis. In certain colleges, teachers demanded payoffs from students wanting to pass exams and some policemen earned extra money by selling their bullets. On the Karachi Stock Exchange, brokers sometimes vanished with their investors' portfolios and no investor had ever won a case against a crooked dealer. In the courts, it was common for a defence lawyer to pay off witnesses, the judge and even the prosecutor to obtain a favourable verdict for his client. In the end, some would-be litigants found it was cheaper and more effective simply to hire a hit man. Karachi today was like Chicago in the days of Al Capone, but mixed in was the English Middle Ages. It was a dangerous place and, with terrorism breeding in enclaves across the city, it was poised to spread its menace not only throughout Pakistan but also far beyond its borders.

At ground level, Karachi suffered a geographical division. The poor, who tended to be more fundamentalist, lived in dust-blown shanties on the outskirts of town. There, they polarised, Pathans with Pathans, Baluchis with Baluchis, seeking to replicate the tribal life of their homelands. In some ghettos the clergymen banned television, women wore burqas and the only education on offer for youngsters was the mesmeric recitation of the Qur'an at religious schools. Elders imposed strict Shari'a law on their communities and punished crimes accordingly, and the police never heard about the rough justice.

The rich and influential lived in the Defence and Clifton suburbs, the latter featuring Californian-style mansions strung along a wide crescent-shaped shoreline. Every few years their walls grew taller, concrete evidence of the rising tide of instability that engulfed Karachi. The rich kids would hang out at Karachi's only mall listening to Western pop while they ate burgers. There are no burqas here; the girls wore short skirts and low-cut tops, their mothers diamante Chanel sunglasses. Bombs were exploding, journalists beheaded and politicians kidnapped, but for the people of Clifton and Defence, this violence seldom penetrated their cocoon. They remained blissfully unaware when a Qur'anic teacher with piercing eyes and a coal-black beard walked by and saw them, and a deep and sinister rage rose within him. That same teacher was a member of an outlawed extremist group associated with a string of killings and bombings across the city.

The problem plaguing Pakistan was that its founders had never agreed whether it should be a relaxed country whose citizens happen to be Muslims or an austere Islamic state adhering to Shari'a law. As with so many countries, this ambiguity was responsible for the ongoing tug-of-war between the country's religious extremists and Westernised moderates. As a city, Karachi embodied these contradictions. For Karachi's youth it was said that there were just two choices, embrace the West or join the jihad.

In 1947, when Britain spilt the Raj into India and Pakistan, modern Karachi, more than any other city, was a by-product of this upheaval. Before partition, its inhabitants included Hindus, Parsis, Muslim traders, Goans and Sheedis, descendants of African slaves shipped over in chains during the eighteenth century. At partition, most of Karachi's half a million Hindu inhabitants left, replaced by a million Mohajirs, or Indian migrants. They, too, followed the dream of Pakistan's founding father, Mohammed Ali Jinnah, to create a nation for Muslims. The Mohajirs achieved status by conducting vicious ethnic warfare in Karachi; the Pathans and the Sindhis retaliated but the Mohajirs matched them murder for murder. Until recently, Karachi had been under the grip of the merciless Mohajir godfather, Abdul Hassan, but he was now a fugitive in London charged with more than one hundred counts of murder, sabotage and arson.

Arif Edhi was the spitting image of Zaffar, his cousin, and was the chief shipping supervisor at the head offices of the Oriental Shipping Company in Karachi's prime marketing centre near Port Muhammad bin Qasim. Arif began working for the company when it was established in 1970 and had built a reputation for himself as a leading figure in the company, which was the leading component of a worldwide consortium. Arif had a fine reputation for being capable of smuggling anything anywhere and he was well connected to all sections of society including the police, the mobsters, the wealthy, the fundamentalists and also the terrorists. He was considered by everyone as useful and therefore he was untouchable. The consortium provided a variety of integrated shipping services, including shipping, chartering, terminal operations, freight forwarding, crewing, watch and ward security, bonding and warehousing. In Karachi an individual survived by being a member of, or being affiliated to, a group that could protect him. Arif was no exception for he, like his cousin, was a Mohajir mobster and, for a competitive price, Arif would guarantee a complete door-to-door shipping package to anywhere in the world with total discretion. From his office overlooking the Arabian Sea he controlled a workforce of five hundred largely Urdu-speaking Mohajir refugees, most of who were entirely indebted to him and utterly dependant on his will.

Like so much of Central Asia, Karachi was deeply affected by the Soviet Union's 1979 invasion of Afghanistan and the jihad that was declared throughout the Islamic world in response. To fund their campaign against the Russian invaders, Afghan warlords used Pakistan as a transhipment point for heroin and Karachi as a major point of export. Paid for in part by drugs money were the vast shipments of small arms and Stinger missiles passing the other way through Karachi's port, before being loaded onto trucks bound for Peshawar and eventually onto camels and mules headed for Afghanistan's interior. Arif built his reputation on importing weapons of all varieties from the United States for the Afghan war against the Soviet invaders, and by exporting drugs all over the world. He had access to a web of legitimate businesses that employed many of the three thousand newcomers lured to Karachi each day, even if it meant packing tyres in a filthy tyre production factory for a measly eight US dollars per twelve-hour shift before bedding down with the fat and plentiful rats on a stretch of pavement.

On reaching an agreement with Dalia for a cool one million US dollars, Arif put plans in place for the smuggling of two small crates among a regular shipment of vehicle tyres bound for Argentina. The tyres were to be palletised, containerised then bonded for shipping as usual at the tyre production factory that lay on the eastern outskirts of Karachi but packed within them would be the illicit cargo.

The container vessel earmarked to transport the shipment of tyres direct to Buenos Aires was a German-registered ship, the BBC *Columbia*. The ship's regular crew were to remain entirely ignorant of the illicit cargo, but Arif had arranged for two of his own trusted men to enlist as casual crewmen for the journey. Their job was to identify the container and watch as the shipping company in Buenos Aires, Intranationale SA, unloaded it, then hijack the container truck as it left the port to deliver the container load of tyres to Dalia in an old warehouse in the La Boca district of Buenos Aires.

Intranationale SA was Argentina's largest international freight forwarder, shipping agent, customs broker and bonded warehousing operative, and it served the port of Buenos Aires and many other ports throughout Argentina. Arif had already spoken with his regular contact in Intranationale SA and agreed a reasonable price for the simple favour of port officials looking the other way.

Arif was supremely confident with his plan, after all it had worked many times before, though never before for such a high fee. He was confident his plan could not fail because anyone who may have cared was in some way indebted to him or at least to people that he knew. Only those who were poor and uneducated were a threat, for experience told him that these people did not necessarily have the good sense to accept a bribe and forget the deed. His most expensive bribe was to the Karachi port authority inspectors for twenty thousand US dollars. This guaranteed their satisfaction and silence.

Arif's most pressing problem was how to guarantee loyalty and discretion from four Pashtun tyre production factory workers and for that task he chose Zaffar.

Chapter 7

December 10th, Z – 143 Days
East Karachi, Pakistan

Founded by the British in the 1940s, the Corolla Tyre Company owned four factories throughout Pakistan, with its largest situated in a deprived neighbourhood in the east of Karachi. This factory manufactured and exported low-budget tyres for trucks, buses, cars, motorcycles, cycles and agricultural machines to countries all over the world. Its main markets were the United States, Brazil, Argentina, the United Kingdom and France, followed by most other European states. It employed five thousand employees who were largely drawn from the unskilled labour force of the surrounding districts; in adhering to legislation the management encouraged a multiracial workforce, which also provided a clear benefit to them through the prevention of a consolidated and powerful workers' union.

The factory itself had changed little since its construction in 1942 but, despite its Dickensian appearance, its permanent odious and sticky smell and the deafening noise of its old machinery, it was remarkably clean, well organised and efficient. Occupying a huge site, it had been the first tyre factory to open in Pakistan and had been designed to employ over ten thousand workers in support of the United Kingdom and her Commonwealth during and after World War II.

As electricity generators replaced coal-powered steam engines, and as the manufacturing process was automated, so the workforce was halved despite the acceleration in annual demand. Production effortlessly kept pace with demand and, as labour and raw materials were cheap, the long-term future of the factory seemed secure, although as its profits soared, so too did the kickbacks paid to the Mohajir mafia.

One hour after a bribed night guard had confirmed the

workforce had left and that the factory was shut down for the night, a small team of four night workers raised themselves wearily from a rest room situated off the tyre production factory's vast manufacturing quarter. Already the deserted factory was descending into darkness as the daylight faded. They had two hours of unlawful work to complete before hurriedly completing the night duties that justified their presence. The overtime work available to one four-man team each night was highly prized among the workforce and an effort was made by all supervisors to allocate it on a seemingly equal and fair basis. Riots and fatal stabbings were the alternative. Tonight's four workers had ensured their presence by delaying their own rightful turn, by merely swapping or bribing, and in one case by threatening a work colleague with his life. Their task tonight was to replicate a well-trodden smuggling practice that was familiar to many of the Corolla Tyre Company's workforce.

Such was the size of the factory that it took the four workers ten minutes simply to weave their way through the increasingly gloomy manufacturing zone, across packaging and palletising and into the vast shipping zone. The most simple and efficient of the three zones, one side of shipping contained countless rows of palletised tyres, extending as far as the eye could see and with each row towering eight pallets high.

None of the four workers knew the exact nature of the cargo to be smuggled on this occasion and neither did they care. They had assumed it was to be a standard shipment of Afghan heroin destined for the Americas or Europe, as each worker was to be paid a typical fee based broadly on the weight of the drug shipment.

As instructed by his friend Arif, on their arrival into the shipping zone the supervisor, a gaunt, spindly man, chose the most distinguishable shipping container, one that had already been packed and bonded for BBC *Columbia*. All containers bound for the ship were the standard twelve-metre steel type, and although they varied in colour none was unique enough to cause the supervisor to look closer.

Eventually, for the first time since leaving the rest room, the supervisor spoke. 'We will reopen this bonded container and remove the first four pallets. The bottom two will be stripped down as usual then the pallets repacked with the cargo that will be arriving shortly. The cargo will be located in the centre of each pallet and the pallets repacked, rebound and replaced, with everything returned to exactly as it was. The two pallets must look identical to the others. We will take any spare tyres with us tonight. I will check every stage. Do you understand?'

The three men nodded obediently before one spoke up. 'How much are we to be paid, Mohammad?'

'You will each receive fifty thousand rupees for tonight's work and if you work hard you will each be rewarded a fat bonus. You have been chosen because you are fortunate enough to have the bonding, fork-lift and palletising skills required, and you will not let me down. Begin now. I will fetch the cargo.'

The three workers, none older than twenty, eagerly discussed the apparent ease of the task as the supervisor strode away. Laughing over their good fortune, one moved towards a nearby forklift truck as the other two went in search of the necessary tools required to break open the container.

Meanwhile, the white Mercedes transit van with Dalia and her guard of five armed men had been negotiating the eastern suburbs of Karachi and heading towards the factory. Although they had endured an exhausting 900-mile journey with one hurried rest stop at Bahawalpur they were fully alert and had parked within eyeshot of the factory some fifteen minutes earlier at 8:15 p.m. At precisely 8:30 p.m. Dalia spotted a lone man exit a man-sized stable door set within a giant pair of arched wooden doors capable of allowing articulated vehicle access. The man lit a cigarette and after several minutes he began to wave it in a circular fashion, creating a red circular effect in the night.

'That's the sign,' said Dalia. 'Drive towards the large doors and keep the lights off.'

As the van moved slowly forwards, the lone man re-entered the building through the same stable door he had left. As the van reached the large doors, the left-hand door swung open and in the gloom through the opening Dalia could just make out the vast shipping quarter. The van pulled into the building then, without knowing where to go, Dalia commanded the driver to halt. Immediately after the van had entered the building the door was closed behind them and the cavern was plunged into darkness. After relocking the single door, the lone man walked up to the passenger side of the van.

Before Mohammad could overcome his obvious surprise at finding a beautiful woman in command, Dalia had opened the van's electric passenger window and demanded, 'You're Mohammad?'

'Yes,' he mumbled, mesmerised.

'Are you ready?' she shot back, her eyes stony.

'Yes, follow me,' he said quickly, responding to the authority in her eyes and voice. 'There are four of us. I am the supervisor.'

'We're six, armed, and I'm the leader,' Dalia snapped, an unfinished smile frozen on her lips. 'First, tell me about the factory's security arrangements?'

Without hesitation, Mohammad answered, 'The two night guards have been bribed and will ignore us. They normally monitor the security cameras but the system does not work tonight.' Mohammad had checked earlier in the day and found that the factory's nominal CCTV system had not worked for some time.

'Excellent,' Dalia conceded. 'Regardless I will post my own guard at a good vantage point overlooking the front of the factory. Where is a good position?'

'Up there,' said Mohammad, pointing to a long vertical ladder and overhead gantry that hung adjacent to a huge arched glass window located above the giant entrance doors.

Dalia spoke rapidly to someone over her shoulder and an armed man in black fatigues jumped out of a rear door and ran towards the ladder.

Only then did the van slowly creep forward, following Mohammad as he began walking towards a distant light. As they approached, Dalia saw three young men working among a number of weak paraffin lamps and the dim lights of a fork-lift truck, unloading by hand the few remaining tyres from a pallet, another pallet beside it already lying empty with tyres strewn all around. Behind them lay a yellow shipping container with its end doors wide open. As the van halted near the empty pallets, Dalia ordered the men in the back to exit the van and unload the two small sealed crates. The same cautious men assisted the enthusiastic workers with the loading and binding of each wooden crate onto each pallet.

Satisfied that Mohammad was capable, Dalia slung her AK-47 rifle over her shoulder. 'Now show me the distinguishing markings on the container,' she ordered, as the work progressed with the repacking of the tyres.

'Follow me.' Mohammad beckoned Dalia to walk around the container. 'First, it's yellow, which is an unusual container colour. Shipping containers around the world are generally white, green, orange or brown, but rarely yellow. Second, you can see a unique serial number in preparation for this shipment, painted on every side except the bottom. This one is OS WT 780022-3. OS stands for Oriental Shipping. Third, to help with identification my men will paint a large black symbol on every side.'

Mohammad showed Dalia the serial numbers, which consisted of a series of letters and numbers painted three centimetres high, all black on a small patch of white background.

'Surely a symbol would attract attention?' enquired Dalia.

'No. It's common for containers to have permanent or temporary markings on them, and also a lot of graffiti. It's simply a question of choosing a unique symbol.'

'Then I would like a crescent moon on each side, in the top right-hand corner of each side, like this.' Dalia traced a crescent moon with her finger on the container. 'Can you do that?'

'Of course,' Mohammad assured her. 'It will be done immediately we have reloaded the pallets.'

Once satisfied with the simple problem of identification, Dalia and the supervisor watched as the repalletising was completed. Eventually, each pallet looked as if it had never been disturbed.

'Wait,' cried Dalia, as the first rebuilt pallet was about to be loaded into the container. Walking over to the pallets, she took the opportunity to examine each one from close up. Satisfied, she eventually waved to the forklift operator to continue. The onlookers watched as the two crucial pallets were loaded on the bottom front row immediately inside the container doors, followed by the two undisturbed pallets that were placed on top, resting on steel separation posts. Unless forewarned, there was no way that a customs official would consider this container of tyres had been tampered with.

Dalia watched as the workers painted the crescent moons then tidied up. After inspecting the crescents, one of her own men handed her a dark-green holdall that contained a payoff of half a million Pakistani rupees. She immediately handed it to Mohammad and without comment walked back to the nearby van. Taking the bag, Mohammad did not dare to insult the woman by counting it in her presence. Instead he and his colleagues walked towards the giant entrance doors. Satisfied that all was in order, Dalia ordered her men back into the van and after briefly stopping at the entrance door which the workers opened, they left the factory.

As the white Mercedes transit van sped away with its six occupants, the four joyous workers glanced around for any trace of their activity and then returned to the manufacturing zone to begin their night-time duties.

Usually the four-man night team finished by midnight, but tonight their routine duties took them until 2 a.m. to complete. The two night guards noticed their late departure and smiled to themselves as they each fondled their reward.

Another man also watched their departure, but he was in no mood for smiling. He lit a fresh cigarette from the stub of his last.

Chapter 8

December 10th, Z – 143 Days
Buenos Aires, Argentina

As celebrated in tango song, Buenos Aires was the 'Queen of Cities'. Perhaps its secret lay in having everything from culture, architecture, art and music to non-stop nightlife. Together, the complex mix of geography, immigration and European influences combined to form a sophisticated and cosmopolitan city.

Buenos Aires was born mimicking Europe, copying characteristics from London, Madrid and Paris. To many tastes, this cocktail of styles turned out better than the originals. However, Buenos Aires also created its own heritage, adding to the mix some sultry tangos, ubiquitous quaint cafés known as *colectivos* and, most of all, the flair its residents, the proud *porteños*, had for interacting with each other in a myriad of restaurants, coffee houses, discotheques and bars, open until the early hours of the morning. The multiethnic friendly atmosphere of this city largely made up of Spanish, English, French and Italian immigrants, and indigenous native Indians made it the best place on earth to go unnoticed and unrecognised.

Among all the century's dictatorships in Argentina, that of 1976 was the worst. Jorge Videla, President and the Supreme Commander of the Armed Forces, had devised a plan to combat the subversive elements of the population, specifically the extreme left and right of the political spectrum. Under his direction, the Armed Forces created a sort of terrorist state and used it to control and persecute political dissidents. They kidnapped, assassinated and robbed, and left thirty thousand people missing. Even now, despite the huge inroads that had been made towards democracy since the overthrow of the Junta in 1983, there was an underlying legacy of wariness and distrust of authority as relatives still searched for their loved ones. Malik believed that this legacy could only help the anonymity of his terrorist cell and its activities.

Until 1885 the port of Buenos Aires, known locally as 'El Puerto', suffered from unchecked deposits of mud brought downstream. It could not offer sufficient depth of water for vessels of even moderate draught and these had been required to anchor many miles offshore. New docks in the district of Retiro one mile west of the city attracted vessels of the highest tonnage from across the world, with vessels of lower tonnage anchoring at the smaller, modern port of Boca del Riachuelo, which lay one mile east of the city. The original port of Puerto Madero in the city centre was left for the use of pleasure boats and ferries.

Malik met with Mohammad Rafiq Jamali in a coffeehouse on Caminito, a street in the La Boca district of the city. It was the middle of the morning. A mobster from the unruly region of Argentina at the convergence of the Argentina–Brazil–Paraguay borders, Jamali was principally a thug who thrived from money laundering, smuggling, and arms and drugs trafficking. When it suited him he pronounced himself as an Islamic fundamentalist and Argentina's leader of Islamic militants. His last involvement in a terrorist attack, for which he had been handsomely paid by Hizballah, was the bombing of the Israeli Embassy in Buenos Aires on 17th March 1992 where a huge blast destroyed it, killing 29 people and wounding another 242.

Jamali had flown down this morning, flattered to be acknowledged by the Network and keen to be involved in a significant operation surely worth many dollars. Inferences made during his telephone conversation with Malik the night before had satisfied his caution and raised his curiosity and expectations.

It was the height of the summer in Buenos Aires, and the temperature inside the coffee house was already 30 degrees Celsius. A suffocating north wind, humid and warm, seemed to fill the atmosphere with electricity.

'This wind never lasts more than three days,' Jamali groaned, suffering, like everyone else, from the debilitating heat. 'It generally changes to a south-east wind, bringing rain or storm. Then the Pampero comes.' The Pampero was a cold, dry south-west wind. Highly charged with ozone, it purified the sky and helped lift the polluted atmosphere of the thickly populated sections of the city. This healthy wind had provided the city with its name – Buenos Aires, or 'Good Airs'.

After thirty minutes of idle conversation when each man studied the other, both concluded it was time to for business. Malik had decided that, for the right fee, he could trust the man, and Jamali had no concerns other than to be paid handsomely.

'I understand you have many contacts in the city?' Malik inquired.

'Indeed amigo, I have many friends and colleagues but mostly relations. Perhaps even a few I do not know about,' chuckled Jamali.

'Do you know any real estate agents?'

Jamali shrugged. 'Realtors? Lots, but the most trustworthy is one of my daughters. She works in an office off Plaza de Mayo, in a small but influential firm.'

'I require you to rent a factory short-term, with a view to purchase. One of the vacant meat-processing factories down by the docks in Boca del Riachuelo. It is called Iguazú after the waterfalls, I believe. It is opposite a large boatyard on the Avenue Don Pedro de Mendoza and is advertised as being available for hire short- or long-term, as well as for sale.'

The La Boca district of Buenos Aires was officially incorporated into the city in 1998 and had been a section of the busy coastline that had fallen into disrepair. Today, luxurious restaurants, offices and movie theatres were gradually replacing ancient silos and disused warehouses, as they had already done in the trendy district of Puerto Madero. La Boca was slowly being converted into one of the most exclusive districts of the city.

'I want you to arrange for the leasing of this factory for two months, after which it will be left as we found it.'

Jamali was silent a moment. 'Does it have to be this one?' He knew better than to ask what for.

'Yes. I have made some initial enquiries with the agent. You must visit the factory and confirm that it is as they say. You will be leasing the factory in order that you can conduct enquiries for redevelopment prior to a full purchase agreement. After two months you will pull out.'

'And that's all?' Jamali slumped back in his chair and sighed, disappointed he was to be nothing more than a broker.

'To complete this and other minor requirements, you will be

rewarded with one million US dollars.' Malik was prepared to pay two million but instinct told him too much would cause unwelcome interest.

Jamali hesitated for a second, unsure he had heard correctly. 'A million US dollars,' he whispered, immediately before his face burst into a brilliant smile preventing further speech.

'You will pay all the overheads,' Malik added. 'The rent is just thirty thousand pesos a month. I will require all the usual services including water, sewerage and electricity. You will arrange payment of all of these bills.'

'What about a telephone?' enquired Jamali.

'Not required.'

'And when do you wish to have access?' Jamali assumed it would be soon, and was already considering what his daughter must do to secure the agreement.

'Seven days from now.'

'That is very soon,' replied Jamali ruefully. 'Is there anything I need to know that may cause me difficulties?'

Malik understood the question but did not object. He would have enquired too.

'There's nothing that concerns you, though I want you to provide sufficient guards for the site while I am occupying it. The main threat is from the usual hordes of unsuspecting thieves, vagrants and vandals that roam the Boca del Riachuelo docks. I do not wish anyone to stumble across what we are doing and, if anyone should, they're to be terminated immediately and disposed of quietly. The guards must be wise, trustworthy and lethal, and have no interest in my business inside the building.'

'I understand my friend. I will employ my best men. They will welcome a trip down to the city.' Jamali gave a reassuring smile.

'I trust the reward is sufficient?'

'Of course, I serve Allah.'

Malik and Jamali finalised the details over beefsteaks before parting. Malik took one of the city's black-and-yellow cabs to Avenue Almirante Brown, a busy shopping street that connected the city directly to Boca del Riachuelo and the Iguazú factory. On leaving the taxi he visited many shops and noted the items that he and Dalia needed to purchase as they prepared to move into the factory. Taking a left turn at the bottom of the avenue, he walked towards the old factory once more and in doing so he arrived at his destination, the boatyard where the ocean-going yacht he intended to buy lay moored.

Chapter 9

December 10th, Z - 143 Days
Karachi, Pakistan

Karachi was a city of thieves and Zaffar Khan, the assassin, was the prince amongst them. He often complained to Arif that he barely made a profit after he had paid off the police and other contacts, though on this occasion he had not complained to his cousin, the chief shipping supervisor, as there was no one to pay but himself and his small team of hit men.

It was after midnight when his untraceable cell phone rang. After taking the call from Arif, he stubbed out his cigarette and slipped out of the apartment, followed by three armed killers, each a heavy-set, Urdu-speaking refugee. Karachi was not safe at night, not even for an assassin with connections, so his colleagues had two roles; they were to assist with the hit and provide him with protection, with their own lives if necessary.

Thirty minutes later Zaffar watched from outside the factory entrance as four factory workers climbed into a distinctive red Toyota van. The worker entering the front passenger door, probably the leader, was grasping a dark-green holdall that Zaffar knew contained a pay-off of half a million rupees. If all went well that was to be their bonus payment. Zaffar and two of his men were sitting in a battered but reliable long wheelbase Land Rover, a common enough vehicle in Karachi. Its current colour was midnight blue which suited their purpose. One of the men had busied himself earlier in the day by finding an appropriate vehicle before paying a youth to steal it. Later, the same killer had fixed a false pair of licence plates to the Land Rover before giving it a rigorous test drive.

The fourth killer was one kilometre away, sitting behind the wheel of a stolen black four-door BMW saloon, also with false plates, as he waited for instructions via another untraceable cell phone.

'That's them, let's go,' Zaffar ordered eagerly.

The driver of the Land Rover, the same man who had earlier switched the plates and accustomed himself with the vehicle, pulled out some way behind the van. There was little need for conversation as they were all familiar with the simple operation.

En route, Zaffar considered the hit and the unlikelihood of any response from the authorities. Violence in Pakistan's largest city had seldom been out of the headlines in recent years. The major cause was sectarian violence between the majority Sunni and the minority Shi'ite Muslims that regularly reared its ugly head. Only yesterday nine Sunni Muslims had been gunned down on Karachi's Shara-e-Faisal Boulevard. This was believed to be in reprisal to a suicide bombing of a Shi'ite Muslim mosque in Karachi's business district two days before, in which fifteen people died and over one hundred people were hurt, twenty-five of them critically. Only last month, an attack on a Shi'ite mosque in Quetta had left fifty people dead. In the last four weeks there had also been a shoot-out between police and suspected al-Qa'eda terrorists, two bomb attacks on foreigners, an alleged attempt on the life of the nation's president and the kidnapping and killing of a British journalist and a United States Embassy official. There were also a huge number of local murders but such was the competition these failed to make the headlines. Accurate numbers of kidnappings, carjackings and armed robberies were never established. Zaffar knew that if this hit went as planned, there would be no serious attempt by the authorities to find the person or persons responsible for the very reason that most residents of Karachi turned to the criminal groups or mafias for their defence and protection, including the police officers.

As they journeyed through the outer suburbs, Zaffar maintained contact on an open cell-phone line with the driver of the stolen BMW saloon. Thanks to their intimate knowledge of Karachi and only the occasional glance at a street map by Zaffar, each knew precisely where they where.

The BMW had been shadowing the van and Land Rover on a parallel road for several minutes when Zaffar finally saw an opportune moment for the attack. Zaffar hissed the final command to the BMW driver before terminating the call. 'The arsehole has just stopped at a fucking light. Turn next right and you'll find the bastard fifty meters up on the right. Stop them from moving, now.'

The narrow thoroughfare was deserted. As they waited behind the white van at the red light, Zaffar saw the BMW approaching the junction from his left. The three occupants of the Land Rover immediately pulled down their black facemasks. As the BMW came to a sudden and unexpected halt directly in front of the van, boxing it in, he barked the order to attack. All three occupants of the stolen Land Rover jumped out. One dashed to the front of the van and sprayed the two occupants through its windscreen with three magazines from an old but fully functional US-made Ingram 9-mm sub-machine gun. At a thousand rounds per minute and only thirty-two rounds per magazine, it was over in seconds and the driver and passenger were dead. Meanwhile, Zaffar and the second killer, both armed with similar assault weapons, sprayed into the van's thin skin from the side of the road. After emptying his third magazine, Zaffar dropped a grenade through a shattered window in the left rear door and ran for cover behind the Land Rover.

After the loud explosion that was magnified by the narrow street, Zaffar returned to the heavily peppered van and pulled open the front passenger door. Retrieving the holdall from the passenger foot well, he rushed to join his colleagues in the BMW.

Glancing over his shoulder through the rear window as they sped away into the night, Zaffar considered that the hit had taken less than a minute. Soon he lost sight of what remained of the van and he turned to face forward. What sign of life he saw in the vicinity did not trouble him.

Forty minutes later, having abandoned the BMW, torched it and driven home in his own late model Mercedes, Zaffar and the three armed killers re-entered his apartment.

Still laughing, they found the bonus payment intact.

Chapter 10

December 11th, Z – 142 Days
Buenos Aires, Argentina

Before Malik entered the boatyard, he stopped, looked over to his left, and saw the old factory beyond a six-foot-high brick perimeter wall topped with security barbs. The wall gave way to a vehicular entrance that was barred by a pair of tall, arched, wrought-iron gates, also topped with security barbs. The gates were closed, one joined firmly to the other with a large chain that was locked together in the centre. The disused meat-processing factory looked dirty and desolate, but with the exception of graffiti on the outside of the brick wall and over the old factory sign to the right of the main gate, the buildings had not been vandalised and the factory appeared secure. This was more than could be said for many of the other vacant industrial sites in this run-down district. Malik's eyes were drawn to the sign and the name 'Iguazú' and the faint pictures of waterfalls either side of the name. Once again he wondered what, if any, the connection was between the historic falls and the factory. Satisfied with his decision to lease this factory, Malik continued walking to the boatyard that was approachable from land only by passing under the six-lane Autopista Dardo Rocha flyover. As he drew out of the shadow of the overpass, Malik came to the high chain-link security fence that secured the boatyard. He found the entrance twenty metres further down the asphalt road.

The Marina Riachuelo, owned by the world-famous yachtsman Carlos Frer, was a tranquil oasis in the desolate docklands of the Boca del Riachuelo. Malik saw that the large boatyard retained a marketing advantage, as it commanded a prime marina location on the Río de la Plata, and as the development of the La Boca district of Buenos Aires continued along similar lines to Puerto Madero, so the land value of this tranquil dockyard would rise.

The marina was able to accommodate boats both large and small and provided the closest permanent moorings to downtown Buenos Aires.

At the entrance Malik found a high security access system preventing him from entering the boatyard so he used the intercom and waited. With a scheduled appointment, it was not long before a tall, lean and deeply tanned man looking charmingly dishevelled in a red jacket and dark blue flannel trousers – clothing that Malik assumed to be a standard employees' uniform – approached the gate. The man possessed the leathery look of someone who lived his life on the open sea.

Earlier that morning Malik had spent three hours in an Internet café, where he had sent a number of emails to London and Pakistan, before using the World Wide Web to search for a suitable boat. By chance, he had found a promising selection at the Marina Riachuelo opposite the old factory and one telephone call assured him that he would receive a warm welcome at the marina when he arrived that afternoon.

The approaching man was Carlos Frer. What Carlos saw was a polished and businesslike Englishman in his mid-forties, whose handsome face had enjoyed years of sun and sea air. With an unmistakeable English accent, Sean Kent could not have been anyone else. Carlos had no knowledge that Malik was using the identity of a long-forgotten Briton held on a life sentence in a Turkish jail; a cover that had cost no more than a few clothes, some furnishings and an unhealthy supply of cigarettes.

Scenting a wealthy buyer, Carlos intended that Malik receive VIP treatment, treatment that he had refined for buyers and never taken for granted. Before Malik's arrival every detail of his visit had been hastily considered, albeit based on very little information. Desks were cleared, boats washed and staff were briefed and prepared accordingly. Nothing had been taken for granted. Carlos swiftly opened a pedestrian gate and took Malik's hand.

'Please come, in Señor Kent. Welcome to Marina Riachuelo,' Carlos offered politely.

It was a busy and colourful marina fit for a picture-postcard. In the middle of the Argentine summer, the marina was full with a huge variety of boats whose hulls provided a white brightness that would have stung his eyes if Malik had not been wearing dark sunglasses. The forest of yacht masts were silhouetted against the lush green trees of the Reserva Ecológica that lay in the distance on the far side of the Antepuerto Canal. This wide canal was the principal sea lane for those wishing to reach the Río de la Plata from Puerto Madero and the docks of Boca del Riachuelo, and Malik noticed how the wash from numerous passing vessels caused the tangle of masts to bob frantically up and down. He also saw that, despite the sailing season, many boats were raised on stilts propped on the sun-baked slopes of the marina, and that people who he assumed were tradesmen or owners were maintaining their boats. Malik could hear the persistent calling of gulls and the relentless chiming of halliards as each rope repeatedly flapped against its accompanying alloy or wooden mast in the light breeze. He could not help but consider that this picture represented the perfect life for Karima and himself. Malik envied Carlos.

Carlos ushered Malik into a large brick building that looked no more than three years old. It housed the marina offices, a clubhouse with bar and a sizeable restaurant whose balcony overlooked the marina. There was a small, busy shop inside which sold everything from newspapers and milk to vital sea faring victuals. They passed an unmanned and brightly polished wooden reception desk, above which hung a large brass bell, then through a frosted glass door labelled 'Staff Only'. Carlos led Malik through a small open-plan office that consisted of eight desks and two large designer work stations to a room labelled 'Presentation Room'. As they entered Malik was introduced to two senior employees, the chief designer and chief mechanic.

After receiving a cup of coffee, a glass of water and a fistful of brochures, Carlos asked for the lights to be dimmed and he began a short, tailored presentation. 'Welcome to Marina Riachuelo, Señor Kent, and thank you for allowing us the opportunity to address you, and show you the boats we have for sale. We believe that any one of six boats that we currently have for sale will meet or surpass your wishes. I hope that covering all the facts and figures in the comfort of this air-conditioned suite before inspecting the boats will help you narrow down the choices. This will allow you to spend more time inspecting your preferred options when we go outside. If there is anything at all that we can do to assist you during your visit, please do not hesitate to ask any one of us.'

'Thank you, Carlos. It states on your website that potential buyers can take the option of a free charter for up to a day to help finalise their decision. If I choose a boat today, which I believe I may, then I would like to reserve it pending that charter. My wife must help me choose, you understand.'

Scenting a sale, Carlos readily agreed. 'Of course that is entirely satisfactory. To reserve the boat there is a small fee or you can leave a deposit, but it would be a pleasure for me personally to take you on a day charter. First, I would like to take you through some information on my marina, then payment and insurance options, then registration issues, followed by the specification of each of the six boats I believe will suit you.'

'Please leave the payment options. I will be making an immediate payment in full.'

'Thank you,' replied Carlos excitedly. 'That will certainly allow us more time on the boats.'

Malik hoped he had saved at least a few minutes of the lecture. He was tempted to tell Carlos to skip to the specifications but resisted.

'The Marina Riachuelo has forty-five years of experience of offshore sailing and racing, designing, building, selling and equipping sailing and power boats. We are the leading agent in South America for Nautor's Swan, Hallberg Rassy, Catana, and Sunseeker...'

Malik politely listened and watched the presentation, which was, as it happened, very informative. He knew that to take the opportunity of absorbing every possible useful piece of information was vital, for one piece could always make the difference between success and failure. On a personal level he found the topic extremely informative too. At last Carlos got down to the specifications.

'The first motorboat shown here is the very sleek and modern Azimut 46. Constructed by Marten Marine and launched just one year ago, she has a length of 14.9 metres, width 4.42 metres and draught of one metre. She has two powerful Caterpillar 457-horsepower diesel engines fed by two 900-litre fuel tanks and has a maximum speed of thirty knots. She can cruise at twenty-six knots. She has a flying bridge with full instrumentation, automatic pilot, GPS, plotter, radar, VHF radio, satellite TV and satellite telephone. Inside she has air conditioning, a desalinising water purifier to refill the 400-litre water tank, three cabins...' As Carlos continued, Malik rapidly formed the view that this boat was ideal.

'The cost?' Malik asked, enabling Carlos to draw breath.

'Three hundred and ten thousand US dollars, including one year's insurance and one year's free mooring here at the Marina Riachuelo. The insurance and mooring applies to all the boats sold through this boatyard.'

'It's a possibility,' added Malik helpfully.

Carlos quickly continued. 'The second motorboat shown here is a fine Crucero Arax 45. Designed by Pagliettini and constructed two years ago, she has had only 250 hours of use. She has a length of 13.8 metres, width of 4.3 metres and draught of one metre. She has two Cummings 370-horsepower diesel engines fed by four, 400-litre fuel tanks and has a maximum speed of thirty knots. She can cruise at twenty-two knots. She, too, has a flying bridge, automatic pilot, GPS, plotter, VHF radio, satellite TV and satellite telephone. Inside she has air conditioning, two staterooms...'

Carlos paused after completing his description of the second boat, so Malik responded respectfully. 'I prefer the first boat so we need not consider this one further.'

Carlos responded with a polite smile and moved on. 'The third motorboat shown here is a smaller but very powerful and sleek Chris Craft Crown 282. She was constructed in the United States ten years ago. She has a length of 9.03 metres, width of 3.05 metres and a draught of 1.25 metres. She has a single Volvo Penta KAD 44 turbo diesel 260 horsepower engine with 175 hours use...'

Malik politely interrupted. 'I would like to purchase a boat that is run-in, but not more than three years old. She is rather small for my needs and I must have twin engines.'

As it would have been a much cheaper option, Carlos was happy to continue. He presented the specifications of the fourth, a Corvette 320 Europa, and fifth boat, a Stevens Viet 1500, but like the second and third, although they were beautiful crafts, neither satisfied Malik. Carlos respected Malik's forthrightness for he had often spent hours with clients who it transpired had no intention of ever purchasing the boats that he had spent hours presenting.

Still confident that he would satisfy all of Malik's requirements with the last boat, Carlos loaded the slide and paused for effect. 'I feel sure you will love the next motorboat Señor Kent, though I say so myself. I have saved the best until last. The boat shown here is a fast, luxurious sports cruiser, the Eastbay 54 Salon Express.'

Malik gazed at the picture before him. He felt himself leaning forward, placing his elbows on his knees for a closer look. This stunning yacht could be the one.

After a long silence, Carlos passed Malik a portfolio then talked through the specification. 'The successful partnership of Grand Banks Yachts and the legendary C. Raymond Hunt modified deep V-hull design guarantees a proven balance of quality construction and incredible smooth ride, performance and reliability. Constructed by Eastbay and launched just one year ago, she has a length of 16.5 metres and a width of 4.9 metres. She has two powerful Caterpillar 34 Sixty E 800-horsepower diesel engines fed by two 2,000-litre fuel tanks. A maximum speed of over thirty knots is expected. She can cruise effortlessly at speeds of up to twenty-seven knots. She has a generous cockpit with engine room access, and like the Azimut 46 she has full instrumentation, automatic pilot, GPS, plotter, radar, VHF radio, satellite TV and satellite telephone. Inside her configuration consists of a galley, three staterooms, a spacious...'

As Malik listened, he concluded that this boat outshone his only other option, the first one, and in every necessary department. As soon as Carlos finished he asked questions. 'What about her draught?'

'My apologies, I believe I missed that. She has a draught of one metre. This model allows for the same safe passage at sea but its special low air draught of 2.8 metres makes it able to pass safely under many low bridges. It's a safe and seaworthy boat for all weathers.'

'The boat is available immediately?'

'Yes, but if you wish, alterations can be made to suit your specific needs. You may wish items to be fitted or refitted. This would require a little time and we would be only too pleased to do so.'

'That may prove convenient. The boat will be here for much of the next month at least. But first I must inspect her, and my wife and I would like to take up the offer of the one-day charter just to be sure.'

'Naturally. Would you like to see the two boats now?'

'I'd like to see the Eastbay, yes. Probably not the Azimut. How much is the Eastbay?'

'Ah. You will understand Señor Kent that there is a waiting list of at least three years for a new boat in this beautiful design. This one is a perfect and proven example, and just a year old. The new price, fully fitted, is seven hundred thousand US dollars. But I can sell this one to you now for half a million.'

'Agreed, providing we like it,' replied Malik immediately. 'I can arrange to wire transfer a ten-per-cent deposit this afternoon, and transfer the remainder of the payment on purchase. Is that acceptable?'

'Perfectly, Señor,' grinned Carlos.

'Then let's go and take a look,' added Malik eagerly.

Carlos and Malik walked down to the marina in the sweltering afternoon sun. The boat was beautiful and combined modern, high performance with classic good looks and world-class craftsmanship. Malik saw her name was *Last Tango* and that she was registered in Buenos Aires. Any doubts he had immediately evaporated as he thought once more of his daughter and how she would love her. As they stepped on board, Carlos stopped speaking and watched patiently from the cockpit as Malik inspected the boat inside and out, marvelling at her beauty.

The beautiful handcrafted teak workmanship began in the sumptuous enclosed salon that provided a full-circle view of the cruising scenery while it protected those on board from the elements. It was the perfect entertainment and living area with ample built-in storage. Although Malik was no expert, it was easy to feel the power of the boat and appreciate the quality of the construction and its refinements. As he opened every cupboard and lid and peered everywhere, he confirmed in his own mind that the boat was perfect for his operational needs. The generous cockpit with engine room access extended the entertainment area outside for sunny-day gatherings and provided room for a breakfast table and chairs. The internal configuration consisted of a down galley, a navigation and dining area, three staterooms, each with double or twin beds, a spacious office and laundry, a bathroom, and a separate lavatory.

Exiting the salon, Malik found Carlos sitting patiently on the shady side of the cockpit.

'Is there anything I can help you with, Señor?' enquired Carlos knowingly.

'Thank you, yes. I'd like to purchase the boat for the asking price but she will require re-registration to London, full annual insurance and any faults rectified that I identify during the trial. I will contact you regarding a suitable date for the day charter but it will be soon.'

'I'm delighted, Señor. Both you and your wife will be very happy with this fine boat. Shall we return to my office and arrange the paperwork and holding deposit?'

As they walked back to the office building, Malik added, 'I plan to cruise the Mediterranean next year with my own crew but I will need a crew to sail her to Gibraltar non-stop for me, one way, leaving sometime in early February. Are you able to arrange a good crew for me?'

Carlos gave Malik a reassuring smile. 'It's my pleasure. I never have a shortage of trustworthy and capable volunteers. We like to pay particular care of the boats we have sold here at the Marina Riachuelo and only recommend the very best crews. My son captained the last delivery to Europe. I'll fix it.'

'Thank you, Carlos,' replied Malik appreciatively.

Later that evening at the Inter Continental Hotel on Moreno Street, situated in the heart of the gaslight district of the Old Town, Malik relaxed in a deep bath. As today's news on CNN spilled from the television next door, he contemplated the ease with which he could disguise two deadly packages on board *Last Tango*.

Chapter 11

December 15th, Z – 138 Days
Karachi, Pakistan

The Café Zoak on Abdullah Haroon Road in central Karachi was getting busier as lunchtime approached. The café's large and colourful canopy that reached over the pavement shielded customers from the bright but cool winter sunlight. Dalia was sitting at a gallery table immediately behind a large window overlooking the pavement, which was littered with planted pots.

The waiter had already mistaken Dalia for a Westerner who was visiting Pakistan on business or perhaps a holiday. As Dalia stirred her latté she glimpsed out of the window at the traffic, and noticed a boy weaving between several cars and motor-rickshaws held up by the nearby traffic lights. He was selling posters of Osama bin Laden and she could not help but smile when she noticed the expression on bin Laden's face. It was ascetic and yet sensual, as he floated above an Afghan mountain range, where an eagle was ripping its claws into an American F-16 jet fighter as if it was some hapless pigeon. She felt her body quiver as she thought of Malik and how they, together, represented that eagle. Whilst this mission did not involve attacking the United States directly, Dalia knew that the Americans were the strategic goal. After 9/11 the Network would not wish to evoke further international sympathy towards Americans by physically attacking the US mainland again in the near future. The terrorist organisation's vision remained the establishment of fundamentalist Islamic states through the defeat of corrupting infidels across the globe, but their immediate goal had changed and was now the alienation of the US from the remainder of the world. Dalia knew that this mission was the spearhead of an effort to remove her most trusted ally, the United Kingdom, from play. Once the US had been marginalised, the Network would return to targeting the US economy through further direct attacks. Weaken the UK and then the US and the remainder of Western civilisation would capitulate.

Her two contacts were due in another ten minutes. While she waited, Dalia returned to reading her *Dawn* newspaper with leading articles about Pakistan's re-entry into the British Commonwealth after its expulsion during the last military coup and other articles about further steps in Europe towards interstate cooperation.

Just as Dalia completed reading the headline news, two men, each lean, fit, tanned and, Dalia estimated, in their late twenties, entered the café. The high-backed cubicles towards the back of the restaurant were secluded and empty, and it was towards these that they strutted. Dalia watched as a waiter immediately took an order for drinks, she assumed, since they had not bothered to study a menu. Out of habit, Dalia swept her eyes across the restaurant and after contenting herself that no one was paying either her or the two men any undue attention, she rose and approached them.

'I'm Dalia,' she said warily in English as she drew close. To her surprise the two men politely stood up, outstretched their hands and introduced themselves in excellent English. Such was their unity and intimacy that Dalia wondered whether they were more than just colleagues.

'This is Hans, and I'm Fritz,' the taller of the two explained warily.

Despite the cool weather, both were dressed in brown ankle boots, white knee-length socks pulled up, tight-fitting khaki shorts and white sleeveless shirts. They had matching tattoos on each of their arms.

'We're Arif's sons,' the shorter of the two announced.

'And I'm his only daughter,' responded Dalia dryly with a stiff smile. They all knew that Arif had no children and that he liked to play the spy game. Dalia took the bench opposite them in the cubicle and ordered another latté, this time with an additional bottle of still water. During some idle conversation Dalia discovered that both the men were experienced crewmen on board BBC *Columbia*, their first time on this ship, and that they had maintained a close and profitable working relationship with Arif for many years.

After her coffee was served Dalia reached in her jacket for a slip of paper. 'The job is tough but you'll be well rewarded,' she said calmly. 'First, you're to ensure that a particular shipping container with a consignment of tyres is loaded safely on board later this week. Here are the container details.' Dalia unfolded the slip of paper and pointed to a hand-drawn sketch of the container that illustrated its distinguishing features and serial number. 'It'll be delivered tomorrow to the container pound at the port, as part of a consignment of twenty-two containers from the Corolla Tyre Company.' I would like regular confirmation on your progress to Buenos Aires, say once a day. My cell phone number is written here.' Again Dalia pointed to the slip of paper. 'En route nothing untoward must happen to the container. It is not to be tampered with, unloaded by accident at Cape Town, and neither is it to be swept overboard. Do I make myself clear?'

The men nodded and smiled as they continued to study her.

Undeterred, Dalia continued. 'The final instalment of your fee will not be paid unless you deliver the container to me intact. As for delivery, it is to be delivered to me at this address in the La Boca district of Buenos Aires.' Once again Dalia pointed to the slip of paper.

'You're to seize the container and its rig as it departs the port and before it reaches its intended destination in Rosario. The sooner you seize the rig, the less time you will have to travel and be involved. The rig will be concealed at the address I've given you only for as long as it takes to unload my shipment. As soon as you arrive at the address, you will help us unload my shipment from the container, a task that should take no more than one hour. We will then resecure the container and you will drive the rig to a place where it can be abandoned.'

'You wish us to make it look like a simple highway robbery?' asked Hans.

'The police are to believe it to be a hijack that was abandoned when the cargo was found to be tyres.'

'Easy enough,' offered Fritz, shrugging his shoulders.

'Will you kill the truck driver?' asked Dalia without emotion, wondering what they intended.

'I think not,' replied Fritz. 'There's no need to eliminate the driver. That may attract undue attention. Better it's left a simple, unprofitable hijacking with no harm done. We will drug him, leaving him to sleep for at least eight hours. That will provide sufficient time.'

'Good. Arif tells me you two are the best and that's what I'm paying for. I know you would not wish to disappoint us. Now you know what's to be achieved you will understand that my people require complete confidentiality. Do you have any questions?' Dalia's meaning was clear, as were her terms.

Hans had one. 'When do we receive payment?'

'I will instruct Arif to pay you half immediately. As soon as you confirm that the rig has been abandoned and the task complete, I'll instruct Arif to pay you the rest.'

'What about customs, here and at Buenos Aires?' Fritz asked.

'The container has been bonded at the factory. The relevant port authorities at each end have been tipped off to concentrate on the crew and passengers for illegal immigrants and several known terrorists. They will ignore this container,' Dalia smiled, 'especially as the supervisor at Buenos Aires is a friend of Arif's.'

The two men appeared satisfied and nodded their acceptance.

'I'd like to visit on board and watch the container being loaded. Can this be arranged?' asked Dalia.

The two men smiled at one another, both thinking how much they would like to entertain Dalia on board. 'It's acceptable to have guests on board,' replied Fritz. 'I'll contact you soon.'

With nothing planned for the afternoon, and with the two men on their final day's shore leave, they remained in the pleasant café for lunch and enjoyed beef shish kebabs and chicken shashlik.

Chapter 12

December 15th, Z – 138 Days
British Embassy, Kabul, Afghanistan

Afghanistan faced daunting challenges after three decades of war, civil strife, years of severe drought, and a shattered infrastructure. Meanwhile, international peacekeeping forces continued to combat insurgency and terrorism, and the leaders of the Islamic State of Afghanistan struggled to maintain a semblance of government. There was the continuing threat from terrorists and mobsters as well as thugs. Attacks against Westerners, soldiers, Afghan government officials and civilians were commonplace and included vehicle bombs, remote-controlled devices and suicide bombs, as well as kidnapping and violent crime. Nowhere was safe. There was also the real danger from the presence of millions of unexploded landmines and other ordnance, most of them uncharted. A significant problem was the feeding, sheltering, medical care and policing of the large proportion of the Afghan population that was unemployed, many of whom were gravitating to the urban areas, particularly Kabul. The rudimentary or non-existent basic services, an army under training, inadequate border patrols and inexperienced and undermanned Afghan security forces all contributed to the lawlessness.

Situated on the Kabul River at an elevation of about eighteen hundred metres Kabul was the capital city of Afghanistan and one of the highest capital cities in the world. The city's population was around one and a half million people, though this was rising rapidly. The nation's chief economic and cultural centre, it had long been considered of strategic importance to Central Asia because of its proximity to the Khyber Pass, an important route through the mountains between Afghanistan and Pakistan for as long as recorded history. The city's industries included textiles, processed food, chemicals and wood products, though many of these were controlled by gangs and not the Government. The Tajiks were the predominant population group of Kabul, but the Pashtuns were an important minority, the Tajiks owning most of the industry. Kabul University had been the country's most important institute of higher education prior to its closure due to war in 1992. The university was now partially reopened and students had returned, though it needed much more reconstruction before it could operate normally and to any real purpose.

Kabul had been occupied by troops of the Soviet Union from 1979 for ten years, but in 1992 the city went through the toughest and most disastrous civil war in its history lasting until 1996. Over fifty thousand people lost their lives during Mujahidin infighting on the streets of Kabul, and the city was effectively destroyed. The city had been under the control of a Taliban government from 1996 but this control ended in late 2001 after a US-led invasion. Eventually the Northern Alliance gained control of the city as the Taliban withdrew from Kabul and retreated southwards. By now, infrastructures such as the roads and the traffic system, the telephone system, electricity, water sanitation, and most buildings were in shambles and total reconstruction was needed to make Kabul a working city again.

Facilities at the British Embassy in Kabul reflected the years of strife, and more permanent reconstruction work had yet to begin. The once vast and proud Colonial-style buildings had been reduced to rubble during the civil war, and little more than the hospital compound remained. The embassy had once been 'one of the finest UK diplomatic residences east of Suez', according to one seasoned diplomat, but that could not be said now. Reconstruction was currently restricted to British Army Engineers building tall, bastion-style protective walls around the entire compound, and the erection of numerous temporary cabins for use as offices and accommodation, known collectively as 'Tin City'. The embassy was now under the routine protection of the British contingent of the NATO-led peacekeeping force.

The British Ambassador was always surprised and appreciative of the ability of her staff to cope, particularly the locals. The fact that the British Embassy was able to provide limited consular and intelligence assistance was a major achievement for which everyone felt justly proud.

Terrorist threats against British nationals were reported on an almost daily basis and in many instances led the embassy to restrict its own staff to essential travel only. In Kabul at least ten soldiers and thirty civilians, indiscriminate of nationality or faith, had been murdered over the last few days alone. The embassy strongly discouraged visitors from travelling to Afghanistan, and to those that did, they advised not to venture outside Kabul where there was no NATO protection. There was also a long list of places in Kabul that foreigners were to avoid, including hotels, restaurants, shops and marketplaces, particularly at night.

It was mid-afternoon when Amir was standing opposite the entrance to the British Embassy compound with an Afghan boy of no more than ten years of age. They quickly agreed a deal and Amir handed the boy a ten-thousand Afghani banknote and a thin envelope. He then watched as the boy ambled across the dusty street towards the two British soldiers who stood in a bunker overlooking the steel doors of the main entrance to the compound.

The boy passed the letter to one of the highly suspicious soldiers then ran away. Amir studied them as the soldier glanced at the envelope before talking briefly to his colleague who was still aiming his rifle in the direction the boy had disappeared. The soldier left the bunker for the compound, returning seconds later to his post. Satisfied, Amir casually walked away, wondering whether Harry would come.

In the temporary administration cabin situated near the compound entrance the clerk dropped the letter into the crude pigeonhole cut in the surface of the reception desk. Another, more junior clerk checked the tray every hour and it was her responsibility to take all mail to the security cabin for clearance before she could deliver it to the recipient. Within an hour, the unsolicited letter, opened and stamped 'Security Cleared', was placed on the desk of the Ambassador's personal assistant, along with four others of a more routine nature. Scanning each letter, the PA took them into the Ambassador's temporary office and left them for her return from a meeting.

The PA, a serving army lieutenant-colonel, told Diane Broughton of the beige letter that had been dropped at the gate that afternoon as she greeted him on her return. Removing her coat in her cabin, she immediately examined the letter. Consisting of just one page, it did not take long for the Ambassador to read and appreciate the contents. Her first move was to place an internal telephone call to her resident MI6 spook.

Within minutes, George Galway, the commercial attaché and resident spook, was in the Ambassador's cabin, sitting on a stackable armchair.

'What do you make of this, George?' enquired the Ambassador, handing over the letter.

George quickly read the letter, which he found was written by hand in good English.

'As you know, ma'am, Harry was my predecessor.'

'Is this Amir a contact of yours?'

'No. During my hand-over Harry informed me that Amir wished to retire. Due to the success of the Allied operations against what we thought was the last of al-Qa'eda and the Taliban, his retirement was considered acceptable. Despite Amir's valuable contribution we did nothing to dissuade him. I recall that Harry once said that Amir, a devout Muslim, roundly condemned terrorism. Would you like me to pull our file on Amir?'

'Yes, later. I remember Amir very well. He was our best informant for many years.'

'The letter feels right,' George offered.

'His credentials were impeccable. Amir's intelligence was always good and helped us flush out many al-Qa'eda and Taliban fugitives hiding among the tribes. The Americans even captured bin Laden's deputy Mohammed Atef, believed to be the architect of the 9/11 attacks on the basis of his intelligence. Sending a note like this isn't untypical of him. If Amir wishes to speak with Harry then I believe it may be important and we must respect it.' The Ambassador thought for a moment. 'It would be good to see Harry again. I must send a message to Sir Michael. He'll want to engage with this immediately. What time is it over there?'

'Eleven-fifteen.'

Opening the bottom left-hand drawer of her desk, the Ambassador removed a message pad and quickly drafted a note before passing it to George.

'That does the trick, don't you think? I've kept it short.'

'You may wish to add that the letter appears genuine and that the original will be sent across immediately for examination.

Also, that the reliability of the information is rated high and that we rate the priority high, too.'

The Ambassador smiled thinly, took back the message pad and scribbled over it again. The spooks always had to have the last word. Harry was just the same.

'How's this?' the Ambassador asked as she handed over the pad for the second time.

All Foreign and Commonwealth Office message pad users were taught to write concise messages, and the Ambassador was no exception. They were easier to encrypt and decrypt, it provided less opportunity for anyone attempting to break the code, and it saved valuable time.

'Fine. Would you like me to transmit this personally then deal with the letter?'

'Please. I'll let Sir Michael know it's on its way.'

'I'll also check Amir's file for any examples of his handwriting that we can forward along with the letter. That will help London to authenticate the letter if need be.'

George rose and as he walked out of the office he heard the Ambassador pick up the handset of her secure telephone and speak to the embassy operator.

Later, George found one example of Amir's handwriting on file. It was a short, faded and apparently hastily written note on a bar receipt marked for 'H', stating he could not wait any longer. It was simply signed 'A'. Someone, probably Harry, had attached a note to the receipt confirming its provenance.

Chapter 13

December 15th, Z – 138 Days
London, England

MI6 was originally part of the Secret Service Bureau, which in 1909 divided to become MI5 and MI6. Under the command of Captain Cumming, or 'C' as he became known, 'Six' took responsibility for all intelligence gathering overseas while 'Five' dealt with security threats within the United Kingdom.

The roles of MI5 and MI6 changed markedly with the end of the Cold War, as the need for counterespionage in the Soviet Union waned. As with the CIA and FBI, the origin of the threat now determined primacy. MI5 was responsible for security threats that originated in the UK, for example in Northern Ireland, against organised crime, illegal immigration and benefit fraud. MI6 was responsible for threats that originated from abroad, including the threat of global terrorism. There was, of course, overlap, but the Joint Intelligence Committee resolved any conflicts.

Sir Michael Jackson CBE, the MI6 Director General and current 'C', received the telephone call at 11:45 a.m. in his car while en route back to MI6 from the Home Office where he had just completed a routine weekly meeting with his superior, the Foreign Secretary. He was accompanied by his deputy, Rosalind Washington, and driven by his personal driver and ex-Special Air Service bodyguard, Tony.

'Sir Michael? It's Merissa.' Merissa was Sir Michael's affable and thoroughly professional personal assistant.

'Go ahead, Merissa.'

'A flash secure fax from Kabul has arrived, designated Top Secret and marked UK Alpha Eyes Only. It's being decrypted now. That should take no more than five minutes. The Ambassador telephoned as well, just a moment ago, to check you were in. I told her you would call back. She was insistent.'

'We're on Millbank approaching Vauxhall Bridge. You'd better postpone my meeting at noon with the department heads. Reschedule for four-thirty. Call the Ambassador and tell her I'll be in contact after I've read her message, about twelve-thirty.'

Completely used to each other's lack of customary farewells, Sir Michael simply replaced the handset and stared at his building coming up on the left.

Every day brought new surprises, Sir Michael pondered, as they sped across Vauxhall Bridge. He caught sight of the Union Jack fluttering on the rooftop balcony outside his office. What was today's he wondered. The minefield that was Afghanistan was capable of exploding at any time, that was for sure. He looked through the car window down at the river, noticing the tide was out, exposing the foreshore of shingle and mud. The river was muddy as usual but not because it was polluted, quite the opposite. Arguably the river was cleaner now than it had been for centuries. It was naturally brown in colour due to the sediment of the estuary and the twice-daily rise and fall of the tide. Sir Michael saw people walking on the foreshore, up the slipway from the river and around the outside of his building along the South Bank walk. Strangely, to see ordinary people doing ordinary things around Vauxhall Cross pleased him. He despised the evil necessity that was the brick walls, the high metallic fencing and tight physical security that surrounded the MI6 building and made him feel he was up to skulduggery. At least the architects had kept the riverside walk open to the public.

'Probably linked to terrorism,' said Rosalind, reading his thoughts accurately as she so often did. Rosalind was a career MI6 officer who had built up considerable experience from the start of her vocation in the early 1980s, well before the collapse of the Soviet Union.

'Perhaps the Ambassador has found out bin Laden's whereabouts. I can think of no better news at the moment,' said Sir Michael optimistically, after a morning of heavy political news.

The MI6 building at 85 Albert Embankment, named Vauxhall Cross, was a most unusual structure for London when construction was completed in the mid 1990s, though the much-needed post-1990s architectural boost in the vast capital city soon saw her toppled from that throne. The contrasting cream-coloured stone and green glass, the sharply graduating floors, the heavy security railings around the outer wall, the revolving steel security gates, and the large numbers of security cameras, all gave the building a sinister appearance. Built over a labyrinth of underground chambers and tunnels, some dating back to Roman times, the building's apparent size was an illusion for the interior incorporated as many sub-surface as super-surface levels.

On reaching the underground car park, the two MI6 leaders left Tony and caught the lift to the sixth floor. Tony had known his boss for seventeen years and would cheerfully give his own life to save that of the ex-SAS commanding officer. His only other responsibility in his working life was the safe-keeping of the dark-blue fully specified Jaguar with soft hide upholstery that purred through the busy London traffic with him at the helm.

Unlike depictions of its ilk in the Hollywood movies, the interior of Vauxhall Cross was a typical corporate structure just like any other modern, largely open-plan office building. More like something out of the Hollywood movies, Sir Michael's spacious office had wood-panelled walls, comfortable soft leather furniture, a large antique desk, and many fine original paintings and artefacts that had been gifted to the State over centuries of empire building and subsequent dismantling. Settling behind his desk, Merissa placed the decoded message in front of Sir Michael before silently leaving the room. Rosalind sank into one of the two leather armchairs facing the desk, and as he read the message she watched his expression harden. She reached over as, without a word, he passed it to her.

Sir Michael considered his next move as Rosalind read the contents. His instinct told him this was a very real threat of global proportions, but years of experience had taught him not to act on impulse. When she raised her eyes he began a verbal assessment of the sparse facts by asking Rosalind, whose uncanny ability to sense trouble was legendary throughout MI6, a simple question. 'Real or phoney?' he asked flatly.

'I say real,' Rosalind fired back, her logical mind already working the possibilities.

'Me too. We've dreaded a nuclear device falling into the hands of terrorists for some time, particularly al-Qa'eda. It looks as

F101: SIGNAL DECRYPTION FORM #0000089756

TOP SECRET

UK ALPHA EYES ONLY

FLASH

Time Sent:	11:40 Zulu	To:	DG MI6
Time Received:	11:43 Zulu	From:	HM Ambassador, Kabul
Time Decoded:	11:51 Zulu		

Start/// At 09:45 Zulu today I received a hand-delivered note marked for my personal attention from 'Amir'. The original note is en route to you. It translates:

'Osama bin Laden has a nuclear bomb and with others he intends to destroy London on the Prophet's Birthday. Peace be upon Him. This is not the intention of peaceful Muslims. I wish to speak with Harry. Allah is Merciful and Compassionate.'

The Prophet Muhammad's birthday is on May 2nd. I assume the note refers to next year. Amir was one of Harry Winchester's informants before they retired, and he trusts Harry. Amir may have stumbled upon important information. I recommend that Harry meet with Amir. Consider him HIGH reliability, a fact supported by Harry? No one else informed save essential staff (Standing Operating Procedure 602). I await your instructions.

This message refers to a HIGH priority task. ///End

Received by: C Anderson

Decoded by: A Griffin

FLASH

UK ALPHA EYES ONLY

TOP SECRET

though the inevitable has happened. I will inform the Minister. It must go no further until the PM has been informed.'

'We will need the Americans,' stated Rosalind matter-of-factly. 'The sooner they are on board the better.' She and Sir Michael had discussed this scenario many times.

'Agreed. The tightest security will be vital. I will recommend to the Minister that we notify the Central Intelligence Agency and of course our own Joint Intelligence Committee. As for leads, there is not a great deal to go on. Your thoughts?'

'There's Amir, who may hold more information, and also the nuclear device and its source. Harry will be needed to revisit Afghanistan and rediscover old times with Amir. The Americans are best positioned to investigate missing nukes.'

'Definitely, he was our operative in Afghanistan for seven years,' Sir Michael sighed. 'He recruited Amir and between them they provided a vast amount of intelligence that helped defeat the Taliban and track down terrorists. He's still our best antiterrorist field operative.'

'Why London, do you suppose?' Rosalind enquired, predicting the answer.

Sir Michael frowned before answering. 'The Minister will ask that. My guess is that al-Qa'eda has found a way to up the stakes, and that they consider London the optimum nuclear target for maximum effect in the West. London's the largest capital city in Europe, the strongest political link between Europe and the US, of huge Western cultural influence, a vast global financial centre, the seat of UK government, and so on. The UK is a key pillar within the UN Security Council and NATO, she has a Special Relationship with the US, and she adds substantial weight to US Middle Eastern and other global policies.' Sir Michael was silent for a moment. His frown deepened and his voice became edgy. 'The terror attacks in London beginning with July 7th will have provided much intelligence about our security and emergency response operations. And unlike 9/11, there was no retribution on the scale of Afghanistan, or Iraq. Christ, that's all just for starters. Just wait until the global strategists in the Foreign Office get hold of this.'

'The Minister or PM must not think we can play this one alone, Michael. And they may want to as soon as the full enormity of such a strike sinks in. The threat alone can destroy the nation.

Since 9/11 the American approach to intelligence gathering has been transformed. It's vital that we tap into the full machinery of the CIA and their Counterterrorist Centre.'

'I wasn't aware it had changed its name again, Rosalind.'

'The third in two years. It's now known as the "CTC". They're in a much stronger position than us to pick up on any leads from the web of terrorist intelligence sources they have. After 9/11 they reorganised disparate intelligence organisations into one centre and procured the state-of-the-art means to capture, analyse and report on information. As you know I visited the centre at Langley three months ago and it's very impressive. It has already become the CIA's biggest outfit and dwarfs our entire intelligence capability. Who knows, they may already be joining the dots on this story.'

'Maybe, but if London is the intended target then we must retain control of our own destiny. Anything else?'

'Our immediate movements?'

'I'll return to the Home Office immediately. Undoubtedly I will spend much of the afternoon at Number Ten "drawing the roadmap". The Prime Minister will probably want to speak to the President today. If so, I'll speak to the Director CIA, Jim Ridge, immediately afterwards. Schedule a meeting for the team, here, for tomorrow afternoon. Let's have ourselves, reps from the CIA, Harry and someone from Five along too. I would also like that boffin who helped with the sunken Russian sub, the one from the Atomic Weapons Establishment at Aldermaston, and, of course, our Deputy Director Intelligence. I'll brief the department heads later this afternoon and request an extraordinary meeting of the JIC to convene before the end of the week.'

As she walked towards the door, Rosalind paused and turned. They both glimpsed the fear in each others' eyes.

'Mike, as you know, Five has recently completed a study into the effects of nuclear explosions at key targets in the UK. I'll request a copy of the findings. I think we should know what this could turn into.'

'I think we can guess,' replied Sir Michael grimly. 'I suspect the work will be more beneficial to the Home Office and their preparations. Neither does the intended target tell us much, or for that matter the timeframe to May 2nd. I suspect the only significant leads are the missing nuke and Amir. The CIA is best placed to follow the nuke, we will follow Amir. Let's hope that he has more information. We have everything covered for now I think, let's speak later.'

'Sure. By the way, will you contact Harry?'

'Yes, I'll call him sometime this afternoon.'

As Rosalind left, Sir Michael buzzed Merissa through his desk intercom and requested his car.

Chapter 14

December 15th, Z – 138 Days
London, England

The Foreign and Commonwealth Office was situated on King Charles Street between Whitehall and St James's Park, and lay parallel to Downing Street. Nearby landmarks included the Houses of Parliament and Big Ben to the south and Trafalgar Square to the north.

The uniformed doorman on duty began to step out into the heavy rain as Tony drew the Jaguar to a halt outside the FCO's main entrance. But Sir Michael helped himself out of the car and quickly entered the building, nodding to the approaching doorman and to the policeman who stood at the entrance, armed with a Heckler and Koch MP5 personal defence weapon.

Construction of the FCO building, the first purpose-built foreign office, was part of an initiative to centralise the disparate major departments of state residing amongst the squalor in the narrow streets and alleys of Whitehall in 1850. The building was completed in 1868 and housed both the Foreign Office and the India Office. Named Scott House after its designer, George Gilbert Scott, the building was designed in the classical style as a kind of drawing room for the nation, with the use of rich decoration to impress foreign visitors. By 1978 successive amalgamations had transformed the offices into the Foreign and Commonwealth Office and by 1997, after extensive restoration and renovation, the entire building formed one interconnected and modernised office block, while at the same time safeguarding historically significant treasures.

Entering the grand hallway, Sir Michael walked across the antique-style mosaic floor, passing another two armed guards. He passed the portrait of George Gilbert Scott that hung above the magnificent chimneypiece, then a statue of a Gurkha soldier by Richard Goulden. He was met with a whispered welcome at the bottom of the Grand Staircase by one of the Minister's personal assistants before ascending the stairs in silence. As always, he glanced around as he passed under the two great ormolu chandeliers and the magnificent murals by Sigismund Goetze depicting the origin, education, development, expansion and triumph of the British Empire leading up to the Covenant of the League of Nations after World War I. Although no stranger to the building, at the top of the staircase he glanced down the first-floor corridor and marvelled as he always did at the classical pillars and stencilled designs by Clayton and Bell on the walls and high ceilings. A Sybil adjuring 'Silence' was painted above the entrance to the Secretary of State's suite adjacent to the Grand Staircase and he felt, as every person did that passed under it, its steadying influence.

The Secretary of State's suite occupied a quadrant that overlooked St James's Park and comprised his own office that included a bathroom, a reception room in which his immediate staff worked, and a waiting room. The office, known as the Oval Room, was formerly the room of the Secretary of State for India from 1868 to 1947. Apart from its restored gilded dome and fine furniture, one of its notable features was a pair of entrance doors, installed, so it is said, so that two visiting princes of equal rank could be received simultaneously without either losing precedence. Sir Michael was ushered through the reception room directly into the Minister's office by way of one of the two doors, the other providing an entrance from the waiting room. He found the elderly and distinguished statesman on his own, standing in the centre of the room.

'I didn't expect you back so quickly,' the Foreign Secretary said, smiling warmly as Sir Michael entered the room. 'Perhaps you would like that drink I offered you earlier?'

'No thank you, Minister, replied Sir Michael gravely. His voice was like ice. 'Regrettably I have a matter of urgent national importance to bring to your attention. It came in as I returned to my office from your weekly meeting this morning.'

The Minister sensed the urgency in Sir Michael's voice and knew instinctively that shocking news was on its way. He tensed. 'Please, sit down Michael.'

They both sat down, the Minister behind his beautiful antique desk, crafted over two hundred years ago by Bengalese tribesmen, and Sir Michael in one of two English leather chairs. Above the Minister hung the portraits of the Emperor Napoleon III and the Empress Eugenie, painted by Melincourt and presented to the East India Company in acknowledgement of its contribution to the Paris Exhibition of 1855.

'I believe that our worst fear regarding international terrorism may have arisen, but before I continue you should read this.' He handed over a copy of the fax received from the Ambassador to Afghanistan.

The Minister read the flash signal and noted the Ambassador's 'high reliability' and 'high priority' gradings. Turning pale he croaked, 'God help us. Is there any chance it can be wrong, a hoax?'

'Anything is possible at present,' replied Sir Michael calmly. The intelligence has yet to be verified.'

'We all knew it was only a matter of time before a terrorist organisation like al-Qa'eda or a state such as Iran obtained a nuclear bomb. With the collapse of the Soviet Union and escalation in Third World countries, the security of many of these weapons is perilous. That's why I kept hinting at it despite the accusations of scaremongering in government and in the press. Just in case it actually happens. Jesus Christ, Michael, this could destroy the country.'

'We should inform the Prime Minister,' Sir Michael offered, 'then I must get it verified, with the CIA's help.'

'We must start with the Prime Minister, quite so. This Harry Winchester, is he the spook I remember from Afghanistan?'

'He is, although he retired a year ago to run his father's private investigations firm.'

'A good field spook I recall. Will he rejoin us and talk to this Amir?'

'He was and probably still is our best antiterrorist operative. He understands Islamic terrorism better than anyone I know. Harry will return for something as earth-shattering as this.'

'Six will have the lead, Michael, you can be sure on that. You will need to maximise the resources of the JIC, the Home Office and Five.'

The Minister rose from his chair and walked over, as he often did, to the marble chimneypiece by Michael Rysbrack dating from 1730. The fireplace depicted 'Britannia receiving the Riches of the East'.

'If this threat is real it's going to examine, test and question every antiterrorist plan and initiative that we have raised since 9/11. Goodness, some are not properly established yet, not even funded, never mind tested.'

Before the Minister could launch into his favourite subject, underfunding, Sir Michael continued. 'Perhaps you could visit the Prime Minister this afternoon. I could accompany you if you wish. On the face of it we know the who, what, where, when and how, and that is more than usual, though we await verification. We have at least one good lead too – Amir.'

'Al-Qa'eda, a massive and deadly attack, London, May 2nd, nuclear bomb,' the Minister listed using the five fingers on one hand. 'Jesus, the press will love this, and for six months too. We need some news, Michael, and fast. We must have the information verified immediately, then find that bomb. The impact of just the possibility of a nuclear attack on London will have catastrophic consequences. There are eleven million people in this city and every one of them would have to be evacuated. And what about the bloody stock market? London is the target, but the goal is the irreparable downfall of our nation. That much is obvious.' He paused. 'What was that you said about the CIA?'

'Our chances of success are increased tenfold with them on board. In my opinion that is a useful step we can make with the Prime Minister this afternoon. It would be helpful if he could share the problem with the President and secure cooperation between the CIA and Six. The existence of the threat must be kept very quiet too, for now.'

'Who else can be informed?' asked the Minister.

'This threat must be kept top secret, otherwise my job and for that matter the Home Secretary's will be much harder. Protocol dictates that the Prime Minister, the Cabinet, the Cobra Group, and the Members of the JIC are informed. The Americans will need to be sensitive to the security issue too and we will be at the mercy of their own protocol, but that's a risk we must take. With the exception of Sheila and me, no one must divulge the true nature of this threat to anyone else without my approval.' The Cabinet Office Briefing Room, known as 'Cobra', was essentially an executive committee of the Cabinet, chaired by the

Home Secretary, which commanded the response to terrorist and other major incidents in the UK. Its group included Cabinet ministers, senior military advisors, security experts and senior representatives of the emergency services. Sheila Hamilton was Sir Michael's opposite number, the Director General MI5, although she reported to the Home Secretary.

'Al-Qa'eda may go public with the threat at any time of course, but their modus operandi is to maintain security and claim responsibility after a successful attack.' Sir Michael fell quiet for a moment as he wondered whether there was a new MO. He quickly concluded that there was little benefit to al-Qa'eda in leaking the attack so far in advance through Amir. And in any event, Amir was solid.

The Minister looked up, wondering what Sir Michael was thinking. 'Neither we nor the Home Office can afford to let secrecy prevent us from dealing with this. Courses of action will need to be identified and plans activated. This is huge Michael, as big as it gets. We can only respond if all departments, at all levels know what they are about and are given maximum time to prepare.'

Sir Michael sensed the increasing panic in the Minister's voice. He was not surprised. 'We must work without divulging the significance of this threat any further than we have to. After all it could cause panic on a scale we have never seen before, never mind hamper our counterterrorist operation. Perhaps an antiterrorist exercise scenario on a national scale may be appropriate. In any event, it's time we ran a joint exercise to test the worst case scenario against all our procedures incepted since 9/11 and in the aftermath of July 7th.'

It was the Minister's turn to fall silent and think. The possibility of making preparations under the cover of an exercise, a potentially useful one at that, as opposed to widespread panic throughout London and the nation was reassuring. 'That will keep the Home Secretary busy. But can we find the bomb in time, Michael? It will be like looking for a needle in the proverbial haystack.'

'With the help of the Americans, NATO and one or two others, I believe so.'

The Foreign Secretary telephoned the Prime Minister himself and arranged an immediate appointment, something he had never once had to do in four years of office. After the briefest explanation, the Prime Minister agreed to meet them both in one hour.

'Sir Michael, let's go for a walk around Durbar Court.'

Durbar Court was the Minister's favourite spot for reflection when he needed to think. He also liked his staff to see him occasionally around the building. At the heart of the FCO building, Durbar Court was an architectural masterpiece, this time by Matthew Digby Wyatt. Originally open to the sky, the four sides of the court were surrounded by three storeys of columns and piers that supported arches. The Doric columns and the first-floor Ionic columns were of polished red Peterhead granite, while the top-floor Corinthian columns were of grey Aberdeen granite.

After pacing the pavement and staircase of Greek, Sicilian and Belgian marble for thirty minutes, the two men made their way through the ground floor corridors to the secluded Downing Street entrance.

Chapter 15

December 15th, Z - 138 Days
London, England

Under the stolen identity of Mr Sean Kent of Islington, London, Malik landed at London Heathrow Terminal Four on British Airways Flight 246 from Buenos Aires ten minutes early at 8:20 a.m. Flying business-class, Malik experienced a reasonable night's sleep on the novel fully reclining aircraft seat. He had thought that he might suffer jet lag after losing four hours travelling west through three time zones but the club-class facilities were excellent and he felt fine. After collecting his luggage and clearing customs, he refreshed himself in the BA executive lounge where he shaved and changed into a Western-style business suit, before taking the complimentary breakfast. By 9:15 a.m. he was climbing into one of the waiting black London taxis and heading for central London. Allowing for the heavy traffic, he estimated that he would be at the offices of Company Services International Limited on the Strand one hour early.

At 10:15 a.m. Malik strolled through the revolving doors into the imposing old building on the Strand. A smart brass noticeboard told him that Company Services International Limited took up the entire third floor; it also instructed visitors to report to reception in the foyer. A young receptionist confirmed on a desktop monitor that he was expected before she booked him in and provided him with a security pass that he clipped onto his top outer pocket. Satisfied, the receptionist telephoned his host and invited Malik into a waiting room off the entrance hall. Within two minutes a slim, suited man in his early thirties entered the waiting room and approached the only occupant.

'Mr Kent?'

'That must be me,' Malik replied, smiling as he looked up. He stood and they shook hands.

'Hi. Nice to meet you. How was your flight?' Without waiting for a response, the younger man continued, 'I'm Al Ross, one of the partners. I spoke to you on the phone several days ago after receiving your enquiry. Please, follow me. We're meeting in my office.'

Malik followed the executive through the entrance hall to the elevator. Minutes later they entered a small but well-appointed office on the third and top floor.

Refreshments ordered, Ross informed Malik of his progress. 'It's unfortunate but we've made exhaustive enquiries with little success. You see, even though you stressed that money was no problem, there simply aren't any berths available on the River Thames in London at present for a craft of your specifications. The Thames River Authority has informed us that there's a waiting list of at least ten months, and even that's dependent on whether current tenants wish to renew or not. Public moorings are no use to you as boats are not allowed to stay at any one for longer than twenty-four hours and there is a "no return" time. They manage it a little like car parking in London. The river's estate is very carefully monitored as you might expect.'

Malik's face hardened. 'Let me remind you that whatever the cost I simply must have a permanent mooring for my boat, off the bank if necessary, but somewhere in central London. What about buying a lease or a freehold?'

'Well,' Ross stammered. 'I'd already thought of that and there may be a possibility. I have already discussed it with the senior partner. He's our CEO.'

'And what possibility is that?'

Ross removed his glasses and rubbed his eyes. 'We're currently trying to find a buyer, or more accurately an investor, who's willing to save a small to medium-sized company from bankruptcy. It's currently in receivership and requires investment in the region of one and a half million sterling if it's to survive. The company suffered a catastrophe six years ago when its flagship riverboat sank killing six passengers. Although no fault was attached to the company or its employees for the freak accident, the boat itself was inadequately insured and the company has never recovered. We've been looking for eighteen months for a suitable investor and have just eight days left to find one or the firm goes under. I'm not dealing with this case so I must ask the CEO to join us if you're interested.'

'Does it have a berth?'

'It owns several long-term leases, all in a choice location in the heart of the city.'

'Then let's ask him in.'

Ross rang through to the chief executive's personal assistant, who was already aware of the potential interruption to her boss's ongoing conference. On this occasion the PA had strict instructions to interrupt him and minutes later he entered Ross's office. Introductions were limited to a brief handshake during which the CEO introduced himself as Matthew Collins. Malik immediately evaluated him as an extremely capable CEO who was evidently very experienced in mergers and acquisitions, hostile or otherwise.

'So Al, where have we got to?' asked Collins briskly.

Ross explained what had been discussed.

Looking pleased, Collins continued. 'The company in question was founded over a hundred years ago and is called Thames Cruises Limited. It's a family business that owns four boats, with a fifth, a very expensive replacement, under construction over in Amsterdam. There are twelve full-time employees and double that in casual staff. The company specialises in everything from group charters to a floating restaurant. Here's a brochure detailing their operations.'

Ross passed Malik a glossy brochure.

'Al will also provide you with a summary of the company's accounts over each of the last five years including lists of assets and liabilities, and also the projections. The company has an annual turnover in the region of two million sterling. With immediate investment to the tune of one and a half million sterling, the investor would gain a 49 per cent share of the company that should turn a profit sometime after four years. Projections estimate that it would take twenty years for the original investment to be realised in full. The good news for you, Mr Kent, is that the firm owns the freehold to its shipyard in Gravesend further up the Thames Estuary and it owns what remains of a 999-year lease on the historic Signet Quay and Pier, off Sun Lane in EC4, adjacent to London Bridge on the North Bank. There is adequate mooring there for four riverboats. The oldest one is permanently moored as a floating restaurant. We understand from the Thames Water Authority that your boat could be licensed to moor there if it were registered as part of the company's business.'

Malik thought quickly. While he had several months before the bombs would reach London, there was a great deal of planning to be done, beginning with finalising the two methods of entry into the heart of the city. He wanted one to arrive by boat up the River Thames, and the other to arrive by road. Only one bomb was required but two increased the chances of success. 'When is the new boat due to depart Amsterdam?'

'The instalments are overdue and must be paid up to date,' Collins replied, delighted with the very specific question. 'The final instalment is due by the end of February. She will have completed her trials and should be ready for collection by mid-March. The shipyard is prepared to arrange delivery but that issue has yet to be finalised. If an investor is found now and the procurement of the boat continues, she could be operational on the Thames as early as mid-April.'

Malik looked at each executive and made up his mind. 'Here's the deal. Subject to satisfactory accounts, I'm prepared to invest the necessary amount in this company with only minor conditions.'

Collins looked at Ross, who hastily prepared to take notes.

'First, I've no wish to be involved in the day-to-day running of the company. I want nothing more than to be a board member with common voting rights though I may like to work as a deck hand early on to gain a feel for the company. Other than that I will maintain a hands-off approach. Second, I wish to have direct access to the boat in Amsterdam and to all information necessary to ascertain its true value to the company. I alone will decide its future. Third, I want a permanent berth for my boat whenever I require it, which will be seldom. I trust that you will resolve all issues and draw up the contracts.'

The two executives were stunned. Never had they been gifted a deal so amicably, and so quickly.

Collins found his voice first. 'None of that should be a problem. May I draw up the necessary contracts for, say, Thursday morning? Given the situation the current owner finds himself in, I'm sure that both he and the Receiver will agree to a meeting here on Thursday to finalise terms and sign the contracts. Mr Kent, may I ask, is this a private bid?'

'Yes, of course.'

'Excellent. How can I contact you?'
'Here's my card.'
Collins took the offered card which bore an address in Islington and two telephone numbers.
'You will have better luck using my cell phone,' remarked Malik. He had foreseen the need for credible domiciled addresses in Buenos Aires and London. The Mailman had made the necessary arrangements through his global network of contacts.
Playing out the role, Malik reminded Collins about the summaries of the company accounts. Collins rang through to his PA and asked her to bring them over.
'Will you bring any advisors on Thursday?' asked Ross.
'It's unlikely but I'll let you know. I'm sure that you will both look after my interests admirably. I would like to address any issues right now.'
It took the two executives just one hour to identify every issue they needed to bring the agreement to its eventual conclusion. They even telephoned the Receiver with Malik present, to inform them of the imminent purchase and to obtain preliminary agreement. The conversation with the Receiver had taken twelve minutes and it was clear to Malik that there had been no difficulties. If all went well, Thursday would be no more than a rubber-stamping event.
Later that afternoon Malik checked into the Waldorf Hotel in Covent Garden, changed into casual clothes, then took a taxi down the Embankment to Swan Lane, EC4. He found a large, weather-proofed message board on Signet Quay adjacent to the pier with a winter timetable that informed him that only one leisure cruiser was operating that day. According to the timetable, he had thirty minutes to wait for the next boat. Ordering a cup of coffee at a nearby café, Malik sat on the pier and waited.
It was a cold winter's day in London but at least it was dry. As he embarked, Malik paid his fare and was pleasantly surprised to see that today's riverboat, called *British Master*, was a first-class vessel that was luxuriously appointed. It was a long, sleek boat with multi-purpose twin decks, one sun deck and one lower deck, with high quality furnishings and facilities. The fully upholstered teak-panelled entrance hall, with its polished brass wall uplighters and handrails, made an impressive introduction to anyone boarding *British Master*. Leading off the entrance hall was the exquisitely

fitted lower stateroom, complete with fine-quality carpets, furnishings and fabrics. These set off the leather settees and polished oak tables and chairs. For all-year-round comfort the stateroom was equipped with central heating, air-conditioning and double-glazed windows.

As *British Master* passed under Vauxhall Bridge and by the striking MI6 building on the South Bank, the elderly captain interrupted his own public address commentary and walked about the boat. As he passed, Malik struck up a conversation and asked why such a splendidly appointed boat was used for a typical tourist tour. The captain explained that during the off-peak season all company boats were rotated as others received maintenance, and that it was advantageous to periodically give each boat a run through the winter. Its presence also advertised *British Master*'s primary function, formal or informal party hire. All manner of functions could be hosted, even corporate exhibitions and lectures, all serviced from the 240-volt power supply. Malik took an immediate liking to the amiable old captain and could sense the genuine pride that the man had in the boat.

After the brief conversation came to an end, Malik's thoughts drifted back to the mission and in particular the location of Signet Quay. It was ideal for his needs, and its acquisition, along with the boat in Amsterdam, allowed him to finalise his plan.

Chapter 16

December 15th, Z – 138 Days
London, England

Ten Downing Street stood close to the site of what was once the Palace of Whitehall. The palace was an enormous rambling collection of buildings and gardens confiscated from Cardinal Wolsey by King Henry VIII, whereupon it served as the official residence of the monarch until it was destroyed by fire in 1689. Until the 1860s, Whitehall was far from being the select and salubrious home of central government that it was now. In those days major and minor departments of state rubbed shoulders with livery stables, dressmaking establishments, public houses and cheap lodgings for Irish and Scottish Members of Parliament. Whitehall was a very cramped, squalid and noisy district, the houses unstable from boggy ground caused by underground streams. In the 1860s the buildings on the south side of Downing Street were pulled down to be replaced by the Foreign and Commonwealth Office that now overshadows the modest terrace.

The Foreign Secretary and Sir Michael exited through an infrequently used door on the north side of the FCO building and crossed the quiet street. Downing Street was a cul-de-sac, with its entrance into Whitehall barred by high cast-iron fencing and security gates that were manned by armed police. The very ordinary address and modest terraced façade were deceptive and gave little clue to its real size and grandeur, for the Prime Minister's residence at Number Ten actually consisted of two houses. The house that faced Downing Street was a typical late-seventeenth-century town house. But it was now part of a complicated building that was refronted in the eighteenth century and enlarged in the twentieth century. A corridor joined this house to another that was once a mansion in its own right, with a walled garden and a view across Horse Guards Parade. The two houses were joined in 1732 when the property became an official government residence.

The two men approached the world-famous front entrance and the duty policeman saluted casually with a hand to his helmet before he opened the door. They stepped into the entrance hall and onto its black-and-white chequered marble floor as the great door closed behind them. They waited alone for a few moments in the silence, and Sir Michael looked into the small alcove leading off the entrance hall. This alcove, established by Lady Thatcher as a showcase for modern British sculpture, was used to display drawings or sculptures by Henry Moore, by arrangement with the Henry Moore Foundation. He noted that the present sculpture was the *Reclining Figure*. Meanwhile, the Minister, a connoisseur of fine art, admired the paintings of Horse Guards Parade attributed to John Chapman, a portrait of William Pitt the Elder by William Hoare and a portrait of George Downing, who was widely regarded as a profiteering rogue and who built the front part of the house and the adjoining house at Number Eleven in the seventeenth century.

After several minutes the Prime Minister's private secretary broke the silence as he entered the hall and greeted them, immediately apologising for the delay. He explained that the Prime Minister's visit to a scheduled award ceremony for charity fund-raisers in the Banqueting House across Whitehall had been postponed for an hour to accommodate them, and that it was causing considerable administrative difficulty. The private secretary also mentioned that the Prime Minister was working alone, as was his habit, in the Cabinet Room and he escorted them both in that direction.

The Cabinet Room was separated from the rest of the house by soundproofed double doors. The room was now asymmetrical because in 1796 twelve feet was added to expand it, an extension that required the Corinthian columns at one end to support the wall above. The boat-shaped table that filled the room was introduced by Harold Macmillan and was designed to allow everyone round it to see and hear each other clearly. They found the Prime Minister sitting in his chair in the centre of the room and with his back to the fireplace. Even his chair took on significance in this bizarre building, for when he was not in the room his seat was customarily left at an angle away from the table. There were twenty-three chairs around the table, one for each cabinet member, the same chairs used by Gladstone and Disraeli in the reign of Queen Victoria, and of the set, only the Prime Minister's had arms. The windows at the far end were made of glass, three inches thick, and were a precaution taken after the 1991 terrorist mortar attack that shattered the glass. The current Prime Minister was not alone in using the Cabinet Room as his office. Winston Churchill used the room as an office during World War II, and Harold Wilson and John Major liked to work in there. It was the room most commonly used by Robert Walpole whose studio-copy portrait by Jean-Baptiste van Loo hung over the mantelpiece.

The Prime Minister rose as the Foreign Secretary entered with Sir Michael.

'Good afternoon, Prime Minister,' began the senior of the two visitors. 'I apologise for this interruption but I know that you will want to discuss our reaction to this threat immediately.'

The Prime Minister studied his two visitors with piercing eyes. 'I do, John,' he replied, his voice bristling with resentment, not due to the interruption but the threat and its implications. Leaning across the table, the Prime Minister shook hands with the Minister and Sir Michael before offering them chairs. Facing them both he added, 'I expect our discussions today will only strengthen my resolve against terrorism. Thank you for all your recent briefings, too, they are very informative. As you both know, I see the war against global terror as a new, twenty-first century war that the world is not yet accustomed to, or prepared to deal with. It's very different to the localised state terrorism that we were used to dealing with in Northern Ireland.'

The two visitors sat in chairs directly opposite their leader. The personal secretary took a chair next but one to the Prime Minister and prepared to take a record of this private meeting, a task that was not uncommon.

The Foreign Secretary spoke first. 'Prime Minister, nothing has changed since we briefly spoke on the telephone over an hour ago. This is a copy of the fax from Afghanistan for your office. Sir Michael will take the lead and seek to confirm the threat, and if necessary he will find and disarm the weapon. He is aware that he must use whatever means necessary.'

The Prime Minister interrupted. 'There are no restrictions, Sir

Michael, other than human decency which I leave with you, and the rule of law which you must leave with us. If you must test the law, most of which is entirely unsuited to dealing with global terrorism, then you will want my approval. To make the correct judgements in the fight against the threat of global terrorism we will inevitably stretch, break then remould the boundaries of current understanding. It is vital that both of you understand my approach, my doctrine if you like.'

The Prime Minister glanced over to his private secretary to ensure he was not talking too fast.

'In short, I expect you to do anything necessary to disarm and recover that bomb, Sir Michael, and I mean anything. Under no circumstances, and I mean no circumstances, must this bomb, if it is real, be allowed to detonate in London or anywhere else.'

The Foreign Secretary and Sir Michael relaxed slightly. The Prime Minister was obviously of the same determined mind as themselves.

Taking a deep breath, the Foreign Secretary briefed his leader. 'In order to smuggle a bomb into London it is likely to be small, perhaps even small enough to deliver as a parcel. Even the smallest tactical nuclear bomb of less than a kiloton can destroy an area to a radius of three kilometres, not too mention the effects of radioactive fallout for tens of years. Detonation could destroy London and bring down the nation. Prime Minister, you're aware how easily we believe these weapons can be found on the black market, though it is less easy to maintain and operate them safely and reliably. On the face of it we know the who, what, where, when and how, and that's more than usual.'

'I don't just want the bomb, John. This time I want to throw the war on terror back on them. I want the ringleaders. We're not prepared, lawfully or otherwise to cope with this new phenomenon even though I have informed the House on countless occasions that we are at war. Whatever the constraints, we must deal with this enemy appropriately and protect our country. I want whoever is behind this to be identified and shut down.'

'Our leads are few at the moment. Sir Michael will need support from the US. To begin with, they can help with global terrorist intelligence, and help identify the source of the nuclear bomb.'

'Or key components since we may be looking for an RDD,'

added the Prime Minister. 'It's a tall order of course but we cannot ignore that fact.'

Sir Michael marvelled that the nation's political head had absorbed every related intelligence report from MI6 including those that referred to Radiological Disposal Devices or 'dirty' bombs.

The Foreign Secretary nodded in agreement. 'We believe that the terrorists would need expert scientific support. The Americans are best placed to help here too, by narrowing down the whereabouts of scientists across the world available to support such an attack.'

'There's no way we can tackle this without the Americans,' declared the Prime Minister. 'I will talk to the President. What else is there?' As the Prime Minister finished speaking, he glanced down at the Ambassador's message.

'Our best lead is the leak from Afghanistan, the informer, Amir. Harry Winchester, you may recall, was the MI6 operative who discovered and raised the alarm about the Heathrow bomb scare several years ago, and prevented a catastrophe. He retired last September, and was, and still is, our top counterterrorist operative.

'Then let's welcome him back and send him out there. What else?'

'We will increase our international intelligence effort on bin Laden and al-Qa'eda, shake all the trees, and talk to the usual suspects. Five will question all al-Qa'eda sympathisers in the UK.'

'I don't want a witch hunt, John. It's vital we don't alienate our Muslim community. Our enemy is terrorism, not Islam. Anything else?'

'Indeed. An attack like this requires a large budget. Six will follow this up, probably with the support of the world's leading terrorist financial experts at the FBI in Washington. For now, Prime Minister, that sums up the leads we have to go on.'

'Well, it could be worse. The tip-off could have been anonymous for one thing. What about London as the target? Doesn't that tell us anything?'

'A considerable amount of terrorist threat analysis has been conducted since 9/11, and in particular since July 7th. We will revisit the findings, but I believe the fundamental strategic reasons are clear and lead us nowhere. We're a major Western power and member of the G8, and then there's our involvement with the US in Afghanistan against the Taliban and al-Qa'eda, and then there's Iraq and the sleeping giant, Iran. There's our support of pro-Western Islamic states, the close relationship between ourselves and the US, and our well-publicised intentions to attack and defeat global terrorists at every opportunity. Bin Laden may see an opportunity to create divisions in Europe, particularly between ourselves and the French and Germans, and an opportunity to isolate the US. Frankly, the list is only bound by the human imagination.'

The Prime Minister knew all of this and accepted the futility of his question with a curt nod. 'Bastards. London remains an obvious target. Some of us have been stating as much for years. What can I do?'

'It would be helpful if you would speak with the President this afternoon as you suggest, and enlist the support of the CIA and FBI. Sir Michael would like to contact the Director CIA this afternoon.'

'All right. I will let you know of the outcome.'

'It is also imperative we keep this one quiet for now. If the terrorist cell knew that we were aware of this threat it could drive them further underground. Also, public knowledge at this stage would cause chaos and wide-scale panic, the economy would nosedive and our preparations would be hindered.'

The Prime Minister went pale. He was so focused on the terrorists and the probable nuclear attack that he had not fully considered the more immediate impact at home. 'Since 9/11 we have been under the constant threat of global terrorism, demonstrated by July 7th, so the public are not ignorant of the potential threats. Nonetheless you are right, John. A direct threat of this magnitude, far greater than anything we have ever faced in our history, will cause panic and chaos. We will restrict knowledge to the Cabinet, Cobra and the JIC for now. I'll brief the Cabinet tomorrow and set the ball rolling. It's to remain top secret, with control on Sir Michael. Agreed?'

'Yes, Prime Minister. You might be frank on the security issue with the President too.'

'Hmm,' pondered the nation's leader, 'our response to such a massive threat will require the assistance of a great many people, but I do agree in principle.'

'You may wish to consider forewarning the Home Secretary too. Our preparations for an attack will fall on his shoulders. Perhaps you should consider upping the theme of global action against terrorism in the House as well. It will help lessen the shock later.'

'How on earth can we conceal the truth?' asked the Prime Minister, anxious to prevent an immediate slide into panic and nationwide chaos.

'Sir Michael has a plan for that, Prime Minister; I will let him explain.'

Sir Michael, who so far had said nothing, was prepared. 'Prime Minister, as you know new organisations and many procedures to deal with a cataclysmic threat of this magnitude have been formed or established since 9/11. However, our ability to react to such a devastating scenario remains untested, particularly in London. It's precisely this type of scenario, the worst-case scenario, that we should employ in an exercise to test our reaction. I propose that we prepare ourselves under the cover of an exercise that tests London's preparedness for a nuclear as opposed to a conventional attack, and that while the Cabinet and other essential personnel know the truth, the remainder of the Government and the general public consider it nothing more than a prudent, albeit inconvenient, exercise. If need be, the exercise can be ramped up from command only, to a full training exercise on the ground that includes all the emergency services, the Armed Forces, even Londoners. The exercise can be transformed smoothly into real play, if necessary.'

The Prime Minister thought for a moment, somewhat stunned by the magnitude of the exercise his senior intelligence advisor was proposing. 'I like it. It will serve many purposes and is probably something we should be doing in any event. It will also assist my aim of demonstrating the seriousness and importance of redefining the global response to terrorism. Nuclear warfare involves civilians as much as the military, no matter how small the enemy. No one is safe and everyone must be prepared to play their part to resist attacks such as the one we may now be facing. The only credible way to prepare for an attack of this nature is to engage the entire nation. The Home Secretary will lead the exercise. What about a name?'

'Perhaps, Prime Minister, you could suggest Exercise Rapid

Response and if you order it to turn real, Operation Enduring Freedom.'

The Prime Minister smiled briefly.

'Thanks, Sir Michael. Do either of you have anything else for now?'

The Foreign Secretary suggested the Prime Minister make a similar speech to the one that he proposed to give to the House, at the next NATO summit in a fortnight. The Prime Minister agreed.

'You both have my full confidence as you know. If anything I've said, or anything we've agreed today, concerns you, then please let me know before Tuesday when I will address the House.'

The Prime Minister glanced at his wristwatch. 'Well, I am due at the Banqueting House. My office will put a call through to the President and I'll speak to him the moment I return.'

All four stood up and the Prime Minister walked the two visitors to the front door of Number Ten. The private secretary vanished.

'You must find that bomb in time, gentlemen. John, perhaps you and I could meet later this evening with the Home Secretary to discuss tomorrow's Cabinet Meeting. Fix a time, would you?'

'Certainly, Prime Minister.'

Chapter 17

December 15th, Z – 138 Days
The White House, Washington, DC, USA

The shape of the Oval Office was first introduced by George Washington at his home in Philadelphia. With no one standing at the head or foot, the idea was that official guests to his presidential office were an equal distance from him as he stood in the centre. This oval shaped room became a respected symbol of democracy and over successive years it became a powerful symbol of the American presidency. Years later, its design was incorporated into the president's official office at the White House.

The President of the United States of America returned to the Oval Office in the West Wing of the White House during a luncheon and waited for his secure telephone to ring. He had hosted the British Prime Minister and the UN Secretary General at Camp David only six days ago and had been pleased with the outcome. Between them they had bullied the Secretary General into declaring a review of the United Nations Charter in relation to its current inability to confront the rise in global terrorism. Now, all he knew was that the Prime Minister needed to speak with him personally regarding an urgent matter of global security on a related topic.

The President considered that they were close friends. They had got to know each other well over the last five years and held similar forthright views about tackling global terrorism. He also knew that the Prime Minister's Office would not advise presidential staff that he excuse himself from his commitments to receive the telephone call unless it was a matter of importance. He was due to give a speech on 'Weapons of Mass Destruction Proliferation' to the National Defence University at Fort McNair later that evening, a commitment he was still determined to meet, but it was unfortunate that he had to cut short his luncheon downstairs with the US Top One Hundred Industrialists' Club. Fortunately the Vice President was present and able to hold the fort. He intended to return to wish the influential visitors farewell before they left at 3:30 p.m., but admitted to himself that disappointment at his unscheduled exit before the dessert had been limited, particularly as the numerous informal introductions that had taken place before lunch had been achieved and guests had already had a chance to lobby him. Also, there were no speeches and most of them, including the Vice President, were well on their way to drunkeness.

While the President waited, he dropped into one of the two large four-seat cream sofas that faced into each other in the middle of the room, removed his shoes and wriggled his toes into the newly fitted, freshly smelling and specially designed woollen rug that featured the presidential coat of arms.

The secure phone on his desk rang. The President rose from the sofa, walked behind the solitary desk, answered the call, then sat down in his wood and leather armchair.

'Mr President I have the British Prime Minister on line one,' said his personal assistant.

'Thank you, Joanna.'

After brief pleasantries and several remarks about the recent meeting at Camp David, the Prime Minister cut to the chase.

'MI6 has been informed of a probable terrorist plot to detonate a nuclear bomb in London, possibly on May 2nd next year, the day of the Prophet Muhammad's Birthday. The plot was leaked to our ambassador in Kabul this morning via a letter hand-delivered to the embassy from a credible source. MI6 has yet to verify the information, but we believe it to be highly reliable. I do not need to tell you that the impact for London is cataclysmic. Then there is the "ripple" or in this case "wave" effect on the remainder of the country and the rest of the world.'

There was a brief period of silence on the line as the President overcame his shock and evaluated this shattering information, its impact across the world and on his own nation and his policies. His heart reached out to the British Prime Minister, understanding his anguish. 'Damn it, any attack on London is an attack on the free world and will have ramifications for us all. NATO will support the United Kingdom. It's a clear Article Five violation. You and I both know the UN will pontificate. We've been preaching for global action to defend itself against this type of threat since the mid-nineties.'

'Perhaps now people will sit up and listen.'

'They should've done after 9/11. Thank God you found out. Is it for real?'

'We think so. We're sending someone to verify the source.'

'God help us. It was only a matter of time nukes came into play. NATO will set the example and support you on this. Every member knows the target could just as easily be them. In fact every civilised nation has a stake in your defence, but for the time being it will be up to those nations like us in NATO who are prepared to act to prevent the spread of WMD and their use, especially by terrorists and terrorist states. The threat of an explosion in London alone could create a stock market meltdown and rock the world...'

The Prime Minister felt relieved at the President's honest outburst. He had anticipated and hoped for this reaction and he continued to listen respectfully to the most powerful man in the world. He felt like he was listening to his father all those years ago.

'...Hell, they are clever bastards. Recent al-Qa'eda-sponsored attacks on Western oil workers in Saudi Arabia have already had a huge impact on oil prices. Did you know that oil has risen by twenty dollars a barrel in the last four months?'

No reply was expected and none received. This was not the first time this subject had been discussed between them.

'...The unrelenting attacks in Iraq by terrorists linked to al-Qa'eda and insurgents led by extremist clerics continue to cause massive casualties and destruction of property. Imagine what would happen if London was destroyed. Those bastards would not think twice about murdering millions of people. Hell, I would hate to have to evacuate New York. Just imagine.'

'I have to...'

'No doubt the analysts will tell us, but it won't be pretty. Damn it, it makes me so angry. It seems so easy for them to attack us and so difficult for us to seek out and destroy them. We will do whatever is necessary to help.'

The President was becoming increasingly upset as it dawned on him the full horror should this catastrophic terrorist plot prove successful.

The Prime Minister, who had not enjoyed an alcoholic drink all day, reined in the conversation. 'Time is a big factor. Despite the date of May 2nd next year for the attack, our hunt will begin immediately. The longer our delay the more likely the bomb will find itself implanted in London.'

'It may already be in the city, sleeping,' suggested the President.

'It's possible.' The Prime Minister's stomach turned. 'We think it more likely the leak occurred close to when al-Qa'eda first acquired the nuclear bomb. My highest priority is to verify the source, then find the device and neutralise it. I intend to seek out the perpetrators and take the battle to them if I can by neutralising those responsible, though that must play second fiddle for now.'

'Talk to me about that sometime,' offered the President.

'I will. I was thinking of NATO. The best form of defence against al-Qa'eda is attack. If we don't tackle the leaders making these threats, then even if we find this bomb there will be another, then another. Our informant in Afghanistan, who is highly reliable, points the finger at bin Laden and others. Whoever is involved must be destroyed.'

'You can count on us, independently or through NATO. NATO will come through for you guys though. The only sure way to prevent terrorist attacks is to destroy them in their lair.'

'The Director General MI6, Sir Michael Jackson, will be leading the hunt. We hope you will consider assistance from the CIA and the FBI. In particular he would like access to the vital global terrorist intelligence gathered by your Counterterrorist Centre at the CIA headquarters in Langley. But, this threat must remain top secret, at least until we find and neutralise the bomb. If we fail to keep it secret we will drive the terrorist cell further underground where they can sit back and enjoy a steady escalation of fear and panic over the next five months.'

The President understood. 'You've got it. We'll send a CIA liaison team over. Nations like Libya have gotten the message and renounced their nuclear weapons programmes because we worked together. The nuclear proliferation network of A.Q. Khan, that bastard who sold nuclear secrets to Iran and North Korea, is being dismantled thanks to a joint task force comprising the CIA and your Secret Service. Its top leaders are now out of business for ever. America will not allow terrorists and unlawful regimes to threaten our nation or the world with a damn monkey wrench, never mind a nuclear bomb.'

'Thank you. So we must maximise security.' The Prime Minister did his best to keep the conversation on track. 'Privately I'm not entirely confident that we can respond adequately in the UK to a catastrophic terrorist nuclear attack. If it detonates it will change the face of the country for ever.'

'Focus first on saving lives and leave Sir Michael to his job. Trust me on that, I know.'

'We have emergency disaster plans in place but we've yet to physically test our response to a major terrorist threat of this magnitude, so I intend to. It may mean evacuating London.'

The President detected an air of desperation in the Prime Minister's voice as he mentioned evacuation, but was impressed with the idea and said so. 'That's a bold idea. Exercise and training reduces the fear of the unknown. But don't worry, together we'll find that sucker. Don't worry about security either. It's vital to every civilised country that this is kept under wraps for as long as possible.'

Across the Atlanic Ocean, the Prime Minister's nerves calmed as the President continued.

'I'll need to discuss this with my National Security Council including my National Security Advisor, Director FBI and Director CIA, but that's about it. The latter two will need to inform their teams. The FBI has worked wonders tracking terrorist funds all over the world over the last few years. It has transformed itself into a bureau dedicated to the prevention of future terrorist attacks. They can also advise on the best technologies to bring to bear against WMD threats. Our Department of Homeland Security can help your Home Department too. Just a thought, but you might want to consider advice from our Department of Homeland Security border and port inspectors.'

'That's great. Sir Michael will be asking the CIA for support with identifying missing nuclear weapons or material from anywhere in the world, and also the identification of any nuclear scientists capable of assisting such an attack.'

'Jim Ridge will do whatever he can. The man represents a six thousand strong army. After the success of the A.Q. Khan mission we owe you one. We will help you as much as we can, just ask. You can count on our support, as I know we do yours.'

'Thank you. Sir Michael will contact Jim Ridge within hours.'

'Your Home Department might need some help with qualified personnel technology, and equipment too. They will need everything from medics to comms experts, Geiger counters to medical supplies. Maintaining critical infrastructure will be vital. Need any troops? Believe me, over the last two years every possible type of terrorist scenario has crossed my desk.'

'I might like sight of some of those.'

'I'll have them posted. Let me know what else we can do. If we'd thought that the attacks similar to 9/11 could have happened before they did, hell, we may have prevented the attacks and the loss of so many lives. That's why we've done everything possible since to second guess their next move, everything except practice an evacuation of the Big Apple, that is.'

'I know and thanks again. I'm confident the country will pull together across all walks of life and religions. I'm resolved to evacuate London if necessary.'

The two heads of government continued to talk for another two minutes before hanging up.

After he returned the handset the President leant back and thought hard for several minutes. It was real, he felt it. As he so often did nowadays, he quietly contemplated the implications of this threat on his own, before the National Security Council joined the affray, beginning with who should take the lead for the hunt, the US or the UK. He knew that many of his advisors would want US primacy, regardless of the target. Better to support the British who were equally able and whose country, after all, was the one under direct threat. An American-led blunder that caused the destruction of London with a population of eleven million was unthinkable and he would not allow it. In any event the President prided himself on always playing with a straight bat. The overarching need to bring the world together in order to defeat global terrorism was a re-election battleground, but it was better to achieve this without cutting off his right hand and alienating the British. He also reconsidered the need for secrecy, though not for long. The British leader was right, if this threat was real and was made public now, the hunt would be made infinitely more difficult and the terrorists would manipulate the circumstances by escalating fear and panic in London, with the aftershocks being felt all the world over.

The President punched his intercom. 'Joanna, I would like to see the National Security Advisor and the Director CIA in my office this afternoon regarding an urgent national security issue. If they're out of reach, set up a conference call for 4 p.m. and schedule the face-to-face for early tomorrow. I'll be downstairs at the luncheon until three-fifteen.'

'Yes Mr President.'

The President rose from his chair and returned to the grand dining hall. Many guests were financial supporters to his party and the reason for his personal success. They deserved his attention.

Back in London, the Prime Minister fell back in his office chair and quietly thanked the US President for his unequivocal support. Without the President he would have felt very alone in his struggle against the most catastrophic of terrorist threats, a nuclear attack on his own capital city, eleven million people, the centre of Government and the centre of so many other things. After several minutes of quiet reflection, he telephoned the Foreign Secretary and then Home Secretary.

For both leaders, the war against terror had taken a new turn, and they both knew that regardless of the target, they were in it together.

Chapter 18

December 15th, Z – 138 Days
London, England

The United States and United Kingdom governments shut down the Abdul Qadeer Khan network after a successful joint penetration by the CIA and MI6. A.Q. Khan was the father of the Pakistani nuclear programme and had led an extensive international network from Pakistan for the proliferation of nuclear materials and knowledge. Khan and his associates used a factory in Malaysia to manufacture key parts for centrifuges and purchased other necessary parts through network operatives based in Europe, the Middle East and Africa. Centrifuges were metal tubes which spun uranium hexafluoride gas in order to separate out the uranium 235 which was needed to make a nuclear reaction. Libya, Iran and North Korea were customers of the Khan network and several other countries had expressed an interest in Khan's services. Over several years, the two intelligence services gradually uncovered the network's reach and identified its key experts and agents as well as its financial network.

The Proliferation Security Initiative, or PSI as it became known internationally, was proposed by the US President several years after 9/11. It cemented law enforcement cooperation between willing nations who actively expanded their focus and used Interpol and other mechanisms to pursue terrorists and end their operations. Nations focused on taking practical steps to interdict proliferation shipments of WMD, delivery systems and related materials at sea, in the air or on land.

As a result of the US and UK penetration of the A.Q. Khan network, German and Italian authorities stopped a ship as it was heading for Libya from Pakistan and seized several containers filled with parts for sophisticated centrifuges manufactured at the Malaysia facility. The Government of Pakistan had assured the Americans and British that their country would never again be a source of the proliferation. For the directors of the CIA and MI6 the operation had represented a major victory in the war against terror, as it demonstrated what could be achieved with international cooperation under the PSI.

After meeting on two occasions in the last two months, Sir Michael Jackson and Jim Ridge, the recently appointed Director CIA, had formed a deep respect and common understanding of each other's ability. They had never met socially but such was their growing friendship that this was inevitable.

Merissa had left for home and Sir Michael was sitting at his desk when he received the telephone call from the Foreign Secretary confirming that the Prime Minister had spoken to the President. He heard that the US President had offered his country's full support and that the Government's focus would be squarely on public resilience and preparedness, leaving him to his job. Though he did not like to openly admit it, MI6 desperately needed the support of the CIA and FBI. He also knew that soon they would need the support of a great number of other nations, including those hapless nations that the terrorist leaders were holed up in and from which they occasionally emerged like some kind of global killer virus. But Sir Michael felt satisfied for all in all he had achieved much in the short time since he had read the Ambassador's message.

It was 9:15 p.m. when his private line rang for the second time that evening.

'Jesus, Mike, you don't waste time,' Ridge began, brushing aside any formalities. 'I've just finished a teleconference with the President and the National Security Advisor. We have an NSC meeting at the White House tomorrow morning, and, Mike, I need to find something the President hasn't heard already. By the way, what's this I hear about you getting a knighthood? Do I have to call you Sir now or what? I worked just as hard as you on the Khan case and I know foreigners can be knighted. Oh, and er ... how's the family?'

Sir Michael smiled, not sure where to start. Ridge always liked to play things down, whatever the stakes. 'I'm plain old Mike to you. Julia and the kids are very well, thanks. Foreigners have to work twice as hard for a knighthood. Fix this latest threat for me and I'll write your citation personally and have it endorsed by the biggest hitters in the land. How's your family, and north Virginia?'

'I'll hold you to that. We're all good thanks. I've no idea about north Virginia, I rarely get to step out of Langley and when I do it's into a chopper. Three feet of snow at the moment and it's crazy cold. Now, let's cut to the chase, because despite the rumours I do have a home, and at least another three hours', no, better make that four hours' work ahead of me. I was not banking on a 4 p.m. papal bull from the President; normally they're incoming at breakfast.'

'OK, Jim, what's the President told you?'

'The President called it "the greatest single attack on freedom ever". A reliable source in Afghanistan has informed you that al-Qa'eda plans to detonate a nuclear bomb in London probably on May 2nd, next year. We, that's America, are to provide our full support to the motherland in defeating this threat. We are not to conduct unilateral ops unless there is evidence our homeland is threatened. The CIA is to provide immediate support to MI6 in order to find then neutralise the weapon. He wants the perps found and neutralised too. He means to eradicate this source, Mike, with or without anyone else, though he appears hopeful of NATO. The Department of Homeland Security is to assist your Home Department with national emergency planning and resourcing. Oh, and our friends at the FBI are to assist with any financial ops. In a nutshell that's it, Mike, certainly until I meet with him tomorrow morning.'

'Neutralise?'

'To deactivate the bomb and destroy the enemy, Mike. If they give up or get caught they go to jail. If they fight or evade arrest they get killed. Either way, if we can find them the bad guys are taken out of the picture, permanently.'

'Wherever they may be, Iran perhaps?'

'There is nowhere they can hide, Mike. He's not just referring to the cell, Mike, but the leaders.'

'Good. I'm holding a co-ord conference tomorrow evening here at Vauxhall Cross, 4 p.m. How about sending a liaison officer?'

'I'd like to send two operatives, an int operative for your op centre and a cover operative for the ground team. OK by you?'

Sir Michael hesitated for a moment. It would mean full exposure. 'Sure.'

'They both know their stuff. They're very capable.'

'I don't doubt it.'

'I think we can manage this end, but if you would like to send someone over you'd be welcome. Perhaps you should come and see our latest capabilities for yourself?'

'You're ahead of me.'

Ridge detected distress in Sir Michael's voice. 'We will find the weapon and catch the bastards behind it, Mike. We will not allow this to become our Armageddon, the worst parts of the Bible all rolled into one. I was an official cover operative in Beirut in October 1983 when 241 US soldiers were killed in the Marine compound by a horrific terrorist bombing. We had enough knowledge prior to that bombing to prevent such carnage, though we did not have the ability that we do now to find and interpret the information. Nothing moves nowadays without leaving a trail and with a little piece of luck we can find the right trail. We already have a huge amount of information on al-Qa'eda just waiting for common thread like this to make sense of it all.'

'Thanks. That's a great help.'

'The liaison officer is an intelligence expert called Tim Bernazzani. He's married, aged forty-one. The cover operative is a bright woman called Tess Fulton. She's single, aged thirty-six and has just returned from several years in Damascus. I'll send over their bios this afternoon. I'm sending you our best, Mike.'

'They should both tie up with my PA, Merissa. My field operative is Harry Winchester, single and forty. He's not aware of the op yet.'

'Ha! Not your guy in Afghanistan who discovered the whereabouts of bin Laden not once, but twice, only for the rest of us to give up the bastard?'

'The same. Our contact in Afghanistan was one of his most reliable informants.'

'I thought he'd retired. He came to visit our Counterterrorist Centre about two years ago.'

'I remember.'

'He was a natural int officer, good at picking out the wheat from the chaff. The CTC has improved a lot over the last two years not least because of his advice. It's now my busiest outfit and has 1,100 analysts and clandestine agents. Some 2,500 cables pour in every day from CIA stations all around the world, from the Guantanamo Bay detention facility and from foreign intelligence services that have tips on terrorist activity, including yours. It grinds out five hundred terrorism reports a month 24/7; all distributed across eighty US agencies. Every afternoon I have forty senior officers from the Directorate of Intelligence and Directorate of Operations, a team jokingly called the "Small Group", to my conference room on the seventh floor here at Langley for a grilling on the day's terrorism intelligence. Washington's "A" list is no longer the Georgetown glitterati but the two hundred top officials who get their own copy of the daily Threat Matrix that I prepare for the President. This matrix is a running tab of the terrorism threats the CTC are receiving or investigating. On busy days it can be thirty pages long. The idea is to connect the dots to foil a major new attack such as this. Our scientists are running exotic supercomputer programs and artificial intelligence that help analysts link hundreds of thousands of names, places and bank accounts. We have even sent teams to pick the brains of Hollywood scriptwriters who dream up far-fetched terror spectaculars. When the analysts return to Langley, they comb their databases to see if al-Qa'eda has the capability to carry out such attacks. The bottom line, Mike, is that between us we can stop this barbaric threat to London, and hopefully prevent similar acts from happening elsewhere.'

Sir Michael was considering the CTC. It alone held the same manpower as MI6. 'I take it there's no intelligence that al-Qa'eda has obtained a nuclear bomb, or that he's planning a nuclear attack?'

'Sorry, Mike, we know nothing of it, not yet. We may well have relevant information but we have yet to discover how the dots join together and produce an intelligence picture.'

'The President may ask you that question at the NSC meeting.'

'Maybe, but I doubt it. He wants answers not scapegoats. We will investigate any leads that exist including absent nuclear scientists and missing weapons, then combine them and see if we can create a picture. It will be much easier since we have an idea of what we are looking for. One thing concerns me though. There are more lost nuclear bombs than nations would care to admit to, particularly in Russia. I do not hold out much hope with that.'

'Me neither. But thanks Jim, you're a great help.'

'Unless you have anything else, Mike, I have to brief my team.'

'Not right now, Jim.'

'OK, buddy. Hang in there. And don't forget to keep an eye on your own back yard. The bastards responsible for 9/11 were in the country for months, many on student visas. You know the CIA's unofficial motto?'

'Trust no one.'

'You got it. *Ciao*.'

The line went dead. Sir Michael replaced the receiver and made some notes for his conference tomorrow.

Chapter 19

December 15th, Z – 138 Days
London, England

Oxford Street in the heart of London's West End was buzzing with late-night shoppers ten days before Christmas. The narrow road running down the middle of the street was choked with black taxis crammed with weary passengers and red double-decker buses with steamed-up windows. With no discernible wind on a damp and chilly evening, the light and persistent drizzle of rain fell on those pedestrians unfortunate enough not to have hats or umbrellas. It was a dark and cloudy night above the city, although the glowing street lights, bright street decorations and light cascading from shop frontages lit up the famous street. From far above, the European space satellite Stella Three could easily distinguish London amongst the remainder of the half-world in her vision.

As office workers began their holiday breaks, so the crowds on Oxford Street grew until umbrellas could not be raised without fear of harming a fellow shopper. London was vibrant at this time of year, and despite the discomfort caused by the rain, it was compensated for with the well-stocked shelves, exciting shop displays and heartwarming seasonal decorations. Many shoppers were children, excited by the prospect of meeting Father Christmas but getting increasingly tired as their parents searched for those last few, elusive presents.

It did not matter to the man outside the Oxford Street entrance to Bond Street Underground Station whether the mass of shoppers were commuters or out-of-town shoppers, or even tourists, so long as he sold his ninety-five remaining copies of the *Evening Standard.* His task may have been easier if it had not been raining and the crowd preoccupied with shopping. It did not help that the young man just two metres from him was more vociferous selling hot-roasted chestnuts.

As the newspaper vendor stamped his feet and threw his arms around his back in an attempt to keep warm, he pondered whether he ought to move back to Oxford Circus, although by now a colleague would most likely have taken his previous patch. He listened as two parents, surrounded by excited children, debated over whether they had time to eat before the curtain rose on *Dick Whittington* at the Piccadilly Theatre on Shaftesbury Avenue. The children resolved the issue by pointing out the Burger King restaurant across the street.

Meanwhile, down on the cobbled streets of Petticoat Lane, the annual pre-Christmas evening market was in full swing. Locals and more strangers than was usual flocked to the market to purchase their trees, seasonal decorations and cheaper Christmas gifts. Among the throng the smell of steaming clothes, cigarette smoke, fish and chips, kebabs and Indian takeaway food was intoxicating to all but the most seasoned Londoner. Tramps and beggars, thrown out of central London and its Underground railway by strict by-laws, milled around in their old greatcoats, searching for charity. West Ham United was playing soccer in a local derby against Fulham in an FA Cup replay at Upton Park with kick-off at 8 p.m., and the local pubs that advertised 'The Match Live on Sky, Big Screen' were filling with noisy and excited customers.

London was a multiethnic and multicultural society, but there was no doubt in most minds that 9/11 had caused a wholly unfair but nonetheless deep-rooted suspicion between ethnic groups, particularly between the Christian and Muslim communities. Xenophobia, distrust and suspicion between neighbours were escalating and an influx of forty thousand immigrants over the last ten years added fuel to the fire. Illustrating the depth of feeling, the British National Party had recently won their first ever central government by-election in Bradford East and the comfortable victory had set alarm bells ringing. The losing Labour Party candidate had claimed it was a backlash in response to the illicit dealings of a militant Muslim cleric, but few were fooled.

The main terrorist danger to the United Kingdom and her dependent territories was determined by the Joint Terrorism Analysis Centre to be from al-Qa'eda and affiliated extremist groups. Located in London, the JTAC was the county's equivalent of the US Counterterrorism Centre. It brought together all government departments that assessed and reported terrorist threat intelligence into a single entity.

The JTAC's latest threat assessment concluded that Islamic terror groups aimed to attack Western interests worldwide and also Islamic nations they considered to be corrupted by the West. Despite the many successful operations since 9/11 to destroy the terrorists and remove their capability to conduct attacks, it was known that these groups and others maintained the will and means to mount conventional terrorist operations anywhere in the world. Bin Laden had been making statements publicly, naming UK interests as targets, and encouraging attacks to be carried out against the country with evident success, beginning with the killing of over fifty civilians in London on July 7th. The JTAC habitually reported that al-Qa'eda cells and supporters of affiliated groups were known to be active in the UK and preparing for conventional attacks. There had, of course, also been attacks on UK civilian interests overseas, the most recent at the Consulate in Istanbul. Attacks on British workers in Saudi Arabia were also increasing in intensity, demonstrated by the attacks in Al Khobar that resulted in the death of twenty-four people, mostly Westerners.

In light of the threat picture the public had been advised to remain alert to danger and to report any suspicious activity to the police on the antiterrorist hotline.

The Government had moved to strengthen arrangements for emergency planning and civil protection in the years after 9/11. A new Civil Contingencies Secretariat had been created within the Cabinet Office, bringing together the Home Office's former responsibilities for emergency planning with a new capability at the centre of Government to assess and respond to emergencies as they arose. This horizon-scanning capability had been established within the Cabinet Office to anticipate and prepare for the potential impact of any large-scale terrorist incident. Soon after its creation the Secretariat had published a damning report on the emergency planning arrangements in the UK. The Government responded immediately by instigating a comprehensive review of the country's preparedness and contingency plans to deal with terrorist threats, and this ultimately led to new organisational arrangements with all relevant departments working together, coordinated at the centre with the Home Secretary in overall charge, and to the passing of the Antiterrorism, Crime and Security Act.

The Government's programme of work involved the enhancement of eleven key generic capabilities that allowed the nation to respond to the most demanding emergencies. The Civil Contingencies Secretariat managed this programme and drove the progress of organisations involved in delivering each of the capabilities. They were, central response, essential services, local response, decontamination, site clearance, treatment of infectious diseases, treatment of mass casualties, mass evacuation, identification and assessment, warning–informing–alerting, and dealing with mass fatalities.

Guidance had been published by the Government on decontamination of people following a chemical, biological, radiological or nuclear, or CBRN, incident for use by the emergency services and other responders, and a UK national stockpile of countermeasures was established in strategic locations around the country and included antibiotics, antidotes and respiratory-support equipment.

Resilience Forums had been created in the wake of the 9/11 attacks. These were composed of senior officials representing the main emergency organisations and key sectors within the region. They included police, fire and the ambulance services, key utilities such as water, sewerage, gas and electricity, businesses, health, transport, communications, local authorities and voluntary organisations. The Armed Forces could also be included.

In London, the London Resilience Forum was well established to drive forward the resilience agenda. The Minister for London chaired the forum with the Mayor of London as his deputy. Substantial progress had been made, and plans that included revised pan-London command and control arrangements had been drawn up. The programme of work to enhance the eleven generic resilience capabilities in London, coordinated nationally by the Civil Contingencies Secretariat, remained the core framework through which the Government intended to build resilience across all parts of the country. Work was progressing in London, although inevitably some areas were more advanced than others, not least because of the necessity to keep plans under constant review to enable a more effective response to revised threat assessments.

Regional Resilience Forums had also formed throughout the remainder of the country. Though less advanced than the London

Forum, these teams also took the lead in managing key relationships with local responders, communications with each region's partners, and between themselves, each other, and government. Each of them was generating plans for enhancing the eleven generic resilience capabilities.

The Office of Government Commerce had a dedicated Chemical, Biological, Radiological and Nuclear procurement team in place to ensure economies of scale, assist with equipment interoperability issues, and streamline procedures across the country, and with their limited budgets they had done well. The first responders, the emergency services, whose capability to cope with terrorist threats was the key to minimising loss of life, had received major investment in training and equipment since 9/11. Under the New Dimension programme, 4,400 personal protective suits had been delivered, enabling fire fighters to work effectively in a CBRN environment. Purpose-built decontamination vehicles were coming into operation around the country, and fire fighters were being trained in their use. The rolling training programme for police had seen over five thousand officers trained and equipped in CBRN response. The CBRN Police Training Centre had been established at Winterbourne Gunner in Wiltshire, and it had delivered command training to at least four commanders from every force. Every acute hospital and ambulance service now had a stock of personal protective suits, and each was equipped with mobile decontamination units to allow safe working and decontamination of patients. Over three thousand protective suits had been provided for hospitals and over four thousand for the ambulance service. Of the 360 mobile decontamination units procured, 200 had gone to hospitals and 160 to the ambulance service. These units offered shelter, power and water management systems to National Health Service personnel who were required to decontaminate patients. In addition, a central stockpile of protective suits had been established and agreements had been reached between the blue-light services throughout the country for mutual support in the event of a need for mass decontamination.

The Department of Health had funded measures to counter bio-terrorism and was well ahead in its planning. A country-wide Reserve National Stock of vaccines and antibiotics suitable for the treatment of infectious diseases and specialist equipment had been built up over the past year and now stood ready for immediate deployment. Guidance on handling infectious diseases had been issued throughout the NHS. Vaccine was to be offered to volunteer health-care personnel who were to be able to react quickly and work safely with patients. A similar group of specialist military personnel were also to receive vaccination, and laboratories capable of diagnosing diseases had been identified.

Companies operating Civil Nuclear Installations had always been required to have in place robust, detailed and well-rehearsed plans, as well as adequate resources, for responding to radiological releases. These plans involved the emergency services and local authorities in the surrounding area and were regularly checked by the Nuclear Industries Inspectorate. The arrangements had been enhanced following the Chernobyl disaster in 1986, and again after 9/11.

Communication was a vital element in ensuring that there was the ability to respond to a crisis effectively and rapidly, and once again the Home Office had approached the requirement as efficiently as the limited resources would allow. The department engaged with those upon whom it would have to rely in the event of a major or minor incident. This enabled it to make the best use of expertise, not only from within central government, but also from other organisations and sectors such as the business community and the voluntary sector.

The local response capability was one of the key building blocks of the country's resilience. The Government maintained close contact with local responders, including the Forums, Local Authorities and the emergency services, through formal and informal channels. Action was taken to improve communications with local and regional responders through face-to-face briefings at senior level and by presentations from the Civil Contingency Secretariat at the Emergency Planning College at Easingwold in North Yorkshire.

Fourteen military reaction forces had been identified to support the civil authorities, each comprising up to five hundred reservists. Each reaction force was based on a Territorial Army infantry battalion with support from reserve specialists. Army division and brigade headquarters had also been identified to provide a regional planning, liaison and command and control capability. Each military headquarters worked closely with a Regional Resilience Forum, the emergency services and local authorities.

The British people had been used to living with the threat of terrorism for over thirty years and had, historically, demonstrated commendable resilience and common sense when called upon to respond.

But the probability and sheer scale of a nuclear fission attack on the country's capital posed new challenges of which all but a handful of people were ignorant.

Chapter 20

December 15th, Z - 138 Days
Chertsey, Surrey, England

It was 4 p.m. when Harry returned to his office at Mercury. It was rare that he would take the opportunity for a break from paperwork and make the short walk to his home across the gravel courtyard, preferring instead to finish each day at a reasonable time. However, today the firm's premises were unusually quiet and by 2 p.m. he had felt sluggish and craved fresh air. He had decided to take a six-mile jog rather than work through as he often did. Last night the firm had celebrated Christmas by holding its annual party, always a thoroughly enjoyable night spent eating until it hurt and dancing to exhaustion in an annexe to Harry's favourite pub, the Fox and Hounds off the A30. Harry's father insisted on always having the party midweek; that way everybody attended. Sensibly, most of the staff including his secretary, Tally, and all of the directors, had taken today off and by lunchtime everyone who had inescapable reasons for coming in this morning had also gone home. But Harry had been away from the office on business for the last three days and had felt compelled to come in and clear his urgent work for the attention of others first thing tomorrow. So far today he had got through the paperwork which left only the electronic mail.

Harry returned to his office after his run, set his telephone to the answerphone function then tapped his password into his desktop computer. He sighed as he saw that sixteen emails were red-flagged for urgent attention and that a further twenty-six were labelled as routine. Only one was for his information. He sat back for several seconds and smiled, apart from feeding the ponies at 6 p.m., he had no other commitments today so he should be able to polish these off. He relaxed his posture and enjoyed the fresh feeling that only sustained exercise followed by a hot shower could bring.

Harry's electronic mail box was vetted by Tally so he knew that all emails in front of him required his attention. Like the paper files, if it was red-flagged then it would be truly urgent, which generally meant it was a personnel issue or, more likely, it would cost the firm money. Most emails were from outside the firm; company policy limited the number of internal emails.

It was late when the telephone rang and the button for his home line lit up. Harry picked up the handset and pressed the button.

'Harry Winchester, please,' the voice enquired.

'Speaking.' Instantly recognising who it was, Harry asked, 'Sir Michael?'

'Yes, it's me Harry. How are you?'

'Hangover from the office party last night. You?'

'Good, thanks.'

'So, are we safe or should we be worried?'

There was a moment's silence. Clearly all was not well.

'We need you for an important assignment. It's an emergency, Code Red.'

More silence.

Harry did not need to ask any questions. He instinctively knew Sir Michael meant business. 'Will the Government pay Mercury's business rates?'

Sir Michael, who had not even considered Harry's support as a business-to-business proposition but rather as Harry being re-employed as a public employee, smiled to himself. He would have paid far, far more.

'Full non-public terms naturally. Expenses, insurance, the whole nine yards. Everything, except the pension rights. You'll be one of the Increment.'

The Increment was the nickname given to a section of ex-Special Air Service, ex-paratroopers and other experts in specific fields who conducted ad-hoc work contracted out by MI6. Its members rarely knew one another and conducted active or special ops such as assassinations, coups, black propaganda, or psychological operations known as Psyops. It was nearly always physically dangerous work that could be entirely deniable by the Government.

'That sorry bunch of arses,' Harry laughed. 'What can you tell me?'

'It doesn't get bigger. It's Top Secret, Alpha Eyes Only. What I can tell you now is that we have been made aware of a major terrorist threat. We have to act immediately and you were, still are, our leading terrorist expert. The tip-off came from a reliable source known to you personally. I would have driven over for a face-to-face but the ball began to roll at lunchtime and I have spent the afternoon briefing and planning with the Minister and the PM. I've just finished with Jim Ridge.'

'Americans involved?'

'Up to their necks, but it's our show. An old friend of yours is coming over to join the team, Tim Bernazzani.'

'He's a good man. He was a NOC for a while in Afghanistan. Last saw him at Langley two years ago.' A NOC, pronounced 'knock', was a Non Official Cover operative, essentially an undercover CIA spy who did not enjoy diplomatic immunity, acted alone and was unprotected. Although a CIA employee, if caught he would be ignored, regardless of his fate.

'I have a meeting planned for half past three tomorrow afternoon. Merissa will call you later this afternoon with the details and to arrange a car.'

'You're telling me I'm in?'

'Harry, I covered your back for four years while you were undercover in Afghanistan. Come to think of it, I covered your back after you took on the cushy role of commercial attaché, too. I'm not going to bullshit you. We both know you're the best terrorist operative this country has to offer. You speak fluent Arabic and you're dangerous. Most importantly, you know where the lines are drawn. I don't have the time for you to consider this, Harry. This is more important than any op Six has ever run. Millions can die.'

Harry sat up, sensing the Director General's despair.

'Is there anything I need to bring?'

'No. Merissa will book you somewhere close so you can overnight. You'll need to spend sometime in the dungeons after the meeting. I'll join you, and then we'll have dinner. OK by you?'

The dungeon was an indoor shooting range and bunker deep under Vauxhall Cross.

'Do I have a choice?'

'No one has. Thanks, Harry, see you tomorrow.' The line went dead before Harry had a chance to say goodbye.

Already Harry could feel the undeniable excitement rising within him. He sat back, clasped his hands behind his head and reflected on the conversation. The mission was clearly of vital importance to national security, clear from the razor-sharp edge to Sir Michael's voice. Sir Michael had not been in a position to take no for an answer, not that Harry would have declined anyway. Not only because of his loyalty to his country, but because he could guess the identity of the reliable source and that, too, necessitated his involvement.

Unlike the mundane tasks that Mercury had conducted on behalf of the Government's security departments since his departure from MI6, this mission required his personal involvement. Since Harry's early days in the Special Air Service as a troop leader under the command of Lieutenant-Colonel Mike Jackson, he had always craved for and thrived on adventure. Harry had seen the writing on the wall as his military career gravitated towards a life less demanding of field craft and he had eventually agreed to Jackson's requests and followed him into MI6.

None of the tasks conducted by Mercury for the Government had necessitated any employee to visit Vauxhall Cross or practise their bygone weapons skills and Harry knew that this op represented a new dimension for the firm. He mulled over what Sir Michael had told him and after several minutes he deduced that a major terrorist threat had been uncovered in Afghanistan, and that it was likely to represent a substantial threat against the country and Western interests. He also knew the mission would be dangerous though it would be good to see Amir again.

Harry missed being a field operative. Although he wanted a more stable life as the managing director of his father's firm, and even a family, he knew that he was not ready to settle down. He believed that he could still contribute to both worlds by working for his firm in the Increment.

Just as Harry returned to his few remaining emails, his telephone rang again. It was Merissa.

Chapter 21

December 16th, Z - 137 Days
London, England

Malik passed through the smart revolving doors to the offices of Company Services International Limited at 9:50 a.m. He had reckoned that by the time he had negotiated his way through the building's reception and been escorted to the company's offices on the third floor, it would be 10 a.m. He had intended to be on time to cut out the tedious small talk prior to the conference commencing and also to create an air of anxiety among those waiting. He had considered whether he should take anyone with him for appearances' sake, but decided against it as it increased the risk of being found to be something other than a genuine long-term investor. Several days ago Malik had taken a pleasure cruise on the river vessel *British Master* as a member of the paying public, and yesterday, after an invitation orchestrated by Collins, he had been compelled to visit the boatyard at Gravesend. He had felt he must accept, as any investor would. Despite his reluctance, he had been impressed with what he had seen and had wondered whether the trip would prove useful after all.

Declining to wait in the waiting room offered by the same receptionist he met previously, Malik remained in the hall, knowing that by the time he sat down an escort would appear. He removed his coat and made an appearance of studying the large portrait paintings that hung on the walls and the magnificent fresco on the ceiling. He found no obvious connection between the paintings and any of the companies listed in the building. After three minutes he grew puzzled that no one had arrived to collect him and he walked towards a smart cigarette ash stand. He was about to light a cigarette when he heard the smart tapping on the marble floor of footsteps rapidly approaching him from behind. Turning, he found Collins with an outstretched hand.

'Very good to meet you again, Mr Kent, you're right on time. We're prepared in our boardroom upstairs. If you would like to follow me?'

'With pleasure. Is everything all right?'

'Everything is running smoothly, now. I don't expect any more difficulties.'

Malik did not bother following up the comment but followed Collins to the highly polished elevator, wondering about the cause of the delay. He decided that whatever it was, Collins was pleased that Malik had not been too early, and that the matter had been resolved.

On entering the boardroom Malik was greeted with a group of eighteen people, several of whom he recognised from his previous visit to the company and yesterday's visit to the boatyard. But he had yet to meet the current owner who had absented himself yesterday, and also the staff from the Receiver's office. He decided that he should mention his boat trip at the first opportunity, in case it was considered underhand.

Judging by the thick air and piles of papers already littering the highly polished mahogany table, there had already been a considerable amount of discussion. Malik guessed it had probably been a last gasp effort to find an alternative solution that did not involve selling forty-nine per cent of the family-owned company. Collins led Malik around the boardroom as everyone remained standing, most holding coffee cups. In no apparent order he was introduced to each person including a silver-haired man he recognised as the boat captain from his river trip, who was simply introduced as the 'Captain'. It turned out that the elderly boat captain was the owner, and that he had with him a small army of lawyers and accountants. There were several representatives from the official receiver's office and a handful of staff from Company Services International Limited who were stood by to take a record of proceedings, confirm English company law or provide any immediate redraft to the contract. It seemed to Malik that other than himself, the only people who would actually influence the conference were the Captain, Collins, and the senior representative of the official receiver's office.

After greeting everyone present, Collins poured Malik a coffee.

Sandwiches had materialised but Malik declined these and watched as others quickly devour them. Collins ushered Malik to a seat at the centre of the table and sat beside him. The Captain and his team sat on the opposite side with the Captain facing Malik. Once everyone was settled, Collins, who was chairman, spoke up.

'Ladies and gentlemen we're here to reach agreement over a rescue package for a wonderful company, Thames Cruises Limited. As you all know she fell into receivership just under one year ago. As trustee, the Receiver has confirmed that the company may return to independent management in just one month, rather than face liquidation, if an uncommitted sum of 1.3 million pounds sterling is paid to satisfy creditors. After a detailed analysis of the company, Mr Sean Kent is prepared to pay that sum and invest another two hundred thousand sterling specifically intended to aid the company's re-establishment.'

There were a number of appreciable nods from around the table, several from the other side. After Collins completed his introduction and before he launched into the detail of each agenda item, he asked if the Captain or Malik would like to add anything. The elderly man spoke first.

'Shame I didn't get down to the yard yesterday, one of the crew was sick so I was needed on the river.' He stared directly at Malik, finally recognising him as a passenger on *British Master*. 'I expect you think I'm some old fashioned geezer who doesn't want to see his business leave the family ownership no matter what. Well, you'd be wrong.' The Captain paused to gain his breath, and composure. 'We all know that your investment is critical to us; without it there'll be no Thames Cruises. But I know the market and unless the firm can supply what it demands we'll sink, if you get my meaning. We simply must have *Dutch Master* out of Amsterdam; without her we cannot remain a leading company on the river and turn a profit. She's bespoke built and with her we'll meet the most profitable demand of all - private functions. That's all I have to say.'

'I hope you're right,' said Malik with an agreeable smile. 'You'll be pleased to know that based on the information provided, I too agree *Dutch Master* is important for the future of the company, and that despite the outstanding costs I hope to keep her. Having read your arguments, which I'm inclined to accept, I would now like to see her for myself and meet her manufacturers. If I decide in favour of retaining *Dutch Master* I may even travel over in her from Amsterdam, and learn about the vessel and meet some of the crewmen. However, I must inform you that while I'm in Amsterdam I'll also consider her resale value and balance this against my investment. With a long waiting list for similar orders I'm sure the yard will find her easy to resell.' Malik let the thinly veiled threat hang in the air; any leverage might prove useful later.

The Captain back-pedalled. 'Of course, I understand your concern. She's an expensive vessel but she's worth every penny. She'll work for thirty years, probably longer, and she'll be the pride of London. She looks magnificent in the company livery, don't you think?' He slid a photograph of the vessel across the table to Malik. There could be no doubt in anyone's mind, including Malik's, that *Dutch Master* was a beautiful vessel.

Collins pushed the meeting along. There was sufficient opportunity to cover the necessary contractual and financial issues, but further market analysis and talk of vessel specifications that he thought would lead to sea-dog tales would have to wait.

Malik and the Captain spoke little throughout the remainder of the conference, with remarks confined to providing consent to each issue. Malik was repeatedly required to assure all present that, with the exception of *Dutch Master*'s future, his input would be restricted to that of any other board member, although one with a forty-nine-per-cent stake.

As the conference went on it became clear to Malik that the Captain was not only a practical businessman but a realist whose company had evidently been on a sound footing until the tragic disaster. By the end of the first hour it was obvious to him which of the Captain's team had caused the delay to the conference, as they continued to bicker amongst themselves.

The last agenda item before lunch was 'Investment Schedule'. Collins introduced the item and invited the senior representative of the Receiver to comment. The representative reviewed the payment terms and urgency, but it was Malik that dealt with the item by assuring everyone that as soon as the contracts were signed he would contact his bank and order the necessary wire transfers to the Receiver and to Thames Cruises Limited. The excitement increased as people realised that the necessary investment would be made today, and Collins took the opportunity to adjourn the meeting for lunch.

Several staff fled the room to prepare for the next and final agenda item, 'Contract Endorsement'. Malik was grateful that lunch, which was a cold buffet at one end of the boardroom, was over quickly and that the short period was restricted to light conversation. Towards the end of the lunch break, staff laid copies of the revised contract in front of every place at the conference table.

Collins reconvened the conference, and once everyone had settled down he flicked through the revised contract, page by page, asking for comment. With no disagreements, the parties signed, beginning with the Captain.

Immediately the conference concluded, Malik telephoned his bank and arranged the two transfers. For the Captain, who had dedicated his life to the company his grandfather had formed, it was an enormous relief. And so, too, it was for Malik.

Chapter 22

December 16th, Z – 137 Days
London, England

It was overcast, damp and cold on a late December morning as the Prime Minister peered out of the window from the warmth of his private office in Ten Downing Street. In twenty minutes he was to face what would routinely be the last Cabinet meeting before a three-week recess but which would probably be the most important of his political life. He knew that the Deputy Prime Minister, the Chancellor of the Exchequer and the Secretaries of State for Foreign and Commonwealth Affairs, the Home Department, Environment, Transport and Scotland, Health, Defence, and Trade and Industry had arrived and were already seated in the Cabinet Room. Not until all of the twenty-three ministers were present would he receive a message from the Secretary to the Cabinet notifying him that they were ready.

As the Prime Minister entered the Cabinet Room, the occupants stood up respectfully and an expectant silence pervaded the room. The Secretary to the Cabinet, who had followed the Prime Minister into the room, closed the soundproof double doors behind him. As the Prime Minister sat down, he invited everyone to do the same before noticing through the thick, reinforced glass windows at the far end of the room that snow was now falling. Several ministers helped themselves and others to the refreshments that were placed in the middle of each half of the highly polished oval table. Some opened the new bottle of still Scottish water that had been positioned in front of them. Someone commented on the snowfall.

When he was ready, the Prime Minister began in a solemn voice, befitting the gravity of the situation.

'You are all aware that the agenda has been changed to reflect the emergence of a grave new terrorist threat. Before I begin, I must mention that this subject is classified Top Secret, Alpha Eyes Only. A great many lives could be endangered if the details of this threat were leaked. The Director General MI6 is the Originator Controller.'

The intelligence community traditionally used a marking called ORCON, or Originator Control. This referred to the controlling person that limited and monitored the distribution of intelligence material among carefully vetted people. In this instance, the need-to-know list was limited to the Government's Alpha List.

'I appreciate that you're all fully aware and supportive of my stance against global terrorism and the war against terror. We are all aware of the successes in the war against terror that our security services and Armed Forces have had both abroad and at home since 9/11, although attacks continue, even as I speak, on oil refineries in Saudi Arabia. We are also aware that our resilience to global terrorism has been improved across the country, through initiatives led by the Home Secretary and the Civil Contingencies Secretariat. But we also know that this work, while on schedule, is far from complete and difficult to resource. We know too that a chemical, biological, radiological or nuclear terrorist attack could kill millions of people and prove crippling for the country, perhaps providing a situation from which we as a nation would never fully recover. And finally, we know that it is up to us, the people in this room, to protect our people, our economy and our country. It's against this backdrop that we are meeting today. We're already at war against this threat, a new kind of war that's difficult to define, an asymmetric war that many people have yet to come to terms with, a terrible war that has neither boundaries nor rules.'

The Prime Minister took a sip of water, letting his words hang in the air.

'Within the last forty-eight hours I have received unverified but highly reliable information that a nuclear bomb is to be detonated in London, probably on May 2nd next year. This happens to be the Islamic holy day of Malid al-Nabi, the Prophet Muhammad's Birthday. It's also a bank holiday weekend too. Even if the device has a low yield, it has the potential of killing millions of people, perhaps more than the total number of Britons lost to warfare since records began. It's probable that our hidden enemy has armed himself with the most hideous weapon known to mankind, and such is his means, his ability to blend into our multicultural society, that he has a good chance of using it.'

The Prime Minister locked eyes briefly with each minister before focusing on the Chancellor of the Exchequer sitting opposite.

'Whatever resources are required, whatever degree of mobilisation of the population, whatever the cost, we must prevent him from using it, now and for ever.'

The Prime Minister's eyes moved on to the Foreign Secretary, who took his cue.

'The Prime Minister has asked me to update you on the current situation. In front of you is a red folder marked "Operation Enduring Freedom" and marked "Top Secret". We will add to the folder at successive meetings, with minutes of relevant meetings, and so on. There are blank pages at the rear for personal notes should you need to use them. Please open it and read the top document at Flag A.'

Each person opened their folder and read the copy of the message received by MI6 from Her Majesty's Ambassador to Afghanistan.

'The message was received by MI6 midday yesterday. It's our considered opinion that this is a real threat, though it will be confirmed by Harry Winchester, the man named in the message, as soon as possible. However, for now, we must act as if it's a genuine threat. We do not believe that al-Qa'eda is aware that we know of the planned attack and we can use this to our advantage. You will find at Flag B the latest threat assessment from the Joint Terrorism Analysis Centre and you will find at Flag B Side Flag 1 reference to the moderate-to-high likelihood of this nature of attack. We believe that al-Qa'eda has now obtained a nuclear bomb, which is no surprise since there are over three hundred such devices unaccounted for across the world, most from ex-Warsaw Pact stockpiles. So far, we only know who, what, where, when and how in broad terms. The Prime Minister has spoken with the US President who has been informed of the situation and he has offered his support, specifically the CIA, the FBI and the Department of Homeland Security. Sir Michael Jackson is holding a meeting this evening at Thames House, bringing together the key players in the hunt for the device.'

'Thank you,' responded the Prime Minister. 'The US President and I believe passionately that we must be accurate and deadly, not only in finding the bomb but hunting down the terrorists responsible and destroying them. Our mission is to find, neutralise and dispose of the nuclear bomb before detonation in order to defend the United Kingdom. I trust that is clear.'

The Prime Minister broke off and glanced at the faces around him. The atmosphere was tense and serious.

'In outline, I want to conduct this operation covertly for as long as possible to avoid panic amongst the population, to protect the economy, to prevent the terrorist cell from going underground, and to give ourselves more time to prepare. Terror instilled by the mere threat of such an act can cause the breakdown of law and order, destroy our economy, create religious hysteria and bring total chaos. Even without death, these alone would represent a massive victory for al-Qa'eda. The Foreign Secretary will be responsible for finding, neutralising and disposing of the bomb and locating those responsible, and the Home Secretary will be responsible for our resilience, that is, our preparedness for and reaction to a terrorist nuclear attack, and our ability to manage the major emergency after the attack. Given the magnitude of the threat, I consider myself solely responsible to our Sovereign and nation for our combined actions in dealing with this threat. Remaining departments will provide all necessary support.'

The Prime Minister took another sip of water before continuing. Nobody dared make a sound.

'The Home Secretary will bring forward the domestic counter-terrorist measures, with London's measures completed by the end of February. He will also conduct a full training exercise that tests London's Gold Coordinating Group, led by the Metropolitan Police Service and the Government Office for London. The exercise will involve all stakeholders, including the *entire* population of London.'

The Gold Coordinating Group was the Metropolitan Police Commissioner's planning group in the event of a strategic-level emergency in London. Silver represented command and control at the operational level, in each borough, and bronze at the tactical level, at each incident on the ground.

'The exercise is called Exercise Rapid Response and will involve a number of escalating states, ending, if necessary, with the evacuation of the city. The Home Secretary will ensure that London's Gold Group can cordon, control and evacuate the city within one week with just twenty four hours' notice. He will also provide internal security support to the Foreign Office as required. MI5 will continue to conduct its current ops against known or suspected terrorist cells in the UK and advise MI6 accordingly.'

The Prime Minister sat back for a moment before looking towards the Home Secretary.

'The Prime Minister has asked me to provide you with some coordinating issues. These are bulleted at Flag C in your folders. We have a strike date of May 2nd, to be known as Zulu Day. Exercise Rapid Response will take place in the latter half of March, and will be announced by the Prime Minister in the House. At a date to be established, the Prime Minister will inform the House of the real threat, to be followed immediately by a public announcement on live television. The priority of work is first, to find the bomb, second, to provide protection and prepare London for a nuclear attack, third, to prepare for our reaction after any attack and fourth, to track down and destroy the terrorists responsible. You all know that I've recently signed an agreement with the US Homeland Security Secretary. This is leading to unprecedented cooperation between both governments. We were to conduct a major US–UK exercise next year but this has now been replaced by Exercise Rapid Response. Liaison streams between us and the Americans will be between MI6, and the CIA and FBI, and between the Home Office and the Department of Homeland Security. The Prime Minister will continue to liaise directly with the US President of course, and the French and Irish Presidents over border control issues.'

The Home Secretary studied his notes for a moment.

'Command and Control responsibilities are summarised at Flag D and have been determined by the need for simplicity and the need for the utmost security. The Met's Gold Group will report to the Cabinet through Cobra.'

An integral part of the Cabinet Office was the Civil Contingencies Secretariat whose objectives included assisting Regional Resilience Forums in the development of an integrated response, the development resilience doctrine, ensuring that the Government would continue to function and deliver public services during and after a crisis, and the improvement of the resilience capability of all levels of Government. The Secretariat reported directly to the Home Secretary, who chaired each of the three relevant Cabinet committees that represented its work. One committee oversaw work on protective and preventative security, another worked to build the UK's resilience and ability to manage the consequences of major emergencies and the third, the Civil Contingencies Committee, oversaw lead department or group management of major emergencies after they had taken place.

'The nine regional resilience forums will continue to support and advise their respective emergency coordinating response groups. As you know, London's forum is chaired by the Minister for London, with the Mayor as his deputy. Incidentally, the Mayor will be London's spokesperson, working out of the Gold Group. The Joint Intelligence Committee and Joint Terrorism Analysis Centre will continue to operate as normal, informing and supporting the relevant department as necessary. All other protocols and procedures remain extant, including requests for military support, which will be inevitable should we wish to create an impregnable curtain around the country, evacuate London and conduct cordon and search ops. The provision of military support to either Exercise Rapid Response or Operation Enduring Freedom will, from this moment, be a higher priority than any current exercise or operation.'

The Home Secretary paused before raising the next issue in case the Defence Secretary wished to interrupt, but he did not – there was no need.

'The equipment required to tackle a CBRN threat has been identified through the resilience programme, but there will be new, urgent operational requirements. For example, a large amount of Geiger counters of varying shapes and sizes and other radiation-seeking devices will be required I have no doubt, and as soon as possible. A similar situation exists with a shortfall in protective clothing and decontamination equipment. Other equipment programmes, including the use of biometrics to monitor individual movements, iris recognition, immigration fingerprinting with links to the Eurodac system and extensive use of CCTV, all designed to smooth the flow of legitimate travellers while catching illegal entrants and terrorist suspects, must all be considered for fast-tracking. We are introducing the routine screening of all port traffic for the illicit movement of radiological materials, although the speed of equipment roll-out is dictated by availability of funds. I hope to be able to fast-track these now.

'I've already touched on how the Prime Minister and I intend to deliver the news about the real threat. Over the coming months we will be escalating the public's awareness of the war against terror and their own role within it. The Prime Minister will be addressing the House on a number of occasions, and I will be commencing an advertising campaign, among other projects. These initiatives will be designed to inform everyone and thus lessen the shock should the time come to reveal the true threat.'

'Thank you,' the Prime Minister said as the Home Secretary finished. 'Ladies and gentlemen, time is moving on and there is much for you all to consider. I intend to hold regular meetings of the Cabinet on this matter from now on. There will come a time when we may have to meet elsewhere, but I will await the Home Secretary's advice on that. I'd like to close the meeting but before I do there is a final issue I must raise. The country's morale is going to be a key component in overcoming this attack. I've no doubt that all government organisations will pull together but we must keep the public on our side. We must continue to work calmly and effectively and, when the time comes, demonstrate to the public that we mean to provide for their security and safety, and catch the perpetrators. Whatever the immediate future throws at us there can be no let up or loss of momentum. There's to be no politicising of this for we will need the support of all Opposition parties. Plans must be watertight and well publicised, disruption to daily life must be minimised for as long as possible and wherever possible, and law and order must be retained at all costs as we strive to find the bomb. If we bear down on May 2nd not having neutralised the bomb and not having a foolproof response in place, panic will escalate into total chaos, not just for London but for the whole country. Zulu Day is just 137 days away, yet we do possess the wherewithal to survive this threat. But to do so we must galvanise ourselves properly and concentrate our efforts where needed.'

At the end of the briefing the Prime Minister asked for questions. The Chancellor of the Exchequer spoke first.

'Prime Minister, the Treasury will need to treat the expenditure required to meet this threat on a war footing. Whether we like it or not, a national and totalitarian response may well be required to overcome this threat. There will be massive penalties to agreed programmes. Perhaps you could suggest to the House what a major terrorist threat may do to the nation's economy and confirm the footing we are on as soon as you are able. We are either at war, or we are not. We cannot reasonably maintain a fiscal policy and ignore the cost of war.'

'Yes, thank you. Soon after the threat is confirmed I will *remind* the House that I have already declared war on terror under my royal prerogative, that this war against terror remains as real today as it was on July 7th and that we are now facing a specific threat, for which our defence will require the resources of the entire nation. I will seek parliamentary approval, though that will not prove an obstacle. Our nation will be at war, and we will be a War Cabinet. Are there any more questions?'

The Secretary of State for the Environment, Food and Rural Affairs rarely asked a question but felt compelled to ask the obvious. 'How do we know that the bomb is not already in London, set to detonate on Zulu Day?'

'We don't, not yet anyway. That's one of the key questions to which MI6 must seek an answer. A radiological survey of London to establish it's clean, and to establish a baseline, is being considered by the Home Office, but suspicions would be raised in the media if we began immediately, and that we simply cannot risk. We hope that it will prove easier to discover the whereabouts of the bomb by tracking and finding it before it gets to London or, for that matter, the country. A full radiological survey may prove vital but it must be conducted within appropriate conditions.'

The Prime Minister glanced around him but all he saw was pale and drawn faces. There were no further questions. He stood up, gathering his notes as he did so.

'Ladies and gentlemen, if that's all, I must leave for Buckingham Palace.'

Chapter 23

December 16th, Z – 137 Days
London, England

The polished mahogany conference table in the MI6 Director General's office seated ten people. Sir Michael, with his back to the wall at one end, faced the middle of his outsized office with eight visitors to his front. Beyond the far end of the table stood his desk and the wall of windows which provided a panoramic view of an overcast North London. Embedded in the wooden wall panelling to his right was a large flat-screen monitor that he could operate remotely from a small portable consul that lay in front of him. Comfortable swivel chairs on wheels enabled those attending to establish an optimum view of the screen when required.

The visitors had conversed in small groups, helping themselves to light refreshments from a side buffet until it was time for the meeting to begin. Unfortunately Harry missed the preamble and arrived just in time to sit down with everyone at the table.

'Perhaps we should begin with everyone introducing themselves,' suggested Sir Michael. I am Mike Jackson, the Director General of MI6.'

Rosalind Washington was sitting on Sir Michael's right. He gestured for her to continue.

'Rosalind Washington, Deputy Director General.'

'Jack Spearman, Chief of Staff.'

'Dudley Anderson, Deputy Director Intelligence.'

'Harry Winchester, field operative, MI6.'

'Professor Richard Spedding, Senior Nuclear Physicist, Atomic Weapons Establishment, Aldermaston.'

'Tim Bernazzini, Counterterrorist Centre, CIA.'

'Tess Fulton, field operative, CIA.'

'Patrick Asquith, Deputy Director General MI5.'

'Thank you. A contact sheet will be available in the Operations Room from tomorrow,' Sir Michael began. 'In essence you all already know why you're here. This meeting marks the beginning of what could be one of the most important counterterrorist operations that we have ever conducted. It may call upon more resources than any intelligence operation conducted during or since World War II and have greater repercussions than the nuclear stand-offs experienced during the height of the Cold War. Millions of lives may be at stake. This mission is classified Top Secret, Alpha Eyes Only. It begins with confirming the authenticity of an al-Qa'eda threat to attack on London on May 2nd next year. If the threat is real, we are to hunt down the bomb and neutralise it. We are also to identify the perpetrators back to the originator and, if practicable, terminate them. The Cabinet met this morning and agreed the responsibilities between the Home and Foreign offices. Essentially the former is to prepare the home front for the worst-case scenario and the Foreign Office, in effect MI6, is to find and remove the bomb. I won't dwell on the mass of Home Office resilience responsibilities other than to state that it will provide us with whatever police and MI5 support we need within the UK. This group will control the operation to find and neutralise the bomb.'

So far there were no surprises. It was common to put together a small group to control even the most complex and vast operation. Countless MI6 operations had been hampered by burdensome command and control arrangements.

'It's the Prime Minister's intention to put the country on a formal war footing, but not until the threat is announced to the general public. Our mission, quite simply, is the nation's top priority. If we need anything, and it exists, we get it. It's my intention to start the operation small, to minimise the chances of broadcasting our knowledge of the threat to the terrorists and risk driving them underground, and we will ramp up as necessary.'

Sir Michael saw his audience were transfixed.

'OK, first I will deal with each of our responsibilities.'

People poised themselves to take notes.

'I will be responsible for leading and planning the operation. Rosalind will stand back from her current work and coordinate the day-to-day running of the operation, including management of field operatives and all resources. As you can imagine, the operation will snowball if we do not locate the bomb before it reaches London, assuming it's not already here, and as time runs out. Her responsibilities will include the production and endorsement of a daily briefing sheet for the Prime Minister's Office, the Cabinet, Cobra, the US President, the CIA Director, the Joint Intelligence Committee, the Joint Terrorism Analysis Centre, and each member of this group.'

The daily briefing sheet was a standard MI6 operating procedure for each major operation and provided a short synopsis and forecast of activity. It was restricted in size to one sheet of A4 paper.

'My COS, Jack, will continue to coordinate other work within MI6 and shield Rosalind and myself from much of the routine. The DDI, Dudley, who has already conducted a considerable amount of research into terror groups, including al-Qa'eda, will coordinate our intelligence and control a dedicated Ops Room. He will continue to engage with the JIC and JTAC and will be assisted by Tim who will act as CIA liaison. I have spoken with Jim Ridge, the Director CIA, and we have their full support. The FBI will be assisting on this one too.'

Sir Michael took a moment to scan his bulleted notes,

'Professor Richard will be our nuclear advisor, available twenty-four/seven. Patrick Asquith, our senior MI5 liaison officer, will work with Rosalind. He has access to all ongoing missions run by MI5. That brings me to Harry and Teresa, our field operatives.'

'Please, everyone, call me Tess,' she said in a soft southern American voice.

Sir Michael smiled in acknowledgement.

'Harry and Tess will be working as partners, whether joined at the hip or on opposite sides of the world. Both will report routinely to the Ops Room, with Tim updating the CIA. There are no hidden agendas between us, ladies and gentlemen, no back doors.'

Everyone smiled, most with good reason. Sir Michael took a little time to drink from his coffee.

'Harry and Tess are our eyes and ears on the ground. Harry has first-hand knowledge of al-Qa'eda and other African, Middle Eastern and Central Asian terrorist groups. Harry is ex-SAS, and he speaks fluent Arabic, Urdu and Punjabi. Importantly, he is familiar with the source of our intelligence. Tess is a leading world expert in global terrorist networks and their methodologies. She speaks more languages than Harry, and has a Ph.D. from MIT in Global Security. Both operatives have completed numerous assignments and missions in the Middle East or Central Asia, and both have been directly responsible for bringing terrorists to justice over recent years. Their bios are available in the Ops Room, and I expect everyone to be entirely conversant with them. For now, Jim Ridge and I believe that we're best served with a single cell that can move and think independently, worldwide, and that's what we have. As you would expect, we can multiply our resources as necessary.'

Sir Michael glanced at Tim.

'Tim has the best analytical brain in the CIA. He has a Ph.D. from Yale in Information Technology. He likes to use his own equipment, which he has shipped over.'

Tim shrugged and smiled awkwardly. He was a massive figure at six foot two and weighing in at over 220 pounds. Sir Michael handed Rosalind the remote screen control and beckoned for her to continue. Soon an image of Amir flashed up on the screen.

'So far we have one highly reliable source of information, an Afghan known as Amir, last seen outside the British Embassy in Kabul. Harry knows him well and there is a degree of trust between them.'

A picture of the original message, written in Arabic, with a translation beside it, appeared on the screen.

'The message tells us that al-Qa'eda has a nuclear bomb and that with the assistance of other terrorist groups they plan to strike London on May 2nd. We assume that it's next May, the May bank holiday. This morning we received the original note passed to the Ambassador by Amir, and a sample of Amir's handwriting. The handwriting is confirmed as Amir's. Harry and Tess will depart for Kabul to meet with Amir as soon as possible.'

'If it's OK with Tess we can catch tomorrow evening's BA flight from Heathrow?' Harry offered.

'Sure,' Tess agreed with an easy smile.

'Good,' said Sir Michael. 'That will give you both time to prep and tie up any loose ends. Tess, can you fix what equipment you both might need this afternoon?'

Tess nodded. 'Almost done.'

'As for other leads,' continued Rosalind, 'Dudley will begin by giving us an intelligence update.'

Dudley was an intellectual genius and at the age of thirty-eight he was the youngest director in the history of MI6. He was identified and recruited by his Classics professor, Professor Langman of Glanville and Caius College, Cambridge, sixteen years ago. Dudley had the full resources of MI6, one of the most efficient and highly respected foreign intelligence organisations in the world, supporting his work and it included criminologists, sociologists and psychologists from all over the country, as well as a wealth of intelligence and information technology experts. Tess noticed the respect that Tim showed to Dudley and knew that the intelligence director was for real. The screen control was passed to Dudley.

'This threat represents the first time we know that a terrorist group has obtained a fully functional nuclear bomb. There could, of course, be more than one. Perhaps Amir can help us with that, Harry? But first, let us look at the human intelligence, what we call HUMINT. It's enlightening.'

Everyone knew that Dudley's team had not rested since the message had been received the day before.

'Islamic terrorists can be divided into four general categories. The foot soldiers are recruited from refugee camps and poor communities throughout the Arab world. These young people, predominantly men, are impressionable, usually illiterate, and know little if anything of the Western world. They are the front line suicide bombers who "smite" the Israelis, roll heads from the kidnapped, and murder tourists by mercilessly hacking them to pieces. Some are selected as members of the *Shia'heed*, an elite group of martyrs. They speak only Arabic. They blend in quite well in Arab society, but are essentially unable to function outside of it. These are the troops that bin Laden and his lieutenants trained in Afghanistan, and now, in Iran and Syria, many in religious schools known as *madrasahs*.'

Everyone was captivated.

'The second category is the Arabs with better educational skills, usually literate, some with technical skills. The fundamentalists and 'hate preachers' actively recruit these people, appeal to their religious sensitivities and nihilistic tendencies through web sites and religious groups, and seek to convert them to their perverted view of Islam. Since these people have often lived, or live, outside the Arab world as citizens, they understand how to manage in Western society. These people, known as *takfiris*, are dangerous for they are not distinguishable from the majority of innocent Western Muslims, though with sound intelligence they can usually be traced. It's people from this category that hijacked the airliners that crashed into the World Trade Centre and the Pentagon.

'The third category of terrorists can be thought of as generals. Bin Laden and his chief lieutenants, financiers, bankers, technical advisors, and so on. These people are Muslims but may have any ethnic origin. For whatever reason, terrorism appeals to their religious view of the world.

'As for the fourth category, few are Arabs or even Muslims. They see profit in terrorism. Some of them take pleasure in the pain they inflict, but most are mercenaries. These people are enemies of Western civilisation but can be Americans, British, French, German, Canadian, in fact anyone with a grievance, real or imagined, or anyone who craves wealth. These people are the most dangerous of all. As you will discover, the successful and covert transportation, planting and detonation of a nuclear bomb requires considerable expertise, and considerable cost. Our belief, supported by the CIA, is that al-Qa'eda has recruited a specialist outsider to lead this mission, someone from the fourth category who is highly intelligent, patient, commands respect across religious and ethnic divides, is unknown to the global terrorist intelligence communities, ruthless but not religiously fanatical, and can blend into all manner of societies. We are looking for a Carlos the Jackal character, but with one exception. We don't believe that he, or she, can be operating alone. It's likely that we are looking for one cell of two or more like-minded assassins. We are, of course, improving on this preliminary profile as we speak.'

'Everyone agreed?' enquired Sir Michael.

Everyone nodded.

Dudley pressed on. 'Next is the issue of the target. In all my years of intelligence I have never seen a terrorist operation as successful as the 9/11 attack. Quite remarkable. It was possible because our American friends put their constitution and individual rights before security. That, of course, has changed in America, but not to the same degree in London, despite the attacks in the city on July 7th. London remains a weak terrorist target, regardless of the Government's recent efforts, because we remain so trusting. The terrorists' aim is to attack Western civilisation and a successful nuclear attack on London will instil fear into every living soul in the Western world and further polarise support among Islamic fundamentalists. London is a founding partner and a conduit for capitalism that the Islamic fundamentalists seek to destroy. At the same time they prove their strength and strike a blow against America by isolating them and fostering hatred. They want to create fear and chaos, and inspire a holy war, or jihad, between Western civilisation and Islam. Bin Laden is intent on creating a clash of civilisations. In the new Dark Ages that will follow from the destruction of capitalism, they will build their holy empire. These fanatics wish to shatter the primacy of rich, unholy nations. They think that the struggle will radicalise the Islamic masses and destroy the Islamic governments that attempt to straddle the cultural divide. The goal is to build fundamentalist Islamic nations led by the Qur'an, not by democratically elected governments. Think of it. Billions of ignorant, starving people bowing to Mecca three times a day. Bin Laden sees himself as an Islamic messiah sent by Allah.'

'So what does all this tell us?' enquired Sir Michael. No criticism was intended as so often in intelligence work there was no clear solution supported by facts, simply assumptions followed by possibilities. But the best, often the bravest, in MI6 voiced the possibilities and provisos, particularly Dudley. Unfortunately politicians all too often wanted just one possibility and referred to it as a conclusion, but that was up to them.

'Appreciating the target is necessary, but in this case it exposes little that we don't already know. A terrorist might conclude that a massive attack against London would rock America's single most important ally and leave the US isolated diplomatically. Only the top dog would make such a decision and therefore we feel sure that bin Laden is behind this plot. Frankly, we don't believe that any other terrorist organisation has the will, finance or clout. Not on its own anyway. London is a highly credible and high-value target for bin Laden. It leads us to think that the plot is real, and that it has been very carefully considered for maximum impact on Western civilisation, more so perhaps, than targeting a second American city.'

Sir Michael thanked Dudley. 'I think it would be useful if we examined the impact of a nuclear attack on London now. Professor?'

Professor Richard Spedding leant forward and rested his elbows on the table.

'I've also been considering what little we have so far. A nuclear bomb can be anything from a dirty bomb, a conventional explosive packed with radioactive debris, to a nuclear fission bomb. Terrorist organisations have had easy access to radioactive debris for some time but now we're inclined to believe they have their hands on a nuclear bomb.'

'What about taking the plutonium out of a weapon and making a new nuclear bomb. Is that possible?' asked Harry.

'The configuration would be limited, but yes it is. Plutonium is the deadliest substance known to man. It is unlikely to be critical, but it's decaying, radiating. Anyone who opened a warhead would need a clean room, body suits, containment devices for the plutonium, scrubbers, all of that. They would have to have the facilities and equipment with which to work or they would be dead within days of getting to the plutonium.'

'Why bother opening the warhead, why not just blow it up?' Harry asked.

'Why not indeed? I think the answer lies in the magnitude of the destruction they wish to cause. It's unlikely a terrorist cell would wish to open them up, not without a well-equipped expert. Setting it off would spray microscopic bits of plutonium over an area dictated by the force of the bomb, the worst kind of dirty bomb. The stronger the wind, the greater the area of contamination. It would be nearly impossible to clean up. The half-life of plutonium is about a quarter of a million years. It would be the worst ecological disaster in the history of the world. But, the damage caused and the terror factor in the case of the dirty bomb is minute compared to that of a nuclear bomb.'

'And as you say, terrorists have had access to radiological material for years. If a terrorist got his hands on a nuclear bomb after many years of trying, surely he would strive for a nuclear explosion,' suggested Rosalind.

Dudley added, 'I agree. Only if nuclear fission could not succeed would they resort to a dirty bomb. Frankly, I think they would rather wait until they could succeed.'

Dumbfounded, no one spoke, so the professor continued. 'There are believed to be a number of nuclear devices available on the black market ranging from one-kiloton artillery shells to two-hundred-kiloton warheads used in long-range missiles. At the height of the Cold War the Russian KGB used a small proportion of their armoury of nuclear artillery shells in the one to ten-kiloton range to make over two hundred suitcase bombs. Many were spread strategically around Western Europe and up to one hundred and thirty-four are believed to be unaccounted for. To give you an idea of the devastating power of a single ten-kiloton bomb, it approximates to the nuclear explosions suffered at Hiroshima and Nagasaki. Each bomb is quite small too. Nuclear warheads in the 200-kiloton range could be as small as a football, so they are easily transportable. Nuclear bombs can also be unstable, and therefore unreliable, unless properly maintained. In my opinion, any terrorist cell with the serious intention of detonating a nuclear bomb, not least of all to preserve their own lives, would need an expert, a nuclear scientist, to prepare the bomb.'

Tim cocked his head. 'The CIA is already tracking all known nuclear scientists worldwide. A huge undertaking, but it might throw up something. They're also investigating whether anyone has noticed any missing nukes, or parts, but that is far less promising. Countries just don't like to admit to that sort of thing.'

'Thanks,' said Sir Michael. 'Professor, it might help us to know what we're fighting to prevent. Remind us of the effects of such an explosion.'

'OK,' the professor began briskly, 'let's consider a ten-kiloton bomb exploding at Charing Cross. Remember the photographs of Hiroshima? Ground Zero would be about four miles in radius razing everything within that distance to the ground. Sitting on the edge of Ground Zero at the outer edges of London, say Wimbledon, the initial concussion would be terrific. Windows would be blown out and the flying glass and debris would kill. If you survive that, a few seconds later the thermal pulse would arrive, the heat would fry flesh from the bone. As the rising fireball consumed all the air around it, air would rush in from surrounding counties to feed it, creating a hurricane.'

The professor paused unnecessarily for effect. He certainly held their attention. His audience did not appear to be breathing.

'With an explosion that size, two to three-hundred-mile-an-hour winds could be expected. These winds would cause most damage outside Ground Zero to a distance of about ten miles. Buildings weakened and twisted by the initial blast and perhaps set afire by the thermal pulse would be destroyed by the hurricane rushing towards the vortex. The air would become semi-solid, full of glass fragments, dirt, stone, and metal, everything the hurricane could lift. That debris would sandblast structures, shred and abrade anything standing.'

Faces paled and eyes widened. Several people merely gaped, others around the table felt a wave of nausea.

'Then there's the radiation. The radiation would be lethal, that's death within days, to any human being left standing within a range of twenty miles, or downwind of maybe one hundred miles. To escape the radiation effects completely you would want to be at least two hundred miles away. A dirty bomb, even plutonium, is peanuts in comparison to the real thing.'

Everyone present looked shaken. They were all thinking the same thing, mass casualties, corpses blackened to a crisp, and even without them, the radioactive and political fallout would deal the nation's economy a devastating blow from which it would probably never recover. And then there were the national treasures, people's possessions and so on. What a legacy it would leave to future generations.

Harry was the first to break the silence. 'Without prior warning, a ten-kiloton bomb could kill, maim or poison twelve million people, that's a fifth of the nation. It will cause serious Islamaphobia across the Western world and probably a backlash ending in World War III and annihilation.'

'The Government has a massive problem with the mere threat of a bomb of this lethality.' Rosalind added, her quivering voice betraying her calm exterior.

The mood around the table was one of shock.

'OK everyone, let's stay focused,' said Sir Michael quietly. 'Professor, what can you tell us about detection?'

The professor was prepared for this question and answered confidently.

'The detection range will vary widely depending on the type and strength of the radiation. And that will depend on the amount of shielding around the emitter or source. A well-shielded reactor, such as one in a late model nuclear powered submarine would probably be undetectable unless you were within a few dozen metres. Missiles don't have much shielding because it makes them too heavy. The plutonium inside is decaying, radiating. Given the low amount of shielding in a missile warhead, it would be detectable at about five miles. The radiation emitting from nuclear devices of man-portable size can be screened relatively easily using lead, making detection difficult. A low emitting device could be fully screened by just one inch of lead. Our detection equipment is almost exclusively the Geiger counter, which can be as small as a mobile phone and worn on the belt. They are simple and unsophisticated, but limited by the ease with which emissions can be shielded. Generally the bigger the Geiger counter, the bigger the catchment for emissions and the more chance of detection. We also have a small number of gamma ray and neutron flux detectors but they are big and bulky, and not necessarily any better. We have the means to build and test the next generation of detectors at Burghfield, but no funds.'

Sir Michael saw the opportunity. 'Professor, you must raise that with the Home Office. We may need them.'

'Tess and I will need to familiarise ourselves with the component parts of a nuclear bomb,' added Harry.

'An inert training aid will be here later this evening for us to examine,' answered the professor. 'I will instruct both you and Tess on it personally. It's a full-scale model of the ten-kiloton warhead used in our submarine-launched ballistic missiles. I also have some slides to show you.'

Professor Spedding took the meeting through his short slide show, which illustrated various sizes of nuclear bombs, and how readily they could be concealed.

'Essentially every bomb is similar. There will be the bomb itself including the neutron generator, and attached to it will be a number of detonators that are all wired to a capacitor, possibly through a junction box. The capacitor will receive an electrical current from a battery, usually of low voltage. It's easy to attach a timer between the battery and the capacitor. Of course, any circuit can be booby-trapped, particularly through the recognition of a voltage drop due to the cutting of wires. The arming mechanism will normally be placed between the battery and the capacitor. Bombs can be set off remotely, in situ by hand, or by timer, or a combination of all three.'

With no more questions for the professor, Rosalind returned to possible leads.

'The next lead is computer tracking, some serious short cuts can be made here, assuming no violation issues. We're at war after all. Tim, perhaps you could expand?'

'The CIA's Counterterrorist Center has state-of-the-art equipment for hacking into databases and servers that no one else can. Even terrorists leave tracks, whether it's credit cards, telephone calls, car rental, flight tickets, hotel bills, that kind of stuff. I'm having some kit shipped over that will help me work hand-in-hand with Langley. I can run that lead with the CIA?'

'Do it,' ordered Sir Michael. 'Perhaps we should send some people to assist in the CTC, and maybe have Tim oversee our work here. We don't want overlap.'

'I'll fix something,' replied Rosalind. 'Patrick, do you have anything to add from Five?'

'We're already stepping up our surveillance of all known sympathisers and possible terrorists throughout the UK. We're well served by a large number of willing informants and are in close contact with Customs and Excise and Immigration as you would expect.'

'I don't want to discourage entry or drive anyone underground just yet. We must stand off and observe until we establish the whereabouts of the bomb,' ordered Sir Michael.

'Understood,' replied Patrick.

'What of the financial trail?' Sir Michael asked Tim.

'The FBI has done a lot of work with the CIA on sourcing and denying the funding of terrorist activity across the world. This attack will cost a great deal and there will be a trail. I suggest we let my chums back home run with that. I'll keep you informed.'

'Thanks, Tim.'

Sir Michael considered that Dudley and Tim were going to be inseparable.

As the meeting progressed, Tess studied Harry and found him different to what she had imagined, not least of all because his official photograph was of a boyish young man in his late twenties. But he was considerably more handsome in person. Sporting a natural tan that she figured came from his deceased Italian-born mother and many years in Afghanistan, his thick sandy hair curled over a smooth forehead. His face, with strong cheek bones, wary denim-blue eyes, a determined mouth and lean, curved jaw line seemed somehow at odds with his casual dress of fresh jeans, clean blue gingham shirt and a loose brown leather jacket that could so easily hide a pistol. At a little under six feet tall she guessed he weighed 180 pounds. She figured he looked after himself and imagined a soldier's body type, powerful thighs, lean muscular hips and a torso that broadened toward flat shoulders designed to provide the upper-body strength essential in special operations. From what she had gleaned from his file and from first appearances, Tess concluded that Harry was one of the most intriguing men she had ever met, an understated man who bristled with anomalies.

Thirty minutes later the meeting broke up and Harry approached her for the first time. He had already been struck by her beautiful sun-kissed face, soft brown eyes and straight dark hair that curled under at the shoulders.

'Hi. It's a pleasure to meet you. I'm sorry we couldn't introduce ourselves before the meeting. I made it just in time.'

They both smiled politely.

'No problem. Tim and I arrived mid-morning so we had time to find our way about. I was even given your bio to study. It reads like fiction.'

'I'm sure yours is no different. Tim speaks very highly of you,' Harry continued. 'It looks like we've a knockout evening of guns and bombs to look forward to.'

'Sounds like a great night out. Your people have prepared three sets of IDs. Did you know we're married in two of them?'

'No. I suppose it's worth a trial should I ever see the real thing,' joked Harry before steering the conversation back to business. 'Have you everything you need?'

'I think so. Someone is to organise a diplomatic pouch on our flight for our weapons and other essential items. I brought some of the CIA's future-generation satcom wireless notebooks with me, one for each of us and the Ops Room. They've been approved by Sir Michael. Your comms system is good, but a little too current. It still relies on the Web and the encryption and decryption of messages, and it's cumbersome. Nor does it allow the user access to the firm's latest classified intel compartments. Our latest system is no larger than an average paperback and has its own cellular modem that's permanently activated into the CIA intranet via our own network of global satellites. It's a little like Broadband but wireless. Comms are fully secure, instantaneous and untraceable. Each satcom provides access to the finest classified intelligence sources, libraries and encyclopaedias in the world as well as the Web, and each system comes complete with compatible camera equipment and cell phone. As for Geiger counters, despite what was said in the meeting, the small Geiger counters Professor Spedding brought with him today are the best currently available.'

Harry was impressed. 'Sound's great. Where are you staying?'

'Same place as you.'

'That's helpful,' Harry replied, as impressed with the accommodation arrangements as he was with the newest advances in microtechnology. 'Perhaps we can fit dinner in later and I can catch up. Unfortunately I must return to Chertsey first thing in the morning to clear my desk. I'll be back here by three o'clock at the latest.'

'Dinner sounds great.'

Harry and Tess were collected from Sir Michael's office by an assistant and taken to a briefing room for a lesson in nuclear weapons. On the way down the corridor Harry watched her walk ahead of him, and admired her athletic figure and graceful walk. Meanwhile, the assistant, who was leading the way, kept the conversation going.

'Sir Michael sends his apologies but he will not be able to join you for training or for dinner tonight. But he asked that you make time to see him before you leave tomorrow.'

Harry, walking behind, smiled to himself. So, too, did Tess.

Alone in his office, Sir Michael finished his telephone conversation with the Ambassador in Afghanistan and reviewed the afternoon's meeting in his mind. The CIA was best placed with a worldwide network over twenty times the size of MI6's to search for missing scientists and nukes, to find and follow any terrorist money trail, and also infiltrate databanks with their superior technology. Each day the Counterterrorist Center would share the wealth of information they gathered, leaving MI6 to concentrate on controlling the operation and chasing its key lead, Amir. He knew he should focus on what Six was best at, overseas field operations, and he felt secure in the knowledge that within twenty-four hours he could multiply by twenty-fold the number of operatives they had deployed in the field. Content that nothing else could be done, he left the office for Windsor and a rare evening at home with his wife, Julia, and their three children.

Chapter 24

December 17th, Z - 136 Days
Port Muhammad bin Qasim, Karachi, Pakistan

The port, like Karachi, was a large, dirty city often obscured by a noxious pall of smoke, engine exhaust, and the smell of rotting rubbish. The sewage floating in the blackened waste of the harbour didn't help matters, especially on a day like this when the wind blew from the sea.

Dalia met Fritz outside the well-guarded main entrance to Port Muhammad bin Qasim at 10 a.m. She climbed into the ship's Jeep and Fritz drove her to Dock C. In contrast to the port, Dalia could not help but be impressed by the huge ship that appeared in front of her as she approached. Due to set sail tonight, the loading of the ship was well underway but with most of her hull still high above the waterline the ship dwarfed the dockside. En route Fritz had explained that this giant, three-year-old, medium-sized, twin-screw freighter of twenty thousand tons was capable of sailing up to 25 knots or 480 nautical miles every day. Since her launch the ship had apparently been kept busy between the Indian subcontinent and the Americas, and although she was still young her owners had obviously spent money on retaining her original splendour. Dalia considered this boded well, as it represented a degree of efficiency not always common amongst shipping lines.

Fritz parked the Jeep next to the only gangway that led onto the vessel. They sat and watched for a moment as a huge orange gantry crane hunched over the dockside like a voracious insect, sucking the corrugated metal containers up off a procession of railroad trucks or articulated rigs that were lined up in two neat columns on the dockside. As they sat, Fritz explained to Dalia that, until the 1960s, the loading and unloading of ships was a slow, expensive process. Then, the emergence of container technology made it possible to rapidly shuttle standardised boxes from ship to train or truck and back again. The time required to load and unload a big ship like BBC *Columbia* reduced from upwards of a week to as little as eight hours and now the entire loading operation could be conducted immediately prior to sailing.

'Remember what the nature of container transit is,' Fritz explained as Dalia watched. 'What it sells is speed and predictability. Virtually everything that travels in a container is something of fairly high value. The whole system evolved very quickly because it was a safe, fast and relatively cheap way to get cargo from continent to continent. In other words, if you're moving commodities that aren't worth very much and your margin is razor thin, then unless you can get a very good deal in containers, you won't move them that way, you'd go some other route. However, high-margin consumer goods like running shoes, electronics, food, clothes, furniture, automobiles and auto parts, they go by container.'

'Fritz, I am confident you know your business. Now where's my container?' enquired Dalia patiently.

'Hans is keeping an eye on yours now. I don't suppose it's arrived from the compound yet. Let's go and see. We must not get in the way though as we're both off duty right now.'

Fritz and Dalia climbed out of the Jeep and she followed him up the steep steel gangway onto a lower deck. Hans greeted them and told them that their yellow container was to arrive by lorry in the next few minutes as he led them quickly through a maze of gangways and up several flights of stairs.

Soon they arrived at the Cargo Control Centre that was situated over the ship's bridge where they found the ship's cargo officer, by chance an Argentine, and several of his division working steadily controlling the loading operation. No one seemed concerned about their presence at one end of the wide upper bridge, and from their own vantage point they had clear visibility over the entire loading operation. Loading was being conducted simultaneously fore and aft of the gleaming white accommodation tower in which they stood, and Dalia watched the cargo officer with admiration as his orders were transformed into a buzz of coordinating radio traffic and physical activity amongst the crane operators, the deckhands, the dockhands and the port authorities.

Minutes later Hans spotted the yellow container and calmly pointed it out to Dalia as he handed her a pair of binoculars. She was impressed that he had identified it so quickly and at such a distance. She could identify a crescent moon marking and through the binoculars she read the unique serial number, OS WT 780022-3.

As the container was unloaded from an articulated lorry they descended to the main deck and walked forward towards a group of deckhands that were waiting for the next container's arrival. Keeping their distance, they watched as the yellow container was unloaded onto the centre of the foredeck. Without telling how he had arranged for it to be stowed here, Fritz explained that this was the most secure location for a container for it would be surrounded by other containers also destined for Buenos Aires and that it could not be swept overboard. Just as crucial, their container was located third from bottom so it could not be crushed.

'Can that really happen?' asked Dalia, who had not considered crushing as a possibility.

'It happens often. The cargo officer must calculate each load and position each container carefully. The ship's centre of gravity and its handling is also important, not just the strength of each container. It's been estimated that as many as ten thousand containers a year are lost in transit. Container ships like this one often stack those things eight high. A stack like that can weigh eighty tonnes. Normally only the outer stacks on both sides of the weather deck are secured with steel turnbuckles. In a heavy sea the bottom containers can be crushed as the ship rolls, creating slack in the system that causes the fasteners to fail. Sometimes the fasteners aren't properly secured when the ship is loaded. Sometimes the fasteners just fail catastrophically. If the outboard stack goes over the side, very occasionally the inboard stacks go too.'

Hans saw a look of concern on Dalia's face and smiled.

'On the other hand, over a hundred million containers are delivered annually across the oceans. Most containers are lost through ships sinking, and this lady will not sink.'

Once Dalia was satisfied the container was safely stowed, Fritz drove her to Arif's office on the quayside opposite Dock F, where, after briefly greeting Arif and assuring Dalia he would keep in touch, he left them to their business.

'You are content with the arrangements, Dalia?' enquired Arif as they climbed the polished and ornate Victorian stairs to his office.

'Hans and Fritz are excellent. Let's hope that they have a smooth crossing and that they arrive on time in three weeks.'

'Nowadays, shipping times are like train times. The company prides itself on collecting and delivering goods on time, and so do I. Schedules are very important in our business as profit margins are so tight. It can only be nature that prevents us from delivering your cargo on time. I hope the salty environment will not cause you corrosion problems.'

Dalia glanced at Arif for a moment, wondering if he knew more than she had told him.

'I doubt it. My cargo is well insulated, and the container safely positioned on board.'

'*Insh'Allah,*' replied Arif. If God wills it.

Chapter 25

December 17th, Z – 136 Days
Chertsey, Surrey, England

Merissa had ordered a car and driver to take Harry home from London. As he completed his packing in his room, he received a telephone call from the doorman of the Park Lane Hotel at 7:55 a.m. to let him know that it had arrived. Rising two hours ago, he had taken a refreshing early-morning swim before enjoying a full English breakfast, including black pudding, his favourite. Harry was a great believer in eating breakfast like a king, lunch like a prince, and supper like a pauper, but like most people he found the adage difficult to maintain. Nonetheless, maintaining a healthy diet and plenty of exercise, he knew he was physically prepared for the operation. As he left the hotel, he wondered what Tess was doing, having not seen her since they parted company in the first-floor corridor at midnight last night.

Unknown to Harry, Tess had been in the gymnasium as Harry swam but she had not seen fit to disturb him, or her exercise. Instead she had continued to cycle as she watched him power up and down the length of the pool.

As Harry was driven back to Mercury, he pondered on Tess and their discussions the previous evening over supper. It was 10:15 p.m. by the time they had returned to the hotel and the dining restaurant was closed, so they had ordered food from the saloon bar where they had eaten and shared a decent bottle of red wine.

Harry admitted to himself that he had been, and still was, intrigued by her beauty. During the evening Tess explained that she had inherited her unusual colouring from her mother who was Persian and her father, now dead, who was descended from Native Americans, and who had worked in Saudi Arabia for many years as an oil drilling manager before an accident had killed him. Harry wondered whether her spellbinding appearance could compromise a mission and guessed that she had learned to use it to her advantage. Afghanistan was not the ideal place to have a female partner if one had to have a partner at all. Afghanistan was backward, women were third-class citizens after men and boys, and there were frequent terror attacks on foreign women who were seen as weak, wealthy and shameless. Harry told himself he was acting like an overprotective parent and had to remind himself that she was intelligent and experienced enough to know the risks and that she could clearly look after herself. She had told him that she was recruited by the CIA while at Yale University where she double-majored in Physics and Information Technology, and that she had served in the CIA for fifteen years before completing her Ph.D. at MIT. Tess had been a little reticent about discussing her past although she did mention that she had not previously visited Afghanistan. She had explained that her bosses in the CIA did not consider that a problem as Harry knew the ground intimately, and the CIA did not expect either of them to remain in Afghanistan for long. It transpired that she had worked in almost every other Islamic state, particularly Syria, where as part of a non-official cover team, she had spent the last two and a half years hunting down al-Qa'eda suspects. He also remembered her telling him of her active enjoyment of ju-jitsu, or at least a form of it that Harry had never heard of. Neither had she said how good she was. He tried to remember more but could not, and checked himself as he admitted that he had a crush on her.

Harry remembered telling Tess much about himself, though little more than she would have gained from his bio. She had appeared genuinely interested and had asked many questions. He had even pondered on whether he should invite her to Mercury this morning, but decided against it, as they both had plenty to do before the evening flight.

Harry broke from his thoughts and asked the driver to pass him the car phone.

'Tally, hi, it's Harry.'

'Hi, boss.'

'I'm on my way back, and should be with you at about nine-thirty. I have a job with Six and will need to absent myself for a while. I'll clear my desk and leave any outstanding issues with

Jarrad or Pat. Please ask them to pop in at ten o'clock. What else? Yeh, I must leave, packed and with the house straightened by one o'clock. I have a car and driver from Six. She'll wait for me.'

'OK,' she replied blithely. 'Is there anything I can do?' Tally and everyone else had already suspected that Harry would be off on a job.

'Beyond what you do already? You're superb and I don't deserve you. There's Max, the ponies, the house...'

'Flattery gets you everything. Of course I'll look after them.'

Back in July, Tally had offered to look after Harry's home whilst he was away for several days and he had gratefully accepted, insisting that he pay her as he would have done the Animal Aunt firm he had previously employed. Tally had her own flat in Woking but she loved staying in Harry's little house. She never looked back as she left for Chertsey.

'You better come in with Jarrad and Pat. See you in about half an hour. Bye.'

'Bye, Harry.'

Tally enjoyed staying in Harry's house. She loved its quaint exterior, decor, furnishings and its distinctly bachelor smell. But she always felt it empty, a house that would benefit from her presence. Then there was Max and the ponies. Everything reminded her of Harry. The one thing she did not like was being paid.

Harry leant back into the soft leather seat in the back of the Mercedes and his mind drifted back to yesterday afternoon. The instruction on nuclear bombs from Professor Spedding had lasted a little longer than an hour. Both he and Tess had been struck by just how simple the final construction of a nuclear bomb actually was, and how easily it could be deactivated.

The range practice down in the bunker under Vauxhall Cross had become competitive. It transpired that Tess had brought her personal weapon from home, a subcompact Glock 26 pistol. Among the family of pistols it was small but Harry knew it had the power of a Magnum. As she unloaded it from its casing, Tess had chillingly explained how she liked a target to go down with one high-velocity round. Harry could have chosen from the vast array of weapons held at Vauxhall Cross but as usual he had chosen the trusted Browning High Power 35 Luger which he had used since his days in the SAS. It had not taken long before both discovered, to their mutual advantage, that not only did each weapon use the same NATO 9-mm round but that they were equally good marksmen.

Last night, Tess had demonstrated the CIA satcom notebooks to Harry, and several other items of equipment she had brought with her from the US. Both satcoms were identical and as he had surfed through the software, Harry had seen for himself that they provided access to an encyclopaedic database somewhere in the depths of the US National Security Agency that held a vast wealth of information on nuclear bombs.

There was a sudden increase in noise as the Mercedes left the tarmac road and drove onto the pebble drive that swept for thirty metres to the manor and Harry's home. Harry jolted back from his thoughts and asked the driver to pull up outside his converted barn house.

'See you back here at one o'clock, Anna, and thanks.'

'Right-oh, sir,' replied the pert young blonde.

It was a bright, clear but cold winter's day as Harry unlocked the front door to his home. The central heating provided a warm welcome.

Fifteen minutes later Harry walked into his office in the manor house.

'Hi, Tally, how's it going?'

'The usual. We saw you arriving. Jarrad and Pat are waiting in your office. We're on the edge of our seats. You sounded so secretive.'

'Come on through,' replied Harry, 'this may take a while.'

Harry greeted Jarrad and Pat, and they all sat around his conference table.

'Six have asked us to complete another job. They need me to go back into the field. It's a matter of national security and requires me because of my work as an MI6 operative in Afghanistan. Before I continue, each of you must sign a copy of the Official Secrets Act. The operation is classified Top Secret, Alphas Eyes Only and so despite the Act, I am restricted with what I tell you.'

Harry quickly passed around the forms that Merissa had given him.

'Tally, the three completed copies are to be given to Anna,

the MI6 driver who's grabbing a coffee in the anteroom downstairs. She'll pass them to Merissa, Sir Michael's personal assistant.'

Each of them had, on various occasions in the past, been required to sign the Act, and it was no surprise that Sir Michael required them to be updated. Each person signed and dated the bottom of the reverse side of a single sheet of size A5 paper, and added their home address. This government form, signed by thousands of servicemen, civil servants and government employees, spelt out in headline fashion what the signatory was agreeing to.

'No one else is to know the nature of what I'm about to tell you. Millions of lives are at stake.'

They all realised that Harry was not exaggerating.

'MI6 has received a message from the British Ambassador in Kabul. The message stated that…'

Harry provided a synopsis of events so far. One of his parting conditions with Sir Michael was that he must be able to trust his closest colleagues in Mercury. Sir Michael had agreed, providing each person signed the Official Secrets Act, and that Harry was equally responsible for them.

'…I will be flying out this evening with Tess Fulton, departing Heathrow this evening. That's about it'

The three Mercury employees stared at Harry in amazement. After several moments spent composing herself Tally asked, 'Can we contact you?'

'Not directly. Official, urgent operational traffic may be passed to Merissa for onward transmission but, unless it's related, they will hold any messages for my return. Tess and I will be in regular contact with each other and Vauxhall Cross using state-of-the-art satcom electronic notebooks provided by the CIA. So, anyone any questions? I'm afraid I have no idea how long I will be.'

'Jarrad and I have already discussed everything, we'll be fine,' said Pat. This is your function, what else do you think we employ you for?'

The dry laughter that followed did little to ease the tension.

After the meeting Harry and Tally went to his house. She watched as he placed several items into two grips, explaining as he packed that most items he required he would purchase on the job using credit cards provided by Six. He always took some things from home, principally second-hand, old, and comfortable items like his well-worn shoulder holster that he barely noticed wearing, his hiking boots, a small pocket knife and an old address book. With both grips not even half full, they went downstairs and discussed caretaking arrangements over coffee. Tally insisted on making some sandwiches.

At 1 p.m., Tally accompanied Harry back out to the staff car.

'Did you manage to get some lunch?' Harry asked, as Anna flipped the boot.

'Yes, thank you, sir. Several of your staff took me to a local pub.'

'Good, let's go then. Tally, thank you again.'

Harry hugged and kissed her lightly on both cheeks. Before she had time to respond, he was climbing into the rear of the car and closing the door.

'Good luck, Harry,' she mouthed, not wishing others to hear the intimacy in her voice. 'I'll be thinking of you.'

'Don't worry about me Tally, I'll be fine,' replied Harry through the open window.

Anna turned the ignition and Tally waved as the car gently accelerated down the pebble drive.

Tears rolled gently down Tally's cheeks.

Chapter 26

December 18th, Z – 135 Days
Karachi, Pakistan

Early in the morning the day after the container had been loaded onto BBC *Columbia*, Dalia and Arif sat in his office and watched through binoculars as the harbour pilot boarded the ship. A man carrying a clipboard who Arif knew to be a port official walked down the gangway, then motioned the dockworkers to remove it.

Obeying orders from the ship, the dockworkers removed the final ropes that held the ship to the quay. Soon after the last rope was released, the ship slowly began to move. She backed away from the quay under her own power as two tugs hovered near by, prepared to provide assistance. Eventually she began to creep forward and her head began to swing as she answered her helm. Slowly increasing her speed, she made her way between the anchored ships into the harbour, heading for the sea beyond. The two tugs fell back and disappeared.

Noticing a small boat following the tanker, Dalia asked its purpose and Arif replied that it was routine for a pilot boat to collect and return the pilot to the quay once the ship was safely outside the harbour. Dalia knew then that this phase of the operation had been successfully completed.

Dalia took a taxi back to her hotel where she completed her packing before sending a short electronic message to Malik from his room. Within one hour of arriving back at the hotel she had checked out and taken another taxi to Quaid-e-Azam International Airport some twelve kilometres from central Karachi. She boarded the first available Airblue flight to Islamabad, collected her car then drove home.

Chapter 27

December 19th, Z – 134 Days
Amsterdam, Netherlands

Not a week seemed go by in Amsterdam without its media grabbing onto another story about drugs or sex or some other aspect of the city's seedier side. It was true that Amsterdam was a liberal city. Over the years the city had been a safe haven for those who felt persecuted. Amsterdam's tolerance was often viewed as a development of the last few decades, but in reality, it went back several centuries. In the sixteenth and seventeenth centuries, Jews and Huguenots bolted from France to this Dutch capital to escape oppression. And, during World War II, many people came to Amsterdam to hide out from the Nazis. Amsterdam made its mark in other ways as well. The city's famous diamond trade began in the sixteenth century and brought wealth and culture to the nation. Amsterdam held the title of having cut both the largest diamond in the world, the Cullinan, and the smallest, which, at the minuscule size of 0.00012 of a carat, was fully faceted with fifty-seven polished surfaces.

Amsterdam was, without question, the Netherlands' cultural, historical and commercial hub. Known as the Venice of the North, it was a marvel. A lively, liberal and vibrant city, it was built on ninety islands in what used to be a marshy bog. The city boasted 1,300 bridges, nearly a third of them historic stone structures, and over 160 miles of waterways. Bicycling residents zipped through the narrow cobbled streets of the old city centre. Grand Gothic structures sat side by side with Baroque beauties, and its incredible number of intact historic buildings made Amsterdam a huge, open-air museum of architecture.

Today, the Netherlands was one of the most open countries in the world on issues that are perennial hot potatoes in other places. The open availability of 'soft drugs', same-sex marriage and legal rights, the legality of euthanasia, and the Government's stand on prostitution as a taxable business, were all alien to both Malik's religion and his country. Nevertheless, these were to be Western qualities that the jihad would benefit from in the months ahead.

Malik heard a 'ping' and looked up. He saw the 'Fasten Seat Belt' sign light up and before the announcement was made he had done so, in preparation for the early-morning landing at Schipol International Airport. As the aircraft descended, he continued to ponder his moves over the next few days and reflected on the excellent opportunity that Thames Cruises had presented him in *Dutch Master*. He saw an opportunity to avoid losing *Last Tango* after all.

After landing, Malik quickly negotiated one of the most efficient and compact airports in Europe. It was only a short walk to the baggage area, through customs and immigration then on to the railway station. Malik took one of the many fast trains from the airport to Central Station in Amsterdam, a journey lasting less than fifteen minutes. From there a cab carried him through the busy traffic to the La Meridian Park Hotel on Stadhouderskade 25 in the vibrant city centre between the famous Leidseplein cafés and the Museumplein.

Malik checked into the hotel, went to his room then contacted the receptionist and enquired whether a Mr Rashidi, an Egyptian, had checked in. On hearing that he had arrived yesterday, Malik asked for his telephone extension number, thanked the receptionist and rang Mr Rashidi.

'Hello,' Malik said in English when the phone was answered, 'is that Mr Rashidi?'

'Yes,' was the sleepy response, 'can I help you?'

'Would you like to take a cruise on the Museum Boat?' Malik asked.

Recognising the identifying question, Mr Rashidi immediately sat up in his bed.

'Your friends tell me it's wonderful. You're Malik?'

'Yes.'

'Then I would be delighted. I'll be in the lobby in ten minutes. Please, call me Baba.'

'All right, Baba, see you then.'

Most of the museums in Amsterdam were situated quite close together and the Museum Boat offered a shuttle service that linked over twenty of them and other sightseeing attractions together. The boat trip took two hours and would give Malik ample time for discussing his plans with Baba, as well as providing a private and easily securable meeting place.

Thirty minutes after meeting they boarded the riverboat, and found a quiet spot near the stern.

'Thank you for travelling to Amsterdam to meet me, Baba, your work is vital to us.'

Baba, a giant for an Egyptian, owned a small cruise and shipping business that operated out of Cairo and across the eastern Mediterranean Sea. He was a very experienced seaman and not fussy whom he worked for provided it was well paid.

'How could I refuse such a generous offer? And Amsterdam, such a good place to visit. Your friend Abu Saudi can be very persuasive. I fear though that Amsterdam may be a little far for my old boats. So, what does Allah require of me?'

Malik felt confident that Baba was trustworthy and capable. 'This afternoon I'd like you to see a boat I am planning to buy, and in several months I'd like you to help me deliver a small package from Gibraltar to London via Amsterdam. You'll provide a small crew to meet me and sail my motor boat from Gibraltar to a shipyard here in Amsterdam, then on to Cairo. It will be carrying a discrete package hidden in one of the boat's fenders. At Amsterdam I'll transfer the package to another boat, a recently built riverboat that will make its maiden voyage to London this April. I'll take the riverboat to London, and you will deliver my motor boat to Cairo.'

'But where is the danger, my friend?'

'There may or may not be danger. I cannot be certain yet of the threats, so we must address them later. Regardless, the package must arrive in London undetected. We must be prepared to do anything to protect the package, anything at all.'

'Aha. As you journey to London, you wish me to act as a decoy?'

'That's a possibility, yes. Amsterdam is well known as a major smuggling route into England. You see, I must assume that by April, the British will be expecting this package to be smuggled in. If so, they will cordon their mainland at sea with their Navy. I would like you to escort the riverboat using my boat and if need be respond in such a way as to divert attention onto you. There's only one opportunity for the ruse but that's better than none. If you tease them and turn away, they will chase you down. And if they catch you in international waters and discover nothing they'll not detain you for evading their search.'

'That may be,' considered Baba as he fondled his deep cleft chin. 'First, tell me about these new boats of yours.'

For the remainder of the trip the two men discussed the details of their plans beginning with Malik describing the two boats. Baba relished the prospect of skippering *Last Tango* with his crew. So immersed were they in the details, they were completely oblivious to the gabled houses that lined the waterways and did not leave the riverboat at any of its stops.

The two men ate a late lunch together at the hotel before taking a cab. They arrived at the boatyard on the southern bank of the North Sea Canal at 3:10 p.m., ten minutes later than planned, delayed because of dense traffic. As they drove into the gravelled courtyard they saw a woman of about sixty, with a fitness and ease of movement that belied her age, waving to them as she strode purposefully in their direction. She gestured to the cab driver who turned in her direction before stopping. Malik paid the driver and they got out.

'Hello, you must be Mr Kent?' she said in English as she offered her hand.

Baba glanced at Malik and smiled.

Malik answered before introducing Baba as a colleague.

'I think it's wonderful you have purchased a share in Thames Cruises. It's a very good company and does not deserve to fail. You'll find *Dutch Master* a truly beautiful vessel of the highest quality, Mr Kent. She's the first of a new design but we cannot begin the final stage of construction until the issue of her ownership is resolved.'

On noticing her hardened hands and listening to her forthright manner, Malik guessed that much of her own time, dedication and skill had been invested in *Dutch Master.*

'Come. Follow me. First, I'll take you on a tour of the boatyard. Then you'll inspect *Dutch Master.*'

As they followed, Malik discovered that her name was Anita and that she and her husband owned the Jachthaven Aeolus and had done so for nearly thirty years. Her husband was currently in Marseilles where he was purchasing two new engines for a catamaran.

As they walked, Anita commentated and Malik was shown a vast hangar over a dry dock, with another in the open that was currently flooded. There was also a large expanse of ground littered with boats of all ages and designs, a long and vacant quayside, and a marina which was only half full of yachts and other vessels. Malik guessed that the boatyard's location near the Central Station would ensure that it was very busy in the summer months.

Although the huge rolling doors of the vast hangar were opened two metres, Malik and Baba were not prepared for the strong smell of fibreglass, varnish, paint and other toxic substances that assailed them as they entered. Despite its cavernous size, much of the space around the unoccupied covered dock was filled with the clutter found in any boatyard, including the remains from a newly built boat. Huge prefabricated moulds were suspended above the dock from the tall ceiling and smaller ones were left propped against walls. A large number of wooden crates were stacked in another corner. The only people Malik noticed were gathered together around a table in a prefabricated office that had windows overlooking the driveway and the covered dock.

'Well, that just leaves *Dutch Master*,' said Anita as they completed the tour.

They departed the hangar through the same massive doors and turned left. As soon as he turned a corner, Malik's eyes fell on a tall, sleek vessel floating in the still water, resplendent in its smart livery of royal-blue hull and white upper decks. Anita continued to talk proudly of her boatyard's achievement, but both men were only half-listening as they looked at the twenty-metre vessel.

The combined sea- and river-going, three-decked *Dutch Master* was a beautiful all-weather vessel with its spacious covered and open deck areas making it suitable for a variety of functions at any time of the year. Arriving guests stepped directly aboard into a large entrance hall that had ample room for clients to set up welcome reception facilities. Off the hall were the toilets. Leading from the entrance hall was the large, impressive enclosed lower saloon, complete with its own wooden panelled bar. The all-round windows gave the lower saloon a light and airy atmosphere during the day while the inset ceiling lights added intimacy for evening events. Tables and chairs awaiting the vessel in London could be arranged around the perimeter of the deck leaving a large central dance and entertainment area. From the entrance hall a flight of stairs led up to the mid-level deck that was split into open and enclosed areas. The forward enclosed section also had its own bar, space for tables and chairs, and a central open balcony feature that looked directly into the lower saloon. This section was ideal for those guests wishing to rest with a quiet drink but still remaining in touch with the party. Set into the ceiling, also inset with subdued lighting, was a large fanlight linking up to the top deck. The open stern section had non-slip decking and was large enough to accommodate open-air barbecues. From the mid-level deck another short flight of stairs led up to the wide-open expanse of the top deck. This totally open area was a fresh air platform that would provide an excellent view of London's world-famous riverside attractions. Baba, in awe of the craftsmanship and design, estimated that the vessel would easily accommodate in excess of three hundred people.

After inspecting the boat, Malik understood the Captain's frustrations with his company's receivership, as this craft would prove a huge success in London. It was the answer to the company's prayers if only they had had the financial support to back up the bold recovery plan in the face of a disaster resulting in loss of life several years before.

During the tour, Anita had skipped over the stowage lockers and the propulsion system, explaining that her husband was far more knowledgeable. Baba asked if he could have a second look at the latter while Malik asked to see all the lockers. Anita accompanied Malik, and Baba sauntered off. Twenty minutes later Anita and Malik were joined by Baba who looked contented.

'Perhaps you'd like to finish by inspecting the seaworthiness certificates and licences over a cup of coffee,' invited Anita.

'We would, thank you. And may I congratulate you on designing and constructing and equipping such a first-class vessel. She's beautiful,' replied Malik. 'Perhaps my colleague and I could have a look at some drawings too. If all is well, I'd like to contact the company and inform them of our progress. Will that be possible?'

'Naturally. But are you happy to proceed with the purchase, Mr Kent?'

'I'll let you know very soon, but first I must see the drawings and speak to the Captain,' Malik replied. Baba, who was clearly impressed, grunted his satisfaction.

Inspection of the certificates and drawings was necessary, and Malik noted that final sea trials were scheduled for mid-February. He also noted the specification of the fenders to be provided with the vessel. Allowing for the outstanding minor work and defects that had yet to be rectified, *Dutch Master* would be ready for delivery from the end of March.

Satisfied, Malik phoned the Captain.

'You're right. *Dutch Master* is perfect, Captain. I understand your eagerness to continue with the purchase and I'm delighted to say that I agree.'

Malik felt the man's relief flood down the telephone line.

'I knew you'd like her. Will you now pay for her?'

'I will. I'll inform Anita that the outstanding payments will be made immediately and the next payment withheld subject only to completion of all extant construction provisos. I still want to travel home in the vessel, but perhaps you can organise a crew and whatever escorts she needs.'

Later, as they waited for their cab, Malik confirmed with Anita that he would return in early April with escort vessels to deliver *Dutch Master* to her new home. Anita assured Malik that she would resolve the outstanding work and that *Dutch Master* would be ready.

On their return to the hotel, Malik and the affable Baba went directly to the bar and ordered drinks. They talked of *Last Tango*, *Dutch Master*, and the sea until the early hours of the following morning.

Chapter 28

December 20th, Z – 133 Days
CIA Headquarters, Langley, Virginia, USA

When the Director of the Counterterrorist Center, Major General Tom Carter, US Marine Corps, entered the CIA Director's office on the 'seventh floor' of the Old Headquarters Building he found Wayne Ewart and Bob Howard were already settled in and in deep discussion with the Director Central Intelligence.

'Tom, grab a seat,' offered Jim Ridge, the DCI, as he pointed the CTC Director to a low-backed easy chair.

General Carter held considerable respect for Ridge who had successfully fought a long and bitter campaign to retain the multi-agency Counterterrorist Center at Langley. It had not been a victory won, as cynics claimed, because of the close relationship between Ridge and the President, but a hard battle fought and won, in Carter's opinion, for the right reasons.

'My apologies, sir. Delayed landing into Dulles, heavy snowfall.'

Carter had just returned from a UN meeting in New York. A career soldier, he had joined the Marines as a private soldier straight from college. Both he and Ridge were appointees, though Ridge had been political, and Carter had led the Joint Military Intelligence Centre at the Pentagon for three years before his promotion and posting to the CIA four months ago. Wayne Ewart, the Chief Analyst and Deputy Director Intelligence and also Carter's boss, and Bob Howard, the Deputy Director Operations, were both career men, each having joined immediately after graduation. Both went to Yale, which was no surprise, for in those days the CIA recruited heavily from the Ivy League colleges.

Ten years ago the CIA's organisation was founded on two principal divisions, intelligence and operations. The operations division had consisted of just under two-thirds of the entire CIA's workforce of over six thousand personnel. Then, a branch of the intelligence division, the precursor to the CTC, was formed which caused a swelling in the ranks of intelligence collectors and analysts while it robbed experienced officers from the Directorate of Operations. The pendulum swung in favour of the Directorate of Intelligence.

Carter's responsibility was to lead this relatively new department within the Directorate of Intelligence, a large department that was fully established several years ago and whose mission was to pre-empt, disrupt and defeat terrorists. Now, reams of terrorist intelligence was collected and analysed daily. The CTC gathered primary information from the CIA's official and non-official cover operatives and its vast number of foreign intelligence sources that included the UK's Secret Services. It also gathered secondary information from the remainder of the US intelligence community, including the FBI, the National Security Agency and the National Reconnaissance Office. The Patriot Act underpinned the requirement for all US Government departments to share data with the CTC and no department was to knowingly withhold potentially relevant information without prior Presidential approval.

The Terrorist Threat Integration Centre within the CTC was the conduit for all this information, and it was here that it was combined and formed into useful intelligence. The TTIC provided the 'joined-up' view. Not only did the TTIC provide analysis that forewarned and protected the US Homeland and her global interests, but its analysis allowed the CTC and CIA to go on the offensive.

It was 3:30 p.m. and the DCI had ninety minutes before his daily briefing from the 'Small Group' in the conference room just down from his office. This daily briefing usually attracted about forty senior personnel, predominantly from the CTC. After each day's briefing, Carter would order the issue of the top-secret 'Threat Matrix' to over two hundred of America's highest security officers including the President. In effect, the Matrix informed its readers what terrorist threats the US intelligence community had uncovered and were currently investigating.

'Tom, I was just explaining to Bob and Wayne where we are with the nuclear threat to London. Can you expand?'

'Yes, sir. Right now my department is focusing on four issues, namely the tracing of missing nukes or nuclear and radioactive material, whether there are any errant scientists, the identification of suspicious activity using our supercomputer technology, and, with the help of the FBI, whether there are any associated money trails. But right now there is one issue that concerns me above all others.'

'Security?' guessed the DDI.

'That's right, sir,' replied Carter, 'specifically the Matrix.'

The wide distribution of the top-secret Matrix, vital for integration of the US Intelligence Community, caused the CIA sleepless nights. Although the Matrix had never knowingly been compromised, the risk of exposure of its secrets, whether malicious or innocent, was always there. Carter felt compelled to explain his concern to the new DCI.

'If we red-flag the terrorists the consequences could be massive, sir, directly for London, and indirectly for the world. The Matrix provides an insight into our knowledge and thinking. It details our intelligence and what we're doing. In the circumstances, I believe we must sanitise the information we release on the Matrix.'

'We can't trust anyone,' exclaimed the DDO, who had never supported the Matrix. 'This may become the biggest disaster since 9/11, and bigger than any of our ops overseas including A.Q. Khan and his nuclear network. We would be damn foolish to risk compromising this operation at an early stage. After all, we're not the direct target, the Brits are, and they have asked that we maintain maximum security, and that means keeping it tight. We all know that Capitol Hill leaks like a sieve, never mind the Intelligence Community across the US. This story would be worth a lifetime's salary and there are plenty of people in D.C. that need the cash.'

No one disagreed.

The DCI nodded. 'OK, I agree. We cannot take that risk. I will talk to the President after our conference, but for now let's assume he agrees and that it will remain a classified CIA intelligence project. What's the CTC doing, Tom?'

'We're contacting every nation who holds or has held nuclear weapons, and we are reinvestigating those nations who have the ability, or may have the ability, to manufacture a bespoke nuclear bomb. We already know that bin Laden has been searching for a nuclear bomb for many years. Just what bin Laden has in his stockpiles, and what he plans to do with it, and what can be done to stop him, have been our most pressing questions since 9/11.'

'Airborne anthrax and hijacked planes are little more than a tease compared with the prospect of rogue nukes, and bin Laden knows it,' added the DDO. 'The goal of terrorism is to spread panic and just the threat of a nuclear attack will guarantee that. Psychologically there are no constraints in a terror campaign. It could all be a bluff.'

The other three men considered this for a moment.

'But this threat was discovered through the back door,' replied the DCI. 'My belief is that it's real. Bin Laden may intend to publicise the attack prior to detonation and accelerate the panic. It's also unlikely bin Laden would want to compromise his credibility amongst his followers; if he says something he follows it through. It's also been an open secret that bin Laden and his al-Qa'eda organisation have long lusted after nukes.'

'A terrorist group like al-Qa'eda obtaining a nuclear bomb is as inevitable as evolution,' said the DDI. 'It's the ultimate terror weapon and that's the business they're in. I think it highly likely that bin Laden has recently stolen or purchased a nuclear bomb. We know al-Qa'eda had links to scientists in Pakistan. Perhaps Khan provided them with the material and they have since constructed one?'

'It's possible,' said the DCI, 'but more likely, I think they've stolen or purchased one.'

'First London, then Washington,' the DDO mused. 'We cannot afford to delay the search for terrorist nuclear stockpiles for long. We should deploy more operatives.'

'No. Not yet,' answered the DCI. Neither the President nor I will compromise London and act unilaterally. They want to take a subtle approach that does not drive the terrorists underground. We will support MI6 and cooperate through our operatives, Bernazzani and Fulton.'

The three subordinates nodded.

Carter glanced at his watch and continued. 'We know bin Laden has been searching the black markets of Europe and Asia for some time looking for pirated Russian warheads. We also know that al-Qa'eda has been looking for components including enriched uranium. Relatively new to the free-for-all thieving of the post-Soviet republics, bin Laden has been fleeced at least twice, getting fooled by black marketers who tried to sell him low-grade, radioactive rubbish.'

'Perhaps that forced him to redouble his efforts to seek out and buy or steal a ready-made nuclear bomb?' the DDI suggested.

'Quite possibly,' answered Carter. 'Bin Laden has certainly been a patient shopper. Jamal al-Fadl, one of the four al-Qa'eda terrorists convicted of planning the US embassy bombings, informed us about bin Laden's numerous attempts to get hold of nuclear material. Bin Laden paid one and a half million dollars for a cylinder of South African uranium, though it's not certain whether he received it. He also paid at least one million dollars for nuclear waste to be brought from Bulgaria through Moldavia and Ukraine but, again, there was no evidence he actually received any shipments.'

'What about nuclear bombs from ex-Soviet states?' enquired the DDO.

'We know that Russia and the former Soviet states are leaking like a sieve,' Carter answered. 'The Soviet Union produced more than 140 tons of weapon-grade plutonium and a whopping 1,000 tons of highly enriched uranium during its nuclear peak. Russia's internal security agencies admit that on hundreds of occasions they have had to seize fissionable materials or technical documents that had fallen into the wrong hands. The United Nations' International Atomic Energy Agency reported at the conference I attended this morning that there had been 175 known cases of trafficking in nuclear material since 1996. In the late 1990s, Afghan and Pakistani smugglers were sneaking so much nuclear material out of the former Soviet Union that they had to stockpile it in at least one warehouse in Peshawar, Pakistan.'

'I remember that case,' offered the DDI. 'Andrew Smith, an American antiquities dealer familiar with Pakistan's black markets, claimed to have been in a Peshawar warehouse where dozens of canisters of nuclear contraband were stored under the floor.'

'Our investigations led us to believe that was radioactive waste scavenged from hospitals, certainly not weapons-grade stuff,' the DDO added.

'All right, I get the picture,' the DCI interrupted. 'Tom, what about the scientists?'

'If nuclear bombs are trickling out of the former Soviet Union,' replied Carter, 'nuclear scientists and engineers are too. A year ago, Russia intercepted a planeload of missile scientists leaving the country to go to work for North Korea. Since then, redundant scientists and engineers have become more desperate, and Russian borders are more porous, meaning that the brain drain has worsened. But detonating a nuclear bomb won't require much technical assistance if bin Laden can get his hands on an off-the-shelf weapon. Just one technician would probably suffice. After the East–West thaw, Russia claimed to have secured all the weapons but we know that's not true. In the late 1990s, a Russian General Alexander Lebed claimed that his government had lost track of 134 mini-nukes alone, and stories have circulated that bin Laden bought twenty of them from Chechen warriors for thirty million dollars and two tons of heroin. Some may be duds but even a partial detonation of one of these weapons could destroy the heart of a city and release a lot of radioactivity.'

'Presumably a dirty bomb requires no nuclear skill either?' asked the DDO.

'That's right, though like the true nuke you may need a nuclear technician to check it over,' answered Carter. 'It's the home-made full-blown nuclear bomb that requires the skill, making this a very unlikely option for the terrorists. Even a low-grade home-made nuclear bomb is an enormously complicated business, unlike the ready-made weapons, which are simple. We're probably looking at either a true nuke or a dirty bomb, and perhaps just one or maybe two technicians. Dirty bombs are very simple. Detonated in a crowded city like London, a dirty bomb would pack an explosive punch no greater than its ordnance but the radioactive debris it would scatter could sicken and kill large numbers of people and contaminate a vast stretch of real estate.'

'The upshot is,' added the DDI, 'we believe we're looking for a nuclear-fission device supported by at least one competent nuclear technician. And if we find the cell, they will likely lead to the weapon.'

'If they do that, they may also lead us to bin Laden,' said the DCI optimistically. 'What else have you got, Tom?'

'The NSA and NRO are intercepting telecommunications throughout the Middle East and Central Asia. The NSA's state-of-the-art voice recognition systems at Fort Mead are monitoring any conversation that refers to the two key words "bomb" and

"London". If we can narrow down the search pattern we will increase our chances. The Brits are hoping Winchester and Fulton will help with that.'

'Does that include email?' asked the DDO.

'We're intercepting email too, but there are many excellent encryption packages available nowadays and the NSA's systems do not capture them all. A user can simply avoid using key words too, or even translate messages into obscure languages.'

'Essentially, unless we are very lucky, we must locate the computer terminal or the dial-up number using traditional methods,' added the DDI. 'Only then can we monitor them.'

'That's right,' confirmed Carter. 'If we knew which terminal the terrorist was using for email we could monitor it. The same goes for telephones. The location of cell phones can be triangulated to within several metres, but for that we need a number. Unfortunately there are millions of unregistered cell phones. On the plus side, if we can narrow a source down to a single country or region, and have someone's voice print taken from say, television, we can pinpoint the number.'

'I see,' said the DCI. 'Can we maximise foreign intelligence sources?'

The DDO nodded. 'The support we get from allied security services geographically close to bin Laden is vital, particularly from the Pakistan Secret Service, the ISI. Requests have been made for specific intelligence information that will not raise the alarm.'

'Good. We have thirty minutes,' noted the DCI.

'We're running a supercomputer search of thousands of known or suspected terrorists and monitoring their movements through just about everything that leaves a traceable record,' continued Carter. 'The usual things are bank accounts, credit cards bills, hire car transactions, flight bookings, and so on. We have a huge database that can cross-reference thousands of names and places.'

'I assume we'll be simulating the attack to examine how they might conduct such a strike?' asked the DCI.

'We are, sir. We're feeding in the probabilities as we speak, but that will take some time, at least a week. Even then it will not give us anything useful until we narrow down the variables with hard fact, and refine the probabilities.'

Nobody spoke, so Carter continued with the next issue.

'A major avenue to follow up is the terrorist's financial trail. We have learned a considerable amount about bin Laden's financial network from the likes of Zacarias Maoussaoui, the twentieth hijacker in the 9/11 attack, the al-Qa'eda terrorist, Ahmed Ressam, and a bin Laden bagman for the 9/11 terrorists, Ali Abd al-Aziz.'

Carter paused for effect, then looked at the DCI. 'Frankly, sir, the way I see it is that we're at war against the first truly global terror operation. Our nation understands that, even if many nations in the international community do not. Once you cross that invisible line and declare war, you should win and restore order as soon as possible, using any means at your disposal. No one wants a protracted war against terrorism, and applying overwhelming force or conventional tactics alone is not going to beat them.'

'Al-Qa'eda does not recognise any rules. If we're to beat them, then it must be on the same playing field,' said the DDI helpfully.

'Bringing bin Laden to justice has been the non-negotiable US war aim since 9/11,' added the DCI, 'when the President publicly declared that he wanted the al-Qa'eda leader dead or alive, as well as the eradication of the global terror network. The implication being that we must do everything within our power to stop this man, by whatever means is necessary.'

'Precisely,' said Carter. 'There are financial operatives in the FBI who claim they can go much further than international law allows, if only someone would give them that authority. They claim to be able to hack into known terrorists' banking records unnoticed and follow money trails. A nuclear attack would cost a considerable amount of money to support and the FBI may be able to identify and trace that money. Who knows, the international community may even be able to recover it, prevent its use to fund terrorism and use it instead to support the victims. It should also lead us to terrorists. It's too valuable not to follow up, and in the circumstances...'

'Why on earth haven't we hacked in already?' asked the DCI incredulously.

The DDO smiled then answered. 'The Director FBI won't allow it as it infringes international monetary law.'

'There was another reason,' said the DDI. 'Your predecessor discussed the issue with the President at a time when we were not faced with a nuclear threat. There were specific concerns involving the Egyptian and Saudi governments and also Pakistan. During the Afghan war against the Soviets, a number of Western countries including ourselves, and the intelligence services of the Egyptian and Saudi governments, funnelled aid, equipment, training and financial support to the Afghan Mujahidin jihad against the Soviet invasion. It's believed that this financial support now funds al-Qa'eda and its attacks on the West. Worse, any investigation will reveal that steady financial support still finds its way to al-Qa'eda from some Islamic states, including several allies, as well as wealthy Arab heirs, princes, oil sheikhs and businessmen who either support bin Laden's ideology or are inclined to hedge their bets on the outcome of his protracted battle with the West.'

The DCI sighed. 'Anyone think we shouldn't hack in?'

Everyone remained silent.

'OK, I'll raise this issue with the President on the video link after the briefing. My advice will be that we, rather than anyone else, hack in, then deal with each consequence as and when it arises. The Brits will certainly attempt it if we don't. This way we get to control the skeletons.'

The DCI stood up, and the others followed. 'The Brits have named their response "Operation Enduring Freedom".'

'Classy,' remarked the DDO.

They broke up with just ten minutes to go before the briefing. The three subordinates were relieved that the new DCI had the courage to do what was needed to combat this new type of global warfare. Despite any prejudices, it was clear to each of them why the President, after his recent successful election campaign, had chosen to promote the Homeland Security advisor into the CIA's top job.

Chapter 29

December 19th, Z – 134 Days
Kabul, Afghanistan

Harry and Tess flew into Kabul International Airport on an Azerbaijan Airlines Tupolev TU–154. Both were feeling tired after a twelve-hour journey from Heathrow via Istanbul and Baku on the Caspian Sea; it was necessary to change flights at Baku due to the refusal of most international carriers, including British Airways, to fly into Kabul until stringent international air safety regulations were met. A junior officer from the British Embassy in Kabul had taken the same journey, and it was he who carried the two matching cases which contained the belongings of both operatives.

Travelling as Western journalists working for the UK branch of an American-owned independent television company called United Media (UK) Limited, Harry and Tess were confident that their covers were watertight and would not attract suspicion from anyone including NATO's peacekeeping force. Knowledge of this MI6 operation, like many others, was to be minimised.

Routinely clearing customs and immigration, the two operatives were met in the airport foyer by a driver holding up a card bearing an alias. Ahmad, the driver, greeted Harry and Tess like any other fare and led his passengers to a yellow-and-white four-by-four Mitsubishi that was parked directly outside the entrance. The junior officer, who had enjoyed diplomatic immunity, followed them to the car and simply handed them the cases before he melted away.

'*Chi toor hasty*,' Ahmad greeted Tess, enquiring after her health. He merely glanced at Harry without any recognition, concerned that he might give something away that he shouldn't.

'*Khub os tom. Ta shar koor*,' Tess replied in fluent Dari, an Afghan-Persian dialect. She thanked him and then told him that they were fine.

The look of astonishment that spread over Ahmad's face made Harry smile. He was glad that the Embassy had seen fit to employ Ahmad as their driver and guard.

Ahmad was a Tajik and Sunni Muslim who spoke Dari, Persian and excellent English. He possessed typical Tajik features that combined a slender build with light skin, an aquiline nose and black hair. The four million Tajiks in Afghanistan, accounting for approximately twenty-five per cent of the population, were a sedentary people who lived in many sections of the country but maintained a strong sense of community loyalty. They made up the bulk of Afghanistan's educated elite and possessed considerable wealth and political influence. They were also the principal inhabitants of the republic of Tajikistan across the northern border.

Ahmad was regularly recruited by the British Embassy from Jamshady Services in Ariana Market, Kabul, a Western-style company that provided translators, drivers, airport pickups, bodyguards and anything else of a similar nature. Their customers were predominantly foreign government workers, aid workers and journalists. He had been regularly employed as a British Embassy driver, guide and minder for over four years and he loved the job that earned him respect from the British and Tajiks alike. In his mind it put him in the centre of the universe.

With his numerous contacts throughout Kabul, the north-east and the west of the country, Ahmad was also of considerable value to the British Secret Service. Harry had known Ahmad for three years and he knew that the Tajik was born in the north-eastern mountains of Afghanistan to poor village-dwelling farmers and had remained there until the fall of the Taliban in 1996. Harry also knew that Ahmad had emerged as one of the canniest Tajik guerrilla fighters during the war with the Red Army, that he was fiercely patriotic and that he had come to Kabul with thousands of other Tajiks to help restore order to a devastated city and country in the post-Taliban era. Ahmad was as trustworthy as anyone in this region.

Although the Tajiks were the second-largest group after the Pashtuns they had survived the two decades of war and strife in a far less fragmented state and were now in a much better position to challenge for power.

As they left the airport, Harry pointed out to Tess the rusting heap of vintage planes and collection of trashed aviation memorabilia on their right, known locally as the Ariana Graveyard. Some of the devastation was the result of coalition attacks in late 2001, but the real damage was done between 1991 and 1996 as rival Mujahidin factions had battled for control of the city. Gulbuddin Hekmatyar, the leader of Hezb-i-Islami or the Islamic Faction, had launched constant attacks on the airport right up until the Taliban had taken control of the city.

On the sixteen-kilometre journey to the city, Harry caught up with events in Afghanistan; there was little of newsworthy value that Ahmad did not know. Above the commentary emitting from the dashboard radio, recognisable as the BBC World Service, and the noise of the fan emitting hot air, Harry and Tess heard how violence was spreading across Afghanistan amidst preparations for national elections.

Ahmad explained passionately how the killings had worsened again since Harry had departed the year before. That very morning a remotely detonated roadside bomb had exploded in Kunduz 150 miles north of Kabul, as a convoy of international peacekeepers had driven through the Gandum Bazaar Market. Three civilian bystanders, all Tajiks, had been killed. Yesterday eleven Chinese workers and an Afghan guard had been killed in Kunduz province, and five members of the medical relief agency Médecins Sans Frontières had been fatally shot in the remote north-west last week. According to Ahmad, Government propaganda prevented the real news from being told, so if they wished to hear the truth, they must ask him. Apparently over five hundred people had died in violence across the country this year, most in Kabul by armed factions. A high number of casualties were aid workers and government officials. Most were the victims of the ongoing Taliban insurgency, though some died in fighting linked to the country's booming drug trade.

As they drove past acres of flat fields blanketed with snow, Ahmad explained to Harry and Tess that there had been a half-hearted nationwide campaign to eradicate part of the country's bumper harvest of opium poppies this year, but that drug traffickers had fought back. In the end one thousand acres had been destroyed, and Ahmad speculated that this was a token effort, destroying little more than barren fields.

According to Ahmad, the fugitive Taliban leader Mullah Omar

and Osama bin Laden were hiding in Africa and they were together, biding their time before they returned to crush the West as they had done the Soviet Army. Neither Harry nor Tess gave his theory much credence, though they did admit to themselves that Ahmad had as much idea as anyone else.

'What makes you think that, Ahmad?' enquired Harry.

'It's what is said on the streets,' replied Ahmad with a shrug of the shoulders. 'You Westerners underestimate the amount of support they have in this country, especially amongst the Pashtuns.'

'Where exactly?'

'In the coffeehouses. They pass word through the coffeehouses.'

'But where in Africa?'

'Sudan. He was expelled and came here for several years, then went back.'

Harry let it go.

The conversation, as it always does with drivers in Afghanistan, turned to the state of the roads. The numerous off-road car wrecks were a reminder of the dangers of travelling anywhere in this war-torn country. All traffic was in danger of landmines that had been planted on and near roadways. An estimated five million landmines and large quantities of unexploded ordnance existed throughout the Afghan countryside and alongside its roads, posing a danger to travellers. Robbery and crime were also prevalent on highways, even in Kabul. With the odd exception that included Ahmad's Mitsubishi, vehicles were poorly maintained and often overloaded. Traffic laws were not enforced and driving was erratic. Vehicular traffic was chaotic and had to contend with numerous pedestrians, bicyclists and animals at all times of the day and night. Many urban streets had large potholes and were not well lit, and most rural roads were not paved. The road conditions were dreadful, made much worse by the icy conditions. As a result it took Ahmad over an hour to drive the sixteen kilometres to the Intercontinental Hotel. While weary, Harry did not consider it time wasted, but time to absorb information, to acclimatise.

The whole of West Kabul summed up the wanton destruction the city had seen over the last three decades. West Kabul was once a huge residential area with a grand avenue that led to the Darulaman Palace and Kabul Museum. Thousands of people had been forced to flee, however, as the rival Mujahidin factions rained shells at each other across the avenues and villas from their strategic positions in the surrounding hills. As a result of that sustained shelling, the area had been reduced to rubble and dust. Today it was a haunting reminder of Kabul's recent history, with the palace and the museum being the most striking evidence of the bitter legacy of war. Just beyond Kabul Zoo was a roundabout with the Maiwand Memorial Column in the middle. The column and the completely destroyed surrounding buildings were what most TV crews now filmed to emphasise the destruction of Kabul.

The Intercontinental Hotel, situated on the outskirts of the city heading into West Kabul, was probably the best-known hotel in Kabul; this was the place for all the international conferences, and a temporary home to many journalists, diplomats and Afghan government ministers, many of whom had chosen to live here when they returned to Kabul after the expulsion of the Taliban. The hotel was being restored to its former glory and work had just commenced on the fifth of eight floors. There was a new fitness centre and swimming pool that were only open to men, a sauna, tennis court and barber. The busy internet café in the basement advertised high-speed connection, printing and scanning facilities.

The first thing Harry noticed as they drew up to the Intercontinental Hotel was the protective perimeter fencing that had not been there when he left. The second was the attempt at reconstruction. A squad of mean-looking US soldiers from the NATO peacekeeping force were guarding the entrance to the hotel's compound and cursorily checking identification. Ahmad explained that many of the provincial government ministers were staying here now and that the hotel's manager, another close friend of his, had demanded NATO security. The hotel, popular amongst foreign visitors and local dignitaries, had suffered a bomb attack four weeks ago causing minor damage and several casualties. Ahmad claimed that the manager was more concerned about the ongoing rebuilding than the guests.

Asking Ahmad to wait, Harry and Tess entered the hotel with a porter following behind carrying their bags. Twenty minutes later they returned to the car refreshed, and Ahmad drove them through the busy midday bazaars of central Kabul to the British Embassy in the west of the city, off Salang Wat. Although Harry was prepared for the destruction and grime of mid-winter, he could see that Tess was shocked. It was impossible for a first-time Western visitor not to be struck by the shear waste of what was once a beautiful city.

'Where have the inhabitants gone?' asked Tess solemnly.

'Most are dead, the rest are living in the camps outside town, or in the cellars,' answered Ahmad. 'The lucky ones live in the hotels or hostels. Only a very lucky few have some kind of house to live in.'

Sporadic gunfire could be heard in the distance.

'Don't worry,' said Ahmad, calmly viewing his passengers in his rear-view mirror. 'It's not important. It's people fighting over land after an unfavourable ruling. You may claim what's yours in Kabul, but you must fight for it. If you win, the mines are next, then the kidnappers, eh?'

International communication was very difficult in Afghanistan. Most foreigners relied upon satellite communications even to make local calls. Although the equipment was expensive and often bulky, it was dependable. Cell phone services were offered in Kabul and were inexpensive in comparison to satellite communications, but the network availability was extremely erratic. Distressed foreigners could face long delays before being able to communicate their situation to family or colleagues outside of Afghanistan. Internet access through global service providers was limited and also unreliable, and when it was up and running, free terminals were hard to find. On the other hand, Harry and Tess would have no difficulty with their satcom systems, whose remote stations were directly above them in space.

As the two operatives entered the British Ambassador's makeshift office, they were welcomed by Diane Broughton who was accompanied by George Galway. Diane was delighted to see Harry again, and they kissed each other on both cheeks before everyone sat down.

'So how is my loveable rogue?' asked the Ambassador.

'Still loveable, I hope. This is my partner, Tess, she's CIA. Tess, this is the Ambassador, and George Galway, the local official cover operative.'

'Call me Diane,' the Ambassador said to Tess. 'So what's the latest, Harry?'

Harry quickly brought them up to speed. '...So you see, I must find Amir as soon as possible.'

'I think we can help there,' said the Ambassador. 'Rahim Mullah, the Christian Cemetery guardian, has sent word that he must see you when you come back.'

'The body snatcher. Are we still paying him? And what, I wonder made Mullah think I was coming back?'

Everyone smiled. Even Tess had come to know that Harry liked to create names for people who stood out.

'Precisely, and yes we're still paying him. He holds many keys and his information is worth every rouble.' The Ambassador leaned toward Tess. 'It's rumoured that Mullah Omar once offered him a lifetime of Taliban protection but that he turned it down.'

'You should catch him this afternoon if you leave now,' suggested George.

'Harry, this place is *less* secure than it was a year ago,' added the Ambassador. 'The rumours of progress are little more than spin. Trust no one and be careful, both of you.'

'Thanks, we will,' answered Tess gratefully.

Harry glanced at his chronometer. 'Diane, we'd better go. I'm not sure how long we will be staying in Kabul but perhaps we could call back, maybe tomorrow?'

'Any time, Harry. Tess, it was nice to meet you. If you need anything contact George. He is remarkably resourceful.'

'Any news on the Embassy rebuild?' asked Harry as he made his way to the door.

The Ambassador chuckled. 'None. I was just replying to some idiot in Whitehall who's proposing a concrete monstrosity, when you arrived. Truth is, a generation will go by before its worth considering a rebuild. There are far higher priorities out here.'

'By the way, thanks for arranging Ahmad,' Harry added.

'You're welcome. Call back OK?' replied George as he opened the door.

Harry and Tess followed George out of the office and through the compound.

After they had left, the Ambassador sat down and wondered about Harry and Tess. Lucky girl, she thought.

The Christian Cemetery was open every day and was a walled graveyard of around one hundred and fifty graves behind large arched wooden doors about one hundred and fifty metres beyond the martyr's shrine on Char-i-Shahid. Christians had been buried there for more than a hundred years. More recent additions to the cemetery were the NATO memorial plaques. To the right of the entrance there was one to the British officers and soldiers who died in the Afghan wars in the nineteenth and twentieth centuries, which was placed in the wall last year. Opposite at the other end, there was a memorial plaque to the German officers and soldiers who lost their lives in Afghanistan placed by the German contingent. Other plaques to NATO soldiers could be spotted on the perimeter walls.

The cemetery guardian, sixty-year-old Rahim Mullah, had been tending the graves for seventeen years, one of which was rumoured to belong to his wife. For Mullah, the Taliban period had been a difficult one, for he had been heavily criticised during that time for continuing to tend the cemetery. And though he was salaried, his income dried up after the international agency that was paying him, the International Organisation for Migration, was bombed and pulled out of the country. Money was sent in from Peshawar in Pakistan, but it was an uncertain trickle of funds. Today the British Embassy in Kabul paid Rahim's salary and he looked forward to passing the mantle of service to the British Embassy on to his eldest son.

Harry entered the graveyard on foot with Tess. They found Mullah taking a break in his old stone shed, and after several minutes of pleasantries between the two acquaintances, Harry asked what he wanted. The body snatcher nodded thoughtfully then with a toothless smile he turned away from them for a moment. On turning back, he handed Harry a small, tattered envelope.

'*Ta shar koor, Khuda Hafiz,*' Harry responded as he took the envelope. Thank you and goodbye. Harry put the envelope in his pocket and handed Mullah a ten US dollar bill as they left, the equivalent of three days' wages.

Harry waited until he and Tess were back in the security of his hotel room before retrieving the envelope from his pocket. The note was written in Dari and both operatives read simultaneously.

My dear friend,
Forgive my caution but these are trouble times. I know you understand. Be at Kabul Zoo at eleven o'clock in the morning

and Babur Gardens at three o'clock in afternoon, and eat at our favourite eating place each evening from eight o'clock until I contact you. Allah is Almighty.
A.

In Kabul you can eat almost anywhere and catch almost anything. There are kebab stalls on every corner. Restaurants were slow to open after the Taliban fell, but there were now several places that served good foreign and Afghan food. Wealthier Afghans and the international community particularly enjoyed the Golden Lotus and Khyber restaurants. But the Anaar had always been Harry's favourite though security was more of a concern there. For a small price, Harry and Tess employed Ahmad to watch their backs.

Amir had introduced Harry to the Anaar which offered a wonderful, warm dining experience. Located down a lantern-lit alleyway, the restaurant reception and dining rooms were hung with beautiful Afghan carpets. In fact, all the decor was local. A magnificent, carved wooden doorframe to the dining area furthest from the draught of the reception area was a fabulous work of art. In this room, diners sprawled on Afghan cushions and ate from low-level tables while everywhere else there was seating. In the centre of the main seating area, on to which all other rooms converged, there was a vast fireplace that, along with the kitchen, heated the building. The cuisine was described as Indian, Chinese, Thai or 'Local'. Indeed the restaurant was co-owned by an Indian and Afghan who had brought their culinary experiences to play there very successfully. The Thai green curry was particularly good. There was no alcohol served there, but you could bring your own as long as you were discreet about consumption and requested permission from the management first.

Tess accompanied Harry to the Anaar where he chose a quiet corner table in the main dining area that overlooked the door from the reception. As they ate, folk music drifted from a trio of local instruments in another corner close to where Ahmad sat with some colleagues. Harry recognised a guitar-like *rubab*, a *dhol*, similar to miniature drums, and a *richak*, which was similar to a violin. After an enjoyable starter of *maushawa*, a local pulse and yoghurt soup, Harry and Tess waited fifteen minutes before the main course arrived. They shared a meal of Afghani lamb, *chelo nachodo*, a chicken, chickpea and rice dish, and *kadu bouranee*, sweet pumpkins. Harry told the waiter he would try the Thai green curry, their speciality, tomorrow night. Soon after they tucked into the main course, Tess asked Harry what he thought about the war on terror then immediately apologised. But with at least another hour to fill, he happily replied.

'OK, the war on terror aims to destroy global terrorism. A laudable aim for sure, but I'm not certain whether our strategy of armed response can be successful. Punishing the terrorists is necessary but will not resolve the problem; indeed it may encourage others. This strategy suggests we do not understand what has happened. We must find an enduring solution through a combination of military and political means. The grievances of the terrorists who committed the horrendous attacks on America on 9/11 have deep and persistent roots going back more than one hundred and fifty years. The terrorists harbour a hatred that will not die without a lasting commitment to political and religious enlightenment, respect and tolerance from both sides, Islam and the West. Islamic opposition to the West is far from being a phenomenon invented by Osama bin Laden, or the Taliban, or for that matter Iran, Iraq or the Palestinians. It has grown consistently since the beginning of the nineteenth century as an effective oppositional force both to the West and to local secular rulers. We have to look back centuries to see how it began and to discover what we must do to put it right. In my opinion Western powers were blind to the increase in Islamist opposition forces throughout the late nineteenth and twentieth centuries because they were overshadowed by a greater power rivalry during this period.'

The waiter arrived to ask if all was well with the meal, so Harry broke off. Tess poured more juice and an extra glass of still water. She took a sip as he continued.

'The original leader of the opposition to the West was Jamalludin al-Afghani who lived to about one hundred years ago. He was called the "Father of Islamic Modernism" and was educated in Iran, Afghanistan and India. He travelled throughout the Islamic world promulgating Islamic reform. Using an Islamic ideology helped him to transcend ethnic differences in the region and preach a message all Islam would understand. He sought to mobilise Muslim nations to fight against Western imperialism but also gain military power through modern technology.'

Tess knew much of what Harry was saying and said so. Both of them found it helpful to establish and understand each other's views. They ate as Harry continued.

'Al-Afghani claimed that Britain, France and Russia in particular were operating in collusion with Arab rulers to rob the people of their patrimony through sweetheart deals for exploitation of natural and commercial resources in the region. As a direct result of the efforts of al-Afghani and his followers, groups such as the Muslim Brotherhood evolved throughout the region. These groups generally espoused three methods in their political and religious activity: personal piety coupled with evangelism, religious modernisation, and political resistance to secular regimes.'

'Not violence?'

'No.'

'So, many of the rulers were considered Western puppets?' asked Tess.

'Many were. On the face of it, the three methods in al-Afghani's political and religious activity appeared reasonable to many Islamic peoples, most of who thought the Western nations had committed a litany of crimes against the Muslim world. After World War I, many Arab nations were treated as war prizes to be divided and manipulated for the good of the militarily powerful Europeans. The British and the French, without consent or consultation on the part of the residents, took every nation between the Mediterranean Sea and the Persian Gulf for their own benefit. This further increased the resentment of the fundamentalists against the West and against the rulers installed and upheld by Westerners.'

Tess knew where Harry was going. 'Seeking out and eliminating the terrorist thugs is one thing but extinguishing the historical resentment is quite another.'

Harry thought for a moment. 'My task is the former and nothing more, but it helps me to distinguish the good guys from the bad if I understand their motivation. A religious nut does not equal a terrorist.'

Tess said nothing. Harry paused to eat before continuing.

'But the meddling of the infidels got worse. After World War II, the US and the Soviet Union fought over Arab nations.

Governments such as those of Egypt, Sudan, Iraq and Syria were constantly pressed to choose between East and West. The choice was often prompted by "gifts" of military support to sitting rulers, their people entirely unaware. With ready sources of money and guns from either Washington or Moscow, Arab rulers easily oppressed the religious fundamentalists who opposed them. This added to the anger of the religious reformers. At this point the frustrated oppositionists abandoned political action through conventional political processes and turned to non-legal methods or terrorism to make their dissatisfaction felt.'

'Christ, did we, the West really cause all of this?' asked Tess incredulously.

'Ultimately terrorists are entirely responsible for their own deadly actions. For them there can be no excuse. As well as protecting ourselves, which incidentally is our job, politicians and rulers must establish the conditions where everyone can live side by side. But to achieve that, everyone must compromise and there are many, I know, who won't because they have too much to lose. In that respect we doom ourselves.'

A silence followed while Harry finished his meal.

'Your country became the sole representative of the West after 1972, when the UK, poor and humbled, could no longer afford to maintain a full military force in the region. Anxious to protect oil supplies the US propped up the Shah of Iran and the Saudi Arabian Government despite internal unrest. The people were subjugated.'

'The ill-fated "Twin Pillars" strategy,' pondered Tess. 'That ended with the Iranian Revolution, leaving us with a messy patchwork of military and political detritus.'

'That's about right,' responded Harry, grimly amused. 'And when Iran went to war with Iraq, the US supported Saddam Hussein to prevent Iran from winning. Then, anxious about the Soviet invasion of Afghanistan, it propped up the Taliban. These two monstrous forces, Saddam and the Taliban, were supported by the US for their own purposes. The final blow came when the US finally had to confront its former client, Iraq, in the first Gulf War. The US established a military base on Saudi Arabian soil considered sacred by pious Muslims. Saudi officials had been resisting this move for years, knowing that it would be politically dangerous for them. This specific action provoked the Saudi Osama bin Laden's opposition to the US.'

'All of this meddling gives credence to the assertion that the West was out to rob the Muslim people of their prerogatives and patrimony,' Tess said. 'Twentieth century and current terrorists in the region, including bin Laden, can be said to have political pedigrees leading directly back to the original reformer, Al-Afghani.'

Harry took the conversation a final step. 'He is, of course, simply a thug, no better than a mafia boss. But that cannot necessarily be said of all those thousands of people who are prepared to lay down their lives for his cause. I believe that bin Laden does consider himself a messiah as will others after him, and therefore I consider it essential that global leaders find a way to break this pattern, or we will be mired in these troubled waters for ever. But first, you and I must prevent a catastrophe that will probably prevent a solution for all time. Worse, it could trigger hatred and annihilation never experienced before on this planet.'

'Let's say we prevent the strike, then what?' asked Tess, seeking the next unanswered question.

'That is up to the leaders of the world. In my opinion they need to be united, probably under the UN banner, if they are ever to address and eradicate this global threat. They must achieve two things. First, the world must get to the root of the problem and without being selfish, insulting or condescending to any one nation state, its religious beliefs or its system of government, remove the rationale for terrorist support. Second, if terrorists are to be dealt with adequately by a progressive world, every nation must accept that terrorism is a crime against international law and hunt down the perpetrators.'

'I think they can achieve the second step,' said Tess.

'So do I,' replied Harry, 'but I worry the first may be impossible.'

Finishing her main course, Tess asked a waiter for the menu. They decided against desserts but ordered coffee, which they lingered over for another thirty minutes. The conversation turned lighter as it became clear Amir was not coming.

Tomorrow Harry and Tess would spend time visiting the Kabul Zoo and Babur Gardens and if necessary they would return to the Anaar Restaurant.

'Tomorrow night it's your turn to speak for the blue corner,' laughed Harry as they left the restaurant with Ahmad.

There was a great deal for Harry and Tess to see in Kabul as they waited for Amir to contact them, even though most of it was wrecked. They both understood that Amir would be stalking them, watching and biding his time. Amir would have no wish to be caught by Taliban sympathisers and beheaded.

Harry purchased a Nancy Dupree pocket guidebook for Tess at the Intercontinental Hotel and in one morning she read it from cover to cover. Kabul had changed dramatically since the book was first published in 1972 but it gave an incredible insight into what the city was like. Despite the freezing weather over the next few days, Harry and Tess, accompanied and protected by Ahmad, visited some of the must-sees such as the Darulaman Palace, the Kabul Museum, King Nadir Shah's tomb, the attractions of the money market, the Ka Farushi bird market and the wealth of arts, crafts and carpet sellers at the bazaars. It was surprisingly easy among the snow-covered rubble to forget that Kabul was one of the most mined cities in the world.

Chapter 30

December 23rd, Z – 130 Days
Buenos Aires, Argentina

It was another hot, humid day in Buenos Aires. Malik drove up to the rusty wrought-iron gates of the old meat-processing factory in his rented Toyota Land Cruiser. Through the rear-view mirror he saw Jamali pull up immediately behind him off the Avenue Don Pedro de Mendoza. Behind Jamali in a third car was Jamali's daughter, Nadia, a realtor. Nadia had been delighted to trace the factory owner and negotiate a short-term let with a view to buy, and for once she had the additional satisfaction of undercutting one of her ruthless competitors. As it turned out, the factory had been empty for three years, and her credible offer was warmly welcomed.

Nadia opened the large lock, released the heavy chain and left the two men to open the twin iron gates. Returning to their cars, they drove into the factory compound, parked at the rear in the parking lots which were out of sight from the road, then returned on foot to the gates to close and relock them. The factory had not changed since Malik last saw it several weeks ago before his trip to London and Amsterdam, and he still felt the same air of abandonment that pervaded this part of the city.

As they walked back to the main pedestrian entrance at the side of the vast building where the offices were situated, Nadia saw Malik's expression and interpreted it as doubt.

'The factory is split into three parts,' Nadia explained in English, 'the undercover loading bay where vehicles can drive in then out, the offices and the meat-processing area. I negotiated with the owners to have the offices cleaned and for the remaining machinery to be disposed of as a health and safety consideration. I've not seen the finished product yet, but they have provided assurances that the work has been done.'

'Thank you, that's very considerate,' Malik replied gratefully.
'You're welcome. Fortunately there were legal grounds as it was a meat-processing factory.'
Nadia wanted to ask what he planned to do with the premises, but she knew her father would disapprove. Instead she referred to the contract. 'If you're content you may sign for the lease today. I have the documents with me.'
'That's excellent, thank you.'
As they entered the foyer, Malik was surprised by the warmth inside and made a mental note to buy some air-conditioning units and fans. It was the first time that he had been inside the building, and he hoped to find that the advertising literature and particulars were accurate. Nadia showed Malik around the offices off the foyer first. Malik noted that it would be easy for him to allocate sleeping accommodation for himself, Dalia and the scientist, Baloch. He wanted Baloch somewhere where he could keep an eye on him. Despite the sun's rays pouring through the opaque windows, Nadia insisted on trying each light switch as they went and to their surprise, every bulb worked.
'I made them check all the electrics too,' Nadia explained.
The final room in the office suite was a small kitchen. Although it lacked useful items, including any cooking facilities, it had been recently cleaned. Nadia was unnecessarily apologetic and suggested that the cleaners had probably decided it was easier to dispose of the cooker rather than attempt to clean it. But overall, Malik was delighted with the office complex as it suited their living and security requirements perfectly. He still had a week before Dalia was due to arrive, then another before Baloch was to join them, so he had plenty of time to prepare for their arrival. Malik had already prepared a list of items that he would need and as he viewed the factory he added to it.
Departing the office complex through an inner door, they walked into the vast meat-processing room. The empty room was broken by rows of equally spaced steel pillars that supported the roof. Malik knew from the particulars that it measured seventy by thirty metres. There was a drive-through roll-down door at one end that led to the front of the factory. The room was surprisingly light despite the rows of dirty skylights, and unexpectedly it smelt of diesel fuel.
Nadia explained that until a short while ago the room had

housed wide steel tables that ran the length of the room and large, gruesome meat-processing machines but that the owner had sold and removed these under a separate arrangement. The only evidence that remained of the meat-processing era was the automated track that hung below the rafters in the high ceiling. From this had once hung the thousands of carcasses that had made their way into the vast butchery from the loading bay next door. In the distance, above a pair of large inner doors that Malik guessed led to the vehicle loading bay, he saw hundreds of large hooks hanging down from the track, all concertinaed together. The tracks led to a brick-built windowless structure that stood in the centre of the meat-processing room. This dominating structure was long, narrow, and flat-roofed, and had large steel doors at each end through which the tracks from the ceiling ran. Nadia followed the two men as they walked towards it.

'This is the old refrigeration chamber. It's made of concrete and steel and has a forty-millimetre lead lining,' said Nadia as she read the particulars. 'The refrigeration unit has been removed.'

Malik walked through one door left ajar and into the cool darkness. Feigning lack of interest, he asked whether there was electric lighting. Nadia felt her way over to the bank of light switches and switched them on. Slowly the bank of overhead strip lights flickered on. Malik noticed that someone had stripped much of the lead lining at the far end of the chamber. There were a number of palletised loads of lead panels that appeared to be awaiting collection, and piles of discarded panels on the floor that Malik assumed were waiting to be palletised. Unwittingly, the owner had helped him out.

'I'm surprised the owner has not sold the lead. Surely it's valuable?' asked Malik.

Nadia shrugged. 'I know that he has no intention of removing anything else from the factory, unless we demand it. Perhaps he hoped to sell the lead but was unable to find a buyer.'

'Maybe he quit reclamation when you came along,' offered Jamali.

'Maybe,' replied Malik. 'Please tell the owner to leave the lead. I don't expect him to remove anything else from the property until I've decided whether or not to purchase.'

'I'm sure that won't be a problem.' Nadia reached for her cell phone.

Content, Malik walked out of the refrigeration chamber, and the others followed, turning off the lights as they went. Nadia ushered them to the loading-bay doors Malik had noticed earlier. The wide loading bay ran the length of the vast single-floor building and consisted of a roadway and a long, raised platform which could accommodate up to three container trucks. Malik noticed the electric engine that operated the roof track in the meat-processing room and wondered whether it still worked. He doubted it since it was still there. Natural light poured from the large side and roof windows, but as with the remainder of the factory the windows were opaque, more from dirt than design. Malik spent several minutes inspecting the large wooden outer doors at either end of the single roadway and saw that they were locked from within by massive bolts. Satisfied, he wandered back to Nadia and her father who had remained near the inner loading-bay doors.

With the exception of the false ceilings in the office complex there was no upper floor or lofts, so the party toured the outside and perimeter of the factory. Malik was delighted with the security the outer perimeter provided. It was made up of either tall neighbouring buildings, or a six-foot brick wall topped with broken glass and razor wire. What's more, there was no unnecessary clutter outside behind which people could advance unnoticed.

As Nadia went into the kitchen to complete the paperwork, Jamali remained with Malik in the foyer.

'I've arranged six guards for you, three two-man shifts. Each man will be armed with an automatic rifle and a pistol. They will all arrive together in an old white transit van at three o'clock.'

'I'll be here to meet them.' Malik pointed towards the large reception room. 'They can use that room, next to the office entrance, but they are not to venture any further into the factory. Their job is to provide a covert guard of the building from the outside. What goes on inside is none of their business.'

'They'll do exactly as you command. They're all good men.'

'Can you help with some items that I need?'

'There's little I cannot find. What do you require?'

Malik passed him a handwritten list of items. Jamali read the short list and raised his eyebrows.

'I'm intrigued, my friend, but I know better than to ask. I've many friends in the canned foods and plastics industries. Give me three days.'

Malik smiled. 'Thank you, Jamali.'

After Nadia and Jamali had left, Malik had an hour to wait before the guards arrived. He took another trip around the factory and sited the locations of the new security cameras. With two weeks to prepare, he knew he had time to complete all his outstanding tasks, beginning with the installation of a simple closed-circuit television system inside and around the factory. He planned to move in as soon as the electrical contractors had finished the work.

Chapter 31

January 2nd, Z – 120 Days
Buenos Aires, Argentina

Dalia flew into the heat of Buenos Aires' Ezeize International Ministro Pistarini Airport on a British Airways flight from London on the morning of January 2nd. She had telephoned from the airport and booked her own room at the Caesar Park Hotel where she knew Malik was staying. After catching a taxi to the hotel, she showered and changed before meeting Malik in the hotel foyer at 1 p.m.

The thirty-six hour journey from Karachi to Buenos Aires via London Heathrow over the New Year had taken its toll on Dalia but the thought of her planned meeting with Malik reinvigorated her. They had met only a handful of times before, on each occasion in a safe house near Islamabad where they had met one of bin Laden's top lieutenants, the Mailman. On the last occasion they had spent a long and methodical day with him sitting cross-legged at a low table coordinating their communication and supply requirements. After they had left the heavily bearded older man with his muscle-bound bodyguards, the two of them had spent the remainder of the evening together at a secluded restaurant before parting at her hotel room door. She had enjoyed the rare feeling his physical presence had given her and since their last meeting she had often thought of his steady confidence, intelligent face, well-toned body and Mediterranean complexion that she admired. She found him infuriatingly handsome. Dalia also knew that he was not an extremist but a heartbroken man who wanted a new life for himself and his remaining daughter. Purchasing an outfit at Heathrow Airport between flights, she was determined that Malik would take notice of her, and not simply her skills.

Malik's lungs seized as he watched Dalia walk across the hotel foyer towards him, but he managed to constrain his outward emotion. He took in her lush dark hair, smooth café au lait skin and slender figure. Lithe and graceful, she was taller than most women, about five foot eight, and in excellent shape. Her appearance was distinctly Western, a nicely fitted light-brown suit that seemed to exude sensuality, smartly cut, low-heeled shoes, diamond earrings and a distinctive Louis Vuitton bag. She looked every part a stunning and successful Argentine business woman. Despite the long flight from Karachi her skin glowed with health just as he had remembered it did and her deep brown eyes glinted with intelligence and something else that was hard to identify, something appealingly enigmatic. She had a symmetrical face that was a perfect combination of sculptured jaw, high cheekbones and smooth forehead. Her smile, which Malik could see was genuine, was radiant.

Dalia smiled inwardly, for she felt she had won this round despite Malik's best efforts to conceal his attraction. Not knowing what to do when confronted with each other, they simply shook hands. Her fingers felt so wonderfully smooth that Malik did not want to release her hand and held it for a fraction of a second too long. As they walked to an awaiting taxi, Malik struck up a conversation in English.

'We're booked into a Mediterranean restaurant called Tramezzini on the Santa Fe Avenue.'

'That's a coincidence.'

'Pardon?' responded Malik with a puzzled expression.

'Never mind,' teased Dalia as she wondered if there was more to his complexion and choice of restaurant.

'How did it go in Pakistan?'

'No difficulties. The packages are on time.'

'When did you last hear from the couriers?'

'A message arrived immediately I switched on my cell phone after landing.'

They both climbed into the taxi and kept quiet until they were seated in the restaurant and drinks were ordered. By choosing a secluded table at the back of the restaurant, Malik had an excellent view of the restaurant, its door and through its windows into the street. He was confident no one was tailing them.

With no one within earshot Malik switched to Punjabi, their native tongue. He told Dalia what he had been doing since they had last met, days before he went to Cyprus. He told her about his trip to the banker, *Last Tango*, his trips to London and Amsterdam, his meetings with Baloch and Jamali, and the factory. He went into detail about their remaining preparations for Baloch's arrival in another eight days and what he wished to achieve while they lived and worked at the factory.

Dalia updated Malik on what she had accomplished, and included news from home and her visit to their homeland of Kashmir and her mother and sick father. She described in detail Harakat ul-Mujahidin's assault on the train which she had been appointed to lead, the two nuclear weapons, the trip to Karachi, the tyre factory, her meetings with Arif, Fritz and Hans, and the loading of the ship.

The two mercenaries remained at the Tramezzini restaurant until late in the afternoon, enjoying watching and listening to each other.

'Everything is going according to plan but we should leave,' Malik concluded as he noted the time. With a brilliant smile he added, 'Would you like to come and see our new home?'

'Tomorrow,' replied Dalia feistily. 'First I need to do some shopping, then, I must sleep.' She thought she saw a look of disappointment cross Malik's face and looked forward to their time together.

Chapter 32

January 3rd, Z – 119 Days
CIA Headquarters, Langley, Virginia, USA

The Counterterrorist Center, or CTC, was situated in the New Headquarters Building at CIA Headquarters, Langley, Virginia. Langley was in fact a neighbourhood of the town of McLean. Originally Langley was a hamlet near another called Lewinsville but both grew into one and on the amalgamation of the post offices in 1910 the area became known as McLean, after the man who helped the area grow and prosper. Despite the CIA Headquarters residing in the neighbourhood of McLean, the name 'Langley' still lingered.

The new DCI was one of the first to go on record and state that none of the US Government agencies had penetrated the 9/11 attack. After lengthy investigation by US legislative committees it had been concluded that the lack of communication between the various US Government departments was at fault. Yet the CTC had enjoyed numerous successes both before and after 9/11 with over seventy terrorists brought to justice prior to 9/11, and hundreds afterwards. Several plots, including the Millennium Plot and Ramadan Plot, had been foiled and numerous other attacks and kidnappings stopped or disrupted. But to further improve communication between US Government departments and to exploit the success of the CTC, the Patriot Act was passed to facilitate the sharing of data and the Terrorist Threat Integration Center was formed within the CTC at the New Headquarters Building, Langley.

The mission of the CTC, enhanced by the new, multi-agency TTIC, was to pre-empt, disrupt and defeat terrorists. Essentially the CTC analysed terrorist intelligence, warned of impending terrorist operations, and pursued major terrorists across the globe. It received a massive boost in the aftermath of 9/11 with the formation of the TTIC, which provided a Government-wide ability that combined knowledge, data systems, expertise, mission and capabilities - all critical weapons in the fight against terrorism. For the first time in their history, a multi-agency entity had access to information systems and databases that spanned the intelligence, law enforcement, homeland security, diplomatic and military communities. In fact, the TTIC had direct access to twenty-four separate US Government networks. The TTIC had developed integrated information technology architecture so that sophisticated analytic tools and federated search capabilities could be applied to the many terabytes of data now available to them. This unprecedented access to information allowed the US to gain a comprehensive understanding of terrorist threats originating from anywhere in the world. Most importantly it provided this information and related analysis to those responsible in the US for detecting, disrupting, deterring and defending against terrorist attacks.

The CTC had been fighting terror since its formulation a decade ago, drawing together counterterrorist experts from across the CIA, principally from the Directorate of Intelligence and Directorate of Operations. It had conducted its own collection, analysis and operations, and now, like many other departments, it could benefit from the integrated intelligence provided by the TTIC. Since 9/11 the CTC had never been busier and, despite its notable successes, hundreds of innocent lives had still been lost in terrorist attacks in Tunisia, the Philippines, Saudi Arabia, Indonesia, Turkey, Spain and Iraq. Many of these attacks had been attributed to groups associated with al-Qa'eda, and for this reason a specific bin Laden Issue Station had been established within the CTC. The station even had its own dynamic plan for dealing with bin Laden, known as 'The Plan', and when news of the possible nuclear attack on London surfaced and that bin Laden was suspected, General Carter ordered its immediate review. With this new threat identified, standard procedures resulted in the station doubling in size overnight.

General Carter had two designated car parking places, one at either end of the massive CIA Headquarters complex. Unless he was pressed for time, he usually parked outside the Old Headquarters Building on the low ground, despite the lengthy walk to his office in the New Headquarters Building that backed onto higher ground.

On a cold, grey and blustery winter's morning, with snow drifts of up to two metres in places, General Carter, the Director CTC, walked from his car and passed the bronze lifesize statue of Nathan Hale that overlooked the entrance to the Old Headquarters Building. Nathan Hale had been the first CIA agent to be executed for spying for his country and General Carter, like all other CIA officers who passed this spot, could not help but be moved by the encryption of Hale's last words, 'I regret that I have but one life to lose for my country.'

The Old Headquarters Building, completed in 1963, had been the brain child of former DCI Allen Dulles who had a dream that the CIA would operate from a calm, college campus-like atmosphere in which intelligence officers could work near the policymakers eight miles away in Washington, DC, yet remain in a safe and secure environment that spanned 258 acres of land.

Carter walked with a purpose. He was to begin the morning with an update from his senior staff on Operation Enduring Freedom immediately before joining the DCI and DDI for a trip to DC where each of them were to address the Senate Select Committee on Intelligence. The Commission Hearing had been scheduled for over a year, and the DCI intended to take this opportunity very early in the New Year, and before the next budget-round, to impress on the Commission the importance of the CTC and CIA operations to world peace, not only to US homeland security. The latest threat to London, known to those who received the Matrix, would prove a powerful example.

Many of Carter's staff had returned to work after a long Christmas break only yesterday, but he was confident that every one of his dedicated staff would be up to speed by this morning. As work in the CTC stopped for no man, many desks were double staffed, allowing for sickness, shift and out-of-office work. Over twenty per cent of the CTC's posts were manned 24/7.

Walking into the Old Headquarters Building through the formal main entrance to the CIA's buildings, Carter strode over the large granite CIA seal that had been the emblem for the Central Intelligence Agency since 1950. It comprised three representative parts: the eagle which stood for strength and alertness; the shield which stood for defence and the sixteen-point compass star which represented the convergence of intelligence data from around the world. As he walked over it, Carter always wondered if anything new had been uncovered while he had been away from the office. Taking off his hat before he walked passed the CIA memorial wall to his right – a memorial in honour of those members of the CIA who had given their lives in the service of their country – he glanced at all the stars, each one representing a life lost. General Carter continued the morning's ritual walk to his office by making his way to one of the two main first-floor corridors connecting the Old Headquarters Building to the New Headquarters Building, a massive extension to the Headquarters that was completed in 1991. He always chose the portrait gallery corridor, which housed a chronology of portraits of previous directors of the CIA or its predecessor, the Office of Strategic Services.

The New Headquarters Building consisted of two six-storey office tower blocks built down into the hillside behind the original Headquarters Building. Entering a new block on the first floor, Carter was greeted by a huge atrium covered by a skylight ceiling. Criss-crossed by two escalators that carried employees up and down between the four office floors, and with planters providing greenery on each floor, this atrium between the two towers was where pedestrian traffic between the Old and New Headquarters buildings converged. Between the two towers high up on the upper floor was the main entrance to the New Headquarters Building which most of Langley's employees routinely used. Anyone entering this entrance was greeted by a spectacular view of the Old Headquarters Building through the atrium's skylight ceiling and the new inner courtyard enclosed between the two. Suspended from the ceiling of the atrium were reminders from US intelligence history – three one-sixth-sized reconnaissance aircraft. Carter quickened his pace through the atrium's first floor and made his way to the escalators and his upper-floor office where he found the Director TTIC.

The CTC consumed acres of space in the CIA's New Headquarters Building, with computers whirring, telephones jangling and TV sets switched on twenty-four hours a day, not only to CNN, the favourite of US and NATO command centres, but also to al-Jazeera, a Qatar-based TV network that was usually the first to broadcast videos from Osama bin Laden. The warren of offices and cubicles that made up its main section was so large that street signs named after dealers in terror were erected to guide visitors. The crossroads that drew the most smiles was Saddam Street and Osama bin Lane.

Carter and the Director TTIC made their way through the corridors that linked the CTC's open-plan offices and down a level to the CIA's Employee Awards and Events Suite that most CIA departments used for larger meetings. They entered the room and the sixty or so senior officers respectfully stood as the noisy conversation ebbed away. As he and his senior staff took to their chairs on the small, low stage, everyone sat in silence. The room accommodated 150 seated guests but, as Carter had expected, less than half the seats were taken. The small stage intended for presentations had the CIA and US Intelligence Community seals and a thick row of flags as a colourful backdrop. In Carter's opinion, the simple, stately elegance of the room provided the perfect environment for the type of informal, collective and creative thought that he desired. He remained seated and spoke.

'Ladies and gentlemen, we have no more than one hour. Before we delve into the operation I would like to wish those of you I have yet to meet this year a Happy New Year. I know that it's been a busy period for us all but hopefully we're now suitably organised and can settle down to the detail. In the Marines we hold what are known as "bird table" briefings, and many headquarters staff turn up to stay informed. It can save on time spent cascading information. I intend this meeting to be as advantageous, but with one crucial difference. I've no wish to circumvent routine command streams, but I've learnt after many years in this line of work, that the devil is in the detail. It's the front line, you guys, the ones who confront it daily, that only together can create a meaningful intelligence picture.'

Carter surveyed his audience and was satisfied that he had their complete attention and, judging by the number of nods, their approval with the new-style regular briefings. He was making these senior collectors and analysts feel unique, and deservedly so. Under his command, he had many of the brightest and highest-qualified specialists in the country. They, in turn, were armed with the most up-to-date information systems. The CTC comprised people from nearly all fields of study. Scientists, engineers, economists, linguists, mathematicians, accountants and computer specialists were but a few of the professions. Much of the CTC's work, like that in academic institutions, required careful research, careful evaluation and the writing of reports that ended up on the desks of the nation's policymakers. Carter was very aware that the leaders within the CIA were not the ones who found the dots or even knew where to look for them. What Carter wanted to achieve this morning was to check that he had the right asset focused on the right part of the problem, for every department of the CTC had a role to play. He was quite prepared to shift collection and analytical resources on fairly short notice to areas where they were most needed.

'There are some aspects that set this operation apart from others we have undertaken to date, and that require a special approach. First, this is the first time we have received intelligence that al-Qa'eda is actually intending to conduct a devastating nuclear strike on democracy. Second, for the first time the CTC has been provided with a broad picture, too broad, and we have no detail, not yet. Put another way, we do not need to join the dots, we need to find them. I want the CTC to establish as many of those dots as possible. Third, London is the target facing the first nuclear strike from global terrorists, not the homeland, but the President has pledged our support to our friends across the pond. In his words, "It might as well be us". Fourth, we believe we know the intended strike date so the clock is ticking. All that means that the US intelligence community and in particular the CTC will be under the spotlight from around the world. We're the best and that's why the UK has asked for our support.'

The meeting continued with short briefings and interactive discussions led by department heads and station chiefs.

It was generally agreed that while the search for missing nuclear weapons could be narrowed down by size and age – that is, by practical parameters appertaining to terrorist use – it was not possible to be thorough in the search as so many nukes were believed to be unaccounted for around the world. Between Russia, China, North Korea, India, Pakistan and Iran, the CIA believed that at least four hundred nuclear warheads of varying accuracy, yield, survivability and reliability were unaccounted for, with at least two-thirds of these capable of reaching the hands of terrorists. Nonetheless, the CTC was to continue to gather intelligence from the hundreds of operatives deployed around the world who were already making discreet enquiries. On the plus side, all countries that had been notified had expressed willingness to comply with the audit. The problem was that there was no way of independently verifying the answers and the CIA believed that some countries would not want to admit to missing nukes. Unsurprisingly no missing nuclear weapons had been declared, not even from Russia, so there were no leads, not yet. The situation regarding losses of radioactive material was on an even greater scale of impossibility. Although some losses had been reported, every one of these had been quickly identified and accounted for.

Other leads appeared a little more promising. The CTC had compiled a list by nation of all scientists and nuclear engineers believed to be capable of constructing or maintaining a nuclear weapon. With dual use in both the military and civil nuclear sectors, the numbers of nuclear scientists across the world wishing to take advantage of the rapidly expanding market, and in some cases weak or unenforceable national export controls, was huge. Exhaustive enquiries were being made of the whereabouts of each person on the list by their country of residence. The UK alone had over one thousand, of whom 130 had yet to be located. Pakistan had 102 of which over eighty had yet to be found. Carter agreed that the list needed to be refined further by home nations before the CIA attempted to trace the unaccountable. It was agreed at the meeting that since the three major suppliers of WMD-related technologies and providers of extensive support to countries like Pakistan, Iran and India continued to be Russia, China and North Korea, unaccounted personnel from these nations should be short-listed for CIA investigation first. Russian scientists and engineers would top the list as their state-run defence and nuclear industries were still strapped for cash. Everyone present knew the search was a tall order but that it had to be conducted. Sensing a feeling of helplessness Carter ended the bleak conversation by informing everyone that the US and UK had a team of operatives on the ground in Afghanistan awaiting contact with a credible source in order to verify the threat, and possibly produce a name.

The supercomputers and 'superanalysts' in the TTIC were sifting through incalculable amounts of data to establish any pattern that would help in the search. Already there were a large number of faint leads for the relevant international intelligence agency to follow up. Someone from the back commented that it was like looking for a proverbial needle in a haystack and someone else responded with 'what's new?'. Most people simply shrugged since that was their job. The TTIC also maintained a single 'Watchlist' of all known international terrorist identities and to date there were approximately 106,000 known or suspected identities catalogued. A short list of over two thousand possible terrorists had been drawn up and superanalysts were working hard to narrow them down.

A list of terrorist groups from a large number of countries who might be involved in such a plot had been drawn up by the CTC and over seventy official and non-official cover operatives and agents had been tasked to use whatever means possible to discover whether their target was involved. Al-Qa'eda was believed to have influence in sixty-eight countries, though the CIA believed bin Laden himself was in a sanctuary somewhere in the Middle East, Central Asia or North Africa. Fifty staff in the TTIC, including officers from the FBI, imagery officers from the National Geospatial-Intelligence Agency and signals intelligence or SIGINT officers from the National Security Agency, were working flat out to collect and process signals intelligence information from countries identified or believed to be sympathetic to al-Qa'eda.

The Director CTC took an opportunity to confirm that the National Reconnaissance Office were reassigning satellites over the Middle East, Central Asia and North Africa to increase their coverage in support of the investigation and that the NRO was to urgently receive new imagery architecture to help in the search.

The computer model for a terrorist nuclear attack on London had already been played out over four days during the Christmas period, but, unfortunately, until the variables could be refined, the planning options available to the terrorist were too numerous for the results to be meaningful. Nevertheless, the senior simulation analyst, a red-haired Yale graduate known as Callie, outlined the three most plausible options available to the terrorists, which, according to 'Jane', the CTC name for the multi-million dollar computer simulator, were head and shoulders above all the other options. Carter was not sure just how much use the simulator could be but everyone around him was taking it very seriously. I must ask her to brief me on it, he thought to himself, as she spoke up from the back of the room.

Progress on the money trail was more positive. A competent FBI liaison officer called Chuck Berry, after the rock 'n' roll singer, briefed the meeting on work over at the J. Edgar Hoover Building in DC. The FBI, with advisors from the Businesses for National Security and the International Bank, had already compiled a short list of probable terrorist money-laundering banks and accounts placed across the world. Starting from the top, formal requests were being made to gain access through front doors. Meanwhile, with the approval of the President, the FBI had commenced hacking in through back doors. A small but widening network of suspicious accounts with dubious transactions were already being traced and monitored. It was methodical work that many in the FBI had longed to begin. No stone was being left unturned.

The meeting ended exactly an hour after it had begun. Carter concluded by thanking everyone for their efforts and said that he was delighted with progress so far, particularly given the festive season. He paid a special tribute to the Bin Laden Station, which had provided everyone such a head start.

Everyone stood as Carter left the room. He would update the DCI and DDI in the car en route to Washington.

Chapter 33

January 5th, Z - 117 Days
Kabul, Afghanistan

The Pashtun people formed Afghanistan's dominant ethnic and linguistic community, accounting for just over half the population. The Pashtuns mostly spoke Pashtu, although some residing in Kabul and other urban areas spoke Dari and were generally Sunni Muslims. They were divided into tribal and sub-tribal groups to which they remained loyal, but these divisions had been the source of conflict among Pashtuns throughout their history. Even today, the Pashtun political parties were divided along tribal lines. The majority of Pashtuns made their living from agriculture and traditionally lived in the south of Afghanistan, though enclaves of Pashtuns lived scattered among other ethnic groups in much of the rest of the country, especially in the northern regions and in the Western interior.

Amir was a Pashtun, but he saw the danger to his country caused by tribal divisions. First and foremost Amir considered himself an Afghan and he loved his country. He loved the change in the seasons, the tranquillity of the countryside and the natural skills and rich artistry of the differing peoples. Above all he loved the history of the Afghan region and the glorious artefacts, ancient and modern, that brought the past to life. He was born into poverty as the only son of a shepherd and his wife in the harsh southern hills of Afghanistan. Both his parents had died before he was eight years old, but he still remembered their simple cattle farm and the enjoyment that they and their kinsfolk had found in the hills. His family's legacy was to teach Amir to respect nature and the countryside, and also the multitude of uses for a dagger. Amir's ancestral dagger had been in the family for generations, perhaps as far back as the once great Moghul Empire when, in 1504, the great Babur had made Kabul his imperial capital. For Amir, this very ordinary dagger that had been bequeathed to him on his father's death represented his soul.

Amir was also a traditionalist. On his head he always wore a cream-coloured *pakol* made of lambs' wool similar to his father's and his father's before him. It was generally worn by the tribal men of Afghanistan, and Amir could not remember his father without one.

After seasons of drought and near to starvation years before the Soviet invasion, a relation had given up Amir to aid workers who had placed him in the care of an orphanage in Kabul. It was here that he was taught to read by a Samaritan, and this skill eased his adoption several years later by the then Director of the Kabul Museum who, after a long and distinguished life, died naturally two years ago. Amir had worked part-time then full-time in the museum since his adoption, spending his free time either practising with his precious dagger or reading the history of his people's once great empire. The museum provided him with all the books he needed, one resource that had been left largely untouched by over three decades of war.

Amir had been forced to witness the destruction of his beloved museum during and after the civil war, by Pashtun then Taliban factions. What sickened him was the tacit authority that so many of the robbers were given by the Government's ministers, the supposed guardians of the once great nation's riches. He had watched helplessly as individuals or gangs of looters had brazenly stolen or damaged over seventy per cent of the museum's collection, a collection that was once famous throughout Central Asia. He could not understand why any worthy Afghan would wish to destroy or steal their own nation's historical and religious treasures. Once, during the height of the civil war, a group of thirty Taliban guerrillas with three trucks stole some three hundred paintings and other artefacts, destroying a further 150 portraits by fire. Later a rival faction had thought it fun to fire at and destroy all the outside statues, predominantly of lions and horses. After the civil war and during the Taliban period of rule, persons would regularly enter the museum clutching papers authorised by the Minister for the Interior that enabled them to choose a prize up to varying values, and the museum staff were powerless to stop them.

A short while before the fall of the Taliban Government a gang of twelve Taliban guerrillas openly forced their way into the museum, shooting dead anyone who got in their way including the Deputy Director and two other staff. Twelve innocent people died in this massacre. Among the many miscellaneous artefacts they removed was the entire collection of forty thousand coins dating back to Alexander the Great.

Three nights later, an infuriated Amir had caught two young men red-handed with loot as they crawled out through a ground-floor window. Pulling knives on him, the two men fought to kill Amir but armed with his ancestral dagger, it was he that left them for dead. No one appeared to care, there was no investigation into their deaths and no one other than the municipal workers attended their funerals. That night, Amir decided that he would stand up to what was wrong, beginning with his own regime. He considered himself a guardian of Afghanistan's heritage and decided that he would do everything he could for his beloved country, by safeguarding the nation's remaining treasures and by helping to destroy those fanatics and terrorists who wreaked havoc and anarchy. For eternity, Muslims all over the world would be able to appreciate his efforts.

Just days after Amir killed the two men, the Director closed the museum. Amir had assisted with the transportation of what remained of the rare and valuable items into secret hiding and he took it upon himself to form a guard for the museum. He even copied the museum's register of lost artefacts by hand then began walking Chicken Street and the bazaars throughout Kabul for stolen items. On those occasions he found an item annotated as missing from the museum catalogue, he either persuaded the possessor to return the item, or as was more often the case, he simply logged the sighting. Soon Amir became widely known and respected as an apostle for the museum, and when the museum recently reopened for extensive renovation, he was promoted to Assistant Deputy Director and Director of Artefacts. Amir became the principal contact with the hugely supportive British Museum and he had travelled to London by invitation to witness first hand the workings of a national museum in a free society.

Before Harry was to announce his departure from the Embassy, Amir had already decided that he would cease taking risks by reporting intelligence to the British, and leave the fight against the terrorists and the criminals to NATO and the new Afghan Government. He and Harry had informed each other of their intended retirements on the same day.

Amir did not consider himself a spy as he only passed information to Harry about outlawed terrorists or criminals intent on undermining the recovery of his country. Harry had often reminded him that were it not for brave people like himself the fanatics would hide unseen by the security forces among a public kept silent by fear, oppression and misplaced tribal loyalties. That way the country would remain forever enslaved.

As Amir watched Harry and Tess wander through the Kabul Zoo with their cameras, he patiently and carefully studied anyone who may be taking an interest in them. Amir knew that Harry was trustworthy and that the Englishman would stick to his rules as it was his life in danger. Observed in the mere act of talking to a Westerner without a chaperon was enough to seal someone's fate in these lawless times. Unfortunately, it was customary for Afghan men to idly discuss other men's unusual movements – that is, unless their own lives depended on it. Amir, like everyone else, also knew that al-Qa'eda and other outlawed groups had many spies in Kabul, all prepared to report but for the want of useful information. It was therefore crucial that any meeting should happen in an open place that both he and Westerners regularly visited and could be readily and simply explained. This was the first time in seven years of association that Harry knew in advance that they would meet and it was the first time that Amir had risked using his old and equally dedicated friend, the Christian Cemetery guardian, to deliver a message to Harry.

As Amir watched the two operatives, he wondered whether they were lovers. He reflected on how he and Harry had met – in the British Embassy compound soon after the civil war. Embassy staff had contacted the museum about stolen artefacts that had been found in an abandoned car near the entrance to the compound. It turned out the old Ford Zephyr had simply run out of fuel sometime the night before. Within the confines of the Embassy, Amir had told Harry how he wished to protect the museum and Harry had offered all the help the British Embassy could give. Days later Amir had discovered who was responsible and, keen to protect the museum, he had sought out Harry and informed him. He had continued to tell Harry about anyone he considered a threat to his museum, and his nation, ever since.

Kabul Zoo was a soulless complex and was not a great place for its more permanent inhabitants. Several years ago China had donated two lions, two bears, two pigs and a wolf. In addition, there were a number of other species, including bears, jackals, birds, rabbits, eagles, wild boars, foxes, guinea pigs, monkeys, owls and six huge vultures. In total, the zoo had over a hundred animals and a staff of sixty to care for them. Conditions were poor but it was a popular place for Kabulis, and up to three thousand people visited each week according to the Director who had worked at the zoo for nine years. A British animal protection group, the Mayhew Animal Home in London, ensured there was enough food for the animals, including the twenty-five kilos of meat the two lions Zing Zong and Dolly ate every day.

Zookeeper Aziz Omar was also an obliging guide with gruesome stories about the fate of the zoo's last elephant, and for a small tip would show visitors the final resting place of the zoo's most famous resident, Marjan, the one-eyed lion. On this, their third, visit to the Zoo, Harry paid the tip to Omar and Tess saw the revered place. It was a cage, located within its own wooden building that had been erected specifically for Marjan by German NATO troops and several local artisans. Once inside, Harry pointed out the small plaque on the far wall that commemorated Marjan's life. Harry explained the significance to Tess.

'In January 2002 the most famous resident of Kabul Zoo, Marjan the one-eyed lion, and veteran of so much fighting, died. Marjan, the only lion in the zoo, was a gift from Germany soon after he was born and he was estimated to be forty years old when he died. Half blind and almost toothless he'd survived all the fighting in Kabul. The zoo had been on the front line and in the direct line of fire from rocket attack from the nearby hills for many years. Marjan lost his eye when a Taliban fighter climbed into the lion's enclosure. The starving Marjan killed and ate the man. But the man's brother returned the next day for a revenge attack and threw a grenade into the cage leaving Marjan blind and lame. In his last few weeks of life Marjan enjoyed this heated cage and plenty of food and medicine. People like Ahmad, the body snatcher, Amir and Omar saw him as a sign of the perseverance within Kabul and that with outside help everything would come good in the end.'

Tess could see that Harry was affected by the story and she could not help herself. She leant closer to him, curled an arm around his back and pulling him towards her, she gently kissed him on the cheek.

Without thought, Harry returned the kiss then immediately broke the spell. 'I think that Amir is watching us from the old elephant's enclosure,' he whispered. The elephant's enclosure had been destroyed in 1996 and had remained untouched ever since.

'Presumably he's waiting to see if we're being followed?' offered Tess.

'I guess so. He needs to be very cautious. He has worked for and fought to defend the Kabul Museum for most of his life and is streetwise. If we can see him it's because he wants us to.'

'Perhaps it's a sign that he'll approach us soon,' suggested Tess.

'Perhaps,' Harry replied hopefully.

On leaving the wooden building Harry scanned the zoo but failed to spot Amir again. Half an hour later they left.

That same afternoon, after a short visit to the US Embassy, Harry and Tess visited the Babur Gardens on the Sarak-e-Chilsitun road, also for the third time. In time, these six hectares of walled gardens were once again going to be one of the most beautiful spots in the city. After the three decades of conflict during which the rival factions fired their rockets either over or into this former imperial park, the place became little more than a wasteland. However, today more than twenty gardeners toiled away at the site every day of the year, regardless of the weather, clearing, rebuilding and landscaping by hand. Already new paths and the layout for a rose garden were visible among the cleared snow. The gardens were built in the mid-sixteenth century at the behest of the first Mogul king, Zahir-ed-Din Mohammad Babur Shah, and remained one of the few cultural landscapes in Afghanistan to retain their original shape.

Harry and Tess entered the gardens from the Sarak-e-Chilsitun main road that ran in front of the Babur Shah Mountain. The gardens started out as a gentle climb up the snow-covered mountainside, but the last stretch was steeper, though it was worth the climb. Tucked away on the final terrace at the top was the tomb of the former emperor himself, Babur Shah. His wife was buried separately, and her adjacent tombstone was possibly even more beautifully carved than that of her husband. Just below them was a wonderful little marble mosque built by Babur's successor, Shah Jahan, dating from the mid-1600s. There was a small coffeehouse towards the top end of the gardens with a breathtaking view over Kabul in the winter and the mountains beyond. Despite their poor state and the weather, the gardens served as a much-needed respite to the inhabitants of Kabul who came throughout the year, particularly on Fridays, the Muslim equivalent of the Christian Sunday, to relax in the relative calm and visit the mountainside mosque, see the tombs and enjoy the spectacular views.

It was a bright but cold Thursday afternoon as Amir sat on the coffeehouse balcony and watched the two Westerners climb slowly up the cleared path to the secluded terraces at the top of the gardens. The coffeehouse, rebuilt by British military engineers last summer, was open and had provided him with a warm drink and an opportunity to sit in shelter away from the wind. Despite the cold, he felt that today's sunshine and exercise in fresh clean air would do him some good. He knew that visitors to Babur Shah's tomb could not be observed by anyone below them, yet they could readily observe anyone ascending the mountainside. It was the perfect meeting place, especially now as no one other than the two Westerners had ventured beyond the coffeehouse and not come down. He also knew that Harry had seen him from afar, and that Harry had understood the need for them to bypass the coffeehouse and venture on to the top.

Amir waited until Harry and his friend were out of sight at the top of the garden before he followed them up the mountainside. Occasionally he glanced behind and far below him, but he could see no one showing any interest. Reaching the final terrace at the top he walked past the woman who ignored him as she continued to take photographs of the scenery. He made his way to the tomb of the former king, a king he knew so much about. If we had a president with his qualities, thought Amir, he would know what to do with rebellious militants who besmirch Islam, Allah the Magnificent and the Holy Prophet Mohammad.

'Greetings, Harry, how are you?' asked Amir formally and in

excellent English as he approached and hugged the man he trusted as a brother.

'*Ta shar koor*,' replied Harry equally formally, telling Amir he was well.

Amir managed a smile despite being out of breath. Although he was only forty-five years old, he felt much older. 'We've little time. The girl?'

'Her name is Tess. CIA. She's a trusted friend. I trust you are well?'

'Thank you, yes. And I trust you and your relatives are in good health too?'

'Yes, thank you. Did you enjoy England?'

'Yes, very much thank you.' Amir was pleased Harry had found out about his visit to England. 'I met many Muslims too. I would like us to enjoy the same peace here.'

'Then let's see if we can help you on your way.'

Amir nodded. 'I traced a painting looted from the museum to a village near Jalalabad. I told the young retainer that possessing an artefact above a certain value without checking its provenance with Kabul Museum was punishable by the cutting off of his hands.'

'Is it?'

'No, but it should be. I showed him my official museum pass and informed him that he must hand over the painting immediately and tell me how he received it. That way he would receive a small reward.'

'And he believed you?'

'That part is true. Allah will reward him. They know more about guns and scary stories than history, politics or law. It's also difficult for someone to sell something like that for a good price without being noticed. He has a big family and a dependable job delivering fresh water around the east of the country in an old relief-agency truck.'

'I take it he sang?'

'Like a parrot.'

'Canary,' corrected Harry gently.

Amir grinned. 'Like a canary. We sell many parrots at the Ka Farushi bird market, and few canaries,' he explained. 'The young man said that he had valuable information and begged to share it with me, for me to take the painting, and to forget him. I said that it depended on the information but if it was true and valuable, then I would give him my word. The painting was payment for transporting three men and their baggage in the back of his water truck from the outskirts of Jalalabad all the way to Qandahar. One day last November he was driving past a car that had broken down. Two men from the car stood in the road and flagged him down for assistance while the third waited on the roadside. The older man handed over the painting and promised to hand him an additional twenty American dollars when they arrived at Qandahar. Initially he thought they were Pashtun robbers from the south, but after they spoke and the offer of money he realised they were Palestinians. He noticed the sacks each of them carried. The sacks looked or felt as if they were packed with weapons, drink, food and money. He did not dare say no, nor question them, for he suspected they were terrorists. As he drove, he was told by the older man to open the rear window of his cab to let heat into the cargo area as it was cold. He also passed them cigarettes to have with their drink when they asked for them. Our driver pretended to be as ignorant as possible and he concentrated on his driving and the radio. He was very scared. As they travelled south, he overheard the older man boasting about a nuclear attack on the West by al-Qa'eda and how weak the West was. They talked of a planned nuclear strike on London that would destroy the city on the Prophet's Birthday and the brilliance of bin Laden. The three men delighted in meeting the "new messiah" and seeing the mighty Islamic forces combine to defeat the West. One of them kept mentioning the name Malik, and how the Prophet would guide him to victory. Another mentioned the name Baloch. The driver was sure these names did not belong to his passengers.'

'Malik and Baloch?'

'Those were the names.'

'Could he have misheard the names?'

Amir shrugged. 'I asked him that of course. He replied "no" but who knows.'

'Did the man get descriptions of his passengers or anything on their car?'

'Again, I asked him, but no, nothing other than they just abandoned it. That's common. This is not England, my friend, and neither was the young man a policeman. The two older men had argued about where they had just been to. One thought they had just been to mountains in Tajikistan, the other to mountains in southern Pakistan, near Quetta. I cannot understand that.'

Amir thought for a moment. 'There is another thing. They were in the midst of the Eid-al-Fitr celebrations.'

'When would that have been?'

'Ramadan ended on November 13th last year so the feasting began on the 14th, the first day of the month of Shawal.'

'How long does the feast last?' enquired Harry.

'Three days.'

'I'd like to meet this man.'

'That's not possible, my friend. He has told us everything and he is, I believe, a good Muslim. I have given him my word that he will be left alone. Any more contact and word would get out, and he would be a dead man and my word would mean nothing, assuming I was not dead also. He has nothing else to tell, I know it.'

'All right. But how did the driver get away?'

'His three passengers eventually went to sleep and he woke them in a crowded bazaar. They paid him his twenty American dollars then left.'

'Why do you believe this story?'

'A combination of three reasons, my friend.' Amir ticked them off using his fingers. 'First, we cannot afford not to believe it. Second, because the young man was not intelligent enough to deceive me, and, third, he would have prepared a much simpler lie.'

'Forgive me, but the mere suggestion of a nuclear weapon exploding in London can strike fear and chaos into the West. We have to be certain. Could you have been deceived?'

'I take no offence with your suggestion. I understand. You see, it was I who found this painting, it did not find me. If it were a plot, someone would have led me to it.'

Harry nodded. He knew it was true.

'You're the only person I know who would trust me and pass on the truth to your Government. I regret I'm not bringing good news, but bad. But it's better that your people know, and better for Islam too. I have thought about nothing else for weeks, Harry. I believe this to be bin Laden's biggest-ever terror attack, this time on London. I've been to the great city and I cannot imagine what the attack would mean, for London and the world. It would unleash an evil never experienced before. Now, I have said enough and we must leave.'

'Thank you, Amir,' said Harry as they hugged each other once more.

'Go now. Leave me to pray.'

Harry departed and rejoined Tess. Tess, walking by his side, left him to his thoughts as they stepped quietly down the mountainside. At the entrance they met Ahmad, who drove them back to the hotel. Thirty minutes after they left the gardens, Amir walked slowly down the mountainside.

As Harry and Tess were driven back to the hotel Ahmad broke the silence.

'Will you be eating at the Anaar again tonight Harry?'

'No thanks, Ahmad, take the night off. Tonight Tess and I will be dining at the hotel.'

Tess knew what that meant. Tonight they would send the routine daily sitrep, or situation report, that provided the standard information required by the Ops Room such as their schedule, contacts and health. But later that same night they would be sending a more detailed oprep, or operational report, which would contain whatever parts of the jigsaw they believed they now had.

Chapter 34

January 5th, Z – 117 Days
London, England

The Home Secretary was sitting at the head of a modern mahogany rectangular table in the spacious private conference room adjacent to his office.

'Ladies and gentlemen, we face a grave threat, possibly the greatest threat this country has ever faced.'

The Home Secretary's office was situated on the top floor of the Home Office building in Queen Anne's Gate, midway between Whitehall and Buckingham Palace. He was chairing a meeting of twenty people that consisted mainly of ministers and senior civil servants from the Home Office and the Civil Contingencies Secretariat. The Minister for London, the Minister for Counter-terrorism, the Mayor of London and the Police Commissioner were also present, as were the Minister for the Armed Forces and the Chief of Defence Staff, the country's most senior soldier. Other departments and agencies represented included the Foreign Office, the Immigration Service, Customs and Excise, the Coast Guard, MI5, MI6 and Professor Spedding from Aldermaston.

In fact, this meeting was the inaugural meeting of the Cobra Group which spearheaded the UK's response to threats against her domestic security. The Home Secretary knew that as the situation gathered momentum some faces around the table would change and certainly the numbers would reduce, but at the beginning of such a mammoth task he was content. In future, he intended to have Cobra meet at the Cabinet Office in Whitehall, but with so many of his own staff included on this occasion, it made sense to begin here.

The Home Secretary spent several minutes bringing everyone present up to speed with events so far. Then he introduced Professor Spedding from AWE Aldermaston who gave a prepared ten-minute presentation on the effects and after-effects of a nuclear explosion. Sir Michael had telephoned and suggested this to the Home Secretary yesterday morning. You could hear a pin drop by the end, and no one was in the mood for argument.

'Thank you, Professor. I take it for granted that you're all familiar with the extant command and control protocols when reacting to terrorist threats to the country. Cobra is responsible for both Exercise Rapid Response and the overarching operation to defend the country against attack, Operation Enduring Freedom. The Committee will co-opt other members or advisors as necessary and will report through me to the Cabinet. The Government's Civil Contingencies Committees that advise on the protection, resilience and our response to terrorist attacks in the UK will continue to act for Cobra as sub-committees.'

'I take it London's Gold Group will report direct to Cobra?' enquired the Police Commissioner, Adrian Walker.

'That's right, Adrian, for both the exercise and the operation.'

'And I assume the Gold Group will have the London Resilience Forum in support,' the Commissioner continued.

'Yes, the Forum will be in direct support of the Gold Group. You may even want to consider combining them.'

'I'll consider that, Minister, thank you. The Mayor will be London's spokesperson as per the protocol, but what of the Minister for London?' the Commissioner asked. The Minister for London was a relatively new ministerial post instituted by the Prime Minister.

The young Minister for London added confidently, 'I've already discussed this with the Prime Minister. He sees my primary role as liaison between Gold and Cobra.'

'Well, let's run with that and see how things develop, Adrian,' added the Home Secretary patiently. 'We can fine-tune roles and responsibilities as we go.'

'That's fine. I'll need all the support I can get,' replied the Commissioner a touch unconvincingly.

'Indeed. That neatly brings me onto Operation Enduring Freedom's command and control arrangements and your tasks. Essentially there are four operational theatres.

'One. The Metropolitan Police Commissioner will be responsible for London, through the Gold Group, unless the state of emergency is such that martial law is imposed until law and order can be restored. The Ministry of Defence must be prepared to provide any support that the Commissioner requires.

'Two. Chief Constables throughout the UK will continue to be responsible for any related or other terrorist activity in their areas of responsibility, and are to provide support to London.

'Three. The Immigration Service, Customs and Excise and the Coast Guard will control all land entry points into the UK.

'Four. The MOD will maintain control of international and coastal waters from the Permanent Joint Headquarters at Northwood, and conduct a cordon and search operation around the mainland effective immediately. The Prime Minister and Foreign Secretary are briefing the NATO Secretary General on the threat as we speak, and we can expect them to come to our aid soon under Article Five of the Washington Treaty.'

Rosalind Fox looked up when it was clear the Home Secretary had finished. 'Minister, you may wish to add a fifth for the sake of clarity. The Foreign Office, more specifically MI6 with the support of the Home Office including MI5, is responsible to the Cabinet for locating and deactivating the nuclear bomb and identifying those terrorists involved, whether overseas or in the UK.'

'Thank you, Rosalind.' The Home Secretary paused. 'You're right. There are five operational theatres. The fifth is the Foreign Office responsibility to the Cabinet, one that's to receive the full support of this Department. I should highlight that MI6 have primacy in finding the nuclear bomb and terrorist cell wherever they may be, and they will require intimate support from MI5 and the Met.'

The Deputy Director MI5, Patrick Asquith, felt compelled to speak. 'MI5 are working closely with Six and the Met's anti-terrorist branch. We're currently maintaining surveillance on three possible terrorist cells in London and four possible cells outside London.'

'And the JIC is to meet tomorrow morning for the first time since the threat was exposed,' added Rosalind. 'The latest threat assessment will be considered then.'

'And I will be represented,' confirmed the Commissioner.

'Excellent,' said the Home Secretary, smiling inwardly as he stretched towards the middle of the table and the fresh coffee that had just been brought in by his personal assistant. 'Now,

I would like to focus on the exercise for several minutes. Cobra will exercise the Gold Group and its preparations for the security of London and safety of its population sometime in March as a precursor to any further evacuation that may be required prior to May 2nd. Adrian, have you had a chance to develop any thoughts?'

'Yes, Minister. If necessary, I propose to physically evacuate London for thirty-six hours from 6 p.m. on Sunday 20th March. 'There can be no half-measures. May 2nd is a bank holiday and that should help. I intend to maximise the obvious opportunities that the long weekend provides and rehearse in similar circumstances. For starters, I would like March 21st declared a bank holiday.'

'I'm sure that won't be a problem,' the Home Secretary replied flatly.

'The exercise will need to be declared as soon as possible so everyone including London's businesses can make adequate preparations,' continued the Commissioner. 'The evacuation of every soul from London will be challenging, and with your permission I'd like to give you a flavour of what's involved.'

The Home Secretary nodded.

'The population will need to be warned in advance that alternative accommodation must be found for the period. Anyone who does not identify somewhere to stay will be sent to temporary camps, set up at vacant military establishments and elsewhere throughout the country. There can be no flights into any of London's airports over the period, prisons must be emptied, and also hospitals. Homeless people and the infirm must be cared for. No one, unless authorised by me or the City of London Corporation, and that includes the Palaces and Whitehall, is to be inside the cordon. Any machinery that requires a human being to keep it going is to be relocated in advance, or switched off. As an exercise concession, I propose that the countless treasures and artefacts in London, business equipment and personal belongings need not be taken, but effective plans should be in place for their rapid recovery. I will examine my support requirements and the question of martial law as the exercise progresses.'

Everyone was shocked, including the Home Secretary, but no one could think why it should not, or could not be done.

'Anyway, I'll let Cobra know of my detailed plans in due course,' the Commissioner said matter-of-factly. 'For now, it would be helpful, Minister, if you could confirm the exercise dates with the PM and Cabinet.'

'And what of May 2nd?' asked the Home Secretary tentatively.

'Exercise Rapid Response will focus on the worst-case scenario, a high-yield nuclear fission bomb, but the exercise evacuation through March 21st will be for a shorter period than May 2nd. Regarding Operation Enduring Freedom, I intend to make preparations for London's evacuation from midday Sunday May 1st to midday Tuesday May 3rd. That's forty-eight instead of thirty-six hours.'

Everyone stayed silent so the Commissioner pressed on. 'The Cabinet will need to focus on communicating the message to the public, through Parliament and the Media Emergency Forum, which, incidentally, I recommend is located at New Scotland Yard. There must be a coherent and joined-up communications strategy, top down. There will also be penalties. The Gold Group, in fact entire Met, must be free to focus on the operation of which the exercise is a useful precursor, not the myriad of initiatives that eat up our resources. Most of them will have to be shelved.'

'Thank you, Adrian,' said the Home Secretary. 'We have the communications strategy in hand, beginning with the Prime Minister's speech to the House in several days. Immediately afterwards he will go live to the nation at a press conference. But remember that until the real threat is formally communicated to the public, it remains top secret. I see no reason why we should not prepare ourselves fully for the exercise without disclosing the real threat.'

'If it's disclosed to the general public now, all our jobs will be that much harder and public safety will be severely undermined,' added Rosalind helpfully.

No one disagreed. At that moment a secretary entered the room and advised the Home Secretary that the Prime Minister wished to speak with him urgently. He made his apologies, ordered a break and left. Ten minutes later he returned, gave a reassuring smile, and everyone resumed their places.

'You will recall that I recently signed an agreement of cooperation between the Home Office and the US Department of Homeland

Security. They're willing to help in any way they can. Requests for foreign aid are to be passed through usual channels.'

'It would be helpful if we could refine the bureaucracy,' commented the Commissioner ruefully.

The Parliamentary Under Secretary looked uncomfortable, but was prepared. 'We'll respond to every request for military and non-military foreign aid within forty-eight hours,' he said defensively. 'Internal support should be quicker. I've already spoken to all major departments, including the DTI and Treasury, and discussed how we can streamline our urgent operational requirements. If the solution exists, then we should be able to meet it quietly.'

'That is the first time I've not heard the word "affordable" in a long time,' the Commissioner fired back testily.

Rosalind exhaled. 'The Gold Group will need as many Geiger counters and protective suits as they can lay their hands on. There will also be a requirement for a large number of mobile teams equipped with Geiger counters, stood by to conduct radiological surveys. These teams will continuously sweep the city, grid by grid. The Royal Navy, Immigration Service, and Customs and Excise will need a large number of Geiger counters too.'

'There are limited stocks,' answered the PUS, 'but I understand the US Army has a large stock of Geiger counters. They also have several large vehicle-borne survey systems that can cover large areas quickly. The important thing is that all urgent requirements are identified by those responsible, and passed through the chain of command as soon as possible, so that effective and timely action can be taken.'

'That's clear. Excellent,' said the Home Secretary. 'I feel we're getting somewhere. Well done, everyone. Are there any other issues for our immediate attention?'

The Mayor spoke for the first time, the voice of the people. 'I'm concerned about an anti-Muslim reaction. It might be helpful if the PM considers this important issue when he addresses the House and country. Our Muslim community is not responsible for this threat.'

'Thank you. I will pass that on.'

As the Home Secretary prepared to call the next agenda item, the Mayor spoke up again. Fixating the Commissioner with an ice-cold stare he continued, 'There is considerable nervousness among Londoners that the police are not adequately governing their "shoot-to-kill" policy.'

The Commissioner looked uncomfortable and glanced across to the Home Secretary for support but the Mayor continued in his indomitable style.

'Londoners must have faith that the armed police are professionals, properly trained, and controlled with accurate and timely intelligence. Apart from the tragic loss of innocent lives, police shooting innocent bystanders is precisely the chaos terrorists aim to achieve.'

The Commissioner sat erect, his face stony. 'Lessons have been learned in the aftermath of July 7th and have been implemented, as we are well aware. Procedures are in place that will help prevent unfortunate incidents yet allow us to protect the general public from suicide bombers intent on mass murder.'

'Not learned from the Israelis I hope,' the Mayor quipped. 'We should be setting the example, not following it.'

The Commissioner reddened.

'That's enough!' barked the Home Secretary. 'The point has been made. Commissioner, I look to you to reassure the community you serve that your officers are prepared, supported and are held accountable to the law. This issue has been discussed on countless occasions recently, and I will hear no more of it now.'

The meeting continued to chew over issues raised during 'Any Other Business', something the Home Secretary did not object to on this occasion as he had achieved his personal aims and there was time before lunch.

One hour later, after some useful discussion on Armed Forces priorities, antiterrorist legislation, medical care and border-control issues, the meeting ended.

Chapter 35

January 5th, Z – 117 Days
Kabul, Afghanistan

It was just after 5 p.m. when the two operatives walked through the foyer of Kabul's Intercontinental Hotel and took the elevator to the executive suites on the fourth floor. Agreeing to meet in Harry's room in several minutes, they each went to their adjacent rooms and took the opportunity to discard their coats and hats, and freshen up before tackling the task ahead.

'Hi, Tess,' said Harry after hearing the gentle tap through the adjoining double door.

'It's such a beautiful city, and such a waste,' said Tess forlornly as she entered. 'I captured some great shots of the city from the top of Babur Gardens. How about you?'

'Me to. The contrast between the devastated city, the blue sky and the blanket of pure, white snow was breathtaking wasn't it?'

As Harry and Tess continued to talk about their fictitious forthcoming TV documentary, she helped him scan the room with her US-made Interceptor 4000 bug detector while he did the same with his UK-made Professional 800 bug detector. Their actions were standard procedure. As each device had a range of over thirty metres, and an ability to scan through walls forty centimetres thick, they had no need to move from the centre of each room unless a bug was detected. It was not long before the tests showed that both rooms were 'clear'.

The US Interceptor 4000 was one of the two leading bug detectors in the world and capable of scanning between 3 megahertz and 3.5 gigahertz. It covered all types of bug, telephone tap or wireless camera in that frequency range. The user was alerted to the presence of an offending device by the LED display and audio indicator. Using both the earpiece supplied and the LED display, the Interceptor led the user to the exact location of the bug, tap or camera. The UK Professional 800 digital bug detector was the other leading bug detector. Used by MI6, it operated between 1 megahertz and 3 gigahertz and it also covered every bug, telephone tap or camera that worked in its frequency range. Like the Interceptor, it pinpointed the location of the offending device, but by using a more sensitive signal-strength indicator and a unique LED display it also showed the exact frequency of the transmitter. This was useful if the user wanted to jam the offending device, or if the user wished to double-cross the eavesdropper. Back in London, Tess had decided to bring both of the small and lightweight bug detectors; for all other equipment she had selected the best on offer.

Harry took his VoxTel 24, twenty-four-hour digital voice and telephone recorder from his coat pocket and examined it. The device used either the in-built or a remote wireless microphone and recorded conversations using either mic from up to thirty metres away. Either mic was capable of picking up room conversations and transmitting them to the recorder which could be hidden away. The VoxTel 24 recorded for an amazing twenty-four hours and had a voice activation facility to save record time. With accessories, it was also capable of tapping telephones. Harry had used the device in its simplest mode to record his conversation with Amir.

Meanwhile, Tess set up her hybrid long-range listening device detector on the desk. The equipment searched for and located any known long-range listening device up to a distance of three kilometres. The most successful long-range listening devices known to MI6 and the CIA could only be placed up to one kilometre from the target.

Although neither of them suspected they were under surveillance, conducting their drills by the book was not only standard operating procedure but good fieldcraft.

'All clear?' asked Harry.

'Sure. What about your Sensor Six?'

'Not a peep.'

Neither of them was expecting Amir to be wired, but it paid to be sure. The personal spy bug detector, the Sensor Six, was a small but clever device, about the size of a small mobile phone, which detected wireless transmissions from bugs or cameras to a range of about six metres. By pressing and holding the button it lit the green LED to show that the device was working. If a bug frequency was detected, the red LED lit up or it would vibrate or make a sound. For a short while, Harry had had a hand in his pocket with the sensor set to vibrate.

'I took several stills of Amir and some video footage of you both at the site,' Tess informed Harry. With her small and powerful telescopic digital video camera lenses, it was difficult for any subject to see or even notice if he or she was the object of any photograph or film, particularly at thirty metres distance. As well as a powerful zoom lens, the combined digital camera and video recorder had a remote capability though Tess had not used this function on this occasion. The camera was extremely small, ideal for body-worn covert application and able to fit into a coat pocket or onto a belt. It was powered by a long-lasting lithium battery and was extremely mobile.

'Well done. Let's compile and send the daily sitrep first, then we'll play the tape, do some thinking and send an oprep. OK with you?'

'Sure.' Tess plugged the mini-dish to her satcom, booted up the system, entered her password, then opened the secure message software and found the relevant template. Between them they quickly completed the routine report that described what they had done that day, who they had met, where they had been and why, any resources requirements and so on. Most of the twenty serials were not applicable, and they left them blank or inserted the comment 'No Change' when a comment against that serial had been made the previous day and remained unaffected. When she arrived at the serial for photographic support, Tess downloaded several portraits of Amir from her digital camera into a software programme on the satcom notebook, made some size adjustments and picture quality refinements, and then attached the finished product to the relevant serial. At the end of the routine sitrep, Tess added that their first oprep would follow in approximately two hours. They read the sitrep through a final time, making several minor amendments as they went, then Tess checked she had a satellite uplink and clicked the 'Send' icon. In ten seconds the sitrep was sent, with a backup copy saved to the hard drive. Ten seconds later Tess received confirmation that the sitrep had been successfully received at Vauxhall Cross.

Harry rang downstairs to book a restaurant table for 9 p.m., then turned to Tess who had already flashed up the oprep template onto her satcom notebook's screen.

'Let's start by listening to the tape,' suggested Harry as he picked up the VoxTel 24 from a pile of electronic equipment next to him on the bed. Tess was sitting at the narrow desk with her satcom notebook at the ready.

Both operatives listened carefully to the taped conversation. Switching off the VoxTel, Harry turned to Tess.

'So what do you think?'

'I think we're in deep trouble. Play it again.'

They listened for a second time. Turning off the VoxTel, Harry spoke first.

'Amir is a highly reliable source.'

'There's no doubt we must consider the threat real. Wars have started for less.'

'I thought the United States was already at war.'

Tess smiled. 'We are. Even CIA operatives forget that. Trouble is, until now it has been a war for some and not for others. This is a very different kind of war, a war without boundaries.'

'We knew that a nuclear strike was being planned by al-Qa'eda and that the target was London on May 2nd. We also knew that other terrorist organisations were involved. All these aspects can now be considered verified and fact.'

Harry paused for Tess to respond, but she waited for him to continue.

'The story about the painting is sound. Again, Amir is a proven source, one that has no purpose in helping terrorists. He knew that I would trust him and take the story seriously without treading on toes. Like Amir, I don't believe that checking out any part of his information is going to achieve anything more but risk lives and expose our knowledge of the threat. I also think that bin Laden is unlikely to want to bluff with his first planned nuclear strike. His credibility is important to him. If the plot is doomed to failure for whatever reason, he will still achieve considerable capital from it. The fear factor will be far greater with future threats if this one is found to be real, even if it fails. I believe we must treat the story as fact and move on.'

'I agree,' said Tess, allowing Harry to continue with his summary and hypothesis.

'The three men were probably Palestinian terrorists, possibly

Hamas, and their loot either funding for, or a pay-off for work they are to complete. They appear to have been at the heart of whatever was going on, well-informed, and on their way back from a clandestine meeting of probably more than one group that included al-Qa'eda and bin Laden.'

'What about searching for these three men?' Tess asked.

'I think that searching for them would be time-consuming and fruitless. We have no descriptions and, if we did, there would be thousands who fitted the description. If that information existed Amir would have provided it. Amir is very thorough.'

'You're right; we can always consider Amir's source and the three men later if need be. What about the car?'

'We'll check but the car is likely to have been removed by now, or if not it will have been stripped bare. Even if it's found it's likely to be untraceable as vehicle tags are notoriously inaccurate out here. As for additional evidence like fingerprints or DNA, there is only a slim chance. I'll contact George Galway and have NATO check it out right away.' Harry immediately contacted the British Embassy using his satcom cell phone. After a quick conversation with the official cover operative he added, 'George will contact the NATO headquarters in the city.'

'And so...'

'And so we have the main issue, the nuclear trail. That's where I think we should be focusing. It would appear that a number of terrorist organisations are involved. Six and the CIA will draw up a short list and monitor recent movements, particularly around November 14th last year. Malik and Baloch are not names I'm familiar with, but they appear to be tied to the al-Qa'eda leadership somehow.'

'Perhaps one of them is the leader of the terrorist cell?' offered Tess.

'Maybe. Bin Laden and his co-conspirators would require a small but very able cell. These people would be revered. My guess is that they would want very capable and determined people each without any terrorist history and capable of blending in in the West, English speaking naturally. But they would want Muslims, people who are not necessarily fanatical warriors of the jihad but cool-headed assassins. They were probably head-hunted.'

'The profilers will love this.'

'A nuclear attack such as this is likely to require an expert in nuclear weapons, a nuclear scientist or engineer. The profilers may be able to match the perfect terrorist suspects for this type of attack.'

'The driver could have misheard the names,' Tess suggested.

'I dare say your analysts are like ours in Six. They will run similar names to these when conducting their searches as a matter of routine. We will send the recording, Amir was very clear.'

Harry considered his next issue for a moment. 'The three men had just been to a meeting that included bin Laden and other terrorist organisations, on or soon after November 14th last year. Could it have been at his hideaway?'

'Unlikely,' replied Tess, understanding where Harry was leading. 'It would have been very foolish of him if he did because people would learn where he was hiding. In this country, information is widely accepted as a tradable commodity and not something that is constrained by a great deal of loyalty.'

'Hmm, the meeting must have been held elsewhere. But why would the three men not know where they had been?'

'For security. Perhaps they were blindfolded?' Tess opened her satcom and dialled into the CIA World Atlas zone. 'Tajikistan and the Quetta region of Pakistan are equidistant from Jalalabad by about six hundred kilometres. Each area covers hundreds of square kilometres. Perhaps the men were wrong, perhaps they were anywhere along here.'

Harry leaned over Tess's shoulder and examined the screen. Tess traced her hand over the screen along the southern border of Afghanistan and Pakistan, all the way to Tajikistan. 'The whole of that region looks alike. Perhaps it was night, or a combination of both. Perhaps they experienced a long journey in the dark.'

Harry thought for a moment. 'To travel as far as the three men thought, would take weeks on foot. They must have travelled by air to wherever they went, necessarily by helicopter. London will have to check air traffic over the period. That may lead us to the meeting place and from there, and with a date, the movements of other people attending the meeting may be traceable.'

'Even bin Laden,' suggested Tess hopefully.

'The less than Holy Grail,' answered Harry.

The two operatives continued to brainstorm ideas, often

repeating themselves until they had exhausted every avenue. They decided to recommend to London that they prioritise on the nuclear trail, rather than spend more time verifying the story and potentially exposing their knowledge of the intended terrorist strike.

Tess plugged Harry's VoxTel into the satcom using a USB cable and began to complete the oprep by finding the appropriate serial and downloading the recorded conversation between Harry and Amir. Once downloaded, she played the copy back to ensure it had loaded successfully. Tess then plugged in her digital camera video recorder and downloaded the still pictures of Amir and the film of the short meeting that she had taken. Again, she checked the copies. London could take more still pictures from the film if they wished.

Harry and Tess carefully completed the remaining serials of their first oprep together. It began with many questions that required short answers such as serial number, time, location, reporting operative and subject title. They completed the background serial next, and then a review of new information that included ratings for reliability. In the following serial they were required to provide their own analysis of the information. Next they had the opportunity to suggest what action London might take and this left a serial requiring them to state their own intentions. Tess skipped this serial for the time being and scrolled down to the end of the electronic template. Once again, many serials were left blank including one asking what the opposition or enemy may be intending. There was no point in guessing.

'That'll keep them busy in London. Any thoughts on what we might do while we await further leads?' asked Tess as she prepared the oprep for transmission.

'I would like to revisit the UK and US embassies and receive int briefings on the current politics and terrorist activity in the country. A thorough understanding of the situation out here may prove invaluable. I would also like to visit to the NATO headquarters. George will fix that.'

As Harry telephoned George, Tess scrolled up to the serial referring to their 'Future Intentions' and poised to type in the appropriate text.

'OK,' said Harry after completing the call. 'We'll visit your embassy on the Great Masoud Road tomorrow morning at 10 a.m. followed by the British Embassy where we can grab some lunch. We can visit the NATO headquarters at 3 p.m. by which time we should have received a response from London.'

Tess finished the oprep and sent it, receiving the usual confirmation of receipt within minutes. Then she made arrangements with the US Embassy.

Satisfied, Harry and Tess prepared themselves for the hotel's busy restaurant and dinner.

Chapter 36

January 10th, Z – 112 Days
London, England

It was 4 p.m. in the packed Lower Chamber when the Speaker demanded silence as the Prime Minister was going to make a statement to the House. The assembled MPs quietened down, though not entirely, and the Prime Minister rose to the despatch box. Should anyone have had a mind to notice, the galleries overlooking the debating chamber not only included members of the public but some important guests, including the Director General MI6.

'With permission, Mr Speaker, I will provide the House with an update on the progress that we are making in improving security for the United Kingdom against terrorism and also with combating terrorism worldwide. Since the 9/11 attacks in America and the attacks in this, our capital city, on July 7th, we have made significant progress in developing effective counterterrorism and resilience measures, focusing on a range of fronts such as threat assessment, infrastructure, exercises and joint working. I discuss the assessment of threats frequently with the heads of our security services and it is clear to me that we must accept the realistic possibility of unconventional terrorist strikes on the United Kingdom. By "unconventional" I am referring specifically to clandestine chemical, biological, radiological or nuclear strikes. This is why we as a nation have invested significantly in prevention and in our resilience and also in our post-emergency procedures. The greatest responsibility of this House is to provide security to the nation. The killing by terrorists has continued relentlessly since 9/11, in Bali, Jakarta, Casablanca, Riyadh, Mombassa, Jerusalem, Istanbul, Madrid, London and Baghdad. Terrorists continue to plot against the civilised world and only by our combined will and courage can this danger ever be defeated.

'Creating security against terror requires effective Government, effective services and effective international cooperation principally through the UN, EU and G8. This means having the right organisational arrangements. We must be vigilant and well prepared across the nation by working on border security and having the right equipment and expertise available. We must use exercises to train for a range of risks including worst-case scenarios. We must tackle terrorism at home and abroad by seizing and stopping terrorist finance and by making arrests and detentions where necessary.

'I am proud to be a Prime Minister of a country of so many cultures and many faiths. Islam has given birth to a rich culture of learning, literature and science, and in Britain the Muslim community has contributed across the board to our history, culture and economic prosperity. All Britain is at war with terror and this Government will ensure that innocent British Muslims have nothing to fear.

'We and our allies must help to ensure that all nations are taking measures to combat terrorism and that terrorist groups can find no safe haven. Now that we have progressed in providing security against terror it is vital that we test our own reaction if we are to gain the public trust, a vital ingredient during a major emergency. So today I am announcing to the House that a large-scale counterterrorist exercise to a nuclear attack will take place in mid-March and that it will involve the complete evacuation of London from 6 p.m. on March 20th for thirty-six hours. The exercise will be called Exercise Rapid Response and it will be led by the Home Secretary. Monday March 21st will be a national bank holiday but with a difference.'

The Prime Minister turned and smiled reassuringly to his cabinet colleagues and own backbenchers who were poised to break the unusual silence in support.

'With the exception of the thousands of emergency personnel being exercised, the public will not be able to visit London and Londoners will be required to vacate the city.'

Low murmurs of discontent could be heard from several parts of the House.

The Prime Minister looked up, confident.

'I realise of course that there will be many questions, queries and concerns, and these will be addressed by the Home Secretary and others in the following weeks.

'Since the end of the Cold War we have undertaken a sweeping reorganisation of our counterterrorist capability. Our Secret Services have transformed themselves into services dedicated primarily to the prevention of terrorist attacks on the United Kingdom. The Ministry of Defence has established new regional commands whose priority is to protect the United Kingdom's home base. The MOD is also training servicemen from most Regular Army and Territorial Army home-based units on specialist counterterrorism tasks should they be required to provide military aid to the civil authorities or powers in the event of a terrorist strike. We have established the Joint Terrorism Analysis Center, to merge and analyse in a single place all vital intelligence on global terror. The Home Secretary has established a robust group of committees and groups that advise upon and control preventative and resilience measures and provide post-emergency command and control through to the Cabinet and myself. Costed measures are also in place to support this preventative and resilience action in the Budget, and emergency funding is now to be treated on a war footing.

'Even with all these measures, there's no such thing as perfect security. So we've continued to work to improve the ability of the nine regional authorities to respond quickly and effectively to emergencies. First responders at all levels of Government will know their responsibilities, will follow a clear chain of command, and will be able to work with each other effectively in a time of crisis.

'We'll face the terrorist threat for years to come. We are prepared to meet that threat. We've strengthened the infrastructure, we've taken steps to protect the people from dangerous weapons, and we have helped prepare our first responders for any emergency. Beginning with the 9/11 attacks in America, we've taken significant steps to ensure the safety of air travel. The Home Office is strengthening control of all our borders and ports of entry, to capture or keep out terrorists and criminals and dangerous materials. We're using technology to allow law-abiding travellers to cross the border quickly and easily, while our immigration officials concentrate on stopping possible threats. Customs and Excise personnel are checking ships and analysing manifests to prevent high-risk cargo from entering our nation by sea. Our secret services have established a national cyber security centre to examine cyber security incidents and track attacks and coordinate responses. We've greatly expanded the strategic national stockpile for drugs and vaccines and medical supplies.'

The Prime Minister could hear low cheers from behind him and knew he was gaining the understanding and support of his party. Now he wished to secure the support of the remainder of the House.

'Legislation that we have brought in is paying off. Two precedents have been set in the fight against terrorist financing, convictions have been obtained under Section Seventeen of the Terrorism Act and cash forfeitures made under the Antiterrorism Crime and Security Act. There have been twenty-four cash seizures under this Act so far. An example of this is an extremist support cell convicted of terrorist finance offences, with two men sentenced to eleven years each and a network disrupted that has raised in excess of half a million pounds through cheque and credit-card fraud. Internationally we continue to develop new standards and best practices to counter terrorist financing. With our allies we have made significant progress in tracking down and freezing the funds of international terrorist groups. Much of the 200 million US dollars frozen in the United Kingdom after 9/11 has been made available to the legitimate governments of Afghanistan and Iraq for the reconstruction of those countries.

'Now we have so much in place, we must test our counterterrorist drills and procedures. Exercise Rapid Response will provide confidence to the public that we in this House are doing everything necessary to provide security from a worst-case scenario nuclear attack on London.

'We are in mortal danger of mistaking the nature of the new world in which we live. Everything about our world is changing, its economy, its technology, its culture and its way of living. We must not let down our guard or take anything for granted. If the twentieth century scripted our conventional way of thinking, the twenty-first century is unconventional in almost every respect. The new terrorist threat is asymmetrical and very real, and so must be our response.

'I have recently become concerned with two recurring phenomena. The first is the increasing, not decreasing, amount of information about al-Qa'eda that is crossing my desk. The extremism seems remarkably well financed. It is certainly very active. The second is the attempts by nations, some of them highly unstable and repressive, to develop nuclear weapons programmes, chemical and biological material, and long-range missiles. What is more, it is obvious that there is a considerable network of individuals with expertise in this area who are prepared to sell it. The point about 9/11 was not its detailed planning; not its devilish execution; not even, simply, that it happened in America, on the streets of New York. All of this made it an astonishing, terrible and wicked tragedy, a barbaric murder of innocent people. But what galvanised us was that it was a declaration of war by religious fanatics who were prepared to wage that war without limit, as we ourselves experienced on July 7th. They killed three thousand in New York. But if they could have killed thirty thousand or three hundred thousand they would have rejoiced in it. Al-Qa'eda's purpose has not changed. It still intends to cause such hatred between Muslims and the West that the world is engulfed by a religious jihad. Make no mistake, al-Qa'eda is prepared to bring about Armageddon to achieve its ends.

'A subject of considerable concern throughout the world is the problem of secret acquisition of nuclear weapons. Numerous treaties and agreements have been made between the nations of the world to restrict the spread and deployment of nuclear weapons and to formalise the resolve by many nations not to acquire them. Even if all nations were to join, the concern would persist that one or more nations might break their agreement. A number of regulatory regimes have been set up to circumvent this, but none of them are foolproof. The question arises then, what sorts of weapons could be acquired secretly or illicitly? International regulation aimed at proliferators impose significant restrictions on the types of activities in which a non-nuclear nation can engage in an effort to acquire weapons. The nuclear-weapon nations have the advantage of being able to pursue whatever weapons designs or technologies they wish, and to build the best weapons they know how to build, in whatever numbers they feel they can afford. For nations seeking to develop weapons in secret, the technologies and industrial capabilities employed are lacking in whole or in part. Design and development decisions must be made to circumvent these disadvantages. Of course, fears of clandestine proliferation are not limited to what a nation-state might do. There is reasonable ground to believe that any nation or national leader can be deterred from using weapons of mass-destruction, since the nation itself is also a hostage to others. But this assurance does not exist if the party possessing these weapons is not a nation, and in fact has no identifiable homeland. Sub-national groups, that is, rebels, guerrillas, criminals and especially terrorists, are cause for the gravest concern.'

The House was silent again, broken only by the Prime Minister's voice. The Members of Parliament were spellbound.

'The House will remember the activities of A.Q. Khan, the former leading Pakistani nuclear scientist, and of an organisation developing nuclear-weapons technology to sell secretly to nations wanting to acquire it. There were plants to manufacture nuclear weapons equipment in Malaysia, in the Near East and Africa and companies in the Gulf and Europe to finance them. Training and know-how was provided, all without any or much international action to stop it. It was a murky, dangerous trade, done with much sophistication and it was rapidly shortening the timeframe of countries like North Korea and Iran in acquiring serviceable nuclear-weapons capability. It didn't matter that the Islamic extremists responsible often hated the regimes. Their actions could have destabilised the West and achieved their goals.

'The House has realised where I am bound. We know that al-Qa'eda has sought the capability to use weapons of mass destruction in their attacks. Bin Laden called it a "duty" for al-Qa'eda to obtain nuclear weapons. We know that al-Qa'eda has experimented with chemicals and toxins for use in attacks and that it has received advice from at least two Pakistani scientists on the design of nuclear weapons. It is only a matter of time before somewhere in the world finds itself under such a cataclysmic attack and as July 7th demonstrated, we are not immune. We must not wait for an emergency to take place then wonder why, but act on intelligence beforehand...'

Sir Michael, looking down at the Prime Minister from his seat in the balcony, thought that the latter had strayed a little too far. Surely a Member of Parliament would ask if the Prime Minister had received specific intelligence of a pending nuclear strike? Then he realised that in light of the large number of threats the country received daily, if asked, the Prime Minister already possessed a stock answer.

'Decisions about how we respond to this asymmetric war are seldom easy. Let me give you an example. As you now know we recently received specific intelligence warning of a major attack on Heathrow. We did not know until it was foiled whether or not the threat was real. But when we received the intelligence beforehand we immediately heightened the police presence. At the time it was much criticised as political hype or an attempt to frighten the public. But sit in my seat. Here's the intelligence. Here's the advice. Do you ignore it? But, of course, intelligence is precisely that, intelligence. It's not hard fact. It has its limitations. On each occasion the most careful judgement has to be made taking account of everything we know and the best assessment and advice available. But in making that judgement, would the public prefer us to act, even if it turns out to be wrong? Or not to act and hope it's OK? I for one do not mind being wrong.

'Mr Speaker, this is the struggle which engages us. It is a new type of war and so far we are responding well. It is resting on intelligence to a greater degree than ever before. It forces us to act even when so many comforts seem unaffected, and the threat so far off, if not illusory. With our allies we are taking action to stop the spread of chemical and biological, radiological or nuclear weapons. We're working together to prevent terror groups from gaining the means to match their hatred. We're confronting nations that develop deadly weapons. We're shutting down groups that trade in the means to produce the technologies of mass murder. Nations like Libya have renounced their weapons programmes. The proliferation network of A.Q. Khan has been dismantled and its top leaders are out of business for ever. We need to remember also that our security can only be assured through a sustained long-term effort that includes work to address the political and social conditions that terrorists exploit and to ensure that CBRN materials and know-how do not fall into their hands. This is just as important as building resilience at home.

'I will end by emphasising the need for balance and of not letting terrorism disrupt daily life any more than is necessary. We have lived with threats for over three decades and they will be with us for years to come. We need to find a way of carrying on normally while taking sensible measures. One such sensible measure is to exercise the very measures we now have in place. Exercise Rapid Response will be a challenge to us all and is designed to save lives, our way of life, and to demonstrate to terrorists that we cannot be defeated. These things it will do. I commend this exercise to the House.'

As the Prime Minister sat down, loud cheering broke out from all four corners of the House.

Sir Michael knew the Prime Minister had cleared the first hurdle.

Chapter 37

January 10th, Z – 112 Days
San Carlos de Bariloche, Río Negro, Argentina

Baloch's manager readily gave him permission to leave work early for his seasonal holiday and rare visit to his family in Pakistan. He had found it easy to book his chosen holiday period despite the unusual time of year as he had volunteered to cover for his colleagues and work alone in his section throughout the festive period. Also, as a result of Baloch's hard work the project was deemed to have passed a major milestone immediately prior to the Christmas break and could manage without him for a short time. His manager had noticed his distressed and increasingly dishevelled appearance of the last month and put it down to loneliness and stress, though Baloch knew differently. Among other things he had worried ceaselessly about what to do with half a million US dollars in cash. Eventually he had decided to simply hide it until after the job, when he would travel to Panama and open an offshore account.

Baloch, a short and stout man, was sweating profusely as he drove his old Fiat saloon home. Not for the first time in the last month he promised himself a brand-new car, something German with efficient air conditioning, just as soon as this job was over. Parking in the driveway, he switched off the Fiat's engine and glanced once again beside him at the two large heavy grey grip bags each embossed with a large company logo, one placed on the passenger seat and one in its foot well. Fellow employees of Investigación Aplicada had not thought it unusual for Baloch to requisition and remove tools, equipment, protective suits and instruments from his workplace over the last month; this was common practise for a scientist who regularly travelled to sites across the country. He had already held on loan much of the equipment he required for the job in Buenos Aires, most items from many months ago which he had simply not got around to returning to the appropriate store or acquisition departments. The remaining equipment had not proved difficult for him to obtain from the custom design science technology division as the stores or procurement staff had no real idea of their purpose, simply their value.

Baloch smiled to himself as he sat at the wheel and stared at the old shack that was his home. Most importantly, this job in Buenos Aires represented the one big break he needed to recover his life and bring his family to a new, better home and life in Argentina. He would retire and they would be proud he had saved so much money.

Climbing out of the car, Baloch removed the two grey bags and his jacket that lay crumpled on the back seat. He took the trouble to lock each door of the old Fiat that he thought his eldest son might like as a first car. No way was Baloch going to tell anyone, including his family, about the value of his windfall; it was going to last.

As usual the outer mosquito door at the top of the front steps to the porch flapped gently in the warm breeze. Baloch had vowed never to fix it himself. It was the landlord's job, like everything else that was wrong with this fleapit of a shack. At five hundred pesos a week and apparently furnished, Baloch had no choice but to accept the place, though grumbling made him feel a whole lot better. According to the neighbours, the last people to live there had been two hookers, before they were both arrested and sent to prison. Good luck to them, he thought.

Baloch had two hours until the taxi arrived to take him to San Carlos de Bariloche airport. He left the two holdalls on the covered porch where they temporarily restrained the mosquito door, unlocked the front door and found the half-empty Jack Daniels bottle and used glass he remembered leaving on the hall table that morning. Grabbing them in one hand, he wandered through into the lounge, threw his jacket onto a chair, removed his already loosened tie and collapsed onto the old couch. After pouring and quickly finishing a large drink, he began to think of the things Malik had asked him to do on leaving home. He wished he had bothered to make a list. In three minutes he was fast asleep.

Baloch awoke with a start as the increasingly loud knocking

on the front door eventually entered his consciousness. Suddenly realising where he was and glancing at his wristwatch, he dragged himself up, swore at himself in Punjabi for being so foolish, then opened the front door. It was the taxi driver as he had supposed.

'Taxi for Doctor Baloch,' said the driver in Spanish, politely ignoring the doctor's dishevelled state. He had seen far worse.

'That's me,' replied Baloch. 'I'll just be a minute. How long have you been knocking?'

'Several minutes. I could see you through the window.'

'Thanks,' mumbled Baloch apologetically.

'You want me to take these bags?' said the driver, pointing to the two large grip bags.

'Thanks,' Baloch repeated, this time nodding.

Closing the front door, Baloch walked back through his living room and down a short dark corridor to his bedroom where he found another grip, this one blue, above the wardrobe. Tossing it on the unmade bed, he rifled through drawers and hastily packed some casual clothes. He fetched toiletries from the bathroom across the corridor, then hesitated before remembering to recover from his bedside drawer the cell phone and its charger provided by Malik. Seeing its charge had run-down and that the cell phone had turned itself off, he realised he could not recharge it until he reached the hotel in Buenos Aires later that night, despite Malik's instructions that it be kept fully functional from the moment Malik left. He wondered whether Malik had tried to contact him in the last few days but thought it unlikely as Malik could have rung his home line or worse, turned up on the doorstep. Anyway, Baloch reasoned, the cell phone had to be switched off during the flight.

Grabbing his last unopened bottle of Jack Daniels as he passed through the kitchen, Baloch glanced at the untidiness for a moment and decided there was nothing that could not wait for three weeks. He completely forgot about the fridge, larder and refuse bins, and could not have cared less about the overflowing ashtrays. However, he did check that the back door was locked and windows closed. Finally he patted his back pocket for his wallet, picked up his sun hat and house keys, then grasping his blue grip he made for the front door. As he left the house he wished he had left time to change, only to remember Malik's instruction about his telephone answer machine. He returned to the house and checked it was off. Content, he walked out of the front door once again, locked it, and made his way to the waiting taxi. Unlike his home and car, this taxi welcomed him with air-conditioning.

As instructed by Malik, Baloch purchased a ticket with cash and caught an internal Aerolineas Argentinas flight from San Carlos de Bariloche to Ezeiza International Ministro Pistarini Airport, Buenos Aires. The flight took off on schedule at 4:45 p.m. and was only half-full. Baloch, to the relief of many of his fellow passengers, found himself allocated to an otherwise vacant row of economy-class seats towards the rear of the Boeing 737. Pleased that he had made the flight despite being more rushed than he intended, and that he had remembered to ensure his luggage received careful handling, he ordered himself a steady supply of whiskey from the stewardess for the duration of the two-hour flight.

During the flight Baloch considered Malik's instructions, or at least, what he could remember of them. He was confident he had thought of everything regarding the technical job and equipment required, but less confident about his security arrangements at home. A man of few possessions and a lifestyle that discouraged visitors, if anyone chose to break into his house, all that would greet them was an unmade bed, dirty laundry and plenty of full ashtrays, not to mention an abundance of unwashed dishes and grime. No one should find his money, not where he had hidden it.

As Baloch sat back and stared at the Pampas plains far below he thought of what could lie ahead. All that remained was for him to make his way from the airport to the Plaza Francia hotel in Schiaffino, Buenos Aires, and wait there for up to three days. Malik was to collect him from there, and then the job would begin.

The job did not concern Baloch. Morally, he justified that any nation who developed and maintained nuclear weapons and forced their will on others by bullying them had no right to expect not to be targeted. In truth, he did not know whether he could complete the job or not, for he had not seen the weapons, but if not, then he would simply lie in order to secure the second payment of half a million US dollars. As far as everyone else was concerned the weapons would be working when they left his hands.

Baloch's lasting anxiety had been whether one million US dollars was enough to hide and start a new life with his family. More immediately, it was whether, in his rush to leave, he had brought enough cash with him on this trip. Though the hotel was being paid for by Malik, Baloch had not taken any money from his hoard to buy the whiskey he needed to help him through the nightmares that such weapons raised. Perhaps, he considered, Malik would advance him some cash against his final payment.

Soon the doctor fell asleep, leaving the stewardess to rescue his glass.

Chapter 38

January 10th, Z – 112 Days
CIA Headquarters, Langley, Virginia, USA

Carter stood waiting patiently in the DCI's outer office holding his hat under his arm in the classic military style. Although it had not always been the case, all military staff working at Langley now wore uniform, normally the more comfortable and practical Works Dress. They only wore the smarter, more cumbersome Parade Dress on the special occasions such as medal ceremonies.

After several minutes, a businesslike thirty-something personal assistant called Summer answered her intercom with a crisp Virginian accent. 'General, they've just finished up, you can go in.' She rose from behind her desk and opened one of the double doors that led into the DCI's spacious and recently redecorated office.

'Thank you,' replied Carter with a friendly smile as he made his way through the open door.

The office was on the south-west corner of the top floor of the Old Headquarters Building and overlooked acres of glorious Langley parkland dotted with memorials. It was bright with natural light, and the scent of fresh paint lingered in the air. As Carter entered, he felt the charged and warm atmosphere of a busy office and saw four men, the DCI, DDI, DDO and the CIA's Executive Director, all standing in the middle of the room around a large coffee table surrounded by lounge chairs.

'Apologies for keeping you waiting, Tom,' offered the DCI.

As the Executive Director made to leave, the DCI explained. 'We've just spent an hour juggling our human and technological resources as a result of Operation Enduring Freedom. We've had to accept slippage in some important projects. The DDI and DDO are already feeling the pinch, Tom.'

The fact was, Operation Enduring Freedom was the President's highest priority and the CTC was receiving everything it demanded at the expense of other operations.

'It's unfortunate, sir, but the good news is that we should have seen the last of that. I'm confident that the CTC is now optimised to support the Operation. The wider intelligence community is pulling its weight too, particularly the NSA and NRO.'

'Good,' replied the DCI. 'I would not wish another hour like the last one. So, is there progress?'

'Maybe,' said Carter, a man who was not known for jumping the gun.

The three senior men listened intently.

Carter had been revising his verbal brief outside in the foyer. He had decided not to dive straight in with the breakthrough, but ensure they got a full and proper update. 'It's unlikely that we'll get a trace on the nuclear device, despite our hard work in attempting to quantify those missing across the world. There are more errant nukes and radioactive waste materials out there than we previously thought. The international community will need to address this whole issue, but right now that doesn't help us. However, we've also been screening nuclear scientists and engineers worldwide, a massive undertaking. To date just over one thousand remain on the most-wanted list but the list is reducing. Meanwhile, Winchester and Fulton have interviewed the Muslim informant in Afghanistan, the man called Amir, and come up with two names, Malik and Baloch.'

'That's a name from the past,' said the DCI.

The DDO and DDI also sensed the breakthrough.

'We ran the two names through the computers and got three hits on the name Baloch. Two of them checked out, but the third, a Pakistani named Doctor Sultan Hussein Baloch, was not at his home near San Carlos de Bariloche in Argentina. This Doctor Baloch left Pakistan for Argentina after being accused by ourselves and the Pakistan ISI of passing nuclear expertise or materials on to the Taliban. We have much information on him, including a dossier sent over by the ISI. Apparently his wife and four children are still living in Pakistan but hope to join him one day.'

The DCI smiled for the first time in a while. 'It's a small world. When I was in your job, Baloch was high up on our worry list for a time. As US forces invaded Afghanistan in 2001, at our request the Pakistan ISI detained Baloch and two of his colleagues for questioning. It was suspected he was a part of A.Q. Khan's inner circle, though he never confessed. They were outspoken Taliban sympathisers, but nothing could be proven so they were let go.'

'We're assessing the dossier at the moment,' Carter continued. 'Apparently he has a job, working for Investigación Aplicada, an Argentinean State-owned company that develops custom design technology in the nuclear field among others. We began full surveillance on his house, work, telephones, etcetera this morning. His current whereabouts are unknown, though his employer has informed us he's just taken three weeks' vacation.'

'Has his house been searched yet?' asked the DCI.

'No, but someone should. Given the sensitivity of this project and the fact that it's run by the Brits, I suggest Winchester and Fulton check it out. I have a hunch this is our scientist.'

'Everyone agreed?' asked the DCI.

Everyone nodded.

'What about the other name, Malik?' the DDI enquired. 'That one is new.'

'It's a common Arabic name. It means the "Master",' added the DCI.

'Master or leader of the attack?' offered the DDO.

'It's possible, sir,' replied Carter. 'It's probably a codename. We have run the name against our most-wanted scientists and our most-wanted terrorist list. No joy with either. London also believes that this name could apply to the leader of the terrorist cell. Their profilers think he may be a mercenary rather than a militant, a professional who can get the job done at the right price. It's a dead end until we receive further intelligence.'

'What about our profilers?' asked the DDI.

'I've not seen the results but I understand our guys agree.'

'Makes sense,' concluded the DDO. 'Bin Laden would have difficulty finding the right man to lead this attack. He would have wanted an expert who would succeed, not some militant raghead raised since childhood in one of his funny farms. A militant might blow it, if you pardon the pun.'

Nobody disagreed.

Carter paused, then continued with his briefing. 'The NSA hasn't found any leads despite throwing their hardware at the

Middle East, Central Asia and North Africa. This and other indicators suggest that this attack is based on a highly developed plan. We normally capture bucket loads of unidentifiable traffic, but on this occasion there's nothing tangible and that's rare. The NRO are obtaining some excellent footage of a number of terrorist lairs and their incumbents, but all locations and most faces had already been identified. Computer simulations are too vague to be of use and the FBI is still working at the money trail.'

'I spoke to Bill Darling this morning on that,' added the DCI. 'We'll be receiving their preliminary report by ten tomorrow morning.' Bill Darling was the DCI's opposite number at the FBI.

'His financial operation is quite impressive,' the DCI continued. 'The FBI has lawfully frozen the assets of 257 bank accounts across the world since 9/11. Apparently the whole process became considerably easier after the first Gulf War when the international community wanted to seize Saddam Hussein's secret personal wealth and Iraq's lost billions. Of these 257, 127 have been closed to date with assets returned to the rightful owners. The FBI are monitoring fourteen currently "active" terrorist accounts discovered through informants, and these so far have led us to another 37 suspect accounts. The FBI's Financial Division is monitoring all active accounts for transactions that suggest a large scale plot. Darling has also assured the President he only taps in through the back door when there is evidence the bank itself is corrupt.'

'I take it Darling himself removed the chains?' the DDO chuckled.

'I spoke to the President, he spoke to Darling,' replied the DCI curtly. 'The President remained cautious about hacking in.'

'Since when was the Director FBI a saint anyway?' added the DDI, who considered everyone outside the CIA corrupt, including banks. 'The end justifies the means, eh?'

Nobody bothered to follow this up. Right now they were at war, and on this occasion the end did justify the means.

'Unfortunately,' said the DCI, 'although the FBI has a number of financial leads, accounts rarely allow the holders to be traced, unless an account holder is brazen enough, or honest enough, to use their own name. Also, the account holder has been and gone before the FBI gets to see any transaction on an account, and staking out all banks is not an option. They have to rely on detaining subjects and questioning them to discover which accounts they own.'

'Have the FBI matched any of the accounts' profiles to a wide-scale plot, possibly Operation Enduring Freedom?' asked Carter.

'There are several accounts that have seen big money movements over the last six months or so but it's still too early to say with any certainty,' replied the DCI. 'They will continue to monitor all suspect accounts. Apparently we need someone to illuminate any one part of the trail and the rest will light up like a string of fairy lights.'

After the short meeting broke up, Carter returned to his office via the DCI Portrait Gallery corridor, and called for the Director TTIC.

Chapter 39

January 11th, Z – 111 Days
MI6 Headquarters, London, England

Sir Michael Jackson walked purposefully to the Operations Room down the corridor from his office. The ops room was a large, windowless room served by efficient air-conditioning. With the exception of narrow strips of dull light that illuminated individual desk spaces, a bank of three small television monitors that hung from the ceiling and several horizontal and vertical backlit map boards, the room was dark. Every effort was made to create an environment that promoted silence and study. The room was purpose-built to control major operations. When not required for this purpose, it was used as a world affairs briefing room available to all MI6 personnel. Next to the ops room was a large and exclusive living area with a balcony that looked out over the River Thames. In the rest room there were bunks, simple catering facilities, a multimedia suite and bathrooms.

As he entered, Sir Michael saw a group of people huddled over the large 'bird table' that dominated the room. Measuring four metres square, the table was low, back-lit and surrounded by benches. Rosalind Fox, the Deputy Director, made room for him.

Rosalind spoke quietly, since work continued around them. 'We've heard from the CIA. They believe that Baloch is a nuclear scientist who has been previously linked to the Taliban and al-Qa'eda. His full name is Doctor Sultan Hussein Baloch. He's from Pakistan and used to work on their state nuclear weapons programmes. He was detained by the Pakistan authorities several years ago and questioned about his involvement with the Taliban, al-Qa'eda and also A.Q. Khan. Baloch was released due to lack of evidence and he promptly left to live and work in Argentina. He still works in the nuclear design technology field. He has a wife and four children, who, according to the Pakistan ISI, intend to join him.'

'Interesting. Where does he live?' asked Sir Michael expectantly.

'In the suburbs of San Carlos de Bariloche, right here.' Rosalind pointed to the city on a large-scale map of Argentina that was spread over the bird table.

'According to his employers he left work for a three-week holiday yesterday. Nobody knows where he's gone.'

'Does his wife know where he is?' asked Sir Michael.

'The ISI checked. She doesn't.'

'I see. What do the CIA suggest?'

'That Harry and Tess search the house. The CIA has his home and mobile phone numbers, provided by his employer. The NSA is tracking them. So far nothing.'

Sir Michael considered the search. 'Send Harry and Tess on a covert search. It's just possible that Baloch may return. Do we believe Baloch is still in the country?'

The DDI, Dudley Anderson, had been pursuing this line of enquiry. 'We've checked with Argentina's Immigration Service. There is no record of him leaving the country for over a year. Either way, a search of his home may lead us to him.'

'Then let's get to it,' replied Sir Michael. 'Anything on the name Malik?'

'Nothing yet,' Rosalind replied. 'Both ourselves and the CIA have cross-checked against our databases. Nothing's come up.'

'We believe it to be a codename for a professional,' added Dudley.

'You mean a mercenary, not a terrorist?' asked Sir Michael, raising his eyebrows at Dudley.

'A mercenary working on behalf of al-Qa'eda. Someone without principles and whose loyalty can be bought. Someone who will not be traced through databases or watch lists. Someone who is not blinkered by fanaticism or ideology, someone who will blend in.'

'The worst kind then? Our immediate enemy is not only dedicated and ruthless, but he is likely to have been specifically chosen for the task.'

'Almost certainly. Of course, there may be more of them in the cell and Malik may not be the leader.'

'With a codename like the "Master" I think we can consider him to be the leader for now. Do we have a profile?'

'I have a team downstairs working on Baloch and Malik as we

speak,' Dudley continued. 'They are working with the CTC on that one.'

'Good. Let me see the results as soon as you can.'

Seeing her chance, Merissa, the Director's private assistant, walked through from the rest room with four mugs of coffee and a plate of biscuits. Placing the tray on the bird table, she whispered in Sir Michael's right ear about a telephone call from the Foreign Secretary, then left the room.

'Anything else?' the Director enquired.

Dudley motioned to an analyst named Lansing Casey who joined them from his nearby workstation. 'Lansing has been working on a theory. His idea has considerable support, including mine.'

Sir Michael knew that within the confines of Vauxhall Cross Casey was considered an intelligence guru. Middle-aged, pallid and overweight from years of sitting on his backside hunched over maps and charts in dark rooms like this, he was a specialist in cartographical, geospatial and air and satellite intelligence. In fact, Casey was one of the most highly respected intelligence officers of his field in the world.

Everyone looked at Casey expectantly.

'Well sir, it's a matter of elimination really. I think I know where the terrorists met, to plot as it were.'

'Now that would be very useful,' offered Sir Michael excitedly. His eyes rested on another large-scale map in front of him on the bird table, this time a map of the entire Middle East and Central Asia.

'Although we do not know where the terrorist groups met on or soon after November 14th, we do know where they could not have met, and therefore we do know if you see what I mean.'

Everyone was gripped with anticipation.

'In front of you is a map of the Middle East and Central Asia with Afghanistan in the centre.' Casey oriented everyone by outlining the border of Afghanistan with a laser pointer.

'I have taken what little we know from Amir, and a large amount of information from air traffic authorities in Afghanistan, Uzbekistan to its north, Tajikistan to its north-east, China to its east and Pakistan to its south-east, and we also looked closely at the ground. Essentially we believe that the three suspects who were taken from Jalalabad to Kandahar must have been carried by helicopter to somewhere within a radius of no more than six hundred kilometres. This includes Quetta to the south, and the Pamir mountain range to the north. Now, if you eliminate no-go areas that are well populated, and you eliminate areas we know that were properly monitored and policed by air traffic control or military surveillance, then you end up with this area.'

Casey swiftly placed a trace over the map and aligned grid lines so it fitted exactly over the underlying map. Suddenly the huge area was reduced to a far smaller area of the Pamir Mountains in Tajikistan, and several narrow corridors that led to it. There was one corridor in Afghanistan, over the Khyber Pass from Jalalabad.

'How would the terrorists get hold of this type of information?' asked Sir Michael hoarsely.

Casey shrugged as if the answer was obvious, and then answered confidently. 'Traffic control systems regularly check their own area of operations to identify any gaps or weaknesses in their coverage. It's a simple matter of obtaining these for a region, overlaying them, then considering any additional factors such as avoidance of populated areas. Drugs traffickers pay a lot of money for this information.'

'And why on earth is the Khyber Pass a blind spot?' asked Sir Michael incredulously.

'*Was* a blind spot,' Rosalind corrected. 'NATO is deeply appreciative of our find, and just a little embarrassed too.'

'In fact, for most of each day it was not a blind spot,' Casey added. 'AWACS aircraft flying over the region are currently responsible for providing the coverage required but between midnight and 4 a.m. local time there was a gap. Anyone plotting the AWACS flight pattern over successive nights could have established this. This trace is for the four-hour period only.'

Everyone present felt Casey had hit on something.

'So where does this lead us?' asked Sir Michael, ignoring his need to call to the Minister.

The senior officers waited for Casey to respond.

'Well, sir, it's my belief that the meeting took place on the night of the 14th, the only night that there was a gap in the air surveillance *and* the weather was good enough for flying. I think the meeting took place in the Pamir Mountains, a place littered with remote buildings and caves, many given over to drugs cartels.

I also believe that the air corridors were used to pick up and ferry those attending.'

'Lansing, this is outstanding, straight out of the left field,' exclaimed Sir Michael. 'Does the CIA know this?'

'Not the full picture, no, not yet,' answered Dudley, unsure whether or not they should have been notified.

Sir Michael allowed himself a smile. This was outstanding intelligence work.

'There are two leads that open up,' Dudley offered. 'I suggest the CIA conduct enquiries in Tajikistan with a view to finding anyone who may have been associated with the meeting, border guards and mountain patrols, the locals and so on. They have more experience and influence in that region than we do. Someone may know where the meeting took place and who was there, and be prepared to speak out. Meanwhile, we conduct a search of air traffic records and identify any aircraft that flew in the vicinity of these blind areas between midnight and 4 a.m. on the 14th, only to disappear and possibly reappear. Our mystery helicopter or helicopters must have flown into those areas from controlled air space and should therefore be identifiable and its flight path traceable.'

'I think it unlikely anyone would risk more than one helicopter,' added Rosalind.

'I agree,' muttered Dudley thoughtfully.

'Well done, everyone, this is excellent work,' encouraged Sir Michael. 'I'd better go and update the Minister.'

As Sir Michael spoke to the Minister, Bernazzani drafted a message to Harry and Tess, directing them to Argentina.

Chapter 40

January 12th, Z – 110 Days
35° 18′ S 57° 5′ W, Río de la Plata

It was a warm clear night as Fritz and Hans stood together under the bright stars on the starboard outer bridge wing of BBC *Columbia*, some thirty metres above the lapping waves. Only the distant rumble of the ship's engines broke the silence. They stared towards the bright lights of Montevideo as they huddled together in the slight breeze and leant in tandem across the railing. Neither was due to start the next eight-hour shift for another hour, but the excitement of entering the Río de la Plata and nearing their destination had woken them early. It was 1 a.m. and by 4 a.m. they expected to be receiving the harbour pilot; from then it would be a very busy day.

Standing on the deck of the pilot boat, Salvador Lascano watched as the lights of Buenos Aires shrank in the darkness. Soon the city's lights disappeared into the sea haze and they were lost in the vastness of the night. With nothing but blackness in the distance, he averted his eyes to the small crew of the pilot boat who were busying themselves. Ten minutes after watching the lights of Buenos Aires extinguish, a crew member stationed by the radar monitor told him they should soon be able to see the lights of BBC *Columbia* off the port bow.

The helmsman was the first to spot her and called out. Lascano followed his gaze and picked up the flickering light. He watched the ship grow larger and larger in the darkness as the pilot boat continued to hammer through the swells.

As the ship slowed the little pilot boat moved in toward a starboard ladder. Five minutes later Lascano was on the bridge with the ship's captain and the little pilot boat had vanished.

'She's all yours, Salvador,' offered the captain in Spanish.

'Thank you, Captain,' replied Lascano. 'We should be docking in about two hours. You have been allocated Darsena D at Retiro. The port is very busy as usual. How long are you staying?'

'Four days. We sail for Marseilles on the sixteenth. We have just twenty-four hours to unload.'

'Starboard ten, half ahead both engines,' ordered the pilot.

'Starboard ten, half ahead both engines,' repeated the helmsman.

'She's a beautiful ship,' offered the pilot, with sincerity. As he watched her turn, he added, 'The ship is very responsive despite being low in the water.'

'BBC *Columbia* is only three years old and everything a modern freighter should be,' replied the captain proudly.

'I know of many ships that should be scuttled,' mused the pilot.

'I once served under a drunken captain and in a ship whose owners were too crooked to pay for a full crew…' began the captain.

The captain and pilot swapped tales and discussed the appalling state of the world's merchant shipping as dawn broke into a beautiful, bright and clear day. The time soon passed and BBC *Columbia* docked at 6:30 a.m. in perfect morning sunshine.

The customs and immigration officers made far more fuss than was usual over the registration of the passengers and crew so it was not until 9 a.m. that the ship's captain was given the all-clear for them to disembark and for the unloading to begin. Soon, four huge yellow gantry cranes were driven into place on the quay alongside and the process of unloading the hundreds of containers began.

As was customary, the foredeck and aft deck were simultaneously unloaded. Hans, already sweating freely from releasing steel turnbuckles and securing crane hooks at a speed dictated by two cranes, watched from the foredeck as the yellow box with the crescent moon markings and unique serial number was lifted from the deck and successfully placed and secured on a flatbed rail truck on the quayside.

Meanwhile, Fritz, who had been promoted to an unloading supervisor, was standing up in the ship's state-of-the-art Cargo Control Centre waiting for the signal from Hans. As his eyes wandered down to the foredeck, Fritz caught Hans gesticulating towards him. It was now up to Fritz to monitor its progress from his vantage point, which meant watching the container receive a customs inspection on the dockside then move from there to the container compound in the distance. Using his binoculars he watched as the customs official on the dockside walked along the dock and the train of shipping containers. The official did little more than walk up to each truck-laden container, glance at the serial number and check it against his manifest, then continue towards the head of the train. As the customs official passed the yellow container of tyres, Fritz telephoned Dalia.

A cargo ship's unloading schedule and the order that containers were delivered to the secure collection compound adjacent to the docks had to be strictly monitored by port officials. The logistics were impressive particularly at Buenos Aires where real estate was at a premium for what was unloaded last had to be collected first from the arrivals compound. Last in, first out was the simple rule that drove many ports and heavy fines were handed to shipping and transport companies if containers were not delivered and collected from the port within the strict timings agreed with the port authorities. The short time span imposed by the need to clear the dock and compound before the next ship was due also caused a problem for the small number of customs officials who only had time to focus their attention on high-risk containers, those usually identified by a tip-off or a known threat. Only those of concern would be diverted, opened and checked, before being allowed to enter the compound. The harsh reality was that only five per cent of inbound containers were checked by customs officials at Buenos Aires and this was not untypical the world over.

By 8 p.m. that night the last of the containers had been unloaded and the crew prepared for the next shipment that would begin loading in two days' time. Tomorrow was liberty day and everyone was looking forward to a run ashore, particularly Fritz and Hans.

Just before 10 p.m. that night, Fritz answered a call on his cell phone from Arif in Karachi.

'My friend in Buenos Aires has confirmed that our container is to be collected between three and five tomorrow afternoon,' Arif said, after greeting Fritz and enquiring after the journey.

'That's fine,' Fritz replied casually.

'Where are you bound next?' asked Arif, always looking to the next deal.

Fritz smiled. With contacts like Arif, soon he and Hans would be able to retire. 'Marseilles, France. We're due to arrive on the 23rd.'

'Mm, that could be of use. I will contact you.'

'Outstanding payment will be made as usual I trust?' asked Fritz offhandedly.

'Naturally. As soon as I receive confirmation from Dalia. *Adiós.*'

Fritz phoned Dalia for the second time that day and told her when she could expect the container to be delivered to the factory.

Chapter 41

January 12th, Z – 110 Days
Buenos Aires, Argentina

The British Airways flight from London touched down at Ezeiza International Airport in Buenos Aires a little after 9 a.m. The long flight from Kabul, with two short stopovers that included one for two hours at London Heathrow had taken its toll on Harry and Tess. They both felt tired despite their final leg in the luxuriously appointed first-class cabin of the Boeing 777 and looked forward to taking some exercise at their hotel, each of them following it with a long hot bath. As they entered the arrivals lounge, it was Tess who first spotted their contact among the large and expectant crowd that had assembled outside the exit from customs and immigration. She also identified the man who stood directly behind their contact.

The contact, Conchita, was an American from Chicago who cherished her Latin American roots. Conchita had worked at a number of CIA stations throughout South America since her training ended twelve years ago and she was now the senior official cover operative at the US Embassy in Buenos Aires. Much of Conchita's experience had been drawn from the continuous war against the drug trade, the CIA's involvement in tracking down Nazis still wanted for war crimes committed during World War II, and the hunting down of some of the world's most wanted fugitives who saw cosmopolitan Latin America as the New World. As Tess had flicked through Conchita's résumé during the flight, she guessed that this was to be the first time Conchita would be knowingly engaged in the war against terror. Given Conchita's character and obvious competence, Tess knew that she would be determined to play her part. Tess was intrigued by Conchita, whom she had never met, as their résumés, appearance and ages were, despite the CIA's constant denials to potential recruits, stereotypical of the Agency. They could have been twins.

Conchita introduced the man with her as Encizo, a Special Agent from the Argentine Secret Service, rising star, and commander of the sizeable Counter Subversion and Counter-terrorist Center. While they remained in Argentina the Anglo-American team was to fall under his tactical control.

Harry and Encizo were surprised by the likeness between the two women but tried in vain not to show it. The two women hugged each other by way of greeting and simultaneously laughed aloud as they noticed the curiosity they drew from both men. Conchita made the introductions.

'Are you sure you're not twins?' asked Harry sceptically.

'Perhaps the CIA has begun cloning their most successful operatives,' added Encizo.

'No relation I can assure you,' offered Tess.

The group laughed. It was a good start.

'Encizo works for the Argentine Secret Service,' explained Conchita. 'It's similar to our FBI and the British MI5. His first assignment was the Mengele-cloning case back in the 1980s. As you were flying over, the diplomatic wires were hot setting everything up. I should explain from the offset that Encizo is responsible for ensuring we all play by the local rules. He has also been tasked with ensuring we have everything we need.'

As the group followed Conchita to the airport's underground short-term car park, Harry studied his new partners. They clearly knew each other well and there was an obvious closeness between them. He already knew that Conchita was a very capable operative and Encizo certainly sounded the part. Tess, already content with the arrangements, noticed Harry's gaze fix onto Conchita's gently swaying hips under her thin cotton dress as the group descended a marble staircase. Tess glared at him, and received a blush as reward.

'Good flight?' Conchita asked simply and without looking back. She could feel their eyes burning into her back. She had already noticed that Harry and Tess did not touch, but she felt the energy between them, like an electric field.

'The car is for you guys,' said Conchita as she approached the car and used the keyless remote control to unlock it. 'It's one of Encizo's. BMW five series with all the usual refinements, run-flat tyres, Kevlar armoured panels, bullet-proof glass, even an engine shield.'

Encizo loaded the luggage into the boot as Harry and Tess opened the rear doors and each of them dropped into the comfortable leather seats. Soon Conchita pulled the car out of the car park and headed north towards the city centre.

'You're both booked into the Sheraton Libertador Hotel, Avenue Córdoba y Maipú, adjoining rooms,' said Conchita with a barely concealed smile. She glanced into the rear-view mirror for any discernable reaction from her colleagues but saw nothing.

'Tess, there is a file in the pouch behind my seat. It's everything that the Argentinians have on Doctor Baloch. A copy has already been transmitted to Langley. Naturally Encizo has a copy of ours too. You may be armed, just let Encizo know and call in to the embassies when you have a moment.'

The CIA was the master at gathering and analysing information on people. Operatives all over the world collected information on individuals, information that was rapidly amassed at Langley into one dossier and routinely analysed. Every field operative was required to memorise each face on the CIA's most-wanted list in the event their paths crossed and information gained or action taken. If the face was wanted for unpunished crimes, a hit team or snatch squad could be dispatched.

Tess knew that information on Baloch had been assimilated by CIA field operatives for over twenty years and that the information they had compiled had already proved useful in preventing his continued liaison with al-Qa'eda, until now at least. Tess had received an electronic copy of the CIA's files on Baloch two days ago, and both she and Harry had already spent hours familiarising themselves with its contents. If the information had been provided in hard copy like the old days it would have been very bulky, taking a while to reach them and much time to read. Without the two satcoms and all the useful electronic links that had replaced old-fashioned cross-referencing, Tess reckoned the same task would have taken three full days. Nevertheless, she felt for Baloch's file and pulled it out. It was quite thin, and usefully, she noted, it contained contact and other information about their trip to Argentina. Tess knew from her own experiences as a local operative, her last tour being in Amman, the Jordanian capital, that this was sound procedure for an efficient local official cover operative. With sincerity she thanked Conchita, and her mind wandered to Jordan.

Tess had been in Jordan for three years as a local official cover operative. It had been a hard place for an American woman to excel but she had done so, leaving with a commendation. She believed it was a reflection on Muslim society and not her ability that she was compelled to advise that her replacement be a man. When she had arrived in Amman it had been the place where Saddam Hussein's henchmen had come to replenish the ruler's military supplies and shop for his grocery list of weapons, as well as enjoy themselves. Once Saddam Hussein was removed from power, far from Jordan's neutrality protecting the country, its neutrality meant that Amman's economy fast filled the void left by the toppled Iraqi leader and it became the Middle East's crossroads of terror. Amman became the Casablanca of World War II. But thanks to Tess and her small network of Jordanian agents, the CIA received excellent intelligence.

As the car sped down Avenue 25 de Mayo Tess scanned through the additional file. Tess knew that Harry would want them both to analyse the additional file thoroughly, and together, later that day.

'Baloch is still a heavy drinker,' Tess stated, to no one in particular.

'According to his employer, and also his neighbours,' added Encizo, the first time he had spoken since the airport.

'Just the person you want tampering with nuclear devices,' Conchita chipped in.

'It says here he's often visited by young women at home on the weekends. That's new,' Tess continued.

Encizo twisted his face. 'We tracked one of them down, a hooker from San Carlos. She offered an interesting insight into the doctor. There's a summary in the folder.'

Conchita turned the car left into the wide Avenue 9 de Julio and headed towards the town centre. Encizo spent the remaining journey briefing the two rear passengers on progress.

Baloch had not been sighted for three days since he landed at Ezeiza International Airport where he had flown in on an internal flight from San Carlos de Bariloche. All national law enforcement organisations including Immigration and Customs and Excise had been alerted as a matter of routine. His employers had been questioned and his home, so far left intact, was under surveillance by local law enforcement. His employers had every reason to believe that the scientist would be back at work in several weeks and had furnished the authorities with a list of the equipment the doctor had currently signed out on loan, much of it in the days prior to his departure. At the request of the CIA they had not been in contact with Pakistan's security services, nor had they sought the services of any other international organisation or foreign country. By their reckoning Baloch was most likely to be hiding out somewhere in Buenos Aires, but the truth of the matter was that, with the right contacts and papers, he might easily have left the country.

Harry was impressed with Encizo's efficiency and told him so. Although Harry had visited the country two years ago, he remained amazed that there was never any hint of animosity towards the British as a result of the Falkland's War of 1982. It was always considered by those Argentinians that Harry had met as a needless war fought for the wrong reasons that only served the selfish purposes of a corrupt junta government. Although people held strong nationalistic feelings about the sovereignty of Las Malvinas it was accepted by these same people that the future of the islands did not justify war. Harry had always been saddened by the war, as he considered the Argentinian nation a close relation to Europe, if not the UK herself. Harry fuelled the conversation. 'How large is the Muslim community in Argentina?'

'Eighty per cent of our thirty million population are Catholic, ten per cent are Protestant and five per cent Muslim. The only religion on the increase is Muslim. Our Immigration Department cannot cope with the numbers of asylum seekers and immigrants, particularly from the Middle East and Central Asia. We are being swamped with illegal immigrants who resort to crime to feed themselves. The situation is worsening. There's a huge black market in human cargo, particularly across our land borders to the north.'

'Do you know the ringleaders?' Harry asked.

'*Si*. We have many successes but never enough evidence to nail the ringleaders.'

'Maybe they would like to assist the Islamic jihad in Argentina,' suggested Harry.

'The Muslim population numbers about one and a half million, with most living in the north. Several clerics are hardline and make no secret of their fundamentalism but they have always stopped well short of violence. There is no localised or orchestrated ideological terrorism that I am aware of, though there are a number of Muslim hard-men, mobsters who use their faith as a cover.'

Harry thought for a moment. 'There was the huge bomb blast that completely destroyed the Israeli Embassy in Buenos Aires in 1992. I recall hundreds were killed and injured.'

'That was global terrorism, not local. Hizballah was behind that, though we believe they used local Muslim mercenaries to assist.'

It was clear to Harry that Encizo held Islamic militants and terrorism in utter contempt.

It was equally clear to Encizo where Harry was going. 'Of the Muslim hard-men I can think of only two that would have the balls to get involved with al-Qa'eda and the Islamic jihad,' he said. 'The rest would not want to endanger what they have, of that I'm certain. I'll have these two checked out at once, discreetly of course.'

There was a short period of silence as Encizo became visibly concerned. 'I must stress that the majority of Muslims here are genuine Palestinian, Iranian or Iraqi refugees who have fled from tyranny and seek nothing more than peace and freedom. The ones I know work hard, very hard. Like any Christian country we will welcome as many of these unfortunate people as we reasonably can.'

The other three smiled, appreciating Encizo's discomfort with speaking English. With the language barrier to overcome it was easy to be misinterpreted. Harry sympathised with Encizo and said so.

The four operatives spent the remainder of the journey to the Sheraton Libertador Hotel discussing the lighter side of Buenos Aires.

Chapter 42

January 13th, Z – 109 Days
Buenos Aires, Argentina

It was liberty day and Fritz and Hans disembarked at eight a.m. and made their way on foot to the heavily guarded main gate to the docks on Avenue Castillo. Here they caught a black-and-yellow cab to the downtown offices of Avis where they hired an Audi for one day. Fritz and Hans, who were not strangers to Buenos Aires, reconnoitred the remote wasteland in the districts to the west of the docklands before spending the remainder of their time before lunch wandering the streets and parks of the Recoleta district close to the port. That district, unlike those to the west, was renowned as 'a piece extracted from Paris'. It was famous for its French-style buildings, large parks, exclusive thoroughfares of upmarket stores and boutiques, aristocratic bars and first-rate restaurants. It was also a great cultural quarter.

The two Germans were dressed in their favoured warm-weather liberty wear of boots, long socks, shorts and open-neck short-sleeved shirts. Both of them carried binoculars and cameras, and Hans held a heavy shoulder bag. At 2:30 p.m., feeling tired after a long morning's touring largely by foot, they sat in the parkland to the south of the Recoleta Cultural Centre along with many other couples. While other people looked no further than their partner, the two men surveyed the entrance to the port and the arrivals container compound beyond. There were other gates, but it was this main gate that all road haulage rigs were required to enter and leave the docks. They saw considerable activity around the compound as containers were being collected. As their car was conveniently parked nearby facing south on Avenue Pueyrredón and the main gate, they decided they could afford to take a late lunch in the tall Hard Rock Café building behind them. This building afforded an even better view of the compound and, more importantly, of their container, which was currently lying on top of a stack of three near the back. So far no one had gone near it, but the trucks were slowly getting closer. The two men walked over to the Hard Rock Café, climbed to the top floor, took a table by a south-facing window and ordered a lunch. Even without binoculars it was easy for them to keep watch on the yellow container with the crescent moon markings. At 4 p.m., just as they were wondering whether they should return to the park, Hans noticed a crane swing towards the yellow container and a light-blue articulated truck pull up beside it. Lifting their binoculars, they established an accurate image of the truck and its driver. Once they had memorised sufficient features so they would not be mistaken, Fritz told the young waitress in Spanish that they had to leave immediately and on handing her five hundred pesos to cover the bill he told her to keep the change.

Excited, Fritz pulled on his gloves and drove the Audi through the one-way system around the mainline railway station towards the main gate to the docks. They parked on the far side of the wide Avenue Castillo opposite the main gate and waited for the big, sky-blue Mercedes tractor-trailer articulated rig with distinctive yellow container to appear. Less than thirty minutes later, the rig showed up and as it pulled out across the busy road heading towards Rosario, Fritz started the Audi. Letting several cars pass, he pulled out. Fritz was no stranger to following a vehicle covertly and he knew the artic driver would frequently use his rear-view mirrors in the busy late-afternoon traffic. As the yellow container was hard to miss, he could afford to vary his position behind the trailer and pull back. Soon they found themselves heading west on the Ruta Panamericana.

Their plan was very simple. At the first opportunity they would either flag down the tractor, acting as helpful passers-by warning the driver of a problem with his load or rig, or they would wait until he halted for a break. The latter was more likely – at one of the many rest stops on the journey to Rosario. Then they would abduct the driver and his rig.

It was another forty-five minutes before the rig pulled into a large service area, somewhere east of Ibicuí. Leaving his rig in the quiet truck park, the driver walked over to the small shopping arcade and rest area. As he did so, Fritz found a suitable parking place in the car park that overlooked both the shopping area and truck park. With no surveillance cameras in sight they saw an opportunity and rehearsed the plan again as they waited. It was not long before the driver reappeared and, as he did so, Fritz and Hans slid out from the car, which they left unlocked, and followed him back to his rig. Rather than climb into the tractor as expected, the driver first walked around his rig, kicking the tyres and inspecting the vehicle. As he circled the rear and walked up the sheltered side, the two Germans crept up behind him and Fritz bludgeoned the hapless man across his head. The driver immediately collapsed unconscious, but Hans was quick enough to break his fall. Taking the general anaesthetic from his bag that he had earlier stolen from the ship's medical supplies, Hans, who was a qualified anaesthetist and part-time ship's nurse, pulled back the man's trousers sufficiently to allow him to administer an injection cleanly into the exposed backside.

In silence and with the calmness of professional thieves, Hans returned to the Audi while Fritz located the keys to the tractor in the driver's upper shirt pocket. Hans drove the car through the sparsely filled truck park to the rig, flipped the trunk from his sitting position and waited as Fritz manhandled the limp body into the boot. Checking once again that there were no witnesses, Fritz opened the tractor, climbed in and corrected the mirrors. Soon the Mercedes diesel engine roared into life, spewing smoke from the chromed stacks. When the engine was running smoothly, Fritz slipped the tractor into gear, released the air brakes and accelerated. Within minutes they were back on the autopista and after turning at the next junction, they returned to Buenos Aires.

As Fritz steered the rig through the city perimeter, the digital clock on the dashboard showed 6 p.m. He took the next slip road down the Avenue Gral Paz and back towards the docks. As he approached the vast and secluded wasteland to the west of the docks, he took a sharp right turn up Avenue Sarmiento and pulled over on the right under a long, dark railway tunnel that they had found that morning. Hans overtook the rig, pulled over and reversed up to the tractor, then turned off his lights and flipped the boot. Without ceremony they looked about them in the gloom then manhandled the driver's body into a comfortable position on the muddy pavement in the darkest section of the tunnel. To satisfy any passer-by, Hans removed a half-litre bottle of whiskey from his bag and emptied the contents over the limp body. Given the dosage administered by injection and the darkness, it was unlikely the driver would stir or that anyone would find him until the following day. Within two minutes the two Germans were heading in convoy towards the Avenue de Julio and the Avis office. Parking near the car-hire office, Fritz waited for ten minutes in the tractor before Hans climbed in beside him.

By 6:30 p.m. Fritz, Hans and their rig were pulling up at the gates to the factory known as Iguazú. A guard sent a radio message to Malik then opened the gates. As Fritz drove forward, the guard pointed in the direction they should go, sending them around the back of the building to the entrance to the loading bay. The loading-bay doors were open when the rig arrived and were immediately closed as the rig passed through. Inside the building, Hans saw Dalia signalling and they headed for her. Fritz drew the rig to a halt, with the rear of the container flush with the loading-bay platform, applied the air brakes then switched off the engine. Climbing out, the two Germans joined the onlookers on the platform.

Everyone watched as Baloch walked to the back of the container carrying a small shiny aluminium case. He placed it on the platform then opened it. After flipping some switches, he removed a wand from inside the lid and plugged its long cord into the box. He waved the wand over the rear of the shipping container and examined the gauges of his instrument. Soon he turned off the power to the instrument, unplugged and replaced the wand, snapped the cover and lifted it.

Baloch sighed with relief. 'It's safe.'

'Good,' said Malik, his relief obvious. He removed the bonding wires with a pair of steel cutters, then Fritz and Hans heaved open the two heavy steel container doors. The distinctive smell of fresh rubber greeted them.

'Our crates are in the lower pallets,' said Dalia. 'There's no need to unpack the top pallets as they are supported on pallet posts.'

Malik cut the metal webbing that held the tyres in place on the two lower pallets, then Fritz and Hans burrowed through the tyres into the left-hand pallet. They soon found the crudely painted black crate and carefully dragged it out. Placing the crate on the platform, they returned to the second pallet and retrieved its twin.

'You must leave immediately,' Dalia said to the two sailors. 'You have done an excellent job. Thank you.'

'You will contact Arif?' enquired Hans.

'Immediately. We are entirely satisfied. There will be no lose ends with the rig?'

'None,' answered Hans confidently.

Dalia stepped back and the trio watched the two men methodically place the loose tyres and debris back in the container before leaving. As the guards locked the exit doors to the loading bay behind them, Malik grasped a carrying rope attached to the end of each crate and signalled for Dalia and Baloch to each grasp a free rope. In tandem, they carried the two crates the short distance to the refrigeration room.

An hour later Fritz and Hans abandoned the rig in a lay-by that was regularly used as a rest-stop for trucks, off Ruta 3 to the south of Buenos Aires between the city and San Justo. They checked the rig thoroughly then shut the tractor's curtains to suggest the driver was asleep before hiking into San Justo. After locating a taxi to take them to downtown Buenos Aires they chose the El Olmo bar, a well-known gay-friendly bar where they spent three hours drinking before finding another taxi that returned them to the dockyard.

'I think they were nuclear weapons,' whispered Hans as they walked across the deserted docks to the ship.

'It's none of our business,' replied Fritz, who had also been rattled by the Geiger counter used by Dalia's friend. 'There are so many nuclear weapons in the world, what's another two? Do you remember last year when we smuggled those nuclear devices from Cairo to...'

Hans put a gentle finger to Fritz's mouth then smiled suggestively. 'Not now Fritz, maybe we can use it all later.'

At midnight Hans telephoned Dalia. She was awake and talking with Malik and Baloch over a bottle of whiskey as she stripped and cleaned her Sig Sauer .928 pistol provided by Jamali.

Chapter 43

January 15th, Z – 107 Days
Buenos Aires, Argentina

Baloch would not risk opening the crates until the lead chamber was complete. Using the lead bricks that had been dismantled from the far end of the refrigeration room, the three terrorists had spent many hours building a thick partition wall across one end of the refrigeration room, reinforcing the inner walls and constructing a tunnelled entrance to create a small lead-lined and well-insulated chamber that met Baloch's specifications. Two days after the weapons had been delivered, the lighting and equipment was installed and after a successful check of the hard-wired telecommunication system, Baloch announced the chamber was ready.

Dressed in white protective suits with black respirator masks Baloch and Malik crawled into the chamber through the makeshift tunnel, leaving Dalia to monitor their progress from the outside. After the scientist surveyed for radiation with his wand and recorded the reading on a dosimeter, Malik grabbed a crowbar and levered open the top wooden panel of each blackened crate as they lay on the floor. Discarding the lids, the two men used their hands to carefully lift the steel cases from their beds of polystyrene foam onto the wooden workbench situated along the length of the newly built partition wall. Baloch took more readings from his wand before he attempted to open the first case. Using his gloved fingers to open each clasp, Baloch found he was unable to release them so he beckoned to Malik to try. Half-expecting the clasps to be locked, Malik had even considered it possible that they may be booby-trapped, before he remembered how Dalia had obtained them. Malik was also unsuccessful, so Baloch handed him a small electric cutting saw and signalled to him to cut through them. In a matter of seconds the locks broke and the first spring-loaded clasp flew open, soon followed by a second. Malik repeated the action with the locks on the second case. To Malik's surprise, Baloch appeared excited, and without any sign of fear the scientist slowly cracked open each casing on their hinges. Leaving the lids fully opened and without touching either interior, the scientist visually inspected each weapon using a small, powerful flashlight.

'First we must ground the weapons,' Baloch shouted through his respirator. 'If electromagnetic energy builds up in one of these things, it's conceivable that we will be blown to hell.'

Malik watched the scientist carefully ground the two weapons by simply wiring each one to a stake in the ground. Both cases were lined with several layers of aluminium foil and there was an instruction sheet glued onto the inside of both lids which the men instantly recognised was written in two popular languages, English and Hindi. The two compartments were reduced in size by an outer ring of lead about three centimetres thick.

'That explains the weight,' said Malik in a muffled voice as he pointed to the lead.

'The plutonium is denser,' answered Baloch matter-of-factly, before reverting back to his intense study.

Each case had a cylindrical tube measuring about eighty centimetres fitted snugly between the top left- and bottom right-hand corners, plenty of wires, a large alkaline battery in the top right corner and two black plastic boxes with screw-down lids. Malik thought that what was in view was uncomplicated, and he could not understand what Baloch found so absorbing.

Malik broke the silence. 'So how do they work?'

Baloch was reluctant to answer and shrugged. 'Pure fission bombs like this one operate by rapidly assembling a sub-critical configuration of fissile material like plutonium into one that is highly supercritical. They only use fission reactions as a source of energy. In fact, these are the easiest nuclear weapons to design, manufacture, refurbish and also to modify, because of their stability.'

Occasionally Baloch would compare one suitcase with the other. With both men deeply focused, Baloch on the weapons and Malik on Baloch's work, neither remembered the timer set by the scientist as they had entered. They jumped when it set off with a piercing ring. Punching the timer off, Malik contacted Dalia on the land-line and told her they were on their way out.

Minutes later Dalia closed the makeshift lead door to the tunnel and the two men removed their respirator masks.

'It seems your intelligence is correct,' said Baloch as he continued undressing. 'But first you must tell me, why are the instructions written in English and Hindi, and not Russian?'

'Why do you ask?' demanded Malik.

'Scientists from different countries often apply different design and manufacturing techniques. As a scientist it helps to know the manufacturer. I know individuals who produced Russian case-sized nuclear bombs like these under orders from the KGB in the 1970s, specifically for the European theatre. These people have certain methods which they refined over the years, these I can replicate. Also, if I can identify the manufacturer it will give me an idea about the quality and reliability of the weapon.'

Malik considered this for a moment. It had been agreed with the Mailman that Baloch would live to fight another day in the event he was required. He could be trusted on three counts – first, he loved and valued his family; second, he was being paid a vast sum of money and third, if he did talk he knew he would be killed.

'All right,' answered Malik reluctantly. 'These weapons were made by the Russians perhaps as long as thirty years ago, but we believe they were purchased, then refurbished in India about three months ago.'

Baloch brightened up. 'That is good. Did you know there are hundreds of these in existence? Because they were originally produced for the KGB they were not taken into account in the Soviet general nuclear arsenal. If you would like any more I know people who would be delighted to help.'

'That is very considerate of you, Doctor. Let's see how we get on with these first,' answered Dalia as she waved towards the chamber.

'Right now, Doctor, our only task is to get these weapons functioning. Your job is to ensure they work, that the timers are set, that they are disguised, and that they are safe prior to the intended detonation,' added Malik.

'So,' asked Dalia. 'What do you think of the weapons?'

Looking at Malik, Baloch replied. 'It is as you said. They are the same. Yes, they are very good weapons, very efficient. Each is a pure fission nuclear bomb fuelled by plutonium with an active tritium trigger and neutron initiator, power source, arming mechanism with a very simple timing device, and other essentials. They have a nominal yield of over ten kilotons, maybe more, enough to destroy any city on earth. Tomorrow I will work the neutronic and hydrodynamic computations for fission weapons on my notebook computer and confirm the yield. They have been manufactured to an effective linear implosion system design and will be very similar in yield to the nuclear bombs dropped on Hiroshima and Nagasaki in 1945. The flying plate line-charge approach is sufficiently simple. I will name our weapons after those bombs. Little Boy and Fat Man.'

Dalia smiled. 'How long will it take you to reconfigure them and rebuild their new containers?'

'Under these conditions I can only work on the weapons themselves for a maximum of forty minutes each day in the chamber. They are currently configured to be detonated by one person with less than thirty minutes preparation. If you wish to set them now to detonate in many months then I will need to replace the receiver and power source with the radio-controlled Zeon Tech 3000 timing mechanism I discussed with Malik. When do you expect these to arrive?'

'Jamali has purchased three from the Internet and expects them to arrive within days. He will bring them over as soon as he receives them,' answered Malik. 'There are other things you can be doing?'

'Of course,' replied Baloch. 'We can prepare the disguises, the ten-litre oil drum – that's Fat Man – and the boat's fender, that's Little Boy.'

Everyone smiled.

'We will need to take some casts and make some moulds. We can remould some lead from the suitcases, and possibly from the refrigerator walls. These will help screen any remaining radiation emissions. The emissions from the cases were already very low so I am hopeful. There is much to be done.'

'How long will it all take?' asked Malik.

Baloch fingered his beard, a habit he picked up long ago and one he associated with a feeling of importance. Malik and Dalia obliged him.

'With your help I will be finished in two weeks.'

'That is good, Baloch,' said Malik.

'You will be rewarded by Allah,' said Dalia.

'Insh'Allah,' Baloch replied.

'Tomorrow we will drive to the large retail centre in the Palermo District to meet Jamali and visit the large hardware stores again. Tonight we will discuss the work to be done and identify what we need. We will buy the items we require from several shops.'

'I need whiskey to calm my nerves,' Baloch added quickly. 'Now I must go back into the chamber and take some measurements and tell you what else I need.'

'Then let's go. We have ten minutes of chamber time left,' Malik said.

Later that night the three terrorists went to a Mediterranean restaurant, this time the Sorrento Corrientes on Avenue Corrientes in central Buenos Aires. Two doors down was the entrance to the Guido Internet Café that was situated above a leather shop.

As Baloch and Dalia waited for their main course to arrive, Malik excused himself and went to check for electronic messages. Malik had found that Internet cafés were very popular in Buenos Aires, he presumed because there were perhaps less home users than were found in other cosmopolitan cities across the world. Certainly there was less chance of having to wait if he visited late in the evening.

Despite the hour, Malik found there were only two booths vacant and the Internet café was humming with activity. Waving to the young assistant as he passed the counter at the top of the staircase, he sat at one of the vacant booths and logged onto an anonymous MSN Hotmail account. Malik was not expecting any messages and there were none. He opened up a new mail window and quickly wrote a simple electronic message to his contact who Malik knew lived outside Islamabad. To be addressed as Muhammad, his contact was in fact Abu Zubaydah Saudi, aka the 'Mailman', bin Laden's top communications officer.

Muhammad,
We have arrived safely and met up with your old friend, Rasheed. Rasheed was delighted to meet us and he is pleased you are well. He is thrilled with his gifts. I think he will do wondrous things with them. We will be moving on soon. PBUH.
Mohammad.

Malik read the message through several times to make sure the Mailman would understand it and that it conveyed the necessary information, no more and no less. Essentially it informed Muhammad that Dalia and Malik were with Baloch, who was loyal; that the two weapons were in their possession and in working order; that they had enough money and that the operation was on schedule.

The wonders of the modern age, thought Malik. No longer was there any need for complex codes or complex communications hardware. The message, couched in language that a simple tourist might employ while speaking to a friend or relative back home took no more than a few minutes to construct then send, via a remailer service on an anonymous server, to the recipient. Because both parties knew of the mission he was able to avoid key words like 'attack', 'bomb' and 'London'. Although he could send an electronic message from his Wap-enabled cell phone, the additional security afforded by the indiscriminate Internet café was akin to using a nondescript public telephone.

Later that night the three terrorists enjoyed their customary late-night drink together in the factory. While Baloch had excused himself for several minutes, Malik told Dalia about the message.

Dalia's longing for Malik increased as they grew to know and trust each other. She wondered whether she should remain in Malik's room tonight but did not want to risk rejection before she was sure how he felt. *Just a few more days*, she thought to herself.

Chapter 44

January 15th, Z - 107 Days
San Carlos de Bariloche, Argentina

By 10 a.m. it was already sweltering. Those people travelling to work or school had done so and the sprawling neighbourhood had once again quietened down. There was little likelihood that Baloch would return to his home that day although Encizo had seen to it that patrol cars were positioned at the two possible vehicular approaches to the locality, with orders to detain Baloch on sight. As his own car was parked in his drive, the likelihood was he would arrive by taxi.

Harry and Tess were sitting patiently in the front of a white transit van marked with the logo and telephone number of a well-known nationwide cleaning and laundry company as they awaited word from Encizo. They were positioned just under a mile away from the house. Fortunately the late-model van was fitted with air conditioning. An experienced forensics team from the local police department was also stood by, ready to be called forward should Encizo require them.

The search of Baloch's house was to be covert to avoid alerting the terrorists, although this placed huge constraints on any search team entering the house. It had taken all of Encizo's persuasion and several telephone calls from London to bring the Director General of Argentina's Secret Service around to the search, for he had been strongly in favour of waiting for Baloch's reappearance.

On the command from Encizo to go, Tess drove the van slowly through the neighbourhood and reversed into Baloch's dusty driveway, pulling up behind a Fiat saloon. Both occupants jumped out, with Harry making for the front door with a hand-held toolbox and Tess sliding open the side door of the van. Wearing matching coveralls emblazoned with the company logo, Tess prepared cleaning equipment inside the van, while Harry pulled open the fly door, which had been crudely wedged into its frame, and rang the front door bell. As he waited he examined the lock, then reached into his pocket and fumbled in his toolbox. In seconds he had chosen the correct lockpick tool and freed the lock. Although Harry was prepared with a cover story, he was not expecting an alarm in a house of this type and condition, and sure enough there wasn't one. With the front door open, he returned to the van and helped Tess carry several bags into the house.

Fences and hedges that had once marked the boundary of the property had long since shrivelled into nothing more than occasional rotten fence posts and isolated scrub bushes. The unkempt lawns were a continuation of the pasture that lay in the open fields beyond the scrub bushes, and the dusty driveway was little more than parched and scorched earth long since invaded with weeds. Under instruction from Encizo, several of his officers and the leasing agent had secretly searched the grounds, the ramshackle garage and the small dilapidated shed several days ago, but they had found nothing of interest.

The house itself was a sizeable bungalow of a typical timber-frame construction for the area, built on a brick foundation that rose to one metre above the ground. It had a decked and covered porch to the front and a surprisingly intact pitched and tiled roof. The house had been painted white long ago, carelessly, and the sun-bleached paint was in terminal decline. The window sills, bared to the wood, were beyond repair and required replacing and the air conditioning units looked old and broken.

As Harry and Tess entered the house, its unsanitary condition and a sharp, noxious and unidentifiable smell repelled them. The bungalow was unkempt and appeared to have been unoccupied for months rather than days, for thick layers of dust coated most surfaces. The necessity for them to wear surgical gloves was driven as much by the risk of contamination as it was to disguise their entry. Selecting various items of equipment from their bags, and without need for conversation, the two operatives set about their business. Harry took the day rooms, including the kitchen, parlour, lounge and dining area, which he soon discovered doubled as a study, while Tess busied herself in the hallway, bedrooms, bathroom, hall cupboards, roof space and floor space. They were looking for anything that might give them a clue to Baloch's current whereabouts.

The search began with reliance on their intuition and the four senses of sight, touch, hearing and even smell. They put themselves in Baloch's shoes to ascertain likely hiding places. Occasionally they would use one of the items of equipment from the toolbox that they had carried inside the house which included two flashlights, a camera, a Geiger counter, and two hand-held fluorescent lights. The two fluorescent lights were the most popular as they magically highlighted otherwise unseen blood, fingerprints, and more recently or unusually disturbed dust, which helped them distinguish between recent and less recent footsteps on wooden floors and rugs.

An hour after the search began Tess walked through to Harry who was working in the lounge.

Looking up, he noticed her excitement. 'You look like the cat who has just found the cream.'

'Only a bag full of hundreds of US dollar bills,' replied Tess with more than a little nonchalance.

Harry stared at her. 'You're kidding?'

'Come and see for yourself.'

Tess led Harry through to the larger of the two poorly lit bedrooms, the one that appeared to be used by Baloch for himself. Falling to their knees beside the unmade double bed, Tess lifted the cotton valance and loose sheets that obstructed their view underneath. Harry's eyes were drawn to the narrow hole in the floor where Tess had removed three short wooden planks.

'Take a peek,' suggested Tess.

Withdrawing a small flashlight from his chest pocket, Harry crawled under the bed and peered into the dark hole. In the murky confines of the dry under-floor of the house the piercing beam of light fell on a grey bag that had been unzipped to reveal bundles of cash. Stretching down with one hand, Harry fumbled through the wads of banknotes to determine an approximate value. Leaning further into the hole he conducted a 360-degree scan of the remaining dark confines and was satisfied when he could see all the outer walls of the building and nothing more but decades of settled dust over discarded building waste.

'About half a million dollars?' suggested Harry.

'That's what I reckon,' agreed Tess.

'You photographed it?'

'Sure have.'

'We'll leave it and continue the surveillance.'

'Oh, can't I just take a little bit?' said Tess with a touch of sarcasm.

Harry grinned then recovered from under the bed, careful to disturb as little as possible. 'You make good here and I'll finish up in the lounge.'

'OK, boss,' Tess replied, nonchalantly.

Ten minutes later the two operatives had completed the search and begun repacking the equipment into their bags.

'So what do you think?' Harry asked.

'Apart from being a sad, filthy drunk?' replied Tess, contorting her face.

'Apart from those things.'

'Baloch intends to come back, probably soon. The money is a pay-off and represents what someone might expect in payment for preparing a nuclear bomb that could murder millions of people. Odd that he didn't do something sensible with the cash though.'

'Perhaps he had no time?'

'Perhaps. Most of his clothes are still here and he could easily afford to buy new. It might be worth showing his face around the department stores in Buenos Aires.'

'It might. Anything else?' asked Harry.

'Nothing. There's no sign of the equipment he took from his work.'

'It will be with him. Encizo can check with the airline.'

'How about you?' asked Tess.

'I found his passport, and everything else here suggests he intends to return. Bank statements, credit-card bills, telephone records and even his address book are lying about. The kitchen is disgusting, nothing perishable has been removed, and nothing has been cleaned.'

'Many of the best minds have no idea how to look after themselves. Maybe he had had too much to drink on the day he left?'

'He left work and flew within an afternoon. Maybe he chose the bottle instead of the brush. There's certainly plenty for Encizo to go on. Baloch likes his Jack Daniels, buys it by the crate, home-delivered too. We could show his face around the off-licences as well as the department stores. For some reason he saves the empties.'

'Argentinians call them liquor stores, like us, and they usually pay for returns,' Tess said. 'It's an eco thing, something that doesn't happen in enough countries.'

'That's the pot calling the kettle black,' whispered Harry tetchily.

'Pardon me?'

'Oh, never mind. There are fingerprints of course, and a large number of unwashed cups and glasses around. Maybe someone came here to make arrangements and payment. I will ask Encizo to call forensics in to lift some prints and DNA. My betting is that few people other than prostitutes and delivery men ever came here. Encizo may be able to narrow them down. Then we can run them through the ASS, FBI, MI5, Interpol, Mossad and any other database we can think of.'

'Did you notice any tracks in the yard? No one has raised that possibility,' said Tess as she peered through a front window.

'Damn.' Harry considered whether or not Encizo's officers had examined them. He doubted it and it annoyed him that he had not thought to ask.

'Encizo can have them checked out if they haven't done so already,' replied Tess reassuringly.

'At least it hasn't rained here for weeks, the ground is like concrete,' added Harry as he glanced out of a rear window over the parched and cracked earth. The stream at the end of the back garden was a trickle. 'Are we done?'

'Only if you fed the cat,' said Tess as she joined Harry's side, nodding towards an old, home-made cat flap that replaced a bottom panel of the back door. Dirty paw marks betrayed its use.

Harry pointed out of the rear window. 'There's a large grey cat over there gnawing on a rodent. No way does that monster need feeding.'

Chapter 45

January 18th, Z – 104 Days
Buenos Aires, Argentina

Although the marina was little more than a fifteen-minute walk from the factory, Malik decided to drive, as he and Dalia each had a backpack. It was already warm and the traffic was still light. Neither of them wished to exert themselves at the beginning of what promised to be a long day in the sun. They hoped that the inevitable heat and humidity would be offset by a cool Atlantic breeze travelling westwards up the Río de la Plata.

Malik drove the Toyota land cruiser up to the Marina Riachuelo's main entrance at 7:15 a.m. and found the gates open.

Carlos Frer, the boatyard's owner, walked toward them from the marina office as Malik parked the rental in the customer parking area behind the club house. He was wearing a red sleeveless shirt complete with boatyard logo and blue shorts, and his face portrayed the genuine delight he felt in greeting his two guests.

'How nice to meet you again, Señor Kent. Welcome back to the Marina Riachuelo.'

'It's good to be back. Carlos, this is my wife, Diana. Please, call me Sean.'

Carlos greeted Dalia warmly. He took in and admired her beautiful strong features and knew that she was what stood between the two men and a final, lucrative bill of sale. He considered it a done deal and relaxed slightly, for it was obviously an exquisite boat for an equally exquisite woman.

'Before we leave today I will provide you with an electronic entry card so that from now on you will be able to gain access whenever you wish. Please, leave your car parked here.'

'That would be very convenient,' said Malik, pleased he did not have to raise his need for a gate key card. Malik grabbed both his and Dalia's day sacks from the back seat before remotely locking the car, and they followed Carlos into the modern club house.

'Please wait here while I fetch the boat keys,' suggested Carlos politely.

Malik and Dalia wandered around the small shop off the foyer that had just opened, and within five minutes Carlos returned carrying a large box of provisions. He was accompanied by an attractive older woman who Malik and Dalia assumed was his wife. The woman carried two bags filled with cans of beer and bottles of wine.

Malik and Dalia estimated the Frers were about ten years older than themselves.

'Sorry I took so long,' said Carlos unnecessarily.

'I had to walk up and close the main gate. This is my wife, Maria. Since we're short-handed today we thought it would be beneficial if Maria came too. Maria is a very experienced deck hand and a wonderful cook.'

As the introductions were made, Malik transferred the day sacks into one hand and quietly took hold of Maria's bags in the other.

'That would be delightful,' replied Dalia. 'I would welcome Maria's ideas about the boat.'

'Well, let's go,' said Carlos. 'We must catch the morning tide.'

The four of them walked into the early morning sunshine and through the awakening boatyard.

'I hope there is a refrigerator for the drink on board,' asked Dalia mockingly.

'There is a purpose-made refrigerator under the bar in the salon, it was the first thing I checked,' grinned Malik.

When it became obvious which boat they were walking towards, Dalia was stunned.

Both men enjoyed the moment.

'Is that her?' Dalia exclaimed excitedly. 'Wow. What a beautiful boat. *Last Tango*,' she said, reading the name on the stern, 'A lovely name too.'

Despite the impending purchase and any bargaining to follow, Malik was delighted that Dalia liked the boat so much. He felt he was purchasing the boat for them both.

'I'm pleased you like her, my darling,' Malik said loud enough to be heard by Carlos and Maria.

As the men prepared the boat for sailing, the two women explored the boat, inside and out. Occasionally the men heard shrieks of approval and giggling from within, exclamations that were not limited to Dalia.

'Sean, I thought we might sail to Montevideo today. It lies about two hundred kilometres due east of here across the Río de la Plata.'

'Suits us,' shrugged Malik.

'Maria is going to cook lunch on board, if that's OK? I do not propose to go ashore, but to find somewhere to anchor offshore.'

'Perfect,' Malik replied.

Carlos took the helm, inserted a key, flicked several switches and the twin Caterpillar 800 horsepower engines stirred immediately. Malik could sense the sheer power of the sweetly tuned engines reverberating through the hull as they idled. Carlos released the stern ropes, and Malik, who was standing on the bow, released his on command from Carlos and he gently pushed the bow from the quay. *Last Tango* gently accelerated away, leaving the quay behind as Carlos smoothly opened the twin throttles and pointed the boat towards the rising sun.

Once in the channel and safely underway, Dalia and Maria made hot drinks on the four-ring gas stove in the galley before sitting in the cockpit where they could avoid the strong wind. Malik decided to conduct his final inspection before lunch and began searching through the boat. Switching the boat to autopilot, Carlos read a yachting magazine on the fly deck as he kept a look out over the horizon and on the instruments. It was not long before Malik was satisfied that the minor faults he had found on his last visit were rectified. Approaching Carlos on the fly deck, he suggested the skipper show him the instrumentation.

'You can drive the boat from the fly deck up here, where you can find the necessary duplicate instruments vital for the basic running of the boat, or you can drive it from the protection of the cockpit below, where all the instruments are located. The GPS plotter radar, VHF radio and satellite telephone are located in the navigation room as you know, but all of them can be easily relocated to the fly deck or cockpit as desired by plugging them here, here and here.'

Carlos spent the next hour explaining the functioning of the boat to a captivated Malik, pointing out items as he went.

'We are currently cruising at twenty knots, but she will cruise comfortably at twenty seven knots, with a maximum speed of thirty knots.' Pausing to call down to Maria, Carlos continued, 'As soon as Maria and Diana relieve us I want to show you the cockpit instruments, the engine compartment and the navigation instruments.'

Two hours later *Last Tango* was anchored about a quarter of a mile off Montevideo and the party of four were enjoying a delicious, freshly cooked meal on the lower deck in the shade of a temporary awning erected by the two men.

'Carlos, Diana and I have discussed it and we agree we want to buy the boat,' said Malik, as they sipped wine after the meal. 'She is exactly what we have been looking for.'

'I never doubted it. I knew from the first moment I met you that it was not a question of money. *Last Tango* is the most beautiful boat I have ever sold, inside and out. She is well-equipped and easy to handle too.'

'There is nothing to object to, *Last Tango* is a fine boat. Will your son and his friends help us sail her to Gibraltar?'

'Miguel would consider it a privilege.'

Carlos thought for a moment. '*Last Tango* will be re-registered to London within days and I will organise for a sign writer to alter the stern. I would also like to offer you one year's free berth and membership at my yacht club.'

'That's very generous of you, Carlos. I'm delighted to accept.'

Carlos returned Malik's smile. 'When we return to the boatyard we will finish the paperwork.'

'And I will wire the balance of half a million US dollars. Is your son able to fix a mooring for me in Gibraltar, the Queensway Quay Marina, for two weeks?'

'I have friends in every major port in the world, *amigo*. Miguel will fix that for us.'

'Now,' said Maria with a sigh, 'can we please talk about something other than boats?'

The two men cleaned up after lunch while the two women stripped to swimwear and sunned themselves on the top deck. The laughter grew as they cracked open fresh beers and the afternoon wore on, but by 4 p.m. it was time to weigh anchor and return to Buenos Aires on the evening tide. On the journey back Carlos quietly remarked to Maria why he considered Sean and Diana so typically English.

'They do not bicker or argue, and appear so respectful of each other's privacy. They are so reserved,' Carlos suggested. 'I cannot encourage him to get drunk.'

'They love each other,' replied Maria, the romantic Latino who could easily interpret the signals. 'But he is preoccupied, perhaps troubled. Englishmen never know when to relax.'

'Most businessmen I know are preoccupied,' said Carlos, seizing the moment to explain any weaknesses of his own.

Maria ignored his excuses. 'What does Sean do?'

'He owns a riverboat company in London.'

'Mm, they look like they spend much time in the open air.'

'They spend a lot of time in the Mediterranean,' replied Carlos.

Carlos and Maria continued to observe the younger couple who stood close to each other on the foredeck looking out to sea.

A slight swell caused Dalia's unsteady legs to falter and Malik grabbed her. As she stood back up Dalia slipped an arm through Malik's and clung on to him. He turned towards her and she kissed him lightly on the lips. They felt a surge of electricity flow between them. It was the briefest kiss of a couple in the infancy of courtship.

'Which bedroom will you choose?' Dalia whispered to him.

'Oh, the stateroom in the middle,' Malik replied casually.

'That one has the largest bunk. It's my favourite too,' Dalia responded coyly. 'We will have to share it.' She gave him a suggestive smile and squeezed his arm.

He could not help but smile back at her.

'They cannot have been married long,' sighed Maria.

Carlos laughed and hugged her with one arm as he steered the boat with the other.

Chapter 46

January 18th, Z - 104 Days
London, England

The exact origin of 'Scotland Yard', the name given to the headquarters of the Metropolitan Police, is unclear. Either the original headquarters site at 4 Whitehall Place, London, had been a residence owned by the kings of Scotland before the Union and used and occupied by them or their ambassadors when in the city, or the name derived from the land being owned by a man called Scott during the Middle Ages. By 1887 the police headquarters had expanded across Whitehall Place, Great Scotland Yard and Palace Place, and in 1890 it was moved to premises on the Victoria Embankment which became known as 'New Scotland Yard'. In 1967, because of the need for a larger and more modern headquarters, a further move took place to the present site at Broadway, London SW1, which took the same name.

The audience of 250 rose as one when the Commissioner walked into the main lecture theatre at New Scotland Yard, accompanied by the Minister for London and the Mayor. The audience represented the higher echelons of the Gold Group, London's strategic command centre in the event of a major emergency in the capital. Every organisation that needed to be represented was present, including Cobra, the Government Office for London, the secret services, senior military officers from the MOD, and the heads of all the emergency services and other key agencies. Numerous experts had also been invited, tasked with resolving particularly complex subjects such as nuclear effects, consequence and recovery management, mass evacuation, site clearance, mass fatalities and critical infrastructure. The Commissioner walked to the lectern and with his back to his senior planning team he began his address.

'Minister for London, Mayor of London, ladies and gentlemen. In over forty years of police service I have never had to embark on so serious an operation. I do not believe the Metropolitan Police or any other police authority in the United Kingdom has ever attempted a task of this magnitude before. I have been informed by the Home Secretary that London's Gold Group is to be exercised by Cobra in just two months time with a scenario that involves the threat of a large-scale terrorist nuclear attack on the city. The purpose of this exceptional exercise, to be called Exercise Rapid Response, is twofold. First, it is to inspire confidence among the public in our ability to manage in the event of a real threat and, second, it is to identify how we can improve our procedures. I have never heard of such a massive test ever taking place before, anywhere in the world. It will involve the deliberate displacement of millions people. But for the short time the exercise takes, it will have been worth it, as we will be better placed to deal with the greatest ever threat to world peace. Each of you should consider what would happen to the fabric of our society should such an attack occur. The consequences of such an attack would obviously have a massive impact on our entire nation, but nowhere more so than the thirty-three London boroughs and the City of London that are all represented here today. For the purposes of the exercise, and possibly for real, every borough, from Hillingdon in the west to Havering in the east, from Enfield in the north to Croydon in the south will be affected. By just how much I hear you ask? Well, to ensure I have your complete attention I have a number of experts here today who will give you some idea. First up is Professor Richard Spedding from AWE Aldermaston who will inform you of the effects of a nuclear attack.'

The lights dimmed and the professor rose to give his shocking presentation, supported by a doctor and a fireman. Forty minutes later there was a break, after which the Commissioner returned to the lectern.

'Since 9/11 much has been done to improve our resilience and contingency planning, but we have not exercised the worst-case scenario. Well, this is it, the threat of a ten-kiloton nuclear explosion, with Ground Zero at Charing Cross. Apologies to the City of London Police, but there we have it.'

'No loss then,' someone whispered a little too loud.

There was laughter from some of the audience. Even the Commissioner smiled.

'A rose among thorns,' an unidentified woman heckled from the back.

The Commissioner accepted the banter. They thought it was an exercise after all. He knew his audience would produce the goods and that there were many heroes in this room.

'As the professor has already shown us, none of us fare well,' added the Commissioner. 'The exercise begins with this conference, and will culminate in the evacuation of London for thirty-six hours from 6 p.m. on March 20th.'

That last remark shocked the audience back into silence, just as the Commission intended.

'The chain of command will run from the Prime Minister to Cobra to the Gold Group then to the Silver Groups in each borough and the City of London Police. Then there are the local operational command units within each borough at Bronze level. There are a total of thirty-four Silver Groups and two hundred and four Bronze, but just five levels of command. So, Canada Square Bronze Group will be found under command of Tower Hamlets Silver Group and so on. You all get the picture. All blue-light and supporting organisations will be represented at the appropriate level of the operational command chain, with the exception of our strategic assets which will remain under Cobra or Gold's direct command.'

For the next two hours the Commissioner and his command team outlined the procedures and their reaction to the exercise.

After lunch, the chiefs from each borough, the City of London Police, and all the heads of the supporting agencies and services returned to the theatre in New Scotland Yard and received verbal and written orders for Exercise Rapid Response.

Chapter 47

January 20th, Z – 102 Days
Buenos Aires, Argentina

Malik and Dalia established a working area outside the chamber for modifying the plastic fender and ten litre cooking-oil drum. Everything they needed was at hand including work benches, lighting, welding apparatus, stoves, electrical equipment and instruments, hand tools, protective clothing, glues and so on. The inventory was thorough but if they found they required anything more they simply purchased it. Although Malik was a creative man and good with his hands, Baloch had taken control of the entire weapon-making operation, and this included the preparation of the two decoys that were to conceal and protect each nuclear bomb. When Baloch was eventually satisfied with his painstaking reconstruction of the two nuclear bombs, he was determined that nothing would go wrong with the two decoys that existed to protect them.

Malik was pleased with Baloch's determined attitude and also his attention to fine detail. He was content to let Baloch dictate the design and fabrication requirements of the fender and drum, for despite Baloch's expertise there was never any doubt about who was in command. In any event, Malik admitted that Baloch knew considerably more than he did about the application of foam fillers, the moulding of lead, and the vast array of other techniques that were used when fabricating the two items. Baloch had supported the application of a ten-litre cooking oil drum but had openly sneered at the original intention of using the spare wheel from a car, suggesting instead the use of a large boat fender. Malik had seen the benefits and seized upon the idea.

Malik rose early and armed with his entrance swipe card and boat keys he drove down to the marina and his new boat, *Last*

Tango. He recovered four medium-sized, bright-orange, oblong-shaped plastic fenders from the eighteen matching fenders that lay in a forward hold adjacent to the anchor locker. Malik knew that one side of the boat did not need more than six fenders to fend off another boat or protect itself from a quay. The remaining six were effectively spare.

Their plan to disguise Little Boy was simple. They would carefully secrete a nuclear bomb inside the fender then place it at the very bottom of the storage locker on *Last Tango*. Such was the awkward access through the locker hatch that any crewman would only ever grasp those fenders and their tie-lines that lay at the top of the pile. In any event, he planned to accompany the modified fender until it reached its final destination in London and ensure nobody attempted to use it. At Amsterdam, Malik planned to exchange fenders in *Last Tango* with matching fenders in *Dutch Master*.

On hearing Malik return from the boatyard, Baloch and Dalia left their rooms and went to meet him at the workspace outside the chamber. As soon as a guard opened the gate, Malik drove inside the vast meat-processing room and pulled the Toyota up near the chamber. He turned off the engine, jumped out, then opened the boot.

'I brought several spares in case we need them,' said Malik as he lifted the lozenge-shaped fenders out of the Toyota's boot.

'I doubt I'll need more than two,' said Baloch as he took one from Malik and turned it over in his hands. 'It's perfect.'

'So, what must we do first?'

'First we'll cut the fender into two pieces from end to end, along here where you can still see the joint. That will allow the completed fender as much strength as possible.'

Baloch traced a finger around the fender, feeling the joint he was looking at.

'Then we'll configure the weapon for the fender on the bench inside the chamber, measure it, and manufacture a small protective sleeve for it from foam-dried rubber. We will use one of the spare fenders as a mould by cutting it in half and lining it with moulding clay to a minimum thickness of forty millimetres. When the two halves of rubber have set we will carve out the inside for the weapon and sculpt its outer surface. We will then place the weapon and some moisture absorbing grains into one half of the protective housing, arm the weapon and seal the housing by fusing together the two sleeves of rubber.

'How will that deal with any radiation leakage?' asked Malik.

'Ah, yes. Although the radiation readings I obtained from the cases are low, of course I would like to provide additional lead dampening between the housing and the fender wall. I will replace the moulding clay with lead. The fender will be heavy, but one person will manage. Is that all right?'

'That's fine, Doctor. Any difficulties?' Malik asked.

'Not that I can see,' replied Baloch.

'Let's hope not,' added Dalia menacingly.

The other part of Malik's plan was to secrete Fat Man into a ten-litre drum of cooking oil. Unlike Little Boy, which was to remain on board until it reached the heart of London, Fat Man was to be taken to Gibraltar on *Last Tango* with Little Boy, but then transported by car, via a ferry crossing, to London.

'Fat Man is simple enough too,' began Baloch as he examined one of four identical oil drums purchased earlier by Dalia. 'We can place the weapon at the bottom of the drum, and then top it up with oil. We must carefully remove the label then cut off the lower third of the drum.' He traced his finger along an imaginary circular line around the drum. 'It will be heavy but may also be carried by one person. The moulding requirements will be similar to Little Boy.'

Dalia was listening intently to what was to happen to Fat Man for it was her responsibility to take this bomb into the heart of London. Malik's responsibility was to Little Boy. 'That's good,' she said. 'I wish to take three drums with me on *Last Tango*, one of which we may use on our voyage. If more than one is destroyed I will buy replacements before we leave here.'

With renewed energy the three set to work on the last phase of each bomb's construction and they worked well into the evening, deciding not to go out but eat a takeaway Chinese meal in the factory.

It was late when Baloch eventually decided to turn in with his books and another bottle of whiskey. Baloch was looking forward to his release, and pay day. Although he trusted Malik and Dalia, for they were good to him, he did not care or question what they were doing or where they intended to go after the work at the factory was complete. From the information he had heard and from what he had seen he assumed they were sailing directly to England with Little Boy and Fat Man but in truth, he didn't care. Right now he wanted to go to bed, for the way he saw it, the more he slept, the sooner his freedom would arrive. As usual, he would not wake up until midday.

Malik's room doubled as the living quarters for the three of them. Dalia slept next door and the scientist slept in another room at the far end of the corridor. A single table lamp illuminated Malik's room, for none of them appreciated the bright glare of the florescent strip lights on the ceiling and, like the others, he had pinned black refuse sacks over all the windows in lieu of curtains to block the early-morning light. After Baloch left, Malik and Dalia remained on his makeshift camp bed that was an unzipped sleeping bag, two rugs and a cushion, all covering a wide, deep and remarkably comfortable air mattress lying on flattened cardboard boxes positioned against one wall of his room.

It was Malik's room that contained most of the equipment and stores that the three terrorists required to sustain themselves, and among a number of large transit boxes, some of which were arranged as a makeshift table, there was a television supplied by Jamali that received a large number of satellite channels. As the film that they were watching ended, Dalia rose and poured each of them another drink then sat back down with her legs drawn up and her elbows resting on them. Malik was lying with his back against the wall.

'Malik, I'm sorry about what happened to your wife and children,' Dalia whispered gently.

'Thank you,' Malik replied, his voice quivering softly.

'Karima is very beautiful,' she added, glancing at the single photograph tacked to the wall.

'She looks like her mother. She misses her mother terribly.'

'She has a wonderful father.'

'I wish she did. I should see far more of her. Live with her and help her grow up. Last time I saw her I promised her I would make everything right. Soon I will.'

'Your sister is looking after her?'

'Yes, Karima has recovered well from her injuries. That, at least is something.'

'Do you know who bombed your home?'

'The car bomber was killed. But there was no evidence and no one claimed responsibility.'

There was a period of silence before Malik spoke again.

'But I do know who ordered the hit.'

Another silence. This time it was Dalia who broke it.

'I would love a family.'

'You will. Any man would be proud to be your husband.'

'I was captured and tortured by Indian reservists in the last war. I don't find it easy to like men. I can no longer have children.'

Malik was stunned. This beautiful woman was barren and he hated the Indian reservists that had made her so.

'I'm sorry. I didn't know.'

'There's no reason why you should have.'

Another period of silence and reflection followed as they watched a CNN report about another terror attack on Westerners in Saudi Arabia.

An hour later Dalia woke up stretched out on Malik's camp bed with her head on Malik's lap and a rug placed over her. He was leaning on pillows propped against the wall reading a book, with CNN still broadcasting quietly in the background. Malik had watched the reports several times as they recycled. Seeing her stir, he used the remote to turn off the sound.

'Do you want to go to bed?' he whispered innocently.

'No,' she mumbled opening her eyes and looking up at him. 'I want you to kiss me, to love me.'

The next thing Malik realised, he was bending down to meet her as she rose up. The back of his neck tingled from the touch of her hands as she reached up for him. When they kissed, he felt as if his breath had been taken away. She was so beautiful, and it had been so long, so long for both of them. At first his lips remained closed, his pressure against hers tentative. Then his lips parted. Her tongue met his, and she had never felt so powerfully intimate a touch. The kiss lengthened and deepened, and they both began to tremble.

'It has been a long time,' he whispered.

'For me also. Perhaps we should wait,' she offered, not meaning it.

'Hell, no,' he replied.

Malik could not control his reaction. He had risked his life countless times as a member of Pakistan's Special Forces. He had encountered fear in its most powerful forms. What he was feeling now had all the symptoms of fear, but the emotion was quite the opposite. It was ecstasy. His fingertips became numb. His heart pounded with chest-swelling speed. As they shuffled and he lowered his hands to cup her hips that were rising toward him, he trembled harder. He pressed his lips against her neck, aroused by the lingering scent of primal salt and musk, earth, heat and sky. It filled his nostrils. It made him feel that he was suffocating. She straddled him. He unbuttoned her blouse and slid his hands beneath her bra, touching her breasts, her nipples growing, hardening to his touch. Her breasts were firm, the size of his cupped hands. He sank back onto his back dragging her onto him. They embraced and rolled, kissing more deeply. He worked his way down, kissing the silken skin of her stomach. She shuddered. He seemed to float, feeling as if he had been taken out of his body, of Dalia's body. He wanted to go on kissing and touching her for ever, to touch more and more of her. Hurrying, needing, they undressed each other. When he entered her, he felt transported, he couldn't get far enough within her. He wanted to be totally one with her. When they came, he felt suspended in a moment between frenzied heartbeats that lengthened and swelled and erupted.

Several hours later Dalia opened her eyes. The television and table light had been switched off. Malik lay naked next to her, asleep on top of the rugs. Neither of them had spoken since they had climaxed earlier that night. The silence had persisted until she had fallen asleep, and Dalia had felt uneasy, worried that he was in the throes of regret, second thoughts, guilt that he had betrayed his dead wife and his children, three of whom were also dead.

But slowly Malik stirred, and he turned to her and touched her cheek with his lips.

So it was going to be all right, she thought.

Then she felt tears and realised Malik was crying. Dalia leaned towards him and hugged him, then kissed him, the kiss communicating tenderness and affection.

'We will be all right,' she whispered, 'Allah is watching over us.'

He was not sure whether she was referring to themselves or the mission, or both.

They gently held each other, each believing the other was falling asleep.

But Malik could not sleep as he could not relieve himself of the unfamiliar tightness in his throat as he imagined her body. The navel that formed a tiny hollow in her flat stomach. Her dark pubic hair that was soft and tufted. Her body that had the contoured, supple tone of an athlete.

Malik realised that his old life was behind him and that his future was with Karima and Dalia. 'Karima will adore you,' he mumbled as he kissed her forehead

Realising he thought she was asleep, Dalia surprised him by whispering, 'Make love to me, Malik.'

Chapter 48

January 21st, Z - 101 Days
Buenos Aires, Argentina

Harry knew that he was over-thinking this. Perhaps he had been away from the intelligence community for too long. It was six days since they had searched Baloch's house but there was no breakthrough, even though the Argentine Secret Service was doing everything possible to locate the terrorist cell. The stark reality was that the Argentine Government was doing all it could to find a rogue nuclear bomb that could devastate a country, and at the same time demonstrate to the world that its unstable history was behind it and global terrorists would not find Argentina a safe haven. Argentina had developed socially and politically since the early 1980s, and it was not about to be sent spiralling backwards to undemocratic times. Although he had been divorced from any diplomatic activity, Harry knew that it had been considerable and conducted at the highest levels. Sir Michael and Jim Ridge had been in the thick of it and the result was the surprising amount of freedom that both Harry and Tess enjoyed.

The two operatives chose to walk the short distance most mornings from their hotel in central Buenos Aires to the Secret Service building at 100 Avenue del Libertador. The building was somewhat cynically referred to by everyone from Government ministers down to street traders as the 'hotel', for that was what it once was, before the original hotel business upped sticks and moved to the more lucrative San Nicolás neighbourhood in central Buenos Aires. Converted from the twelve-storey hotel, the building's internal plan did not follow the modern trend of open-plan offices but remained a rabbit warren of corridors and offices, most the size of a small double bedroom. But anyone would have been hard pushed to find someone who would wish it different. In an attempt to remove the stigma and suspicion that prevailed from the military regime of the 1970s (a time when the Junta ruled by a fear spearheaded by their 'secret police'), the reborn Argentine Secret Service, or ASS, relocated from the imposing and dreaded office building on Avenue Paseo Colón. To the delight of jubilant crowds, the splendid Victorian building had been razed to the ground and the infamous basement to which snatch squads had dragged their own people, kicking and screaming, and from which they rarely returned alive, was dug up and the whole area replaced by a lake and people's park of remembrance. In the ten years from 1972, twelve thousand lives were believed to have been lost in that building, most under torture. The new location for the ASS on Avenue del Libertador near the Palacio San Martín had two underground floors, but they were car parks.

It was obvious to Harry why Encizo had been chosen above more senior people to lead the Counter Subversion and Counterterrorism Division. He was a young but forward-thinking agent, for that was what they were called in Argentina, eager to lead the ASS from its immoral past. Not only was he experienced, energetic and popular, but he was that rare breed, an agent with an astute political brain. Because of this, he cut the bullshit, hated unnecessary bureaucracy and got hard results. Above all else, he epitomised the honest, open, frank and confident leader that Argentine voters had longed to read about and, if they had the chance, vote for.

Harry and Tess used personal identification numbers to enter the building through the bullet-proof and electronically-operated Perspex security pods then took the elevator to the sixth floor. This floor was dedicated to Argentina's Counter Subversion and Counterterrorism Division. Although the division of two hundred and fifty agents already had its hands full protecting their Government's progressive modernist agenda, the priority right now was finding Doctor Baloch, Malik and the terrorist cell in a country of forty million people.

After helping themselves to coffee outside their allocated office, Harry and Tess checked their satcoms for messages. They were not expecting any, as regular messages were sent at specified times of the day and the MI6 and CIA timetables were synchronised for this op. Unless, of course, someone had made a breakthrough, but no one had. Sighing, Harry felt another frustrating day in the offing, for as they had reported in their daily situation report to London last night, everything that could be done was being done. The reality was both he and Tess were sitting back and waiting for a lead to materialise, and they both felt redundant.

'It's time for the morning update,' said Tess, who was idly studying the maps that hung on one wall of the office.

Holding their coffee cups, both operatives walked down to the large briefing room at the end of the corridor, where they found a room already packed with agents and Encizo deep in conversation with one of his chiefs. Encizo insisted that his chiefs always turn out. Anyone else was free to choose. Usually the room was light and airy, but with so many people, about forty today, it would soon be stifling. With the room so full, the blinds drawn closed and the air conditioning units whirring at maximum, the struggle against the heat was a losing battle. The vertical, wheeled, map boards at the business end of the room were rolled back to the wall; the table that usually sat in the centre had been broken down and parked at the far end, and there was standing room only unless you were lucky enough to find something to perch on. Encizo did not mind the lack of comfort; it encouraged brevity.

It was by no means certain but everyone, including Harry and Tess, believed that Baloch had remained in Buenos Aires. Considerable work had been done to predict where someone who wished to tamper with a nuclear bomb would choose to go, and battle lines drawn on the map. Neighbourhoods had been prioritised and covert surveillance teams positioned. The idea of a public campaign and reward programme had been mooted but quashed by Encizo, not least because a large number of sightings were already being received by the ASS from across Argentina's law enforcement agencies. So far, those followed up had been eliminated.

One unfortunate man, a doctor, and the spitting image of Baloch, had been locked up for six hours in a local police station before the Saudi Arabian ambassador had personally come to his rescue. Of the many reports received on the sixth floor late last night, one was from a young off-duty reserve police officer who stated that he had observed a man he believed was Baloch eating in a restaurant in the San Telmo district. The suspect had been accompanied by a younger man and woman, possibly a couple. The reserve police officer had volunteered to tail them but this had been firmly quashed by the sixth floor, an order he was required to copy back over his cell phone. Twenty minutes later, the officer had watched as an overworked ASS response team on their fourth callout in two hours arrived too late.

The young police reservist, who had not been debriefed since he reported the sighting last night, decided to visit the ASS on the sixth floor and demand to be interviewed. As he sat waiting patiently to be seen, he held the appearance of each of his three subjects in his mind.

Meanwhile, the issue occupying Encizo in the morning briefing was how, between the CIA, MI6 and the ASS, computer systems could be utilised to look for Baloch, now one of the world's most wanted men. A recent headshot of Baloch retrieved from his workplace had already been distributed among all Argentina's law enforcement, customs and immigration services. Interpol had issued a directive and the Americans, Brits and many other countries had also distributed Baloch's picture, though Harry suspected with widely varying degrees of thoroughness. The problem was that this entire approach relied on old-fashioned policing.

Although technically different, the CIA and MI6 were still the sole possessors of vastly superior facial-imaging recognition systems and held agreements to use them in concert with each other's electronic surveillance systems and those of a number of countries worldwide. MI6 had followed the CIA's request that they be granted the necessary authority to tap into Argentina's immigration and customs surveillance cameras, as well as the seven hundred traffic and security control cameras that were dotted around Buenos Aires. What this meant was that Baloch's image would be scanned into computers in Washington and London, which would then monitor thousands of surveillance cameras across the world. If his image appeared on one of these cameras, either the Americans, Brits, or both would know within minutes.

But the political ramifications of allowing the Americans and British to spy on the Argentine public were considerable, for civil rights remained a huge issue in Argentina and the public still maintained a strong suspicion of their Government. The

Argentine public were unlikely to stand for another country watching over their every move. Which country would, thought Harry? But what excited Encizo was the fact that all the customs surveillance and traffic cameras were recorded digitally with records held for a minimum of one year, and therefore the facial imaging systems could check back over the period since Baloch was last seen.

After considerable discussion with his chiefs, Encizo eventually had the ammunition he required to recommend to his superior that it was in the country's interests that MI6 and the CIA be allowed to monitor Argentine cameras until Baloch was traced. They could always pull the plug later, and use the experience to examine the success of facial imaging systems and maybe justify a similar capability of their own. With the support of his superior he knew he would win the battle with the President by nightfall and that the two foreign systems would begin running searches by the time he left for home. Both facial-imaging systems would be monitoring real time within two days.

The morning update continued with Encizo facilitating as usual. Already Baloch's home telephone and address book had led nowhere, and it had become clear that Baloch was no longer using any of his credit or debit cards or his bank account, and that he was either being maintained or was paying cash or a combination of both. In essence, there was no money trail. It had been taken for granted for several days that Baloch was under an assumed identity, although no one supposed any of the terrorists believed they were being hunted down. Public poster campaigns at restaurants and liquor stores, and offers of reward were simply out of the question for that very reason.

Of the DNA and fingerprints taken from Baloch's home, no more than three people remained to be identified, quite an achievement since the house had not been properly cleaned for years. The ASS had begun their elimination by using their national database of known or suspected major criminals and terrorists (a rare benefit from the days of the Junta), and managed to discount all but five which had come up blank. Further enquiries with neighbouring countries, including Uruguay and Chile had reduced this to three, and now the ASS were to turn to the international community through Interpol.

The meeting turned to the reports of sightings. As one of the chiefs finished summarising and Encizo was about to move on to the next issue, Harry spoke up from the back.

'Sir, why not lift prints at the restaurant and compare them with Baloch's? I'm assuming he wasn't wearing gloves to eat and as it was late he was probably one of the last to eat off that table last night?'

Encizo looked at Harry, disappointed that someone other than the Englishman had not thought of it before now, even himself. 'An excellent idea. Forensics will have the reporting officer accompany them.' Encizo looked scornfully at one of his chiefs at the front. 'I understand the young police reservist has come in under his own volition and demanded to be interviewed?'

Everyone noted the rebuke in Encizo's voice.

The chief from the front nodded guiltily, as only thirty minutes earlier he had been heard telling loud jokes at the reservist's expense.

Tess, who was standing beside Harry, added confidently, 'If it was Baloch, the chances are we have the faces of two more terrorists, including Malik.'

The room fell silent. This could be the break everyone was looking for. Encizo smiled and calmly ordered that this potential lead receive top priority. One agent quickly left the room to find the reservist.

Thanking Harry and Tess, Encizo moved onto another potentially embarrassing mistake. After exhaustive searching, several of the tyre tracks lifted from outside Baloch's house could not be accounted for and there were no more leads. The ASS had no choice but to wait until suspect vehicles were identified, then have those vehicles checked against the prints.

The meeting ended with Encizo informing everyone that the surveillance team monitoring Baloch's home had reported nothing unusual.

Harry and Tess re-entered their sterile office considering their next move. Tess turned to Harry. 'Fancy coffee at that restaurant?'

'Definitely,' replied Harry with a mischievous smile.

Just as they were about to leave the telephone on Harry's desk rang.

'Harry, it's Encizo. I know where you're going and I'm coming too. Be in my office in five.'

'OK.'

The line went dead. Tess guessed the nature of the call, and Harry shrugged.

'It was Encizo,' Harry confirmed. 'He's coming too.'

'Great, clout is always useful.'

The telephone rang again and Harry answered a second time.

'Harry, its Conchita.'

'Hi,' replied Harry.

Conchita noted the urgency in his voice. 'Wow. I hope it's not me. You busy?'

'We're just on our way out. We might have had a sighting of Baloch in a city restaurant last night.'

'Wow. He must feel confident. Was he accompanied?'

'Two others, a man and a woman.'

'Makes sense. Hell, that could be the whole cell on a jolly night out.'

'I guess,' said Harry, wondering if it made sense for there to be a man and a woman with Baloch. 'I have to go, Conchita. Sorry. I'll call you later.'

'Harry, would you mind playing in a polo match, the foreign player in a charity team, for me? Please?'

This was the last thing Harry had expected, and he could not help smiling. Why not? he asked himself.

'When?'

'First of Feb at the Buenos Aires International Polo Ground. Premier event.'

Harry had always wanted to play there, just once in his life. It was probably the finest polo ground in the world.

'I'm interested, no, make that very interested. But right now Tess and I have a lift to catch. Speak later, OK?'

'Sure.'

Later that afternoon forensics confirmed that it had, indeed, been Baloch at the restaurant. Additional prints had also been matched to one of the two sets of previously unidentified prints at Baloch's home, now believed to be the unidentified male, possibly known as 'Malik'. Other prints taken from the restaurant may have belonged to the unidentified woman accompanying the two men.

The search increased from one person to three.

That night MI6 worked tirelessly at persuading countries worldwide to drop everything and search all known databases for the male print, but the search was fruitless. More surprising, the reasonable artistic impressions of the unidentified male, for whom they had a probable print and possible alias, and the unidentified female, both provided by the reservist officer and restaurant staff, also failed to produce a single hit. In Harry's mind it reinforced MI6 and CIA profilers' joint finding that they were searching for dedicated mercenaries, professionals who knew how to hide their tracks.

Chapter 49

January 26th, Z – 96 Days
Buenos Aires, Argentina

Outside the factory the city of Buenos Aires had reached a hot and humid 34 degrees Celsius by midday. Doctor Baloch and Dalia had been inside the unventilated chamber for twenty minutes when she saw that the inside temperature had risen by 3 degrees to 26 degrees. She noticed the doctor's perspiring brow and considered that his visual discomfort had as much to do with drink and his poor health as the warmth, though to his credit he remained entirely composed despite the deadly nature of his attention. Although she was wearing a similar protective suit to Baloch, she felt fine.

Dalia was compensating for the shadows produced by the single bare ceiling light bulb by holding a powerful flashlight up to his work. She focused on where the beam of light fell and watched as his gloved fingers wove the fine wires through a hole carved in the foam dried rubber sleeve to where the Zeon Tech 3000 control unit was to be fitted.

'Now all I have to do is set the year, date and time, and the detonation time, and then I can connect the control unit and arm the device,' said Baloch, his voice muffled by his respirator. 'I must set the time outside.'

Dalia followed Baloch and crawled out of the chamber. Soon they were standing outside with Malik, removing their hoods and respirator masks.

'It's common for the timer to be the most unreliable part of an improvised explosive device but this control unit is the very best,' Baloch explained. 'The clock is radio-controlled. Whenever it picks up the right radio signal it readjusts itself to the local time. When would you like detonation to occur?'

'May 2nd, midday,' replied Malik without hesitation.

Baloch, who had removed the back of the control unit, withdrew a slip of plastic to activate the power source. 'There, look, the signal is good. The clock has set itself to 1:15 p.m. You can see the date and month, and even what day it is.'

Malik and Dalia peered at the small LED screen. They looked impressed.

'That black triangle with the radiating lines means that the clock's radio-control capability is active,' Baloch explained. In several seconds he had set the timer for detonation.

'Will the control unit receive radio waves through the lead?' asked Malik cautiously.

'Of course, it operates on short wave. Don't worry yourself, Malik, I have thought of everything.'

As soon as Baloch and Dalia re-entered the chamber, the doctor installed the Zeon Tech control unit and the bomb was complete.

'You wish to arm the device?' Baloch asked Dalia.

'Why not?' Dalia reached over and with her small, gloved index finger she pressed the small red button recessed into the cover of the control unit. 'The button has not lit,' she observed with alarm.

'But it has remained depressed. Don't be alarmed; I have removed the bulb. It operates from a redundant electrical circuit and I don't wish the light to create heat that may be detectable, even through forty millimetres of lead. The red light merely confirmed the switch was active, nothing more. It will also help conserve power though that is hardly a concern.'

Baloch grabbed a circuit tester and spent several minutes checking the bomb was armed. 'And now, we have the first of two ten-kiloton nuclear bombs,' Baloch mumbled as he checked the last circuit.

'How long does the power source last?' enquired Dalia.

'This model is used by scientists to drive explorations and experiments in the harshest conditions the world has to offer.' replied Baloch. 'It's also used on many highly technical weapons systems like this one where the power source will last between ten and fifteen years.'

Baloch placed three small packets of absorbent material into cavities in the rubber sleeve around the bomb then liberally painted a toxic rubber solution onto the exposed surface of the rubber. 'Pass me the other half, quickly,' he demanded.

Dalia groped under the bench, retrieved the unused half of the rubber sleeve and passed it to Baloch, who immediately cleaned the upper surface, then pressed the two halves together concealing the weapon. He strapped the two halves tightly together, and then the two terrorists crawled out of the chamber for the second time that day.

Outside, Baloch warned the others what he was to do next, and after several minutes he and Dalia returned to the chamber. Dalia watched incredulously as Baloch removed the straps, then picked the rubber-coated bomb up from its cradle on the bench and shook it with increasing force. Worse was to come. He dropped the heavy weight onto the floor from increasing heights but it simply rebounded.

'Well, you don't want a sea storm to set it off do you?' laughed Baloch confidently as he saw the fear in Dali's eyes. 'Don't be alarmed, there are many myths about nuclear bombs. The bombs themselves are usually designed to be very stable, like these. It's the nuclear reaction between the neutron generators and plutonium that is unstable. No amount of movement will cause this bomb to detonate, even if it were crushed.'

Baloch then lit a blowtorch, but to Dalia's relief he simply sprayed the rubber with flame, particularly around the joints. 'This will seal the rubber sleeve, preventing moisture from entering the weapon. Corrosion is the biggest fault with nuclear weapons, particularly on ships and submarines,' he explained.

'We're out of time,' Dalia reminded the doctor.

'We can take Fat Man out with us now,' Baloch suggested. 'The sooner we place him in the drum the better.'

The temperature in the chamber was now a stifling 32 degrees Celsius, and they both left the oppressive chamber for the last time that day, Dalia with the radiation detection equipment following Baloch who eased the bomb ahead of him.

As the bomb emerged from the tunnel, Malik, who was dressed in his own protective suit, picked it up and placed it on the bench. The ten-litre oil drum in its component parts was already laid out and prepared. It took him less than twenty seconds to place the rubber sleeve into its pocket inside the lead-lined drum and place the lead-lined cover on top.

Baloch was prepared with his wand. 'Look, no reading at all,' he exclaimed proudly.

Malik and Dalia looked at the stationary pointer, then at each other. Neither of them saw any relief or pride in the other's eyes, simply recognition that a potentially problematic phase of the mission had passed.

Once out of the protective clothing, it took another two hours for the three terrorists to seal the lead cover, carefully rejoin the top of the drum leaving the sealed plastic cap undisturbed, and reglue the printed advertising scroll back around the drum's body. By the time they were finished there was no discernable difference between the two remaining drums in front of them, even their weight was similar.

'We will recommence work on Little Boy tomorrow,' said Malik enthusiastically.

'How long will that one take?' asked Dalia.

'The bomb is the same but the formwork is a little more complicated,' replied Baloch. 'We must allow for additional preparation time. Two days at the most, no more. Then my work is done.'

That evening they ate dinner in a secluded Spanish restaurant recommended by Jamali called La Recova de Posadas on Julio Avenue. On their way, Malik stopped at an Internet café to send another brief electronic message.

> Muhammad,
> We have enjoyed our holiday but will move on as planned in seven days. PBUH.
> Mohammad.

It was no surprise to Baloch that Dalia had moved in with Malik. Frankly he had wondered what had taken the man so long.

Malik and Dalia had spent every night together since that first night of lovemaking six days ago and often, after Baloch had left and they had exhausted themselves from discovering each other, they would spend until the early hours discussing the future, with topics ranging from each other and Karima to their faith and the future of the world. Tonight was no exception.

Chapter 50

January 27th, Z – 95 Days
London, England

'Thank you all for considering my thoughts for the monthly press conference on Saturday,' the Prime Minister began, as he settled into the only armchair at the Cabinet table. It was Thursday morning, the day Cabinet meetings were routinely held.

'I trust you are all aware that the threat of a nuclear attack on London by al-Qa'eda has been authenticated by MI6. Operation Enduring Freedom represents our response to this threat and involves the seeking and destroying of the nuclear threat *and* its perpetrators.

'The operation is to remain top secret, until I declare otherwise, in the hope we can avoid panic and encourage the terrorists to bury themselves further underground. The Foreign Secretary and I have already held secret talks with the NATO Secretary General and he has offered his conditional support. When we go public he will, on behalf of all members, immediately invoke Article Five of the Washington Treaty. Article Five, as you know from 9/11, states that an attack on one member shall be considered an attack on all members, and from that time we will receive NATO's full and unconditional support. What this all means is that we can take whatever action is necessary, including the use of armed force to restore and maintain our security, and after Article Five is invoked, we can call upon the military might of our allies including the Americans. I hope that out of all this we can find a lasting cure for global terrorism.

'We will hear in a few minutes from the Foreign Secretary who will update us on progress with finding the nuclear bomb and from the Home Secretary about London's preparedness. First I would like to emphasise that this is a new type of war that requires us to act in secret, for now at least. The impact on our society from knowledge of the threat will be disastrous and play right into our enemy's hands. I have discussed this in depth with the Lord Chancellor, who has confirmed that my actions are entirely legal.

'I do not choose to go to war without Parliament's consent or without the knowledge of the people. For now that is forced upon me by the need for secrecy. We are in a war against people who wish to attack our ability to protect our people. That is the most basic function of government. Any government that can't accomplish this forfeits its legitimacy. Our enemies won't attack with a conventional armed force because they don't have one. But millions could be killed, and we have a responsibility to provide the best possible protection.'

The Deputy Prime Minister drew breath, and then addressed the Cabinet. 'You are all aware why we cannot go public with the real threat right now. We wish to avoid chaos and do not wish to drive the terrorist cell underground. Also, we need more time to prepare. Do we need to spend more time on this issue?'

No one felt they did.

'We are trying with every means at our disposal to find the bomb,' he continued, 'and the terrorists. What we can't do is watch the terrorists run for their burrows or stop the economy stone dead while we hunt for them. If we do that, the terrorists have already won a victory. Our way of life, our democracy and civilisation is at stake. This is a war we must not lose.'

'So,' said the Prime Minister as he looked towards the Foreign Secretary, 'where are we with finding this nuclear bomb?'

'Prime Minister, as you know we have a covert team comprising Harry Winchester and a CIA agent called Tess Fulton tracking the terrorist cell. Having verified the threat with the original source, Amir, and picked up one or two leads, our team has left Afghanistan for Argentina. The CIA, FBI and other security services across the world, including Argentina, are proving extremely cooperative. The CIA believes that an ex-Pakistani nuclear scientist called Doctor Sultan Baloch, who currently lives and works in Argentina, is helping the terrorist cell with the manufacture of the bomb. The doctor was associated with al-Qa'eda and the Taliban during the Taliban rule of Afghanistan, though nothing was proven and he was released. Later he turned up in Argentina, where it's believed he still is and a manhunt is underway. This leads us to believe the terrorist cell has moved to him.'

'It sounds to me as though he could be anywhere,' said the Home Secretary doubtfully.

The Foreign Secretary stayed calm, his voice controlled. 'It's also a question of tools, equipment, supplies and somewhere suitable to hide, not to mention timescale. Baloch works in the Argentine nuclear industry and has access to the type of equipment required to manufacture a nuclear bomb. We believe the mountain came to Muhammad because the latter was less moveable.'

The Prime Minister frowned. 'Do you think there is more than one weapon?'

'So far we have no idea. It cannot be discounted. The CIA is conducting a thorough worldwide search for missing nukes on our behalf, but I'm sorry to say it's a thankless task. It's unlikely this will lead to anything as we cannot be certain how open some countries will be about any lapses of security, but we must explore this avenue. The manhunt for Baloch continues in Buenos Aires, where he was last seen disembarking from an internal flight at the start of a three-week holiday. The circumstances surrounding his movements are very suspicious. Most importantly, Baloch's recent trip to Buenos Aires leads us to believe that the nuclear bomb is not in the UK but that it's still in Argentina, probably Buenos Aires.'

'It's not certain though,' the Prime Minister rebutted.

'We are convinced,' responded the Foreign Secretary, his voice flat. 'Baloch left work with a large number of specialised tools and other equipment in his possession. As a senior nuclear design scientist working in the nuclear industry this is not unusual. What is unusual is that, according to the airport authorities, he took these tools to Buenos Aires on holiday. Furthermore, with the tools in his possession, he would have attracted interest on an international flight, what with the increase in airline security the world over.'

'OK, that's more convincing. What else?' asked the Prime Minister more confidently.

'Our team in Argentina found half a million US dollars in cash stashed under the floorboards in his house. For a man on a moderate income this is likely to be some kind of down payment or pay-off. Our belief is that it was a down payment from our terrorist cell for work on the bomb. Clearly Baloch expects to return to retrieve it and his house is now under surveillance by the Argentine Secret Service. Our team is now in Buenos Aires helping the locals search for Baloch. Finally, the terrorist cell and the bomb would have to depart Argentina by air or sea. The Argentine authorities are monitoring all airlines and shipping, as one would expect.'

'Some progress. Thank God for the agent Amir; he deserves recognition. Thank you, Foreign Secretary.' The Prime Minister turned to the Home Secretary. 'So, what's your plan to prevent the bomb, or bombs, from entering the country?'

'Prime Minister,' replied the Home Secretary carefully, 'Cobra has established immediate plans for three static defensive cordons in support of the offensive counterterrorist measure provided by MI6. First, by the end of next week we will have a ring of steel around the United Kingdom provided by all available Royal Navy and Customs and Excise shipping. The US, French and Irish navies are providing immediate support, but as you alluded to earlier we hope this requirement will be met as part of a wider NATO operation within the next few weeks.'

The Prime Minister glanced toward the Defence Secretary. 'I am sure there is no misunderstanding, but if necessary we will call all our ships back from overseas, including those currently committed to NATO's Standard Naval Forces in the North Atlantic and Mediterranean. As it is, I feel you must consider whether armed forces personnel with families and homes in London should return.'

'I agree entirely, Prime Minister. We are already acting along these lines,' responded the Defence Secretary patiently. 'But we must also remain wary of revealing the true seriousness and nature of the threat.'

'Good. We'll come back to the question of balance between secrecy and action later.'

The Home Secretary continued with his report. 'Second, Customs and Excise and Immigration have increased vigilance at all points of entry into the country by increasing personnel and stepping up electronic border controls. They also have increased support from the relevant constabularies and from Interpol's counterterrorist branch. Third, London's Gold Group is preparing to establish a cordon around Greater London. All three defensive cordons are currently being justified by Exercise Rapid Response and as precursors to the evacuation of London. Frankly, the idea of physically evacuating London has absorbed the media's full attention and will probably eclipse anything else we do for some time to come.

'All three defensive cordons will necessitate the use of a considerable number of Geiger counters and other radiological detection devices to screen for radiation. Obviously more and better sensors are part of the mix, and we are working to establish availability by tapping into the experience of the US Department for Homeland Security. They have recently procured bespoke vehicle-borne radiation detectors and they are happy we borrow some of them. Each vehicle works independently and can search a small town in several days picking up radiological sources. They are far quicker and more reliable than any other known search method, though time can be lost checking out every reading as the devices are ultra-sensitive. Quite simply, the Americans advise checking out the higher readings first. Ten radiological search teams are being shipped over to us by C130 as we speak.'

The Secretary of State for the Environment, Food and Rural Affairs saw his chance to add to the discussion. 'The problem is that our society is full of radiation. Nearly every electromagnetic device is radiating on some frequency. We need these American devices because, although they ring fire alarms when they drive past a dental centre X-raying teeth, they put the emphasis on searching every source. Nuclear bombs can be insulated from radiation spillage and therefore easily missed with conventional hand-held Geiger counters. The downside with the ten units is that we will need a large number of radiological detection teams to check out every source that they find.'

Everyone was listening intently so he charged on about the loads of radioactive waste across the nation. Hospital waste, medical and industrial isotopes, even some types of building materials gave off radionuclides.

'Thank you,' responded the Prime Minister somewhat bemused. 'Surely known sources should already be categorised, and we can expect the local authorities, industry and the general public to ensure they are?'

'Yes, Prime Minister, and that will speed up the process, though each source will need to be re-checked by our teams.'

'Thank you. I trust a plan is being drawn up for London?'

'We're putting together a plan for Cobra,' replied the Environment Secretary.

'Excellent.'

'The MOD has been extremely helpful too,' added the Home Secretary, leaving the Defence Secretary to take up the reins.

'Yes?' the Prime Minister enquired.

'Prime Minister,' said the Defence Secretary, 'I've had lengthy meetings with the Chief of Defence Staff and the Service Chiefs. Apart from the naval cordon and as part of Exercise Rapid Response we are currently putting together a plan that uses the Territorial Army to assist the British Transport Police and Metropolitan Police with the searching of all train and road passengers travelling through the proposed cordon around Greater London. The MOD will also provide Radiological Detection Teams in mobile analytical laboratories accompanied by EOD to investigate every source of radiation. All military units will remain under the operational command of the MOD and the operational control of Gold Group. It will take up to a fortnight to train the service personnel and three days to deploy the forces and become operational.'

'We should maximise use of the Territorial Army,' the Prime Minister stated.

'We need your authority to begin activating territorial servicemen and specialist reservists,' the Defence Secretary requested.

'Then you will have it,' confirmed the Prime Minister, with a slight shrug of his shoulders.

'We'll search with conventional Geiger counters in support of the US equipment. The SAS will be on standby should the terrorists be found with the nuclear bomb. On this last issue, I have listened to many deployment options and scenarios in the event a nuclear bomb is discovered in London. The options are all risky, with horrific consequences if anything goes wrong.'

'I'm sure the SAS will do everything they can when called upon,' replied the Prime Minister levelly.

'Those are the military tasks identified so far by Cobra and the Gold Group, but of course it's early days,' said the Defence Secretary. 'Independently the Defence Crisis Management Organisation within MOD is examining other scenarios that may require military assistance, including the temporary declaration of martial law, the provision of additional pre-emergency and post-emergency support, including medical care, population control, provision of shelter, CBRN expertise and equipment, etcetera.'

The Chancellor thought he should stir up the economic issues. 'The challenge will always be to prevent panic. We don't want a stock market meltdown or everyone hoarding what food they can find, causing inflation to rocket and low-income earners to suffer. The press will learn we are deploying troops with Geiger counters before they leave the barrack gates and ask questions.'

The Prime Minister was silent for a long moment. 'The situation is clear. We must do our best to keep the country functioning and find the bomb. If necessary, we will close the Stock Exchange and freeze wages and prices. We could impose martial law in London, but there is a long way to go before we even consider the implications of that. We'll tell the public everything we can, when we can. I have faith in our ability and in the resilience of the British people. We have survived a huge number of threats over the last century alone, and we will weather this crisis too.

'Exercise Rapid Response is to prepare us for the worst and it will work. It will require robust leadership from us all, and that's what we must provide. There must be no public discord between us, the public need to see strength and confidence in their leaders. My live TV interview here at Number Ten on Saturday will continue this theme.'

'It's when we tell the public about the real threat that I'm worried about,' the Chancellor remarked. 'I'm not concerned about the exercise.'

'Thank you, Chancellor. Together we must continue to do everything we can to increase our preparedness by making the public part of the solution, not the problem. Everyone must know they have a stake in this new kind of war. Any panic or lawlessness merely helps the terrorists achieve their goals. The timing of the exercise does concern me, but it's unavoidable if we are to instil public awareness and confidence, and be adequately prepared for May 2nd.'

The Home Secretary, sitting patiently, saw his chance to complete his briefing. 'This is not simply one isolated and limited incident that Cobra is dealing with; it's war. Having already discussed this with the Prime Minister, with his leave I would simply like to make it clear that it's this Cabinet, not Cobra, which is responsible for the conduct of this war. Cobra, acting as a sub-committee to the Cabinet, is responsible to this Cabinet for the county's preparedness for a terrorist attack, and for our joint response to any terrorist attack within the country.'

'Does anyone have any concerns regarding the Home Secretary's statement?' the Prime Minister challenged.

'No,' said the Foreign Secretary politely, 'but I would like to emphasise that MI6 is responsible to the Cabinet for finding the bomb and terrorist cell wherever they may be, and that Cobra's assistance may prove vital if that is to be achieved.'

'Essentially MI6 is the aggressor and Cobra the defender,' added the Deputy Prime Minister.

'Thank you,' replied the Prime Minister gratefully. 'I could not have put that more clearly myself. Home Secretary?

'An issue of concern to Cobra is that we are a nation at war, and as such there is an acute need to devise a plan to collectively control information. When the news of the real threat breaks, if we do not manage it correctly we will face panic that may lead to political and social meltdown.'

The Deputy Prime Minister added, 'We could also face World War III. Imagine how outraged the public will be. Who knows what might happen if London goes up in a mushroom cloud. The people could elect some implacable bastard who will lead a holy war against Islam. Every British Muslim could find him or herself interred, and that's if they are lucky. Could this spell the end of another Middle Eastern empire, like the Mesopotamians, Babylonians, Assyrians, ancient Egyptians and the multitude of Persian empires before Islam rose in AD 622? Think genocide.'

The Prime Minister allowed himself a brief smile. 'Rather than appoint a specific Minister for Information I would like to appoint my Deputy Prime Minister for that responsibility.'

The Cabinet broke into a subdued laughter at the Deputy Prime Minister's obvious discomfort.

For the remaining thirty minutes of the meeting, the Prime Minister asked the Cabinet to consider how the threat of global terrorism could be defeated. It concluded that for the foreseeable future, NATO, and not the United Nations, was the only international organisation capable of adequately defending and protecting the United Kingdom, and that if the war was to be won it must be taken to the terrorists in their own backyard.

Chapter 51

January 27th, Z – 95 Days
London, England

Standing alone in his sparsely furnished rented flat in Hackney, Muhammad bin Mustafa grinned as he stared south out of the window over London at night. He lived fourteen floors above street level in a run-down council-owned tenement block. His mother, a British Muslim, provided him with UK citizenship, although he believed his Iranian father had given him far more. His father had died for the jihad on direct orders of the Ayatollah twelve years ago, but not before he had raised his only son as a militant in the Islamic Movement. Mustafa still spent as much time as the British authorities would allow in Iran, restricted only by his social security commitment.

Mustafa played an important role within the extremist wing of London's Muslim community. Paid informally, it provided him with additional upkeep and considerable respect, a respect based on fear. And it was respect that Mustafa craved, not money. His unofficial jobs included the planning and coordination of visits by prominent Muslim clerics to the United Kingdom on behalf of mosques and their communities. Listening to the preachings of Abu Hamza, Yusuf al-Qaradawi and other Muslim clerics had revealed to him the right path, and he thanked Allah daily for their guidance. Mustafa also provided assistance to Muslim 'refugees' with overcoming the UK's immigration and citizenship bureaucracy, and he explained to them how they could manipulate their ethnic-minority status and intimidate young government employees. As another sideline, he provided short-term lodging to strangers and tonight he was to welcome three brothers from Iran.

Mustafa did not believe in luck but fate. He had been entrusted with the leadership of an attack upon Canary Wharf Tower at

One Canada Square because he was smart and a meticulous planner who left nothing to chance. Too many holy warriors believed that since Allah was on their side, they would succeed. *Insh'Allah*, 'God willing', was their creed, the road map for their lives. What they forgot was that the forces of evil were everywhere, eternally at war with the forces of Allah. It must be so, Mustafa reasoned, or the world would be a paradise where Allah ruled. It wasn't. Victory went to those who earned it. Allah had arranged the universe that way, and Mustafa intended to earn his ticket to paradise. His previous responsibilities for Islam had been rewarding but this, his first and last battle, was going to be sublime.

Many people in this country thought that money was the way to keep score in life. People with money always thought that. He had plenty of cash in his flat, over a quarter of a million British pounds, but it meant nothing to him other than as a commodity necessary to complete his final mission. He preferred to count the number of infidels he would kill in the name of Allah, just like his brothers who so successfully struck America in September 2001. On that day, three thousand had died, but he planned to at least double that toll in London. Mustafa laughed aloud as he so often did, an insane laugh that could easily be heard elsewhere in the tenement block. He should have bet money that Canary Wharf Tower would eventually be attacked, for it stood so proud and symbolised the arrogance of the West.

Mustafa had been chosen to lead the attack and was to be provided with sufficient mines and explosives, most procured from redundant and cash-poor Irish Republican Army cells in cities throughout the UK and Ireland. On his own initiative, an idea born from 9/11, he had decided to complement the explosive force with a tanker laden with vehicle fuel. At first he hadn't believed this attack would actually take place, although he had eagerly volunteered to lead it and give his life. But that was a long time ago now, a year before 9/11 and many years before the *takfiris* had struck in London on July 7th. Now, he knew that the years of waiting had been worthwhile as his mission was of vital importance to the jihad. He marvelled at the patience of al-Qa'eda. Having seen those twin towers collapse, he fully believed anything was possible, and when he had seen the money, half a million British pounds, he knew the messenger at the mosque was deadly serious, for with such money in his home country a man could have anything he desired. But the mission was more important to Mustafa. A successful mission could win him a place in paradise for eternity. Mustafa was a believer. He knew that life was a few years but that eternity was for ever.

The messenger from Yemen had known who he was. Mustafa had been singled out by the most important terrorist leaders in the Islamic world for a mission of huge importance to the armed jihad. The team of nine terrorists had been carefully chosen for him, several of them *Shia'heed*, the elite group of martyrs, and the messenger had ordered each of them to come to Mustafa's flat tonight between 8 and 9 p.m. Three required accommodation for the duration, and all of them were Islamic militants like him; like him they had been chosen for their preparedness to die for Allah.

One of the team was an ex-security guard from Canary Wharf Tower, someone who had been falsely accused and publicly exposed and ridiculed as being a rapist by the very national newspaper he was hired to safeguard. Another was an explosives expert from Germany known as 'Turk' who specialised in demolishing buildings with minimal explosives. Everyone in the team, including the three women, was prepared to die for Allah. As Mustafa waited for everyone to arrive for their first meeting, he contemplated his own death. He did not fear it; he only cared that he was worthy of paradise. After years of abuse from a very early age by gangs of infidels, he relished the prospect of retaliation. He looked forward to handling the weapons and explosives promised him by the messenger, and the moment when nothing more would matter.

It was not until 9 p.m. that the last of the group arrived. Mustafa was annoyed that he was required to entertain the others until the last had arrived, but he decided not to begin their mission on a bitter note. These believers had sworn to lay down their lives for Allah, and there was no greater sacrifice. No one had been invited for refreshments and no one expected any, though Mustafa did suggest the three that were staying place their bags in the two bedrooms to make space in the living area. The two women were to share one bedroom and the man share the other with Mustafa, at least initially. As soon as everyone was settled in his small, shabby living room, he stood.

'I am Mustafa, your leader,' Mustafa began proudly. 'I don't know you yet, but soon I will. We have all been chosen to die as martyrs for the glory of Allah. We have been chosen by Allah for this honour and guided by our most illustrious leaders. On September 11th, that glorious day in America, three thousand *kafirs* were slain. On April 10th we will slay six thousand *kafirs*, more than has ever been achieved in the history of the world. The entire world will tremble at the mention of Allah's name when it understands our determination. The holy war will continue, and eventually everyone in the world will convert to Islam, just as the prophet wished. And for this great service we will be rewarded with eternal paradise.'

Their faces were determined. Mustafa looked at each of them as they nodded firmly. They all understood. The mission was fantastic, glorious beyond description, a service to Allah that would change the history of the world.

'Our plan is simple. We'll seize control of Canary Wharf Tower on April 1st at 3 p.m., then a demand will be made by our leaders for the release of Muslims held captive under terrorism charges in America, Russia and elsewhere in the world. The tower will be very busy that day, with up to six thousand occupants. We'll be heavily armed and will kill without fear. We must clear the ground floor and first floor of people. Some will be killed but most will be allowed to flee the building or climb to higher floors.'

Mustafa sniggered at the idea of those fleeing upwards, and most of his audience smiled dutifully.

'Remember, we have to live in the tower for a week. Regardless of those who flee, we'll trap thousands of *kafirs* above us by sealing the first floor with our weapons and explosives. The same goes for securing the staircases and the elevators from above and below. We'll obstruct the first floor entry and exit points as our brothers did at Beslan.'

Mustafa let the tension build.

'We'll also have a tanker full of fuel, as much fuel as brought down either of the Twin Towers. It'll smash its way into the building through glass and remain on the unmanned ground floor set with remote detonated explosives. If any of the hostages jump, they will jump to their deaths. If we are to be overrun, we will destroy the tower shouting "*Allah Akbar*" as we do so.'

The living room, which was already hushed, fell deadly silent. No one except Mustafa wished to break the silence. Mustafa was enjoying the control he had over these people, their very lives.

'My orders are to delay firing the explosives until midday on April 7th. That will achieve complete success. Brothers, we have two months to prepare to die.'

Nobody looked shocked, and nobody thought to ask a question.

'Good. These are my initial orders. Turk, you'll control all the mines and explosives. You will be helped by Haddad, Qasim and Musa. You must seal the first floor with mines and prepare all entry and exit points for demolition. Then, you must prepare the tower for its destruction. You will have already prepared the fuel tanker on the morning of the attack.'

Turk grinned insanely and explained how he would destroy the tower. 'There will be a ring-main of mines and explosive devices placed around the steel core of the tower, all designed to explode simultaneously when they receive an electrical charge from a capacitor linked to a battery. Detonation will be controlled by any one of several simple initiation devices. The entire demolition will also detonate should any drop in voltage occur in the circuits from cut wires. The resulting explosion will bring down the entire building, of that you can be certain. We will all have instant, painless but heroic deaths.'

'We are fortunate to have you,' added Mustafa respectfully.

'I serve Allah, the Magnificent.'

'We will all be responsible for purchasing supplies from different locations all over London. One backpack per person will be carried for supplies, including food. Each of us will have a personal radio. Hanna is to coordinate the supplies, and she will provide you all with further instructions and money to buy everything.

'Ahmed has worked in the tower as a security guard. He will drive the tanker. He will also take each of us to look at the target over the next few weeks, beginning with me, then Turk. He will familiarise us with the layout and construction.'

Ahmed nodded.

'Mahmood will organise the weapons with help from Essa and Kalil.'

Mustafa had chosen the three believers who arrived today from

Iran, the three he knew would already be familiar with all the weapons they were to be provided.

'They are to be cleaned and we must practise with them. Each of us will have two sub-machine guns, two pistols and four grenades. There will be as much ammunition as we can carry. Mahmood will provide us with a training plan. Can we practice firing with them, Mahmood?'

'It would be too risky to fire the AKs and Uzis here. We may be able to fire live with the pistols. Let me consider it. We may have to fly to Iran.'

Mustafa nodded. 'So be it.'

'The weapons, mines and explosives will be delivered to me within two weeks, in two vans that we will keep. Everything will be kept in my lockup below us on Forest Road.

'Haddad and Mahmood will drive the two vans. They will each be fitted with front protection bars, and we will use them and the tanker to smash our way through the glass doors onto the ground floor of the tower. Surprise will be vital. Some of us will use a staircase to reach the first floor. We will force the *kafirs* from the first floor then secure it. Some of us will remain with the vans until the first floor is secure then bring up the mines and explosives, and our supplies, in an elevator. Then the elevators will be deactivated and the mines and explosives prepared.'

'That is enough of the plan for now. We must consider other issues, starting with the likely response from the British authorities...'

Later, Mustafa's final issue was security. He informed everyone including the three who were staying, how they must approach and depart his flat. The council tenement block in which he lived, with its warren of passageways and staircases provided many opportunities for discrete entry and exit. It was just a matter of knowledge.

As the clandestine meeting drew to a close, Mustafa sat down. 'If any one of you betrays us, that person will be hunted down and killed like a dog.'

His audience looked shocked at the mere suggestion of betrayal.

'Allah is everywhere and watches over us. He has granted us the chance to succeed and become martyrs,' Mustafa added.

The threat had not been necessary. By midnight the ten terrorists had learnt each other's names, and to Mustafa all of them appeared to be at ease with their impending martyrdom. It was obvious to him that each of them had been carefully selected by their leaders, and that all of them were worthy.

Chapter 52

January 29th, Z – 93 Days
London, England

The Prime Minister held monthly press conferences at Ten Downing Street, organised by the head of the Delivery Unit. He would begin with a short briefing on a particular issue and encourage questions relating to it, though it was usual that a broader range of questions would be raised by the press corps. Today, however, was to be an exception. The press had been informed that terrorism would be the subject, and it was precisely that subject that they wished to probe. As was customary, no other Government ministers were present, for its purpose was for the Prime Minister alone to face the music, and for one whole hour.

The Prime Minister began by reminding the packed room that last month's subject was asylum and the Immigration Service, and that on this occasion he intended to focus on the latest counterterrorism developments. He took twenty minutes to review the current terrorist threats across the world, and he highlighted those that were a specific threat to the United Kingdom and her allies. He explained that Exercise Rapid Response was intended to replace a well-publicised exercise that was to have taken place this year with the Americans and other allies, and that improvements in resilience and preparedness had reached the stage where they needed to be tested in realistic circumstances.

Surprisingly, it took some time for the questions to centre on Exercise Rapid Response. Initially, questions were fired at the Prime Minister regarding the appropriateness of the Minister for Immigration also being the Minister for Terrorism, and the arrest of predominantly Muslim men, known by MI5 and the Metropolitan Police as 'racial profiling', and the ensuing damage that was done to race relations. He was grilled on the apparent selectiveness in the war against terror, particularly against Islam. One journalist suggested the Prime Minister should go and live for several weeks in the Russian Caucasus or Israel, both of whom had suffered considerably more than the death toll experienced on 9/11. Only then could he possibly understand the double standards across the civilised world when it came to dealing with terrorists and their leaders. One journalist asked why it was wrong for them to seek out and execute terrorist leaders, when America and Britain hoped to do the same to bin Laden and al-Zawahiri. Another journalist, a Muslim, suggested the Prime Minister should live with the so-called terrorists, so he could establish whether in fact they were terrorists or not. Did the Prime Minister consider Hamas a terrorist organisation, the Muslim journalist asked? If not, then what did the Prime Minister think about Israel blowing away its leader, Sheikh Yassin? There followed an argument among the journalists about who was, and who was not, a terrorist. It was not the Prime Minister's best conference, but a civil war within the press corps had ensured his survival.

Eventually when order was restored, the Prime Minister was asked a question that allowed him to steer the conference to safer ground. A broadsheet journalist in the centre of the throng established his right to ask the next question by standing up. 'Prime Minister, do you think the international community, possibly the United Nations, should modernise international law and the rules of engagement regarding global terrorism?'

'Yes. As international and national laws stand, particularly the UN Charter, if there was a specific terrorist threat against this country today, those responsible for the security of the country, including myself, would face difficult decisions if they wanted to protect the country and defeat terrorism, but also remain legitimate. It's important that any state obeys the international rule of law, but we are living in a new world, with a new threat of global terrorism that many international treaties and charters simply do not address. And neither do the law-makers fully comprehend this threat. But any elected Government that fails to protect its own people is not acting legitimately, and the appropriate action may not always be supported by charters and treaties. Perhaps you can consider the case of Israel that was raised earlier.'

'Are you suggesting the Government would break international law to protect the public?' asked another journalist.

'If the law was inadequate or simply wrong, then yes. Our current UN Charter was designed for conventional warfare and conventional criminals, not the clandestine operations of the global terrorist. Current international law may even protect the enemy. Clearly it would be necessary for us to be open about any intended non-compliance, and we would wish to ensure that we were in the right and that it was international law that must evolve.'

'Can you give us an example?' asked a woman from the back row.

'I'll try. If I had knowledge of a specific terrorist threat, I may find that I'm legally bound to inform Parliament and the public before dealing with it. Obviously our intelligence and intelligence sources are secrets and they must stay that way too. To publicise specific threats may drive the perpetrators underground, making them more difficult to deal with it, or it may cause panic among the public which would itself achieve a main terrorist objective.'

'Why not revise our own constitution and law?' asked a man from the front row.

'We've been working hard since 9/11, but there is much more work to be done, both at home and within the United Nations. It takes time to evolve to meet new threats, and the more nations that are involved, many with different agendas, the more difficult the task.'

Another Muslim journalist stood. 'A number of Muslim community leaders are blaming radical preachers in some mosques. How concerned are you about this, and what is the Government going to do about it?'

'I'm very concerned about it. I think everyone is concerned about it. The good news is that senior Muslim leaders are concerned about it. We have to challenge these people, and we have to take on their ideology, their rhetoric, their extremism, their fanaticism and we have to defeat it. But there is going to be a limit to what a political leader in my position can do in respect of that. There is the balance between protecting our basic freedoms, such as speech, and preventing incitement. I would like to see the solution for this come from the Muslim community itself.'

'Do you think Israel is a terrorist state?' asked an Australian working for a UK broadsheet.

'No. Israel is a democratic state, and its elected Government defends its electorate under extreme conditions. I think we must all recognise what Israel is going through and realise that what they have suffered for decades is only now becoming a reality for others.'

'Why do you think Exercise Rapid Response is necessary? Surely the cost and disturbance far outweigh the usefulness of the exercise?' asked a journalist from London's *Evening Standard*.

'As I mentioned earlier, the United Kingdom has spent a huge amount of time, effort and cost over the last few years ensuring that we have the procedures and resources in place to prevent and deal with a major terrorist attack. With potentially countless lives and the nation's economy involved, it's vital to test the procedures and our resources in realistic circumstances, and also to educate the people, to ensure our combined response is as effective as it can be. Exercise Rapid Response should not be considered a burden but a sensible precaution from which the entire country will benefit.'

'Are you really contemplating evacuating London, clearing hospitals and prisons, and bringing London-based troops home from abroad?' asked the same journalist, who received condescending looks from around the room. It was considered rude among the press corps to ask more than one question in this unique circumstance.

'Yes. I will not put a price on people's lives. Any Government must take every security measure that it deems appropriate. This exercise must be challenging and as realistic as possible. Only then will it be truly worthwhile and make a real difference. It's for everybody's benefit, yours, mine, our families, everyone. It's the job of Government to ensure it's conducted as seamlessly as possible, and that every possible lesson is learned from the opportunity.'

'What will it cost?' shouted a tabloid journalist from the rear corner of the room.

'Estimates suggest one hundred pounds for every evacuee.'

'That's over one billion quid,' the same journalist retorted.

'A little less than half the defence budget for a single year,' the Prime Minister responded.

'Where will the money come from, Prime Minister?' asked another eager journalist.

'We consider the exercise will teach us valuable lessons lasting at least twenty years, so one-third of the money will be drawn from the Defence and Home departments' budgets over the same period and two-thirds from a small increase in Income Tax over the same period. London alone will not foot this bill. Regrettably there is a price to pay for safety, and global terrorism is without doubt the nation's biggest threat for the next two decades.'

'The public haven't received much by way of advice on how to deal with chemical, biological, radiological and nuclear attacks. How do you propose to tackle that?' someone asked.

'Thank you. Essentially there will be three divisions – at home, at the workplace and for transport, for example, the London Underground. The Home Office is to issue guidelines for the home, through a nationwide mail drop. Employers will be given guidelines to distribute at the workplace, and they will be required to add additional instructions of their own. Likewise, the Government will be issuing instructions to the transport sector. Guidelines and instructions will be distributed by the Government within the next month, and radio and TV broadcasts will begin shortly afterwards as part of the build up to Exercise Rapid Response.'

'Do we currently face any specific threats?' asked another male journalist from the front row.

'Yes, we are currently under threat from seventeen different terrorist organisations including al-Qa'eda and bin Laden's fatwa, the Islamic Jihad, the EIJ, and several Irish groups. Details of these organisations can be found on the Home Office web site. Now,' the Prime Minister glanced at his watch, 'there's time for one more question.'

After a momentary silence a journalist from a Sunday broadsheet stood up.

'Prime Minister, if there was one thing you wished from us what would it be?'

The room filled with laughter, and the Prime Minister was able to smile for the first time. A paradox, it never helped to take this important conference seriously.

'Well, I'm speechless.' He pretended to find the answer among his papers. 'I'm sorry, that's one question I wasn't prepared for.'

Several comments were thrown from the floor. More laughs.

'I'd like you to assure the public that we are doing everything we can to ensure their safety, and that if, or perhaps when, there is another terrorist attack on this country, the public should remain calm, adhere to Government guidelines and public warnings issued by the Home Office, report suspicious circumstances, stay clear of target sites and let the emergency services do their job. We all have a role to play in fighting terror attacks, and that is theirs. Thank you all very much.'

With that the Prime Minister picked up his papers and left, pondering how he might use his next press conference in one month's time.

Chapter 53

January 31st, Z – 91 Days
London, England

Mrs Wendy Evans passed her seventy-seventh birthday three days before. She considered herself a model citizen of Great Britain. With the exception of a short period during World War II she had lived in Hackney since she was four, when her father had moved from the South Wales coal pits to work as a tunnel man under London.

Over the last twenty years she had seen the friendly and predominantly Jewish community around her squeezed out by bullish Muslims who had no intention of respecting British society. She hated the way the Muslims had destroyed the neighbourhood by making the streets gaudy with their cheap shops and tacky restaurants at the expense of the bakers, the butchers and the her old dressmaking shop, which had been pulled down and replaced by a mosque.

If you were white, you were fair game for street robbery. If you were Jewish, you could expect to be harmed as well as robbed. Mrs Evans, a Roman Catholic, had been attacked and robbed on five occasions in Hackney in the last three years alone, each time by young Muslim men who considered and treated her as inferior.

When she was forty-six, the council had seen fit to move her into a brand-new apartment on the fourteenth floor of what was then their pride and joy, a newly built high-rise concrete tenement block that provided 120 homes. Oddly, there had been no attempt to break into her home for at least three years, whereas beforehand it had been a regular occurrence. She assumed it was the fortified door fitted by the council that had made the difference.

Her dislike of Muslims stemmed from the death of her husband in Palestine shortly after World War II. They had only been married a year and she had loved him very much, so much so that she had never wanted to marry again, though she could have done so. He had survived at the spearhead of the Allied advance on Berlin since D-Day on June 6th, 1944, only to be shot in the back by a faceless Muslim terrorist several years later. The killer was never identified.

Mrs Evans considered it her civil duty to report the activity of Muslims in her neighbourhood. It did not seem peculiar to her that she only ever reported Muslims, as everyone knew they were the ones who caused the crimes in Hackney. She had had her eye on the man opposite since he moved three years ago into 1406. Indeed quite literally, as fortuitously the spyhole in her fortified front door overlooked the entrance to his apartment.

Hanging on her fridge door was a long list of telephone numbers. The Department of Social Security's Benefit Fraud Hot Line, the Metropolitan Police's Criminal Hot Line, and Counter-terrorism Hot Line were her favourites. The TV told her all she needed to know about Muslims, and to her it was clear what they were doing. There were the Muslims, and the rest. Within the rest, there was an enlightened minority and in her mind she was a part of that minority.

Mrs Evans would choose the most appropriate number, dial it, and then keep the conversation going for as long as possible, even if that meant embellishing a little. She craved for the sympathetic voice of the telephone operator, and the company was free.

Her next call was taken by a young female police officer on the first floor of New Scotland Yard. There were only fourteen on shift answering public calls at the time, with another three responding to emails. Three booths were vacant due to manpower shortages. If, like most call centres, they had an electronic counter telling them how many calls were waiting or how many had hung up before being answered, they would have known they were answering one in four.

The telephonist took the caller through a form of questions, and then felt compelled to ask why the caller suspected they were terrorists.

'Did I say terrorists?'

'Yes, ma'am.'

'Oh dear, I'm sorry. It's benefit fraud, I'm sure of it. He has all these different people staying there, and it's a council flat you know. They haven't sold any of these flats. They only have two bedrooms and he has five other people staying there.'

'Thank you, ma'am.' The telephonist smiled to herself and thanked Mrs Evans for calling, and promised to have the observation forwarded to the local Benefits Office. Then she scribbled 'for local DSS' on the form and filed it in a basket marked 'Other'.

It was the telephonist's responsibility to answer calls, take the details, make a decision, then file each one from 'Immediate' through 'Urgent' and 'Priority' to 'Low', or 'Other' if it did not relate to terrorism. She doubted whether Mrs Evan's complaint would be forwarded to the DSS, as the forms that lay in the 'Other' tray had never been cleared in her time on the 'phones, but that was not her responsibility. Within minutes she had forgotten all about Mrs Evans.

Chapter 54

February 1st, Z – 90 Days
Buenos Aires, Argentina

The three terrorists had celebrated the completion of the second weapon, Little Boy, well into the early hours. Apart from its weight, there were no obvious signs that betrayed the bright-orange fender had been tampered with. They had been out for their evening meal, after which Malik and Dalia had joined a merry crowd and danced the tango for several hours, as Baloch got drunk at the bar with some very loud new friends. Whether it was the excitement of departing for Gibraltar, or for Baloch his pay day and all that that meant, none of them were certain, but they had been full of energy.

On their return to the factory, they opened another bottle of whisky, but at 3 a.m. Baloch decided to turn in as he knew that the two lovers wished to be alone. As he staggered down the corridor, he thought of his wife and how one day soon they too would be able to hug each other to sleep once more, financially secure for life. He hoped his wife would bring their family to Argentina soon and felt a strong desire to call her on the unregistered cell phone, despite his promise to Malik that it would only be used for contact between the three of them and none other.

I will be leaving in the morning. What does it matter if I make one call now? Baloch thought to himself as he entered his room, clinging on to the walls for support. I will make it quick. Baloch grabbed his phone from a jacket pocket and collapsed on his bed.

Just a short call, thought Baloch. It's 11 a.m. in Pakistan. Tomorrow I'll have left this miserable place. Desperately missing his wife, after fumbling with the key-pad he finally dialled the international code for Pakistan followed by his wife's telephone number.

It was answered on the third ring.

'My darling, it's me, Sultan.'

There was a brief pause on the line.

'Why haven't you called for so long?' his wife asked. 'Are you all right?'

'I have been on business. I'm fine, really, how are the children?'

'They miss you. You said you would call sooner.'

'I must be quick. Tomorrow we can speak for longer.'

'Why? Have you been drinking?'

'It's not my phone.'

'Oh.'

'I've designed a new invention that has been accepted by the authorities. It will make us very rich. I'll tell you more tomorrow. I just wanted you to know. Very soon we will have everything you have ever dreamed of. Trust me.'

'What have you designed?'

'I'll tell you tomorrow. You will come to Argentina to live. It's a wonderful place. You'll love the country, cities, schools, shops, everything. It's a great country in many ways, and it's safe for us.'

'I want us to leave here now. There's so much misery.'

Baloch realised the importance of what she had just said. She had never so plainly stated her desire to leave before. Perhaps, he told himself, something had happened, or perhaps it was the opportunity his assurance of wealth provided.

'We'll all be together soon. I will find a house as we dreamed, somewhere nice. I must go. I love you all.'

'We love you too. May Allah protect you.'

Baloch sensed despair in her voice but pressed the red button and threw down his phone. He had been less than one minute.

Malik and Dalia fell asleep on their bed soon after Baloch had left them and did not wake until 11 a.m. Dalia had been a fabulous dancer, envied by everyone at the restaurant. For the first time since they had slept together they did not make love; even Dalia was too exhausted.

After waking, they showered in the old worker's shower block, then after a light breakfast they packed their personal belongings. Everything else was cleared into the shipping crates that had been used for a makeshift table. Finally, they dismantled the chamber.

At 3 p.m., just as Malik and Dalia were completing the dismantling of the chamber, Baloch appeared.

'I have packed up my room as you requested,' said the dishevelled doctor.

'Help us with this, and then we will be on our way. I'll leave you at the Hyatt Hotel with the remainder of your fee. After that you are on your own,' said Malik.

Baloch grumbled but helped anyway.

By 4 p.m. they had finished clearing the factory to Malik's satisfaction and the Toyota Land Cruiser had been packed with all their personal belongings. He knew that the factory was not forensically clean, but after Jamali and his men had removed the crates and swept the factory there would be little if anything of importance for anyone to find.

Malik walked around the factory one last time before climbing into the Land Cruiser. As he drove past the two guards who were loitering by the gate, he pulled up and handed them the keys. Jamali had arranged to collect the guards within the hour, and would remove any traces of their occupation of the factory before disposing of the crates. Tomorrow, Nadia would return the keys and cancel the lease.

As they drove towards the town centre, Malik looked towards Baloch who was sitting in the passenger seat. 'You know that if you ever betray us it will mean your certain death?'

'I know,' replied Baloch nervously. 'But we both know there would be no advantage, quite the opposite. I have plenty of money and would only be sealing my own fate if I talked.'

'Dalia, pass him his money.'

Baloch turned and took a black leather holdall from Dalia. Placing the bag on his lap, he unzipped the top, opened it and saw the wads of US banknotes.

'You have done a good job, Baloch. Don't take risks. Stay alert, disappear and forget us.'

'I will, my friend, I will.'

'I hope so, for your sake,' Malik replied.

Malik and Dalia left Baloch at the entrance to the Plaza Francia hotel in Schiaffino. Fifteen minutes later at 6 p.m. they finally arrived at the boatyard, yet it was busy with a large number of boats with their crews seeking a berth for the night. Conveniently, everyone appeared to be minding their own business.

The two terrorists casually unloaded their luggage and cargo from the Land Cruiser onto the aft cockpit of *Last Tango*, glad that they were able to reverse the vehicle right up to the stern of the boat that was backed onto the quay. First, they placed the three lozenge-shaped fenders back into the forward stowage locker, with the heavier one at the very bottom, underneath the other sixteen matching fenders, then they stowed the three ten-litre cooking-oil drums in a locker under the galley stairway. Malik had already ordered an additional matching fender to replace the one destroyed during the bomb-making process, and planned to collect it tomorrow.

Dalia followed Malik into the larger stateroom to drop off their personal gear. Most of it was new, reflecting the move from factory to motor cruiser.

It was not until after they had unpacked and stowed their luggage that they realised that someone may have come aboard since their last visit.

Malik walked back into the beautifully appointed salon, where he looked for signs of entry and wondered briefly about an extra set of keys, while Dalia went to inspect the other two staterooms further forward.

'The two forward staterooms have people's belongings in,' Dalia said as she re-entered the salon.

'It's the crew. They are certainly efficient,' responded Malik, as he clattered around in the galley undoing clasps and opening locker doors. 'We already have everything necessary for a long voyage.'

Before long, they found themselves standing in the aft cockpit wondering what to do.

Dalia felt the need for a kiss and flung her arms around Malik's neck before kissing him hard. 'Let's lock up, return the car to the depot, have dinner then come back early for a wild night of passion before the crew arrive tomorrow,' she suggested.

'I like you more and more,' replied Malik as he locked the doors and prepared to leave the boat. 'Can we get some sleep too?'

'I'll let you have a little sleep, for selfish reasons you understand. So, who exactly are the crew?'

'There are two women and two men, all of them young. One

of the boys is Carlos's son, Miguel. He is first mate and knows *Last Tango* well. We'll meet the remaining crew tomorrow morning. They are due to arrive at nine.'

Chapter 55

February 1st, Z – 90 Days
Buenos Aires, Argentina

'Do you think I'll enjoy it? Sipping Pimm's or champagne and mixing with the elite of Buenos Aires is not exactly my thing, not unless it's business anyway,' asked Tess as Harry weaved the silver BMW through the sparse Saturday morning traffic to the Buenos Aires International Polo Park.

It was 9 a.m. on what promised to be a blazing-hot Saturday, the day Harry had been asked by Conchita to play in a charity polo match for the El Boyero Cup. Conchita had invited Encizo and his family, but he had had to decline, not due to work but a family wedding. Encizo promised he would try to escape the reception and catch the big game on television.

'I'm sure you'll love it. They say that polo is the sport of kings and the king of sports,' replied Harry. 'What sports do you play?'

'Oh, just a little recreational ju-jitsu and one or two dangerous sports when the time allows,' answered Tess, deliberately understating herself. 'I have ridden horseback but never played polo. I remember watching a game once at Palm Beach. You had better tell me something about the rules unless you want to risk me making a fool of myself. I'm not too good at sticking to the obedient wife thing.'

'You'll enjoy it, I promise you,' said Harry light-heartedly as he glanced across at Tess. 'Lots of wide-shouldered, thin-hipped brown-eyed Argentine men with wealthy patrons egging them on, not that they need the encouragement. Rich patrons converge to annihilate each other at these meetings. They do it in the city and they want to do it on the polo field as well. Argentina produces the best players and polo ponies in the world. You'll see some first-class polo today, that's for sure. The Argentines play as if their lives depend on it. They are very competitive. There can be a lot of sledging between opposing players, particularly the Argentinians and Australians. The language is unbelievable, that's why the polo field is so big.'

Tess laughed. 'Why did Conchita invite you to play?'

'Good question. It turns out her father is down here sponsoring the game I'm playing in today, the only charity game in the fixture. This is the club's top tournament day of the season, with four games in total. The charity game is just a bit of fun really, a bit of light relief after the stock exchange versus city bankers game and an Argentina trials game, and before top billing, the Argentine Club Cup. We're third on, at 4 p.m. I've played in Argentina before, during a tour with the Beaufort Polo Club, though I was entirely forgettable. I'm only playing today because there's supposed to be one foreign player in each team and according to Conchita the Earl of Tyrone had to pull out at the last minute. Apparently he broke his shoulder blade in a car accident. Somehow she found out I had a handicap of two.'

There was a pause in the conversation for several seconds as Harry negotiated some traffic.

'Do you know the foreign player in the opposing team?'

'According to Conchita, he is a rather attractive Aussie called James. Has a handicap of three.'

Harry smiled to himself, remembering Conchita's recollection when he asked her the same question.

'I know he is tall, well muscled and tanned but that is about it. No, I don't know him.'

'So how's the game played?'

'It's a team game of four players who try and score by hitting the ball between the goalposts. The line of the ball takes priority over everything. Once the ball has been hit and is travelling on its way, no other player can cross the line it has made. If you do cross it, you've fouled and can be subject to a penalty.'

Another pause as Harry overtook an old truck.

'It's full of jargon like "riding off".'

'What does that mean?'

'It involves bumping sideways into another rider to get them out of the way. The two guests will be the number-three players and take the title of "captain".'

'You like to have your own way.'

Harry smiled. 'In polo, arguments are not arguments, they are "debates". The captains are the only players who can discuss questions with the umpires that arise during a game. The number three is similar to a "centre-half" in football or soccer. The captain should attempt to control the speed and direction of the game and usually his passes to the forwards start an attack.'

'Ah, now I'm getting the picture.'

Sensing her mild sarcasm, Harry felt a need to remind her of the dangers. 'But, of course, when you've got eight players all chasing after a ball, each rider on half a ton of horse going at forty miles an hour, it can get a bit dangerous.'

'Now that's more like it.'

'You hold the stick a bit like a tennis racquet, and luckily you don't, as many people imagine, have to hit the ball with the small end, but with the whole side of the head.'

'Not that difficult then?'

Harry smiled at Tess, letting her know he knew her game and that he was not rising to the bait.

'How on earth do games like this ever get invented?' Tess mused.

'Well, this game doesn't have its roots in colonial India as is commonly thought. In fact it originated in Central Asia, and was first played in China and Persia more than two thousand years ago. The first recorded game took place between the Turkomans and Persians in 600 BC. It was actually used as a form of training for cavalry units, with as many as one hundred warriors on each side. Because it was such a valuable method of training cavalry, the sport was soon played all over the world. Do you remember the Emperor Babur from Kabul? He was responsible for establishing the game in India, four hundred years before the British played there. In the 1850s British tea planters discovered the game in Manipur, on the Burmese border with India, and they founded the world's first polo club at Silchar. Today, the oldest club in the world, founded in 1862, is in Calcutta. The game took off in England in 1869 thanks to a British army officer from the 9th Hussars and was better known then as "hockey on horseback." English and Irish ranchers took the game to Argentina in about 1875 and it reached Australia and the USA in 1876. In fact, your country usefully introduced the concept of handicaps in 1888. Kings, queens and emperors have played the game for centuries.'

'Have you ever played with the royals?'

Harry turned to Tess once again. 'So you do know a bit about the game.'

'Only what I read in the magazines.'

'Never, though I would like to. The great thing about polo is that unlike most sports, it's played somewhere in the world all year round. It gets me out and about. There's an old joke, wherever a polo player goes in the world, he's mounted within half an hour.'

Tess smiled but sensed something else.

'Wherever you get lots of attractive people who are very fired up about something it happens, and the Argentine men are especially attractive. It's just fun for them to clean up with all the girls. I, of course, miss out.'

'I was eight when I watched polo at Palm Beach,' Tess added more happily, changing the subject. 'It looked fiendishly difficult, like playing golf on a skateboard.'

Harry smiled. 'It's very complicated. All you really need to remember is that the teams change ends after every goal. The Americans are very strong now, and rank alongside the Brits and Argies, with the Aussies and Kiwis following close behind. The game is enjoying a renaissance in many other countries including India and I guess it's played in about eighty countries around the world right now. It was even an Olympic discipline from 1900 to 1939 and has recently been recognised once again by the International Olympic Committee.'

Tess felt she had heard enough about the game and wanted to find out more about Harry. 'Presumably you play often?'

'Not as much as I'd like. I have three polo ponies at home in Surrey, and share them with a close friend who also has three. He is a much better trainer than me and puts in the time. You really need four to play a match you see, each one playing no more than two chukkas.'

'And a chukka is a period of play, yes?' asked Tess.

'Yes. A full game is eight chukkas, but often four or six chukkas are played. Each chukka lasts seven minutes. Ponies can play two chukkas in an afternoon, with a rest of at least one chukka in between.'

'Wow,' said Tess, as Harry turned the BMW off the main road through the grand entrance to the Buenos Aires International Polo Park.

'As I said, they take their polo seriously here,' commented Harry as he, too, looked out over the grand stadium whose vast main stand rose eight storeys high.

The polo ground would have made any country or sport proud. Open to the roadside, the beautifully kept lawns that made up the vast grounds were immaculate, a lush, perfectly smooth green swathe of grass. Harry knew that, despite its appearance, the quick-drying turf would prove very dusty in the Argentine summer heat. The boundary of the primary field of play was distinguishable by the two pairs of tall goalposts, the low boards placed down either side designed to keep the ball in play, and the playing surface already marked out with the penalty lines that ran in parallel across the field of play. The eye, however, was drawn to the three huge, uncovered grandstands that surrounded the two ends and far side of the playing area.

'Today is the biggest day in the Argentine polo club calendar. By 1 p.m. all the stands will be full. It was only after I agreed to play that Conchita told me that over ten thousand spectators will be watching.'

Harry followed the small temporary road signs that took him behind the stadium and through the bustle that was the huge administrative effort involved in setting up an event of this scale. Behind the stadium, the grounds extended far into the distance, with another three playing areas spread across the foreground. Two of them had been taken over by a large number of trade stands and a children's fairground. The third had been taken over by horseboxes of varying shapes and sizes. The acres of space behind the market and fair were allocated for parking, so Harry made towards that. Showing his players' car pass to a parking steward, he was redirected to an alternative parking area back towards the rear of the stadium.

As he parked the BMW, Conchita drove into the car park and pulled up alongside.

Harry, Tess and Conchita pinned on their lapel badges in the car park, then walked over to a large, white marquee behind the grandstand. A smart sign hung over the entrance that stated "Players' Lounge" in English. As they entered the sparsely populated marquee, they were greeted by a typically handsome Argentine in his late thirties. He introduced himself as one of the home team players, Silvestre Garros.

'Conchita, my darling,' exclaimed Garros as he grappled with her in a bear hug ending in what Harry considered to be an unnecessarily long kiss of greeting that was not restricted to both cheeks. Harry wondered whether they were more than just friends. Once released from his welcome grasp, Conchita made the introductions. His heart leapt as Garros greeted Tess in a manner not acceptable back home.

'Conchita did not tell me you were so beautiful,' Garros said to Tess as he released her from the bear hug and stared intently into her eyes. Harry felt distinctly uncomfortable as a mild jealousy ran through him. Tess matched Garros's stare, smiling broadly as if she was already smitten. Harry was offered the handshake of a supremely confident and nauseatingly handsome young man.

As Garros turned and walked towards a bar at one end of the marquee, Tess felt Harry's anguish and took his hand and squeezed it secretively in the manner of lovers the world over. He correctly interpreted this as some kind of reassurance and pondered on why she should feel the need.

'You will be riding several of my ponies today,' Garros said, looking over his shoulder as they went. 'Our team consists of us, my brother Ramiro and my cousin Salvador Socas. No reserves. They are both sixes like me. We will start two up.'

Harry felt a little honesty was in order. 'I hope Conchita told you I have not played for a month. I will try my best for you all, of course.'

Garros glanced at Conchita, then Harry. 'Ha, Conchita told me you were brave, someone who can look after himself, and she knows what to look for in a man. Your lower handicap is worth another goal too. Don't be fooled by the charity status; today we play our patron's biggest rival. We must win for him, as well as ourselves, but our opponents are very, very good. This game is like no other charity game, and the Argentina team selectors are here today too. You will not let us down.'

'No pressure then,' replied Harry lightly as he pulled a face at Conchita.

'After a drink we'll get you some kit, then I will introduce you to your ponies. You must not worry; they are very experienced and obedient.'

Tess asked after Ramiro Garros and Salvador Socas, the other two players on the team.

'They will be here in an hour, which will give us plenty of time to discuss tactics with Harry and take a little practice. It's very hot already so there will be little that we can do with the ponies. After a lengthy discussion it was obvious to everyone present that Garros had two passions in life, polo and women.

It was just as they were leaving the marquee that Garros got round to asking Tess to accompany him to the Buenos Aires Polo Club annual ball that evening. It was a very exclusive, red-carpet event for which every one of the thousand tickets was highly prized, a society event in the Buenos Aires social calendar. Fortunately Conchita, who understood the chemistry between Harry and Tess, stepped in.

'Harry and Tess are already coming along as my guests, Silvestre, and I happen to know you have already invited Sascha, your patron's beautiful daughter.'

Silvestre caught a look between Harry and Tess, and immediately understood. He smiled knowingly.

'Of course, such a beautiful lady as yourself is bound to be spoken for.'

Graceful in defeat, he wrapped an arm around Harry's shoulders and walked him towards the entrance.

'You are very lucky. She is beautiful, a real prize. If I were you I would hang onto her. I have known her for twenty minutes and I can already see the quality in her breeding. I was tempted to ask Andre to tag you for the game. Now, we must go to the team trailers and get you kitted out.'

'Who is Andre?'

'He is their defender. An absolute bastard who breaks bones to win matches. Pony or rider, he is not fussy. You will need to watch him.'

An hour later Harry was standing with the other three members of his team in brown leather riding boots, white breeches, and a bright-blue team shirt with a white horizontal stripe that was emblazoned with their patron's logo, Jordach Diamonds. As they discussed tactics and commands, the much larger team of background staff busied themselves with the ponies.

Conchita and Tess stood under an awning pinned to one of

the trucks, watching anxiously, as neither of them had actually seen Harry play.

Harry saw several ponies that were tacked up being led towards them, and not for the first time he wondered whether he was good enough for this. It was clear that this was no ordinary charity match; rules and etiquette would be harshly debated and considerable honour was at stake. But he was the captain and more importantly he couldn't afford to get injured. He had already decided the best move would be to attack, despite Andre's reputation – he would simply live for the moment and enjoy the battle. Harry was handed the reins of the pony that he was to ride first during training, the one he would ride in the first chukka. Under fifteen hands, she was a chestnut lovingly prepared with a plaited tail and bandages. Harry had never seen such a well-turned-out pony in polished leathers and praised the stable lad. He made a mental note of praising the team to the owner of Jordach Diamonds when they met later in the day at the sponsors' social. Once he was mounted, the team made their way behind the trailers to the practice playing area where they warmed up and practised moves.

Later that afternoon Jordach Diamonds won thirteen points to twelve in a gripping match of six chukkas. The spectators were left roaring with delight and wanting more. Harry scored two goals himself and assisted with seven, before receiving the El Boyero Cup on behalf of his team.

That evening back at the Sheraton Libertador Hotel, Harry and Tess spoke to the concierge who happily arranged for the couple to be escorted to a gentleman's outfitters and several exclusive ladies' boutiques, where they purchased, or hired in Harry's case, appropriate eveningwear. Returning to the hotel and their adjoining rooms, they prepared for the evening's ball, at which they, much to Conchita's delight, had been re-seated with her on her father's table.

The gleaming white-tiled shower room was spacious, doubling as a steam area. It had an in-built bench with steam jets on either side. It was his third shower of the day, and this time Harry let himself enjoy the steamy heat, relaxing with his head thrown back, eyes closed, the jet of water drumming on his chest and shoulders. They were not due to arrive at the ball for another two hours. He briefly considered the stalemate over the mission, but there was nothing to be gained by worrying about it, so instead he ran over the day's game in his mind. When he had agreed to take part he had considered the game a gentle distraction, but he now knew the risk he ended up taking had been foolhardy. He had been lucky to come away with little more than bruises and a sore groin.

'My steamer is broke. Can I share yours?' said Tess seductively.

Harry's eyes snapped open at the sound of Tess, her naked body obscured from him as she stepped into the steam-filled shower room and closed the sliding door behind her. 'Sorry, I did not hear you, I was trying to unwind,' he replied. He was self-conscious but did not wish to appear so, as if her unexpected appearance was the most natural act in the world.

'That's my job. I don't think we need play games any longer, do you?' she beamed.

'I guess not...' Harry stammered, a little nervously.

She moved into his arms, her body moulding tightly against his with the fast-flowing water soaking them both. She raised her lips to kiss him, and he felt her firm breasts flattening against his chest, her nipples standing out. They separated moments later, Tess standing in the circle of his arms and reaching for the soap. He felt an urge to speak, but she stopped him with a gentle index finger pressed against his lips.

'Not now.'

And so he stood in comfortable silence while she worked up lather on her hands and started washing him, beginning with his chest and shoulders, working downward, finally kneeling at his feet. Her fingers took their time and Harry concentrated on the sensations they evoked, his mind as close to blank as it would ever be. She felt him brace whenever she drew close to a bruise and softened her touch.

Another moment and he bent to slip both hands beneath her arms, lifting her to face him, feeling her thighs clamp around his waist. He moved them and pressed her shoulders back against the warm, wet wall tiles.

'Oh God!' A primal sound erupted from Tess's throat, somewhere between the realms of pain and pleasure. 'Hurry, Harry!'

Harry hurried, wanting the passion to be shared equally and knowing they would have many opportunities to explore each other in the future.

Tess clung to Harry's neck when they were finished, legs still wrapped around his waist, half drowned in steaming water and sensation. Neither felt the urge to separate.

'I think I need a shower,' he said at last.

'You did work up a sweat.' She smiled into the hollow of his shoulder, nipping at his flesh.

'Whose fault is that?'

'Yours. It should have happened days ago. You're very shy, Harry. I had to make the first move.'

'I was concerned about Company regulations,' he joked.

A trained professional, Tess wouldn't let her feelings interfere with the performance of her duties in the field. Her smile went dreamy. 'Hmm. MI6 or CIA?'

'CIA, of course, I'm freelance.'

'That's OK, the CIA have no such regulation any more. In fact nowadays, teamwork is actively encouraged,' she beamed.

They lathered and sponged each other as the spray of hot water streamed over them and the steam billowed around them. Then they kissed, caressed and explored each other's slippery body before they sank to the bench to make earth-shattering love once again.

Later that night they left the ball as early as etiquette would allow.

NEW WORLD ORDER

Chapter 56

February 2nd, Z – 89 Days
Buenos Aires, Argentina

Last Tango dipped unnaturally and Malik woke immediately. He realised that people were climbing aboard. Not only could he sense the transfer in weight towards the stern, but he could hear the metallic clatter of footsteps across the aluminium-alloy gangplank that someone had repositioned. First locating his Sig Sauer 9-mm P228 pistol from his side locker, he glanced at his wristwatch and saw that it was 9:05 a.m. Their muted but businesslike conversation indicated to Malik that they were indeed his expected crew.

Leaving Dalia to sleep, Malik replaced his handgun then slid quietly out of the bunk, pulled on a fresh shirt and shorts then went out to greet them. He surprised Miguel by unlocking and opening the doors to the aft cockpit from the inside, before the Argentine had found find the right key.

'Hi,' said Malik. 'I'm Sean Kent. You must be my crew?'

They all looked twenty-something and rather bewildered.

'It's good to meet you, sir,' Miguel replied in English, with a Spanish accent. 'Sorry if we woke you but we were not expecting you on board until later today.'

'It's no problem; I was awake anyway. My wife, Diana, is still asleep though.'

'No I'm not,' said Dalia, who stood behind Malik wearing a bathrobe.

Dalia surveyed the four visitors and saw they were harmless. She wrapped her arms around Malik from behind.

'I'm Diana, and we are delighted to meet you too.'

Everyone laughed amicably at the awkwardness of the situation, and Miguel introduced the other crew as they put down the supplies they were carrying.

'This is my partner, Amata. This is Jaime, and this is his partner, Elisa. If you like, we can come back later?'

'There's no need,' Malik said amicably. 'Please, carry on with whatever you doing.

Malik and Dalia drew back into the salon, and the others entered.

Amata carried several bags of supplies down into the galley and called up, 'I usually make fresh coffee first thing. Would everyone like some?'

Everyone eagerly assented.

'How about I make breakfast too?'

'I'll take a quick shower then come and help,' said Dalia keenly. 'We'll eat on the aft deck,' she decided on everyone's behalf. Not only did Dalia feel hungry, but she considered that a meal would help break the ice.

'I'd like to tour the boat with Miguel this morning,' added Malik. 'Then Dalia and I must take a last opportunity to do some shopping. It looks as if everything is under control, but if there's anything else we can get for any of you, and I mean anything, let us know before we leave.'

'We have the fresh provisions to collect this morning. Other than that I hope you'll find we are ready,' Miguel replied.

'What about the tides?' asked Malik.

'If you wish to leave today and benefit from the tide we should depart by 4 p.m.'.

'Excellent. Let's leave this afternoon,' Malik ordered.

With no need to rush, the six crew of *Last Tango* sat and chatted over a large breakfast. Amata established some of Malik's and Dalia's likes and dislikes before producing her final provisions list, which she handed to Jaime and Elisa who were to pick up the fresh supplies. This left Malik and Dalia to focus on themselves and Miguel and Amata to complete any outstanding issues with the boat and boatyard.

As Dalia and the others cleared breakfast Malik inspected the boat with Miguel. Though Malik was certain Miguel had noticed the three ten-litre drums of cooking oil in the galley ladder locker, he had not seen fit to mention them, so Malik did.

'We promised some Argentine friends who own a restaurant in Gibraltar. Apparently Spanish oil is not the same and this gives them a competitive edge.'

Miguel nodded in agreement. 'My mother uses a lot of our oil in her cooking. It's important to have the best.'

The casual inspection took less than twenty minutes.

'I cannot thank you enough. You have all done an excellent job in preparing *Last Tango*. Diana and I are thoroughly looking forward to this cruise. How long will it take, to Gibraltar?'

'It's about six thousand miles. It should take twelve to fourteen days. By day we should cruise up to twenty knots, and at night, half that.'

'Take as long as you need. Do you like to fish?'

'I love to fish, we all do.'

'Good, let's buy some tackle from your father's shop later and you can teach me. Is the length of cruise a problem for any of you?''

'I'll ask them, but I doubt it, skipper. You know that you are paying by the day?'

'Good. Let's go via Bridgetown, Jamaica and aim to arrive in Gibraltar in three weeks.'

Miguel smiled broadly and rushed off to tell the others.

Twenty minutes later Malik and Dalia took Miguel's Jeep to the city centre, picking up the replacement fender from the chandlers en route. Sitting in the front passenger seat, she was dressed in a vest, tight shorts and trainers, clothes that exhibited her beautiful long bronzed legs. Dalia understood the effect her body was having on the driver and enjoyed his discomfort.

'They are good people,' remarked Dalia.

'They are, and so are you,' responded Malik looking over at her. 'Now, where would you like to go for lunch?'

'How about a motel,' Dalia teased.

His heart leapt at her words and the longing in his groin increased.

At 3:30 p.m. in glorious sunshine *Last Tango* slipped its mooring and headed out of Buenos Aires for the South Atlantic.

Chapter 57

February 2nd, Z – 89 Days
CIA Headquarters, Langley, Virginia, USA

'Go on in,' said Summer, flashing her Hollywood smile at the DDO and Director CTC as they walked into the DCI's outer office. 'The DCI is expecting you.'

'Thanks, Summer, he'll like this one,' said the DDO confidently.

'In thirty minutes you should ask for that extra time off that you deserve,' added General Carter with an equally broad smile.

Summer liked the new CTC Director, Tom Carter, but like most of the men that she met and was attracted to in her small world which was the top floor of CIA's Headquarters, he was already spoken for.

'Hold on, Wayne,' the DCI said to his telephone before he held his hand across the mouthpiece and looked up at the two men entering his office. 'Gentlemen, take a seat. I'll be with you in a minute.'

The two visitors sat quietly on one of the two comfortable couches placed either side of the low oak coffee table which looked to Carter as if it dated back to George Washington. Several minutes later the DCI rose from behind his desk and joined them.

'Either of you like some coffee?' asked the DCI.

Both visitors accepted. The DCI called Summer.

'That was Wayne,' the DCI explained. 'He's over at the J. Edgar Hoover Building talking to the FBI about global terrorist financial networks. Tom, he asked that you fill him in after our chat.' Wayne Ewart was the DDI and as Carter's boss he would normally have been present at this briefing.

'Yes, sir.'

'So Tom, what's this about a breakthrough?' asked the DCI as he settled into his customary place on the opposite couch.

'You're aware that we asked the Pakistan ISI to tap the home telephone of Baloch's wife?'

'Sure.'

'They intercepted an unidentified call made from an unregistered cell phone shortly after 1 a.m. EST this morning.'

'Doctor Baloch?'

'Almost certainly. They traced the source of this call through a network of masts to Buenos Aires.'

'Can we refine the location of the call?'

'The NSA is narrowing it down now. One call will hop between a number of masts in its locality and the area coverage of these masts can be triangulated to provide an approximate source of the call, in this case considerably less than a square mile. There are a large number of masts in Buenos Aires which helps.'

'What about the conversation?'

'The ISI has forwarded the transcript. It's a pretty damning conversation.'

Carter handed a copy of the short conversation to the DCI.

'Now we have the number, the NSA will continue to monitor the cell phone and record any incoming or outgoing calls.'

The DCI was delighted. 'So Baloch is the bomb maker. I'll inform the President immediately.'

'And I'll inform the DDI and Sir Michael,' added Carter.

Chapter 58

February 2nd, Z – 89 Days
Buenos Aires, Argentina

The foyer of the Hyatt Hotel in central Buenos Aires was always busy at 8 a.m. on a weekday morning. No one paid attention as three well-dressed men walked in through the main doors and made their way directly to the elevators.

'He's on the twelfth floor in Room 2006,' said the leader.

Baloch had drunk to excess since Malik had dropped him off yesterday evening and this morning he felt very ill. So much so that he had already contacted reception and booked himself in for a second night, after promising himself that he would steer clear of excessive drinking this evening. He would depart for home with his money tomorrow, sober, and job done.

The three men did not have the luxury of waiting for him to return home as they had intended. The job was required to be done quickly. Not knowing how long Baloch intended to stay at the hotel, the leader had decided to pay him a visit there.

'It's very busy,' remarked another of the three men, casually referring to the number of potential witnesses in the hotel.

'We're less conspicuous among large numbers of people,' replied the leader.

'On average there is one suicide a day in Buenos Aires, six in Argentina,' remarked the third.

Baloch was lying on his bed sipping water and thinking of his life, and how it was all about to change. He had been born and raised in the slums of Karachi, and here he was, a millionaire, lying on a bed in an executive suite of one of the most prestigious hotels in Argentina. In the Islamic world, very few people escaped from the vast numbers of poor to join the few enormously wealthy people, yet he was one of them. The absence of a middle class was near universal except for the few oil-rich countries that had spread the liquid gold around in the hope of buying social peace for the rich.

Like most people on the planet, he was as loyal and trustworthy a man as money could buy. Honest he was not, but then who was? Even his Ph.D. from the University of Karachi was a little cloudy. He had foolishly supported al-Qa'eda in the past when he had thought bin Laden would secure more support than he had from the Islamic republics, and this, he resolved, would be his last. One million dollars meant that he could retire in style and he intended to do so. He was thinking of the house he would purchase for his family when the knock came at the door.

Baloch glanced at his watch and assumed it was the maid service calling to make up the bed.

'No, thank you,' cried Baloch.

'It's a delivery, sir,' was the meek response.

Still dressed from the night before, Baloch hauled himself off the bed and stumbled over to the door. Without bothering to look through the security peephole, he opened the door and found three men standing there, all of them with drawn pistols fitted with silencers. Baloch stared at the guns. It was several seconds before he recognised Jamali in a suit standing at the back clutching a large briefcase. Before Baloch could react, two of the gunmen barged the door open and forced their way in, reeling him back into the centre of the room. Jamali entered behind them and closed the door.

One of the gunmen pushed Baloch into a chair and watched over him while the other searched the apartment. Immediately finding the black leather holdall on another chair, the gunman pulled it open.

'It's the money,' he hissed. The gunman held up the bag so that the other two could see the cash inside.

'Check it,' Jamali demanded hoarsely as he threw the briefcase onto the bed.

The gunman who held up the bag chose a random bundle and tore it apart. He spread the currency on the bed and fished in the briefcase for a UV light mounted with a magnifying glass. He used this tool to examine random bills. When he had finished he gathered them up, counted them, snapped a rubber band around them, then placed the bundle in the briefcase.

I'm being robbed by Jamali, thought Baloch nervously. *The double-*

crossing bastards. His mind flashed to his money at home, and that it was still enough.

The gunman dived into the leather holdall for another bundle and began the inspection process again. Soon all the money had been transferred to the briefcase and he was satisfied.

'It's real, but only half a mill.'

Jamali turned sharply to Baloch, clearly angry. 'Where's the rest?'

'I don't know what you're talking about,' replied Baloch pathetically, still assuming this to be a robbery.

Jamali cocked his weapon. 'Do not insult me. You told me yourself you were getting a million dollars. Where is the other half?' he barked.

Baloch was no hero and they both knew it. He was terrified and quickly told them what they wanted to hear. 'It was paid in advance. It's under the floor, underneath my bed. It's in a bin liner.'

Jamali studied the sweat forming on Baloch's forehead for several seconds and chose to believe him. In any event their cover story would not allow for the torture of this nauseating coward of a man. He sat on the bed directly opposite Baloch, leant forward menacingly and staring into Baloch's eyes.

'Did the thought never occur to you,' Jamali said insidiously, 'that you might know too much?'

The colour drained from Baloch's face as he suddenly realised this was more than just a robbery.

'What?' he squeaked.

'You're a man of the world, you work it out,' Jamali snapped sarcastically.

Baloch realised that he was in deep and serious trouble, the worst of his life. The sweat began to fall in rivulets from his brow and his shirt became clammy. 'Jamali,' he stumbled, ' I have never whispered a word about al-Qa'eda to any living soul despite all the interrogations I have been through with the Pakistan secret police and the CIA. Why in the name of Allah would I do so now? I know that would be suicide. We all know that.'

Jamali stood and walked around the room, stopping to open the balcony door. He looked out over the largely flat roof tops of Buenos Aires that were littered with clothes lines, giant advertising boards, satellite TV dishes and a mass of other electronic masts. Civilisation was a long way down in the streets that were little more than cracks between the buildings. Jamali let the tension build, enjoying the moment. It was only then that Baloch realised Jamal was wearing gloves, as were the other gunmen.

Baloch tried to speak but found he could not.

'But what if you were arrested now?' asked Jamali. 'In the past you simply remained silent. You have knowingly manufactured weapons that have only one purpose, to kill millions of people. The need for your captors to find the weapons is so great you would face drugs and torture rather than be allowed to remain silent. Then you would betray Allah.'

'Jamali, I swear on my children's lives...'

'You would squeal as easily you did to me about the money. You would say anything to save your own miserable existence.'

Baloch knew he was going to die. 'In the name of Allah have mercy on me. I have done everything asked of me. I'm not a fool! I would never talk.'

Jamali stood in front of Baloch and looked down on him pityingly. 'I would like to believe you for you have served Allah well,' he sighed. 'The reality is that you will be left with no choice. You have appealed to Allah for mercy, so you shall have it.' He glanced at the gunman standing behind Baloch's chair and nodded.

The gunman struck Baloch on the head with the butt of a pistol and his large frame collapsed forward in the chair.

'Throw him over the balcony,' ordered Jamali coldly. He checked Baloch's pockets, filled the briefcase with cash and then turned and walked from the room, removing his gloves as he went. Within seconds the two gunmen joined him in the hall, the last to leave pulling the door closed. On the floor below they caught the elevator to the ground floor.

As the three gunmen walked onto the street they saw people looking upwards, pointing and talking in horrified excitement.

'He was a jumper...'

'He jumped from up there...'

'...landed on the roof of the foyer...'

Jamali heard sirens approaching from a distance, and after casually crossing the busy street he figured he could look back in safety. He saw that the body was perfectly still and that nobody had yet been able to reach it.

Across the street the three men met another man sitting in a parked car. They climbed in, and the fourth man pulled the car out into traffic.

Chapter 59

February 2nd, Z – 89 Days
Buenos Aires, Argentina

It was forecast to be another hot day in Buenos Aires and by 9 a.m. the temperature had reached 28 degrees Celsius in the shade. The morning update had been running for ten minutes when the agents inside the stuffy briefing room of the Counter Subversion and Counterterrorism Center heard the short sharp rap on the door. Without waiting for an invite, a young agent interrupted the briefing by opening the door and taking one step into the room.

'Sorry, sir,' he apologised in Spanish to Encizo who was caught mid-sentence addressing the assembly.

'Metro has found Baloch.'

'Well, that's excellent,' exclaimed Encizo excitedly.

'He's dead sir!'

The room was stunned into silence. Everyone's eyes moved to Encizo as they realised the enormity of the final statement.

'Where?' asked Encizo, as he rapidly assimilated the news.

'The Hyatt.' For the first time since joining the division, the young agent was the centre of attention. He enjoyed the nervous thrill and tried in vain to look calm. The eyes of every chief in the division were upon him for these few precious seconds and he heard himself exaggerate his knowledge. 'He's lying in a pool of his own blood, on the roof to the main entrance. It looks like he jumped from the twentieth floor.'

It would not have been the first time someone had jumped from the Hyatt, one of the tallest and most commanding structures in Buenos Aires. Despite the young agent's comment, no one in the room believed he had jumped of his own accord.

Encizo turned back to the assembly. 'It appears that today's update is superfluous,' he said calmly. 'We will cancel and reconvene tomorrow.' Encizo looked at one of his chiefs. 'Maxim, mobilise a team. The investigation will be our jurisdiction, and you will lead. I will be thirty minutes behind you.' The commander concluded, 'That's all, thank you.'

Maxim hurried out first, followed by several of his staff. The remainder filed out behind Encizo, talking excitedly as they went.

Several minutes later Harry and Tess found Encizo at his desk, absentmindedly rotating a pencil through the fingers of one hand as a poker player might shuffle his chips.

'I love and hate these moments,' Encizo explained, feeling frustrated. 'Love them because they usually represent a breakthrough and hate them because we have failed to prevent the death that occurred. I also hate waiting.'

Harry knew that Encizo would have wanted to visit the scene of crime immediately, but that it would have been construed by his divisional staff as micro-management at best. It would not have been appreciated. Better to wait then travel down and receive a meaningful briefing from his capable subordinate, Maxim. Then he could ask questions and offer ideas.

'Mind if we tag along?' asked Tess.

'I would be disappointed if you didn't,' was his curt reply.

Harry decided that London could wait for an update. He needed to know more.

The Hyatt Hotel could not be reached by car. Encizo's driver double-parked the car and remained with it while his passengers walked the last three hundred metres. Organised chaos was how Encizo viewed their reception, for what they were confronted with was considerably worse than was usual at a crime scene. He, like most law enforcement officers around the world much preferred surreptitious work outside the glare of the media. The average number of unnatural deaths per year in the city over ten years ran at thirty-six and it was very rare that the ASS was involved. On this occasion the nest that was the city's media had been violently prodded and they scurried about like aggravated ants.

It was obvious where the body lay. As they approached the hotel they saw a mass of frustrated photographers, journalists and inquisitive passers-by massing around the front entrance, all of them looking upwards. All entrances to the hotel had been sealed off by the Metro police so no one from the press could enter the building and take their shots. Nor could anyone other than officials gain access to the upper floors and view the porch from above. But Encizo knew it was only a matter of time before the flying ants arrived in the guise of helicopters. The sooner the screens were erected the better.

The road outside the hotel had been closed in both directions by Metro, who was still in the process of erecting barriers in a semicircle some twenty metres from the entrance doors. Only then could they force the gathering crowd to the far side and restore full control. Despite the apparent chaos at this busiest time of the day, the police on-site commander was content, for securing the scene of crime was his highest priority and already the body and the deceased's room were inaccessible to all but those with official status.

As Encizo approached the hotel entrance first one then the remainder of the press pack turned toward him. Tess then Harry tucked in close behind Encizo keeping their heads low in an attempt to remain inconspicuous. Carefully pushing through the jostling bodies, Encizo declined to answer any of the rapid-fire questions, despite the multitude of microphones and cameras thrust into his face. Neither did he respond to any of the usual tricks designed to get the extraordinary snapshot. There were no rules for the Buenos Aires press and the scuff marks on his steel capped shoes proved it. Miraculously, on this occasion he avoided any tears to his clothing.

'I hope you didn't wear your best clothes,' growled Encizo once they were safely inside the front entrance of the hotel.

'Our countries have much in common,' Harry replied as he brushed himself down.

Maxim, who had witnessed the commotion outside, was waiting in the hotel foyer to greet Encizo on his arrival.

'What have you got?' the Commander asked.

With Harry and Tess present they spoke in English.

'It's him, sir. The police have set a ladder onto the porch from the first floor. Follow me.'

As they walked to the grand staircase that led from the foyer, Harry noticed the long lines of impatient hotel guests waiting to be interviewed before they would be allowed to leave the building and continue with their day. Six Metro officers were taking statements, one per table placed by hotel staff at the end of each queue. He hoped the police were asking the right questions for there was often no second chance. Investigations were much smoother when a little thought was applied to the immediate questioning of potential witnesses.

As they climbed the stairs, Maxim continued. 'He jumped, or was pushed, at eight-twenty this morning, and pronounced dead *in situ* by the police doctor several minutes ago.'

'Could he have been dead before the fall?' Encizo enquired.

'He could,' replied Maxim. 'There are plenty of witnesses who say they heard a crashing thud as the body landed on the porch. According to many witnesses there was no sound either before or during his fall. The deceased had stayed for one night and was booked in for a second. That's the big picture. I suggest you see the body first, then his room, twenty-o-six.'

Encizo nodded in agreement and they made their way to a staircase.

'According to the hotel staff he had been drinking heavily. Three bottles of whiskey in less than twenty-four hours. That's a bottle every five hours if you allow time to sleep it off. He was not seen leaving the room in the period, always ordered room service. Tipped like a millionaire in US dollars, according to the waiters. Kept bragging about how he had struck lucky and that his family were to come and live with him in Argentina.'

Maxim led them into a suite on the first floor then over to its balcony which overlooked the porch above the hotel entrance. Encizo was first to descend the ladder that had been lashed to the balcony railings.

'Fully dressed,' he commented when Maxim, who had descended last of the four, arrived by his side.

'Looks like he slept in them,' noted Harry.

They watched the busy scene as the scene of crime officers did their work. A cameraman was taking pictures as forensics personnel scoured the vicinity and pathologists prepared to bag the body.

'It's a long way down,' added Tess, encouraging the law enforcement officers to look up to the twentieth floor. An officer was standing on Baloch's balcony, looking down.

'He must have been alive when he fell,' she stated, devoid of emotion. 'I saw a jumper with a similar wound a year ago. There was the same amount of blood. He landed on his head with his heart still functioning.'

A doctor who stood near by appeared to agree. A guest in the hotel, he had been the first medical expert on the scene. They all peered at the horribly contorted neck and deep split in what remained of Baloch's skull. It was cracked smartly from the top of his head, through his nose to his upper lip.

'I believe he was alive but unconscious when he fell,' explained the doctor. 'The pathologist will find additional trauma at the back of the head where he was knocked unconscious.'

'Is that possible, Doctor?' Maxim asked.

The doctor pointed to the back of Baloch's balding head and a very recent trauma that could not have been caused on impact. 'I believe the lady is correct but the pathologist must confirm it. You will require a full autopsy as soon as possible.'

'So he was knocked unconscious then dropped,' said Encizo.

'He was alive before he hit the veranda,' agreed the doctor cautiously.

'No way was this a suicide. He was a rich, happy man looking forward to seeing his family,' Maxim added.

'Slugged then dropped?' Encizo glanced around for everyone's unofficial verdict.

Everyone nodded and waited for the doctor to summarise.

'Concussed prior to falling, death on impact. Subject to the pathologist's report, naturally.'

'Did he have any visitors during his stay?' Harry enquired.

'Must have, but none reported to reception,' Maxim replied helpfully. 'No one asked for his room number, not that any of the staff recall.'

'So whoever killed him may have known his room number in advance and simply strolled in,' continued Harry.

'The room was booked in advance by someone other than Baloch. Paid cash.'

'Are there CCTV cameras in the foyer?' asked Tess.

'Yes. Some on each floor too. The hotel keeps recordings for a while. We also have guest lists, and lists of all the staff.'

'Well done, Maxim,' offered Encizo, not wanting Harry's input to be misinterpreted. 'Let's go and visit the room.'

The group waited patiently in the corridor outside Room 2006 for ten minutes before there was enough space for them to enter. Maxim made the most of the time, by updating himself on progress via his hand-held radio, and discussing lines of enquiry with Encizo.

Once inside the three visitors carefully studied the room.

Tess walked out onto the balcony. 'Not something you could mistakenly fall from.'

'My mother used to sleepwalk,' Maxim observed.

'When she was drunk and concussed?' asked Tess with mild sarcasm.

'You know my mother?' Maxim smiled.

Harry found two grey grips laden with tools and a black suitcase half-full of clothes that lay open on a luggage rack. 'Better check the tools for radiation exposure.'

'They have been,' Maxim replied. 'Nothing harmful but they have been exposed to radiation recently. No surprise given the purpose of the equipment.'

Harry noticed a black leather holdall lying as if discarded on the floor. 'I wonder what this was used for,' he enquired, holding up the bag and turning it upside down. Scanning the room with his eyes he added, 'All his personal items would easily fit in the case with space to spare. His tools appear to be accounted for. Could there have been something else, maybe money, a final payment perhaps? An amount equal to that found at his home would have fitted in here.'

Maxim liked the idea and expanded upon it. 'Perhaps he was paid the other half for a job well done. CCTV will show Baloch entering the hotel with his bags.

'Perhaps the assassin brought a bag with him for the loot,' Maxim suggested.

'Maybe the assassin was an opportunist, a hotel guest intent on foul play before he checked out this morning?' offered Tess. 'Perhaps Baloch bragged to someone?'

They left the issue there. There was no point in speculating, not until they had seen the CCTV footage.

'May we have an inventory of his personal items?' Harry asked politely.

'Sure, it will be available in a day or so,' shrugged Maxim. 'Forensics will be sifting through all the items first.'

'Thanks. How do we think the assassin got in?' Harry mused. 'These are secure door locks.'

'Baloch must have let the perp in,' answered Tess as she inspected the one open area of the carpet in the room that the SOC team had taped off. 'Perhaps Baloch was tortured first.'

'All right, this is excellent brainstorming, people, but now we must give Maxim and his team some space,' Encizo said with authority. 'We'll have the lab reports in several days and then we will piece together what happened.'

Harry and Tess walked into the corridor. Satisfied they had seen enough the three visitors thanked Maxim and left the hotel, leaving a relieved Maxim to finish his job. In fact, he had welcomed the input he had received.

On returning to their temporary office on the sixth floor, Harry sat behind his desk and switched on his satcom electronic notebook as Tess fetched two coffees. They planned to prepare and send an unscheduled operational report to London. As soon as the miniature computer was booted up a 'Message Received' window flashed up upon the screen. Selecting the 'Read Now' icon, the satcom automatically loaded the message software and opened the newly received message. There was only one, which had originated from the CTC and had been copied to London. Just as Harry started reading the message, Tess entered the room with a mug of coffee in each hand.

'We have a message from Langley, received about an hour ago,' Harry informed her as he scanned the content.

Tess hurriedly discarded the two steaming mugs, walked behind Harry and read over his shoulder.

The morning just got better. Harry and Tess went in search of Encizo, who Tess had just left at the coffee machine down the corridor. Finding him and ushering him to their office, Harry briefed Encizo on the new development.

'The Pakistan ISI has intercepted a call made from a cell phone somewhere in Buenos Aires shortly after 3 a.m. local time this morning to Baloch's family home in Islamabad. The cell phone is unregistered.'

'Do we have its number?'

'Yes. The NSA is already monitoring for future calls.'

Harry showed Encizo a transcript of the telephone conversation recorded by the Pakistan ISI.

'That confirms it,' stated Encizo. 'There is no question Baloch is our guy. Is anyone tracing the call?'

'The NSA is checking it out now,' replied Tess. 'It should be possible to trace the source to within just a few blocks. It depends on the location of the masts.'

‘Brilliant.’ Encizo nodded, impressed. ‘Good for the NSA. As soon as we know the source of the call we can, how do the Americans put it, get our sorry arses down there.’

Tess smiled. Encizo was so *yesterday*, definitely too much TV. But she and Harry shared his excitement.

Chapter 60

February 6th, Z - 85 Days
London, England

The Gold Coordinating Group, led by the Metropolitan Police Commissioner Adrian Walker consisted of fifteen people who represented the full range of front-line organisations in the capital city. They were charged with the responsibility for coordinating the response to any attack by terrorists.

It was in the Commissioner's private conference room adjacent to his office on the top floor of New Scotland Yard where they plotted and coordinated London's response to the nuclear threat. Although the Commissioner was empowered with considerable authority, today he wanted the group to identify those issues that required ministerial approval.

The meeting began with a briefing from each commander around the table. They represented the British Transport Police, the London Fire Brigade, the London Ambulance Service, the National Health Service, the Greater London Authority, the Corporation of the City of London, British Telecom and, at the Commissioner's insistence, the Salvation Army. The Ministry of Defence, the Commissioner's Media Officer, whom he introduced as Chief Inspector Jane Walsh, and a Civil Service liaison officer from the Cabinet Office were also present, along with a crisis management expert, a secretary, and the inevitable financial guru.

'Thank you. I have been delighted with how much has been achieved in only a few weeks. The political and national acceptance that the economic and financial heart of the country must be protected at all costs is reassuring, and it appears that the media and public accept that each and every one of us has a responsible part to play in our response to a threat of this magnitude. However, one has only to peel away the surface and visit each borough's police force and speak to the public, businessmen and, dare I say, the junior officers under our command to find that there is considerable alarm and confusion. To deal with this, it's vital that we continue to provide robust leadership and communicate clear plans and directions.'

The Commissioner looked down at his pad. 'Clearly there are a number of strategic issues that we must address and if possible resolve today. I would also like to identify any that require ministerial approval.'

Everyone nodded, eager to grapple with the problems.

'First though, Chief Inspector Jane Walsh will introduce you to a public information campaign that she has prepared in association with your departments. The tape you are about to watch is a half-hour television documentary that will be supported by a series of shorter television adverts and a poster campaign. It's aimed at the general public and businesses, and it informs people what they must do in the event of a generic terrorist threat and how Londoners are to test national procedures during Exercise Rapid Response. The programme illustrates the national security state mechanism and the necessary response to each level of alert, the need for personal vigilance, who the authorities are, methods of communication, the need to identify alternative accommodation and the need to secure homes, ensure adequate vehicle fuel, clear the fridge, eliminate fire hazards, leave the curtains closed, not to forget the pets, that sort of thing. For businesses it discusses additional measures such as the need to secure equipment for the period their businesses will be unmanned and so on.'

The Commissioner sat back and the Chief Inspector dimmed the lights with one remote control before picking up another that controlled her presentation.

Forty minutes later the lights flickered on, and the Gold Group committee members sat back up. They were clearly impressed by the advertising campaign, which was brief, simple, reassuring and, above all, informative. After minor discussion, the Commissioner moved onto other issues.

'The first is command and control. Our Alternate Headquarters is being established at Watford and we will meet there after evacuation. There must be no misunderstanding among anyone that the Gold, Silver and Bronze groups represent the Strategic, Operational and Tactical levels of command in an emergency.

Of course, every service and supporting organisation will have its own administrative structure, but overall authority will always remain with the police. I know it sounds obvious to us, but it's clear from what you have reported today that there's still some confusion. There are a great many advisory committees and forums too, and they have their part to play but every one of them must ultimately report to a body represented in the Gold Group. I look to you all to make sure the command and control arrangements are made perfectly clear to everyone.

'That leads me on to my second point. Communication. You've seen Chief Inspector Walsh's presentation. It's vital that our message to the public is concise and unambiguous. I don't expect anyone in a position of authority, including members of every think-tank, sub committee or forum, to communicate publicly unless they are authorised by the media operations branch. If anyone, and I mean anyone, starts issuing unauthorised statements or making unguarded comments through the media or otherwise, have no doubt that I'll have them removed.'

Chief Inspector Walsh spoke on cue. 'The Emergency Media Forum will convene here at New Scotland Yard and will include a daily press conference beginning next Monday. There will be days when any one or more of you will be required, or you may wish to use the opportunity to get a particular message across to the public. We don't want the media to speculate and so we will be open, frank and honest with them on a daily basis. We need them to encourage people to help one another, to encourage people to listen to the authorities, to encourage an ordered evacuation and to encourage businesses to prepare. The same press centre will be used to facilitate the emergency broadcasting system, which will allow us to provide urgent information or warnings through a whole range of radio, television and on-line services. We will have a dedicated web site where intelligence updates, press releases, public and business instructions and other guidelines and so on will be available.

'We have hot lines to a call centre in Watford. It will deal exclusively with general public and business queries, and will be operational from next Monday when the advertising campaign begins. Leaflets are also being printed and distributed across London by Royal Mail and by other means.'

'Thank you, Chief Inspector. Please also note that we are to produce and distribute a directory of all key contact details. You will all be asked to provide names, posts and numbers for your organisations sometime tomorrow. I have one last point of detail. Multi-point video teleconferencing facilities are to be established between here, the MOD, Cobra, the Prime Minister's Office and Cabinet, all the boroughs and the City of London police.

'The third issue is centralisation and commonality. The more simple our plans, the more likely they will succeed. Every good idea must be encouraged and passed up the chain of command in order that it's considered for application across the thirty-three boroughs and the City. You don't need me to tell you that our resources will be massively stretched, and the more commonality we have across the City the better. No mavericks who think they can do better alone, please. For the fourth issue, I would like to hand you over to Brigadier James Jarvis from the Defence Crisis Management Organisation at the Ministry of Defence. Brigadier.'

'Thank you, Commissioner. The issue is military support. You are all aware, of course, that you will be desperately short of properly equipped and trained personnel for the myriad of tasks that must be completed, in particular with our response to a nuclear attack. The Commissioner intends to request ministerial approval for the use of troops to assist with cordoning London, the provision of fire-fighting teams and medical services, the provision of radiological detection teams in support of the ten search teams from the US, and also decontamination teams. Helicopters from the Joint Helicopter Command are to assist with the evacuation and security. Finally, the Army and Royal Air Force, with the assistance of a large number of local authorities, are to set up temporary accommodation for a hundred thousand people who we estimate will be unable to rehouse themselves for the period. A temporary detention centre will also be constructed by the Sappers at Colchester. Initial plans suggest about twenty thousand service personnel will be required, including regular soldiers and reservists from all over the country. There are also plans to supplement our military support to the civil powers with NATO troops including the positioning of NATO's Nuclear Event Response Team in the event the worst happens.'

Several Gold Group members shifted uncomfortably as they felt increasingly inadequate. This was all becoming very real.

'My final issue is sensitive and involves use of appropriate force and the authority to use firearms. Of course we must strive to maintain law and order with the minimum necessary force, but while the Commissioner has the authority to deploy as many armed police officers as he considers necessary, this does not include armed soldiers.'

The Brigadier looked up from his notes. 'The Ministry of Defence recommends that your authority extends to include any military personnel under your operational control.'

'Thank you, Brigadier, I will follow that up with the Home Secretary.'

The Chief Fire Officer spoke next. 'What about arrest and detention? Do you hold sufficient powers of arrest to deter or detain troublemakers?'

'An excellent question,' the Commissioner sighed. 'I hadn't envisaged the suspension of habeas corpus, though the Cabinet may want to prepare itself by reconsidering the issue. We can currently detain people without charge for seventy-two hours and for up to fourteen days if their actions are related to terrorism, but frankly, these powers may not prove sufficient in the circumstances. I will raise this issue at the next Cobra meeting.

'The final issue is one of coordination. By next Friday we will issue a final set of orders and overlays for Exercise Rapid Response that will detail the augmentation of the emergency services, the whereabouts of the cordon around Greater London, access points of which there will be eight roughly on the points of the compass, main arteries to be used to and from London, locations of the alternate police and other headquarters at all levels and so on. As some of you know, I deliberately avoided asking the authorities bordering London to provide blue-light and other mobile resources, only sites for alternate headquarters. Without knowing the size and effect of the blast or prevailing weather conditions no one can be certain how they may be affected, so I've found support from further afield. Now, I will take any of your questions.'

The Gold Group spent the next hour raising and considering the wealth of issues that arose from the reports. Each member had brought along their own set of problems, and each was encouraged by how robustly they were received and addressed. It was clear to everyone that nothing, absolutely nothing, was to hinder progress.

The Commissioner had the last word. 'Thank you all for a very productive meeting. I realise that we have focused largely on the pre-strike issues today but be assured that once we are satisfied with our pre-emptive plans we will focus on the deserted city and its repopulation. Of course, for real the aftermath could be devastation and contamination, and we must also plan in detail for that eventuality.

'For now I would like you to ensure that everyone under your command understands the significance of this exercise and applies themselves to their responsibilities. This exercise is to be played out as if it were real, ladies and gentlemen, for *real* it could so easily become.'

Chapter 61

February 6th, Z – 85 Days
San Carlos de Bariloche, Argentina

The rookie police officer would not accept that his first plainclothes assignment was mundane despite over three weeks of shift work in the same godforsaken dark and dusty room overlooking the same godforsaken ramshackle homestead across the street. With the exception of the recent addition of cigarette smoke, litter, body odour and surveillance equipment, the room had not been touched for twenty years since its young occupant had died in a road accident.

Finally, as the afternoon drew to a close the rookie known as Antonio saw a black Mercedes cruise up and down the residential street three times before it eventually sped away in the direction it had come. He thought this odd and told his senior partner, Paulo.

'Did you get a photo?' Paulo snarled.

'Yeh, but the car had darkened windows.'

'Did anyone get out?'

'No.'

'Did you get a licence?'

'Yeh.'

'Well fucking log it then.'

'Should I call it in?'

'Don't be daft. Orders are to call in if someone enters the house, report everything else in the log.'

'I think we should call it in.'

'Nobody gives a shit what you think, rookie.'

The senior officer turned away from the only window and attempted to get back to sleep on the one single bed in the darkening room. He had another six hours before he would be relieved and he had an all-night party with a new girl to attend.

Thankfully the rookie seemed to enjoy the spy game and appeared content to stag on for the next two hours until his relief arrived. Paulo would get the next guy to do the following four hours and in return the senior officer would let the man smoke, providing of course the cigarettes were dished out. The room already smelt like an African jail but he did not feel for the old couple downstairs. They looked like they needed the compensation.

The state police had had Baloch's house under surveillance for over three weeks, and everyone from the chief down had had enough, everyone except these rookies who still dreamed of transferring to the Secret Service. This was a special op on behalf of the Argentine Security Service, and with the exception of the rookies, everyone thought they were being crapped on. It was worse than cruising for hookers, and that, Paulo knew, could ruin your sex life. The local ASS station in San Carlos had provided several teams for the first week and most of the aged equipment, including the night-time image intensifiers and the infrared cameras with x80 magnification, but the excuses soon flowed in.

It was an hour later and darkness had fallen when the rookie saw the same black Mercedes return to the neighbourhood and this time pull up on the dirt driveway outside Baloch's house.

'Paulo, the Mercedes has returned. Wake up,' warned Antonio. There had been no need for him to whisper as their hideaway in a bedroom on the first floor in the house opposite Baloch's was at least a hundred metres away.

Paulo woke from his light sleep and reluctantly pulled himself up from the bed to peer through the image intensifier. Meanwhile, Antonio was busy operating several high-specification cameras. The picture through the image intensifier was grainy and grey, but Paulo could easily make out three men, with a fourth who remained seated behind the wheel. He watched as the three men walked to the front door and without pause, causing Paulo to think they must have had a key, they entered the house and the car reversed before speeding away.

'Two of them are carrying assault rifles,' said Antonio, 'and they're not turning on the lights. Whoever they are we had better call this one in, Paulo.'

'It's them all right. You watch, I'll report the bastards and log it.' Paulo reached for the team's cell phone. The insecure state police radios were never used for covert ops.

Antonio listened to the conversation between Paulo and their headquarters as he studied the target.

'...then the Mercedes buggered off and left them... It will probably return when it gets the go ahead... By phone I guess... You want more stills of them with the money coming out?... Yes... We've not got a video camera... Sure.'

Finally Paulo cancelled the call and pondered for a moment. 'We're to sit tight and continue the surveillance. The chief wants pictures of them on the way out with the money. HQ thought we had a video camera. Pissed them off when I told them we didn't.'

'What's the chief planning to do?'

'How the fuck do I know? They want us to tell them if we see the Merc again and when the men come out. They also want to know if the men have the money with them, and anything else we think might be useful.'

Twelve minutes later the Mercedes returned and smoothly reversed into Baloch's front yard, the hot engine causing havoc with the infrared camera. As the car came to a halt, the front door opened and the three men swiftly left the house. The first two men to exit casually surveyed the dark neighbourhood, keeping their assault rifles hung ready by their sides. The third, the man who was evidently the leader, was carrying a black refuse sac filled with what the two police officers guessed was cash. It looked heavy.

Paulo wasted little time reporting the event, while Antonio witnessed the moment and captured it on the sensitive cameras.

'You've to take the film back to HQ on your relief,' said Paulo.

'What about the surveillance?'

'It's to carry on for now. I guess it'll be over tomorrow. Thank fuck.'

The Mercedes had just two options when leaving Baloch's house, to drive south towards the airport of San Carlos de Bariloche or north into the wilderness. Though both routes were covered by a pair of unmarked cars each of differing makes, only one of the eight officers had put money on the northern route and he won the pot. He and his partner became the 'eye', the car earmarked to follow the Mercedes which was referred to as the 'rabbit'.

It was an easy task on a moonlit night and on the moderately busy road to Paso Limay. Soon all four cars settled into the routine tailing of the rabbit alternating responsibility for the eye with simple drills routinely used by law enforcement agencies across the world.

Just forty-five minutes into the journey, soon after passing over the mile-long suspension bridge over the southern tip of Lake Nahuel Haupí, the Mercedes turned a sharp left into a wide gravel driveway that after three hundred metres dead-ended at an emerald mine owned by the Río Negro Mining Company. The four police cars were forced to remain on the main road so that they didn't alert the rabbit, and the leader was left with no choice but to contact HQ and await instructions. But within minutes they heard the unmistakable sound of rotor blades turning with increasing velocity and seconds later they watched helplessly as a dark helicopter with no distinguishable markings rose noisily into the sky and swung north over the Cordillera de los Andes.

Despite the obvious conclusion, the four police cars swept into the mine, just as they were receiving confirmation by radio that the Mercedes was a rental booked with a stolen licence. First they found the vehicle abandoned on a short airstrip, a short-cropped field of grass with a telltale wind sock that lay outside the perimeter fence. Minutes later, they found two security guards and a dog, all brutally machine-gunned to death.

It was 10 p.m. when the state police chief rang Encizo and briefed him on the activity and loss of contact. He also explained, with obvious embarrassment, that the money had gone. Encizo cursed and received assurance that a full surveillance report, and forensics report on the car and house, would be passed to the local ASS station immediately. He knew that trying to trace the helicopter through air traffic control would prove fruitless as over seventy per cent of Argentinian airspace was not monitored, particularly at low altitude. Encizo reflected on the situation, as the police chief expressed several times how his force had done everything they could. Before long Encizo realised that the man was still living in fear of the old Security Service.

'There can be no doubt that your force has done everything that could reasonably have been expected of it,' Encizo heard himself say. 'There is one other thing though. May I speak to the officer who watched the men enter and leave the house?'

'Of course, Director, his name is Antonio, a young but effective officer. He was in my office just a moment ago. Please wait a moment.'

Encizo held onto the line as he stepped impatiently around his kitchen searching for a pen and paper.

'Hello ... sir?' a young voice said uncertainly down the telephone line.

'Antonio, my name is Encizo and I work for the ASS.' Encizo had decided to drop all formalities, it was enough that the young police officer knew he was more senior than the police officer's own chief, and that he was ASS. 'Good work tonight. Please tell me what you saw, and take your time.'

'It was dark of course, but...' the young officer stammered.

Several minutes later Encizo could picture the scene as if he had been there himself. He was very impressed with the young officer's observational skills and said so.

Encizo was certain the man on the hotel CCTV and the man taking the money from the house were the same man. This man, Encizo knew from a thick file, was known as Jamali, an Arab Muslim who considered himself a rising force among the gangsters of the wild Corrientes borderland region of northern Argentina.

Jamali had been convicted of a string of minor offences since he arrived in Argentina as a teenager fifteen years ago. He had been naturalised as Argentine courtesy of his Argentine mother who, when an aid worker, had had no more than a brief physical acquaintance with Jamali's Palestinian father in a Beirut hospital as missiles had pounded and gunfire rained. It appeared that his father had convinced a young Jamali to stay in Lebanon when his mother had been expelled, as she had been suspected, along with hundreds of other hapless aid workers, of spying. At the age of fourteen, someone or something had made Jamali decide to emigrate from Lebanon, probably his father's unexpected death in an Israeli jail.

Since his arrival in Argentina, Jamali was suspected of orchestrating several murders including one police officer, kidnapping, gang warfare, drug trafficking and smuggling. He was also believed to have played a major part in a number of unrelated bombings, one of which was on the Israeli Embassy in Buenos Aires in 1992 that left hundreds dead and injured. It was also suspected that he maintained close contacts with the

Middle East and the terrorist group Islamic Jihad. But despite many attempts by the authorities to nail him, nothing had stuck, and he remained one of the ASS's most wanted men.

Chapter 62

February 10th, Z – 81 Days
London, England

Abdul Mahmood was thirty-two years old and believed in the jihad against the *kafirs*, the infidels. He grew up in a small village on the edge of the desert, a son of a tribesman. He wasn't sure precisely what the American infidels had done to Islam, but all his life he had been told by bearded holy men who had never been far from their village that the infidels were the enemy, and he had never questioned it. It was a fact of life, like the desert and the presence of Allah.

Nor did he question it these past two weeks which he had spent in London enduring the worst kind of cultural shock. He knew nothing about the country, couldn't speak the language, didn't like the food, hated the music, and was horrified by the women who were everywhere, in every public place and private shop. There was nowhere to escape them. They paraded their bodies, wore revealing clothes, painted their faces and nails, tried to tempt men into sin. They were brazen sluts of the worst sort. And he had been forced to eat with them, deal with them, sit beside them, watch them tempt men they did not know, even tempt him. He felt as if he were visiting the country of the devil where evil prevailed, where the greatness of Allah and the words of the Prophet were despised. He had seen the children smiling, sniggering, and pointing at him and his friends. He felt their amusement, their contempt. And he hated them. *Kafirs*.

This morning he rode with Mustafa and the two women, Essa and Kalil, in Mustafa's car. He did not know where they were going and the leader hadn't told him. It didn't occur to him to ask, and he thought only about the weapons that he had assumed they were on their way to collect. He had helped prepare and load the personal weapons, anti-personnel mines and hand grenades onto a truck in Iran over two months ago. He knew that there were enough weapons in the van to start a small war and he knew exactly how they all worked. He also knew that the *kafirs* had made most of them, then traded them for oil. He would enjoy using the weapons against their makers.

Al-Qa'eda would show the world that they had the courage and the power, Abdul Mahmood thought. The infidels would soon appreciate the fury of the jihad and the power of Islam. Embrace Allah or be destroyed was the prophet's message to the unbelievers, and it was their message now.

As they drove, Mustafa briefed them. Mustafa had been told that morning that the weapons van and explosives van had been parked outside Mustafa's lock-up last night. The keys for each van had been left on the front offside wheel, under the wheel arch, and the vans and their contents were now his responsibility. Fortuitously all four of them were in the flat when the telephone call came from the Yemeni messenger. Mustafa had demanded they all depart for the vans immediately.

Despite the heavy traffic, it took just six minutes for Mustafa to drive to the lock-up. He spotted the two vans and continued driving past before pulling in and parking. Adjusting his rear-view mirror then wing mirrors, he surveyed the area surrounding the lock-up before ordering the others to stay put. He got out of the car and walked up and down the side street several times. Mustafa had chosen the lock-up well, not only was this one large and reasonably clean, but it was secure and any unwelcome surveillance would be easily spotted. The three terrorists in the car watched attentively as Mustafa unlocked the garage doors, checked inside then reappeared. After he had reversed both vans into the lock-up, he returned to the car and reversed that inside before ordering Mahmood to close the doors.

As the doors slammed shut, the inside of the lock-up plunged into darkness, until the overhead lights flickered then eventually lit. Mustafa stood back and let Mahmood take charge of unpacking and checking all the weapons and grenades in the first van. The mines and explosives in the second van were left for Turk, who was due to arrive in less than an hour with the remainder of the group.

After unlocking the van, Mahmood passed out the weapons' rolls. As the three terrorists unrolled the blankets and cradled the weapons, Mustafa caught the emotion on their faces. He watched as they each grew in stature, and for the first time since he had met them he realised how supremely confident they all were. These people were warriors, conditioned for one thing – killing.

For the first time it was Mustafa who felt like the weakest link. He admired the clinical handling of each of the three terrorists as they stripped, cleaned and rebuilt each weapon and magazine before turning their attention to every round of ammunition. Mustafa reflected that someone had provided him with elite fighters from the *Shia'heed* for the greatest of purposes. He felt honoured and once again vowed not to fail Allah or the Prophet. He wondered where they had been trained and knew that any one of them could teach him much about weapon handling, as indeed they must. It occurred to him that he was only the leader of this group because of his local knowledge and language skills and for no other reason. He felt humble. From now on he would show these martyrs the respect they deserved, for in less than two months they would all be in paradise.

Mustafa needed to learn as much as he could about the personal weapons that Mahmood had allocated for him. Starting the day after tomorrow, the terrorists were to fly in pairs to Iran for three days of live personal weapons handling and Mustafa had no desire to travel as a novice.

Chapter 63

February 10th, Z – 81 Days
Buenos Aires, Argentina

Each satcom included a state-of-the-art video cell phone that used standard text messaging to warn the operator of incoming messages. To connect the satcom to the CIA's Intranet and retrieve secure messages, the operator plugged a mini satellite dish to the satcom and pointed it in a direction dependent on whether it was in the northern or southern hemisphere.

Several minutes after 3 a.m. Harry's cell phone alerted him of an incoming secure message with the sound of a single beep followed by the vibration of the phone against the wooden cabinet. Harry stirred from a light sleep in his comfortable hotel bed and reached for the phone to his left.

Tess also stirred. She anticipated the identical sound and vibration that erupted seconds later from the phone to her right. Tess reached out too.

'Maybe we should change one of the alert tones,' said Harry sleepily as he hauled himself up.

'Maybe we should lower the volume at night,' replied Tess. 'These are loud enough to wake the folks next door.'

As they each began to read their identical messages, both phones shrilled again, denoting the receipt of another message.

'Just in case we slept through the first?' offered Tess.

'They probably forgot something,' replied Harry, unimpressed.

They fumbled with their phones and cleared the brief text messages. Without another word the two operatives got up. Harry covered his nakedness with his bathrobe, grabbed his satcom, then slid open the balcony door and placed the case on the wooden table. For several seconds he marvelled at the stillness of the well-lit streets of Buenos Aires and enjoyed the fresh, light breeze in his face before erecting his mini-dish to face outward from the north-facing balcony. Then he connected it to his satcom, switched the notebook on and waited for it to boot up and dial-in.

Tess returned from her room through the inner connecting door carrying her satcom. She was dressed in her bathrobe with her hair now shaken from its plait. Without saying a word she joined Harry on the balcony and set up her satcom and mini-dish at the other end of the table. As she waited, her eyes were drawn over the seventh-floor balcony and she admired the cosmopolitan appearance and calmness of Buenos Aires at this early hour.

Harry glanced up and saw her looking around them.

'Argentina has a promising future. Nice people, too, providing you hang on to your wife.'

Tess smiled.

'I have both messages on my satcom, I'll take the first.' Harry suggested as Tess continued to wait for her satcom to dial-in to the CIA's Intranet.

It was common practice among security services the world over to provide unidentified and most-wanted suspects with codenames. The first message informed Harry that a codename had been assigned by MI6 to the unidentified male, possibly known as Malik, who had dined with Baloch and was placed at Baloch's home. His female dining partner had also been assigned a codename, though her significance to MI6 was currently restricted to aiding the identification of the unidentified male. The male was to be known as 'Fox' and the female 'Vixen'.

The second message, first read by Tess, had been sent from Langley and copied to London. It informed them that the cell phone call made by Baloch to his family home in Islamabad had been made from the La Boca neighbourhood of Buenos Aires. A map was attached to the electronic message that marked the locations of the phone masts that were used during the call. The operating area of each mast was sketched onto the map, each interlocking with the other. The message stated that there was a ninety-seven-per-cent probability that the call had been made from a static location from somewhere within the interlocking operating areas. The interlocking area was remarkably small.

Tess looked over her screen at Harry. 'The Agency has

triangulated Baloch's cell phone call. They believe it was made within a couple of blocks in the La Boca neighbourhood.'

'That's great.' Harry's mind assimilated the possibilities. 'We've received codenames for the man and woman too.'

As a precautionary measure, each operative checked all messages received by their own satcom before saving them, even if they considered their partner had dealt with it.

'Nifty names,' expressed Tess as she opened then quickly scanned the first electronic message.

'That's Sir Michael. He believes people will find simple names more memorable. There was a case where two codenames got switched. Now that was a buggers' muddle. The Russians launched a global manhunt for one of their own undercover agents, and handed classified information about Russian mineral reserves to a Moscow warlord. I'll tell you about it sometime. It was a simple mistake, a simple misinterpretation.'

After packing up the equipment, they withdrew to Harry's bug-free room and closed the sliding door to the balcony. Only then did they speak about the way ahead. Despite the hour they decided to contact Encizo immediately and inform him of the breakthrough.

As they had hoped, Encizo was thrilled and demanded immediate action. He decided to have Counter Subversion and Counter-terrorist Center surveillance teams on the ground covering the entire area by 5:30 a.m. and organised a briefing for everyone involved for 4:30 a.m. at the ASS headquarters. Harry and Tess were to produce an overlay map beforehand, and they were both to attend the briefing.

The two operatives quickly dressed and drove to their office, reaching it in less than ten minutes. Harry searched and found some map marking pens in a desk drawer while Tess obtained sufficient clear plastic overlay. Taking Harry's satcom they walked down to the briefing room with its large-scale up-to-date street map of Buenos Aires that hung on a mobile map board. The area of Buenos Aires they required was in the middle right of the display. As Harry opened the electronic message with the map attachment, Tess fixed the overlay onto the map. Harry watched as Tess carefully marked out the boundary of each operating area.

'I guess we start by searching the interlocking area and work outwards,' offered Tess.

Harry was standing beside her, studying the evolving area, thinking. Before Harry could answer, Encizo entered the room accompanied by Maxim and several of his chiefs.

'What do you think, Harry?' Encizo asked, knowing Harry would be prepared with some ideas.

Harry had the beginnings of a plan, a low-profile cordon and search operation. 'It looks like an industrial area of six warehouses or factories in the La Boca district. It should be quiet at this hour. We have three groups of teams. The first group maintain tight covert surveillance of the entire area starting immediately. Eight teams of two will be sufficient to cover every access route. The second group of six teams of two investigates the factories. Each team investigates one factory, its ownership, its security, purpose, key holders and so on. The third group is the Metro armed response. Two armed SWAT teams must be stood by to gain entry and make the arrests, to be immediately followed by crime scene techs. Afterward Metro will need to go knocking on doors, question everyone in the vicinity.'

'Each factory should be considered contaminated, and everyone will need a picture of Baloch,' added Tess.

'Metro will want jurisdiction,' confirmed Maxim.

'And they can have it,' responded Encizo, more interested in the result than the glory. 'I would like Metro to set up a tight outer cordon, before people start turning in for work. Ops like this never stay secret for long, Harry, not here. Metro will need to handle the press with a cover story. I will speak to the Commander of Metro's Special Branch first, then the Commissioner. The Commissioner's Office tends to overreact, and when it comes to the press they leak like a sieve.'

As they continued to discuss the finer details of the plan, the briefing room filled with ASS agents.

Two hours later the operation was unfolding. The six locations had been investigated and they had had a hit. One of the sites, a disused meat-processing factory managed by a real estate agent, had recently been let on a short-term lease under an alias. The real estate office manager for whom Jamali's daughter Nadia worked had given a description of Jamali and identified him as the tenant. Since Jamali was one of Baloch's assassins, the connection had been made. It transpired that the tenant was midway through a three-month pre-purchase letting agreement and that all services to the property were up and running under the same alias. Despite the early hour the real estate agent had provided sufficient information, including accurate and detailed floor plans, to satisfy the investigating team. Oddly, no one thought to question Nadia who, throughout the entire period of investigation, had been left to sleep.

The ASS surveillance teams that had been redeployed to overlook every angle of the factory had reported no movement. The factory appeared deserted, but no one was certain. One person in each of the security firms employed to guard the two neighbouring factories had chatted recently to security men guarding Iguazú and were aware of some activity, but neither of them had noticed anything untoward. One guard remembered he had heard the premises were to be purchased then levelled to make way for luxury apartments as had happened extensively at Puerto Madero. No, they did not know who the occupants were or whether anyone was still there.

The terrorist cell, believed to number two or more, was considered heavily armed and highly dangerous. Metro's Special Branch controlled the assault which involved establishing an inner cordon around the immediate area, securing the ground using police snipers, securing the air space with several police helicopters and sending in a Special Weapons and Tactics team to apprehend the hostiles. The police commissioner was to handle the press consistent with a raid on a holed-up armed criminal gang, for that was the cover story. Regardless of the real outcome, the assault was to have been reported as too late, and the factory found deserted.

Now, a single SWAT team comprising eight heavily armed men were stood-by in their final assault positions to conduct a weapons-tight entry on the factory complex known as Iguazú. It was approaching 8 a.m., the time of the attack. They were overlooked by six police snipers who between them had all possible enemy firing positions covered. Despite the daylight, the electricity was cut off as the attack commenced. A pair of men abseiled down a high building adjacent to the premises as another pair negotiated a wall at the rear of the building. Both routes were obscured from view from within the building. Two more pairs approached seconds later in a low-flying helicopter hovering for ten seconds at either end of the main building as the men abseiled down onto the roof. Off-loaded, the assault helicopter immediately returned to its pick-up point leaving police helicopters to maintain control of the airspace above the target. The attack would only become weapons-free if any one of the highly trained police officers assaulting the building considered it necessary. No one did. In ninety seconds all buildings and rooms had been cleared and secured and not a concussion grenade had been used nor a weapon fired. The terrorists were gone.

Encizo, Harry and Tess watched the assault unfold with a number of other onlookers from the rear of the command vehicle, a truck known as CV1, that was parked beside an identical truck in the yard of a neighbouring factory. The second truck, CV2, was responsible for controlling the inner cordon and administration, while CV1 controlled the assault itself. On the far wall of CV1, above a bench, was a bank of fourteen small colour monitors, and underneath the bench were banks of recording machines, all whirring away with red lights glowing. On the left a group of six monitors screened static pictures of the outside of the factory, the same picture as the arc of fire available to each sniper, and on the right, a second group of eight monitors each received a picture from a camera that each member of the SWAT team had fastened to his helmet. An operator sat in front of each group of monitors keeping their eyes fastened on their screens. The lone assault commander stood behind them with a headset, his eyes everywhere. No one dared stand close. If the commander wanted to speak to the outside world, he would turn around or use one of the available communications devices.

Harry felt the relief flood the CV, a relief that was quickly followed by disappointment. No people killed, no booby traps, but no enemy.

The assault commander turned around to the spectators that included his divisional commander and the local Metro commander and gave the all clear for Metro to take over the security of the old factory. The Metro commander immediately left the CV barking orders as he went. Moments later the assault commander spoke into his headset mic and gave the command for the assault team to withdraw. Harry soon heard the approaching helicopter then watched it hover just above the roof as the eight men climbed in. Soon it had spirited them away as fast as they had come, just as he had done years before in the SAS.

A group comprising Encizo, Harry, Tess and four of Encizo's chiefs walked over to the factory and waited outside the gate that was open to allow authorised vehicles in and out. An apologetic Metro patrolman standing guarding the gate informed them he was under strict orders not to let anyone in other than crime scene techs. Encizo nodded his acceptance and watched patiently as he saw a couple of techies carry in some crates marked with biohazard warning signs.

After thirty long minutes Encizo was politely informed by the patrolman that they had been given the all-clear and could enter. Encizo thanked the officer and the group split up, visually inspecting the empty factory inside and out, including the office accommodation, the loading bay, the meat-processing floor and the large refrigeration hut, careful not to interfere as the crime-scene techs conducted their meticulous work.

They all met where Harry stood at one end of a large cold store located inside the factory, in what Harry assumed to be the main butchery shed. He saw that the cold store was built like a long, rectangular ammunition bunker with steel doors large enough to be driven into with a fork-lift truck. It was brick-built and lead-lined, at least at one end. The large steel doors at each end had been swung open, and the far end resembled a building site for someone had stripped much of the lead lining. At the same end a number of crime-scene techs wearing latex gloves were working under the harsh electric glare of a half-dozen mobile arc lamps. Others were busy taking photographs, while six techs wearing white disposable overalls were on their hands and knees, moving up the hut in a line, sweeping the floor for the smallest trace of evidence.

'They were here,' stated Tess.

No one disagreed.

'They lived and worked here,' she added.

Some nodded their agreement, others stood still, but no one disagreed.

'It looks as though it's been sterilised,' observed one of the chiefs. 'I'm betting forensics won't find much.'

Encizo found it hard to deal with his disappointment. 'I agree, but there should be enough to confirm their presence at least, maybe even assist with identification of Fox and Vixen. Whoever cleaned up will not be able to deceive our forensics. Obstruct them, perhaps. I don't suppose the terrorists ever thought we would actually find this place.'

Harry grimaced as he looked down. 'They never clean the drains.'

The group looked towards several unfortunate technicians who were preparing to take swabs from the drains. No one in their right mind fancied burrowing into the drains and sewers of an old meat-processing factory.

'Any one care to guess why they came here?' asked Encizo tightly.

Harry's voice was determined. 'Fresh lorry tracks in the loading bay, accommodation, fresh water, excellent security, and above all, this,' he said as he slapped one of the large metallic doors to the cold store. 'Add in the ease with which an Eastern European or Asian can blend into Buenos Aires society unnoticed and the excellent trading links throughout the world and you have your answer.'

'There's more. There's a bathroom, hot water, a kitchen and electricity, even showers,' added Tess. 'It's a regular apartment.'

'But what about the cold store?' asked one of the chiefs.

'It's in the kitchen, stupid,' replied another, causing several of the group to snigger.

A forensic scientist looked up from his work with an annoyed expression.

'Do you see those stacks of loose lead bricks at the far end?' asked Harry quietly as he pointed towards the techs at the far end of the hut.

'Worth a few dollars,' someone quipped.

'There are enough loose bricks to construct a decent-sized lead-lined chamber this end of the hut.'

Tess understood. 'And not for storing half-cuts of meat.'

'Anyone got a Geiger counter?' Harry asked grimly.

Several chiefs looked at their hands, as if expecting the skin to peel off.

Chapter 64

February 15th, Z – 76 Days
London, England

The Prime Minister looked down at his handwritten notes. 'I would like to begin by thanking the Defence Secretary for laying on such a useful visit today. All the presentations were excellent. It was certainly an enlightening visit. I had no idea that, thanks to our Defence Academy, we are the leading nation in Europe on advancements in resilience to disruptive challenges, whether natural, accidental or deliberate.'

Most of the Cabinet had been to Shrivenham in Oxfordshire that morning to visit the Defence Academy, a faculty of Cranfield University. There they received a series of short but intellectual briefings from the country's leading academics in subjects including global security, crisis management, nuclear effects, and security management.

There were general murmurs of agreement from around the Cabinet Room, although the Chancellor, who sat opposite the Prime Minister, mumbled something about media headlines and the Cabinet returning to school.

'Now,' said the Prime Minister. 'You all know our purpose and it's getting late so let's get started.'

The Deputy Prime Minister was first. The Prime Minister had appointed his deputy responsible for the Government's Communications Strategy, and for the Government's own Evacuation Strategy.

'On the whole, Exercise Rapid Response has been well received by the House, the press and, it would appear from polls, the public. The Home Secretary and the Media Emergency Forum working out of Scotland Yard will continue to inform the public of progress. The most significant event will be the point at which the Prime Minister declares the real threat, and the reaction of the public and economy. A top-secret analysis of the country's response to this threat has been conducted by the Home Office, a synopsis of which is included in your folders. It makes grim reading I'm afraid, but it does unequivocally support the decision to withhold the real threat until MI6 has had every opportunity to locate the bomb. It also makes hardnosed recommendations for law and order, price and wage freezes, and the suspension of trading on the Stock Exchange.' The Deputy Prime Minister gave everyone time to find and scan the bullet points. 'Only when absolutely necessary will the Prime Minister inform the House and nation on the real threat, and our plans for tackling it.'

'Any thoughts anyone?' asked the Prime Minister.

'Al-Qa'eda may choose to announce this threat,' said the Chancellor. 'I would if I was them, though perhaps not until the bomb was in place. Question is, will we be ready before they do?'

'We will be as ready as we can be,' the Prime Minister replied grimly.

'I have one other issue,' added the Deputy Prime Minister. 'As we draw closer to Zulu Day the Government will need to evacuate London along with everyone else. It will be the responsibility of each department to move itself out of London, direct to temporary accommodation that Environment has identified across the Midlands. The Environment Secretary has provided a list of locations in your folders. The Prime Minister's Office and the Cabinet Office will be moving to temporary accommodation in Victoria Barracks, Windsor before moving to more permanent accommodation in Birmingham.'

'Will it be necessary to evacuate for Exercise Rapid Response?' asked the Defence Secretary.

'For the exercise only people are to be evacuated, and that includes the sick, homeless, and prisoners,' the Deputy Prime Minister replied.

'If we are required to evacuate London permanently, time and transport will be vital,' stated the Health Secretary. 'Perhaps there should be some form of priority evacuation plan?'

'That's being considered under plans for Operation Enduring Freedom,' responded the Transport Secretary. 'I expect the Government's transport requirements, including the National

Health and Prison services, to be provided by the Armed Forces, and that industry and the public will resource themselves. If necessary, my department will requisition commercial assets and allocate them on a priority basis. We have the whole country to source from and the EU if need be. It will be the biggest lift ever undertaken. Land transport will include road vehicles and trains, and there's the air option with five accessible airports around London. We hope to ship via the Port of London and the River Thames too.'

The Prime Minister noted the time. 'Perhaps we can move on to an update on Operation Enduring Freedom. Foreign Secretary?'

'Thank you, Prime Minister. The terrorist cell of at least one man and one woman codenamed Fox and Vixen have been traced to Buenos Aires where a nuclear bomb-making factory has been found. A Pakistani nuclear scientist known as Doctor Baloch who is linked to al-Qa'eda moved to Argentina soon after the Coalition invasion of Afghanistan. He was found dead several days ago in suspicious circumstances. We believe that nuclear bomb components were imported to Argentina from the Middle East or Asia, and that Doctor Baloch re-engineered them in a local disused factory prior to his death. The bomb is now believed to be en route to the UK by sea. Unfortunately no one has been able to identify the source or current whereabouts of the nuclear weapon.

'Our NATO allies are supporting the Royal Navy with a cordon around Britain that stretches as far as the Caribbean Sea in the south and the Arctic Ocean in the north. It's being run as a covert NATO operation that utilises their standing naval forces, augmented by additional Royal Navy and other ships. There are ten European navies involved, over eighty ships, each conducting board and search operations on any vessel destined for the UK. The results so far have been startling, but no nuclear bomb or radioactive material has been uncovered. I have one final issue, but before I continue I would like to ask if there are any questions.'

'Do we have an ID on Fox or Vixen?' asked the Defence Secretary.

'We have a picture of the woman, that is all. The profiles of the two subjects suggest they are not idealists, militants or suicide bombers but well-educated people who can readily blend into Western society. Neither of them has featured on any of the huge number of terrorist and criminal databases that we, Interpol or the CIA have access to worldwide. We believe that they are mercenaries who were headhunted for this attack. These people have been chosen because of their clean records, for their intelligence, for their Western appearance and, we presume, for their misguided loyalty, ruthlessness and complete disregard for human life.' The Foreign Secretary waited for any further questions but there weren't any.

'My final issue is highly sensitive, but the Prime Minister, Home Secretary and I consider that it's something on which the Cabinet, not Cobra must decide. We all know that there is little doctrine and precious few conventions that govern this nature of total warfare. In short, if we are to maximise our chances of preventing this cataclysmic event we are going to have to play dirty in comparison to a more conventional conflict. As you all know we have employed an ex-Six operative, someone who is prepared to do whatever it takes to not only find the bomb and deactivate it, but find the terrorists and eliminate them. This man has already had considerable success tracking the terrorist cell through Afghanistan and Argentina and we intend to continue to run this physically dangerous special operation, what the spooks call a "Black Op", here in the UK. Winchester will remain under the full control of MI6, but he will be working on MI5's patch. He and his CIA partner will soon be back in the country, both armed of course. It is noteworthy that the CIA now has a "Special Recovery Unit" that eliminates or kidnaps terrorists anywhere around the world, as their legal barriers have been removed. Not wishing to understate this, both the CIA and ourselves intend that this team of two will be our very own highly trained and dependable assassination team on the streets of London and they will do *whatever* it takes to locate the terrorists responsible and discover the whereabouts of the bomb. They will have impunity, and we, if necessary, will have plausible deniability.'

The room was hushed, but the Foreign Secretary sensed no resistance.

'We have discussed the legality or otherwise of such impunity on many occasions in recent years. Many of you will remember the lengthy discussions the Cabinet held over our attempts to eliminate the presidents of Yugoslavia and Iraq, and more recently our "shoot-on-sight" debates when dealing with suicide bombers here in the UK.'

The Prime Minister took up the reins. 'The simple fact is, we have a responsibility to do everything we can to prevent the destruction of London, our economic heartland where one third of the country's valuable artefacts and possessions are held. Most importantly, there are over ten million people, and it's their safety and continued well-being, not any perceived rights of terrorists or mercenaries, that are of paramount importance. Current laws, treaties and charters do not adequately cater for this nature of warfare, and neither can we afford to respect the rights of individuals intent on this level of destruction, not until we have stopped them dead in their tracks.'

The Chancellor surprised everyone by speaking up for the Prime Minister and Foreign Secretary. 'Economically speaking our country, our small but highly populated country, will not be able to withstand the destruction of London. I promise you that. These bastards must be stopped, at all costs, or we will slip back five hundred years.'

'We must put our trust in these two operatives,' the Prime Minister continued. 'They are both outstanding, proven operatives and as anxious as we are to avoid bloodshed. That's all I have to say.'

The Cabinet carried the issue unanimously.

'You're aware,' continued the Home Secretary, 'that all entry points to the UK have been reinforced. Every person that enters the UK now requires eye and fingerprints to be taken and every one is checked against UK, US and Interpol records. Unfortunately hand-held Geiger counters are still being rolled out to Customs and Immigration officials and will not be fully deployed for another week. But thanks to the Americans we will soon have enough. The Commissioner is to brief you on progress with Exercise Rapid Response at the next Cabinet meeting, and among the wealth of issues, he will inform you about progress with obtaining a footprint of all radiological emissions in London, to be established during the thirty-six hours that the capital is evacuated. He will also have several issues that will require Cabinet approval.

'The first we have already anticipated. He requires support from the Armed Forces to the tune of twenty thousand servicemen.

Many will come from the Territorial Army and Reservists. Support requirements include the provision of radiological search teams, decontamination teams, cordon and road-block security, provision of temporary accommodation for the homeless beyond that which local authorities around the country can provide, fire and ambulance support, transport and traffic support, and so on. Gold Group and the Defence Crisis Management Organisation have already drawn up preliminary plans that Cobra have approved.'

'And you have left the neighbouring authorities to Greater London intact?' asked the Prime Minister.

'Yes, we have.'

'We should seek parliamentary approval for the additional numbers of TA and Reservists required, but that shouldn't be a problem,' added the Defence Secretary. 'With them, the Ministry of Defence can meet the Commissioner's requirements from our own resources and with few additional penalties. So far we have two-thirds of the Royal Navy assigned or reassigned to the NATO cordon operation and six thousand service personnel who live in London have returned home on leave. What is currently taxing us is the cost of invoking martial law over the Greater London region should we ever have the need, including military involvement in a post-nuclear scenario. In the latter case, the NATO Secretary General has already offered NATO's unconditional support.

'The Commissioner's second issue,' continued the Home Secretary, 'is the authorisation for use of firearms by the police and Armed Forces. I'm already empowered to authorise the police to bear firearms, as is the Commissioner, albeit with some limitations. Should the Prime Minister or Parliament approve the deployment of troops to aid the civil powers, then the Cabinet should authorise the use of firearms by those service personnel. We will be debating this issue at the next Cabinet meeting.

'My final point involves internment. It may prove necessary to arrest and detain suspected terrorists, looters or just plain troublemakers for longer than is currently possible. My department is considering an emergency proposal for us to put to Parliament, which will cater for these extraordinary emergency conditions, immediately the real threat becomes known.'

'Thank you, Home Secretary,' said the Prime Minister. 'I look forward to your proposals. I have just one more issue involving communication with the press and public. Other than the terrorists, our greatest enemy in the lead-up to May 2nd will be fear followed by panic. It's vital that all media releases are accurate, honest and timely. You are to ensure that Cobra is kept fully abreast of your departments' operations in order that they can be accurately coordinated and projected at the Media Emergency Forum.

Chapter 65

February 15th, Z – 76 Days
13° 9′ N 56° 17′ W, North Atlantic Ocean

Commander Miguel Nicanor of the Portuguese Navy stood on the bridge of his command, the recently commissioned frigate PONS *Vasco da Gama*. The captain was watching a seaman sitting transfixed by the primary radar screen that was sunk into the station to his front. The badge on the seaman's right arm signified he was a Radar Technician First Class and Nicanor knew him to be very capable and reliable. The orange screen of the radar that swept thirty-six miles in every direction from the ship was littered with bright dots, each highlighting a vessel of differing type.

Out of the historic naval docks at Lisbon, this was the Portuguese fighting ship's second visit to the Americas and Caribbean in this its maiden year. But on this occasion it was not another diplomatic and flag-waving trip. Nor was this unscheduled mission a multinational training exercise, but it represented the ship's first operational voyage as part of NATO's Standing Naval Force Atlantic or STANAVFORLANT. Under the umbrella of supporting the routine counter-drug smuggling ops between the Americas and Europe, the ship had secret orders to intercept any vessel regardless of flag that may hold weapons of mass destruction, conventional weapons, terrorists or illegal aliens bound for the UK. His ship's marine detachment had even been provisioned with hand-held Geiger counters to detect radiation. Although the hunt was easy to explain to his crew in this nuclear age, it meant one thing to the ship's captain, the hunt for a rogue nuclear device.

PONS *Vasco da Gama* was a MEKO 200 type, US-built frigate of 3,200 tonnes. She was approximately 116 metres long, 14 metres in beam and had a draft of over six metres. She had been commissioned ten months ago and was the youngest ship in the Portuguese navy. She was fast too, capable of thirty-two knots from her two gas-turbine engines or twenty knots from her two auxiliary diesel engines. Armed with eight Harpoon surface-to-surface missiles, eight NATO Sea Sparrow missiles for air defence, six torpedoes and an impressive array of guns and cannon ranging from 20 to 100 millimetres and also small arms, she was well-equipped to deal with compliant or non-compliant board and search operations. PNOS *Vasco da Gama* was the pride of the modern Portuguese navy, which had a long heritage of fast, sleek yet well-armed naval ships back to the year 1524.

The primary radar was sufficient for maintaining control of the close operation, but the captain relied on his highly technical operations room in the heart of the ship to provide wider and more detailed radar coverage, deeper sonar, and control of the ship's strike and counter-strike weapons. With three radar systems, radio and satellite communications and additional information from the Naval Operations Headquarters outside Lisbon, the ship's ops room was able to rapidly identify vessels in her area of operations. Those that could not or would not be identified were pursued and dealt with.

PONS *Vasco da Gama* was holding station across a busy sea lane from the Americas to Europe, approximately two hundred miles east of Barbados. She had been on station for thirteen days and to date had identified over four hundred vessels of which thirty-one had been 'suspect' vessels and necessarily boarded. Only one vessel, a 'target' vessel, had to be chased and warning shots had been fired. The target vessel turned out to be a floating bordello, with passengers and crew high on drugs and no one but the autopilot left in charge.

In addition to the floating bordello, the ship's haul had included seventeen uncertified firearms, some explosives, a little over three and a half tonnes of mainly cocaine, one tonne of which had been fished out of the sea, and a smaller quantity of refined drugs, but no nuclear device.

The early-morning sea mist and the listing of a ship going nowhere did not help Nicanor's mood. It promised to be a hot, relatively calm day with good visibility, but right now he had sixteen vessels, over twice the normal number on his radar, and all on a bearing for Europe. He knew that the best way to smuggle across the ocean was to hide among other vessels with more questionable flags, and any one of them could be doing just that. Also, a light, fast vessel could plead ignorance because of poor communications in just three foot of swells, and in international waters would feel untouchable among a number of larger, slower ships. On the other hand, Nicanor knew that his two boarding parties could thoroughly search ten smaller vessels in the time it took to search one larger cargo vessel.

This morning the search was underway of a Syrian-registered cargo vessel owned by an Arab shipping cartel that had departed from Buenos Aires via Caracas and was destined for Southampton. The search would occupy both his boarding crews for at least another three hours. Meanwhile, any vessel intent on smuggling would slip through his thin net, and all he could do was hope that one of the other 115 fighting ships or 415 other coastal vessels employed in this NATO operation was presented an opportunity to board them. If not, then it would be down to the customs officials. It also frustrated Nicanor that the true nature of this classified operation could not be divulged to anyone other than his second-in-command. He felt sure his boarding crews would work more purposefully if they knew more precisely what they were searching for.

Nicanor empowered his operations staff to decide which vessels to search, though occasionally he or his second-in-command picked one for themselves, often on nothing more than instinct. Choosing the most likely smuggler was not an exact science. Nicanor knew that NATO's current hope was that the net was deep enough across the breadth of the oceans and seas to frustrate the smugglers into a nervous reaction or mistake, and thereby signal their presence. It was surprising how many smugglers gave themselves away by running. Either that or NATO receive some intelligence, a tip-off maybe.

To help Nicanor decide whether a vessel was suspect or not, he listened to the international radio channel, VHF Channel 16, and then other channels as required. VHF Channel 16 was patched through to one of a bank of loudspeakers hanging from the bridge bulkhead as well as to a speaker hanging in his quarters next door. Nicanor would listen in and gauge the verbal response of the vessel under examination.

Nicanor walked over to the radar technician and looked down at the radar screen which identified the next target. He watched for any sudden change in course. At the same time, he listened intently to the forthcoming Right of Approach questions from his ops room, broadcast in English.

'Hello, unidentified vessel at thirteen degrees nine minutes north, fifty-six degrees seventeen minutes west, travelling on bearing thirty-three degrees, at speed ten knots. This is Portuguese Naval Ship *Vasco da Gama*. Our position is three miles due east of your current position. Please acknowledge, over.'

The radio traffic had been busy that morning, but with the request from a warship in the area left open and requiring a response, the international channel remained quiet and obedient. Thirty seconds later the same message echoed around the bridge once again, this time in Spanish. There was no need for impatience, the delay in response was quite normal. On the third request, once more in English, there was an immediate response in what sounded to Nicanor as an unmistakeable English accent.

'Hello, *Vasco da Gama*, this is *Last Tango*, over.'

'Thank you, *Last Tango*, please switch to VHF Channel 38 and identify master, port of departure, port of call, flag, passengers and nationality, over.'

Seconds passed and the situation remained entirely normal. The captain was passed a steaming mug of coffee as he listened out for a response through another speaker that had been hastily reset to VHF Channel 38.

Meanwhile, down in the ops room another radio operator from the cramped bank of eight operators took control of this conversation as the first operator remained on VHF Channel 16 and addressed the next vessel on his list.

'Hello, *Vasco da Gama*, this is *Last Tango*, a pleasure cruiser. The master and owner is Mr Sean Kent, Bridgetown, bound for Gibraltar. We are London-registered and have six passengers, two British and four Argentines over.'

'Thank you, *Last Tango*, maintain course and reduce speed to two knots. Stand by, over.'

Without Right of Innocence passage that a vessel would normally enjoy in territorial waters of up to twelve miles off shore, any civilian vessel had no choice but to obey or risk becoming a target vessel.

'Roger, *Vasco da Gama*, maintaining course and reducing speed to two knots. Standing by, out.'

The Operations Officer, who stood behind the bank of radio operators in the ops room considered the information for a moment, saw nothing immediately suspicious, and in accordance with standard operating procedures he ordered a third radio operator in constant contact with Lisbon to verify registration and ownership. The operator could also have demanded verification on the port of departure, but given their current proximity to Bridgetown it seemed superfluous. The Portuguese Naval Operations Centre outside Lisbon routinely checked flag and ownership of *Last Tango* with the Royal Navy's command centre at the Permanent Joint Headquarters based at Northwood outside London.

With dozens of requests for checks to be made from a large number of Royal Naval ships across the Atlantic, it was thirty minutes before a reply was received via Lisbon. *Last Tango*, which had by now passed PONS *Vasco da Gama*, was circling obediently. The registration and ownership of *Last Tango* was confirmed, and in the midst of seven other incomplete radio conversations, the radio operator working the *Last Tango* was ordered to stand the vessel down.

'Hello, *Last Tango* this is PONS *Vasco da Gama*. Thank you for waiting. You may stand down. Have a good voyage, over.'

'Thank you, *Vasco da Gama*, roger-out,' the English voice replied.

For a brief moment Nicanor pondered over the vessel's registration and Argentine passengers, but she had been entirely compliant. He felt no unease, unlike the lumbering cargo vessel he could just make out in the mist, three points to starboard.

For as long as the search of the Syrian-registered cargo vessel continued, PONS *Vasco da Gama* was fully employed. Within minutes *Last Tango* was forgotten when a heat-seeking device uncovered six unregistered Arab passengers hidden in a shipping container with two tonnes of cocaine, five hundred kilograms of plastic explosives, one hundred thousand US dollars in cash, and a large cache of unlicensed small arms and ammunition.

Chapter 66

February 20th, Z – 71 Days
Buenos Aires, Argentina

The last few days had been frustrating for Argentina's Counter Subversion and Counterterrorist Centre. Their only material breakthrough had been to establish matches between three sets of fingerprints found at the restaurant with identical sets found in the factory. These prints were known to belong to Doctor Baloch and the as-yet unidentified Fox and Vixen. Although the Argentine Security Service had a record of Jamali's prints they had not been found at either location.

Since the discovery of the bomb-making factory law enforcement agencies throughout Argentina had been conducting a nationwide search for Jamali and the unidentified man and woman. However, the intelligence was sparse. Police forces had little more than an electronically enhanced but inadequate CCTV picture captured by a street camera some way from the one restaurant the terrorists were known to have used, plus a host of contradictory identikit pictures and the fingerprints.

Encizo had deduced that they were looking for two global terrorists and that the deceased Baloch, although a terrorist, had been no more than a temporary and expendable addition to the cell. Similarly, support to the cell in Argentina had been organised by the local man Jamali, who was now wanted on terrorism charges as well as for the murder of Doctor Baloch.

With the information they had, Argentine Immigration officials had searched back three months through the records of all known arrivals and departures into Argentina, but there was no match with their description of the Fox. Nor was there any evidence of any of them departing the country.

However, yesterday evening the Vixen's entry into the country may have been found. According to the ASS's powerful indentikit computer software, the same equipment that was used by the CIA, MI6 and Interpol, there were only three women who had entered the country in the last three months and could match the Vixen's blurred features on the CCTV footage with a ninety per-cent probability or higher. Agents had quickly traced and questioned two of the women and they had proven genuine. The third woman had travelled under the identity of a middle-aged Pakistani woman to Argentina for the first time on January 2nd and had been provided with a ninety day visitor's visa. There was no record of her residence, or departure.

His heart racing, Encizo reread the urgent message from the Pakistan ISI that stated the middle-aged woman had in fact died four months ago at the age of thirty-six in a motor vehicle accident somewhere in Karachi. Apparently the death certificate had not been requested. He buzzed for Harry and Tess who had also just arrived at their office for another day and were about to recommence sifting through videotapes and other evidence from the Hyatt Hotel, Doctor Baloch's home, the Iguazú Factory and elsewhere. They hadn't relished the prospect and both rose gratefully from their chairs and hurried to the Director's office.

'We've heard back from Pakistan. Our third woman was killed *four* months ago.' Encizo handed Harry the facsimile message received overnight from Pakistan. 'The passport is false but it's difficult to see how her features could have been altered.'

'It's a certainty that she's our Vixen,' agreed Harry as he read the message then studied the headshot provided by Argentine Immigration. Encizo was right, thought Harry. The facial features of the person entering the country were indisputably clear and striking.

'But that headshot doesn't come up on any of the searches,' replied Encizo in frustration. 'Interpol, CIA, MI6, nothing!'

'We shouldn't be surprised after zero results from the prints. These people are professionals, of that we can be certain.'

'But few professionals of this calibre are unknown everywhere,' added Tess disbelievingly.

'I agree. It's most likely that she has no criminal record, and that whatever electronic records may have existed anywhere have been removed,' Harry puzzled, thinking he might discuss this theory with London. 'I'm afraid that might be a dead end, for now at least.'

'I'll have the picture distributed immediately,' Encizo stated, pleased that Vixen's image if not identity had been established from the line of enquiry.

At 9 a.m. Encizo, Harry and Tess went to the briefing room as usual. With the exception of the message received from the Pakistan ISI, which was met with a chorus of 'I told you so', the briefing was depressingly void of new leads. The daily briefing could have been over in just two minutes but Encizo had other ideas.

'It's been several days now since we discovered the factory and we have nothing on their current whereabouts. We believe they have achieved what they intended in Buenos Aires and although we originally thought they would intend to hide here a while longer, with Doctor Baloch's murder they may consider the risk of capture too great. Therefore I believe it's probable they have left Argentina, despite our tight border controls.'

There were mumbles of agreement and Tess saw Harry nod. He had come to the same conclusion.

'Perhaps they are in the United Kingdom already?' asked Maxim.

'They could be, but I doubt it unless they flew and I don't see how they could have passed airport security,' replied Encizo, 'but I still consider they are unlikely to want to spend too much time in London before they deliver the bomb, and they will not wish to do that until nearer the time of detonation. More likely they have decided to stop off somewhere en route, mainland Europe perhaps.'

'And the bomb?' continued Maxim.

'The Army have been searching the district for several days and found nothing. I believe the terrorists have removed the bomb. On the one hand, even a terrorist may want to keep his distance from a nuclear bomb. On the other, they would want to keep the bomb close until they reach its final resting place. But the fact is, as we continue to search for the terrorists here, they and their bomb could have left the country.'

Encizo sighed and looked over at Harry. 'I think London should face the greater probability.'

Harry nodded in agreement.

'There are so many ways that one or more people could leave our country,' said Maxim, 'but less for the safe and secure transportation of a nuclear bomb.'

'I agree. How would you do it?' Encizo asked him directly.

'I would accompany the bomb and not attempt to fly the Atlantic Ocean. Maybe travel across the border by land or maybe charter a small plane, then I would send the package by sea. Yes, I would slip across the border then make shipping arrangements from somewhere in Uruguay.'

'So either send the bomb by sea and fly across yourself, or take a cruise and accompany the bomb,' Encizo summarised. 'Anyone else any ideas?'

The assembled group of forty staff considered the multitude of options.

Harry spoke up, seeing where this was leading. 'I think it more likely the terrorists will accompany the bomb and protect its passage. This means a cruise, for which they have time. But to where I have no idea. They could attempt to sail or even drive into England from anywhere in Europe.'

'I agree,' said Tess. 'They would not risk flying transatlantic. They would have to travel by ship or boat, commercial or private.'

'OK,' said Encizo. 'So they take an oceangoing vessel from Argentina or Uruguay across the Atlantic. Where are we with our check on all shipping departing Buenos Aires?'

A section chief in the middle of the assembly stood up, someone known for his humour no matter how dire the circumstances. He was an expert in counter-smuggling operations. 'The port authorities are already doing everything they can to search shipping and cargo leaving Argentina. Immigration is checking every crewman and passenger leaving the country too. But,' he smiled, 'the system is not watertight.'

People groaned at the poor attempt to joke, then laughed at his discomfort.

The amusing chief battled on, used to the ribbing. 'Shipping is far less secure than flying, though you can rule out cruise liners because their security is comparable to airports. It will always be easier to smuggle something on a cargo ship, in a shipping container, perhaps one destined for the heart of London. The port authorities are already doing all that they can. But this is not the easiest and most dependable option for the terrorists because shipments can be unreliable and planning a shipment involves time and people. Small transatlantic jets can take off from private airstrips all over the country but flights are registered and monitored by air traffic controllers, and any flight that leaves our airspace can be searched immediately it lands. The same cannot be said for private motor cruisers or yachts. Thousands of yachts leave the country each day from hundreds of boatyards and many do not register their departure. Nevertheless, boatyards are being questioned about our three suspects but so far, nothing.'

'A private yacht does seem the most likely option,' stated Encizo. 'How long before every boatyard is investigated?'

'In the country?'

'Starting with those closest to Buenos Aires, yes.'

'It'll take three weeks to complete working flat out. There are thousands of boatyards, small harbours, jetties and private moorings.'

Encizo considered this for a moment. 'We must try. I want to find their method of departure, the name of a boat, something. I believe that the terrorists have fled our country and that they have taken the bomb with them. Maybe Jamali has gone too, I don't know. It's most likely that they intend to cross the Atlantic by boat, probably a private boat. I want to know how and when the terrorists departed Argentina, starting with private shipping then inland border crossings. Am I clear?'

Everyone nodded.

'Do we contact our neighbours?' Maxim asked.

'No. We cannot involve other countries any more than we already have. We cannot risk a leak. If we find nothing internally, then we have come to the end of the road.'

Back in his office Encizo looked forlorn. He turned to Harry and Tess. 'You know what I'm going to say. We know when Vixen entered the country, but not Fox. We also know the true identity of Jamali and what Vixen looks like. But that's all we know for sure, other than that the threat is real. There are hundreds of ways each or all of them may have left this country. There is little else we can do other than maintain the hunt along our border and continue to investigate all other possible means of departure, particularly by boat.'

Encizo looked away for a moment. 'We need a stroke of luck over the next couple of weeks, after that the trail will be cold and there will be almost nothing more I can do. Then, you may be better off searching in England or Europe.'

'There is already a massive cordon and search operation underway across the Atlantic by NATO,' Harry remarked.

'Let's hope they are lucky. What will you do?'

'There's not much that Tess and I can do in England at the moment. If it's OK with you we would like to stay on the trail for now.'

'I would be sorry to see you go.' Encizo looked pleased that they were staying. 'The least we should do is determine how these bastards left our country.'

'Assuming they have,' added Harry.

'In truth, we've learnt a considerable amount,' Tess offered flatly. 'The intelligence, particularly Jamali's identity and Vixen's image, will help us find them.'

Early in the afternoon Harry and Tess left for the hotel and went for a run but it did nothing to ease their frustration. In the deserted hotel gym they each did a hundred push-ups, then the same amount of sit-ups, sweat dripping from their toned bodies. They practised several martial arts moves before swimming and showering.

Later that evening they discussed the way ahead and found themselves agreeing with everything that Encizo and his team had said at the morning briefing. Both the CIA and MI6 taught their operatives that the best place to begin or continue a manhunt was at the end of the trail. Agreeing between them that they should stay on to exhaust all possible leads before returning to England, they informed London.

London agreed that the two operatives were to continue to assist the ASS with their investigations and find out when and how the terrorist cell and nuclear bomb left the country.

Chapter 67

February 21st, Z – 70 Days
FBI Headquarters, Washington DC, USA

From its inception in 1908 as the Bureau of Investigation the offices of the Federal Bureau of Investigation had been housed in the Department of Justice Building and eight other locations across Washington. This was impractical and expensive, so in 1962 Congress approved a new FBI Headquarters, and the following year a site was found in north-west Washington bounded by Pennsylvania Avenue and E Street and North and Tenth Streets. The Headquarters of the FBI moved into the new building in 1975 when it was dedicated by President Ford. The building had been officially named through Public Law as the J. Edgar Hoover FBI Building, signed by President Nixon two days after Director Hoover's death in 1972.

Because major parades marched down Pennsylvania Avenue, all new buildings were required to have open first floors to accommodate spectators. The new FBI Headquarters was to be no exception, especially as it was the first Government building to be erected on the revived north side. A pipe dream in 1962, the north side of the Avenue was now lined with shops and buildings with open arcades and courtyards.

The FBI Headquarters building had an open mezzanine and courtyard, but access to the courtyard was limited, and most of the ground floor was closed to facilitate security. Recessed concrete panels along the ground floor were spaced to give the illusion of two-storey columns, thus producing an arcade-like façade. With over seven thousand employees, the building along Pennsylvania Avenue reached the maximum allowable seven storeys and along E Street it reached eleven.

Special Agent Clinton Blake had been one of the first FBI employees to move into the new building in the summer of 1975, thirteen years after Congress had approved construction on the Pennsylvania Avenue site. Approaching full retirement, Blake had worked with the FBI in a number of differing roles since 1970 and was one of the few remaining employees to have worked in the Department of Justice Building. He was also one of the few special agents who had received a letter from the President in recognition of his long and dedicated service.

Blake considered that, with the exception of the growth in the FBI's counterterrorism and cyber work, the primary role of the FBI had changed little over the years. The FBI was responsible to the Attorney General and Department of Justice for investigations into violations of federal criminal law and to protect the United States from foreign intelligence and terrorist activities in a manner that was faithful to the Constitution. To achieve this task, the FBI Headquarters was supported by fifty-six field offices and four specialised field installations, as well as forty foreign liaison posts known as legal attachés.

The organisation included eleven thousand special agents and another sixteen thousand support personnel. But even after thirty-five years of service Blake had remained low in the pecking order. He had always been a loyal and steadfast employee of the Federal Government but had been unable to check his growing resentment that he, like many other specialists, had been bypassed for promotion by the politically motivated mainstream agents they called 'vultures'.

Blake could recall the first banks of computers being installed among the central core of files in the main part of the building facing E Street and remembered it was 1977 when he first joined that elite band of twenty explorers. Apart from three years in the Training and Development Division at Quantico, Virginia, where he taught cybernetics at the FBI Training Academy, he had spent his career at the FBI Headquarters. He was almost always found in his office, but that was the nature of his specialism within the field of cybernetics, the science of communication by computer. In his sizeable office which he shared with one colleague he had some of the most powerful computers in the world, and from them he was able to investigate cyber crimes wherever he chose. Now called the Cyber Division, it was some three-hundred-strong and benefited not only through the synergy created by amalgamating the nation's top cyber agents but by the centralisation of some of the world's most powerful information-technology systems. Essentially the Cyber Division coordinated, supervised and facilitated the FBI's investigations of those federal violations in which the Internet, computer systems and networks were exploited as the principal instruments of criminal, foreign intelligence or terrorist activity.

Blake was charged with investigating computer-related crimes involving both criminal acts and national security issues. Examples of criminal acts would be using a computer to commit fraud, or using the Internet to transmit obscene material. In the national security area, the FBI investigated criminal matters involving the nation's computerised banking and financial systems, the various '911' emergency networks and also the plethora of telecommunications systems. Blake was one of the division's most experienced operatives, and usually, during his mid-term or end-of-year appraisal interview, he was told by his young manager that he was being retained in the department because people with his skills were rare. Blake knew that he could command a much higher wage outside the FBI, but he did not want to change careers; he simply wanted to be recognised, valued and rewarded. What he always asked, but never got an answer to, was why did he not receive commensurate pay for his experience, and why did the FBI managers get paid so much more than their peers who were doing the actual work – investigating? After all it was the agents who always took the full responsibility for their investigations; the managers were simply that, not leaders. Of course, the FBI had pay bandings in each rank and trade, but the relevant increments were pitifully low and in Blake's opinion did not reflect ability, experience or responsibility. Despite his near constant complaints, his work was held in the highest regard by the Director FBI, the legendary Bill Darling. Sadly, the line managers had never told Blake.

The FBI's Counterterrorism Division consolidated all federal counterterrorism initiatives and worked closely with the Counter-terrorist Center at Langley. Among a vast array of counterterrorist tasks the Division's primary responsibilities were to detect, disrupt and dismantle terrorist sleeper cells in the US before they acted, to prevent acts of terrorism by individuals with a terrorist agenda acting alone or in a group, and to target terrorist support networks in the US, including their financial support networks that by their nature lay across the world.

The CIA's Counterterrorism Center and FBI's Counterterrorism Division often sought the assistance of the Cyber Division as it was here that the country's top cyber security experts investigated global networks in order to disrupt federal violations and protect the US homeland.

On receiving the case, it had been immediately clear to the Assistant Director, Cyber Division who should lead it. Although they would continue to work out of the FBI Headquarters, Blake and whatever team he required were reassigned immediately to Operation Enduring Freedom. The significance of the operation became clearer to Special Agent Blake the moment he received a briefing on the operation at Langley.

Until now Blake had been working on the decoding of a robust encryption system, a system used by one of the top three US defence contractors whose directors who were believed to be communicating with countries embargoed by the US Government despite their public denials. Blake knew that for every cyber code there must be a decode programme, but the harsh reality was that, unless you knew the code, there were only two methods to break it. The first was to place a chip into the transmitting computer that would send the decoded message or the code itself to him. He had used this method successfully when the US sold computer systems to Iraq in the early years of Saddam Hussein's regime, but for this case they had had no premonition. The second and only other method meant getting a copy of the encoded messages, perhaps even a copy of the hard drive, and working out the code. Although Blake did not have a hard drive, he had plenty of messages to work on. Nowadays this method could not be relied upon, unless there was sufficient repetition or mistakes made during the encoding and it was these that he was still waiting for. With a feeling of failure, Blake had reluctantly passed this problem on to the FBI's Investigative Technology Division to see if they could break the code or invent something that would. With that done, Blake had cleared his desk.

Conversely, it had taken Blake just one week to break through the firewall established by the Premier National Bank of Cyprus though already the vultures were beginning to circle when, on the back of a lucky guess, the breakthrough came. Mawdsley had been delighted and relieved, and to Blake's utter amazement he was congratulated first hand by the Director who personally visited Blake in his office. It was at this moment that Blake truly appreciated just how important Operating Enduring Freedom was to global security. This breakthrough was the catalyst, and as the floodgates opened Blake and his growing team of cyber experts worked around the clock to unscramble a global web of terrorist funding by backtracking every transaction.

Rebecca Greenberg had been a journalist for the *Washington Post* for twenty years this summer. Divorced twice, she began dating Clinton Blake, who was ten years her senior, two years ago. They enjoyed a mutually convenient relationship, particularly in Washington where, unlike any other city in the world, if you were not involved in politics or crime or a combination of both, your prospects were limited. Greenberg, wanting to avoid marriage for a third time, and Blake, who had never been married, sold their shabby apartments, and together they purchased a larger, more luxurious apartment off Pennsylvania Avenue just two blocks from 935 Pennsylvania Avenue, the Headquarters of the FBI.

At the same time and by coincidence, Greenberg received the first real break of her long and undistinguished career when her savvy editor informed her she was to go and work full-time in the White House. The effect of having over one thousand journalists from all over the world working in and around the White House could not be underestimated by any reporter, and Greenberg knew that to succeed she would have to be patient and when an opportunity arose, ruthless. Within this number, just twelve worked for the largest newspaper in the District of Columbia, her newspaper, the *Washington Post*. Although delighted with her new role, Greenberg was still waiting for her first big scoop and her editor was already beginning to wonder whether her relationship with an FBI Special Agent actually warranted her position, or whether she should return to the street.

As Blake and Greenberg dressed and had breakfast on another cold, gloomy and wet Washington morning, Greenberg scented a story. She would never ask Blake to reveal secrets from his work, but in her increasing desperation for her first breaking story, something truly new that would demonstrate her worth and maybe propel her through the glass ceiling, she was prepared to listen to what he had to say and act upon it. After all, how could any reporter ignore something born out of innocence? Blake, of course, had no deliberate intention of telling stories out of school or for that matter state secrets, but it was easy to consider that the woman he woke up with each morning had his interests and not her own at heart.

Greenberg began the morning's conversation. 'Your toast is ready. Why so many late nights all of a sudden? It was three o'clock when you turned in.'

'Christ, I feel it too,' said Blake blithely as he stepped into the kitchen rubbing his shoulders. 'Did I wake you?'

'Yes, but never mind. I was asleep again in minutes. Coffee?'

'You bet. Have you seen my cuff links?'

'They're on the windowsill. So what's up?'

'Just the usual,' Blake shrugged. 'Another possible terrorist threat that requires cyber support.' He sat down at the small table and bit into his toast.

'Hardly usual,' she smiled, 'I've never known you work beyond seven.'

Mildly irritated with any suggestion that he may be predictable, he cleared his mouth of toast and sipped his coffee. 'We've never had the threat of a nuclear strike before.'

If he'd considered what he'd said for a moment he would have realised his mistake but he did not, and twenty years of experience prevented Greenberg from showing any emotion or excitement.

Not wanting to reveal her eagerness she kept the conversation going as she danced around the kitchen. 'I'm interviewing the First Lady this morning. She's redecorating more state rooms.'

Blake thought for a moment. 'Remember several years ago? Cost two million bucks for four rooms I seem to recall. It caused a national outcry.'

Greenberg smiled. 'This time it's four million, same rooms.'

Blake smirked and walked toward the sink to wash the few dishes. 'What's she doing, covering them in gold leaf?'

'There'll be a reason,' she sighed, 'there always is. How I would rather be you.'

'The grass is always greener on the other side. You'd loathe it. The feeling of always being owned, and working with selfish political vultures, most of them grossly overpromoted.'

'Sounds like the *Washington Post*. Quality doesn't cut it any more. If you want to compete and survive then it's shock and awe you provide, or you get fired. So who or what are those terrorists targeting this time?' asked Greenberg indifferently as she finished her coffee and grabbed a drying cloth.

'Oh,' he replied offhandedly, 'the usual high-calibre targets that represent civilisation. Government buildings, financial institutions and so on, who knows? Law-enforcement targets will not be immune.'

Greenberg feigned a look of concern. 'It's only a matter of time before the Hoover Building is targeted. You must be careful, Clinton.'

Blake gave her a quick hug, holding his wet hands from her back. 'Don't worry yourself unnecessarily. Perhaps London will attract the bastards' attention, and not the Eastern Seaboard.'

With the apartment tidy, they made their separate ways to work, Greenberg via the subway and Blake on foot.

As Greenberg journeyed towards Georgetown, she considered what she knew, or thought she knew. With all her years of experience as a journalist, nothing had prepared her for such a potentially explosive story, one which she felt the public had every right to know. If terrorists were to target a nuclear weapon on US interests, as she assumed, then this story could be big, bigger than anything she or anyone else had ever known. Considering Clinton's words and his behaviour, she was certain he was being candid. She had never known him try and outsmart her when talking about his work, or for that matter attempt to mislead her. But how should she proceed? She would not inform her editor, for he would merely overreact and probably pull the story from her anyway. She would rather face being fired. She would interview the First Lady this morning and carefully ask after the President and see, more by her reaction than words, whether anything specific may be troubling him. She would also attend the daily White House press briefing at 11:30 a.m., which the President was to due to attend today. Greenberg smiled to herself as she arrived at her stop for today; for the first time she would have an opportunity to bushwhack the President, without of course giving too much away to anyone including her fellow reporters. Immediately after the press briefing, she would contact her editor with her proposed front-page exclusive.

Greenberg's twenty-minute interview with the First Lady was sufficiently thorough, but provided for a rather dreary feature. It seemed that the annual decoration budget of ten million dollars for the entire White House had not been overspent and that it could cater for the First Lady's latest refurbishment plans. After all, stated the First Lady, who would want the United States to be represented by a tatty White House? Greenberg had bigger fish to fry, so she had continued to pleasantly nod and smile as she prepared for her follow-up questions. There had been hesitation and a defensive reaction when she had enquired about the cause of the current strain that the President appeared to be under. The First Lady covered herself by blaming any apparent strain on a recent bout of food poisoning but then instantly appeared to regret it. Hardly surprising, as the President's health was a matter of continuous public debate and the remark was so blatantly untrue.

By 11:25 a.m. the press room in the White House was full and Greenberg sat near the back, fiddling with her pencil nervously. She had already chatted to a number of journalists and had concluded that there was no other breaking news lurking in the wings. Today the President was to address the press corps on the economy which, along with the war against terror, was dominating this administration. Yesterday afternoon the Chairman of the Federal Bank had forecast a decline in US economic growth for the first time in this administration, causing the Dow Jones to fall a massive 240 points in the day.

The room fell silent as the President, followed by his Chief of Staff, a senior economic advisor and two Secret Service personnel entered the White House press room through the stage entrance to the left of the podium. The President stood behind his famous lectern that was situated centre stage and shuffled his papers before he looked up and offered a calm welcome and warm smile. Silhouetted against the seal of the President of the United States of America, he began to read his prepared response to the Chairman's statement of yesterday afternoon.

Greenberg knew that the entire briefing would last exactly twenty minutes and that intentionally, the President would take up most of the allotted time. There was normally time for at least five questions of which hers must be one. It was vital that she attract the Chief of Staff's attention and be allowed to ask the President a question. In her favour, she had never asked one before.

On time, the President finished extolling the virtues of the current US economic outlook by suggesting that the American economy was to receive a smooth landing to an entirely predictable and expected dip in the economy that lay among a wider period of sustained growth. He answered a related question with ease. As was customary, the questions soon diverged from the President's statement, this being an issue of continual frustration between the Chief of Staff and the White House press corps. With the cameras rolling live for an allotted time, the President had no choice but to answer every question. He could not back away.

'There's time for one more question,' called the Chief of Staff who had already spotted Greenberg and considered her tame; maybe a question about decorating, she thought. A sea of hands swept skyward. 'Ms Greenberg,' she announced, pointing towards the fortunate reporter.

'Yes, Ms Greenberg,' the President added.

The room fell silent as usual. Questions from other reporters were often better than your own.

Like a novice, Greenberg cleared her throat and with obvious nervousness asked her question that she had spent the morning considering. 'Mr President, there's a rumour that there's a possible nuclear strike being planned by terrorists against targets along the Eastern Seaboard or against American interests in London, England...' In the following microsecond the atmosphere in the room changed and she could have heard a pin drop. The air could be cut with a knife as she poised with the killer question. She hoped her editor was watching the live broadcast. '...Will you confirm whether such a threat exists and, if so, why the American public or, for that matter, the British have not been informed?'

This was the first question today regarding the war against terror, and although the President had not expected one, particularly this one, he was always prepared for the unexpected and he was experienced enough to know the pitfalls. With only the tiniest pause, he answered with passion.

'Thank you, Ms Greenberg. I can assure both you and all

Americans that the Department of Homeland Security and all security and law-enforcement agencies throughout the country are constantly on the look out for possible chemical, biological, radiological or nuclear attacks against our mainland or United States interests worldwide or, for that matter, against our allies. We not only look out for worst-case-scenario strikes using WMD but we actively seek the perpetrators of such strikes. As you know, we have excellent warning procedures in place to forewarn the public of any potential strikes through the media, and also the military alert state system across states and districts across our great nation. In principle, I'm a believer in informing the public immediately we know of any terrorist threat in order that they might help by preparing themselves and thus relieve pressure on our first responders and other finite resources. Should I receive definitive information about a particular threat, then be assured, Ms Greenberg, that I will respond in the best interests of our nation, our people and our allies.'

'Thank you, everyone,' said the Chief of Staff curtly, her eyes on fire, 'that will be all.'

The Chief of Staff followed the President as he returned through the corridors and stairs of the White House to the Oval Office. The President always preferred to take the stairs rather than the elevator. Not only did it give people the opportunity to see him, and he them, but it kept him fitter. He was alarmed but not, to the Chief of Staff's relief, angry.

'I want to meet with the National Security Advisor, Director CIA and Director FBI in my office as soon as possible. I will need to speak with the British Prime Minister afterwards by telephone, no later than two o'clock.'

An hour later the four men and one woman were discussing the final minutes of today's press briefing in the Oval Office.

'Not a bad answer, Mr President,' the National Security Advisor offered. 'The rumour will be front page across the states tomorrow of course, though not for the first time.'

The President stiffened. 'If the true facts leak out then the terrorists could dive for cover leaving a nuclear weapon on the loose. They could dump it anywhere they chose. It could also make them more careful and more difficult to catch. If they succeed in bombing London, I don't need to tell you the impact it will have on the world. Hell, it may well start World War III.

I want this bomb found and the bastards caught whatever the cost.'

The room fell silent. The President glanced at each of his advisors, his eyes finally falling on the Director CIA.

'Mr President we must maximise our chances of catching the cell and finding the nuclear bomb. First, I believe we should honour our agreement with the Brits to keep this under wraps for as long as possible. Their capital city is the intended target not ours, and they would never forgive us if we put ourselves before them in the face of such an attack. One of al-Qa'eda's goals will be to estrange our allies from ourselves, let's not help that. Basically, sir, it's their call not ours to release the details of this attack, and frankly if I was them I wouldn't, not yet. Second, we don't know that this rumour refers to Operation Enduring Freedom. The rumour could be nothing more than a media fishing trip. I suggest that the FBI issue a statement which clarifies that they are investigating this rumour along with many others, every one of which they take seriously. Meanwhile, as a matter of precaution and until the source and credibility of this highly publicised rumour raised during a Presidential press briefing has been established, the Department for Homeland Security should raise the alert state on the Eastern Seaboard to amber.'

'I take it, Bill, that you agree with Jim?' the President asked the Director FBI.

'Jim and I spoke together briefly a moment ago and, yes, I do,' replied Darling. 'We should be very glad the rumour is so inaccurate. It may even help us.'

'How so?' asked the National Security Advisor.

'It'll strengthen public awareness on the Eastern Seaboard and in London but shouldn't alarm the bombers. Rumours of terrorist nuclear attacks have been commonplace for the last decade.'

Everyone understood the simple logic.

The President remained tense. 'I'll inform the Prime Minister. Are we sure this isn't some elaborate decoy in support of an attack against the United States? What if this cell moved from Buenos Aires to the United States instead of England?'

'Mr President,' answered Darling reassuringly, 'every intelligence agent and law enforcement officer in the country is engaged in the fight against terror. We're doing everything we can and, so far, no one has uncovered any suggestion of an imminent nuclear attack on the homeland.'

The President relaxed a little then stood up before shaking their hands firmly. 'Thank you all for coming along at short notice. As you all know, the next National Security Council meeting is in three days. I'll expect a full update then. Meanwhile the White House will deal with the media.'

After the short meeting, the President informed the British Prime Minister by telephone about the rumour of a nuclear strike on the Eastern Seaboard and on US interests in London. He informed the Prime Minister that the FBI was establishing the source of the rumour and that as a precaution, and until the source had been investigated the terrorist alert state along the Eastern Seaboard had been raised to amber. The President stressed there was nothing to suggest the rumour was related to Operation Enduring Freedom, but both leaders agreed that it was only a matter of time before the British press seized upon the rumour of a terrorist nuclear strike on US interests in London and the rumour of an attack on the city escalated. The fact that the rumour originated as an attack on American interests in London was largely irrelevant.

In London, the Prime Minister knew it was only a matter of days before he must inform the country of the real threat.

Chapter 68

February 22nd, Z – 69 Days
London, England

The lead story in the *Washington Post* was out of this world and spread like wildfire across the North Atlantic Ocean. It was broadcast as the lead item on the midday television and radio news throughout the United Kingdom and Europe.

The news was just too late for the midday edition of London's *Evening Standard,* so that afternoon the news editor and his staff reconstructed their lead story in time for the evening edition, consciously switching from the tediousness of the imminent Exercise Rapid Response to a real attack. The editor was aware that he had to shock the reader into paying renewed attention, as Londoners would simply not consider this a new story since the possibility of terrorists armed with nuclear weapons had been told and retold on so many recent occasions. The *Evening Standard* was determined to steal a march on tomorrow's nationals and produce an evening headline that begged attention. The editor eventually plumped for 'London Faces Total Nuclear Devastation' over a full-sized picture of a huge mushroom cloud that rose upwards from a silhouetted skyline of London running along the bottom of the page.

That morning national media headlines had focused on the arrest of four men yesterday on suspicion of terrorism offences. Three of the men had been seized in a preplanned operation by officers from the Metropolitan Police antiterrorist branch at a hotel in Brent Cross, North London. A fourth man was also arrested at his North London home. All four had been arrested under Section 41 of the Terrorism Act, on suspicion of the commission, preparation or instigation of acts of terrorism. Police had been acting on a tip-off received by a Sunday newspaper from an anonymous source that the four men were plotting to buy radioactive material for a dirty bomb. But the lengthy story in that day's *Washington Post* was much worse and spoke of huge nuclear explosions and fission reactions.

The news editor's early instinct had led him to rapidly assemble his staff and decide on the eye-catching headline before setting them to work. Forty journalists had just two hours to replace the lead story for the evening edition and it was to fill eight pages. The *Washington Post* had provided the most believable and chilling evidence yet that al-Qa'eda was targeting London as well as America with nuclear weapons, and that it had been planning on doing so for years. It quoted an irrefutable source from within the US Government's intelligence community who had confirmed that US financial interests in US cities along the Eastern Seaboard and in London would be targeted by a 'colossal and simultaneous nuclear attack in the near future'. There were a whole host of quotes from credible and less credible sources including radical Muslim clerics, professors, politicians and even doomsday prophets. Even the President was quoted as recently saying, '...a nuclear attack on America is inevitable.' The story stated how a journalist from the *Washington Post* had challenged the President yesterday afternoon during a press conference in the White House after a tip-off, and that the suggestion had been unconvincingly denied by an anxious President. Suspiciously the alert state in New York, Newark and Washington had been raised to amber within hours of the White House press briefing. Today's article in the *Post* boldly challenged the President to come clean over this latest threat and tell America's citizens what they had a right to know. This, the news editor of the *Evening Standard* decided, would be his line too, but targeted at the British Prime Minister.

As he waited for the next knock on his door, the editor surfed through the *Washington Post* web site and found much more. What appeared to have convinced his opposite number at the *Post* yesterday was the speed with which counterterrorist action had been taken by the President immediately after the press briefing and the ensuing effect on the streets of Washington. Within hours streets had been closed, trucks banned from parts of the city, and police armed with sub-machine guns were standing guard over key Government and financial buildings. By 3 p.m. there were more police cruisers around public buildings than tourists' cars and after nightfall, security spotlights replaced the glow from the lamps around Lincoln Memorial. It was reported that the famed National Mall resembled a city under siege. There were pictures of police everywhere, some carrying automatic weapons, others walking bomb-sniffing dogs. Concrete barriers blocked roads and security checkpoints dotted Capitol Hill. Curtained-off steel fences had been erected to block the view to many Government buildings including the White House and an anti-aircraft missile site had been placed on top of the FBI Headquarters. The odd thing was, it was reported, in the years since 9/11 Washington's alert state had been raised to amber on a number of occasions yet this level of reaction had not been seen before.

The *Evening Standard's* news editor, like many other editors across the country, was convinced something big was blowing in the wind. *Just what is going on?* he thought to himself. *Was Exercise Rapid Response a precursor to a real, cataclysmic attack only known to a few? What were the Metropolitan Police up to?* Despite conventional terrorist attacks in the capital, with the exception of concrete barriers surrounding the Houses of Parliament and the rare armed police officer around Westminster, London today was the same as it had been for the last fifty years.

A colleague poked his head around the office door, disturbing the editor's thoughts.

'No comment from Number Ten until tomorrow at the earliest, boss. The Home Office said it was '... continuing to monitor real and serious threats from terrorist groups ...' but would not comment on specifics.'

'That's pathetic. There's something brewing.'

'Someone has caught them with their pants around their ankles. Me, my money is on a nuclear threat and all this exercise shit is a way of preparing the public without causing panic.'

The editor believed his colleague was right. He was renowned for his nose for political deception.

'You're probably right. The only way we'll find out some semblance of truth is to rattle some cages.'

The colleague smiled. 'So let's rattle.'

Most Londoners felt secure in the knowledge that the Metropolitan Police antiterrorist branch could apparently catch terrorists with ease, but that of course was the point of high-profile arrests and the ensuing press releases and leaks.

But those in contact with the US Eastern Seaboard, the global business leaders, bankers, financiers, media chiefs and some politicians saw a more immediate situation developing. The Dow Jones had ended 135 points down the day before yesterday and 210 points down yesterday. Both falls were attributed to the gloomy US economic outlook by the Chairman of the Federal Reserve Bank and despite the optimistic statement from the President yesterday afternoon. But late yesterday dealers began pouncing on stock affected by global terrorism such as travel companies and airlines.

Today the public suggestion of an imminent al-Qa'eda strike, this time a full-scale nuclear attack, did nothing for market confidence. By 2:29 p.m. the FTSE 100 had plunged down 140 points, commensurate with today's Dow Jones futures and adding to the fall of the last two days of 242 points. At 2:30 p.m. the opening bell on Wall Street rang without a buyer in sight. The Dow Jones plunged another 660 points before meeting any resistance, the biggest-ever one-day fall. UK stocks trading in New York and London took the brunt. At 3:27 p.m. trading was suspended in London for the remainder of the day, with the FTSE 100 down 590 points before an automatic stop, introduced to the market after 'Black Monday' to check such a freefall, was able to break trading and take hold. Quite simply, every US investor wanted out of the UK immediately, and panic at the London Stock Exchange was widespread. Although several UK companies with predominantly global assets and interests retained over seventy per cent of their value of that day, other stocks that were UK-dependent had as much as two-thirds their value wiped out. Insurance stocks were decimated and associated banking stocks suffered.

One trader, who pooh-poohed the idea of London being destroyed and the UK economy being thrown back into the proverbial 'Dark Ages', thought he saw a buying opportunity and bought into the slide on behalf of twenty thousand unsuspecting savers. He purchased over twenty million pounds sterling of shares in a London-based insurance company, only to see his huge bid filled instantly and the shares decimated in three minutes. Worse, he was unable close or reverse his position. Resigning immediately on a Post-It note, he disappeared only to be fished out of the River Thames three days later.

The market signal was clear to the *Evening Standard's* financial editor and all the other corporate and business executives who took a global and necessarily cynical view of the world. The fact was, US corporate investors, who next to the President were the most connected and informed people in America, considered the UK incapable of surviving a terrorist nuclear attack on its capital. There was no better indicator in the world than the global financial markets.

The *Evening Standard's* vendors manned their patches as usual but sold a record thirty per cent extra newspapers that evening. Yet despite the shocking story, most Londoners that were polled said they felt safe. London's global business leaders, bankers, financiers and media chiefs felt differently; they were scared, very scared.

Chapter 69

February 23rd, Z - 68 Days
Gibraltar, Iberian Peninsular

After their long voyage via Barbados and *Last Tango*'s brush with the Portuguese warship PONS *Vasco da Gama,* Malik and Dalia felt a mixture of sadness and relief that the four Argentines would soon be leaving.

With the Gulf of Cádiz to stern *Last Tango* was rounding Cape Trafalgar in fair weather, and Malik estimated they would be through the Strait of Gibraltar and entering Gibraltar Harbour in about three hours, at approximately 11:15 a.m. Both Dalia and he had enjoyed the carefree company of the four Argentinians, and more than once Malik had wondered whether it was practical to postpone Baba and retain them for the next leg of his journey to Amsterdam.

Since the crew had been listening in to Channel 16, it came as no surprise when *Last Tango* had been requested to identify herself to the Portuguese man-of-war. Malik had decided that the best policy in the circumstances was to act as honestly as possible and that, it appeared, had paid off. However, this morning's BBC World Service broadcast had concerned him, and it was clear that a second challenge, while employing a crew of four Argentines, would present an unnecessary and foolish risk.

The four Argentines had considered it their responsibility to ensure both Dalia and Malik had a relaxing and enjoyable cruise. Both Amata and Elisa were incredible cooks and delighted in swapping experiences with Dalia. The preparation and eating of either Argentine, English or Mediterranean dishes was always accompanied with considerable banter and laughter. On one occasion Dalia had openly joked with Malik whether they had brought enough cooking oil, and for several seconds she had been rewarded with a deep frown. On several occasions Miguel had hinted how they would like to crew for Señor Kent in the future. Certainly, Malik would have no objections as they all worked hard, shared a range of excellent skills including seamanship, catering, safety and cleanliness. Malik and Dalia also found them friendly and entertaining, and there was no escaping the effect that the youthful love between each of the two couples had on Malik and Dalia. Throughout the three-week cruise via Barbados they had all played a multitude of games, many childish, some very adult. During these games Malik had often thought of his developing relationship with Dalia, and what his nine-year-old daughter Karima, who also enjoyed playing games, would make of Dalia. He thought they would get on well.

Malik had just finished clearing the galley after breakfast, a task that appealed to his sense of order and need to contribute, and now sat at the rear of the boat in the aft cockpit. The journey to Europe had been pleasurable, but Malik yearned for land and the opportunities that presented. He promised himself that one of the first things he would do after finding a hotel and fixing the return flights from Gibraltar via London to Argentina for the crew, was to take a long run around the historic rock of Gibraltar. As he ran he would compose the message that he must send to the Mailman.

Looking out to his left towards the Spanish mainland on the horizon, he pondered his next step as he listened for further news on the radio. He assumed that Dalia was also listening in as she sat alone at the helm on the fly bridge clearly enjoying the morning's winter sun pouring down on her face and shoulders. The four Argentines were busying themselves preparing the boat for port and, typically, they appeared entirely uninterested in anything outside the boat other than the regular shipping forecasts. Malik and Dalia, on the other hand, kept abreast of the major stories from across the world, something that the crew appeared to expect of the older couple. Of late, news had been dominated by the US President's foreign policy towards the Middle East and Central Asia, universal disquiet with the latest Israeli and Palestinian peace plan, and concern over the downturn in the world economy due to OPEC's insistence on capping oil output despite demand.

Last Tango had small and discreet loudspeakers situated around the boat, even in the heads, and one was attached to the bulkhead adjacent to the salon door on the aft cockpit. As the crew of *Last Tango* were breakfasting in the aft cockpit that morning, the breaking news broadcast by the BBC World Service had sent a chill down Malik's spine. The female BBC newscaster reported with characteristic eagerness that the previous day the *Washington Post* had uncovered US Government knowledge of a chilling nuclear strike believed to be by al-Qa'eda on the US Eastern Seaboard and London, England. Apparently the CIA had issued a statement confirming that 'Counterterrorist advice and support continued to be provided to allies of the United States.'

The White House had stated through a press release earlier that morning that secret messages discovered on a terror suspect's computer in Washington showed US financial institutions in America and London were being targeted by al-Qa'eda for attack. The terror suspect, a Pakistani thought to have studied in Washington, was behind the major alert currently taking place in the US, as it was said to list five specific financial buildings in New York, New Jersey and Washington as well as a further four in London, indicating they could even be hit by a tactical nuclear weapon. The President had declared, 'We are nations in danger', as his Homeland Security Director raised the security alert in the cities of Washington and New York to its second-highest level, amber, for only the third time since 9/11. In New York, streets had been fenced off and closed, trucks banned from parts of the city and black-clad police armed with assault rifles were standing guard. Security had already been raised at key Government installations in both cities including the New York Stock Exchange on Wall Street, the landmark Citigroup Center famous for its sloping roof, and the key bridges in and out of Manhattan including the Williamsburg Bridge and the Holland Tunnel. The Prudential Plaza Building in Newark and the International Monetary Fund and World Bank Headquarters in Washington had also been cordoned off under tight security.

According to the BBC newscaster, the response in London was more subdued. The Home Office had stated that it was monitoring a '... very real and serious threat...' but that it would not comment on specific targets as that information was 'sketchy'. The Prime Minister was expected to make an announcement in the House later today before issuing a press statement. The newscaster had speculated that the US targets in London could possibly be the financial giants Bank of America, Citibank, J.P. Morgan Chase and Morgan Stanley, all situated in the vicinity of Canary Wharf, and that possible methods of delivery for a conventional attack were considered to include suicide bombers, car bombs and aircraft. The newscaster speculated that some form of CBRN attack on a major European city that exemplified capitalism was always a possibility, then briefly recapped on the British Government's *in-situ* preparations to exercise their response to a WMD attack in London over the weekend of Sunday March 20th.

The news broadcast had continued with a financial expert relating the effects of the renewed fears of an al-Qa'eda strike on the world's financial markets. The price of crude oil that had reached a record high in New York several days ago was expected to rise further today. London's Stock Exchange was to remain suspended for a second day today and Wall Street was already braced for another turbulent day.

Somehow a BBC journalist had managed to interview the Mayor of New York who said, 'New York City is not going to be cowed by terrorists, make no mistake about it. The people of New York know that giving in to terrorists is exactly the wrong thing to do.'

The bulletin had ended with the promise of a phone-in programme to be broadcast tomorrow after the morning news at 9:05 a.m. Malik had made a note to listen in from his hotel room.

Sitting in the aft cabin Malik reran the broadcast through in his mind. What bothered him most was the reference to a nuclear attack in London and the UK Government's low-key response in the face of substantial preparations. *How much if anything do the British and Americans know of my plan?* Malik thought to himself. There was no such student linked to his operation, not that he was aware of. He concluded that someone had probably picked up something of his mission and that the student was irrelevant. *Yes, my operation has been compromised somehow. But what do they know? Do they know about the source of the weapons, Doctor Baloch, or Last Tango?* Malik had learned to believe in his own instinct. It told him they knew enough about his attack to take it seriously and take the necessary precautions. *But how did they find out?* The truth was, there were many who knew about the attack, but thankfully only Dalia and Malik knew how it was to be conducted.

Passing one nautical mile west of Europa Point, Malik overheard Miguel contact the Queen's Harbour Master on VHF Channel 12 and establish that the Southern Entrance was clear of large traffic. The reply was immediate and final. Malik guessed they were swamped with larger shipping that as a rule used the North Entrance. He could see that several oceangoing tugs were busying themselves with a large commercial tanker, and Malik he continued to watch he saw a pilot's vessel speed out towards an approaching American warship, which he guessed belonged to the US Sixth Fleet that was permanently stationed in the Mediterranean Sea. In addition he counted at least six other warships either at berth or anchor, and also a submarine that according to the *World Harbours Compendium* was located in the Z berth, a berth used exclusively by nuclear submarines. Most warships were flying the White Ensign of the British Royal Navy, but there were other flags that Malik recognised. He could not believe this level of activity was normal and his instincts sharpened.

The increased level of naval activity was of concern to Malik, as it was more usual for one, possibly two, warships to be docked at Gibraltar. As all ships underway to or from the harbour were to remain in contact with the Queen's Harbour Master on VHF Channel 12 at all times, Malik was able to listen and maintain an accurate idea of the comings and goings in the historic harbour. As Malik found no outside interest in *Last Tango* and could see no reception committee awaiting them he began to relax.

On impulse, he fetched the *World Harbours Compendium* from the salon and a pair of binoculars from the navigation room. Returning to the same seat he flicked through and found the pages for Gibraltar. The Gibraltar port facility was located on the west side of the Rock of Gibraltar and was adjacent to the town. The port was composed of a commercial harbour, and three marinas for leisure craft where they were now headed, a Royal Navy base and a ship-repair complex owned by *Cammell Laird*. Malik had planned long ago that he wanted to berth in Queensway Quay, where fuel diesel was delivered to the quayside and where they would have their stern to moorings on floating pontoons. It was the smallest of the three marinas with just 120 berths. On Malik's request the Queensway Marina Master confirmed via Channel 73 that *Last Tango*'s berth, prebooked by

Miguel prior to departing Argentina, was available. The main reason for Malik choosing Queensway Quay was the differing customs arrangements. Unlike Marina Bay and Sheppards that both required yachts to visit the Customs' Reception Berth, crews from yachts berthing at Queensway Quay were required to report to Customs in the marina office.

As Miguel steered towards the quayside, Malik thought back to his last meeting with the Mailman, aka Abu Zubaydah Saudi, aka 'Muhammad', his sole point of contact to the end of the operation. A pragmatic man, the Mailman had made it extremely clear that the operation was to be completed whether it was compromised or not – that was why al-Qa'eda was paying Malik and Dalia millions of US dollars. Only their combined capture could prevent success, with both staking their lives, and the lives of their relatives, on not being captured.

Malik climbed up to the fly bridge, glanced down at the GPS on the instrumentation panel and noted that their destination coordinates, Latitude 36° 08' North Longitude 05° 21' West was flashing. It still amazed him just how accurate the system was, as they cruised among a number of warships towards the inner harbour of Gibraltar. Malik raised the binoculars to his eyes and scanned the jetty. Perhaps it was the Red Ensign flying off the stern, or perhaps all the harbour officials were simply too busy, but he was confident no one was paying *Last Tango* undue attention.

With *Last Tango* neatly secured stern-to, and sandwiched between two smaller yachts, the crew sauntered across to the customs office. The one customs official who met them glanced at *Last Tango*'s papers and after establishing there was nothing to declare he stamped all six passports. The name *Last Tango* of London clearly meant nothing to the customs official and Malik finally relaxed. If they were to be seized, now would have been the time. There was nothing to declare and as there was nothing in the customs officer's thirty years of experience that told him there could possibly be a danger with the six cheerful people who were standing in front of him, he politely reminded them that they must report on departure and waved them on their way.

Built in the Colonial style, the Rock Hotel on Europa Road was on the seafront off the town centre business and shopping areas and adjacent to the airport. The room which Malik and

Dalia shared overlooked the sea and the two continents of Africa and Europe. The hotel nestled in the side of the Rock itself, with panoramic views of the town, the Spanish mainland and the Moroccan coastline, and usefully it was only a ten-minute walk to the airport.

Malik and Dalia booked themselves in for seven nights. Once in their room, they had five hours before they were to meet the crew in the hotel bar off the foyer. Malik had chosen to repay the crew for their commitment by taking them to the International Casino for dinner and entertainment, before they flew home to Argentina the following morning. As they unpacked, the two terrorists considered the merits of the hotel gym or a run outside.

Malik switched on the television before dressing for a run. Choosing CNN, they were confronted with speculation about planned terror attacks on the US Eastern Seaboard and London. There was no fresh news, merely plentiful advice from an army of experts.

It was Dalia who first raised the news broadcast from earlier that morning. 'What are you thinking?' Dalia asked in Punjabi on noticing Malik's grave expression.

'I think the attack has been compromised, and that the British are planning to avoid panic. The Washington student and American targets could be a convenient smokescreen. The fact that London is mentioned, that *all* of London is fortuitously being tested for a nuclear attack, the mere mention of a nuclear bomb, and the warship outside Barbados, are too many to be coincidences.'

'The level of naval activity in Gibraltar is strange too,' added Dalia. 'It's as if they are looking for a ship but they do not know which one.'

'I'm certain they suspect but don't want to cause panic so have made up a cover story.'

'I think so too,' said Dalia as she hugged Malik. 'What will we do?'

'We'll contact the Mailman. I'll consider this further as I run down to the mosque at Europa Point and back. Later I will walk into the town, surf the Internet for news, then contact Muhammad. Do you want to come running?' Malik asked, knowing the answer would be 'no'.

Dalia returned his smile. 'I'll use the gym. Maybe I'll go with you into the town later and find some newspapers.'

'*Insh'Allah*. I'll be back soon.'

Two hours later Malik was sitting with Dalia at a computer terminal in the busy Med Web Café in the centre of the small town of Gibraltar. They had drafted a brief message for Muhammad.

Muhammad,
Our safe arrival in Europe was met with unexpected news.
We appear popular and await your guidance. PBUH.
Mohammad.

Content, Malik moved the cursor over the Send It Now? button and clicked the mouse.

Back at the hotel, Malik and Dalia read a selection of that day's British national newspapers.

'Just more of the same in the British papers,' offered Dalia.

'It's much the same as the Internet,' observed Malik.

'The media want the threat to be real because it's a more profitable story, but they have no proof.'

'The US or UK governments may have the proof,' suggested Malik.

'We will find out soon enough,' Dalia answered warily. 'No government can keep this from its people for long.' She pushed the newspapers off the bed before Malik could get engrossed, then reached up and pulled him towards her.

'We still have two hours,' Dalia whispered as she struggled at Malik's clothes.

'But you've had a bath and I have showered.'

'There's plenty of hot water and the bath fits two,' she whispered, as he succumbed to her.

Chapter 70

February 23rd, Z - 68 Days
London, England

The Prime Minister woke from another nightmare. He had become adept at waking quickly to the soft ring and answering before it disturbed his wife lying beside to him.

It was the duty officer. 'Prime Minister I have the US President on the telephone. He says it's urgent.'

'What time is it?' whispered the Prime Minister. It was easier to ask than risk moving the books and magazines that obscured his bright bedside clock.

'It's six minutes past five, sir.'

'Thanks,' he whispered. 'Tell him I'll be down in a moment. I'll take it in my private office.'

'Would you like some coffee sir?'

'Please.'

The Prime Minister rose then pulled on his dressing gown and walked through the silent corridors to his private office, before picking up the handset and pressing the one lit button.

'Sorry to keep you waiting,' the Prime Minister answered in a raspy voice.

'Sorry to wake you,' offered the President. 'I guess it's early for you guys.' His voice sounded agitated, tired.

'That's OK,' replied the Prime Miniser, suddenly tense, his mouth dry. 'I usually rise at five but it was a late one last night. What's up?'

The President, who was sitting behind his desk in the Oval Office was about to turn in when information originating from the Washington FBI Field Office reached the Chief of Staff to warn her of the next front page headline in the *Washington Post*. The first newspapers would hit the streets in Washington in just a few hours. 'The *Washington Post* is breaking news in several hours. It seems that their reporter, a Rebecca Greenberg, is very well informed.'

The Prime Minister noted the President's bitterness and guessed at her source.

'Apparently her partner is an FBI Special Agent who is, or should I say was, working on Operation Enduring Freedom. There is no evidence so far but the FBI's Office of Professional Responsibility is investigating. The traitor is near his pension too.'

The Prime Minister had not been far from the mark. 'I had an incident like that recently,' he said grimly. 'Despite all the warnings, an MI5 officer allowed himself to be tricked by an attractive young journalist. I take it the *Post* is expanding on yesterday's story?'

'It reveals the intended target is London, not the Eastern Seaboard. Worse, they are saying the city is to be attacked with a nuclear-fission bomb of ten kilotons. They have various experts claiming how easy it would be and what detonation would mean for the city. I'm told the results are described in graphic detail and they ain't pretty. A ten-mile radius obliterates downtown and destroys the suburbs, not just for now but for the next thousand years or more because of the nuclear fallout and radiation.'

The Prime Minister clenched his teeth. 'Damn it. I'll have to go public. We're simply not ready.'

'It'll add credibility to anything they write.'

'Uh huh. Do they know anything else?'

'Yes.' The President sounded apologetic. 'They also say the bomb may already be in London and state that it's set to detonate on May 2nd. One article is dedicated to the importance of the Prophet Muhammad's Birthday in the Muslim calendar. They pretty well tell the whole story as we know it.'

'What about the threat to US interests?' asked the Prime Minister, grateful he had not fuelled the cover story.

'Wait a sec.'

The Prime Minister heard the President talk to a woman he assumed was his Chief of Staff. '...The *Post* states that there is no direct evidence of a nuclear threat to the Eastern Seaboard, and there's no mention of US interests in London.'

The Prime Minister suddenly felt ill. He knew what he had to do, and it was not a matter for debate. 'I'll go public today. I'll inform the House at eleven o'clock then hold a press conference at Westminster. Would you consider releasing a full press statement by nine o'clock, that's 4 a.m. EST?'

'Sure. You'll receive our full support throughout this, and we'll make damn sure others provide it too.'

'Thanks. NATO are already helping out as you know. What about your alert state?'

'That will run its course. The Department for Homeland Security will control it. I expect them to reduce later today. What will you do?' asked the President sympathetically.

'Search for the terrorist cell and the bomb, and prepare to evacuate London. What else is there to do? We must find it, or we're finished,' the Prime Minister replied determinedly.

'All pretty defensive but I guess those are the priorities right now. What we really want to do is fight back and crush them once and for all. The UN Charter is inadequate, but NATO holds the necessary ways and means to fight back, if only we knew where the bastards were holed up. This will be declared by NATO as an attack on itself within days and then you will have all the support you need.'

The Prime Minister could not help but smile, not only at the change in the President's mood but also at the similarity in their views. 'If we find the ringleaders you'll be the first to know. What I fear though is that if we cut off one head, two will grow. Destroying the perpetrators is essential but won't solve the problems we have with Islamic fundamentalism. What we need are twin-track long-term political and strategic solutions that enable us all to live together in peace, regardless of our religious beliefs.'

'I know,' the President said hoarsely. 'But for as long as much of the world is in poverty and living in unbearable conditions, there will always be a breeding ground for terrorists. You and I have a responsibility to protect our citizens now, and that must mean fighting the terrorists now and allowing time for the political agenda to develop and for progress to be made. Hell, it took us hundreds of years to develop societies in which every person can expect basic freedoms and a decent standard of living. Those in poverty around the world, including millions in Islamic countries, should not wait for Shari'a law.'

The Prime Minister was reluctant to be drawn into such an

important debate now, but couldn't afford to let it go. 'Poverty-stricken countries have many problems. Lack of education, corruption, religious beliefs, fear of suppression by minorities, abuse of natural resources, to name but a few. I agree that terrorism, the indiscriminate butchery of innocent people, cannot be the answer, is not lawful and has no place in any worthwhile society. It must be stamped out and NATO can play its part as the opportunity arises but soon the UN, not NATO, must address the fundamental global problems if we are to win the war on terror. If it does not, then we will merely maintain the status quo that includes the threat of massive nuclear strikes.'

Now it was the President's turn to smile. 'I would love to see the UN grapple with global terrorism but first you need to look to NATO for support. I'll have a copy of the *Post* article sent to you, along with my press statement.'

'Thanks.'

'You're welcome. Remember, no one can do any better than you're doing, OK?'

'I hope not. The country needs my very best right now.'

'We all need your very best right now,' the President shot back.

The Prime Minister knew that going back to bed was out of the question as he had an important speech to prepare for the House, a speech that would be broadcast live to an expectant nation. After that he must speak with the NATO Secretary General, then visit the Queen who was in residence at Buckingham Palace. Deciding to leave everyone, including the Home Secretary, Foreign Secretary and his press advisors, undisturbed for another hour the Prime Minister finished his coffee and set to work in the quietness of his private office at Downing Street.

At 6:45 a.m. a press release from Number Ten confirmed that the Prime Minister would make an emergency statement to the House as it opened that morning and that there would be a press conference at Westminster immediately afterwards. By 7 a.m. the London Stock Exchange had confirmed that trading would remain suspended for another day. The press release had come as no surprise to the world's media who had already picked up on the front-page story in the *Washington Post*. By 8 a.m. the full horror of the impending nuclear attack on London was being reported by the world's news agencies.

As Londoners settled into their daily routine it became clear that their worst nightmare, predicted by so many, was a reality. What no one had previously considered was that they would be left with over two months in which to act and dwell upon their fate. The more responsible broadcasts stressed the need for calm and a measured response. But normality was impossible for most of the country's population. In London a small percentage of people immediately turned back home or to their children's schools, as others sat dumbfounded listening, watching and wondering what to do. It did not help those in the multitude of office towers to see on their television monitors the final minutes of the twin towers of the World Trade Centre replayed time and again. People in their homes from Hillingdon to Bexley, and Barnet to Croydon, were deciding whether to stay in their homes and remain tuned in pending further information or whether to collect their children from school, or be early at the food and DIY stores to purchase those emergency stores they thought would prove vital. A large number of people picked up their recently delivered Government booklet 'Preparing for Emergencies' and read it for the first time. But the vast majority of Londoners listened to the advice of the media; they stood fast at their workplace, college or school, or they stayed at home, all of them waiting for information.

It was the police, business leaders and embassy staff who first demonstrated outward signs of coordinated command as the country awaited the Prime Minister's speech to the House. The former doubled the number of officers and police vehicles on the streets of London, and every police crisis management centre in each borough and at Scotland Yard was fully manned and prepared.

Barriers were erected in Parliament Square and up Whitehall to Downing Street, and it was not long before the predicted crowds began to gather. There was an eerie, trancelike calmness about the people of London. The police acted with care and understanding, most of them holding the same anxiety. It was as if everyone in the massing crowds understood the stakes and no one wanted to be an additional burden or provoke others at a time when everyone's well-being, possibly their very lives, depended on an appropriate response from the authorities and each other. A senior police officer remarked to a television camera in Whitehall that there was a certain Blitz-like camaraderie among the people, a belief in the safety of numbers. The senior officer in Whitehall knew the crowds were in shock, but that that shock could so easily turn to frustration, anger and violence. He contacted Gold and provided an update.

It did not take long for most business leaders to evaluate the catastrophe that they were facing. They spent the morning hastily considering their responsibilities and working hard at contingency plans which many considered they would have to introduce within days if not hours. Meanwhile, managers and secretaries busied themselves by cancelling, postponing or simply altering the venue of countless business meetings arranged for the coming months. Workers were requested to continue work as normal and as best they could pending further announcements. Some businessmen identified an opportunity for profit as others saw the need for charity.

Estate agents wondered what would happen to the housing market and how they could maintain their profits. Debates among board members got heated as they discussed whether to shut down DIY stores, supermarkets or transport operations in London, or whether to risk the lives of their employees and remain open to provision and feed the population until the last possible moment. If they remained open, there was the question of volunteer staff and pay in the face of danger from an early detonation and an increasingly desperate public. Many business leaders were unable to determine whether they had the right to expect workers to remain in the city in such conditions. Some remembered the Government Instruction issued to firms in the event of such an emergency and found time to read it. This made them responsible for their employees, and after yesterday's slaughter on the stock market few businessmen were optimistic about compensation from the shattered insurance industry. Most firms, large and small, opted to close their London stores in the following few days.

As people thought deeper into the situation and its consequences, they saw a cleverness in the delay to destroy London. Unlike 9/11, July 7th and other world-wide terror bombings, if al-Qa'eda could divorce themselves from any loss of life but maximise the chaos that ensued over a long period of time, then they may receive a more profitable response to the pure hatred they received after killing thousands of people. Just as this fact dawned on many people, so it dawned on the Prime Minister, still working in his private office. The fact was that most people would not wait to be told to evacuate London and there would be a rush for the gates.

The Foreign Office quickly issued a warning against tourists visiting London. By 10 a.m. every one of the 112 foreign embassies and consulates in London had issued their own strong warnings to their nationals not to visit. Within hours, foreign flights destined for Heathrow Airport and City Airport were diverted to Gatwick, Stansted or Luton. Travel agencies and tourist offices rapidly filled with foreign visitors wishing to amend and advance their return tickets before fleeing to their departure airport.

Several minutes before 11:00 a.m. the Prime Minister's cavalcade, which comprised double the usual squad of protection officers, cars and outriders from the Metropolitan Police, with the Prime Minister's Jaguar sandwiched in the centre, drove slowly through the iron gates at the entrance to Downing Street and down Whitehall to Parliament Square and the Houses of Parliament. Hundreds of police officers in yellow vests were standing shoulder to shoulder in front of barriers lining the route.

By now thousands of Londoners had gathered in Whitehall and Parliament Square, but the crowd was patient and expectant, not hostile. The Prime Minister wanted to see and be seen by the crowd, but he chose not to wave, instead adopting a rigid demeanor. He noticed that the crowd was calm, that there was no riot equipment in sight, and that many people held a radio. The crowd would listen to his speech live, as would London and the world, including, he assumed, the terrorists. He could not help but think of how London's mob had had so much influence on state policy since its earliest days.

At 11:30 a.m. the Prime Minister rose to the despatch box, and complete silence fell over the packed chamber. Without notes, and speaking from the heart and with resolve, he began.

'Mr Speaker, Honourable Members, it is my grave responsibility to stand before you and make a short statement at the start of a debate in which my Secretaries of State and I will engage, in the knowledge that the world and also our enemies, are listening. My Government is fully aware that our greatest responsibility is to the safety and protection of our people. Our people have a right to know about threats made against them and what we are doing about such threats. But they also understand that sometimes information needs to be kept secret to protect both themselves and the lives of those who work hard behind the scenes. As we have always made clear, if ever there is a need to issue a specific warning we will do so without hesitation. And that, Honourable Members, is what I am about to do today.

'I have to inform you that the Government has received intelligence which confirms that a terrorist cell with links to al-Qa'eda is intent on detonating a nuclear weapon, possibly of considerable destructive power in this, our capital city. We believe that the terrorists intend to detonate the weapon on May 2nd this year. We are not certain whether the weapon is in the city or even in the United Kingdom. Be under no illusion. This threat represents a massive attack on our homeland and the very fabric of our society, and is an attack on global democracy. It is an act of war by a clever, manipulative and unseen enemy.

'You are all aware of Exercise Rapid Response and the plan to evacuate London over the period 20th to 22nd March this year. The Metropolitan Police has benefited from the experience so far which has included a considerable amount of liaison with many other police forces, Government departments and our allies. Of course, it is that same service which is responsible for coordinating London's response to this threat. None of these preparations have been in vain; they will stand us in good stead for what is to come. With immediate effect, Exercise Rapid Response is cancelled and its achievements to date will be channelled to meet this new threat under the designation of Operation Enduring Freedom.

'As the House knows we have been working very closely with our American allies on emergency planning and response, and we have learned a great deal from each other. I spoke to the President of the United Sates earlier this morning, and I am delighted to inform the House that the US has promised its full support and all the resources at its disposal to allow us to meet this threat to London, the country and Western civilisation. Indeed we have already received a considerable amount of cooperation and equipment from all over the world, and in particular the United States which has provided survey equipment, dosimeters, protective clothing and portable decontamination chambers. Naturally this support was provided for Exercise Rapid

Response, but I have already received assurances it will be increased for Operation Enduring Freedom. Among others, I spoke with the NATO Secretary General this morning and he is to convene an emergency meeting of the NATO Council to discuss the single motion that the cornerstone of the NATO alliance, Article Five of the Washington Treaty, has been breached for only the second time in its history, the first being on 9/11. The House is aware that Article Five states that an attack on one or more of its members shall be considered an attack on all its members. It also confers on each NATO member the right to take whatever action is deemed necessary, including the use of armed force, to restore and maintain security. All morning we have been receiving renewed and new offers of help from all over the world. I would also like to assure the House that we are receiving unparalleled support and cooperation from every international intelligence service we have approached, including Interpol. We are certainly not alone in our hour of need.

'As I speak the intelligence services and police are busy seeking out the terrorist cell and their nuclear bomb. I am confident that we will find the terrorist cell and neutralise the bomb before it is activated, but as a sensible and necessary precaution the Metropolitan Police Commissioner will be revising and issuing plans for the timely evacuation of the city as a necessary precaution and as a key part of Operation Enduring Freedom. We have a little over six weeks to achieve this momentous task in order to save life and secure our private belongings and this nation's valuable treasures.

'Right now one thing is more important than anything else. I would like to take this opportunity to inform the House that in order for us to meet this shocking threat and ensure public safety it is vital that every single person remain calm, react positively and supportively to instructions from the authorities, help themselves where at all possible, and also help others. London's emergency services will be severely stretched, but with the help of the public, the Armed Forces and local authorities across the nation I am confident that we can respond effectively.

'London has risen to similar challenges in the past. Many people will remember the Blitz of 1940 and how Londoners pulled together during World War II. What we face as a nation now, what our capital city faces, is a war of enormous destructive power that from 9/11 has been fought all over the world in the Far East, Middle East, Central Asia, Africa, North America and Europe. I have no doubt that this country and in particular Londoners will respond with equal bravery and vigour to this battle as others already have. No one must be in doubt that we are at war against terror. Let us all be clear that the attack we now face is potentially catastrophic and economically speaking it could throw this country backwards by five hundred years, a situation from which we may never recover. It is up to all of us, united together, to defend ourselves against this threat. Honourable Members, in the event I may be misunderstood and since in recent years it has not been fashionable to declare war, understand that on this occasion I am declaring a state of war on behalf of the United Kingdom against the perpetrators of this attack.'

As the Prime Minister sat down, he received wild applause and cheers from all sides of the House. He hoped the unifying response from Parliament would provide a singular and positive message to the crowd outside the Commons, to all Londoners and the British people. Letting the commotion subside, he rose to his feet again to answer the inevitable follow-up questions. The Leader of the Opposition set the tone by offering the Prime Minister all the support that he required. Other party leaders followed suit. After twelve minutes of Prime Minister's questions the Home Secretary rose to speak, followed by the Defence Secretary. The Foreign Secretary remained seated.

At 12:50 p.m., the Government requested and received an unopposed majority in support of the declaration of war and of their action that included the use of regular, reserve and territorial Armed Forces personnel in support of the civil powers.

Buoyed up by the morning's debate in the House, the Prime Minister went to the press conference with renewed vigour. It was a time for robust leadership and he was ready to provide it. He also felt confident that he was on his way to securing a positive culture for dealing with the threat, defensively and offensively.

The press conference was broadcast live, and the Prime Minister received a more hostile barrage of questions that probed deeper than the House of Commons and its show of unity would allow. Fielding all the questions expertly, his most difficult moment arose when he was asked about the possibility of the bomb detonating earlier than expected. He responded that he considered it unlikely due to the significance of the Prophet Muhammad's Birthday, the likelihood that the bomb was still not in the country, and experts' beliefs in the terrorists' new strategy of delaying detonation in order to maximise chaos and fear prior to causing long-term destruction. He also ventured his own opinion that the terrorists may perceive a lower death toll as being an advantage, particularly as some nine per cent of the population of London, 700,000 people, were Muslim.

Chapter 71

February 24th, Z – 67 Days
London, England

Over the previous two weeks most members of the terrorist group had visited an al-Qa'eda mobile training camp near Mahmood's village in Iran for several days where they received training in their personal weapons and in explosives. Every member had visited the Canary Wharf Tower at One Canada Square accompanied by the ex-employee Ahmad, who showed them everything he could.

The Canary Wharf development in London replaced the derelict dockland area with fine offices for commercial and financial institutions. Canary Wharf Tower was the centrepiece at 236 metres high with fifty floors. It was the tallest building in the United Kingdom built by steel-frame construction. The building had a compact steel core and an outer perimeter tube formed by closely spaced columns with floors that were of composite construction over metal decking. It had been built at a rate of three complete floors every two weeks, the same rate as the twin towers of the World Trade Center.

Ahmad and Turk's visit to Canary Wharf Tower was the last and began early in the morning when they met outside Tower Hill Underground Station. The two men were dressed like any other junior office worker, and they took the Docklands Light Railway to Canary Wharf where they walked through the labyrinth of corridors and elegant shops under Cabot Place, up an escalator and through revolving glass doors that let them into the ground floor of Canary Wharf Tower. Turk, like so many other visitors, had marvelled at the simplicity of the ground floor of the skyscraper and even he, an experienced building demolition expert, wondered how the building stood. What greeted him was a single cavernous room dominated by two identical inner cores that housed a bank of elevators which faced each other. The walls and flooring were decked in rich marble tiles of various shades of brown, and fifteen metres overhead a ceiling made of large composite prefabricated blocks and bright steel girders. Glass windows stretched from floor to ceiling on three of the four outer walls, and natural light streamed through, reflecting off the highly polished marble to create a brilliantly lit space. The elegant furniture was sparse and designed to dissuade anyone but the briefest of visitors.

Turk counted four unarmed male security guards, two of whom hovered between the twin banks of elevators in the middle of the ground floor as the remaining two chatted up the reception women who were manning a highly polished black marble Information Desk. Near the desk was a chrome pole on which hung a flat television screen broadcasting BBC World news.

Walking over to an engraved marble display stand, Turk read the gold leaf lettering that told him which companies were housed in the skyscraper and on which floor. Ahmad pointed out the national newspaper group and the Canary Wharf Tower security section, both on the first floor, which he knew housed a multitude of televisions and radios, and the building's CCTV monitors.

Without wanting to appear unduly interested in the marble display, Ahmad led Turk over to the windows that overlooked the main entrance to the tower from Canada Square Park and speaking English, he quietly explained his plan. 'I will drive the tanker down that road, known as the North Colonnade, through the shiny steel pillars and large flower tubs, then smash through this glass into the building.'

There was a good line of approach and ample distance between the stainless steel columns and large flower tubs to drive a tanker through; it was abundantly clear to Turk that the thickened glass would provide little resistance.

'Where is the best place to leave it?' Ahmad asked.

Turk thought about the question and whispered, 'You will have no difficulty smashing your way in. You must stop the tanker between the elevators. That way it can be used to fight off an attack from below and its destructive power will weaken both inner cores. I would like to take an elevator to a higher floor now.'

'No way. Only pass-holders are allowed,' replied Ahmad bluntly.

Turk nodded then sat down on one of the comfortable leather sofas that faced the middle of the tower and lit a cigarette. He spoke quietly to Ahmad, who was sitting opposite. If anyone had bothered to watch they would have assumed the two men were waiting for a host or visitor.

'That's unfortunate but not vital,' Turk reasoned. 'The tower is constructed around two inner steel cores that rise up through the building, each an independent hollow section that houses the elevators. We will gain access through the elevator shafts and cut each steel section on the first floor. This alone will cause the building to collapse. Come, show me outside.'

They walked through one of the revolving doors to the main entrance and immediately turned right following a line of highly polished steel columns that surrounded the outside of the tower. These columns supported the outer walls of the tower and were of little interest to Turk.

Entering Smollensky's café opposite the tower, Ahmad ordered espresso coffee at the bar before striking up a conversation with the pretty Asian waitress whom he had come to know well. As he took the two cups of fresh coffee from the counter they exchanged smiles, then Ahmad joined Turk who was sitting by a window on a bar stool facing the tower. Turk was looking up at the skyscraper, deep in thought.

Ahmad broke the silence. 'I suppose the martyrs of 9/11 had no need to examine their targets before they boarded the planes.'

'No one planned for those towers to collapse; it was Allah's will. He has shown us the way,' replied Turk.

Turk continued to stare at the outside of the skyscraper. On the upper two-thirds of the building the evenly spaced windows reflected the greyness of the clouds that blanketed London and on the lower third the windows mirrored the surrounding modern metropolis.

'My information about the structure is accurate,' said Turk. 'It's fully occupied with two hundred people per floor; that's ten thousand people.'

'This will be a great attack and we will be martyrs,' replied Ahmad happily.

'I would like to see the basement now,' said Turk a few minutes later as he finished his drink, 'though I am content with the method of its destruction. It's a truly magnificent building and it will be an honour to die in it for the glory of Allah.'

After finishing their coffee in silence, Ahmad led Turk down some steps to Nash Court and an entrance to the lower ground floor of One Canada Square.

Ahmad explained where they were going. 'This is the far end of the underground shopping mall we walked through earlier to get to the tower.'

Ahmad led Turk through the set of glass doors into the busy shopping mall and back towards the Docklands Light Railway. Turk considered that anyone down here might survive, but he did not really care.

From 9 p.m. there was another meeting of the terrorist cell, this time held in the lock-up, as Mustafa's apartment was over-crowded and inadequate. Also, he did not trust his prying neighbours who had nothing better to do than mind his business.

'Ahmad has a job selling fuel from a garage near London City Airport,' Mustafa was explaining. 'Fuel deliveries are scheduled a month in advance and take place every second or third morning with a full load, so we will soon know if there is to be one on April 1st. We will assault on that day or the day after, whichever day the fuel delivery takes place. As soon as we have captured the tanker we will fasten the explosives and strike. Ahmad will drive the tanker and Turk and his section will be ready with the explosives. And now you will listen to Hannah.'

Hannah, already prepared, continued. 'I will be at the lock-up next Monday and Tuesday. You are to bring your equipment and supplies, and I will help you check them. Remember that all clothing is to be black or dark in colour and this includes the pull-over headgear that we must all wear during the attack. We are soldiers and must not act or look like crazed fools.'

Mustafa cut in. 'They must think we fear being recognised. The *kafirs* must believe that we wish to escape.'

'I intend to dress as the men,' said Essa. 'It's more practical and it's what we have been taught.'

Mustafa was taken aback by the apparent challenge from the Black Widow, as the women jihadi fighters who had lost their husbands or families had become known in the West. He glanced towards Hannah who nodded her agreement. 'Naturally,' he replied coolly. 'We will meet again in two weeks and run through the plan in detail. By then I want all personal equipment stowed here, weapons and equipment rechecked and explosives prepared. Nothing will be left to chance.'

Kalil, another Black Widow, smiled. 'Can anyone accommodate Qasim before Mustafa slits his throat?' Everyone laughed. Qasim was the youngest of the group at seventeen.

'The boy can stay with me,' offered Turk easily. 'He's on my team and can help with the explosives.'

'Thank you,' responded Mustafa with obvious relief.

The two women staying with Mustafa, Essa and Kalil, smiled at each other. Although Mustafa considered himself fortunate, neither of them had any interest in anyone but each other.

Chapter 72

March 2nd, Z – 61 Days
Gibraltar, Iberian Peninsular

It had been seven days since Malik sent the message to Muhammad but there had been no response.

Maintaining their aliases as Sean and Diana Kent, Malik and Dalia passed their days visiting a number of sights on the small rock of Gibraltar, in southern Spain and also on the continent of Africa, and their evenings either at the casino or on *Last Tango*. They visited the Moorish Castle, the siege tunnels, the 100-tonne gun, the Barbary Apes and Europa Point where Gibraltar's mosque stood. They talked of living in Gibraltar, a convenient yet modest place that demonstrated how the West and Islam could live side by side.

On one day they journeyed into Spain and visited the royal city of Alhambra at Granada. They were in awe of the fortress city that, rising up above the Red Hill in the heart of Granada, stood proud and eternal as one of the most important architectural structures of the Middle Ages and the finest example of Islamic art left in the world.

On another day they took the thirty-minute flight from Gibraltar's international airport to Casablanca, the town made popular by Humphrey Bogart and Ingrid Bergman in the film of the same name. Malik and Dalia found this old Moroccan port to be both sophisticated and cosmopolitan, and they promised to return to Africa and visit the charming city of Tangier and the spectacular Marrakesh.

They were kept well informed by the world's media of the unfolding events in London. Already newspapers were labelling May 2nd as 'Doomsday', 'Armageddon' or 'Judgement Day'. They were provided with a thorough insight into London's preparations, progress on the manhunt for the terrorists and more expert advice than they required. Every British and foreign newspaper they picked up was dedicated to reporting the attack. To Malik and Dalia, it was as if they had their own army of intelligence experts gathering and reporting information on their behalf. Reports included masses of expert opinion regarding the preparedness of the country and its capital, criticism of the emergency measures, and gory detail about the pure fission explosion, its effect and the aftermath. Vigilante gangs were reported to be indiscriminately assaulting and terrifying Muslims and people who simply looked Muslim. Terrorists were vilified in the West and condemned in the East, and huge ransoms declared for bin Laden, dead or alive. One British newspaper reached out directly to the terrorist cell responsible, asking them to give up the bomb for God and humanity.

Malik and Dalia remained detached from the hysteria and focused on heir mission. Both had known precisely what they were agreeing to at the outset and what was required of them. Both had lived through pointless suffering and witnessed devastation and death first-hand, and notwithstanding their huge financial reward, they believed in the cold logic of shocking the corrupt world to its senses.

Disregarding the effects of the explosion, of particular interest to them was the UK Government's investigation into the terrorists responsible and the security and protection afforded to the UK and London.

It was clear that from the moment the Prime Minister had stood in front of the nation's press in Westminster that no one in Government would attempt to dodge or underplay the gravity of the situation. Several articles went as far as praising the Prime Minister for his frankness and leadership. Overall, the media appeared to agree that such was the gravity of this attack, so total for the country, that everyone must pull together to fight it.

The two terrorists had assumed that the delay in the Mailman's response to Malik's message was because of the need for him to report to the council and for them to reflect on the sheer magnitude of what was happening. Bin Laden would want to know the source of the leak, establish how much information had been divulged, and whether his weapons were at risk. Neither Malik nor Dalia expected the operation to be cancelled, but they did think that the target could change, possibly to Paris, Brussels or Berlin. After all, it may now be foolhardy to infiltrate the UK and risk losing the bombs, when there were so many softer targets within easy reach.

When the terrorists had read the UK Prime Minister's latest interview with the media, they were surprised. It transpired that he had known for a while that London was the target of an al-Qa'eda sponsored nuclear strike, and that the country had been preparing to defend itself. There were plans to evacuate London, and the UK's Secret Intelligence Service had been tasked with finding the terrorist cell and a bomb. It transpired that the ISI, which Malik knew as MI6, had been on their trail for over a month, and had traced the cell as far as a disused factory in Buenos Aires. There were also reports that a Pakistani nuclear scientist had made the bomb, and that he had committed suicide soon afterwards. One well-informed UK national newspaper, the *Daily Mail*, printed Doctor Baloch's long and sordid association with the Taliban and al-Qa'eda. The two terrorists also read of the declaration of Article Five of the Washington Treaty, and NATO's sea cordon around the UK mainland.

Today was no different to the last six for the two terrorists as they waited to hear from the Mailman. Mid-morning they purchased the same wide selection of newspapers that included one-day-old issues of the *Washington Post* and *New York Times*. They found that today's leading stories were dominated by the impact that the threatened attack was having on the UK and world economies, but it was another story that caught Malik's attention.

'Front page of the *Daily Telegraph* has an article about a retired spy who has been redrafted into MI6. A man called Harry Winchester. Apparently he served in Afghanistan for seven years, and was a captain in the British SAS. The newspaper speculates that the warning originated from a source of his in Afghanistan as Winchester was spotted in a Kabul hotel by journalists a week before he flew to Buenos Aires. Apparently he has been tasked to hunt down the terrorist cell. It reads, "…it remains to be established whether the terrorist cell or nuclear bomb are in the country. MI6 would not confirm Winchester is assisting them, and declined to comment further." There's a picture of him too.'

'Hmm,' offered Dalia seductively as she inspected the photograph.

Malik chuckled as he cut out the article and threw the remainder of the newspaper on the growing pile already on the floor.

Dalia spotted something that alarmed her. 'Bastards!' Her heart pounded.

'What is it?'

'On page three of *The Times* there's an article that reads, "Bomb Maker Murdered. Doctor Baloch, the man believed to have constructed the nuclear bomb destined for London, did not commit suicide but was murdered by three men as early as February 2nd. Argentine police investigating his death believe the nuclear scientist did not commit suicide after all but that he was unconscious when thrown from the twentieth floor of the Hyatt Hotel, central Buenos Aires. They also believe he was murdered after preparing the bomb. It's not known whether his murderers are members of the terrorist cell intent on destroying London." '

Malik was rarely stunned into silence, but this was an exception.

'The Network has silenced Baloch,' said Dalia with incredulity.

'Bin Laden must have known of the assassination,' Malik agreed.

'The Mailman must have known too. But why not order us to kill Baloch?' There was a nervous edge to Dalia's voice that Malik had not heard before.

'Perhaps it was Jamali and his thugs, though it could have been anyone intent on stealing his money,' Malik speculated. 'He may have got drunk and boasted about his wealth. It's also easy to see why the Network would consider him a liability and want to make his death look a local affair. We, after all, have a greater mission.'

'Which do you believe?'

'Either is possible.'

'If it was a hit, why not inform us?'

Malik understood Dalia's unease. They both realised that someone may have orders to kill them both; perhaps soon after the bombs were delivered. What neither of them could comprehend was why.

'We must be careful what we tell the Mailman,' said Dalia.

Malik nodded thoughtfully. 'Do you think the Network wants to kill us?' he asked.

‘After detonation, the Network will claim responsibility for the attack,’ Dalia said. ‘But we know where they hide, how they operate, how they are funded. I think the Network no longer trust us with their secrets.’

‘What makes you think they ever did?’

‘The same reasons as you,’ Dalia answered. ‘Our profiles, our lives and the lives of our loved ones, the money they paid…’

Malik sighed. ‘Let’s finish with the newspapers then go to the Internet café.’

The two terrorists walked to the Med Web Café, the only Internet café in Gibraltar and famous for its cocktail, the ‘Black Pig’. As usual they ordered drinks and shared a terminal. Malik opened the electronic mail host and typed in his username and password. He was warned he had received a message, which he opened immediately.

There was no mistaking the reply. Rage spread over Malik’s face as he read the short and blunt message. Without realising it, Dalia reached across to Malik and placed a hand over his. Staring at the screen, Malik felt the hatred rising within him. He read the message, written in Punjabi, for a second time.

> Mohammad,
> We are pleased you are having such an enjoyable trip. I have spoken to your family and everyone agrees you must continue as planned. Meanwhile, I have taken it upon myself to look after your beautiful daughter so you have no cause for concern. Our reward will be your safe return. The Prophet will watch over you. It is God’s will.
> Muhammad.

Not trusting himself to remember every word of the message, Malik printed a hard copy, and without a word he logged off and walked out into the cool street. Dalia followed him and together they made their way in silence back to the hotel.

For Dalia, it was Malik’s decision, and as her hand found his in the elevator, she told him so. For her there were no children, no family of her own, and she would help, whatever he decided. He, and his daughter, represented her future now.

As they entered the hotel room, Malik made for the balcony were he knelt facing Mecca. He prayed for his daughter, Karima, and thought of what she had already experienced in her short life, and what she was enduring now. He imagined her being kept prisoner in the Mailman's fortress home outside Islamabad. The Network must have snatched her from his sister, Yasmin, whom he also prayed for. Malik blamed himself and knew that he would do everything within his power to rescue his daughter, and then make up for all the sadness and inadequacies he had imposed on her short life.

Offering a final prayer to Allah for his only two remaining living relatives, Malik re-entered the room, sat down and for the next thirty minutes he formulated a new plan. Dalia eyed him occasionally as she lay on the bed watching CNN, unsure what to do.

Malik knew that for now he had no choice, and that regardless of the risks, he must continue with the operation. He could not fight the Network single-handed. Sitting on the bed, he turned to Dalia who he knew was waiting expectantly.

'You're right,' Malik said finally. 'They no longer trust us to see it through.'

'Baloch's death was arranged to look like suicide,' Dalia reasoned. 'He was not supposed to be connected to the bombs. The Network knows we'll hear of his murder and that we'll think we may be next. They believe that there is a good chance we will cut and run on the news of Baloch's murder, maybe even make a trade with the British.'

Malik considered that for several seconds, then surprised her. 'Do you think the evacuation of London removes the terror inflicted?'

Dalia thought for a moment.

'No. I believe the victory is greater if the city is levelled but the death toll is low. If millions die, there is a greater chance the West will respond by attacking Islam, possibly wiping us out. It's even possible that the Network caused the leak in Afghanistan to reduce the chance of a massive nuclear counterattack.'

'It's probable the Network intended to announce the attack in advance, but after the bombs had been placed. Perhaps they intended to use al-Jazeera television, but a premature leak wrong-footed them.' Malik looked desperate, lost, his voice quivering. 'Do you think they will ever release her?'

Dalia felt hers eyes welling, and looked away. 'I'm sorry, Malik,

I don't know. But you know that I will do anything I can to help Karima.'

Malik surprised Dalia for the second time in as many minutes. 'Then we will continue. I will send a message back to Muhammad, then we'll find you a car, right-hand-drive with British registration.'

As they travelled back down in the hotel elevator, Dalia wondered how Malik intended to rescue his daughter as he surely would, but instead asked about the car.

'And where do you propose to find a British-registered car?'

'In Gibraltar or Spain. There are several British-registered cars for sale here, but there are many more to choose from in Spain. I found just the place on the Web, somewhere about ninety minutes drive from here, in Malaga. Apparently British home owners in Spain, ex-patriates on the Costa del Sol, exchange and upgrade their cars there. They like to keep the British registration, presumably in case they decide to return home.'

'I want a sporty Western car that is fast and will attract a hitchhiker.'

'I know.' Malik forced a weak smile.

'I'll need an address for the registration?'

'You'll be living as Diana Kent at our home in Islington. We'll use that.'

'You've thought of everything.' As soon as the words spilled from her mouth, Dalia regretted them.

'Not quite,' responded Malik tersely.

The two terrorists were silent a moment.

'Since the Argentine police know about Baloch,' said Malik, 'what do they know about us, our identities?'

Dalia paused for a moment in the street outside the hotel. Her legs felt rubbery. 'It's unlikely. Our plans have been faultless. We didn't enter Argentina as Sean and Diana Kent, and no one can be searching for them otherwise we would have been detained by the Portuguese warship or the police would have been waiting for us here. And even if the police visited the boatyard and questioned Carlos, it would come to nothing. Our new disguises are immaculate; Arabs don't have blue eyes.'

Malik smiled for he felt she was right. Their appearance, reflected in their British passports, had been Dalia's idea. She looked stunning with blue eyes, which, once seen, were unforgettable. 'And we're not being followed, despite your beauty,' he added sincerely.

For the second time that morning, the two terrorists entered the Med Web Café where they were offered the same vacant terminal as before. On the off-chance that she may read it soon, Malik wrote his sister, Yasmin, an uncomplicated email asking after Karima and his sister's family. He explained that he was 'busy', in the knowledge she would understand that she was to say nothing and to delete the email. Yasmin was one of the few people in the world who knew the truth about Malik. He promised her he would return as soon as he could. After sending the message, he and Dalia surfed the Internet for British car sales in Malaga.

'We'll buy a car tomorrow,' said Malik as they searched. 'The day after tomorrow Baba and his crew will arrive and you'll leave for Madrid. There you'll have time to buy Spanish goods to pack the car for your journey to England.'

When Malik found the car-sales web site he was looking for, he noted the details.

'And when we have accomplished our mission and hidden the bombs?' asked Dalia.

'Then we'll rescue Karima, take her to Cairo and decide what to do.'

'I have the perfect plan.' Dalia reached up and kissed Malik.

'Does it include *Last Tango*?' asked Malik, knowingly.

'Definitely. I'll tell you tonight, but only if you promise to tell me how you propose we rescue your daughter.'

Malik promised her he would, then composed a message for Muhammad.

> Muhammad,
> Despite the busy season our journey is on schedule and our resolve unchanged. We will be home for the celebrations soon and look forward to seeing our family and friends after all this time. Please pass my love to my daughter of whom I know you will take great care. Allah is Almighty.
> Mohammad.

That evening, Malik received a reply from Yasmin. Malik read the fear, apology and anger behind her words, some of the anger directed at him. Karima had been snatched from school two days ago and the police were doing what they always did.

Malik's short reply told Yasmin everything she needed to know.

Chapter 73

March 4th, Z - 59 Days
London, England

The extraordinary thing was that many residents would not leave the doomed city. It was not that people were being belligerent; most sincerely believed they could be of more help to themselves and others if they stayed in their homes for as long as possible. Conversely, the Home Office's Instructions for Residents advised the earliest-possible evacuation. However, it was only mandatory that everyone was outside the cordon by midday Friday April 22nd, and only in exceptional circumstances would authority be granted by the City of London Corporation for an extension of one week to midday Friday April 29th. Obviously there was no indication in the instructions for when people might return and the very last paragraph stated that failure to comply would result in forcible removal and possible detention.

For businesses the instructions and penalties for non-compliance were more complex. All businesses were to consider the immediate relocation or closure of London-based operations, and the laying-off of non-essential staff in the capital. With the exception of necessary public and private industries identified by the City of London Corporation, which included food and fuel retail and other basic services, including water, sanitation and limited transportation, businesses were to close within the thirty-four boroughs and the City of London by midnight Thursday April 21st. Remaining services were to be withdrawn by midday Saturday April 30th, the final evacuation deadline. Although the plan was simple, the Home Secretary believed that common sense among business managers and the simple but weighty effects of supply and demand would encourage and accelerate their closure. Based on the recent closure of the London Underground Central Line for maintenance it had been calculated that the capital's prime shopping mall, Oxford Street, lost over one million pounds per hour of trading. It was clear to everyone that the financial impact of the terrorist threat was already greater, possibly as much as ten-fold. And as the nation's economy was influenced by Government spending, so too would London's ability to trade reduce as central, and local, Government-funded operations closed down.

The last census held one year ago confirmed the residential population of London was a little over ten million. On a weekday this figure would rise by half as much again as up to five million commuters and visitors poured into the city. The Metropolitan Police estimated that since the announcement of the nuclear attack by the Prime Minister the residential population had already dropped to eight million, with the population swelling to twelve million during the day.

Unsurprisingly, the impact on London from this sudden change in population was most noticeable with a reduction in traffic and space on public transport. Visitor attractions including the Tower of London, Westminster Abbey, London's museums, the British Library, the Tate Galleries, and many others, had already made the decision to close, the trustees quickly deciding to concentrate on saving the vast array of priceless artefacts, antiques and works of art that made the historical capital one of the world's finest tourist attractions. It was a similar story for the countless cinemas, theatres, casinos, clubs and other entertainment outlets, most of which relied on the late-evening and night-time trade that had all but dried up. As a result, the thousands of restaurants and bars throughout the capital were noticeably quieter, particularly at night, and owners and managers were wondering whether they, too, should close. The Home Secretary was right. Once the Orwellian downward cycle had begun, it would accelerate under its own momentum.

In compliance with other Home Office instructions, all boroughs had established street-level Neighbourhood Emergency Response Teams that consisted of volunteers who could be called upon at any time to assist the emergency services in their neighbourhood. They were to produce a list of human and physical resources in their neighbourhoods that may prove useful, and draw up a simple pyramid warning system that would be used to cascade down information to every resident. They were also required to implement simple first-response plans of their own in the event the emergency services could not reach them quickly. Neighbourhood volunteers included retired doctors, nurses and police officers, St John Ambulance employees, British Red Cross employees, qualified first aiders, Women's Royal Voluntary Service members, owners of generators and in some areas owners of boats, as well as child carers and other able-bodied volunteers.

Unfortunately, many NERTs developed a siege-like mentality, so Gold Group ordered that borough police forces, supported by local authorities, establish community briefing teams that visit each NERT and brief them on the threat and the appropriateness of their responses. Police community briefing teams soon discovered that most NERTs had advised the stocking of food and water, the construction of Anderson shelters in gardens and the nuclear hardening of houses. As a result, supermarkets and shops were short of basic critical products, including food and the DIY equipment necessary to secure their property in compliance with Home Office instructions. Slowly the community briefing teams convinced the most obstinate NERTs that the priority was safe and ordered evacuation not entrenchment, and that although enhancing the security of each abandoned home in the city was appropriate, hardening those homes against nuclear attack was futile.

The evacuation of London's population was the highest priority assigned to Gold by Cobra, but they had other priorities too. Each police borough was also responsible for establishing the whereabouts of all known radiological hazards within their boundaries. As soon as this was achieved, mobile radiological search teams attached to the Army from the US Government moved in and swept the area to determine if any previously unidentified radiological emissions existed. If any were identified, radiological detection teams comprising military Explosives Ordnance Disposal personnel, scientists and other radiological experts and professionals were called in to identify, and if necessary neutralise, each source. Slowly, a complete footprint of the radiological hazards throughout London was mapped then plotted onto a master in Gold's briefing room at New Scotland Yard. The thirty radiological detection teams were already overwhelmed with the spiralling number of radiological hazards and other suspicious packages that were being reported all over London.

Sitting at his desk, the Commissioner was concerned about one worsening problem among his responsibilities for which he had no effective response. London's seven hundred thousand Muslims were becoming increasingly polarised. In the two weeks since the Prime Minister's announcement, the Muslim Council of Britain had worked hard to disassociate British Muslims and the Islamic faith from the attack, and despite the Commissioner's personal pleas to newspaper editors, jingoistic articles frequently inferred that London's Muslim community were providing a safe haven and breeding ground for terrorists. This morning one tabloid newspaper had printed the front page headline 'War against Islam', and although the Commissioner had just been informed that the editor was unceremoniously sacked thirty minutes before, the horse had bolted. The sacking had taken five telephone calls beginning with the Deputy Prime Minister. On a live daytime independent television chat show broadcast yesterday, a member of the British National Front had suggested what he considered many millions of Britons now believed, that all Muslims should be interred like the Germans in the United Kingdom or Japanese in the United States during World War II, then sent packing back to where they belonged. He had been arrested on the South Bank at the studio for inciting racial hatred. Alarmingly, sixty per cent of the phone-in poll supported the man's view.

Unfortunately the perceived liberal acceptance by the Government of immigrants, refugees and asylum seekers over the last few years, and the ease with which Muslims in particular appeared to gain British citizenship, had had a much greater impact on the general public across the country than the Government had imagined. The attack was the catalyst, and now the xenophobia was surfacing.

Two well-attended marches through London organised by the Muslim Council of Great Britain which denounced terrorism, nuclear warfare and racism had not helped because both marches had been met head-on by counter-marches organised by the British National Party and others. They had ended in bloody riots. Two Muslim youths had been kicked to death at the second riot, and as a result the Commissioner had acted swiftly within his State of Emergency powers to ban all marches in London.

But now he was afraid because for the first time, he was looking at new figures that supported a bigger and even more frightening picture of racial discrimination that was accelerating out of control. The figures were startling. Muslim children were being systematically victimised in school and could no longer attend for fear of their lives; Muslim women were being attacked and stripped of their traditional clothes while out shopping or working; and Muslim men were being beaten up, many half to death, some to death. Their homes and businesses were being targeted too. Age, the Commissioner saw, made no difference either. The violence was spreading beyond the British Muslim community too. Many white shopkeepers had had their doorways daubed with anti-Islamic slogans or premises had been torched, for nothing more than serving Muslims or people thought to be Muslims. But it was the final set of figures that shocked him the most. An escalating number of police men and women and other emergency services' officers called to assist Muslims were being targeted. The night before, two police officers had rescued a young Muslim woman from an assault and the three of them had only just got away with their lives as the patrol car sped away in flames having been torched with petrol bombs then shot at.

The Commissioner knew that his force required more resources and additional powers to deal with the escalating violence. He could not help but remember the haunting pictures that illustrated so horrifically how the German people had treated the Jews both before and during World War II. Not for the first time that day he lifted his telephone handset to speak with the Home Secretary. He would present the shocking weekly figures he had just received to the Home Secretary then to the media, and demand that the Prime Minister speak publicly on this issue. Most importantly, he decided to widen training and begin arming the entire Metropolitan Police for the first time in its history. Currently he had less than three thousand armed officers at his disposal, about ten per cent of his force. But with the exception of one thousand 'authorised shots' and five hundred more in the specialist firearms unit, SO19, the remainder were dedicated to royal and Government protection. The alternative was to call upon the Armed Forces, and he had no intention of requesting that, not yet. Every officer under his command had a right to personal protection against deadly force, and each one had a duty to effectively protect the public from the same fate. The only way to achieve this now, he reasoned, and within the rule of law, was to begin training and arming every officer before it was too late.

Chapter 74

March 4th, Z - 59 Days
Gibraltar, Iberian Peninsula

Malik watched as the four men walked down the portable staircase and stepped onto the apron of Malaga International Airport. It was a bright, sunny day and difficult for the spectators to find somewhere to stand on the outer viewing balcony that was not affected by the brilliant reflection of sunlight from the silver Royal Air Maroc Boeing 737 fuselage. Malik did not know three of the men, though he trusted Baba's judgement and was confident they would be experienced sailors. He watched as they walked the short distance across the tarmac to the Immigration and Customs lounge and saw that the three men were young and fit. With Baba looking older and more wizened, together they appeared to onlookers to be no more than what they were, another hired boat crew for the Mediterranean. They did not look like the seasoned smugglers Malik knew them to be.

Twenty minutes later Malik greeted his crew in the arrivals lounge of the Pablo Picasso Terminal. Baba hugged Malik, then warmly introduced his men. They were all unmistakably Egyptian and made Malik, as Sean Kent, appear West European. It was obvious that none of Baba's men spoke much English, something else he suspected Baba had planned.

'My friend, before you ask, it was an awful journey,' exclaimed Baba. 'The Egypt Air flight from Cairo was two hours late arriving at Casablanca Mohamed. Then the connecting flight was delayed by eight hours because the baggage handlers were on strike. They should cut their lazy hands off. That will stop their pathetic Western whinging. No in-flight movies either, only cosmetics advertisements.'

'So the food was good?' Malik asked with a friendly smile as he led them to his hired minibus in the short-term car park.

'Hot food was cold, cold food was hot. All of it unfit for pigs,' answered Baba grimly.

It became a competition between them both to find something good about the journey from Cairo, a journey that Baba had tried to convince Malik should be made by sea, with Malik collecting Baba and his men from Limassol in Cyprus or possibly Palermo in Sicily. The Egyptian hated flying, particularly the cramped seating that barely accommodated his massive figure.

It took another hour for Baba to calm down and the remaining thirty minutes of the journey to Queensway Quay for him to return to being the jovial character he habitually was. On arrival at the quayside, they emptied the minibus of luggage and Malik led them down the wooden quay passing many smaller yachts. On arrival at the stern of *Last Tango* of London, Malik walked across the gangplank and turned when he realised that his four crewmen were not following.

'What's up?' Malik asked, a look of bemusement on his face.

Baba and his three colleagues looked stunned and somehow reluctant to board as they surveyed the boat with glazed eyes.

'Mr Kent,' Baba said, barely managing to remember his orders, 'she's beautiful.'

Malik grinned and waved at them. 'Just wait until we get her into open water. Come, we'll have a drink, then I'll show you your cabins and the rest of the boat. I wish to leave by three o'clock.'

Baba crossed the gangplank and followed Malik through the cockpit into the salon where he dropped his luggage. He saw his colleagues were out of earshot standing on the aft deck talking excitedly. 'You must be a very rich skipper, very rich indeed,' said Baba, habitually fingering his fleshy chin. 'I fear I have undersold myself, and my men,' he added, as his eyes surveyed the luxurious salon. Baba had been at sea all his life and never before boarded such a fine vessel.

'Then if you all do your jobs well I will double your salary,' laughed Malik, as he handed Baba a locker key before walking behind the bar.

'You'll find the Red Ensign in the rearmost locker in the aft cockpit. Please have someone raise it while I fix some drinks.'

Over the next three hours Malik familiarised his crew with the boat, took them for lunch and returned the minibus to the hire company. On his return they made the mandatory visit to the customs office and by 3 p.m., just as Dalia was arriving in Madrid, they slipped their mooring and made headway for the Strait of Gibraltar.

Chapter 75

March 4th, Z – 59 Days
Madrid, Spain

To Dalia's surprise she found the route by car from Gibraltar to be populated with British expatriates as they migrated to the port of Bilbao on the north coast of Spain, leaving behind their villas that they had hired out over the spring and summer months. At Bilbao, in the heart of Spain's Basque country, passengers and their vehicles would take the Pacific and Oriental ferry to Portsmouth on the south coast of England. In early March, Madrid hotels and the P&O ferry were rarely fully booked, so Dalia had experienced no difficulty in booking a superior hotel room and a Premier Class cabin before she left, at the Gibraltar Travel Centre on Europa Road.

Two days before, Dalia had purchased her first-choice car with cash, an Audi A3 Sport that was seven months old and with 14,552 miles clocked. The wide range of British-registered cars available at the Malaga British Car Sales showroom opposite Malaga International Airport's Pablo Picasso Terminal had reflected the claims on the company's web site. Ebony black, it was fast, reliable and sufficiently large yet innocuous for London. To Malik's delight, the car not only had British plates but it still had its badge signifying it had another five months of British road tax paid. That had left the simple task of obtaining insurance which Dalia had arranged at the showroom with a British insurance company.

The five-hour drive through Spain to Madrid's Ritz Hotel was relaxing for Dalia, as her immediate destination was well marked from Gibraltar and the roads were uncluttered. Attentive to the speed restrictions, she enjoyed the effortless power of the two-litre petrol engine as it ate up the miles, allowing her mind to drift to Malik. With minimal rest breaks, it took twelve hours to reach Bilbao from Gibraltar, but a break in Madrid would refresh

Dalia and keep her alert, as well as provide her with time to shop and plenty of time to catch the ferry.

As Dalia looked out of her hotel room window over Retiro Park and the Prado Museum, she considered whether she should attempt to pick up a hitchhiker as additional cover for her arrival in England. It was something Malik was undecided upon and had chosen to leave to her. She decided to take the opportunity if it arose and if the right person was available, concluding that a British woman with the proper credentials who urgently required a lift through to London would be ideal.

Meanwhile Jamali, who spoke Spanish and was travelling as a Spanish tourist, was sitting in Retiro Park facing the hotel. He pulled hard on his cigarette as he considered his next move. The Network had paid him two million US dollars to ensure that at least one of the bombs made it to London, and then to kill Malik and Dalia. The difficult task was not to lose track of Dalia, as he knew that the chances of finding her again would be slim. Immediately Jamali saw the car and witnessed their separation he knew that the car and boat would each carry a bomb to England. He had been forced to follow Dalia rather than the boat, but he felt confident she would soon lead him to Malik after her drop. If he were to fail after accepting the risks, making promises and being so well paid, he knew he would spend the rest of his life looking over his shoulder. Nonetheless, Jamali enjoyed the moment as he sat in the empty park, and he could not help but consider how this mission and its reward would propel him forward as one of the most powerful underworld chiefs in Argentina. This was the last time he planned to get his own hands dirty.

Jamali had been surprised but relieved that the Argentine authorities did not discover Malik's interest in Carlos Frer's boatyard. He had been concerned that any investigation by police of the boatyards in Buenos Aires would have uncovered *Last Tango* and its intended journey to Gibraltar. The guards that Jamali provided for the Iguazú Factory had told him of Malik's and Dalia's frequent visits to the yard, and it had certainly proved easy for him to discover from one of the yard workers about the boat's recent sale to an English couple and their departure for Gibraltar. Although the yard, and presumably the police, had been fooled by the disguises, Jamali had not.

For ten days he had waited patiently for the arrival of *Last Tango* into Gibraltar, and when the boat finally arrived he was able to pick up his targets' movements. He had followed them to Malaga then back with the Audi A3, and watched as they had loaded Dalia's belongings and, he thought, one bomb, into the car. It had been an easy task to place the magnetic transmitter under the car as it sat in the hotel car park, and with a range of up to twenty kilometres and batteries that lasted for over seventy-two hours he was confident the sophisticated vehicle-tracking equipment would not let him down. So far it had worked perfectly.

It was not easy to follow someone across Europe in such clandestine circumstances, especially on your own and when you were well known to the target. He must be invisible, infinitely flexible and always prepared to respond immediately to any move the target may make. With these principles in mind, Jamali travelled light on a fast Yamaha 1300cc motorbike with aluminium chassis and a powerful four-cylinder fuel-injected engine that combined high performance and a comfortable ride.

Apart from the clothes he was wearing, his wallet, his motorcycle helmet and the vehicle tracking device, his only other possessions were crammed into a small backpack. Most of the contents were highly sophisticated surveillance items, including movement sensors, wireless listening and telephone-tapping devices and personal tracking equipment, should he be able to get close enough to Dalia or her possessions. It was the surveillance equipment, all of it obtained legitimately, that gave him the edge.

Jamali rose stiffly from the park bench to look for a foreign money exchange bureau, a travel company, and somewhere to purchase some alkaline batteries. He would need plenty of British currency, as well as euros, and ferry timetables from Spain to England. He also required ferry timetables from France including Eurotunnel train times, though he was already confident that Dalia would take a ferry from Bilbao.

Staying in the same hotel as Dalia was risky but no worse than boarding the same overnight ferry. It also provided him with immediate access to Dalia's Audi in the hotel car park, and also her room.

Chapter 76

March 4th, Z - 59 Days
London, England

The last two weeks in Buenos Aires had yielded little more information, and with no more leads Harry and Tess were at a dead end. London agreed that the trail had gone cold and ordered them to return home. It was believed the terrorists had left Argentina and that there was a far greater chance of finding the terrorist cell as they crossed the Atlantic Ocean or as they entered the United Kingdom.

The Argentine Security Service traced Jamali as far as Madrid Barajas Airport where he had flown from São Paulo, and although European law-enforcement agencies were now searching for him, he had subsequently disappeared, they assumed under a new identity. The ASS had apprehended the two men who were filmed with Jamali in the Hyatt Hotel on the night that Doctor Baloch had been murdered, but apart from finding conclusive evidence of the doctor's assassins they were satisfied the two men knew nothing of the bomb factory or the terrorists.

Although Argentine law enforcement agencies continued with surveillance at all border points, Encizo's Counter Subversion and Counterterrorist Center had begun to scale down their search to find the terrorists in Argentina. The reality was that if the terrorists wanted to leave Argentina undetected, then they could have done so with ease.

But their time had not been wasted, for Harry and Tess had collected a vast amount of information, including Jamali's identity and an excellent image of the Vixen, and growing dossiers on all three fugitives. They hoped that by combining this intelligence with information obtained by MI6 and the CIA, new leads would follow.

Harry had telephoned Tally last night to tell her he would be home within the next couple of days though he would still be working on the case. She had appeared at ease with Harry's mission. He knew that the media reports would have helped fit the pieces of the jigsaw together and was pleased that his firm had greater knowledge of his involvement. So far Tess had not been named publicly and MI6 hoped to keep it that way. Tally had enquired whether Harry had a partner, and he told her as much as she needed to know, which included that he intended to invite his partner to stay at his home for the duration of the mission. After all they were partners and would be working all hours, not to mention sharing the same car. The case did not need the added complication of them living far apart, and Harry had no intention of staying in a hotel in London when he could easily travel outside the cordon and home to his own bed. Tally had sounded businesslike and told Harry she would ask Maureen, Harry's cleaner, to make up the spare room. Harry had left it at that.

As they prepared for landing at Gatwick on the long British Airways flight from Buenos Aires via São Paulo, it was Tess who broached the subject of home. 'Will you introduce me to your ponies? How many did you say you have?'

'I hope you'll help me look after them,' Harry replied light-heartedly. 'I have three – Jupiter, Saturn and Neptune. Not quite enough for a string, but three is all I can manage right now. Together with a friend we make up a string of six. We help each other to train and exercise them. Fortunately he is rarely away from home, although I'm always in his debt. It's not ideal sharing but it's one way to survive in the game, especially as I'm away so much. It's pre-season in England now; I should be busy exercising.'

'Perhaps I can help. I've done a little horseback riding.'

'That would be great. The hacking and gallops are easy enough, but the moves, sharp turning, and so on, are tricky.'

'I'll pick it up,' said Tess nonchalantly.

'I don't doubt it.'

'Will you stay at your home?'

'I think we should stick together,' replied Harry hopefully.

'I guess we'll have to stay in London.'

Harry looked crestfallen. 'Chertsey is very close to London.'

'Are you asking me to stay?'Tess asked, supressing a giggle.

Harry cheeks flushed. 'I kind of hoped you would. Would you like to stay?'

Tess had made up her mind days ago when she had checked a map. 'I guess so,' she replied off-handedly.

Harry kissed her. 'That's great. I hope you like Maureen.'

'Who's Maureen?' replied Tess, raising her eyebrows.

'She's my housekeeper. Tally is the company secretary and lives near by. Together they keep things running when I'm away.'

On leaving the arrivals lounge, Harry and Tess were hailed by an MI6 driver and driven to Vauxhall Cross.

"Harry, Tess, come on in,' said Sir Michael as he rose from behind his desk. 'Minister, this is Harry Winchester and Tess Fulton.'

Harry and Tess realised that the Foreign Secretary had been waiting in Sir Michael's office for their arrival, though it could not have been long since Merissa walked in behind Harry with the first tray of coffee and other refreshments.

'Please, sit down,' Sir Michael said to no one in particular.

The office had been rearranged with the right number of chairs, all facing the desk.

'Minister?' began Sir Michael.

The Foreign Secretary cleared his throat. 'Harry, Tess, I hope you don't mind me calling you by your first names but I feel I know more about you both than my own family. First things first. Tess, the Director CIA has reaffirmed that both yourself and Bernazzani will continue to operate this side of the pond until Operation Enduring Freedom is resolved.'

Tess felt a wave of relief. She had dreaded the possibility of returning home.

'You have both done an excellent job in discovering what you have, information that will undoubtedly help us find the terrorists. What you don't know is that we're now actively pursuing a second front. Sir Michael will explain more in a moment, but before he does, I want to make it clear that the Government considers you both as its vanguard in this entire operation. It's not only vital that you neutralise this terrorist cell and the bomb but highly desirable that you capture one of them alive. We believe that Fox is the leader and he would be ideal. You'll both have all the resources that we can provide at your disposal, and I'm hoping that you'll find we haven't been sitting still.

'MI6 is to continue to control the offensive arm of Operation Enduring Freedom here in the UK, and is receiving the full support of the Home Office and all other Government departments. Within the Home Office close support is being provided by the Gold Group who have the full support of the Armed Forces, as well as MI5, Customs and Excise, and the Immigration Service. Anyway, I'll let Sir Michael explain why we need one of these people alive.'

Sir Michael leaned forward, resting his elbows on his desk in front of him. 'Thank you, Minister. You'll be briefed on the detail in the ops room by Rosalind immediately we've finished. With the help of the CIA, NSA, NRO and our own GCHQ, we believe we have established where the leaders of terrorist organisations met to plan this attack. Tracking air movement to and from a heroin factory high in the mountains of Tajikistan, we have so far established the whereabouts of six different terrorist organisations. The organisations represent some of the most hardline Islamic terror groups in the world, all united by al-Qa'eda. We believe that bin Laden and al-Zawahiri masterminded the attack, though their personal whereabouts remains to be established. Either we or the Americans have surveillance on each of the known hideouts from the air and ground.

'Now that Article Five has been invoked, NATO is secretly preparing amphibious and airborne rapid reaction forces that will act with surgical precision and destroy these organisations, and others should they be identified. NATO's problem is that the political risks associated with violating sovereign territory to engage with the terrorists are considerable. However, NATO has received personal assurances from the leaders of each of the six states so far involved that should there be irrefutable evidence that these organisations are responsible for orchestrating the nuclear attack on London, each will grant NATO the authority to proceed.'

Harry and Tess realised where this was going.

'Current air and ground intelligence is effective at locating and watching the terrorists, but neither is likely to provide proof of complicity. We need inside information and despite the efforts of every Western intelligence service we believe that only an insider close to the operation can provide the evidence we need. Unfortunately, we cannot seize a suspected leader, without risk of compromising the NATO response.'

'You mean to capture one of the terrorist cell?' whispered Harry in amazement.

'I appreciate the responsibility on you both is huge,' the Minister nodded gravely. 'We must prevent this attack on London and its inevitable repercussions. But we must also prevent further attacks by neutralising those responsible, and establish a firm basis upon which all nations can properly address the root causes of the growth in global terrorism. This attack on London provides the ultimate rallying cry.'

'Has my country bought into this?' Tess asked, surprised that the CIA had not attempted to lift suspects from known sites.

The Minister sipped his coffee. 'Soon after we had located several Islamic terror groups, your President proposed the wider plan at a secret NATO summit. He supports rapid and decisive NATO-led retaliation against all groups involved, quickly followed by aid packages and economic support to states infested with terror groups, and then UN action intended to identify and implement long-term global solutions.'

Sir Michael's office fell silent.

'Is there any chance of finding bin Laden and his lieutenants?' asked Harry, excited by the possibility, however remote, of destroying the terrorists' hierarchy and preparing conditions for peace.

Sir Michael had foreseen the question. 'Other than by seizing an insider? It's doubtful. We still have a number of unidentified flights out of the mountains of Tajikistan. Currently, we believe that bin Laden and his lieutenants are hiding out either in tribal areas near Afghanistan in the rugged South Waziristan district of Pakistan or near the north-western city of Peshawar. Casey is working on the possibility of a connecting flight that may have been taken from Peshawar into Sudan, somewhere near Khartoum. We're not hopeful about confirmed sightings from the air, or word from our people on the ground.'

Sir Michael glanced at the Foreign Secretary then stood up. Harry and Tess followed suit. 'Harry, Tess,' Sir Michael concluded, 'I'd like you both to catch up in the ops room this afternoon, then sleep on the problem and come back and see me tomorrow morning. I'll have the key players assembled, then we'll consider how we might capture at least one of the cell.'

'Thank you, sir,' responded Harry, plainly doubtful.

No one thought anyone else looked particularly confident.

As he walked towards the door, Harry faced the Director.

'Sir, just one thing.'

'Yes, Harry?'

'I take it our intelligence on the terrorist cell has not been released?'

'No, but there is pressure from Number Ten and the Home Secretary to release the headshots to the media, with as much supporting information as we can provide.'

'We must not, sir. That may be the only edge we have left.'

Looking puzzled, Sir Michael assured Harry that nothing would be released without his knowledge and that they would discuss the issue at tomorrow morning's meeting.

Four hours later, after an exhaustive briefing and debriefing in the ops room with Rosalind, Dudley and a host of other operatives including Bernazanni and Casey, Harry and Tess recovered their luggage and made their way down to the foyer. Here Harry collected the keys for a car that was waiting for them in the underground car park under Vauxhall Cross.

Once inside the Range Rover, Tess spoke up. 'So what are you thinking?'

'That on the face of it we are doing all we can, using every resource available to us. We have the tightest border controls I have ever seen, MI5 are conducting a massive internal search for the terrorists, and the Metropolitan Police with the help of the Armed Forces are searching hard for the bomb.'

Harry pulled the Range Rover up the ramp, through the heavy green-metallic electric gates and out of Vauxhall Cross before heading west.

'How long until we get home?' Tess asked feeling a change of subject was in order.

Harry liked the way she said 'home' and told her so. 'We should be there by three. There will be time to show you around before people knock off. Do you mind, there won't be time in the morning?'

'Can't wait.' Tess smiled. 'I really can't,' she followed up, kissing him on his left cheek.

Harry knew it must be said. 'Tess, I don't want you to take this the wrong way but...'

'I know,' Tess interrupted. 'In public we must remain entirely professional, at least for now.'

Harry sighed with relief. 'I thought you'd understand. I just had to be sure.'

'I also know that it goes for your firm as well as the operation, in fact everyone. I didn't ask for this, my feelings aren't just physical.'

They glanced at each other.

'I feel the same. Let's see where it leads us, OK?'

After several minutes Harry broke the silence. 'On the surface everything that can be done is being done on land, by sea and in the air. But it's all symmetrical.'

'You mean predictable?' queried Tess.

'Yes. You and I have followed this cell for weeks now. They are not predictable. This cell is clever, well resourced, and well motivated. On the surface their plan has been faultless. We may get another lucky break, but we can't rely on that. We need to think outside the box, we need an asymmetric response to this attack.'

'Something new?'

'I guess.'

Tess gave a confused look. 'Can you give me a for instance?'

'We can improve our chances of success by increasing vigilance among the public, searching for bombs, and by everything else that is already being done. But our responses are predictable, reactive. What we don't have is a proactive plan that, if played out, provides an opportunity to win.'

'Is that possible?'

'I'm not sure. What is it that we have that the terrorist cell does not know we have?'

Tess thought for a moment. 'Some intelligence, our pictures, profiles.'

'That's right. If our profiles of these people are correct then perhaps we can win.'

'OK. I'm listening.'

'I'm thinking psychological warfare.'

'You're kidding?'

'Psyops has contributed to the winning of more wars than any other strategy in the last two thousand years, probably in the history of mankind. We could gather a group of the world's leading experts.'

'But you need to communicate with the terrorists to have an effect on them.'

'And for that we have the best media machine in the world,' Harry concluded.

At 3 p.m., Harry pulled the Range Rover into his driveway.

'Impressive,' said Tess as she looked around her and admired the old Tudor manor house, the smaller house adjacent to it that was attached to a stable block and a barn, and the long pebble drive with paddocks either side. 'You own all this?' she asked incredulously.

'According to Tally, I do now. On paper at least. My father and I are rather hoping he will live considerably longer than the period necessary to avoid inheritance tax.'

Tess frowned. 'Why put your life at risk when you have all this?'

Harry glanced at Tess, realising she was teasing him. 'Material goods are poor substitutes to health and happiness. I know some very wealthy people who are also very unhappy. It's people, people like you and the people who work here, people who want to make a difference, who make me happy.'

As Tess entered the house ahead of Harry, she was confronted by a grinning black Labrador sitting patiently on a large soft cushion in an oversized basket.

'This is Max,' said Harry with affection. 'He's the only being in the world who believes I can do no wrong, apart from leaving him behind that is. He will not leave his basket until I have apologised.' Harry dropped everything he was carrying and made a fuss of Max. Within seconds Max was thumping his thick black tail beside himself with joy. Leaning forward, Max gave Harry several slobbery licks before leaving his basket and greeting Tess with an equally enthusiastic welcome.

Chapter 77

March 8th, Z – 55 Days
50° 08′ N 3° 21′ W, English Channel

Eleven Type 42 Destroyers form the backbone of the Royal Navy. The primary role of the British destroyer was to provide area air defence to a group of ships, although it was also effective against surface targets at sea. In addition to their role as an air defence platform, the Type 42 Destroyer operated independently conducting patrol and boarding operations, enforcing UN embargoes as well as providing humanitarian assistance across the world. Each destroyer was capable of a maximum speed of thirty knots from two combined gas turbines. As well as holding Sea Dart missiles each ship had a 144-mm gun, two 20-mm close-range guns, two Vulcan Phalanx close-in weapons systems, and anti-submarine torpedoes and decoy launchers. Each ship was also equipped with a range of sophisticated sensor radars and sonar and maintained a Lynx helicopter that was armed with missiles, anti-ship and anti-submarine torpedoes and machine guns.

The first HMS *Nottingham* commissioned in 1703 was a fourth-rate cruiser with 365 men and 60 guns. She had formed part of Shovell's fleet that sailed with Admiral Rooke to attack and take the formidable Rock of Gibraltar in 1704. Since then every *Nottingham* naval ship had had a close association with Gibraltar.

It was the sixth HMS *Nottingham*, commissioned in 1980, with her D91 pennant number emblazoned in large black letters in the middle of her sharp grey hull, that was on station in the English Channel, with HMS *Cardiff* forty miles to her west and HMS *Liverpool* seventy miles to her east. At a state of operational preparedness, the first since she had returned to duty from a repair period, her orders were to patrol the English Channel within boundaries and conduct board and search operations on vessels from foreign ports of departure that were capable of smuggling a nuclear bomb into the United Kingdom.

Twelve nautical miles due north of Alderney in a blustery English Channel, *Last Tango* was to receive its third request for identification or Rights of Approach questioning since leaving Gibraltar. It was unfortunate for her that HMS *Nottingham* had a boarding crew available, and remarkably there were no other suspect vessels in the vicinity. In *Last Tango*'s favour the boarding crew considered her to be low-risk, particularly as she had a British owner, she was destined for Amsterdam, her registration verification had checked out, and she was entirely compliant. The captain also understood that there was no woman on board, contrary to his brief. However, the boat was in UK territorial waters and a simple search would keep his crew active.

Malik had already discussed with Baba and his three crewmen the possibility of being boarded, though he need not have worried. All of them were seasoned professionals when it came to smuggling, and as far as they were concerned there simply was no cargo. The three Egyptian crewmen who spoke very little English showed a touching faith in Baba, who in turn was visibly confident that Malik knew what he was doing. Despite Baba's considerable efforts, he had been unable to find any illegal cargo either inside or outside the boat, and if he could not find it he surmised no one would. Naturally he could not tear up the boat in the search process so he had quizzed Malik repeatedly, but to no avail.

Barely making steerageway in parallel with HMS *Nottingham*, *Last Tango* was boarded by a sublieutenant, a petty officer and two ratings on the aft deck. No one was surprised to see the sailors carrying personal side arms holstered on their waist bands. Two ratings, each armed with assault rifles as well as their side arms, remained in the boarding vessel with a coxswain where they maintained a covering position supported from a distance by HMS *Nottingham*'s 4.5-inch gun and starboard 20-mm close-range gun. The two ratings on board *Last Tango* each held a wandlike sensor that was attached to electronic equipment carried on straps over their shoulders. Malik recognised them as Geiger counters similar to the cased sensor and wand used by Baloch at the Iguazú factory. As Malik considered what Baba and his men would make of the irregular equipment, the sublieutenant offered his hand, introduced himself then asked for their passports and papers. Malik had them to hand and was relieved to see that they received no more than a cursory glance.

Returning the passports, the sub-lieutenant continued, 'You are within twelve miles of the United Kingdom and are therefore in UK territorial waters. Do you have anything to declare?'

'Nothing at all,' Malik replied confidently.

'Are you carrying anything for anyone other than yourselves?'

'No.'

'Will you comply with a search of your boat?'

Malik had little doubt the search would continue, regardless of his reply. 'By all means, please do. My crew don't speak English but will assist in any way they can.'

'Thank you, sir.'

The sub-lieutenant signalled to the petty officer and ordered the search, then stayed on the aft deck with Malik, as Baba escorted the petty officer and two ratings below deck to begin the search.

As the search continued, Malik struck up a conversation. 'This morning I was asked twice to provide identification, once by a French naval ship and once by HMS *Cardiff*. We were in international waters on both occasions and neither of them boarded me. This the first time I have ever been boarded by a military vessel. Is it to do with the terrorist threat to London?'

'I can tell you it's a NATO counterterrorist operation, sir. We are aware you have been challenged already though not searched.'

'But why search us if we are not destined for the UK?'

'I apologise for the inconvenience, but our orders are to search all ships entering UK territorial waters.'

After twenty minutes neither Geiger counter had registered anything more than normal background radiation and the petty officer signalled the all-clear to the sublieutenant.

The sub-lieutenant handed Malik a form attached to a clipboard and pen, then pointed to where Malik must sign. 'I would be grateful if you would sign this declaration, then we will be on our way.'

'What's this for?' Malik demanded, as he prepared to sign.

'It simply confirms that you were fully compliant with the search, and that no damage was caused, or that anything was seized.'

Malik shrugged casually, then signed and handed back the clipboard and pen.

'Well, sir, we're finished. Thank you very much for your cooperation. Providing you do not call in to any port en route to Amsterdam or make any unexplained detours, it's doubtful you will be troubled again.'

Malik escorted the sub-lieutenant back to the boarding vessel. 'What happens to those who don't cooperate?' he asked off-handedly.

'They find us in hot pursuit,' the sub-lieutenant replied bluntly. 'We will deploy whatever assets are necessary to stop them.'

'Ever sunk one?'

'Not recently,' the sub-lieutenant grinned.

'Well, good luck,' offered Malik.

The two men shook hands.

'Thank you again for your cooperation, sir. Have a safe voyage.'

'You're welcome, thanks.'

Malik watched as the heavily laden boarding vessel skipped over the three-foot swells towards HMS *Nottingham*, outboard motors whining. He responded to a perfunctory wave from the sublieutenant in the manner of all sea captains.

Last Tango worked back up to fifteen knots and continued towards Amsterdam.

Chapter 78

March 9th, Z - 54 Days
London, England

Harry drove the Range Rover onto Thorney Street from the car park under Thames House, the home of MI5. Soon they were heading down Horseferry Road to New Scotland Yard.

'Do you really think it'll work?' asked Tess sceptically.

'There were three hundred politicians, global security strategists, psychologists and spin doctors in that room, Tess. Politicians, professors, doctors, journalists, religious leaders. Everyone necessary was there, even the most sceptical of newspaper editors. I can understand people's cynicism but, vitally, everyone accepts that we should give it a try.'

'But how do we know the terrorists will watch the television and read the newspapers?'

'We don't, but it's highly likely they will. After all, how else do they get to find out what we are up to and whether their campaign of terror is succeeding? Terrorists are narcissistic too; they like to read about themselves in newspapers and watch their exploits on TV.'

'There must be risks,' asked Tess, mystified by Harry's strong belief in this fluffy and public plan. 'What do you consider are the risks?'

'The first was exposed at the conference,' Harry said patiently. 'I believe the principal risk is that the fringe media and the public will think the Government has gone soft just when they believe a hard line is required. As we heard today, and despite most people's protestations, people do believe the written word and what they watch on television, regardless of whom it was written by or who produced it, or to what degree a story tells or conceals the truth. Right now public opinion is firmly against Islam. If my plan is to work we need to turn public opinion and encourage people to actively differentiate between Islam as a faith and political terrorism.'

'There are some who are speaking out for the terrorists.'

'They speak out to inflame the situation and maximise chaos. It's precisely the opposite effect that I seek, and that's why certain radical clerics and other extremists must be detained and their personal freedoms removed. If the public rebel against the more compassionate and conciliatory tone suggested by our panel of experts, then the mass media may turn, and then too will the Government. It's down to Cobra and our propaganda experts to keep the momentum going.'

Tess looked doubtful. 'OK, I'll buy that for now. What's your second risk?'

'That they don't speak English.'

Tess chuckled. 'The nation's great and good discussing the issue for seven hours and not one person mentioned the obvious.'

'Fox and Vixen are very intelligent and they most likely speak English, but we don't know to what degree they can pick up the nuances. What we can be confident about is that they are mercenaries who will not die for bin Laden. Jamali, on the other hand, is a thug who is less sophisticated and is therefore extremely dangerous. If his finger is on the trigger, which I doubt, then we're in trouble.'

'Why doubt Jamali has access to the bomb?'

'The killing of Doctor Baloch was too clumsy. Jamali is well resourced, but I don't believe he has the credentials to pull off such an important mission. He's nothing more than a common criminal. I'm surprised he has travelled to Europe, and can only conclude he is following Fox and Vixen.'

Tess immediately considered the possibility Jamali was following Fox and Vixen. 'You think he means to kill them?' she asked incredulously.

Harry nodded, then pulled up to give way for a bus.

'Jamali has probably been entrusted to tie up loose ends, which means Fox and Vixen are considered dangerous by al-Qa'eda. That proves they could be useful to us.'

Tess sat back and thought about this for a few moments. It made sense. 'Why must you be publicised as the hunter? By raising your name as the person responsible for hunting down the terrorists you are presenting yourself as a target to those who wish them to succeed. The terrorists can give themselves up to any police officer.'

'That one was down to the experts, but I have to agree. If this plan is to work the terrorists must know that there is someone out there they can trust, someone who the UK Government will respond to, and someone who understands them. By going public I will be offering myself as the facilitator.'

Tess looked down at her notebook open on her lap. 'Surely the counterterrorist operation that MI5 and the police are planning on March 20th, raiding twenty-six different locations throughout the capital, will discourage conciliation.'

'That's why we must all carefully distinguish between good Muslims and the political subversives within Islam. We must be conciliatory towards the faith but damning about the violence. Our terrorist cell must be encouraged to understand that we consider this attack an act of war and that it will have grave and long-lasting repercussions for all Muslims and Islam. They must be informed by their own clerics that our future goals are compatible with the correct interpretation of the Qur'an, not conflicting. Importantly, we must remind them that the West will not negotiate with terror organisations and, as the UN discovered recently in Turkey, neither will anyone else. I will, however, leave the door open for them to talk to me.'

'Are we going to double-cross them?'

'I doubt it. If we show we can't be trusted then the next terror attack may prove unstoppable.'

'It sounds like you're advocating negotiating with terrorists.'

'I hope that Psyops can turn the mercenaries.' If we can find and deactivate the bomb, learn from the cell, destroy their leaders, and seek a new beginning with the Islamic world, we will have achieved a massive victory against global terror.'

Tess thought a moment. 'You've been studying Sun Tzu's work, the *Art of War*. "Know your enemy better than yourself and understand his battlefield".'

'Those two factors help explain why your country lost the Vietnam War, despite massive superiority in firepower. The North Vietnamese were not concerned with a high body count and knew how to fight in the jungle. The US politicians and public could not come to terms with the human cost, and the GIs could not overcome the fear of simple booby-traps in the jungle laid by children no more than six years old. You heard the psychologists today. Sure the ground is the world, land, sea and air, but the battlefield or battlespace of global terrorism is not limited by anything but the human mind. People herald global terrorism as a new type of war although it was first discovered thousands of years ago. Progress in the art of war over the last two thousand years has been anything but progressive. Science on the other hand...'

'The end justifies the means,' Tess concluded.

'And so said the terrorist,' replied Harry. 'War is limitless, it's as simple as that, and nowadays if you start applying your own boundaries you will exclude consideration of options available to your enemy and probably lose. Fox and Vixen are not motivated by ideology in the same way the 9/11 hijackers or London bombers were, and that, along with the knowledge they are coming, is one of their very few identifiable weaknesses that we have to exploit.'

Harry and Tess left the Range Rover in New Scotland Yard's secure car park off Victoria Street. Over the next four hours the Deputy Commissioner introduced the two operatives to the Commissioner, then gave them a series of briefings on the preparations for London's evacuation, the search for, identification and mapping of radiological emissions, and the ongoing operations against London's known or suspected terrorist cells.

The most visually inspiring part of the tour was their visit to the vast Metropolitan Police Command and Control Centre which was fed live pictures from over five thousand powerful zoom cameras positioned at key locations around the capital. Originally intended to support traffic control, it was not long before its value in preventing, detecting and solving crime was realised. Astonishingly, the system could lock onto an individual's image and track him or her throughout most of the capital.

Their visit concluded with another short discussion with the Commissioner before the two operatives were taken to the Media Press Forum and introduced to the Commissioner's Media Officer, Chief Inspector Jane Walsh. Here they watched with interest as the daily briefing unfolded, the public face of the authorities' response to the nuclear attack. The room was packed full as usual and today, among the more routine briefings, the Mayor of London spoke and took questions.

Harry knew that it was just a matter of time before he stood at the same podium.

Chapter 79

March 9th, Z – 54 Days
52° 30′ N 4° 59′ E, North Sea

Last Tango's V-hull sliced cleanly through the surface of the smooth sea. The tips of the gentle surface ripples broke into white cusps only in the boat's wake. Despite the familiar throb of the two Caterpillar 800-horsepower diesel engines, the calm that greeted Malik as he left the salon surprised him. Yesterday evening his watch had been gusty, but wet and now the new dawn was calm and with heavy fog.

Malik climbed to the fly bridge. He knew the crewman at the helm to be a quiet and efficient seaman and they exchanged an amicable glance. There was no need to break the magic that every morning at sea presented. Surveying the dials, Malik saw they were maintaining a steady five knots. At that speed from their current position he estimated it would take two hours to reach the Jachthaven Aelous boatyard on the south side of the North Sea Canal. Amsterdam harbour was off one of the busiest shipping routes in the world, and until the sun rose higher in the east and burned off the fog they remained reliant on radar.

Feeling the cold and damp, Malik reached for his tin of miniature cigars, lit one with his Zippo lighter then sat on a cushioned seat out of the breeze. Considering his mission, he knew that *Dutch Master* would be ready to make her maiden voyage to London in a few weeks where she would be immediately brought into service to help with its evacuation. Dwelling on Dalia, he knew that every day she would be monitoring the news from London as she made her way towards its heart. He also knew that she would be constantly re-evaluating the best site for Fat Man, not for maximum impact, as that was irrelevant for such a devastating bomb, but for its security prior to detonation. Not wanting her to take any risks, he had suggested she simply leave the bomb at the house in Islington, maybe in the kitchen or larder. Drifting back to his own plans he reconsidered *Last Tango*'s role during the next phase of the operation, *Dutch Master*'s safe passage to London.

Malik knew that it would be a simple operation to exchange the fender, in fact a whole set of fenders, between *Last Tango* and *Dutch Master*. He would do this task himself one morning when his crew were at the hotel sleeping off a late night at the Vondelpark Casino that Baba had enjoyed so much the last time they were together in Amsterdam. After the search by HMS *Nottingham*, Malik was confident that Little Boy would make the voyage across the North Sea to the heart of London, but nevertheless he decided that Baba and his crew should stay in Amsterdam as planned and escort *Dutch Master* at least as far as UK territorial waters before turning and making headway for Cairo. Throwing his cigar overboard, he went in search of Baba whom he heard swearing in the galley.

Malik found Baba attempting to light the stove. 'Here, let me,' he offered. 'You fill the kettle with water.'

Baba and two of his crew had been up until the very early hours that morning drinking ouzo and playing cards while Malik had taken the helm.

'How long until we reach Amsterdam?' mumbled Baba, feeling ill.

'Another two hours. There is a heavy fog.'

'I'm not well.' Baba looked white, pale.

'So I see. We will wait for breakfast and eat on shore.'

'That is wise, my friend.'

Malik made coffee while Baba sat nursing his head in the salon.

'I'd like you to stay in Amsterdam as planned, then escort *Dutch Master* at least as far as UK territorial waters,' Malik instructed. 'You'll attract any attention shown to *Dutch Master* prior to turning for Cairo. Understood?'

'It'll be a pleasure my friend,' Baba groaned.

Malik handed a steaming hot mug of coffee out from the galley, and Baba carried it to the helmsman before returning to take his own.

Chapter 80

March 15th, Z – 48 Days
London, England

In the United Kingdom, the Home Office was responsible for counterterrorism policy, and the lead for ensuring domestic security lay with the civil authorities, particularly with the police. Support from the Armed Forces, especially the use of force, was provided on the specific request of a civil authority like the Metropolitan Police to the Home Office. When deploying forces overseas the Ministry of Defence had to ensure that military capability remained available to these civil authorities should they require support in response to terrorist incidents or other emergencies at home.

The MOD played a major role in the management of any crisis involving national security, be it a terrorist incident, a regional conflict, or transition to major war. The department's most important role, established by Oliver Cromwell in 1646, was the maintenance of the Government when threatened. At the highest level of the national crisis management system was the Cabinet with Cobra in support. The Chief of Defence Staff, the highest-ranking military officer, sat on Cobra and attended Cabinet meetings when necessary.

The Cabinet had political control over the various means at the Government's disposal, including diplomatic, political, economic and, if necessary, military action. It was the Cabinet, with the Prime Minister in charge, who were at the helm, not the MOD. The MOD was responsible for the defence aspects of crisis management, including the high-level direction of military operations. It ensured that Cabinet and ministerial decisions were translated into clear and unambiguous direction to the subordinate military headquarters which undertook the day-to-day running of military operations.

The Chief of Defence Staff drew on the expertise of the chiefs of the Naval, General and Air Staffs as the professional heads of their services, normally through discussion in frequent Chief of Staff Committee meetings. Below the Chief of Staff Committee was the heart of the MOD, the Defence Crisis Management Organisation. Here, integrated contingency planning of crisis commitments was undertaken and advice prepared for ministers.

The Permanent Joint Headquarters located at Northwood was a subordinate headquarters to the MOD and was responsible for the execution of specific military operations. The Permanent Joint Headquarters commander, the Chief of Joint Operations, was normally appointed Joint Commander for operations assigned to the powerful military headquarters.

In essence, crises were met on a day-to-day basis by the DCMO, which was located in the MOD Main Building in Whitehall. The DCMO fell under the direct responsibility of the Minister for the Armed Forces and was organisationally joined up to all the necessary strands of Government and other bodies by a network of secure electronic communications. During crises, the Foreign Office, the Cabinet Office and representatives from other key organisations met regularly in the MOD in order to formulate policy and exchange information. The MOD was also the forum for assisting other Government departments with crisis-management techniques and procedures.

Given the current geopolitical environment and Britain's continuing global interests, discussion and negotiation through numerous international bodies played a vital part in preserving international security. The UK contributed to this through her membership of the United Nations and with her seat on the UN Security Council as a permanent member. Her current chairmanship of the UN Security Council's Counterterrorism Committee had already proved useful in gaining worldwide support for Operation Enduring Freedom, and for worldwide condemnation of the terrorists. The UK was also a member of the EU, which provided cooperation on civil protection measures, a common European arrest warrant, strengthened air security, and cooperation with the sourcing of terrorist finances.

But it was through NATO that the UK expected support in defence of external threats to her security. After 9/11, NATO had declared that terrorist strike to be an attack on all its members and invoked Article 5 of the Washington Treaty for the first time in its history. After the nuclear attack on London had been verified, Article 5 had been invoked for the second time and now the UK could formally count on the support of all member states. NATO had already deployed airborne warning and control system or AWACS aircraft to help patrol UK, European and North Atlantic airspace, deployed NATO standing naval forces to the Atlantic Ocean, Mediterranean Sea and North Sea to conduct cordon and search ops, replaced UK troops on overseas commitments, attached specialist CBRN troops to enhance the radiological detection force in London, and provided considerable intelligence on terrorist groups with links to al-Qa'eda. NATO also had its Response Force of twenty thousand soldiers on 72-hour stand-by.

Lieutenant Commander Chris Marshall of the Royal Navy was one of a small number of staff who worked in the Defence Logistics Operations Division of the DCMO within the MOD. Aged forty, he had joined the section of four officers that represented each of the three services almost two years ago to work in the 'Commitments' area. His main role was to provide logistics advice to the MOD's DCMO. During his tour he had been involved in the planning and conduct of a large number of operations throughout the world, mostly in the Middle East, Central Asia or the Far East. Less often he had been called upon to provide logistics advice to operations at home, in support of civil authorities overcome by the absence of firemen or ambulance workers, a foot-and-mouth disease crisis among cattle and sheep, and on one occasion, a response to a potentially hazardous traffic incident involving the transportation of nuclear fuel. This latter operation had involved the MOD's Nuclear Accident Response Organisation, which Marshall had controlled since he was the only naval representative in the team and it was his service that maintained the UK's nuclear deterrent. The aim of MOD's NARO was to ensure, in conjunction with civil authorities, an effective response to a nuclear accident or incident, including those arising as a result of terrorist acts involving nuclear weapons, special nuclear material, facilities or reactors. Their key objective was to protect public health and safety, and they were proving invaluable in supporting both DCMO and Gold Group during Operation Enduring Freedom.

In the aftermath of 9/11, Marshall had been deeply involved in contingency planning for a major terrorist strike against the UK, the worst-case scenario being a nuclear strike delivered by air against a major city such as London. He had been heavily involved with Exercise Rapid Response and had continued responsibility for planning the logistics behind NATO's support to the naval cordon and search operation.

When the Prime Minister had announced the al-Qa'eda threat to destroy London with a nuclear weapon and declared war a month ago, all hell had broken loose. Immediately augmentees were draughted in to help plan, control and cover the watchkeeping requirements in the DCMO's bunker in MOD's Main Building and Marshall's cell increased to eight. The logistic effort involved in planning, sustaining and supporting the huge military commitment to Operation Enduring Freedom was taking its toll on the section, but at last, after one month of intense action and incredibly long hours, a steady state had been achieved.

The Chief of Joint Operations was the nominated commander responsible for the military support to London's defence, and in just one month since the Prime Minister's declaration the numbers of Armed Forces personnel involved had grown to 55,000, half of which were Regular Reservists or Territorial Army personnel. So far volunteers had been drafted, but today the Secretary of State for Defence was to submit a paper to the Cabinet justifying why the compulsory call-up of reservists must be applied to certain critical shortfalls in trades including doctors and nurses.

Apart from the massive NATO naval operation that ring-fenced the British Isles, the Royal Navy and its Auxiliary Reserve were providing two hospital ships at Tilbury Docks north of the River Thames, with another two at Gravesend south of the river. These were surface ships that had been held until now in War Maintenance Reserve. The Royal Navy was also providing personnel in support of maritime integrity by augmenting the port authorities, in particular HM Customs and Excise and the Immigration Service.

The Army had a number of responsibilities that began with the cordon around London that was in place but yet to be enforced, two field hospitals, twenty mobile decontamination teams, thirty radiological detection teams including Explosives Ordnance Disposal teams, and fifty-four ambulances. Forty Green Goddess firefighting trucks were also held on stand-by. A predominantly Territorial Army formation, 2 Signals Brigade had been mobilised to provide the deployable element of a national communications infrastructure that was compatible with the civil police and emergency services. In addition, troops had been provided to secure key Government buildings and installations both inside and outside London and a vast amount of military transport had been provided to help move Government departments out of the capital. The Corps of Royal Engineers were busy building an array of temporary detention centres, temporary camps, water supply points, and decontamination centres throughout the south-east of England. The DCMO had also identified a reserve of troops based on a regional brigade who would be used to restore law and order should it be lost by the civil authorities.

To combat airborne delivery, the RAF was patrolling the skies over London using advanced radar systems and Tornado F3 aircraft that maintained the Quick Reaction Alert capability. These capabilities were supplemented by NATO AWACS aircraft and Royal Navy Sea Harriers. The Joint Helicopter Command provided over two hundred observation and support helicopters to the Permanent Joint Headquarters, a force that provided a fast, flexible and powerful response to any location in London. Several flights of helicopters had been allocated to VIP movement, some for medical evacuation, and many for police and military quick reaction forces.

The only element of the Armed Forces immediately available to Operation Enduring Freedom but not under control of the Permanent Joint Headquarters was the SAS. Remaining under the operational command of the MOD, the regiment was assembling in Hereford, where the assault and sniper teams were preparing for ops.

Chapter 81

March 20th, Z – 43 Days
Bilbao, Spain

Dalia had tired of staying at the Ritz Hotel in central Madrid and had looked forward to continuing her journey north to Bilbao. Her passage to London had been well planned but a sluggish cyclone in the Bay of Biscay had caused the cancellation of her Monday sailing. She had been pleased that she had thought to check the departure in advance of travelling to Bilbao, and since she was in no hurry she had rebooked the Premier Class en-suite cabin for the following Monday's departure rather than accept the reclining seat that was all she could be offered for Thursday.

The previous afternoon Dalia had booked into a hotel in Bilbao some twenty minutes from the P&O ferry terminal at Santurtzi. That evening she had driven towards the ferry terminal and found the roadside diner described to her by the hotel's concierge. It lay on the A8 midway between Bilbao and Santander, and was a well-known spot for hikers en route for England. Dalia was hoping to find an English woman of about her own age, someone who might pass as her partner. She required someone with little luggage who wanted to go on to London but, as she had expected, she found no one waiting.

It was at 10 a.m. the following morning when Dalia pulled into the diner's car park for the second time and saw at least a dozen men and women, many holding makeshift signs for London, Birmingham, Cardiff and elsewhere. It did not take long before she spotted what looked like the ideal partner, a woman holding a sign for London. Dalia pulled up and flicked a switch to lower the passenger window.

'Hi, I can take you to London if you like?' Dalia offered immediately the passenger window was open.

The slender redhead in her mid-twenties stooped down and smiled excitedly. 'That would be great. I'm so desperate to get home. Thanks.' The woman waved at the other hikers, then levered herself and her backpack into the passenger seat of the sports car.

Dalia pulled away, noticing the envious looks on the faces of those left behind.

'I'm Susie, by the way.'

'I'm Diana. I hope you can manage with the backpack for ten minutes. Later we'll stow it behind your seat.'

'Thanks, I'm fine. I can't thank you enough for this. Another thirty minutes and I would've had to start walking to the ferry terminal like those losers behind us.'

'Do they start hitching again when they arrive in Portsmouth?'

'Hikers never stop looking for lifts. They'll start the moment they get on the ferry, some as soon as they arrive at the terminal. Some hustle and give hikers a bad name. I don't have to worry now and can look forward to a good night's sleep thanks to you.'

'You looked desperate,' said Dalia flashing a warm smile.

'I was supposed to be working in Spain until September, but now I have to get home to help my parents evacuate the city.'

Dropping Susie at the terminal building, Dalia followed the road signs to the Premier Class booth and checked in with her revised booking reference number. She had agreed to meet Susie at the information desk on board soon before the ship docked at Portsmouth. There were few cars queuing for customs and the Spanish officials saw her British plates and waved her through without concern.

With just under two hours to wait before departure Dalia left her car locked in the short Premier Class vehicle queue on the quay and wandered over to the exclusive club lounge in search of a coffee. With one attendant and two other passengers in the lounge, Dalia was able to relax for the first time that day. She chose from a selection of freshly cooked snacks and helped herself to coffee at the buffet before sitting and selecting Sky News. She checked her cell phone for messages but there were none. Longing to contact Malik, she knew that she could not.

Jamali watched Dalia drop the hiker off, check in, pass through customs and make her way to the club lounge on the quay. Only then did he swing around his Yamaha 1300 and head back to the terminal building where he booked a berth in Standard Class. The cabins were considerably less luxurious than Premier Class but were en suite, functional and complemented his cover.

As Premier Class passengers received priority boarding, Dalia was the fourth vehicle to board the single funnelled P&O ship *Pride of Bilbao*. Leaving her car secure on the upper car deck, she was pleased to find her cabin so well appointed. En suite, it was located in a quiet section of the ship with easy access to the main passenger deck. It was spacious with a bunk big enough for two, a sea view, a colour television, a mini bar and a telephone. Room service looked promising and was available around the clock.

For a brief moment, Dalia considered finding Susie who she knew would have to sleep on a reclining seat. She felt that in different circumstances she and Susie would have enjoyed each other's company. After days of waiting alone in Madrid, Dalia scanned the ship's brochure for something different to pass the time. She decided on Langan's Brasserie for lunch, followed by the cinema, then later a swim and sauna followed by dinner in her room and perhaps the casino. Tomorrow morning she might have another swim and sauna before a late breakfast, when she would consider how else to pass her time until the ship docked at 4:30 p.m.

As Jamali checked his disguise in his cabin, he decided to establish Dalia's whereabouts on board after all. Just as he was applying the finishing touches, Dalia and Susie bumped into each other in a corridor near the restaurant and as he stepped out of his cabin, Susie gratefully accepted Dalia's offer of lunch.

Chapter 82

March 18th, Z - 45 Days
London, England

As Harry and Tess arrived at New Scotland Yard a little after 4:30 a.m., over five hundred police officers were reporting for duty across London in preparation for a preplanned counter-terrorist operation aimed at Islamic militants and suspect terrorists. At 6 a.m., twenty-six raids were to take place on homes, hotels and business premises by MI5 and the Metropolitan Police Antiterrorist Branch.

Above all, the twenty-six squads, comprising armed police, forensics experts and radiological detection teams, hoped to uncover evidence that would lead the authorities to the nuclear bomb and to Fox and Vixen. Evidence or not, the reality was that those arrested in the early hours of this morning would be detained for terrorist offences and held under Section 41 of the Terrorism Act on suspicion of the commission, preparation or instigation of acts of terrorism. Of the one hundred or so arrested and detained few were likely to be released before the early May bank holiday. The subjects ranged from those on the most-wanted list to hate preachers, members of radical organisations, outspoken terrorist sympathisers and supporters of Islamic fundamentalism.

Because of the potentially damaging appearance of racial heavy-handedness, Cobra had ensured that the Cabinet approved the operation in advance. Apart from finding anything that led to the nuclear bomb, the operation was also intending to deny Fox and Vixen support, and to reduce non-related terrorist or criminal activity. It was also hoped that a successful operation would ckeck the escalating fear that insufficient progress was being made by the authorities.

The planning for the operation had commenced months ago with the initial classification of subjects, their investigation and their subsequent surveillance. The suspects were of nineteen different nationalities, including thirty-two Britons and two Germans. The remainder were nationals from countries that lay somewhere between Libya and the Philippines. All but two of the Britons were known to be Muslim. Some were students and some businessmen, though most were either visitors or asylum seekers.

Harry and Tess made their way to the Command and Control Centre where they met Samantha Eldon, the Deputy Commissioner in charge of the operation. They also met a number of other senior figures hosted by the Commissioner, including the Director MI5, the Commanding Officer of 22 SAS, whom Harry knew well, and several members of Cobra. Every visitor could not fail to be impressed with the banks of monitors in front of them that would soon be provided with live feed from each of the twenty-six raids. A second bank of monitors provided multi-point video teleconferencing facilities with the offices of every senior member of Cobra, and the Prime Minister's office.

For the next twelve hours, until the evening's press conference, Harry and Tess were mesmerised as the Deputy Commissioner commanded her operation with authority, clinical judgement and considerable zeal. The operation began at 6 a.m. sharp with police squads approaching each target location. It was chaotic from the offset, as such operations often are, but as the day wore on the evident success of the operation unfolded. It was easy for Harry and Tess to see how Eldon had risen so quickly through the ranks and against the odds in such a male-dominated force. She quite literally drove the operation from New Scotland Yard, and when a subordinate fouled up she resolved the issue swiftly. Two raids ended in messy armed sieges, one of them not ending until 3 p.m. At a third a policeman was shot and wounded while the gunman was chased across London and eventually caught outside the Regent's Park mosque. Despite weeks of surveillance, one heavily armed team had approached the wrong property, losing the element of surprising the suspects who were holed up next door.

For the luckier squads most of the day was spent painstakingly searching the suspect's property for evidence prior to them being taken to police stations where they were booked in, detained and later questioned. In all, over a hundred and forty suspects were arrested then detained at the high-security Paddington Green Police Station.

By the daily press conference at 4:30 p.m. the Deputy Commissioner and Media Emergency Forum were ready to engage with the eagerly waiting press, who were poised like vultures circling above a carcass. In fact, several of the searches were still on-going and only a few interviews had been conducted, but all the subjects had been detained and their property secured. It was too early to release details of the operation's success, but the confident Deputy Commissioner was armed with the purpose of the operation, what had happened during the day, where, knowledge of what had been seized including guns, explosives and subversive material, and the extent of any injuries and the numbers involved, including those arrested and detained.

Harry knew that so far the operation had not provided MI6 with any direct leads. However, the operation and the ensuing publicity would not only assist their search, but London was undeniably a much safer place tonight. This is what he told a relieved Deputy Commissioner after the press conference as he and Tess departed for Chertsey.

Chapter 83

March 20th, Z – 43 Days
Amsterdam, Netherlands

For the period they had to wait for work on Dutch Master to be completed and for her crew to arrive from London, Malik had arranged for Baba and his crew to stay in the same hotel as himself, the La Meridian Park Hotel in central Amsterdam. This meant he could stay over on *Last Tango* whenever he desired and enjoy some privacy.

Michael and Anita, the talented builders of *Dutch Master* and owners of the Jachthaven Aeolus boatyard, had let Malik tie *Last Tango* alongside *Dutch Master*. At over sixteen metres in length, *Last Tango* held her own against the longer three-decked *Dutch Master*, but what little she lost in size she surpassed in sleekness and beauty. There had been no need to use any of the fenders stowed on *Last Tango* or *Dutch Master* as a yard hand had prepared for *Last Tango*'s arrival by fastening fenders from the boatyard's supply to *Dutch Master*'s brand-new hull.

Last night Malik had chosen to sleep on board, then early that morning he calmly exchanged the eighteen red fenders from their hold in the bow of *Last Tango* with the eighteen similar fenders stowed deep in the hull of *Dutch Master*, fenders that Malik had chosen and had added to the riverboat's inventory on his last visit.

Before lunch Malik enjoyed a long swim in the hotel's fitness centre and reconsidered *Dutch Master* and the hold that now housed the bomb. The hold was dry and dark and with restricted access, and the bomb was buried at the very bottom.

Chapter 84

March 21st, Z – 42 Days
London, England

Brigadier James Jarvis, the liaison officer between DCMO and Gold, looked across the desk at the Metropolitan Police Commissioner, realising for the first time just how tired the commander of the Gold Group looked. The Commissioner seemed to have aged ten years in the last six weeks.

'If you don't mind me saying so, you look as though you need some rest.'

The Commissioner grumbled something inaudible as he poured his fourth cup of coffee since he had arrived in his office three hours ago at 6:30 a.m. The Commissioner lived in Fulham with his wife and four children, and like so many other millions of people they had just four weeks left to finish preparations and evacuate their home.

'You will be no good to anyone if you continue like this, and we have more than a month to go before Zulu Day, never mind the aftermath.'

The Commissioner ignored the Brigadier and stared into his cup of steaming black coffee. 'Do you know how hard it is to find gaffer tape? My home cannot withstand a simple burglary never mind a nuclear blast, but can I get the materials I need? No. Just imagine how many people are in the same boat. No wonder people are reluctant to evacuate the city.'

The only other person in the Commissioner's office was his deputy, Samantha Eldon. She had discussed the Commissioner's well-being with the Brigadier minutes before they had entered the office, and at the toss of a coin the army officer had taken responsibility for expressing their concern. Despite the Commissioner's evasion, both the other senior officers could see the observation had hit home.

The Deputy Commissioner stood to examine the large map board that filled one entire wall of the office. The map illustrated the police boroughs, locations of all key headquarters, alternate headquarters, the cordon and its crossing points. Flagged pins of differing colours littered the map, the pink and red ones denoting unofficial radiological emissions. Red flags denoted unexplained sources, the pink flags explained sources. There were considerably more red than pink, though slowly the picture was changing as the detection teams identified each source. The map was a replica of one maintained in the Command and Control Centre two floors below and was kept up to date by two efficient clerks.

'My neighbour's house was ransacked last night, the third house on my street this week. He evacuated last week,' commented the Deputy Commissioner as she took time to check the map. 'Burglary stats rocketed this month too, doubling the previous figures. It's the highest ever monthly figure by some margin and will rise as more people evacuate their homes. And just think how many burglaries are currently lying undiscovered.'

'If the cordon, curfew and increased control measures are implemented then we will stem the rise,' replied the Commissioner, as he considered his own reluctance to evacuate his home. In the security of his own office, the Commissioner dropped his guard with his deputy and the DCMO liaison officer, the two people whose overarching thoughts he valued more than any other in the Gold Group. Each of them knew that he was seeking their support and were happy to wait until he got to the point. He wanted their opinion before the end of the Cabinet meeting and the telephone call he was expecting from the Home Secretary.

'Quite simply, we have two huge and potentially catastrophic law and order problems to resolve aside from the nuclear bomb. The first involves the polarisation of the Muslim community and the racial attacks. Although levelling out, possibly in response to our media campaign and success with arrests and detentions, the attacks could increase again at any moment particularly as we approach Zulu Day. The second problem is the huge leap in burglaries, looting, muggings and robberies across London which remains unchecked. Both are a huge drain on our resources, which should be otherwise engaged searching for the terrorists and their bomb.

'I would like to discuss how I intend to address these two problems. I've asked the Home Secretary to raise the issue of the cordon, a curfew and increased control measures across London in the Cabinet meeting this morning. I expect his approval for me to introduce them whenever I deem them necessary. Well, I consider them necessary now, and I intend to invoke them as soon as practicable. Closing the cordon will allow us to control access into London at the eight crossing points. We already believe that much of the crime is committed by outsiders, opportunists making the most of the conditions. It will help stop them.'

The Brigadier's blue-grey eyes brightened. 'The cordon is in place and can be established within twenty-four hours,' he said, 'but I feel we should provide some warning and guidance or we risk causing chaos and alienating hard-won support.'

'Hearts and minds, eh, James?'

'Worth thousands of police officers, Commissioner.'

'We haven't resolved how to control the crossing points,' the Deputy Commissioner added. 'Issuing a form of pass would be a burden we could do without.'

'I asked this question downstairs yesterday,' replied the Commissioner reassuringly, 'and the answer was simple. We'll require that every person wishing to enter or leave carry their passport on them at all times. In several days we'll have sufficient scanners available for each of the eight crossing points. The intelligence services like the idea too. The scanners will patch through to the Passport Agency and log all human traffic in and out of London, including time. A passport to confirm identity, and adequate proof of business should be sufficient.'

'And if we give everyone warning, say a week, it will give them a chance to pack up and move outside,' added the Deputy Commissioner keenly.

'Exactly, and at the same time we raise the cordon we begin a curfew. No unauthorised movement inside the cordon and outside buildings from 9 p.m. to 5 a.m.'

The two subordinates took a while to consider this. Both liked it.

'It won't be long before curfew breakers are reported by the public,' offered the Deputy Commissioner.

'To be encouraged,' replied the Commissioner heartily. 'We

will advertise and request the public report any violators, expel them and confiscate their passport.'

The Brigadier nodded. 'Night-time businesses will close down.'

'Exactly.' The Commissioner was smiling now. 'In the last month the population has only decreased by another two million. We still have five million residents in London, peaking at seven million during the working day. We need to encourage faster evacuation, not only by making people feel their possessions will be secure, but also by reducing the reasons they have for remaining here. There will be little social life or fun to be had in London, just work, and even that will be increasingly limited, despite the Chancellor's contrary attempts to minimise the effects on the economy.'

'Most of the temporary accommodation sites we've been building are due to be completed this week,' said the Brigadier. 'We can begin to evacuate the homeless.'

'That's great,' said the Deputy Commissioner. 'I'll get people on to that. The Salvation Army has been badgering for weeks.'

'Good for them,' said the Commissioner. 'My wife is one, did you know that?' Without waiting for an answer, he continued. 'I don't subscribe to martial law yet, but I would like to heighten the security presence on the streets by patrolling in groups of four, each one with a suitable vehicle. Each of these squads will comprise two armed policemen with two armed soldiers in support. According to our analysis it'll require four thousand soldiers working in three shifts around the clock. They'll be attached to each borough police force.'

'When do you envisage starting?' asked the Brigadier, who had introduced this idea to the DCMO several weeks ago, based on his own experiences on the streets of Belfast.

'Midnight on Sunday March 27th, six days' time. My response to the rising criminal element is simple, cordon, curfew and control. The "Three Cs" is what Inspector Walsh intends to call them when briefing the media.'

The Deputy Commissioner was bristling with ideas. 'Sir, talking of control, with your authority I'd like to arrange for an immediate weapons amnesty. It's been seven years since the last one. I think we should try once more before people think there's cause to retain banned weapons.'

'You have it, Pat. Tell Inspector Walsh to blend that into her Three Cs campaign.'

Rapidly reaching consensus, it was clear to the three of them that there was little alternative in response to the rising levels of crime, fear and panic.

As they waited for the end of the Cabinet meeting, it occurred to the Brigadier that it might not matter what the Cabinet concluded. The Commissioner had arrived at the right decision for the way ahead, and thankfully the two police officers appeared determined to effect the plan that afternoon for inception the following Sunday evening, regardless. The Brigadier reached for his mobile phone and spoke to the DCMO.

'Commissioner,' said the Brigadier several minutes later, 'I've been asked to enquire about the Met's plans for moving from London, and how you intend to police the capital once it has been evacuated. I've told them that you're likely to want to evacuate Scotland Yard for Watford only after the capital has been evacuated of all people. As for policing, we've an idea if you would like to hear it.'

'James, thank you. You're right on the first point. All of London's police forces have an alternate location to withdraw to on the morning of Sunday May 1st. Neighbouring constabularies are making suitable accommodation available as close to each police force's area of operations as possible, with the cordon crossing points in mind of course. The alternate headquarters are marked with the blue flags on Pat's map board behind you.'

The Commissioner stood up and walked towards the board. 'As for your second point, we have not firmed up any plans, but the preferred option includes aerial reconnaissance patrols and airborne rapid-response units including teams of emergency services personnel.'

'Good. The DCMO agrees. We have over two hundred helicopters from the Joint Helicopter Force to support the emergency services. I suggest our planners combine and thrash out the detail. Other than the blue-light services, there are the radiological survey teams, the detection teams and the whole gambit of service engineers and so on to consider, not to mention the intelligence services.'

Silence followed before the telephone rang for the first time since Brigadier Jarvis had entered the Commissioner's office. He suspected that all other calls had been diverted by one of the two secretaries outside.

It was the Home Secretary. After curt introductions the Brigadier and Deputy Commissioner saw the Commissioner smile.

'Thank you, Home Secretary ... yes ... goodbye, sir.' The Commissioner fell back in his chair and looked at his military advisor and deputy. 'The Cabinet agreed unanimously to the Three Cs. It seems someone has them by the balls. Should we impose the Three Cs as planned?'

'Yes, sir,' replied the Deputy Commissioner determinedly.

'The MOD is ready,' added the Brigadier.

Chapter 85

March 28th, Z – 35 Days
London, England

'Are you sure none of you are being watched or followed?' Mustafa asked agitatedly as soon as the last terrorist had arrived at the lock-up.

Each one of the nine terrorists looked him in the eye and nodded.

'Then what the fuck is going on? Essa, Kalil and I stayed in a Luton motel last night on our way back from Iran so we could figure out what the fuck was going on. It was fortunate for us we had our identification papers and I could prove I lived in London. The bastards only let the women in because they're lookers.'

Turk chuckled mischievously. 'Triple or singles?'

Mustafa scowled. 'Single and a double. You work it out.'

Essa and Kalil blushed. They were both widows who enjoyed each other's company, were doing their duty and were prepared to die for Allah. Nobody knew for sure and nobody bothered to comment, what was the point.

Turk looked up calmly and spoke of what was bothering them all. 'On TV it said the police know of a terrorist strike, but they think it's a nuclear attack. There's now a cordon around London, there are armed police everywhere, there's a curfew, and soldiers are searching the city for nuclear weapons. Muslims are being beaten in the streets and the *kafirs* are panicking like this big nuclear holocaust is going to happen. I was chased two nights ago by four men who trashed a newsagent's shop owned by Sunni Muslims and spotted me watching. I stopped and cut the fastest bastard, slashed his face good and deep.'

'At the mosque it's said that London is to be destroyed by a nuclear bomb as a birthday present to the Prophet on Milad al-Nabi,' added Mahmood.

'But that's in a month, May 2nd. Not this fucking week,' Musa exclaimed.

'I'e heard and seen no mention of our plan, only this nuclear strike,' added Qasim defiantly.

Turk held his hands up and everyone hushed. 'We know nothing of this threat, if indeed it exists. It may be a ruse by our leaders to increase the terror we inflict. More likely it's real and we are part of a bigger plan. If a nuclear attack is to happen we will already be martyrs and it will be another massive victory for Allah and the glory of Islam.'

Turk was the most experienced terrorist in the cell, and despite his specific responsibility for the explosives Mustafa had appointed him second-in-command. Turk rarely spoke of his past, but it was rumoured he had been involved with numerous attacks on capitalist targets that stretched from Central Asia to the Far East. Mustafa had heard a rumour in the mosque that Turk had learned to fly in America in preparation for the attacks on 9/11 but that he had missed the flight destined to destroy the White House. Mustafa had noticed Turk's grim determination and wondered if that was what drove him on. Perhaps Allah had provided Turk with a second chance of martyrdom.

Mustafa relaxed. 'Turk is right. If the nuclear attack is true, then we must be a decoy for the main strike in another month.'

Everyone respected Turk and his comments made as much sense as anything else. The ten people gathered in this dry but grimy garage off Forest Road in North London could be part of the biggest-ever assault on the infidels of the West. There could be no greater cause. No one felt their pre-emptive strike was any less important and, with their arsenal around them, they felt invincible.

'We will continue as planned, but we must all be careful. No one must leave London and risk the cordon,' ordered Mustafa.

'I read that if London was nuked it would destroy the city for a thousand years. I would like to be remembered for that,' Musa added excitedly. 'It would strike at the heart of capitalism, better our assault on America, and extend the glory of Allah.'

'Yeh. All that fucking hardware and the Americans can't win shit,' added Musa.

'We must only concern ourselves with the impact that the nuclear threat has on our plans,' their leader concluded.

Mustafa dressed in his assault gear and waited. As the others finished changing Turk turned to Mustafa and with Hannah's help they checked over every part of his clothing, weapons and equipment. They asked him a series of questions, and the inspection ended with Mustafa jumping up and down to test for loose items. With the exception of a pistol that was over-oiled, he was ready. Next Mustafa and Hannah checked Turk before leaving him to inspect the explosives. Soon, everyone had been checked.

Laying down their weapons, the terrorists sat in a semicircle on their backpacks to listen to Mustafa's plan. Some of them began to smoke.

Mustafa opened up a scrap of paper and read from it. 'First, I have a message from the Emir. He praises us for defending the Islamic faith against evilness and corruption, and tells us that God will guide us to a magnificent and unforgettable victory. We will all receive martyrdom and be praised forever by all true Muslims.'

There was a collective whisper of excitement and gratitude.

'We're Islamic warriors, ruthless and dedicated,' added Mustafa. 'We're the elite of al-Qa'eda and next week we will all die for the glory of Allah.'

The group responded by shouting praise to Allah.

Mustafa studied their faces and saw no fear. He felt proud. When they settled down he continued. 'Ahmad has confirmed that the assault will take place on Friday, April 1st. Despite the planned evacuation of London, we can expect over five thousand *kafirs* and Muslim martyrs in the tower on that day. We'll meet here at midday and prepare, then depart in the two vans for Ahmad's garage. Fuel deliveries have already been reduced because of the nuclear threat, but there's one scheduled for that afternoon at two-thirty. Just before the tanker arrives at the garage it will have to stop behind Haddad's van. Mahmood's van will be behind the tanker with Ahmad in the passenger seat. Ahmad will enter the cab then kill the driver and hijack the tanker.'

'I know what to do,' added Ahmad, grinning insanely. 'I was trained in Iran. We must make the tanker halt on a hill so the air brakes are applied, then I'll strike from the rear. The driver will recognise me in my garage jacket and offer me a lift. He will not see my knife.'

Mustafa nodded. 'We will drive towards Canary Wharf for about ten minutes then stop at Clyde Wharf, which is deserted on Friday afternoons. Here Turk will tie the explosives to the tanker and Ahmad will dress in his assault gear.'

'And if anyone sees us?' asked Kalil.

'All they will see is Turk inspecting his tanker. If anyone interferes, we will kill them,' Mustafa sneered.

'Everyone must watch from the two vans but not get out,' Turk added levelly. 'I will pass Ahmad his gear then fix the explosives to the tanker. I need two minutes, but Ahmad will need three. I'll kill anyone who interferes.'

Everyone accepted the plan as if it was an everyday occurrence. All they wanted was the idea, for if Allah wanted them to succeed they would. As well as Allah on their side, and despite the nuclear threat, they also had surprise and the shocking reality of massive and brutal firepower.

'It will take another ten minutes to reach the tower at Canary Wharf so the attack will be at three o'clock,' continued Mustafa. 'The area will be busy with people leaving early for the weekend, so the flow of people and vehicles will be outwards. We should find no more than fifty people on the ground floor of the tower. The tanker will smash its way in first, followed by Mahmood's van with me, Essa, Kalil and Hannah, then Haddad's van with Turk, Qasim and Musa. I don't want shock, I want fucking terror. I don't want people frozen still but people fleeing. Kill anyone who is not moving out of the building. That will encourage the others. My team including Ahmad will secure the ground floor. Turk's team will secure an elevator.'

'What about the tanker?' asked Qasim.

'Shoot at the fucking tanker and we die early idiot,' hissed Ahmad, smacking Qasim over the head. Everyone laughed.

'My team will take one staircase, then sweep through and clear the first floor which is open-plan. Our objective is to secure and hold the first floor with no hostages. Kill anyone who resists or does not leave immediately. Meanwhile, Turk's team will unload the mines and explosives from Haddad's van onto the elevator and accompany them to the first floor.'

'Can we use grenades?' Kalil asked.

Turk was steadfast. 'Not unless you have to. We want to secure the objective by getting people out of the ground and first floor.

The less dead bodies the better. Later in the week you'll be grateful.'

Mustafa was shaking with excitement. 'As soon as the first floor is secure Turk and his team will disable the elevators. The remainder of us will secure the staircases. Once the elevators are disabled, Turk's team will block the staircases with explosives and then mines. There are only four, one in each corner of the building.'

'And then we get to rig the building for demolition,' added Turk, overwhelmed with anticipation.

No one thought him insane.

Their enthusiasm encouraged Essa. 'What about the hostages above us?'

'What about the fuckers?' replied Mustafa, his voice quivering.

Essa answered coolly, 'We just leave them, right?'

'I don't care what they fucking do, who they talk to on their phones, whether they have water and food, or how they shit.' Mustafa paused. 'I only hope they watch TV.'

'And if they try to escape?' asked Kalil.

'Fucking hero jumpers can jump if they can break the glass. The second floor is over twenty metres above the ground. We can wave at them as they fall then watch to see if they limp away. Maybe Qasim can shoot the fuckers that live with his telescopic rifle.'

'Do we have any demands?' asked Hannah.

Mustafa grinned again. His team would love what he has to say next. 'We have demands, but we will not be the ones to make them. All demands are to be made by Ayman al-Zawahri on TV. As soon as it's known that we've taken the tower al-Zawahri will broadcast our demands on al-Jazeera television. Ayman al-Zawahri was Osama bin Laden's ruthless deputy. It was obvious to Mustafa that every terrorist, even Turk, was impressed. The fact was, they did not require communication with the outside world until the moment of their glorious deaths.

'And what will be demanded?' asked Qasim.

'Does it matter?' growled Musa. 'It's the attack, and the destruction of the tower that's important to us.'

Mustafa beamed, enjoying the intimacy of the knowledge he possessed. 'A list of Islamic warriors held in captivity around the world and to be released will be delivered to the Prime

Minister. Every holy warrior is to be released by midday on April 10th. We're to be provided safe passage to a destination in Central Asia via London City Airport. All arrangements are to be made to al-Zawahri's satisfaction, and he will tell the *kafirs* that if they fail to comply with any of his demands he will destroy their tower by remote control from outside the building.'

The terrorists glanced at Turk, mystified. This time it was Turk's chance to grin mischievously. They knew this could not be true for there were no remote receivers.

'Don't be alarmed, my friends, that part is not true,' said Mustafa. 'Only we can destroy the tower.' No one interrupted and there were several nods of understanding, so he continued. 'All negotiations with the security forces will be held publicly for everyone to enjoy, including the hostages above us. All contact is to be broadcast through al-Jazeera. There is no way the arrogant West will agree to our demands, and then they will see our determination.'

There was a steely silence in the lock-up.

'And what demands will al-Zawahri make of the British security forces?' Turk enquired.

'The demands made on them will be simple. They will be informed of how the tower has been prepared for remote demolition, and that if security forces come within fifty metres of the building including the basement, al-Zawahri will know it and the tower will be destroyed. If anyone attempts to enter the first floor from above, or any of the hostages attempt to escape we will destroy it. If we feel threatened from above or below we will take our feet off the pressure switches and destroy the building.'

'Do we speak to the British security forces at all?' asked Turk.

'Only to tell them to fuck off. Once we are in the building and we have prepared the explosives I will provide further instructions. We are prepared for, and must last, one week. Then, regardless of the demands, we destroy the building as we shout "*Allah Akbar*". We have the best drugs that this decadent city has to offer and these will help us stay alert and help us pass into glory. If anyone thinks of something, you all know where I am. Are there any questions, brothers?'

There were no questions, only excited chatter as the group undressed and carefully prepared their equipment for their final visit to the grimy lock-up on Forest Road.

Chapter 86

March 28th, Z – 35 Days
London, England

With a little over a month to go before Zulu Day, the population of London had reduced by over thirty-five per cent. The entertainment industry had all but closed down, and a large proportion of small businesses had ceased trading. London's transport services were running at fifty per cent of their pre-threat levels. Ironically, due to high numbers of closures and demand currently outstripping supply, those restaurants, retail outlets and transport services that had chosen to remain open were busier than ever.

Notwithstanding the widespread devastation and horror that a nuclear-fission bomb would cause, many Londoners remaining in the city were fully occupied with their families and homes, having already chosen or been forced to quit their jobs. Others were still waiting to discover what their employers intended before firming up their own arrangements. On receiving consistent advice from the Home Office that there was no indication that a nuclear bomb would be detonated before May 2nd, many of the larger firms had made the decision not to close until the last moment. Similarly the majority of Londoners were resolved to remain in the city for as long as practicable.

Other than the bomb and the need to evacuate, there were three other issues that dominated Londoners' thoughts. The first was the massive rise in crime rates, particularly violent crime against Muslims. Although protest and other marches had been banned, the numbers of street gangs professing some kind of cause or political persuasion had increased alarmingly. Consequently, an increasing number of men and women of all races and creeds were armed as they travelled through the capital. Few spoke of their weapons and even less had any intention of turning them in to law-enforcement agencies under the terms of the latest weapons amnesty that came into effect for seventy-two hours from noon yesterday.

The second issue was the unknown effect that the long-term suspension of the Stock Exchange and the wage and price freeze imposed by the Government would have on the economy, people's savings and investments and their employers' businesses. In essence, Londoners were not sure whether they were wealthy or whether their assets were worthless. There were many businesses, large and small, which would not survive unless they continued to function for as long as possible in the hope the bomb and terrorist cell would be found. Meanwhile, they attempted to compensate for loss in trade by cutting overheads and seeking new trade.

The third issue was the sharp decline in a housing market that was not controlled by fixed retail prices but the supply and demand of the moment. The simple fact was that there was very little demand and, if anyone wanted to sell, they could expect up to a ninety per cent reduction in pre-threat prices. The only price that was fixed was the commission charged by estate agents. Of course, the vast majority of Londoners took the advice of the Home Office to sit out the market, expecting their property to recover its value in the aftermath of the threat. In any event, there were no buyers, and so London's estate agents closed. But this did not stop mortgage lenders and banks from raising plans to pursue mortgage holders and cover themselves in the event of catastrophic negative equity.

It was with some relief and renewed determination that Londoners returned to work this Monday morning. Last night at 9 p.m. the first nightly curfew had commenced, ending at 5 a.m., and at midnight the cordon had been raised. Commuters travelling by car were now required to take one of the eight cordon crossing points into London and show their passports on demand. The fact that traffic flow on many routes into London had been altered to facilitate the inflow of commuters through the crossing points helped speed the process. Most drivers destined for the city found their journey only a little slower than usual due to the reduction in cars on the road. Commuters arriving by overground train at London's rail terminals had to show passports as well as tickets, but they too were surprised at the minimal delay.

Nor could commuters miss the increased presence of police and army patrols that continually paraded the streets. To Londoners, the arrival of more police and troops on their streets was not before time and they felt safer. Most Londoners saw no reason to fear the terrorists or the criminals when they witnessed so much protection and no one, they thought, apart from their own Government, was going to push them out of their city.

One decision that the Government feared would create a backlash was the release of all non-violent prisoners from London's jails who had demonstrated good behaviour and had less than twenty per cent of their custodial sentence remaining. This resulted in the release of over four thousand inmates from London's prisons and not only simplified HM Prison Service's evacuation to the shires, but allowed those Londoners who were freed to go home and assist with the evacuation of their families. The residents of HM Prison Belmarsh were to prove the most difficult to relocate, as this prison contained many of the country's most violent criminals, murderers, paedophiles and rapists, as well as terrorists. But there was only one option, and slowly the occupants were transported to other high-category prisons across the UK.

London had some of the largest and most specialised hospitals in the country. Emergency measures instigated early in the crisis ensured that outpatients were reallocated to regional hospitals as they evacuated from the capital. Admissions had been reduced to Accident and Emergency only with thousands of operations postponed, and plans were made with other hospitals for those patients who required hospitalisation over the May bank holiday. Most doctors and nursing staff were allocated temporary postings to the outlying regional hospitals, to one of the four temporary hospital ships at Tilbury and Gravesend, or to one of two field hospitals established by the Army. The medical schools fell in line with all other universities, colleges and schools that had closed for an extended Easter holiday. The Education Department had decided to postpone the beginning of the summer term by a month, to recommence the week beginning May 17th.

The larger chain stores throughout the capital showed a remarkable responsibility towards the public. Despite the cost of increased security, volunteer staff, and increased resilience, including the improving of their facilities for the protection of their staff and customers, all major stores declared their intention to maintain a high level of emergency provisioning for as long as they were able. Despite restrictions on the transportation of flammable liquids, fuel stations also remained open for as long as they held reserves. Maintaining timely supply chains, and with frozen prices, Londoners were able to purchase sufficient provisions at the larger stores without fear of inflation. Somewhat surprisingly, the willingness of many supermarkets to help Londoners in their time of need was to result in a downward effect on the cost of key food products such as milk, eggs, fruit, sugar, tea, cereals and fresh vegetables. Due to the success of the larger chain stores and the closure of Smithfield's and other wholesale food outlets in London, most smaller retail outlets had already closed.

Gold's requirement to establish all known radiological emissions throughout the capital had been a constant story in the media and gained considerable attention at the Emergency Media Forum's daily press conference. The Commander of the Metropolitan Police's Antiterrorist Branch usually had a slightly easier time than the Deputy Commissioner herself, whose responsibility it was to brief the assembled press on progress with finding the nuclear bomb, but today was to be different. Today the Deputy Commissioner was able to impress even the most critical journalists with the thoroughness of the search for radiological emissions, with credit due as much to the helpfulness and compliance of the public and businesses as it was to the efficiency of the radiological search and detection teams.

Many previously unknown radiological sources had now been discovered. Areas that remained cordoned off pending identification by a detection team numbered less than forty, and new sources found by the radiological search teams had finally tailed off. Progress was definitely being made and was there for all to see on a vast radiological map of London, although so far no nuclear bomb had been found. The Deputy Commissioner explained that this was predictable, as their intelligence suggested the bomb had not yet arrived in the capital. Given the equipment at her disposal and the accuracy of the radiological footprint, she explained that when the bomb did arrive, they should quickly locate it.

Yesterday's arrests of another thirty-five foreign nationals and alleged supporters or members of terror groups linked to al-Qa'eda were to dominate today's press conference at New Scotland Yard as it had the previous evening. The suspected terrorists who had been arrested under Section 17 of the Terrorism Act included Lebanese, Saudis, Palestinians, Syrians and Afghans as well as two Pakistanis. According to the Commander, the thirty-five suspects had been arrested and detained in connection with suspected plots to bomb or poison indiscriminate targets in the city in order to create additional chaos and fear in the run-up to May 2nd. One of the detainees, an Ismail Abdurahman al-Khatib aged twenty-seven, had died in custody this morning, from what the Commander informed the press was a heart attack.

In response to the arrests and death, a protest had been threatened by the supporters of al-Khatib, to be held outside Bow Street Magistrates' Court tomorrow morning, where the thirty-four were due to appear before being sent to detention camps in Middlesex.

The press conference turned ugly during the Commander's briefing, and journalists were left with the impression that no more was being done to find the terrorists who threatened London with a nuclear bomb beyond rounding-up the usual hapless suspects. After what Londoners and the Muslim community were facing daily on the streets, the press did not take kindly to the Commander who, the Deputy Commissioner decided, was addressing this press forum for the last time.

The feel-good factor generated by the implementation of the Three Cs, and progress with the ability to detect a nuclear bomb, was largely nullified by the news published in the *Evening Standard* and broadcast on television and radio throughout the country that evening. Most headline news reflected on the plight of the almost universally innocent British Muslim community, but the remaining news was also dire.

An attempt by Turkey to produce a powerful gathering of European Union and Islamic nations, aimed at improving relations between the two blocks by securing unanimous condemnation of the imminent terrorist attack on London, and identifying a method by which al-Qa'eda and its partners could be persuaded to halt the move into nuclear warfare and World War III, had failed. An alarmingly high number of Islamic nations had refused to attend, most citing threats of terrorism and personal death threats to their leaders if they chose now to be conciliatory to the West.

London's law enforcers were accused publicly of incompetence in the search for the terrorists responsible for the nuclear bomb and much of the media criticised the indiscriminate arrest and detention of Muslims, fuelling public sympathy for their plight.

But it was this evening's broadcast on the Qatar-based al-Jazeera television station that was to chill Londoners to the bone. The latest audio tape to be released by al-Qa'eda to the Gulf satellite station featured Ayman al-Zawahri, the Egyptian-born surgeon and the closest aide to the al-Qa'eda terrorist leader, Osama bin Laden.

In a short, four-minute broadcast al-Zawahri addressed all Muslims. He said: '...not to wait any longer, otherwise we will be devoured, one country after the other. Muslims cannot wait and must resist the West with renewed vigour. The jihad against the Americans, their British cousins, the Jews and their allies is being won, and if our soldiers die as martyrs during our assault on London, continue the path after them, and don't betray God and his Prophet, and don't knowingly betray the trust.'

Al-Zawahri then issued an edict in the war against the infidels: '...all believers not involved in the battle must leave London before Milad al-Nabi, for on that day the corrupt city will be struck by a force from Allah that will crush the infidels. Before then, He will send a sign of his genuineness and on that sign you must leave. You must live to plan and execute the next battle. If you fall during that battle you will be a soldier and a martyr.'

That same evening the CIA confirmed that the recording was authentic and NATO raised the bounty leading to al-Zawahri's killing or capture to equal that of Osama bin Laden's – twenty million US dollars.

Chapter 87

April 1st, Z – 31 Days
London, England

As Ahmad pulled the fuel tanker onto London's Lower Lea Crossing he relaxed, despite the five pounds of plastic explosive that Turk had attached to the belly of the sixty-thousand-litre fuel tank hidden behind the outlet valves. He was also grateful the tanker driver's dead body was now lying face down in the back of Mahmood's van.

As Ahmad had expected, the tanker driver had seen the company fleece he was wearing, then recognised him as the friendly employee from the garage. The driver had happily waved Ahmad into the cab for the remaining journey up the long hill to the garage despite company regulations. If the driver had not offered the lift, then Ahmad had planned to force his entry by beckoning the driver to open the cab door or window by enticing him with a parcel, then shoot the man once in the head with his silenced handgun.

Ahmad was a vital member of the terrorist cell, almost as vital as Turk the heavy-set arms expert. As they had waited to leave the garage on Forest Road that morning Turk had revealed his true identity as he had heard rumours and felt the truth would give them strength. They had all heard of the famous 'Demolition Man', labelled so by the US press, but none of them had thought for one moment that Turk and he were one and the same. Turk, aka Azahari Husin, was a Malaysian who had trained as an engineer in England. He had spent several years studying Mathematics and Structural Engineering at Reading University before completing a doctorate in 1990. He had first been drawn to Islamic fundamentalism during the Iranian Revolution, and when he returned to Malaysia after his doctorate he fell under the influence of Abu Bakar Bashir, an Indonesian preacher who spouted the notions of holy war and who was one of the founders of the terrorist group Jemaah Islamiyah, a close ally of al-Qa'eda. Turk travelled to Afghanistan to train and fight with the Arab Mujahidin under Osama bin Laden, and after the war against the Soviets, his first mission against their new enemy America had been to learn to fly then help pilot a US passenger aircraft into the White House. But days before 9/11 and after months of training in the US, he had been forbidden to take part by Osama bin Laden as he was considered too valuable.

A year later it was a terrorist cell from his native group led by himself that masterminded the Bali bombing which killed nearly two hundred including twenty-six Britons. The following year he was to mastermind the attack on the Marriott Hotel in Jakarta where another twelve people were killed. Now one of the world's most wanted, at thirty-seven years old, he had been chosen to plan the demolition of Canary Wharf Tower. Turk craved a glorious death and martyrdom and not to grow old in hiding or to rot away in a US prison cell. He considered the destruction of the capitalist monument a fitting end to his life.

His control over the wondrous power of the deadly tanker, and the renowned company he was in made Ahmad feel proud. He had already played a vital part in the operation and remained the only one of the ten to have set foot on the first floor. As a security guard for the national newspaper where two hundred journalists worked and lived for half their lives, he had had the freedom to walk over the entire floor plate looking for suspicious packages. Ahmad had lost count of the times he had considered the irony. He knew the response that the thousands of occupants would take to such an attack, what the counterterrorist measures were and the roles and responsibilities of the integrated security staffs throughout the building. As someone who once took his job seriously, there had been little he did not know. He knew which television monitors on the first floor must be protected at all costs in order for them to receive the al-Jazeera TV channel and keep abreast of developments during the siege, where the water coolers and refills were situated and how quickly the elevators operated. He had been content in his job in Canary Wharf Tower and felt huge bitterness towards the woman whose advances he had rejected. After two entirely unfounded claims of sexual harassment and one of rape from the same woman, upheld by her friend, he had been dismissed and publicly humiliated by his employers. Ahmad was not just bitter, he was livid that corruption had destroyed his life and that he had been humiliated. He longed for the opportunity to avenge the evil he had suffered and prayed that both she and her lying friend were working this afternoon.

Ahmad knew that as soon as he pulled the tanker off Aspen Way and down Trafalgar Way that cut between Billingsgate Fish Market and Heron Quays, the sight of his fuel tanker would be considered unusual and suspicious. There was no logical reason for a fuel tanker to ever take this route as it led to nowhere other than the cosmopolitan office heartland of the rejuvenated West India Docks and Canary Wharf.

The two vans driven by Haddad and Mahmood had already overtaken Ahmad and would now be close to the tower waiting for his arrival. They were to be prepared to support his entrance in whatever way they could. It was most important he remained unimpeded as he gained momentum down Churchill Place and Canada Square. Joining Trafalgar Way he mumbled a prayer to Allah as he pulled down his face mask and a pair of goggles, and increased speed. Choosing with calm deliberation to drive the shortest route through a roundabout and only vaguely aware of the sound of horns and screeching of tyres, he maintained his speed down the north side of Churchill Place passing Citibank on his left. Here the robust tanker had its first collision with a car, quickly followed by a second, collisions that Ahmad would have liked to avoid but simply could not. But the hefty tanker was unaffected and Ahmad remained confident the explosives were not dislodged. Turk had told him that the force necessary to render the firmly fastened explosives inoperable was so great it would be catastrophic for the tanker.

The tanker was travelling at thirty miles an hour when it entered the north side of Canada Square. Ahmad had time to notice impotent passers-by staring at him with incredulous expressions, including two black-clad policemen armed with Heckler and Koch sub-machine guns standing guard outside JP Morgan Chase to his right. Ahmad swore at them and drove up the kerb and onto the pedestrian pavement in front of Canary Wharf Tower, causing the cab then trailer to shake violently. The tanker settled immediately and Ahmad steered it between two steel pillars towards the main entrance doors. Ahmad knew now that he would succeed and shouted '*Allah Akbar*' as the tanker ploughed through the revolving glass doors and a group of pedestrians who were attempting to leave the tower at that very moment. The deafening sound of a high-pitched alarm, crunching metal, shattering glass and screams invaded the cab, and Ahmad looked up to find the cab and its windshield had remained intact. With no time to notice the people he was chewing under the tanker's heavy tyres Ahmad plunged his foot on the brake pedal, keeping the tanker on its final course between the two large inner columns that was the compact inner core of the building.

Mahmood's van wasted no time in joining the assault. Sitting in the back, Mustafa noticed that the time was 14:56 p.m. When the van screeched to a halt inside the building no one was disoriented for they knew Mahmood had stopped immediately behind the tanker. The rear doors were flung open, and Mustafa was the first to unleash hell on the unsuspecting workers, many of whom were looking forward to a leisurely weekend after a boozy lunchtime celebrating the end of another stressful week. The four occupants who jumped from the back of the van were joined by Mahmood and Ahmad, and within twenty seconds all four security guards and the four tower staff were shot dead. So were another dozen or so office workers, and to Mustafa's satisfaction every worker within view was fleeing out of the building for their very lives.

Mustafa watched Turk and his team of three arrive in the second van to the front of the tanker, jump out, and secure their immediate ground by firing indiscriminately. Four workers were machine-gunned to death in an elevator as the doors slid mercilessly open. The air was filled with screams, smoke and the smell of cordite as the dead and wounded littered the marble floor. All ten terrorists maintained their arcs of fire, occasionally shooting as a diminishing number of workers fled before them via the elevators and stairs to the exits. Not surprisingly no office workers nor armed policemen were willing to venture onto the ground floor. With no one left standing to shoot at, the terrorists shot the wounded.

In seconds the elevator closest to Haddad's van stopped at the ground floor. Turk gunned down the two hapless businessmen inside as the doors opened then shouted to his team to unload the mines and explosives. Haddad and Qasim quickly positioned the narrow ramps from the back of the van as the others held the ground floor. Pulling out two four-wheeled handcarts, one carefully prepacked with the mines and explosives, the other with their backpacks, Haddad and Qasim steered the carts into the elevator.

As soon as Mustafa saw Turk's team were in control, he shouted to his own team to follow him to a single stairwell. The three men and three women dashed after him, firing at anything that moved.

Ahmad and Kalil led the way up the stairwell gunning down six suited men as they went. The six terrorists regrouped on the landing outside a pair of heavy fire doors, which to his surprise Ahmad found locked from within. Without hesitation Mustafa ordered Essa and Mahmood fix small pre-prepared charges onto the four hinges, setting the remote detonators to 'A'. Taking no more than fifteen seconds to place the charges, the team retreated and protected their ears before Kalil, who held the shrike, switched the circuit switch to 'A'. Ignoring the 'Test Circuit' button she pressed the firing button. After an expected millisecond delay there was a single deafening explosion within the confines of the landing. Using the ensuing smoke and shock effect as cover the six terrorists burst into the vast first-floor plate. Avoiding the corner of the room where the precious television monitors were situated, they systematically and noisily advanced in a line past the elevators in the centre of the building, firing above the heads of the retreating occupants and killing any who offered resistance and some who did not. The six terrorists advanced swiftly, clearing all before them, forcing the hysterical occupants to flee to the stairwells behind them. Aware of gunfire from the ground floor minutes before, most chose the lesser of two evils and fled upwards.

In sixty seconds the floor plate was clear, and as the stairwells and the elevators were guarded, Kalil searched the floor for CCTV cameras and the wounded, both of which were to be neutralised. Her comrades listened to her sporadic gunfire, preceded on occasion by cries for mercy or screams of horror. Soon the first high-pitched wail of the police sirens could be heard from the distance.

There was sporadic shooting from the stairwell guards as workers from above attempted to find an open route out of the building. A descending elevator stopped at the first floor and the doors slid open. Mustafa, who was covering all four elevators, stared at the hapless occupants crammed inside. They stared back at him, frozen like rabbits in headlights. Several of them screamed as Mustafa raised his Uzi, but he decided against killing them and watched as the doors closed and the elevator descended to the ground floor.

Turk's team got out of the next elevator that opened on the first floor. After pulling out the carts, Musa and Qasim dragged the nearest two bodies over to jam the sliding doors open. By watching the floor indicators above each elevator door and calling for each of the remaining elevators as they reached the ground floor, soon the terrorists had all four lifts jammed with bodies at the first floor.

It took another hour for the terrorists to demolish the four first-floor stairwell landings, each constructed of steel and finished in wood. US-made Claymore antipersonnel mines packed with thousands of miniature ball bearings that would devastate anything in their path up to thirty-metres distance were set up to overlook the demolished gap on each landing, supplemented by fragmentation grenades. Each deadly device was attached to a web of tripwires spun across the buckled mass of each passageway. Finally the terrorists scattered small, green, butterfly-like Russian-made antipersonnel mines over what was left of the area before carefully constructing barricades and fire positions that overlooked each stairwell.

Eventually the terrorists removed their face veils. The air was dusty and smelled of blood and cordite, but the air-conditioning was still running, fighting to clear the air. Everything was going to plan, and Mustafa wondered for the first time about the state of panic on the forty-eight floors above them, which he considered must be increasing with every explosion. The demolition team rested for while longer and watched as Mustafa's team loaded all the dead bodies into the four elevators. There were thirty-six bodies, considerably more than Mustafa had envisaged, and it took fifteen minutes to clear them from the floor plate. As the bodies were loaded, Turk worked his way through the ceiling of each elevator in turn and strapped a simple cutting charge to the supporting steel wire ropes. Soon, each elevator was sent crashing down to the bottom of its shaft.

As the final explosion was heard every terrorist let out a cry of delight, shouting to Allah and the Prophet Muhammad. Qasim and Musa began firing short bursts into the ceiling. Ahmad wanted to as well, but he was low on ammunition and he knew that Mustafa was watching him. Mustafa had seen Ahmad single out a woman in the fleeing crowd. As Ahmad had fired towards her, she had recognised him and shielded herself behind her comrades. Four people got in the way but Ahmad had mown them down. The woman's head had eventually exploded like a watermelon as his third magazine of thirty rounds found its target.

There was no need for Mustafa to step in and break the jubilation, and after several seconds when the adrenalin had ebbed away, discipline re-established itself. Ahmad went to find the pan-Arab television station al-Jazeera among others, while Mustafa and the remainder of his team surveyed the floor plate for possible entry points and additional fire positions. Meanwhile, Turk and his team climbed into the elevator shafts and laid the ring-mains of explosives that would bring down the steel-framed tower. To deny access from below and to finish the job, they laced each shaft with Claymores and fragmentation grenades.

On Menwith Hill, two hundred miles away in North Yorkshire, passers-by saw a high-security Government establishment within which there were a series of white balls that from a distance resembled giant golf balls. The highly secretive organisation was closely linked to GCHQ in Gloucestershire and also MI5. Less well known was the exact role of the eleven underground floors that descended deep into the rock below Menwith Hill. Here the British intelligence services and the US National Security Agency used British Telecom's telephone network and satellite technology to tap into over one hundred thousand telephone conversations around the world at any one time. They also tapped into and monitored every major television broadcasting channel, including al-Jazeera.

It was widely known that al-Qa'eda and other terrorist organisations used al-Jazeera as their principal method for communicating globally and today was no exception. At 6 p.m. an operator at Menwith Hill flagged another al-Qa'eda video message broadcast on al-Jazeera. Unfortunately for the intelligence services many people across the world watched the same broadcast, and by the time the information was passed through the chain of command the opportunity for a timely response was often lost.

The broadcast picture was of two men with two rifles leaning against the wall behind them. The chief, Osama bin-Laden, was dressed in what looked like a US Marine Corps combat jacket over a white shirt and white trousers. He was heavily bearded and with an immaculate white turban. Sitting with him was his deputy, Ayman al-Zawahri. The deputy was wearing glasses, a white turban and a black vest over a white shirt.

The chilling message spoken by the deputy as he stared into the camera was blunt and to the point. He proclaimed that the US and her allies would ultimately be defeated and that it was now only a matter of time. He called for all of Islam to unite and rise up against the corrupting influence of the West then calmly announced that minutes ago Canary Wharf Tower had been seized by ten heavily armed Islamic warriors who had captured over five thousand prisoners inside. In return for their lives, he demanded that countries across the world release all incarcerated Islamic warriors. To help them a list had been compiled that was being delivered to the British Prime Minister. He was to be responsible for the release of all warriors by midday April 8th and was to ensure that all warriors were safely transported to destinations of their own choosing. The Prime Minister was to give his personal assurance by midday April 10th live on al-Jazeera that every warrior had arrived safely at his or her chosen destination. If he failed to do so, or he was discovered to be lying, then Canary Wharf Tower would be razed to the ground. After the release of all Islamic warriors, the British were to arrange for the warriors inside the tower to be provided with safe passage to an airport in Central Asia. Should this not happen, or if any attempt was made to recapture the tower or release the prisoners, then the charges would be remotely detonated from outside the tower.

Following the verbal threat from al-Zawahri, there were pictures of the arsenal of weapons and material provided to the terrorist cell that included automatic rifles, hand guns, antipersonnel mines, plastic explosives, pressure switches and hand grenades. Then there was a picture of a fuel tanker with a small amount of explosives and a remote detonator attached to its belly, the picture of the ensuing explosion in a desert leaving no one in any doubt as to its destructive capability.

With an air of confidence, al-Zawahri went on to confirm how the tower would be destroyed. No one was left in any doubt about the credibility of the threat. Then he told how radioactive waste material had been attached to the explosives to ensure that what remained was contaminated and would have to be left for many years to provide a fitting memorial to the power of Islam over the capitalist West. Al-Zawahri finished by simply stating that all communication was to be through al-Jazeera television.

The broadcast ended with Osama bin Laden offering a chilling message that condemned the US, UK, Israel and their allies for their arrogance, selfishness, greed and corruption of Islam, and for causing a jihad that required al-Qa'eda and all true Muslims to conduct the deadly attacks on USS *Cole*, the twin towers of the World Trade Center, Beslan School in North Ossetia, and other bombings across the world.

Every terrorist who had made their way over to the bank of monitors was transfixed. Ahmad pointed to another monitor, this one broadcasting BBC1. The network's schedule was interrupted to report breaking news and immediately there was an archive picture of the tower with a frantic journalist providing on-site commentary. No attempt was made to edit or soften the death and destruction, and the bodies littering the ground were vividly described. The programme cut to a replay of the al-Qa'eda video message first broadcast on al-Jazeera. By the end of the replay the BBC's OB truck had settled its differences with the police and had set up near by. Mustafa was mesmerised as he watched and listened to eyewitness accounts of the attack live on television. Before long a number of monitors were showing different pictures of the tower with widely differing and competing commentary. Mustafa studied the broadcasts and felt content. Now the terrorists would know what was going on around them. What they did not see or hear, Mustafa felt confident he could guess for he knew the security services and legendary SAS would not stand still.

Eventually Mustafa ordered that Ahmad continue to watch the monitors while the rest of his team destroy the telephones then maintain guard. Turk's team continued work on the charges.

By 8 p.m., all the shaped charges and detonators had been

fitted, the circuits checked and Turk was satisfied. Only then did the entire cell settle into their siege routine. The terrorists were confident that there was no way the hostages above them could escape, not by jumping through the thick plate glass windows and from such heights, and not through the narrow ducts or wide elevator shafts. They also believed that there was no way the security services could gain entry without risking the destruction of the entire tower.

Chapter 88

April 1st, Z – 31 Days
London, England

The Foreign Secretary stood at Sir Michael's office window and stared down at the River Thames.

'My apologies for springing this visit on you, but the Cabinet is getting anxious. Number Ten and the Cabinet Office were due to move to Windsor at the end of the week, but the Prime Minister's postponed it. He's reluctant to abandon London.'

'Probably the right decision,' answered Sir Michael. 'Any move will be interpreted as failure, running away.'

'The Thames is looking cleaner now than I can ever remember. I suppose any fallout will pollute the entire river, downstream at least.'

'I happen to know that the Thames River Authority has considered that and they have a plan in place. Bathing and fishing would be ruled out, that's for sure.'

'Michael, I don't mind telling you that Government, both local and national, is at full stretch. That's not to say that we have slipped into turmoil or even chaos, not so far anyway, but we are close. It's a terrifying situation for everyone. The Prime Minister is still looking to you to find the terrorists, but he must have something tangible to announce, and soon. Christ, we're not far from the brink, Sir Michael. Is there really anything in this Psyops plan? It appears, well ... too slow.'

Sir Michael leant back in his leather chair and deliberated on where to begin as he looked across to the MI5 Deputy Director, Patrick Asquith, then to Harry and Tess, and on to his own Deputy Director, Rosalind Fox. Finally, his eyes settled on Tim Bernazzini. The Foreign Secretary had asked for this unscheduled meeting, though its purpose had not been clear until now. He had intended to approach the Foreign Secretary on this serious matter this evening, but now would do fine. Much would depend on Harry.

Glancing back at Sir Michael, Bernazzini took his cue. 'The President and the National Security Council agree with the CIA, who entirely support Harry's plan. A Disruptive Operation is the best course, Minister. We have to attempt to bring the mercenaries on side as we try to catch them. The US President isn't willing to pamper the neo-conservatives any longer with a hard line over the Middle East and Central Asia, and at the expense of London. The political implications are huge, of course, and necessitate a massive sea change in the foreign policies of both our governments. But let's face it, it's not before time.'

Sir Michael smiled at Bernazzini who he suspected had held such liberal views for some time. It was always helpful to start with the US President on side. 'It's not this service's responsibility to dictate Government action or future foreign policy, but it's our responsibility to prevent this, and for that matter future, terrorist attacks. Everything is being done to prepare ourselves for the worst. Everywhere you look there are mass decontamination units, military field hospitals, and nuclear-hardened buildings. There's more traffic flowing out of than into London and the gap is widening. Perhaps more importantly, everything that can be done to find the terrorist cell is being done. We need this Disruptive Op; that is, we need to turn the terrorist cell against its masters.'

'And the Psyops plan is out best chance you say?' said the Foreign Secretary nervously.

'We have already begun, as you know, Minister, and it may be our only chance. But it needs to be properly implemented and bought into by the Government if we're to be successful. We need you to take centre stage. Islam is a faith yes, but it's also a way of life and that makes it political. We must politicise our strategy.'

'But is it the right course?' the Foreign Secretary asked as he paced anxiously around the office.

'We, and the Americans, including the President and his National Security Council believe it's the only offensive course available.'

'The only course,' the Foreign Secretary stammered, 'or we're finished?'

'Yes, Minister. We're already doing what we can defensively. The President used the word "righteous" with Jim Ridge.'

'Well?' asked the Foreign Secretary as he sat down.

'Perhaps I should let Harry explain.'

Harry, already prepared for this moment despite the short notice, rose from his chair and walked towards the flat-screen monitor that hung on the office wall, picking up a laser pointer and a remote control off the conference table as he went. Everyone turned in their comfortable chairs, all except Bernazzini who went to dim the lights.

'Minister, Tess Fulton and I have spent a considerable amount of our time since returning from Argentina talking to a vast number of experts from across the world and in your own department about the rise of Islamic fundamentalism and its grievances. An enormous amount of factual research has been conducted by many experts. We have spoken to historians of Islamic movements, the US Institute of Islamic Political Thought, the Muslim Council of Britain, experts at the Defence College, global security experts and many others. Tess and I have even spent two days at the US Embassy in Iran.

'Recent EU efforts in Turkey demonstrated that al-Qa'eda or any other of the likely terrorist organisations involved in this attack will not talk. Our detailed profiles of the cell members lead us to believe that we are dealing with mercenaries who are Westernised, in possession of Western social skills, highly intelligent, well-financed, well-connected and, perhaps worst of all, more European in appearance than many Europeans. We have little to go on other than their intentions, and several descriptions that in any event can readily be disguised. We must now assume that we will not catch the cell using conventional methods. Tim.'

Bernazzini walked to Harry's side and took over.

'Minister, everything we have by way of pictures, sketches, fingerprints and DNA have been passed through every US, UK and other credible international system of records. Immigration checks have been made across the world with no new leads. UK Immigration continues to monitor all entry points with everything we have but so far, nothing. The fact is, there are no names, records or artefacts associated with Fox and Vixen, and we lost Baloch's killer, Jamali, in Spain. Fox and Vixen are top professionals who have the advantage of meticulous prior planning. It's unlikely we'll find them using conventional means.'

'Thank you, Tim,' said Harry. 'We believe that their one weakness is ideology, or motivation. As mercenaries they are paid and no doubt handsomely. Unless they have been coerced their motivation begins and ends with money. Therefore we must undermine their motivation.'

'By intercepting their money?' asked the Foreign Secretary.

'If only that was possible. The FBI has uncovered a considerable trail of terrorist funding but there is still no firm lead to our terrorist cell. Without that trace we must consider another course. Ignoring bin Laden and his co-conspirators for now, we must appeal openly to the hearts and minds of the terror cell, which means publicly to Muslims across the world.'

'You mean we must alienate the mercenaries?'

'Not quite, Minister. We must alienate the terrorists from the mercenaries, and at the same time appeal to all Muslims. With all the security measures we now have in place throughout fortress UK, we still await one viable lead regarding their whereabouts. There's now a very high chance that we will not catch them in time so we have no choice but to convince these mercenaries that they will be worse off, as will their people and the Muslim faith if they allow the nuclear bomb to detonate. The destruction of London would play into the hands of the neo-conservatives across the world and at best, alienate Muslims. At worst, the scenario is apocalyptic. The Islamic faith and every one of its followers could find themselves the enemy of the world.'

'So what can the I do that's not already being done to convince the mercenaries?' asked the Foreign Secretary doubtfully.

'A result would be to convince the terrorist cell to abandon their mission and flee. A victory would be to turn the mercenaries against al-Qa'eda and obtain the information that NATO requires to destroy the enemy and provide the conditions for political change.'

'We cannot and will not negotiate with terrorists, not while I'm Foreign Secretary.'

'Certainly not, sir, and if you don't mind me saying so, we need you to assist us. In your career as a world statesman you have earned a name for frankness and honesty. That will be very useful as we reach out to the mercenaries through the media.'

'I'm not sure I can talk with mercenaries acting on behalf of terrorists either.'

'What if those mercenaries trade the nuclear bomb, London's future for the next thousand years and the whereabouts of their controllers, the masterminds behind the attack? It's not a question of negotiation; it's a question of turning the mercenaries into double-agents, but at a price. In truth, we have been sanctioning similar methods for centuries.'

Everyone in Sir Michael's office was stunned by Harry's distinction, even Tess and Tim Bernazzini, neither of whom had considered this critical issue in this way.

The Foreign Secretary sat up, a renewed determination on his face. 'So, how are the Prime Minister and I to convince them?' he asked again, this time with more enthusiasm.

'Beginning with ourselves and the US, we must accept and embrace the truth, and stop neo-conservative fantasies and fears, distortions and exaggerations from influencing our politics. We must be prepared to promote foreign policies among Western countries that create a fair and new world order, one that all faiths and religions can enjoy side by side. Hindsight is a wonderful thing, and we should use it to learn from our mistakes.'

'Tell me that you are not proposing that we give in to terrorist aims?' the Foreign Secretary asked coolly.

'I'm not, Minister. Regardless of their aims, whether it's military withdrawal, removal of Western influence, or even world domination, we must do the right thing. We must act, not for selfish interest and not because we risk losing face over deeds done, but for future global interests.'

'Go on.'

Harry began his presentation by pointing a hand-held remote control unit towards the monitor and pressing a button. 'Your department already has a copy of my findings, and Sir Michael has a personal copy for you. What I'm about to tell you, Minister, is a shortened version. In essence, it's a story about the increasingly fractured lines between the West and Islam. These fractured lines are caused by fallen ideology and promises from leaders of a better world that has failed to materialise. It requires some Western governments, particularly the US and UK, to re-address their foreign policies.'

The Foreign Secretary smiled. Close to retirement he was more realist than politician nowadays and knew that Harry's point was valid. 'Are you suggesting we helped create global terrorism, Harry?'

'There's no excuse for any terrorist act; it's cold-blooded murder. But the West must shoulder a share of the responsibility for the conditions that foster global terrorism. It's precisely that which we must face up to and take to the UN if we are to defeat global terrorism. We must seek to win the war quickly, not accept a protracted war.'

The Foreign Secretary nodded in agreement.

'Perhaps an analogy is one where Western politicians find themselves as managers of security rather than politicians seeking a new world order. The rise of neo-conservatism and Islamic fundamentalism are both born of failure, and neither of them can be allowed to succeed. Over the last few weeks eminent people have convinced me that the West, suffering from individualism, selfishness, greed and materialism, has sought through neo-conservatism to unify itself and avoid destruction from within by seeking unifying actions, first by focusing on the Cold War, and now by unifying against terrorism. Those with the darkest fears, particularly in the US and UK have become some of the most powerful people in both lands, so powerful are their lobbyists that presidents and prime ministers would sooner listen to their rhetoric than the facts presented by their own intelligence services, in particular the CIA and MI6. We have only to look to the last Iraq war to see what happens when UK lobbyists are determined to have their way and MI6 hold less than convincing intelligence. These same people have altered foreign policy, often on the back of national disasters such as the war in Vietnam, that both countries have been encouraged to support the overthrow of any regime that did not fit with our democratic model. There are of course exceptions to the rule, such as Henry Kissinger who believed in the global society and was responsible for the era of détente with the Soviet Union beginning in the early 1970s. Jimmy Carter was a global as opposed to unilateral player too. But the overall effect of US and UK influence since 1945, in Palestine, Egypt, Iran, Afghanistan, Iraq and so on, has been to export this sense of individualism to collective societies that were fundamentally not Western. These societies wish to live within an Islamic moral framework in which they can use Western science and technology. They don't want to import anything that can destroy their shared values.'

'It's debatable which is more civilised I grant you,' offered the Foreign Secretary.

'Many Muslims did not wish to worship individualism over what they saw as real truth, and thus we saw the rise of Sayed Kotb and the Muslim Brotherhood in Egypt in response to the US-backed Sadat regime. And although it's easy for us Brits to say so after the Suez Crisis, it was a rotten regime backed by a number of US banks and several Westernised Egyptian millionaires.'

'Hindsight is a wonderful thing indeed. I was a junior officer in the Foreign Office back then.'

'But invaluable in understanding where we are now,' Sir Michael responded, knowing where Harry was going and appreciating how important this foreign secretary's public persona was to be over the coming weeks.

'The Muslim Brotherhood saw themselves as the revolutionary vanguard in the fight for true Muslims against individualism, what they called "Westernisation". We termed it a "Force for Good", which with hindsight was arrogant. Sadat was despised and subsequently assassinated, ending with the execution of his assassins, Egyptian Army Officers, and the imprisonment of Kotb and his followers. All prisoners were consistently tortured and were released after three years but with hardened resolve that can only come from a belief you are right.

'Years later Kotb was executed for his part in a failed plot to flood the Nile Delta, but not before he had raised considerable support throughout the Arabic world. In 1979 the Ayatollah Khomeini had Kotb's portrait put on a postage stamp. Another of Kotb's keenest supporters was a very young Ayman al-Zawahiri, bin Laden's right-hand man. By the end of the 1980s, a decade marked by the efforts of neo-conservatives determined to project Western uniqueness onto the remainder of the world, al-Zawahiri had formed the Islamic Jihad group. This group represented a state of mind that despised the West's everyday vision of the world; something Islamic fundamentalists consider at best barbarous ignorance. The constant torture of Muslim Brotherhood suspects by fellow Muslims particularly in Egypt did not help, and this has been attributed to the belief that as many infidels and untrue Muslims as necessary must die in order to reach perfection.'

'The end justifies the means,' said the Foreign Secretary, appreciating the history lesson that would help him fulfil his public role in Harry's Psyops plan.

'Precisely. Western-style leaders and other non-believers could be justifiably killed, Muslim or not. It's also the belief of many Western philosophers that the wish by neo-conservatives to act as "Democratic Revolutionaries" across the world, imposing their world order at will, can be coupled with the rise of Christian fundamentalism across the US. The rise in Islamic fundamentalism is seen by many as a direct response to this rise in neo-conservatism. Then, with the neo-conservatives seeing an opportunity, the US allied itself with the Afghan Mujahidin or "Holy Warriors" and the Arab Mujahidin against the Soviet Army in Afghanistan in the 1980s. It was not long before the Soviet Army withdrew and they were replaced with a fundamentalist Taliban Government that was soon found to be unacceptable to everyone just as Gorbachev had warned, particularly by the Afghans themselves. As you know the Soviet Union imploded just months later, and several years after that the Taliban were ousted by US-led coalition forces.

'Meanwhile a new terror group had been created by al-Zawahiri out of the extremist Islamic Jihad wing of the redundant Arab Mujahidin. It's widely accepted that this new group, after a series of bombings that included the US embassies in Kenya and Tanzania, was labelled "al-Qa'eda" by the FBI as they wished to make the perpetrators of the bombings identifiable as a single group to assist with prosecutions. Al-Zawahiri offered the leadership or role of Emir to the wealthy Saudi Arabian bin Laden. There was never any coherent organisational structure to al-Qa'eda around the world despite the FBI's assertions to the contrary. Groups were bound only by common ideology and dysfunctional postings on the World Wide Web. Al-Qa'eda was always a small, ghostly group that provided funding and assistance to any other group with similar ideals, all conveniently swept up under the single mantle.

'It's important that you know a little about the Arab Mujahidin. They did not actually fight much against the Soviets; they chose not to. The brigade was raised in Peshawar on the Pakistan border with Afghanistan by the moderate Abdullah Hassam in response to a fatwa by many Arab states for their people to rise up and dispel the Soviet Union from Islamic Afghanistan, and it was largely recruited by prisoners released from jails all over the Arab world. In Peshawar the recruits received training in terrorist tactics and they were paid and were armed predominantly by the US.

'With the collapse of the Soviet Union in 1991, the neo-conservatives continued to push for US influence overseas. Throughout the nineties and until 9/11 the spectacular failings of the Islamic Movement throughout the Arab world and their attempts to topple governments and win popular support, particularly in Algeria and Egypt, meant that they were desperate and this desperation led to a new jihad against the US marked by 9/11. That attack signified the beginning of the full-scale war between the US neo-conservatives, who switched their detestation to the Islamic fundamentalists full-time, and the Islamic Movement. Throughout Western civilisation the impression of a grand revolutionary Islamic force was created by the neo-conservatives who suggested a much larger enemy than physically existed, which ironically was al-Zawahiri's dream, and it was represented as al-Qa'eda.'

'So what's the lesson?' asked the Foriegn Secretary, intrigued.

'In order to win we must stop the fight between the neo-conservatives and the Islamic extremists, or al-Qa'eda. The singular conclusion of all experts, including myself, is that we should accept our mistakes, stop exporting "Democratic Revolution" and stop generating enemies. Terrorism will exist for as long as we in the West behave aggressively. If we truly wish to save London and defeat terrorism, we must find the bomb, destroy the current crop of terrorists, and prevent their regrowth through immediate political change and recognise that every country has a right to govern itself how it wishes, individual or collective. Of course, we all need the help of moderate Muslims and their states. What happens to the mercenaries is not my immediate concern, but whether we like it or not, they are the key – the key to it all.'

'You believe we should not inflate our enemies in order that we can fight the epic battle against evil?' asked the Foreign Secretary, having grasped the real issue.

'Yes, sir. Overinflating them merely makes them stronger.'

'A fundamental change in foreign policy you say?'

'Yes, sir.'

'Arguably you are asking us to divert from hundreds of years of British history.'

Harry thought about this for several seconds. 'We have contributed hugely to the evolution of the world for which we as a nation can be justly proud. But with globalisation other nations have caught up and now it's time to move on by setting the agenda.'

'In forty years ninety-five per cent of the world's oil supply will be in the Gulf region.'

'It belongs to them, Minister.'

'Best make friends then?'

'Yes, Minister.'

'Is this the tail wagging the dog, Sir Michael?' asked the Foreign Secretary, a slight grin on his face.

'It's my role to inform you of the threats to our country, and recommend how we may deal with them,' Sir Michael shrugged. 'The devil is in the detail in the file in front of you, and right now, I would say current UK and US foreign policy is doomed to fail. It's up to you whether you choose to action it. But we need this strategic thinking to be exposed right now in order to have a chance of stopping a devastating nuclear strike on London. We need the hearts and minds on our side, including those of the mercenaries.'

The Foreign Secretary looked remarkably calm. He had come looking for answers and he was getting them, however hard to swallow.

'I feel as if I've been found out, like a naughty, selfish schoolboy. Since 9/11 nothing has been off-limits. I wonder how the PM will take it!'

Sir Michael smiled. 'He will appreciate this as much as you do. It's those that can't see the wood for the trees that we need worry about. And if London is destroyed and we get into the blame game you will want right on your side – that's what the President has figured out. If London is destroyed the blame will ultimately fall equally on the West's failure to respond politically to Islamic fundamentalism as it will on the terrorists responsible. The Government must respond effectively, and immediately.'

'Sir Michael is right, sir. This is how the President and his

National Security Council sees it too,' added the American, Bernazzini, as he turned the lights back up.

'It's a long time before the next election,' added the Minister thoughtfully. 'Tell me, Sir Michael, what is the best and the worst that might happen?'

Harry sat down.

'Worst case, the area that was once London is unworkable for a thousand years. There are many casualties, immediate and longer-term, and the country slips inevitably into Third World status. It takes generations to recover. As for the upside, our mercenaries surface and declare the whereabouts of the bomb and provide intelligence on their leaders, leading to the latter's immediate and wholesale destruction. Then the UN, encouraged by the US and UK, promotes a new world order that addresses the causes of disharmony and invokes a new charter that demands nations to respect each other and recognises global terrorism as a stateless force of evil.'

There was a period of silence as everyone considered the situation. It was broken by the Foreign Secretary. 'Harry, just how do you interpret the terrorist network theory?'

Harry explained. 'In the seventies and eighties the neo-conservatives suggested that the Soviet Union were masterminding most if not all of the major anti-West terrorist organisations across the world. The CIA refuted the theory, but President Reagan's closest neo-conservative advisors won the day. After 9/11 it was the FBI who led the charge for the singular and extensive al-Qa'eda network, and now almost all terror attacks against capitalist targets are attributed to al-Qa'eda.'

Harry glanced apologetically at Bernazinni and his partner. 'Our thinking isn't quite so polarised. We consider al-Qa'eda as a stand-alone terror group under bin Laden that consists of fewer than twenty terrorists. But the group has many thousands of supporters, spread widely across the Western world and Asia, who may readily be coopted as terrorists primarily through contacts in mosques and on the Web. Importantly there's no nucleus other than bin Laden himself. He sees himself as the Emir and religious messenger of a group the FBI named al-Qa'eda or "The Network", a group that is more of an idea and an enabler for other groups to conduct terrorist acts against the West, than a force itself. Because of the recognition and credibility afforded to al-Qa'eda by the West, it's beneficial for other globally inclined terror groups to link themselves to al-Qa'eda. Whether they actually are or not is immaterial. When they wish to, any number of these groups may join together and enjoy the synergy that collectiveness provides, but that alone does not make them all al-Qa'eda. Some are idealists, some are revolutionaries, some are mobsters, but all of them are criminal.'

'Hmm, that's how I see it too. Not much loyalty between them?'

'Definitely not, Minister. And the same goes for our mercenaries. There have been many reports of infighting, particularly over territory and drugs.'

'Michael, I'm sold. We'll see the PM...'

Just as the Foreign Secretary was about to move on, Sir Michael's PA entered the office unannounced carrying six copies of a signal.

'Sir Michael, it's a Code Red from Scotland Yard,' she said urgently as she passed the pages to him. 'It's gone to List A.'

'Thank you, Merissa.'

Sir Michael read the first six lines before she had reached the door. His face paled and his throat constricted. 'Oh Lord,' he whispered before glancing at his watch. 'Twenty minutes ago armed terrorists drove a fuel tanker into Canary Wharf Tower. They are attacking the building with an estimated six thousand office workers trapped inside.'

'Crikey,' exclaimed the Foreign Secretary, uncharacteristically tongue-tied.

'This is not our fight,' said Sir Michael suddenly and to everyone's amazement, 'not unless we hear otherwise. Stay focused everyone.'

Sir Michael picked up a remote from his desk and changed channels on the flat-screen monitor that Harry had been using, stopping at BBC1. The BBC was not on site yet, but a frantic journalist was describing via his mobile phone that he had narrowly escaped with his life and that he could see many people had been killed and injured, some crushed to death by a fuel tanker. Screaming, shouting and the distant wail of sirens could be heard in the background. The portrayal in the news studio was one of chaos and terror, but viewers would have to wait a while longer for live pictures.

'Here,' said Sir Michael as he handed the message to Harry. 'Read for yourselves.'

The television interrupted the silence as each person read the message, before looking up towards a news presenter who was suggesting the attack had subsided. The programme cut to an al-Qa'eda message attributed to al-Jazeera.

'God help the people inside,' croaked the Foreign Secretary as the al-Qa'eda message ended. 'Do they mean to kill everyone in the building?'

'Not immediately,' replied Harry coolly.

Sir Michael stared at Harry.

'They will only shoot those who get in their way. My guess is they have seized the first floor, trapping hostages above.'

'Do you think they have the nuclear bomb?' asked Sir Michael, workmanlike.

'Maybe, but I doubt it,' replied Harry.

'If they sent it up the elevator to the top floor and detonated it, it would cause double the devastation over double the area,' offered Rosalind.

'These people are not our mercenaries, no way,' stated Harry.

'I'm with Harry. This cell is conventional,' added Tess. 'No one risks a nuclear bomb brought halfway around the world, and not due to detonate for another month, with fanatics.'

'Harry?' asked Sir Michael.

'This is a side show, I'm sure of it.'

'Gratifying, but why?'

Harry quickly explained. 'It's a feint, I'm sure of it. Wrong profiles, unnecessary risk, no need for hostages, and there's no way out for them. What good is money to a dead mercenary? Our mercenaries are cleverer than this. The height idea is sound but there's simply no other advantage. Tess is correct; these bastards are assorted killers and martyrs. You name it, and it doesn't fit. This is a very clever and deadly sideshow designed to keep us all occupied. Remember al-Zawahri's previous message? In it he said he would send a "sign" as a warning to Muslims to leave the city. Well, this is it, a pre-emptive strike. We had better get back to Scotland Yard before someone screws up and lets the bomb through the cordon.'

'Agreed. You two liaise with the Met. Patrick and Rosalind will deal with Cobra. Keep focused and let's steer clear of the noise,

OK. Minister, you must inform the Prime Minister of our suspicions.'

'Are you sure this is not our cell?' asked the Foreign Secretary unsteadily.

'Nothing's certain,' replied Sir Michael, 'but I would put my last pound on that nuclear bomb being placed and activated while this horror show is played out. Countless radiological detection teams haven't found it yet, because hasn't reached London.'

They stared at the television. Cameras zoomed onto countless dead bodies, and shattered windows at all four corners of the first floor.

'There are only two ways Canary Wharf Tower can play out,' added Harry. 'One is its complete destruction, and the other is the SAS and the use of deadly force. Their demands are a smokescreen designed to attract maximum attention and resources.'

The Foreign Secretary winced as they listened to commentary about the building. 'That tower is built like a fortress. I'm not confident anyone can retake it intact.'

'Minister,' Sir Michael said slowly. 'You must leave the Home Secretary and Cobra to deal with the tower. Right now, both you and the Prime Minister must focus on the bigger and much more devastating threat. The country is depending on you.'

Harry saw a man before him as an elected official, not a leader. 'I grant you it's not Agincourt, Waterloo or the Battle of Britain, but its next on the bloody list and our backs are against the wall. We have always dared to win, Minister, and with your help, that's what we will do.'

Sir Michael's telephone rang. 'It's for you Minister,' he said. 'It's the PM.'

Chapter 89

April 2nd, Z – 30 Days
Amsterdam, Netherlands

Malik rose stiffly from his double bed on *Last Tango*. He shivered as he walked through to the small en suite bathroom, and wondered when he would next sleep on his beautiful yacht. Looking through a porthole as he did every morning he woke up on board, he was satisfied to see a flat, mirror-like sea, the promise of sunshine and a cloudless sky. He knew that it wouldn't be long before the dew that blanketed the outside of boat and the interior dampness would burn away, and that there would be no delay to today's scheduled departure for London.

If all went to plan, Malik, Dalia and Karima would rendezvous with Baba and *Last Tango* in Cairo, but only after he had recovered his nine-year-old daughter from the clutches of al-Qa'eda. For the first time that day, as he did every day, he swore to himself that if one hair on her head be disturbed he would not rest until he had wrought his own deadly vengeance on all those responsible. As he shaved he considered how his wonderfully intelligent daughter would react when he rescued her, when she met Dalia for the first time, and when she first saw their new yacht, *Last Tango*. Together they would begin a new life, one without fear.

One of the few necessities that had been missing on *Last Tango* was a personal computer complete with Internet access. A few days ago Malik had rectified this at a large department store on the outskirts of Amsterdam and at little extra cost he had secured a fast, reliable Internet Service Provider. He had arranged with Dalia before they parted that she would send him a single email informing him of her progress, immediately before he was due to set sail in *Dutch Master*.

After dressing and making some fresh coffee Malik booted up the computer that was now fastened firmly to a small side desk in the navigation room and logged onto the Web. Before long he was staring with amazement at Dalia's simple message written in plain English.

My Love,
I have returned safely to England and will be staying with my mother in Heathrow for a few days before travelling to town. Have you seen the news? Thousands of people are being held hostage in the city by a gang. I cannot wait to see you again. PBUH.
D.

Malik immediately walked through into the salon and switched on the satellite television. Flicking through the mass of channels he found BBC News 24, then watched and soaked in the news until the broadcast began to repeat itself in the absence of any new or shocking development. Although surprised by the secondary attack, he soon realised on seeing bin Laden and al-Zawahri sitting side by side that it was no accident. He concluded that the terrorist attack on Canary Wharf Tower had no negative impact on his mission, in fact, as they had no doubt planned, it was of much benefit to the Network's strategic intent as it would fuel the 'shock and awe' so successfully introduced by the Americans on Baghdad in the last Gulf War, and deflect the attention of London's law-enforcement agencies as both he and Dalia entered the British capital city to plant their nuclear bombs. Increasing the volume, he returned to the navigation room where he compiled a message in Urdu, the official language of Pakistan.

Muhammad,
As we complete our holiday in Europe I think more about returning and seeing my loved one. I trust she is well. Life in the city has taken a number of unexpected turns as you will be aware, but we can still tour where we wish. I would welcome news before we continue our journey. PBUH.
Mohammad.

In three hours Malik was expecting a tugboat and a crew to

arrive from London to fetch *Dutch Master*, and he hoped that within that time he would receive some kind of response from al-Qa'eda's communications officer confirming that his daughter was well. In the meantime, he would telephone London and inform the old Captain of his schedule then pack his necessary possessions. Yesterday afternoon Malik had agreed with Baba over a game of Texas hold 'em poker in Amsterdam's newest casino that Baba and his crew would return to *Last Tango* by midday for he required the vessels to sail at 2 p.m., one bound on a circuitous route for Cairo and the other two direct for London. Nobody wanted any further delay, not even the owners of Jachthaven Aeolus boatyard who were in desperate need of *Dutch Master*'s prime berth at the quayside.

But first Malik took a brisk walk to the hotel. It was only after a full breakfast that Malik returned to *Last Tango* and telephoned the Captain. 'How's London?' asked Malik as soon as the pleasantries, such as they were, were over.

'Bloody awful,' replied the Captain gruffly. 'No tourists but plenty of fuss mind. Police and soldiers crawling all over the place. They're using Geiger counters, waving bloody wands everywhere. They even search boats at random on the river. We've been keeping busy helping firms evacuate their bloody files and computers, until we lost staff or the boats became unserviceable anyway.' He continued for several minutes, talking personalities, boats and business.

Malik let him talk.

'What time you leaving then?' the older man eventually asked.

Malik smiled to himself. He could still count the times he had spoken to his partner using the fingers on one hand, but they spoke to each other as if they had known each other for years.

'In about three hours. The tug is thirty minutes away and the crew for my yacht are turning up any minute.'

The Captain grunted his satisfaction, though Malik sensed relief.

'Good. Despite what's happening I need *Dutch Master* at Signet Quay. No sense you stopping at Gravesend. I intend to have her running for as long as we can. We'll leave London when we have to and not a minute before.'

Malik knew *Dutch Master* would not be leaving London, but said nothing. 'We should arrive in less than forty-eight hours but we have to take it gently and run her in. She's a beautiful boat, Captain. She deserves a good launch party, which will also provide me an opportunity to meet people. I'll fund it.'

'Sounds good enough. But it will have to wait until the emergency ends, if it ever bloody well does. As soon as you arrive we'll set her to work. I've lost two big contracts already. Most of the crew are off work now to prepare themselves for evacuation. I've not got enough people to fix the boats, never mind crew them. You'll have most of my workforce for the next two days.'

Thinking quickly, Malik offered, 'I'll help if need be. I learn quickly.'

'Aye. Sounds good enough. But think about it, mind. If you're going to help, then you have to be reliable. No distractions. I got to go.'

With a click the Captain was gone. No goodbyes. Despite the complications, Malik was hugely relieved that London had somehow been tipped off, and that the threat of a nuclear bomb was being taken seriously.

Malik checked his mailbox. His pulse raced as he opened a new message from Muhammad.

> Mohammad,
> Everyone is well. After your rewarding holiday everyone will be pleased to see you return. Let us hope that the remainder of your trip is rewarding and that you have a swift journey home. The city awaits your arrival. We wish that you make best use of the time. PBUH.
> Muhammad.

Malik was seething and slammed his fist onto the highly varnished wooden chart table. The thinly veiled threat on his young daughter's life was unbearable and his lack of knowledge of the full plan to attack London alarmed him. He knew that the kidnapping had been hastily arranged after news of the nuclear strike had broken, after which the Network had concluded he could no longer be trusted. The underlying message was clear to Malik and he knew that his only choice was to continue with the plan. Deleting the email, he closed down the computer before realising that Baba and the crew had arrived.

By the time the tug had pulled up alongside *Last Tango* and *Dutch Master*, Malik had learned from Baba how to smash *Dutch Master*'s propulsion system with nothing more than a medium sized spanner. He sat on the foredeck of *Last Tango* and watched as the three crews hastily prepared their vessels for departure.

An hour later *Dutch Master* headed out to the North Sea, watched from shore by the employees of the Jachthaven Aeolus boatyard. *Last Tango* was to remain as escort until *Dutch Master* and the tug had passed the naval blockade. Then she would turn for Cairo.

Chapter 90

April 2nd, Z – 30 Days
London, England

Distribution of national newspapers including the *Daily Telegraph* and the *Daily Mirror*, both with offices at One Canada Square, Canary Wharf Tower, were severely affected by the attack though in just days provincial offices would return them to full circulation. The siege was receiving unprecedented coverage in the media, with yesterday's attack reported in exhaustive detail. The statement and ultimatum by bin Laden and al-Zawahiri on al-Jazeera television was reported word for word in every national newspaper, although there was considerable confusion between this attack and the nuclear strike everyone had be warned to expect for May 2nd. With justification, most newspapers took the view that the radiological waste material claimed by al-Zawahiri to be fastened to the explosives was an important but nonetheless secondary issue, and although it provided a hazard to the authorities and locality that deserved a great many column inches, the main story was the destruction of the UK's most prestigious tower with six thousand people trapped inside.

But it did not end there, for page after page was given over to news and views about the organisation and structure of the terrorist cell and those behind the attack. The latest rumours that bin Laden and al-Zawahiri were dead were quashed, and since the media had fuelled the rumours no one could be blamed. The disposition of the security forces around the tower was illustrated in detail along with computer-generated designs illustrating the effects from the combined explosion of a dirty bomb and a fully laden fuel tanker. The whereabouts of explosives designed to bring down the tower, the explosions that people had witnessed during the attack and other methods that might have been employed to prevent access to the first floor, were shown graphically, supported by comment from structural engineers, scientists and retired soldiers.

But the most shocking sources for stories had been those from the hostages themselves. Even as the attack was underway, the diverse mixture of office workers from many different companies on the upper floors had begun relaying information to relatives, friends and journalists. There were stories from visitors to the tower who were attending their first and possibly last meeting in the tower on that one, fateful day. The most vivid stories came from the hundreds of journalists trapped within the tower. Most worked full time for specific newspapers, but none of them allowed their allegiances or contracts to prevent their first-hand experience from appearing in print elsewhere. It was the more civil-minded journalists who called the police and reported that the terrorists had seized and barricaded themselves up on the first floor, and that no one trapped above could pass and escape the terror.

The police had put the early estimate of the numbers of people trapped above the first floor at six thousand. On a more typical working day without Operation Enduring Freedom, it would have been as many as ten thousand. The clear message from every hostage was that they were terrified of dying in a collapsing tower block and like everyone else, they had seen the horrific pictures of the last minutes of the twin towers of the World Trade Center.

Buried deep in each newspaper, journalists tasked with prophesying how the authorities might recapture the tower ran stories with detailed supporting graphics that showed how Special Forces might succeed with minimum loss to life. It was clear to everyone that an assault through the fastened and toughened windows or from the pyramid roof were impossible to achieve with any degree of surprise, so many journalists plumped for an underground assault originating from the out-of-view Docklands Light Railway and through the shopping mall in Cabot Place East.

It was not long before the more plausible stories in each newspaper were picked up by the television stations and broadcast to millions of people across the world, including the world's most wanted terrorist leaders and to the terrorists on the first floor of the tower at One Canada Square, E14. Such was the quality of the media coverage, supported by some of the most respected experts in the world, that it was likely to prove difficult for the authorities to generate assault plans that were unique and surprising to the terrorist cell. Even this observation was reported since it was widely accepted that surprise was a key principle of war.

News of the strike, which most Londoners thought for a time was the one they had been required to prepare for, rapidly permeated throughout the city, and with the exception of the terrorists, the hostages, the emergency services and the media, the Square Mile was deserted. Fortunately most Londoners chose to ignore speculation about the localised effects from the destruction of the tower and adhered to Home Office Instructions reinforced this morning that continued to recommend the earliest evacuation of the Greater London area by all non-essential personnel. The attack was billed by the Home Office as the strongest reason so far to evacuate the city, and people were now doing so in droves. Main routes out of the city had been busy since yesterday evening, and by midday there was still no sign of abatement.

At 10 a.m. the Prime Minister appeared outside Ten Downing Street and declared that all intelligence reports suggested this was a conventional attack and not the predicted nuclear attack. He assured the public that everything possible was being done to secure the release of all the hostages as quickly as possible, and that the search for the nuclear bomb was continuing unabated until it was found. He ended with a plea that all Londoners continue to comply with all Home Office and Metropolitan Police Instructions, and to remain calm.

After taking stock of the entire situation, the media got behind the Prime Minister's announcement beginning with the midday news.

By 5 p.m., a retired British Army colonel had established a form of command structure based on company hierarchy on each floor of the tower, with himself remaining on the fourth floor and assuming overall command. Since it was his idea, and he had military experience, no one objected.

The Colonel's job was made considerably easier with electronic mail, and in the late afternoon he had sent the agreed chain of command and a long list of names and addresses to New Scotland Yard. There were 6,203 hostages.

The services to the entire building including water, electricity and air conditioning were left fully functional, as the authorities puzzled over what to do next.

Chapter 91

April 3rd, Z – 29 Days
London, England

Mustafa was sick of the dusty confines of the first floor but otherwise happy. His loyal followers had proved themselves worthy of Allah and so had he. They had seven more days to hold out before martyrdom, or until the enemy risked an earlier assault. He knew that the enemy could never agree to al-Qa'eda's demands even if they were prepared to negotiate, so an attempt at an assault was inevitable. The conclusion of this shocking act of war would further demonstrate the vulnerability of the arrogant and corrupt West to attacks from the Islamic Movement and also demonstrate their everlasting courage and dedication to the cause.

Mustafa forced himself to think about the next seven days. That was his job, his role fated by Allah. No attempt had been made by the hostages on the floors above to negotiate the smashed and heavily mined stairwells that were impassable without being killed. The four elevators had also been destroyed, and any ducts or shafts were either too small for a human being or had been rendered impassable by Turk. As he had hoped, the security forces behind the cordon two hundred metres away had not made any visible attempt to recover the bodies of those civilians killed during their assault. The wounded had either crawled away and escaped, or they had died where they had fallen. Mustafa estimated that over fifty had been slaughtered so far, most by Ahmad whose frenzied assault on his former colleagues had taken everyone by surprise.

The terrorist cell had reorganised themselves into two groups of five, with Hannah joining Turk's group. Mustafa and Turk had agreed that each group would keep watch in eight-hour shifts, with each member of each group circulating periodically between observation posts, which included a turn on the main pressure pad set up near the elevators. The terrorists maintained watch over each of the four sides of the tower, the elevator shafts and the four shattered stairwells in each corner of the floor plate.

Everything Ahmad had advised about the tower had been accurate, including the locations of the CCTV cameras which had been destroyed by Kalil. Mustafa was surprised that the security forces had not extinguished the services to the building, including electricity, water and air-conditioning, but he knew that that would come, probably immediately before any foolish attempt at an assault. Although forty-eight hours had gone by, he figured that the security forces were still deciding how to respond, meanwhile keeping the thousands of hostages above him as comfortable and calm as possible. Amazingly there was even hot water, as well as flushing lavatories, heating and air conditioning.

The banks of operable televisions were surreal but inspirational. Mustafa watched the heroic events unfold on behalf of true Islam, and he listened to the world's leading figures talk of nothing but him and his cell. It made the terrorists feel special, ordained and very proud. Before the assault the terrorists had all discussed the Western propaganda that would spill from the television channels and radio stations, and they were prepared for the hatred and derision. But far from being undermined they revelled in the attention and found it easy to distinguish the true believers from the infidels. One television monitor was permanently broadcasting al-Jazeera, and it was this channel that gave them the most strength.

Turk repeatedly checked the charges that were to bring down the tower and others designed to protect them from attack. At the beginning of every shift he examined the explosives, mines, Claymores and grenades, the detonation cord and the miles of criss-crossing circuitry that lay over the bloodstained floor. The shaped charges of plastic explosives placed around the central core of the steel-framed tower were to be detonated simultaneously by a ring main of detonator cord and an electronic detonator that was attached by wire to the main pressure pad. There was also a secondary, back-up system – a flash detonator that would be set off by the flash from fuse wire that could be lit should the self-contained electronic system fail. The mines and explosives covering the stairwells were all set to self-destruct should anyone be foolish enough to trip the wires. There was also one remote-controlled detonator fitted to the explosives underneath the fuel truck on the ground floor with the button-activated transmitter lying beside the fuse wire and the main pressure pad on which he currently stood.

Mustafa considered their plan foolproof. Al-Zawahiri had spoken on television of radioactive waste material and had laboured on human bombs before talking of another terrorist hidden near by with a remote transmitter that would be activated if any person or object approached within fifty metres of the tower. In fact, none of this was true but Mustafa knew the threats would hamper the enemy. Perhaps that was why, after two days, the ground floor was still littered with bodies.

He thanked Allah that the smell of decomposing corpses was not drifting to the first floor. Mustafa thought back to his martyred brothers at the Beslan school siege, and how they had wrapped themselves in explosives and how they had kept their feet on pressure switches. Perhaps the security forces were considering the same terrifying scenario and the carnage that ensued. He wondered whether his cell should have been instructed and provisioned to do the same, and whether in fact he should have retained several hostages on the first floor for good measure. But then his orders were to destroy the tower block. He had no need to face his hostages or stare anyone in the eye as he waited to do so.

The only demonstration of impatience so far had been by Turk. A single telephone had rung incessantly, and upon tracing the source he had ripped it from its floor socket and hurled it at a window. Telephone contact with the outside world was not part of the plan.

Time was dragging by. It turned out that Musa was a political fanatic who enjoyed telling stories of Islamic martyrs. He was a huge source of strength for the cell and everyone was spellbound. Musa left no one in any doubt that this was one of the greatest ever attacks on the non-believers who wished to undermine the Qur'an and contaminate Islam with Western selfishness, greed and corruption. For their benefit, he explained how, for the last twenty years, he had fought for his Islamist beliefs and that his increasing desperation as a lifelong member of the Muslim Brotherhood had led him to the *Shia'heed* and this final act of martyrdom.

From Yemen like his father, who was the messenger Mustafa had met on several occasions, Musa had responded to the fatwa that ordered able-bodied Muslims to seek out Abdula Hassam at the Services Bureau in Peshawar and join the Arab Mujahidin brigade and fight in the Afghan jihad to free the country of the Soviet infidels. Musa spoke of how he had been trained by the CIA, probably the best revolutionaries in the world, before moving into the mountains of south-eastern Afghanistan with American-made Stinger missiles, where he personally brought down several of the massively destructive and merciless Hind helicopter gunships. At the end of the war, when the Arab Mujahidin had considered the Islamists had won a great victory over a powerful enemy, Musa described how he and many others had wished to continue the fight for purity across the Islamic world. Initially they were prepared to achieve their aims peacefully through democratic elections, but in several years it was clear to their leaders that this would not be possible because so many Muslims had already been corrupted by the West and because the democratic process throughout the Muslim world had been a sham. Several governments, including Algeria and Egypt, had even banned the fundamentalists from standing in democratic elections. He told of how he remained with al-Zawahiri's Islamic Jihad group in Sudan, and how he had once been a bodyguard for the Emir, bin Laden. Musa was then seconded to Algeria where he fought for the GIA terror group. Ludicrously, in Algeria he had been bribed by members of the military government to commit atrocities against them simply to generate a climate of fear. From there he went to Egypt to continue the struggle for the Islamist cause before returning to al-Zawahiri and bin Laden in Afghanistan. Musa claimed he was offered a senior position in al-Qa'eda, but when he heard of this attack he chose the *Shia'heed* and martyrdom.

According to Musa, it was necessary to fight the jihad against America and her allies in their own territory rather than within Islamic states, as so many Muslims had become so Westernised, so corrupted against their will, that they were forgetting the higher authority of the Qur'an and were mistakenly revolting against their own freedom fighters. They were so blinded by Western customs that they could not see the purpose and necessity of the destructive actions within their own states, actions carried out on behalf of true Islam. These corrupted Muslims who did not wish to experience terrorism first-hand would not rise up against their governments but instead rose up against the fundamentalists. By way of compromise, and in order for these corrupted Muslims to be given the opportunity to repent and take the right path, the Network had decided that the jihad would be fought in the West's own backyard. Once the infidels had departed from Muslim societies, corrupt and autocratic Islamic governments were to be quickly overthrown and governed by true Islamists and the teachings of the Qur'an.

Musa knew all this because he had had an audience with bin Laden and al-Zawahiri prior to journeying to London. The Emir had ordered him to pass his message on to his brothers while they waited for martyrdom in the tower. Musa's stories made clear sense to the terrorists, and provided additional strength. It encouraged others in the group to tell their stories, stories that were not of strategy but death and destruction. Mustafa was mesmerised and, with no stories to tell of his own, he encouraged the veterans to repeat theirs. Their stories and the television broadcasts were the only entertainment they had.

That evening there was another al-Qa'eda broadcast on al-Jazeera. While a guard held up an Arabic daily newspaper, al-Zawahiri provided instructions to the security forces surrounding Canary Wharf Tower. He stated that two women dressed in nothing more than shirts, shorts and boots may enter the ground floor with a single stretcher and remove those bodies they could find, one after another. They could begin at 9 a.m. tomorrow morning and were to be finished by midday. Bin Laden, who was sitting beside al-Zawahiri, said that he was making the gesture as a reward for the compliance the West had so far shown. After the short broadcast, the terrorists wondered what this concession meant and concluded that the purpose was not humanitarian but designed to further shock the world's media and inform everyone who was in control.

Turk muttered to no one in particular about the thirty-six bodies piled in elevators at the bottom of each shaft, and Kalil mentioned the six bodies in the stairwell leading up to the first floor, all of which, they agreed, might be missed. No one had been killed attempting to escape down the stairwells, so they considered any stench from human decay should be limited to that from below. Although the terrorists hoped that all the bodies would be recovered, some, including Mustafa, remained apprehensive of the opportunity provided to enemy reconnaissance.

Chapter 92

April 3rd Z – 29 Days
Heathrow, England

On each day since Dalia had arrived at the London Heathrow Marriott Hotel, she studied all the major national daily newspapers the hotel offered, and watched countless news and television documentaries, American, as well as British. She also scanned the high-speed Internet facility in her room for related articles and opinion. When not studying the news, she either slept, enjoyed a work-out in the fitness suite, or to vary her routine she used most of the facilities the management offered, from massages in her room to her pick of movies from the complimentary satellite or pay-per-view channels. Three people occupied her thoughts and prayers, not only Malik and Karima, but also Susie.

Most passengers on board the P&O ship *Pride of Bilbao* had found the long journey arduous, but for Dalia it had been fun. The weather had been stormy, and the buffeting winds and angry seas had made for a turbulent crossing. Dalia and Susie had chosen to eat a light Langan's lunch before watching an action movie in the small but comfortable cinema. Then Dalia's intentions for the remainder of the twenty-nine-hour voyage changed, the moment she invited Susie back to her cabin.

The following morning, as Dalia and Susie had watched the small television in her cabin, news of the siege and the heightening security around the cordon had broken. Dalia had decided not to risk driving directly into London, but instead the ship's information kiosk had found her a vacancy in a hotel near Heathrow airport. The availability of the exclusive room, given the mass evacuation of London and the presence of the world's media, had been fortunate.

To Dalia's relief, Susie had not appeared concerned about the change in plans; the hitchhiker had been grateful for everything Dalia had done for her. Susie had happily accepted a lift as far as Reading railway station.

Immigration and customs checks at Portsmouth had been considerably more thorough than either of them had been used to, and despite the news, the large numbers of armed police and soldiers patrolling the docks had surprised them. Dalia, as she had planned, had Susie's company to calm her nerves. At Immigration Control, Dalia had been prepared for her passport to be swiped and for fingerprints to be taken, and they had both passed through without incident. The customs inspection had been much tougher for Dalia. Within seconds of Dalia halting the Audi on the yellow line, a group of six men had surrounded the car, four of them soldiers waving hand-held sensors, one controlling a dog, and the sixth, a supervisor with a clipboard. The supervisor interrogated the two women as his team searched the Audi. After four, long and torturous minutes, they had been allowed to pass.

Before parting at Gibraltar, Malik and Dalia had agreed that, unless there was an emergency, she would not contact him until the day he was scheduled to leave Amsterdam for London. Thirty minutes ago, sitting at the workstation in her hotel room, Dalia had received a response, leaving her relieved and fully prepared to continue with her role in their mission.

Leaving Heathrow that afternoon, she drove through the M4 motorway cordon to the Kents' London home, where she would be joined by Mr Kent in forty-eight hours.

Jamali was confident that Dalia had no knowledge of his high-risk pursuit of her on his powerful Yamaha 1300 from Portsmouth to Heathrow via Reading. He knew that the redhead had provided a distraction to Dalia during the voyage and had often seen them talking and laughing together on the journey to Reading.

Securing a suitable room in the same hotel had not proved difficult for Jamali, and neither had hiding a new and powerful tracking system to her car. More difficult had been gaining entry into her room, and the planting of two listening devices, one into the unused interior pocket of a vanity case he found lying in her en suite bathroom, and another inside her remarkably cluttered handbag which, to his amusement, contained an amount of cosmetics that would put an artist to shame.

Jamali had spent most of his time in the hotel reading newspapers, watching television, and eavesdropping on Dalia. His one regret had been his inability to monitor her time on the Web.

Such was the power and range of his equipment that he was no longer concerned about losing Dalia when he took time to hijack a suitable van and its driver at Heston Services on the M4 motorway into London. Passing through the cordon with stolen papers, it was not long before he found her in Islington.

Chapter 93

April 5th, Z - 27 Days
London, England

By the fourth day of the siege at Canary Wharf Tower many of the 6,203 hostages were beginning to recover from the acute stress brought on by the imminent threat of death and their utter helplessness. After the first horrific twenty-four hours, optimism slowly began to increase as the Colonel established command, control and coordination with the outside world, and as the hostages talked among themselves and with their loved ones outside.

The retired Colonel had responded admirably to the terrorist attack and when leaders from each floor gathered together for the first time twenty-four hours after the attack to consider their parlous state, many congratulated him for seizing the initiative. Though he was a middle-ranking partner in his firm, it came as no surprise to the Colonel that the other leaders were directors, chief executives or editors from each floor.

The arrangements that the Colonel suggested had been rapidly established. He kept his first briefing simple, beginning with a hasty résumé of his credentials in counterterrorism, disaster relief and emergency planning, and the need for those present on behalf of all hostages to accept his overall immediate command from the fourth floor. Then he told them what he wanted, for there was no time for discussion. Still in shock, nobody had seen fit to argue and all were keen to play their part. First, all the stairwells had been cleared and everyone returned to remain at their workstations until directed otherwise. Then an accurate nominal roll by floor had been established. The remainder of his instructions took longer to effect and refine, but by the end of the second day there was a semblance of order at the heart of which was the ability to communicate effectively both internally and externally by electronic mail.

The tower's service staff were put under the Colonel's direct control, and all medical trained personnel had been relocated to the largely vacant third floor where the first-aid centre under a qualified nurse had been established. Immediate medical care had been provided to a large number of people in the first twenty-four hours of the siege and included one woman who had been induced into early labour as well as a large number of shock victims.

Each floor was responsible for its own food inventory, and the colonel imposed a strict rationing of two snack meals per day per person, such as they were. The tower's design included for one centralised kitchen per fifty office workers and each was fitted with a fridge and microwave oven. It was building policy that no food was to be kept at workstations, though few people it seemed adhered to the rule. Between most kitchenettes and individual workstations, there were mountains of biscuits, coffee and tea beverages and even the odd birthday cake, though it had appeared that the journalists enjoyed daytime snacking at their workstations far more than lawyers, who, the Colonel presumed, relied more on the local restaurants. The restaurant and snack bars on the upper floors of the tower were found to have a reasonable supply of food, which, when necessary, was cooked and distributed to the Colonel's instructions.

Each floor was also to be responsible for its own collection and storage of water, whether it was from water coolers or the mains supply. The tower's service staff maintained central reserves of fresh water in case the mains supply stopped. For as long as the water mains remained available, sanitation was not an immediate concern as the lavatories were plentiful and in good order, and there were considerable supplies of toilet roll. There were even a number of showers installed, though the opportunity to take one was scarce.

On the third day, much time had been spent by the leaders considering how they might maintain morale in the face of such desperate circumstances. Every leader had people they considered suicidal, and the fear of death was inevitable and infectious. The last thing they needed was a riot, and a bloody rush for the exits as people panicked. At this meeting, they agreed systems for keeping a close eye on each other and how they might fill each day between mealtimes with routine other than television. Aerobics classes or anything else strenuous were not advised as they simply burnt too many calories. Simple games, stretching exercises and other activities were all recommended to occupy people.

Having established contact, the Incident Commander on the ground outside and the Colonel discussed their options. The brutal truth was that the terrorists on the first floor were talking to no one, and their threat to demolish the entire tower was considered very real. Every hostage was quite prepared to believe the television reports that stated the terrorists were not armed with a nuclear bomb because believing the opposite was simply too dreadful, and many obtained solace from reports that the explosives carried in may not be sufficient to destroy the building and that the radiological waste may be contained. The Incident Commander confirmed that no attempt would be made to airlift hostages from the tower, or supplies sent for the time being.

Besides the destruction of the tower and the inevitable attempt to save the hostages, the most critical issue upon which the two leaders agreed was food, and its impact on morale. It was estimated from the latest inventories from each floor that on two snacks a day each and minimal activity the hostages could be sustained for one week. With water, side effects would not become critical for another week. Although this length of time should see the hostages through the crisis, many would become increasingly weakened the longer a rescue took.

That morning, the Colonel had felt buoyant after their daily meeting, for although his resources staff had had a torrid time redistributing food, everyone had recognised the system as fair and sensible. Also encouraging was the fact that the numbers reporting sick had reduced for the first time. But, most importantly, he had broached the subject of assisting with any attack against the terrorists by opening up a second front.

Everyone at the meeting had responded eagerly and looked forward to returning to their floors to ask for people with specific abilities, since this move was bound to have a massive impact on morale. What the Colonel wanted were volunteers who would be willing to fight against the odds, and for people who may be able to create explosives from whatever materials they could lay their hands on. He wanted ex-policemen, ex-firemen, ex-soldiers, and also construction or building engineers or builders, basically anyone who may have an important role to play in some form of attack. For explosive materials the Colonel was looking to the tower's service staff and the flammable material kept in their storerooms and cleaning and maintenance cupboards dotted around each floor. When the Colonel had been pressed for details of the attack by several leaders, he had refused to say more fearing a leak and losing the element of surprise. He reminded all leaders of the need for absolute secrecy due to the very open communications with relatives, friends and the media; communications that had to remain open if morale was to be upheld. No one was to talk to the outside world about his wish to identify fighters and other experts. The official line for the outside world was that they had been ordered to simply sit tight and wait for the authorities to rescue them and not attempt anything foolish.

That evening the Colonel was satisfied that everything that could reasonably be done was being done. According to the Incident Commander the assault on the tower would not take place for at least another three days, and that for the period the building's services, including the air-conditioning, would remain operable. Tomorrow, the Colonel and Commander would speak further on the hostages' participation in any plan to retake the building.

Outside the tower, the city was not as anyone remembered. The monuments, memorials, parks, historic landmarks and entertainment centres that always made London such a vibrant and welcoming place looked desolate and abandoned. Central London's streets were deserted except for police or military patrol vehicles laden with armed officers accompanied by military escorts. Hastily erected security lamps dwarfed the glow from street lamps and what remained of illuminated neon signs, and bomb-sniffing dogs outnumbered whatever other animals could be seen. Even the pigeons appeared to have deserted the stillness that surrounded Nelson's Column and Charing Cross. Crude warning signs at most street corners alerted what remained of the population to keep alert for anything suspicious.

The stretched Metropolitan Police did what it could to maintain a presence. Most of them were armed, many with automatic weapons. But the most unsettling image to the four million civilians who still remained was not the presence of the security forces but the lack of people. Those larger shops and businesses that were determined to remain open until the bitter end resembled airport departure lounges. All bags were hand-searched on entry, and security guards watched over wary visitors. Extra surveillance cameras had sprung up atop buildings, most monitored by security firms prepared to respond in force to any sign of unwelcome entry and attention.

The Metropolitan Police Commissioner had enforced the cordon, the curfew and control through additional patrols, in order to tackle two growing and alarming issues. The first was the racial violence against those thousands of Muslims and non-whites that remained in the city, and the second was the alarming growth in burglary, looting and arson. The policies had been successful in driving down the numbers of incidents but had polarised perpetrators into well-organised gangs of marauding youths who were responsible for most of the remaining crime in London.

Gangs of up to fifty were meeting at prearranged locations, then terrorising any minority group they could find who still remained in the city. In the last three days, two Muslim men and one woman had been beaten to death, and another three Muslim women had been kidnapped, brutally assaulted and gang-raped. Looting was targeted at Muslim-owned businesses in the form of coordinated raids followed by en-masse looting and the torching of the premises. The horror of these marauding and ghostly gangs was well publicised, and without any effective remedy by the security forces other than to arrest on sight, normally law-abiding people from differing ethnic origins chose to band together and take the law into their own hands.

As a result, pitched gang battles took place in the suburbs, battles that so far had resulted in the deaths of seven people and countless injured. Worse, as the results of the battles were reported, people flocked back into the city to support the rival gangs, criminals and vigilantes alike.

It was at one prearranged battle that the first innocent bystander was shot dead by a police officer. This and subsequent deaths at the hands of the police led to reprisals by armed criminal gangs, and the first policeman to be shot dead during Operation Enduring Freedom. This was followed hours later by the death of the first soldier randomly targeted by a sniper. Combined police and military patrols were no longer immune from deadly force, particularly at night.

These incidents, the Canary Wharf Tower siege and the lack of progress with finding the nuclear bomb fuelled the increasing nervousness that was being felt throughout the city, and country.

The Metropolitan Police Commissioner's immediate response was to increase the numbers of patrols, impose a wider curfew, and infiltrate undercover officers into the street gangs. Any unauthorised person found on the streets of London between the extended hours of 7 p.m. and 7 a.m. was immediately arrested and detained. Measures up to and including deadly force were authorised to be used on any person who failed or refused to comply with a verbal order given to him or her by any member of the security forces. For the first time military armoured personnel carriers were deployed in the city, each APC holding snatch squads of eight soldiers. The security forces also fenced off dozens of streets to hamper the street gangs' escape routes, and security checkpoints sprang up all over the city.

Chapter 94

April 5th, Zulu - 27 Days
52° 10′ N 2° 15′ E, North Sea

A squadron of Royal Navy warships were preparing to intercept and escort two Greek cargo ships as they approached the Straits of Dover from the North Sea. Days before, the Greek ships had been alleged by Greenpeace activists to be carrying 125 kilograms of weapon-grade plutonium, enough to make around forty nuclear weapons. The two ships had sailed from St Petersburg on April 2nd and were scheduled for France where their cargo was to be converted into nuclear reactor fuel rods. The plutonium carriers were intending to pass fourteen miles off the Kent coast.

When pressed for information by the UK Government and with EU backing, the Russian National Nuclear Security Council on behalf of the Russian Government issued a statement confirming that plutonium was being transported by sea to a nuclear processing plant at Cadarache in southern France. There the plutonium was to be 'spoiled' and converted into plutonium–uranium oxide fuel rods, which would be returned to Russia for use in a nuclear reactor. Once converted into fuel rods, the plutonium could not be used in a nuclear weapon or for nefarious purposes, and therefore the Russians claimed this move was positive for this batch of weapon-grade plutonium, and for wider usage and world peace. Their statement also confirmed that the US were aware of the move and supported it with a view to them creating a similar nuclear-processing plant as France, but in the US. The movement was considered a one-off exercise and had been kept secret from the remainder of the world as a security measure to prevent sabotage or terrorism. The statement ended by commenting that further details could not be given without compromising security, but that the ships were double-hulled and each guarded by thirteen commandos and armed with a thirty-millimetre cannon.

When he read the potential threat predicted by the Defence Crisis Management Centre, the Prime Minister was furious. Although he held considerable interest in the capability to spoil plutonium, he felt it was grossly neglectful of the Russians and French for not delaying the sailing until the threat to London had been resolved. If one of the ships was hijacked, it would represent a flexible and unstoppable target for a nuclear bomber that could sail up the River Thames at least as far as the barrier.

As if that was not enough, despite all the security measures and intelligence work being conducted in the UK, Europe and across the world, it was Greenpeace that first discovered the plan. As the Foreign Secretary pointed out to the Prime Minister, if Greenpeace could discover the Russian's plan, then so could a well-connected terrorist group. With the cat out of the bag, a disgruntled Prime Minister quickly received the support of the Russian and French presidents. With their support the Greeks were forced to allow the Royal Marines to board the ships in force, search them, and rather than divert them, escort the two ships to a location off Brest where the French Navy would assume responsibility.

As it happened, Malik had known of the intended sailings on April 2nd for over a month. These events unfolded on the radio news as Malik travelled on *Dutch Master* heading west-south-west out of Amsterdam and he hoped that they would occupy the minds of the Royal Navy as *Dutch Master* approached London. As it was, the Royal Navy squadron was almost entirely employed embarking Royal Marines onto each of the two plutonium carriers when *Dutch Master* reached UK territorial waters.

Standing on the bridge on the third deck of the flat-bottomed pleasure cruiser was not a comfortable experience for Malik, but this was where the radios were situated and he considered it essential to keep up appearances and demonstrate the affection that the crew believed he had for her. After all, someone who had spent three-quarters of a million euros on a vessel, and sailed her across the North Sea in poor weather must cherish his property. Rest was also difficult in the flat-bottomed *Dutch Master,* his temporary hammock lashed between pillars – very different to the opulence of his stateroom on *Last Tango*. The worst aspect of the voyage was not the food, which was dismal, but the cold that was exaggerated by the grey darkness of the choppy sea and worsened by the sharp, incessant wind.

As *Dutch Master* steered toward the tug, Malik looked up and saw his yacht, *Last Tango*, about a mile off to starboard on the same tack. Soon she would alter course on a more southerly tack and head for the Channel and on to Cairo, but not before she had attracted a challenge by whatever naval vessel lay in front of them.

It was about fifty miles from London and fifteen miles from the English coastline that a lone frigate of the Royal Navy, HMS *Monmouth*, challenged four vessels in quick succession, including the tug, *Dutch Master* and *Last Tango*. As previously arranged, the tug's master responded on behalf of both his vessel and *Dutch Master*, identifying each vessel and providing details of their voyage. The fourth vessel, a small container ship, did the same minutes later, and Malik smiled with his good fortune when he heard it was destined for Convoy's Wharf, Deptford, in the heart of London. But nothing was heard from *Last Tango*. After three attempts by the frigate to raise her with no success, Malik, who by now had clear sight of the warship, saw a small helicopter rise unsteadily from its rear and fly urgently towards her. *Last Tango* evidently saw her too for her response was clear to everyone. She immediately turned due south toward the frigate and reduced speed. It appeared to Malik that this manoeuvre had satisfied the helicopter for it hovered over *Last Tango* for several minutes as it sent a signal message by flashlight, and after receiving a short acknowledgement in the same Morse Code, the helicopter returned to the safety of its landing pad.

Maintaining course and speed behind the tug as directed by the frigate, Malik watched through his binoculars as *Last Tango* was boarded several miles away by a sizeable party from the frigate. A long but helpful hour later he watched as both vessels pulled apart. Malik was confident that *Last Tango* and her crew were safely on their way to Cairo, and that whatever problems the Egyptian crew had experienced with her communications equipment and lengthy search, they had been amicably resolved.

Minutes later, and now with eight ships waiting attention, the frigate confirmed that *Dutch Master* and her escort vessel may proceed to her destination at Gravesend, but that the fourth vessel, the small container ship registered in Libya and out of Hamburg, must now heave to and prepare for boarding.

Dutch Master was due to dock at Gravesend at 4 p.m. Malik knew that the stop at the Thames Cruises dockyard at Gravesend would only be temporary and that the Captain expected the vessel at Signet Quay by noon tomorrow.

Chapter 95

April 6th, Z – 26 Days
Chertsey, Surrey

The pale-blue moonlight filtered in through the curtains and lit Harry's bedroom. Tess awoke beside Harry, saw it was 2 a.m. and saw that he was suffering a restless night worrying about the bomb and Canary Wharf Tower. He felt warm to her touch despite him having thrown the duvet off himself. She looked over his semi-naked form in the moonlight that accentuated his body so beautifully, and she was filled with love and desire. She hadn't wanted to get in this condition and certainly hadn't tried, but after weeks with Harry she knew she had arrived. It was the first time for her and it felt wonderful. Harry was the man. Some time later a delicate smile crossed her lips when she thought that he had finally fallen asleep.

'I love you, Harry,' she whispered, thinking he wouldn't hear.

But Harry was still awake, feigning sleep as he feared his restlessness was disturbing her. He smiled inwardly for he had recently lost his lifelong affinity for bachelorhood and had hoped for some time that she felt as he did. Until now neither of them had dared be the first to say those magical words. The words were within him, but he just could not say them for fear of rejection, but now he knew he could choose his moment. Feeling a small contentment for the first time tonight, Harry eventually fell into a deep sleep.

Tess sighed softly as she watched over Harry and considered the circumstances. Although Tess, like any other rational human being, felt the shock and horror of what was happening she figured that it was all so much worse for Harry as it was his country that was imploding, his capital city that was under attack and his responsibility as one of his country's foremost anti-terrorist experts to find the bomb and those behind these terrifying attacks. Although the inception of his Psyops plan was in its infancy, Harry was desperate for it to succeed, not least because so many leaders had shown so much faith in him. But in the main it had to succeed because there were three thousand professionals across the UK intelligence community all working 24/7 to identify and follow up every possible lead and no one had had any success. It truth, Harry's idea amounted to the only offensive plan MI6 had.

Harry's idea, which had involved the country's top psychological and global security experts, received the full and unconditional backing of the Cabinet. For the first time, many Cabinet members were forthcoming about their own global views on Western and Islamic relations as if some great burden was being released from their shoulders. The Government worked hard for a fortnight reviewing foreign policy, and yesterday afternoon the Foreign Secretary addressed a rapt House with their 'moderate adjustment' that was to provide greater tolerance and understanding of Islamic ideals.

Unfortunately, despite the Government statements and because of the healthy distrust in al-Qa'eda, most of the media had begun to speculate that the nuclear bomb was in the tower after all, probably in an elevator that was ready to be sent up to the top floor. The belief had some merit, for what would be the purpose of a terrorist attack by al-Qa'eda when weeks later they were to subject the entire city of London to a much greater nuclear attack? And if Harry was right, and the attack on Canary Wharf Tower was a decoy, then why was it truly necessary? The only plausible explanation emanating from Harry was that the nuclear bomb was due to arrive and be hidden in some impossible-to-find place in London as the world was occupied with the tower's destruction. Although the media were willing to cooperate with the Government, the effect of their speculation and attention it afforded to the tower was the dilution of the message that MI6 wished to send to Fox and Vixen.

When considering their future options last night over dinner, Harry and Tess resolved nothing. Now, as Tess lay in the comforting light she considered her total confidence in Harry, the nuclear bombers' profiles and what the enthusiastic Psyops experts had said. She concluded that the Psyops idea must be pushed to the fore, which meant the Prime Minister and Harry must appeal personally to the hearts and minds of Fox and Vixen through the media. Tomorrow they would speak to Sir Michael, then Chief Inspector Walsh at the Media Emergency Forum in New Scotland Yard.

Tess turned and snuggled against Harry's chest. Slowly she covered them both with the soft duvet. Feeling safe in his embrace, the soft thumping of Harry's heartbeat lulled her back to sleep.

Five hours later the room was pierced with darts of warm morning sun and the sound of birds singing outside the windows. It was a beautiful Saturday morning in the spring. Harry woke with Tess pinning him down with one arm across his chest and one of her legs draped carelessly over his. Her naked body felt so good against his as he watched her sleep and thought of what she had whispered during the night. He gently brushed the hair back from her face and kissed her forehead, instantly regretting it as she stirred.

Slowly Tess opened her eyes, smiling as she looked up at him. She could not believe how incredible it felt to wake up in his arms. She had yearned for love for such a long time. He stared into her eyes for what felt like an eternity, unable to do anything but drink in her beauty. The feel of her naked body pressed against his under the duvet began to arouse him more and more. He could feel that undeniable desire to make love to her consume him.

He pressed his lips softly to hers as he rolled her onto her back and slid his body on top of hers. Her arms encircled his neck, as the kiss grew more passionate. Her legs spread slightly, allowing him to slip between them. She could feel his warm smoothness against her. Her hips lifted just enough as she squirmed for him to enter her and she let out a soft moan into the kiss as she felt him penetrate.

With a slow thrust he was inside her. The warmth enveloped him as he stopped for a moment, revelling in the feelings that were engulfing them. Very slowly, they started to work. Their bodies moved in perfect synchrony as the passion between them grew. Their moans began to fill the room. Tess softly raked her nails down his back as he pushed deep into her once again. He pulled back from the kiss and looked down at her beautiful face. It was contorted in such pleasure. He smiled blissfully as he continued to thrust into her. His pace began to quicken ever so slightly as he watched the fiery need building inside her.

Harry rested his weight on one arm as his other hand moved to her chest to caress a perfect mound of flesh. He rolled the distended pink nipple gently between his fingers as he watched her lose herself in the feeling. He knew that it would not be long now. His pace became maddening as her hips bucked to meet his, no longer prolonging the pleasure. Tess let out a sharp cry as her body convulsed involuntary and her chest heaved as an intense orgasm gripped her.

'Oh Harry,' she cried out as her body shuddered hard. 'Oh my God, Harry.'

The spasms of her muscles around him quickly melted his own resolve. Harry couldn't form coherent syllables. The sensations from Tess had him so caught up in the moment that he could no longer control himself.

Tess's eyes locked on his as she gazed up at him in complete amazement.

'Wow, Harry, what has got into you?' she whispered lovingly.

'You have,' he replied softly. 'I love you too.'

The two of them relaxed, their breathing subsiding as they held each other. Harry spun them both around and softly stroked her back as she lay on top of him. His lips sought out hers as they shared another wonderful kiss. Tess rested her head against his shoulder after breaking the kiss and casually ran her fingers through his hair. They both knew what the other was thinking. Everything about them was finally perfect.

Minutes later Tess broke the silence.

'I've been thinking. We must arrange for the Prime Minister and yourself to make a joint appearance at a live press conference. He must introduce you and inform Fox and Vixen that you are someone even-handed, prominent and trustworthy, someone who can be contacted with a high degree of confidence and someone who is empowered by, and not subject to, Establishment constraints. He also has to drive a wedge between the tower siege and the total destruction of London.'

Harry thought about this. He was not in a philosophical mood but knew Tess was on to something. 'I'll be someone who has the authority to work outside the box. The PM can mention Mercury, for I doubt our mercenaries would use the Met's hot lines or contact MI6.'

'Yes, then you must make them feel you're prepared to listen, to bargain, as we all know they hold the nuts. You could even consider some kind of direct request in Dari or Punjabi, or both.' 'The nuts' was the highest possible winning hand in a round of poker, a game Tess had learned from her father.

'I must make them feel they need something from me,' pondered Harry as he considered the idea further.

'They already have money,' stated Tess.

'Our current line that the devastation of London is not advantageous to them or pursuant of their faith is simply not strong enough.'

'You can stress that the destruction of London will not further any cause but trigger an adverse reaction, World War III, the West against Islam and countless deaths and considerable destruction. Their own countries, friends and family will be affected.'

'That's better, not least because it's true. If London is destroyed, the very least they can expect is NATO declaring unlimited war on all Islamic terrorists, and here's the rub, any Islamic state that does not ally with NATO will be considered an enemy of NATO. As for the UN, not one member could defend the terrorists and its Government survive.'

'"You're either for us or you're against us," the President once said to the world as he declared war against terror after 9/11,' offered Tess.

'And he was right,' replied Harry. 'But I must focus on them and their lives after this terrible act. We must encourage them to want out, to be free from never ending pursuit and life-threatening danger. They are mercenaries for God's sake, people who are in this for themselves. If I can make them think they, and all of Islam, will be better off if they come forward, then they might just do so.'

Harry tightened his grip on Tess and kissed her lips. 'You're right. We need to show them the face of someone they can access and bargain with, show them someone who is prepared to offer them their freedom and a brighter future for global relations in return for lives and information.'

Harry jumped out of bed and rang Sir Michael as Tess showered.

After a long day with the spin doctors, the Prime Minister and Harry Winchester were the only two people who addressed the daily press briefing at New Scotland Yard. The Prime Minister simply introduced Harry as the man responsible to him for finding the nuclear bomb. The two men made a powerful combination and the message was clear. Talking for an hour, they explained how London was under attack on two distinct fronts, the tower, which the Prime Minister handled, and the search for Fox, Vixen and the nuclear bomb, which Harry handled.

Helpfully, it had been a quiet day at the tower.

Chapter 96

April 6th, Z – 26 Days
London, England

The 68-year-old Captain and majority shareholder of Thames Cruises Limited was at the helm and turned *Dutch Master* gracefully in front of Signet Quay to face downstream. Malik stood by his side in the bright midday sun and marvelled at the precision with which the experienced sailor manoeuvred the large, unfamiliar riverboat to the quayside for the first time. The journey from the company's dockyard at Gravesend had taken over four hours because of the increased activity on the river. Despite the heavy police presence *Dutch Master* had not been detained, probably due to the familiarity between the police and the Captain. That was a stroke of luck.

On the journey upriver the Captain had remarked on the similarity of London's current state with the evacuation of the Allies from Dunkirk in 1940. He had been two years old at the time, but he remembered his father braving the Channel in his riverboat by joining the flotilla that went to France. The story had been retold to the Captain so many times that he might as well have been there. The Royal Navy was present today too, sailing reserve shipping up the River Thames to dock at Westminster Pier to assist with the evacuation of Government departments. On the voyage upriver the Captain told Malik what was happening to the city, including the terrorist threat to destroy the city with a nuclear bomb on May 2nd, the cordon that the Captain felt did more damage than good as it impeded the flow out of London, the siege at Canary Wharf Tower that was into its sixth day, and the impact on a population that was expected to fully evacuate the city by April 22nd, in just two weeks' time. He also described the effect that all of this was having on their business. Tourist rides had ceased two months ago, when demand had simply dried up. As a result many of his complement who lived inside the cordon had taken paid or unpaid leave, depending on whether they were pessimistic or optimistic of London's chances, to evacuate their families. But over the last four weeks, as road haulage had become gridlocked and unacceptably slow, the demand for evacuation on London's historic river highway had rocketed. Thankfully, he had found temporary crew from out of town.

The company now had a new temporary purpose helping businesses evacuate the city and it was proving more lucrative per hour than tourism ever could. Even the Captain had been amazed when he had seen a UK FTSE 250 company's entire headquarters infrastructure packed into just one of his boats and taken upriver to Maidenhead. The company's involvement in that business relocation had taken three days around the clock and won it over fifty thousand pounds. Better still the order books were full until April 22nd and required two boats which were all they had left on the water, one of which was *Dutch Master*. A third, the Captain's reserve, was still out of commission and not due out of the boatyard for another two or three days.

The Captain also explained that he had applied to the City of London Corporation for the company to remain operational in the city until April 29th, the maximum allowable extension and was waiting for a reply. He was confident the extension would be granted as it was clear that London's evacuation was far from complete.

All the passenger seats had been removed from *Dutch Master* and put into storage before she left the Gravesend dockyard, so she could begin evacuation work first thing tomorrow. Her first commission lasting three days was to be the ferrying of exhibits from the Tate Britain on Millbank to the historic dockyards at Chatham.

Later that evening as Malik made his way in a black cab to his temporary home in Islington, he reflected on Karima and Dalia and the future that he hoped they would have together. For a short while he considered Thames Cruises and found himself hoping that the third boat would make it back into the water before *Dutch Master* must meet with an unfortunate accident. To protect the company and to meet regulations, Malik had insured the new vessel with a reputable Dutch insurance company.

Dalia peered out the window and saw Malik walking up the drive. She quickly turned off the television, looked around then crossed the living room to the hallway and front door. She opened the door just as he was about to knock. Their eyes met, sending a surge of emotional electricity through their bodies. She stepped aside as she held the door open for him.

'Come in. God, how I've missed you,' Dalia cried as she closed the door. Without waiting for him to finish removing his coat she embraced and kissed him hungrily.

'I thought today would never end. I was beginning to think I wouldn't make it here by the curfew,' he managed as they kissed. 'Thank goodness the Captain booked me a taxi.'

'It seems like an eternity since we last saw each other. Come on. Follow me,' Dalia purred excitedly as she took his hand.

Malik followed Dalia to the lounge and the couch, still gripping her hand as they sat. There was no need for words as they stared into each other's eyes. He leaned in and kissed her again. His lips tasted deliciously salty as they met hers. Her eyes closed as her hand moved to the side of his neck. She caressed it softly as she felt the kiss deepen slightly. Their bodies pressed together as the passion they shared for each other grew stronger.

The tension in the air was palpable, and Dalia pulled away reluctantly, breaking the kiss. They searched into each other's eyes, and Malik's thumb softly stroked her cheek as his fingers cupped her jaw line. The scent of her drew him in for another kiss. This time she could not break it. Her arms wrapped around him, pulling him closer as the kiss became more intimate. Her body pressed tightly against his as he urged her onto her back. She gave in completely. Her back landed against the cushioned arm of the sofa as he lay slightly on top of her.

His breathing was as uneven as hers. They both wanted this moment so badly. Her nails raked over the fabric that clung to his back as their bodies remained close. This time it was Malik who pulled back, looking into her eyes for a long moment. But she no longer cared about waiting for a more convenient moment. Her appetite for him was voracious and it needed satisfying now. He smiled at her for a moment, and without a single sound, he stood up, scooped her up into his arms and carried her upstairs to their bedroom.

Malik carefully set her on her feet next to the bed and turned off the bedside light. She smiled at him as her fingers moved slowly as she lifted his shirt, eager not to rush it after such a long wait. Her gaze dropped as she watched more and more of his chest being revealed. She pulled it over his head and tossed it aside. Her hands immediately moved to the bare flesh beneath, caressing it as she longingly gazed up into his eyes. Her lips brushed lightly against his chest as she continued to undress him. Each time he tried to touch her, she pushed his hands away.

Dalia just wanted to concentrate on bringing him as much pleasure as she could. His belt gave her a moment of trouble as she hurried to remove it. Her fingers could not work fast enough. Once undone, she had his blue jeans down in seconds. He struggled out of them and his shoes, leaving him in nothing but his underwear. She smiled as she stared at his muscular body for a few moments.

His hands gripped her waist as he pulled her closer, his lips crushing against hers as they kissed more passionately. He slid his hands slowly up her back, feeling his way to the top of the zipper. One hand rested against the back of her neck as the other unzipped her red silk dress. He pulled away from the kiss, and his hands tenderly slipped the fabric down her shoulders. The sight of the black sheer lace cupping her firm breasts took his breath away. He watched trancelike as the dress drifted down her body, revealing her matching sheer lace panties before dropping to the floor.

'You're breathtaking,' he croaked as he gently turned her face to his.

This time the kiss was passionate and soft. His hands roamed her warm flesh, wanting to touch every inch of it at once. It felt so luxurious. His fingers quickly worked to unclasp her bra. The kiss was broken again as he moved to sit on the edge of the bed. Reaching up as he looked at her, he pushed the straps down her shoulders and arms. He watched as the taut material freed her beautiful breasts. He stared mesmerised for a moment by their dark centres. She watched him timidly, searching his face for signs of approval.

He could not even begin to express what was going through his head. His lips caught a nipple as he leaned forward, his fingers finding the other. The gasp that escaped her was like music to his ears and he could hear the sheer pleasure in it. Her back arched slightly toward him as she felt his tongue and fingers. As her hands clung to his head, another soft moan pushed past her lips. Soon both his hands moved down her sides and ever closer to the top of the lace that now covered the prize he sought.

Slowly, he peeled the edge of her panties down as his lips began to travel down the curve of her breast and down her stomach. He continued to look up at her in an attempt to see the pleasure and approval on her face. Passion raged in her eyes. The scent of her arousal grew slightly stronger as he stripped her of her panties, his lips brushing over the smooth flesh just above her prize.

'Lie down,' he whispered softly as he stood up.

A blush crept across her cheeks as she lay down. She felt like a nervous virgin.

Every kiss felt like it was her first, every touch never experienced before. His hands parted her legs as he climbed on the bed with her. His lips brushed over the same spot they had just left.

A magical surge of pleasure swept through her as he tenderly caressed her with his tongue. Gasps gave way to blissful moans. The sensation was driving her wild with desire. She wanted so badly to have him inside her. It did not take long for her to be completely lost in pleasure.

He was thrilled as she writhed under his attention. He had never seen a woman look so amazingly sexual. As the climax passed, she gently pushed him away then sat up on the bed and pulled him to her. Her tongue pushed past his lips as she kissed him deeply.

When Dalia broke the kiss, a gentle smile curled on her lips. She searched his eyes. 'Now it's your turn,' she purred.

Malik lay down on the bed and watched her as she knelt next to him. Her fingers hooked under the waistband of his briefs and he lifted his hips as she eased them down, revealing his nakedness. She smiled broadly and kissed him as she straddled his legs. He shivered as he felt the moisture from her lips slowly rub over his chest and stomach and downwards to his groin.

Minutes later she straddled his hips, then reached down between them and held him securely as she guided him into her. Once it was nestled inside, she lowered her hips slowly, always staring down into his eyes. As the warmth enveloped him, he let out a low moan. His hips lifted, pushing him deeper inside her.

Her cries soon followed his as their bodies moved in slow but perfect unison. His hands moved over her body, trying to touch all of her at once. He pulled her down against him. She sensed what he wanted and wrapped her arms and legs around him. They rolled over, him pinning her against the bed. His body lunged, each thrust forcing him deep inside her as his pace quickened. Her muscles clenched tightly around him as the waves of pleasure rushed over her.

Malik felt the spasms as he plunged deep inside her. Her nails raked over his back as she stared up into his eyes. It felt so perfect to have him inside her. Her hips rocked to meet his thrusts. The pleasure was overwhelming as their cries mingled in ecstasy. Her nails dug into his shoulders as she let out a loud cry and her body was trembling uncontrollably as her muscles clamped down tightly around him. They soon sent each other over the edge, their moans intertwined as they passionately kissed. It was the most intense orgasm either of them had ever experienced.

Exhausted and completely in awe of the experience, the two remained coupled. Her arms wrapped around him as she stroked his back. His hand gently touched her cheek, stroking it lovingly as he stared down into her eyes.

'I love you' were the only words Malik could force out.

Dalia had achieved what she had longed for. Her hand slipped up, stroking his hair as she closed her eyes. She had neither the strength nor desire to move. She felt him drift off to sleep and softly kissed his cheek as she considered their future.

Chapter 97

April 9th, Z - 23 Days
London, England

The high-rise office tower at One Canada Square, Canary Wharf was constructed by a US company called Cleveland Bridge, which was responsible for creating landmark buildings and bridges across the world including the National Westminster Tower, also in London. Within hours of the terrorist attack on Canary Wharf Tower, the senior engineers responsible for both towers were travelling to London from the US.

Although the Metropolitan Police were responsible for the siege, it was the British Army's 22nd Special Air Service Regiment that the Police Commissioner through the Home Secretary and Cobra turned to as a last resort. The SAS asked for nothing in return and only asked for the assistance of any other national resource if it was essential to complete their mission. The Commissioner, like any other Chief Constable in the United Kingdom, called upon the military specialists from Hereford to retake buildings from terrorists and secure the release of any hostages in order that the police could re-establish law and order.

Within twenty-four hours of the attack on the tower, the police Incident Commander had provided the Commanding Officer of 22 SAS with a wealth of information on the terrorists. The most valuable information came from a security guard who had watched the ground-floor assault from the far side of the row of four heavy glass revolving doors that separated Cabot Place East and One Canada Square. As a retired policeman of thirty-five years the security guard had known that his contribution as a witness would be invaluable, so he had mentally registered every fact that he could during the assault as he protected the public that had continued to approach from Cabot Place East. He had heard the fuel tanker smash through the main entrance, then saw it and two vans screech to a halt before counting ten terrorists, all wearing face masks. He recounted their long- and short-barrelled weapons, the two carts laden with mines and explosives, and the heavy backpacks. He had also noted how the terrorists killed with precision and without a trace of mercy despite the harrowing screams. He explained how the elevator had been used by one group of terrorists to methodically ferry the laden carts to the first floor, and how the other group of six had killed any wounded they found before climbing one of the four staircases. He had recounted the sporadic gunfire and screams that he had heard as the terrorists had disappeared up the stairs, and the sustained automatic gunfire among the combined screams of terrified office workers from the first floor. He recalled how, seconds later, as office workers had poured out of the stairwells onto the ground floor, he had passed through the revolving doors to guide them through the exit that he knew to be safe. He recounted how a number of workers had assisted those who had been hurt, and how he had stopped two fleeing security guards and between them they had assisted several of the wounded. With the tanker apparently laden with fuel, the observant security guard knew better than to linger in the foyer and he had been the last of the living to leave. The man had wept when he recalled for the first time the deliberate and harrowing execution-style shots that he had heard from the first floor as he had left.

It was clear to the CO of 22 SAS from the MO that the terrorists intended to carry out their threat. He also knew that the demands would never be met. This meant that by the Prime Minister's deadline of midday on April 10th, 22 SAS must storm the vast building if they were to save the lives of the 6,203 hostages. Three key observations led the CO to believe that they did not intend to leave the tower alive. First, the cold-blooded use of deadly force by the terrorists was not consistent with a group that would ultimately wish to seek some kind of agreement. Second, it was clear from the inability to obtain direct contact by telephone and hold discussions that the attackers had no intention of negotiating and making exit arrangements, and third, the attackers were backed by al-Qa'eda and were likely to resort to suicide and martyrdom rather than capitulate to the West and be shamed for the rest of their lives.

By the end of the second day of the attack, Cobra had seen

and heard enough for the Home Secretary to authorise a deadly assault by 22 SAS to retake the tower. Not only were the SAS required to rescue the hostages with minimal loss of life and create the conditions for the Metropolitan Police to re-establish law and order, but on behalf of MI6 they were to attempt to capture at least one terrorist alive, though not at the expense of a single hostage.

The regiment's counterterrorism capability included a command and control, or C2 element, together with two teams, Red and Blue, each with assault and sniper troopers. One of these two teams was on call at any one time. In addition to these main elements, various back-up units provided ancillary services such as communications, methods of entry or MOE, and specialised transportation. There was also a dedicated intelligence section. The C2 element commanded by the CO of the regiment dictated the plan, training methods and assault procedures for any one attack.

The CO and his staff communicated on at least one net with the assault troops and on another with the snipers. The snipers were also connected to a highly secure digital telemetry radio link that provided the CO with a target indication capability. On this occasion the CO had co-located his headquarters with the Metropolitan Police Incident Commander's Forward Control Point, and it was from here that he had secure communication with the Home Secretary, who for this assault was at Number Ten with the Prime Minister. The FCP was located on the inner security perimeter and comprised two articulated trailers or mobile support units, one white and one green.

Apart from the headquarters, the fielded elements of 22 SAS had established themselves in a holding area in the lower floors and car park of Citibank's tower block, just outside the Metropolitan Police inner security cordon. Citibank Tower was not visible from the first floor of Canary Wharf Tower, and neither was it visible to the public or media since a second, outer cordon had been established to secure the whole of Canary Wharf and Herons' Quay. The outer cordon was easily defined as both the Wharf and Quay were surrounded moat-like by the West India Docks, and it had been a simple matter for the police to seal off the few vehicular access routes. As soon as the outer cordon had been secured, SAS special assault vehicles and heavy equipment vehicles had begun to arrive in the holding area. Not long after, briefing areas had been set up and communication links established. The holding area was guarded by the regiment's own, and as soon as it was up and running individual training had resumed while the CO and his team planned the assault.

As the plan developed, so the training became more focused. But in order to finalise plans, more intelligence was needed particularly about the terrorists and the site. This was the role of the SAS intelligence cell that had been one of the first elements of the regiment to establish itself in the holding area. Its task was to see that all information on the terrorist incident was made available and that those involved could absorb the resulting intelligence with ease. Some of this information was retrieved from enormous databases, some from individual terrorist files and a surprising amount from the Cleveland Bridge senior engineers. But most information was obtained from the eye witnesses, particularly the observant security guard. As the information was collated, analysed and reported as intelligence, the assault team rehearsed its basic armed Close Quarter Battle, or CQB, drills and rechecked personal weapons and equipment, the sniper team reconnoitred the ground, and the support entry team, who were responsible for producing any specialised vehicles, assault systems and floor or wall-breaching equipment, got busy.

The role of the assault team was to close with and neutralise the enemy. Speed and aggression played an important part, for the basic survival instinct was strong in all humans, and that included terrorists. As someone looked death in the eye there was always a slight hesitation, even with the bravest or most suicidal of terrorists. While they threatened to kill unarmed hostages they were in control, but the moment they were faced with imminent death the situation changed. No matter how dedicated the terrorists were, most ignored the hostages and concentrated on any immediate threat to their own lives. At this stage the winner was the fastest to the trigger, and that was the one that was better trained and prepared and had surprise on their side.

Closing with the enemy was also necessary in order to win, and the faster it was achieved the more likely any hostages would survive. Generally speaking, the more multiple entry points that could be chosen and the more arms that were brought to bear on the enemy, the greater the speed with which they would be dealt a deadly blow.

On this occasion, it was clear from the moment the call-out came at Hereford that the assault team would wear their 'blacks', a one-piece outer garment with a hood that fitted over a fireproof under suit comprising of vest, trousers and balaclava. The outer suit was fitted with a grab handle for easy dragging should a team member go down. The hood was designed to fit a respirator, earpiece and mic, and all neck, ankle and wrist ends were elasticated to ensure a tight fit. Each assault team member also carried a respirator that provided protection against CS gas and other chemical and biological agents. Even if gas were not used by either side on this op, no one doubted that masks would be worn for they projected an anonymous and intimidating image that could cause additional hesitation, and helped filter the thick smoke and dust caused by explosions.

Each soldier also possessed a radio communications harness that allowed each team member to talk to each other or to Control. The mic was connected by a lead to the central switching unit on the front of the body armour that contained a press-to-talk, or pressel, switch.

The body armour was thin and of a low profile that allowed greater freedom of movement. It allowed protection across the entire torso, back and front, and the built-in blunt trauma shield allowed energy absorption to dissipate the effects of the shock energy transmitted by an intercepted bullet. The SAS possessed bespoke body armour that was fitted with a range of pockets and elasticated grips that removed the need for a separate over vest.

Each assault team member was armed with the Heckler & Koch MP5 submachine gun. The gun clipped flush across the chest in the snatch mode, making it ready for use in an instant. A separate low-slung holster system on one side of the body housed a secondary pistol, or 'short', and a number of magazines for both weapons. A knife was strapped to the thigh.

Other equipment varied depending on the nature of the attack but on call-out each member had been informed that the normal allotment of CS gas and stun grenades, or 'flash-bangs', would be required, as well as night vision goggles. Of course, to operate effectively in such equipment and in absolute darkness and in uncertain surroundings, it required high fitness levels and constant training. Even with the respirator fitted, it was vital that the assault team member could identify and act quicker than his enemy.

The role of the sniper team was to provide a long-range capability for taking out X-rays. In essence, snipers dealt with any situation that presented itself. A secondary role for snipers was as intelligence gatherers. Upon arriving at a scene, the snipers would deploy to various strategic vantage points, allowing them an uninterrupted view of every aspect of the target area, in this case the first floor. All movement in and around the target area was reported back to the intelligence cell in the holding area.

Snipers also covered the approach of the assault team and provided extra security once the assault was complete. SAS snipers were trained in a selection of 'longs', or rifles. Most snipers had a preference for the US-made Browning AW50 Heavy Sniper Rifle. Every SAS sniper retained a set of blacks should he be called upon as an assault team member.

The CO knew immediately that this was not an easy or textbook operation. Significant negative planning factors included the possibility of another terrorist with a remote capability somewhere in the vicinity of Canary Wharf overlooking the tower. If found, the CO would allow the Met's SO19 specialist firearms officers to flush him out, although exhaustive searches by the police so far had turned up nothing. The use by terrorists of booby traps, tilt fuses and pressure fuses also had to be considered, as did the use of explosive-laden suicide bombers though there was no evidence of this. Then there was the cataclysmic danger of nuclear or radiological weapons in the tower. The upshot was that the intelligence cell was unlikely to establish the full terrorist capability in the time available and therefore there would be risks, but refusal was simply not an option for the SAS, the country's last resort.

On the positive side, it was possible to gain out-of-sight access to most of the ground floor through Cabot Place East without being seen from outside the tower or from its first floor. It was also possible to control the services to the building, as was usually the case in these circumstances. But among these advantages the CO considered the most positive aspect to be the unrestricted communications that he had with the hostages. Better still, the hostages had organised themselves into a potentially coherent force and they possessed a clear chain of command with a retired colonel at the helm.

CO 22 SAS had instructed that from the fourth day, the Incident Commander was to turn off all the services to the tower every day between the hours of 7 p.m. and 7 a.m. in an attempt to exhaust the terrorists. In fact, the routine was principally designed to disguise the reconnaissance and assault when they went in.

The CO and his intelligence and planning staff spent much time with the engineers from Cleveland Bridge and between them they established the goals of the reconnaissance, the most vital source of information. It was not until after the covert two-man reconnaissance of the ground floor had taken place over eight hours on the fifth night that the assault plan was finalised.

The reconnaissance team had confirmed that no independently powered cameras were placed on the ground floor or in the stairwells, and it established those parts of the ground floor that could not be seen through the vast windows. About a quarter of the ground floor and two of the stairwells were in clear view to any terrorist watching from the outside and therefore quickly ruled out as approach routes. Using high-tech night vision cameras, the two remaining stairwells were soon discovered to be impassable though the team left powerful listening devices on the home side of the man-made obstructions. But there had been no suitable places for electronic eyes or heat seeking devices, so the command team was left to find another way to limit the risks that came from not knowing the locations of each terrorist at the very moment of assault.

That left the tanker and the elevator shafts. The men had checked the tanker methodically, and found the black box strapped behind the inlet and outlet valves under its belly. They had ensured that their night vision cameras captured the box and fuel tanker from every angle before confirming with the FCP that the command team had seen enough. After checking radiation levels on their Geiger counters and dosimeters, they had carefully filmed the ceiling before making their way via Cabot Place East to the lower ground floor.

As the men approached the elevators at the lower-ground level they had smelt the stench of death. Levering and jacking open the sliding doors, their night-vision goggles and cameras had fallen on the masses of dead bodies packed inside. It was clear to everyone watching the monitors at the FCP that many of the victims had been executed with a single shot to the head.

The reconnaissance had finished with the most difficult job of all. Clambering over the dead bodies in the darkness in each elevator in turn, one man used a small ladder and patiently raised a small 360 degree spy camera on an aluminium pole through each ceiling hatch as the other man added extension poles. After two hours the men had established the elevator shafts were impassable to a rapid assault, due to a series of finely set booby trap wires that began at the ground floor.

Although the picture from the camera had been poor, everyone watching had been in no doubt that the core of the tower would be effectively destroyed by the shaped explosives that had been expertly placed between the ground- and first-floor levels in each elevator shaft. The good news was that, as expected, there were no radiological substances in sight and since there had been no adverse readings, cumbersome protective suits would not have to be worn over their blacks during the assault. Just as the two men finished recovering the camera for the last time, they had witnessed an X-ray open an elevator door and shine a powerful torch down the cavernous shaft before climbing in on what appeared to be some kind of inspection.

Over the next three days the bodies were cleared and each elevator shaft was observed. With help of the listening devices in the stairwells, the routine of the single terrorist who inspected the charges and booby traps was established.

There were over seventy people in the briefing room situated on the first floor of Citibank Tower when the CO walked in at 0030 hours for the final briefing. The aids for the briefing were simple and therefore easy to absorb and comprehend. There were three-dimensional scale models of the ground and first floors of Canary Wharf Tower and two magnetic boards etched with scale drawings of each floor, each board with coloured metallic buttons that represented members of the assault teams, terrorists, and hostages. There was no sign of any computerised systems in the briefing room. Computer software was used extensively by the C2 and planning staff, both before the assault, when various scenarios were played out against old operations for reference, and during the assault, when software was used to monitor the 'real-time' movement of each assault team member and any X-rays acquired by the snipers. But these were of no use to the assault team members whose main criteria were agility and speed. The CO preferred people to take as little down as possible during his briefings. If too much was written, then the plan was considered too complicated and was often revised. That was his view and he was in charge.

The CO glanced at a senior officer from the US Delta Force who stood beside a geeky-looking senior engineer from Cleveland Bridge then at Harry Winchester whom he knew better than his own brother, then Tess Fulton, whom he thought of as fit enough. The CO disliked having any hangers-on at his briefings. The only reason Fulton was there was because Harry had promised him an unqualified favour and that favour, whatever it was, would one day be repaid in spades. Finally he picked out the only other alien with his piercing eyes, the Metropolitan Police Incident Commander.

The adjutant breathed a sigh of relief when he saw his CO was content with the five outsiders.

'Are the Colonel's volunteers ready?' the CO asked the police officer curtly.

'Yes, sir.'

'If they fuck up they'll only have themselves to blame,' the CO added without humour. He turned to his audience, the majority of whom comprised fifty or so members of Blue Team who happened to be the team on duty when the call first came in.

'Right, we have the green light,' the CO barked. 'This one is a right motherfucker and makes the Iranian Embassy siege look like an afternoon at Millwall. It's not an Immediate Action. We've been planning this for days and now I'm sick of fucking planning. As always, if there's anything you don't understand, then improvise. And remember, if you can't do it, then no one can, and then where would we fucking be. Ops.'

Within every member of the SAS there is a special determination to achieve the impossible, or die trying. It's this quality that fuels the ethos behind the Regiment, and it was this quality that the

CO knew would be required on this, one of the most dangerous and crucial assignments in the history of the SAS. He also knew how to draw the necessary motivation from his troops, however macabre his methods may seem to outsiders. In the SAS, the training and operational procedures were firmly under the control of the senior NCOs and many of them were promoted to officer status to ensure that the Regiment's potency and expertise remained intact and free from erosion from uninformed outsiders.

The Ops Major took control of the briefing, beginning with the orbat, the military term for the force structure. Blue Team were reorganised into an assault team of sixteen troopers, a second team of another sixteen troopers who would secure the ground floor, assist with forced entry and act as reserve, and a third, smaller team who would secure the lower ground floor and conduct the most dangerous and the most critical job of all, a simultaneous climb of two floors in each elevator shaft and the rapid deactivation of all explosive devices as they went. Meanwhile, twenty snipers drafted in from Red Team would secure the area from high points surrounding Canary Wharf Tower and assist the assault where possible.

Next, the Regiment's Intelligence Officer, ably assisted by the engineer from Cleveland Bridge, described the immediate vicinity of the tower and the tower itself. For the benefit of the snipers, the IO dwelt on the best positions that an X-ray in overwatch might take.

The Ops Major returned to brief on the X-rays and friendly forces before handing the stage back to the CO.

Later, after days of training and endless briefings, the troops were ready for an assault that was to be unique in the history of antiterrorist operations across the world. At 0300 hours the twenty SAS snipers were in place dotted throughout the buildings of Canary Wharf, all with their own arcs of fire, many of which including the first floor of One Canada Square. It was acknowledged by the CO that regardless of the ammunition, sniper accuracy and reliability would be impaired by the toughened and double skinned glass that surrounded the tower, and unless the glass was already shattered by the explosions or small arms fire then no serious attempt by the snipers could be counted upon except in extreme circumstances, though for the SAS those circumstances were common enough.

The preliminary assault was to begin as soon as the terrorist had concluded his inspection of the charges in each shaft which the SAS knew on this occasion preceded him getting some sleep. It happened to be 0332 hours when the CO ordered the preliminary assault and it began with the silent and unopposed securing of the ground floor, and with the simultaneous entry into the elevator shafts by the four EOD experts whose mutual progress was synchronised by a single commander. At the same time the fuel in the tanker was siphoned off with what actually transpired to be 65,000 litres of fuel into a huge rubber fuel pod that had been pre-positioned by the Royal Engineers in the cramped shopping precinct on the lower ground floor. This activity was accompanied by the silent construction of two four-wheeled cup lock access towers.

For the first time in the history of the SAS, an MOE that involved a pair of two-man mouse holes, each formed through a twelve-inch thick concrete floor that hung over thirty feet above ground level, was to be made. At the same moment these breaches were made using necklace cutting charges, the explosive device fitted to the underbelly of the tanker was to be destroyed by a round fired from a remote-controlled high-calibre EOD weapon.

The signal for the main assault from below would be the successful improvised noisy attack on the ceiling of the first floor from the second floor. The command for the top attack was to be made by the CO to the Colonel by telephone and was dependent on progress in the elevator shafts and the removal of the detonators from the charges, and troops reaching their final assault positions. Should the risky top attack fail for any reason, the CO was, in any event, prepared to give the command for his assault team to 'Go'.

The Colonel and his bespoke team of volunteers had devised a reliable way of producing a massive and penetrative explosion using welding gear that had been found on the forty-eighth floor. It included two pairs of acetylene gas and oxygen cylinders. Acetylene was a gaseous hydrocarbon that was highly unstable and produced an intense explosion and very hot fireball when combined with oxygen.

Burrowing down through the carpets and service ducts under

the flooring to the thin concrete ceiling of the first floor, the Colonel's volunteers had positioned the four tanks at the weakest point on the ceiling below before packing the cylinders from above with countless boxes of printing paper. To initiate the improvised device, one of the tower's service staff, a welder who operated the equipment was to light one of the blowtorches and set the piercing blue flame on its own cylinder. He estimated the explosion would occur thirty seconds later, giving him enough time to get clear.

At 0441 hours on the ninth day of the siege a huge explosion tore a six-foot wide hole in the ceiling above the first floor and the following ball of flame engulfed the first and second floors creating a series of small fires. The second floor was vacant, but the ten terrorists on the first floor were struck by the deafening noise, sudden increase in air pressure, flying debris and the intense fireball that hung in the air for seconds. Before any one of the X-rays could distinguish the strong garlic odour emitted by the first blast, there were two more, this time originating from different locations in the floor. The combination of the three explosions and the ensuing flash-bangs that were hurled into the smoke ensured that the X-rays lost all sense of sight, smell, sound and touch. Not one of them was able to register the activation of the floor's emergency fire sprinkler system anticipated by the SAS team.

Before the X-rays could recover and react to the assault, nine were dead, each with at least two taps to the head. The tenth, an unconscious woman dressed in charred clothing, was searched. Despite her injuries, her hands and ankles were flexi-cuffed before she was abandoned in the recovery position for the clear-up team.

The assaulting troops still had work to do and conducted an initial reconnaissance of the first floor for more X-rays, fire and overall condition. Mercifully the sprinkler systems on the first and second floors were deactivated soon after the Assault Commander and Colonel confirmed the absence of fire, and seconds later the services were restored.

As the dust began to settle and the lights came on, the troops opened the elevator doors and recovered their four colleagues from inside the shafts before conducting a radiological survey and search for additional explosives and improvised devices, marking anything they found with red triangles for disposal experts to deal with. Within five minutes the Assault Commander announced his job done and his team departed through the mouse-holes, making way for the clear-up team. They left the sodden floor plate with nothing more than their personal equipment, satisfied they could provide a detailed and thorough verbal report at the debriefing to follow.

At 0530 hours full control reverted back to the Metropolitan Police and with the support of the Armed Forces and emergency services the clear-up operation began. At 5:45 a.m. the Prime Minister and Home Secretary walked outside Ten Downing Street and informed the media of the success of the SAS operation to recapture the tower, that there had been no friendly casualties and that no nuclear or radiological material had been discovered. As they spoke, the SAS were fully recovered into their holding area and preparing to melt away.

At midday the Metropolitan Police Commissioner issued his first press release stating all mines and explosives had been cleared and that the outer cordon had been lifted. The world's media, who had struggled to view what they could of the night assault from vantage points beyond the outer cordon, moved towards the tower in time to capture the first hostages emerging at 12:30 p.m.

That evening the Commissioner led the press briefing at New Scotland Yard and gave a fuller account of the operation. The final death toll was sixty-seven civilians dead and twelve injured, though remarkably none of these were sustained during the tower's recapture.

Chapter 98

April 9th, Z – 23 Days
London, England

'Mercifully there were no more civilian casualties,' the Prime Minister replied, 'though a large number are being treated for shock. The security forces suffered two minor injuries, both from burns. However, sixty-seven civilians were killed and twelve wounded when the terrorists first attacked.' He had rung the US President over breakfast.

'And the terrorists?' asked the President keenly.

'Nine dead and one injured with third degree burns. We won't be able to question her for several days.' The Prime Minister was equally keen with this result, his voice rising from its previously bitter tone.

'What about the nuclear bomb? Any radiological weapons?'

'None found after an intensive search. No radioactivity was detected either.'

'A bluff then?'

'Yes.'

'Bastards. And the interrogation?'

'MI5 can't interrogate her until she regains consciousness.'

The President exhaled. 'Perhaps my people can help? The CIA and FBI will want to talk to her. Maybe we should send her to Egypt?'

The Prime Minister felt a chill run down his spine. He did not agree with coercive interrogation techniques, otherwise known as torture, not only because he believed it was inhumane and sent one's own societal values into a terrifying freefall, but as the Government had experienced from the last Gulf War, the information gained under torture was almost always fiction and simply what the brutal interrogators wanted to hear. The Prime Minister remembered how a previous US Secretary of State had briefed the UN on their reasons for going to war in Iraq post 9/11, based largely on false information from one of bin Laden's lieutenants provided under torture in Egypt, a place where nothing was considered too gruesome. The end did not always justify the means. However righteous the cause, he had no intention of ever again allowing himself or the British public to be deceived by intelligence gained from unreliable information.

'MI6 is concerned that she will dig in if over-faced,' the Prime Minister replied carefully. 'I know Sir Michael will be speaking with Jim Ridge later today to talk it through.'

The President appeared to accept this. She was a foot soldier who had intended to give up her life for her cause and would probably take her life rather than submit to torture. Right now the priority for everyone was Operation Enduring Freedom. 'Sure. Well done anyway. I watched the assault on CNN. I know it's no consolation, but many more lives were saved than lost.'

'I know, thank you.'

'So what now?' the President enquired abruptly

'We return to the main agenda. We continue evacuating the city and keep searching for the nuclear bomb.'

'The National Security Council is behind the Psyops idea and I am speaking to Congress this afternoon. Amazing really, I thought the warriors might object, but they are more liberal-minded than I thought. I was expecting some trouble from the far right too, but they are unusually quiet. I think some of them have finally realised they're part of the problem. Truth is my Administration was intending to change direction on global affairs anyhow. Rather than let the neo-conservatives talk the al-Qa'eda network up, we intend to do the opposite and pull the rug from under them. That is, bring respectable Muslims on side and reflect the terrorists' few numbers and criminality.'

'Even the smallest terror groups can prove to be ruthless, brutal and sophisticated,' the Prime Minister observed.

'Oh sure, their potential impact won't change, and we'll take nothing for granted. Several terrorists and a nuclear device can alter history, that's a fact.'

'I agree that there'll be greater success if we're more honest about terrorist capabilities and intentions, and not talk them up simply to make people take notice. My Cabinet now considers that talking down al-Qa'eda will actually reduce support to the militants and be more beneficial. Meanwhile, we must ensure people understand that just one terrorist still represents a danger to society. The fact is, until 9/11 Islamic terror groups were losing support. But those strikes created a grand revolutionary force in the minds of many Muslims, who together represent a phantom enemy. With the right global strategies and application of force we can nullify the impact al-Qa'eda and other Islamic terror groups have on the world.'

'Good, it appears we agree,' the President said curtly. 'Truth is I need to refresh our foreign policy before the next election or the liberals will win on this battleground alone. Americans are sick of being slaves to terrorism and want it to be addressed globally by the most effective means. I now believe that with a global approach we have a much better and more palatable chance of defeating the Islamist terror groups. The US should be influencing the world through collective, global strategies, however frustrating that may be, not by unilateral action that makes us an easy target for hatred and condemnation.'

The Prime Minister smiled. Never before had they both spoken so candidly. He knew the President must be very concerned, not only for himself, but for his entire country in light of the nuclear attack on London.

'In my humble opinion we will both win our next elections if we distance ourselves from the far right.'

It was the President's turn to smile. 'Can you tell me any more about this Psyops plan?'

'I'll try, but I confess to being a little bamboozled.'

The President chuckled. 'Me too, though the Director CIA brought my National Security Council around remarkably quickly.'

'Essentially we're attempting to play mind games with the terrorist cell, but much depends on the free press. Six believe that the terrorist attack on Canary Wharf was a feint by militants intent on martyrdom, but that the nuclear strike was planned and is being played out by intelligent, Westernised Muslim mercenaries whose motive is money, not ideology. We believe the cell can easily carry out their threat without being caught, though obviously that will not stop us trying. The bottom line is that we must appeal to them through the media and try to turn them by feathering their weaknesses.'

'Christ, that's fluffy,' replied the President gravely. 'There may still be a mistake, a piece of luck, or a tip-off from Deep Throat.'

'But it's unlikely. The CIA helped with the profiling. This cell is believed to be a one-off, consisting of highly resourced professionals who are working alone.'

'I know,' the President replied gravely.

'We're communicating with them, not with half-truths and propaganda but by explaining the unequivocal truth behind bin Laden and his co-conspirators and the impact that the pointless destruction of London will have on the world and its people, including Muslims. We're also labouring on the repercussions.'

'It may be enough,' said the President. 'They have to have something to enjoy after their work is done, after all.

'We're also hinting somehow through the subconsciousness that if they go through with their plan they can never hide, and that should they cease their attack and provide the locations of the bomb and their leaders, in return we will let them go, never to resurface. We're hoping they have been paid sufficient to make them think twice. Easier to hide from them than us, that sort of thing.'

'The CIA has a department dedicated to propaganda, causing revolution and insurrection, turning soldiers against their officers and politicians against their leaders. Its rumoured they can even turn rats against each other. Who's running with it?'

'Sir Michael aided and abetted by Harry Winchester and your CIA operative Teresa Fulton. They have an army of professional advisors, Muslim leaders and the media barons in support. The media are focusing on Muslim anti-terror campaigns, prayers for the sinners and debates about the evilness that is in complete disregard of the Qur'an. You name it, it's planned. Anything that reaches into their psyche.'

There was a moment's silence.

'Is there anything else?' asked the President, sensing more.

The Prime Minister drew breath. 'At the risk of getting beyond ourselves, if we obtain the evidence and we discover where bin Laden, al-Zawahiri and the other terror leaders involved are holed up, I want to destroy them, and quickly, before they disappear.'

'Of course, we do too,' the President added quickly.

'There will be no time for niceties,' the Prime Minister continued. 'The UN will prove too slow and insecure. Then there is the knotty issue of the UN Charter banning the use of force.'

The President felt something tighten inside. He was a well-known critique of the UN's current inability to respond adequately to global affairs. 'But not for defence. As I have said many times, no nation ever signed away its right to defend itself. In any event, terrorists have no rights under international laws of armed conflict. NATO has declared Article Five and can now act offensively on irrefutable evidence and intelligence in order to defend herself. I've had my arse chewed many times by a hesitant Capitol Hill when it comes to the UN though never have they stopped me doing my duty. In any event, a successful strike on key terrorist leaders will present a wonderful opportunity for modernising the UN Charter which doesn't adequately deal with global terrorism. Tell you what. I'll speak with the NATO Secretary General later this afternoon after I've addressed Congress, where I will gauge the mood, and request that he asks NATO's Supreme Allied Commander to work up a number of solutions involving an enhanced NATO Response Force. I'll even have the US Pacific Fleet move towards the Indian Ocean.'

The Prime Minister smiled, remembering the President was the Supreme Commander of US forces. 'NATO can assume an additional British carrier battle group in their calculations too. I'll have them positioned off the Middle East within two weeks.'

'Excellent,' responded the President. 'The UN Security Council are empowered to investigate threats and authorise use of military force to restore global peace and security, but you're right to question its response time and, above all, its security. The organisation is too open and unwieldy for clandestine warfare. Nonetheless, NATO should consider issuing a warning to the UN Security Council immediately before any attack and must be prepared to justify herself afterwards. I'll raise the subject with the NATO Secretary General.'

'Perhaps NATO should lobby several UN Security Council members in advance, particularly the Russians. We may even want the Russians to assist in the assault. They have suffered through Islamic terrorism after all.'

The President was in full swing. 'I was just about to suggest them. They are geographically valuable and can be guaranteed to provide another carrier force. Congress will be concerned about cost and the US military being seen doing more than its share. If our geo-intelligence is correct, to do this properly I reckon we will need six carrier-borne forces. NATO currently has two multinational carrier groups at its disposal, so that will make five. I'm sure the rest of Europe can manage one.'

The Prime Minister paused, not quite sure what the US President meant by the last comment. 'There's also the outstanding political requirement. We'll be assaulting sovereign territory.'

'That's a problem for NATO and its political arm. Damn it, there must be something left for my Secretary of State and your Foreign Secretary to do.'

The Prime Minister paused. 'At least we won't be on our own this time.'

'For sure,' replied the President. 'The UN can learn a lot from NATO's response to this global threat. Let's hope they do.'

Chapter 99

April 13th, Z – 19 Days
London, England

Malik slowed *Dutch Master* as the riverboat passed under Chelsea Bridge. He knew that at the reduced speed it would take ten minutes to reach the sufficiently deep section of the River Thames between Waterloo Bridge and Blackfriars Bridge. Already dressed in his all-weather suit and prepared for the rough weather outside, he spoke to the remaining two crewmen on board through his personal radio and suggested a change-around for the last leg of the journey.

Dutch Master was on the return leg of a trip that had seen her travel thirty miles upriver. Due to today's large shipment, Malik had begun the day with a crew of seven, plus another twenty volunteers from the finance company, which was evacuating the city for leased premises at Henley.

The move had gone according to plan, and as night fell and London's street lights began to sparkle in the heavy wind and rain, Malik had seen his chance. First he had dropped five of his crew at Westminster pier, a common occurrence on the return leg of an upriver trip and as the working day drew to a close. The five disembarked, not because of concerns over the curfew, since all the remaining staff of Thames Cruises now held passes that authorised them to work late into the night, but because it saved them considerable time returning home.

The change-around alternated the remaining three crew positions so that Malik was now stationed at the stern, with the crewman at that station moving to the bow, and the one at the bow now in the wheelhouse. It was customary to change positions in this manner, particularly during rough weather, giving each crewman some time under cover. The crewman at the stern and helmsman were protected from the elements but the crewman stationed at the stern bow no such protection.

As soon as Malik handed over the helm to Bob, he made his way to the stern. Minutes later all three were at their new stations watching out over the busy river. Though it was past 7 p.m. the river was choked with traffic in both directions, with many of the boats incorrectly or poorly lit and providing a significant hazard to themselves and other river users. The increasing number of boats on the river in recent weeks had meant that no one vessel had a clear passage, and despite the best efforts of the river police, every journey was hazardous and filled with sudden changes of course and speed. The danger multiplied fourfold in poor weather conditions or at night.

Five minutes after taking up his station in the heavy rain, the boat slowed for Westminster Bridge and Malik walked forward and opened one of the deck hatches that led to engine room. Out of sight from the wheelhouse and foredeck, he took several steps down a short ladder before grabbing one of several torches that were clipped to the bulkhead. At the bottom of the steps he felt in his pocket for the medium-sized spanner then withdrew it and waited for *Dutch Master* to cross under Waterloo Bridge.

Usually the large three-decker was able to pass under without delay or incident but tonight it was dark and the weather was poor. More boats than usual were queuing up either side of the bridge waiting for their opportunity to pass. Malik's torch picked out the two large prop shafts that each led from a powerful engine down to an underwater propeller. The starboard engine was idling with its clutch disengaged so, unlike the port shaft, the starboard shaft was stationary. Malik jammed the thin spanner through a universal joint at the end of the starboard shaft near the hull, and then sprang up out of the engine deck before flipping down the hatch and returning to his station.

Even Malik was not expecting the carnage to begin so quickly, but as the boat slowly negotiated then cleared the bridge there was a shout from Jack at the bow, followed by an urgent command over the personal radio telling Bob to take evasive action and steer hard to starboard in full reverse. Malik could not see the cause of the alarm from his post on the aft deck, but he guessed an oncoming boat had misjudged their chance and moved toward the bridge too early.

As the reverse gears engaged and the twin throttles opened,

Malik heard a high-pitched squeal followed immediately by a succession of loud thuds and a series of sickening crunches from the engine room. He knew the hull was being torn to pieces by the unleashed prop shaft, just as Baba had said it would. Rather than risk his life dashing down and investigating the source he ran up to the wheelhouse.

'What the fuck was that?' shouted Malik in panic as he entered the wheelhouse. Bob was still listening to the third crewman, Jack, on his personal radio as he quickly shut down the engines and steered straight ahead again, leaving the riverboat to continue forward under its own momentum.

'I don't know, boss,' shouted Bob, terrified. 'It was our right of way in the centre channel but something happened as I powered both engines into reverse gear. There was a lot of noise and vibration through the hull, and then one of the engines ran away with itself. We didn't hit anything. The boat in our way has buggered off.'

'I'll check the engine room. Maybe something's got caught up in the propellers. Stay in the centre of the channel and steer ahead. Don't attempt to restart the engines or cut across the traffic to either bank.'

'Aye, sir.' Bob could think of nothing else to say. They all knew how much this boat meant to Malik and the firm.

Malik waved his arm across the busy river lanes in front of them as if to justify his last point, then grabbed a distress flare clipped to the wheelhouse bulkhead and left the wheelhouse. Outside he fired the red distress flare into the night sky.

Malik was amazed by the destruction. As he approached the aft deck above the engines he immediately noticed the uneven and splintered planks and a hole where a hatch he had closed minutes ago had been torn from its hinges. Glancing through the hole into the darkness, he could hear and smell the water rushing in through the torn hull. Reaching for the same torch that was still clipped to the bulkhead, Malik surveyed the hull and stared for several moments at water pouring in through several massive holes in the fibreglass hull where a propeller shaft, split from its outward universal joint and still connected to its powerful engine, had spun out of control as if berserk.

The bottom of the hull was already covered with water and the level was rising fast. Although Malik was now confident with

Baba's assurance that the boat would be badly damaged it was not until he felt a sudden listing to starboard that he knew for sure the boat would soon sink.

Running to the port side, he took out his personal radio and barked his orders as he went, fighting to be heard above the driving rain and wind. There was no time for debate or heroics and neither did he want any.

'Jack, Bob, we're sinking. A prop shaft has broken loose and made massive holes in the hull. We have no more than a few minutes before she capsizes. Jack, meet me aft on the port side. Bob, lock the wheel amidships, switch on the emergency lighting and fire off another distress flare. Then come down. I'll beckon the nearest boat for rescue.'

'Yes, sir,' they both replied in unison.

Malik felt the deck lurch. It wouldn't be long now. The closest boat was a small motor boat but behind them and approaching fast was a powerful police launch whose searchlights were bearing down on the stricken riverboat and whose blue emergency light was flashing angrily.

A river police officer took immediate control and shouted to the smaller craft to make way and steer clear. Malik called out that there were three crewmen who needed evacuation and that the riverboat would sink in minutes, although by now the listing was such that this was evident to everyone.

The police were already aware of just how quickly these riverboats could sink, with or without passengers on board. There was sufficient time to remove the three crewmen and that was all. The police vessel nudged its wide bow up to the port side of *Dutch Master* and the three men were hauled on board.

It took just four minutes from the prop shaft failure to the sinking of the riverboat. Malik watched with genuine shock as *Dutch Master* finally disappeared under the surface and as he departed in the police launch he stared at several lights still beaming up from deep beneath the water. It was as if she was intent on saying farewell before her life was finally extinguished.

Once on shore, Malik and the two crewmen were taken to a police station where they made the obligatory statements before being collected by the Captain who was distraught, and two of his sons. They took Malik to a vantage point on Waterloo Bridge where they surveyed the location where *Dutch Master* had sunk.

It was only when they got to the bridge that it occurred to Malik that they were there to console him.

'At least we still have two boats working,' the Captain grumbled, as if there was nothing awful that he had not seen or experienced before.

'At least she was under warranty and insured,' Malik responded sorrowfully.

'She's not dead yet,' the Captain offered encouragingly.

'Have you informed the insurance company already?' asked Malik flatly. He had not expected such swift action from the Captain.

'No, but it's the first thing I'll do tomorrow. Everything is up to them and of course the police. The police will send divers down first to investigate the cause. Under normal circumstances that's done in a few days. Once the police are satisfied, the insurance company conduct their own investigation based on the police reports and decide whether it's down to them or the builder's warranty, and whether there's any point in speeding up her recovery for salvage. Someone has to lift her at some stage, and it sometimes pays to do it sooner rather than later. She can't stay down there blocking the river.'

'Surely the terrorist threat will delay everything?' asked Malik quietly.

'I dare say it will, in which case when she's lifted she'll probably be beyond repair. I'm sorry Mr Kent.'

The group continued to watch for a while in silence, as a police launch meandered over the wreck leaving buoys to mark its location.

Chapter 100

April 13th, Z – 19 Days
London, England

The captured terrorist was simply called 'Black Widow' until her name could be established, but she did not regain consciousness in the otherwise vacant medical centre of Belmarsh Prison until the morning of the third day after her capture at Canary Wharf Tower. Because of the medical and surgical attention that had been administered to the barely conscious, heavily bandaged and sedated woman, it was not until the morning of the fourth day that the doctors finally approved her questioning. Although the Black Widow had experienced massive blast trauma to her chest and one leg had been shattered by concrete, it was the burn injuries to the back of her head, neck and arms that had received the most attention. Fortunately her face had been protected from the blasts and fireball, as she had been sleeping face down with her head in her arms at the time of the assault. After minor skin surgery it was the surgeon's prognosis that with time the young woman would make a full recovery.

The single occupancy room was obviously a prison cell, despite its function as a treatment room. The smell of antiseptic, the heavy metal door, the barred window with opaque glass, the magnolia-painted walls and the absence of any personal touches or creature comforts gave away its underlying purpose. The picture that filled the monitor at the security desk down the corridor was of the heavily bandaged woman propped up staring at her untouched breakfast as she lay on an old iron-framed and mechanically operated bed dressed in a simple green medical gown tied at the back. She was covered with monitoring devices and tubes attached to her arms, chest and head, though remarkably her mouth was clear. Of immediate concern to the doctors was the resetting of her right leg which was currently plastered and held in traction at an angle of 45 degrees but with some reluctance they had approved the interrogation before they got back to work.

Having been unconscious or asleep for the last three days, the woman found herself able to lie awake through much of last night recalling what had taken place and thinking of Kalil who had been her lover and only real friend since childhood. Yesterday morning when she had regained consciousness, she had been informed by a large woman who looked as much jailer as nurse, that she had been 'out' for over seventy hours and that she was the only terrorist to have survived. The conversation had been entirely one-way as the nurse had refreshed her bandages around her head though Essa had nodded pitifully. At eighteen years old Essa wished she were dead too, as she knew that she must prepare for the inevitable interrogation by her captors before they exacted their revenge on her. Deciding she would not cooperate unless she liked them, she determined not to provide them with anything unless there was something in return. She considered it unlikely they would kill her and no Western jail could be worse than the Madrasah, a religious school for orphans in Iran that she had lived in with Kalil for so many years. The reality was that she doubted she knew anything of real value anyway.

As breakfast was cleared an elderly Muslim man entered her room, pulled a chair up to her bedside and claimed to be her legal representative. After several minutes alone with him, Essa decided she could not trust the self-important man with a cleft chin as she considered his waistline symbolic of his decadence and corrupt ways. She ignored his rhetoric, and speaking Persian, she told him her first name and nothing else.

The Black Widow took an instant dislike to the two men in suits as they followed the solicitor into her room shortly after 10 a.m. so she resolved to be uncooperative despite the efforts of the round-faced young Muslim man acting as interpreter. As she felt the eyes of the four men pore over her, she felt vulnerable and she knew that none of them would ever attempt to understand her, just want her as all men did. Despite her damaged hearing and poor English, she was able to comprehend most of the rapid-fire questions but she chose to ignore them by simply staring forwards to a point on the far wall and feigning tiredness. In apparent frustration the younger of the two interrogators broke under the pressure he was under to get results from this ill-educated girl.

'Your fate is in our hands,' he barked. 'You know that don't you?'

The question was rapidly interpreted into Persian.

Irritated, Essa replied for the first time. 'My fate is in the hands of Allah.'

'Clever bitch aren't you?' Again the patient waited for the interpretation but this time she declined to respond and went back to staring at her leg hanging in traction.

The older interrogator took over. 'Why make this so hard on yourself?'

Was it hard? I'm more comfortable now than I've been my whole life, she thought to herself as she smiled unintentionally. 'Every hardship I face is a test of my faith and dedication to God.'

'Why destroy the tower?'

She looked with disgust at her interpreter as if he were a traitor. 'It's the duty of every Muslim to defend the Uma.' The Uma was the global fraternity of Islam.

The young Muslim interpreter suddenly felt ill and responded nervously, 'How can this be defending the Qur'an and the Hadith?'

She shot a devilish glance at the young Muslim. His hands were shivering. 'You know nothing of the true faith. You must repent before Allah before it's too late.'

'This attack will not go unpunished,' offered the younger interrogator who believed his initial show of frustration was responsible for the breakthrough.

'Your retaliation will unite us and divide you,' Essa shot back.

The older interrogator heard a metallic command in his earpiece. Someone had decided that the sixty-minute interview was suspended as it had gained nothing of value and there was a danger the woman was becoming entrenched. Unfortunately for the two interrogators they had known nothing of the woman prior to questioning except that she was an al-Qa'eda-sponsored terrorist, she spoke Persian and her name was Essa. This meant they could not rely on the usual leverage techniques they were used to including financial affairs and friends or family, whereas she could play dumb. Neither could they use force, not here with a camera aimed at them all and with so many non-Five personnel watching. Worst of all, MI5 were under massive pressure and she was not.

After the dispirited men had left, the young terrorist lay back and reconsidered their questions. Essa was stunned by the suggestion that her cell had planted the nuclear bomb that was capable of destroying the whole of London. She knew nothing of this threat other than what the ten of them had seen and heard on television. What she knew was that she was the only person who had lived and that whatever knowledge she held was considered vital by the infidels. But she also knew that her knowledge could not harm Islam.

After a lengthy discussion between the Home Secretary and other key members of Cobra in the medical reception area, the Director MI5 reluctantly agreed to hand over responsibility for the interrogation to the Director MI6.

After lunch another two people came to visit her. This time there was no condescending translator and no grossly overweight and odious State-appointed legal representative. Better still, one of them was female and, the young terrorist thought, was only a little older than Kalil but no less attractive. The two visitors, who appeared to care about her condition and vulnerability, sat beside each other on one side of the bed. The man whose eyes never left her face to wander over her body and who spoke colloquial Persian got straight to the point.

'My name is Harry,' he smiled kindly, 'and I work for the British Secret Intelligence Service. My partner here is called Tess and she works for the CIA. Tess speaks Persian too. We are not here to trick you, or to judge you. We are not political or religious leaders. We simply need your help and quickly to save thousands, if not millions, of lives, and in return we may be able to help you. Do you understand?'

The young terrorist studied the man's soft eyes for a moment, then looked across at the beautiful woman who reminded her of Kalil. She pointed to the ceiling. 'The camera?'

Tess smiled warmly. 'That was an oversight. Give me a minute.' Tess left the room, and while she was away both Harry and the young terrorist noticed the red recording light go out. When Tess re-entered the room she stood on her chair and removed the leads from the back of the camera unit, then symbolically wrapped a bandage over the lens.

'The doctors still insist on monitoring your health. I hope that is acceptable?' Tess asked as she glanced down at the tubes and wires running from the young woman.

Essa merely shrugged.

A short period of silence followed while Tess scanned a clipboard. Her eyes lingered over the terrorist's shapely body that lay before her as if considering the extent of the wounds. Harry shrank back, realising Tess had a new plan.

Essa noticed as Tess lingered on those parts of her flesh that were exposed. She also noticed Harry as he studied his notes, eyes turned away. Bedclothes were not practical due to the terrorist's situation and she lay with her green medical gown covering no more than her torso and with her single top sheet crumpled between her spread legs where it had provided privacy from the camera above her. Eventually their eyes met and a hint of recognition passed between them. Tess covered Essa up as best she could with the single sheet.

Harry was pondering whether he should leave, but decided to stay.

Maintaining eye contact, Tess spoke with serenity in Persian. 'May I call you Essa?'

'Yes.'

They stared into each others eyes searching for something. Tess wondered what horrors this beautiful girl had already experienced in her short life, particularly from men.

'Thank you. Essa, as my kind friend said, if you help us then we can help you. I swear to the one God we will do everything we can. We need the answers to some questions. We know you were not responsible but acting as a loyal soldier. Although our friends would like to know more about the attack on Canary Wharf Tower, right now you know we are more concerned with a threat to detonate a nuclear bomb in London. Were you aware of this threat?'

Even Harry and Tess were taken aback by the coherent response.

'I do not wish a public trial or to face the rest of my life in jail. I have offered my life to Allah, and he has chosen to let me live, perhaps to tell you of the heroes who died so close to victory. I wish to go home with a new identity and with some money. Can you help me?'

'If you answer our questions we will help you. Your embassy

and the media can be informed that Essa died of her wounds in hospital. We will provide you with a new identity, but it would be unwise of you to return to somewhere you are recognised.'

Essa's hard shell evaporated. Harry and Tess watched as she softened into a tearful and vulnerable young woman before their eyes.

'I am an orphan and cannot remember my parents who were gassed by the Iraqis. My only friend, Kalil, is now dead. My home was a warrior training camp for orphans. If I ran away, I would have starved, unless they caught me first. Then I would have been killed as an example to others. They even trained me as a suicide martyr, but someone decided my youth and appearance was more important.'

'Will you talk to our colleagues?'

'I will only talk to you.'

Tess nodded in understanding. Harry sat back and smiled warmly at both the women, amazed by his partner's ability to interact with the girl. There was a bond between them that Harry could never have developed and they all knew it.

'How old are you?' Tess continued.

'Eighteen, I think. Kalil thought I was older.'

'Where are you from?'

'Iran. I lived at a religious school for orphans, a training camp for Islamic warriors near Babol.'

'How long where you there?'

'Fifteen years, maybe longer. I was an instructor of weapons.'

'How many people are at the camp?'

'I'm not sure.'

"Over one hundred?'

'More than two hundred children. As people left to join the jihad, others arrived to replace them. Many would die in the first few weeks, most killed by the leaders.'

'How many leaders?'

'Twelve.'

Reluctant to leave the topic, Tess nonetheless changed tack. 'How many of you were there in the cell that assaulted the tower?'

Assuming some of her colleagues had been blown into unrecognisable pieces, Essa answered. 'Ten.'

'What weapons did you have?'

'Each of us had two assault rifles, AKs and Uzis, and two pistols. We had grenades too.'

'What about explosives?'

'We had what we needed to destroy the entrances and the tower, no more. We prepared them in advance. Turk was our expert though we all helped set them up. There was the fuel tanker too. That was Mustafa's idea.'

'Was there a nuclear device?'

Essa looked up, her puzzled frown obvious to both operatives. 'Did you find one?'

'No. Did you ever see or hear of radioactive material?'

'Only on the television.'

'Could there have been a nuclear device that you did not know of?'

Essa thought about this for several seconds. 'No. I have spent the last two months living with Kalil and our leader, Mustafa. He never mentioned it, but he would have done; he respected us and liked to show off. We both stayed with Mustafa since we arrived from Iran.'

'Was Kalil your friend?'

'She was my only friend.'

The two women understood each other. Tess stared into Essa's eyes and smiled softly.

'How did you travel to England?'

'I came in through Heathrow on a student visa.'

'Did any of you ever leave the first floor of the tower?'

Essa looked puzzled. 'No.'

'Who do you work for?'

'Allah.'

'Which terrorist group?'

'Al-Qa'eda.'

'Are you sure?'

'The warriors are sent away when they are ready. Kalil and I were chosen by al-Qa'eda then prepared at an elite training camp. Soon we were sent to Mustafa in England. No one cared who went where, we all fought for Allah.'

'Are there other orphanages that train Islam warriors?'

'I've never heard of one.'

Although Essa hated the orphanage it simply didn't occur to

her that the West would want her camp terminated for lots of countries trained fighters, many from a very young age.

'Was this your first operation?'

'Yes.'

'What is your family name?'

'I don't know.'

Tess had finished her first round of questions. From memory, she asked the same questions, but in a different order, once more. If Essa thought it odd she did not comment. Finally Tess concluded the interrogation.

'Essa, Harry and I have to go now but I will continue to look after you. No one else other than the doctors will speak with you. Soon I will come back and talk to you in more detail about the attack on the tower and the training camp. If you answer my questions truthfully, you will be given a new identity and sent anywhere you wish. Would you like to ask me anything?'

Essa looked deep into Tess's eyes. 'Will I be killed when I am freed?'

'Only if you break with your new identity or threaten the West again.'

Essa thought on this as the two interrogators left. Allah was guiding her. She had shown her loyalty to Islam, lost her childhood lover and with nothing of importance to give the infidels she was to be allowed home to Iran with a new life and money. She would find a man who could give her strong children, many children who would fight for Allah and the jihad.

Leaving the cell, Harry followed Tess up the corridor to a medical reception area, where a great many people, including the Foreign Secretary, Home Secretary, Sir Michael, the Director MI5 and other senior Cobra members, had gathered to listen to the interrogation.

'Well?' asked Harry crisply as everyone turned to watch the two operatives approach.

'According to the polygraph she's telling the truth,' answered the examiner, who strangely, was wearing a doctor's white lab coat.

Harry and Tess were already satisfied. Neither of them felt they needed a lie detector test to determine whether Essa was telling the truth. They were certain Essa knew nothing of the nuclear bomb and was simply the product of a pitiless orphanage near Babol where terrorists were reared to demand from infancy.

Tess withdrew a digital mini tape recorder from her pocket and passed it to Sir Michael. Without ceremony, he replayed the interrogation then hotly discussed the contents with the Cobra Group.

Twenty minutes later, he took Harry and Tess to one side. 'Well done, both of you. Unfortunately she knows nothing of the nuclear bomb but that's no surprise. We need addresses, Tess, particularly Mustafa's. I also want everything you can get on the camp, everything. She is a small price to pay for exposing it and shutting it down, never mind the backlash the ayatollahs will feel from the demands made by the UN for inspections across Iran.'

'We should consider eliminating the ringleaders of that camp and seizing any proof of complicity first,' said Harry tightly. 'Even hell-holes like that keep records.'

Chapter 101

April 14th, Z – 18 Days
London, England

The house at 36 Richmond Avenue, Islington was a typical semi-detached home with three bedrooms and a garage. Brick-built in the 1930s with a pitched roof over two floors, it was the left-hand house of the pair viewed from the road. Its front door lay to the left of a large bay window that extended to both floors and was inset within a small porch of red tiles with an arched red-brick mantle. The exterior of both houses and each of their single garages had been rendered and whitewashed quite recently. Each house had a mirror image front garden, small but mature and split by a six-foot fence, each with a lawn surrounded by large bushes and shrubs, all overhung by the procession of trees up and down the avenue. The established front gardens and fences provided each house with the privacy that was required. Inside, 36 Richmond Avenue was neutrally decorated with woodchip wallpaper and magnolia paint. It had been sparsely but adequately furnished; the lack of personal items gave the house an air of abandonment. There was no telephone, but a reasonably modern television set provided contact with the outside world and the kitchen was well fitted.

Dalia had passed through the cordon without incident and had arrived at the house two days before Malik, collecting the keys from the caretaker at the local mosque on Caledonian Road. According to the Mailman, the house was gifted by an elderly Saudi Arab called Omar ul-Haq. He had purchased the house many years ago for the local mosques to use as a boarding house for distinguished foreign and other guests when visiting London. The local mosques were responsible for its maintenance and upkeep and had appointed a reliable caretaker.

Five months ago the service bills and other mail had been

altered by name to Mr and Mrs Sean Kent. Dalia had smiled amusedly when she picked up the large pile of mail addressed to them from the doorstep that included her Audi's new insurance and registration documents. Mail delivery had ceased a week ago.

The Mailman had also told them that, unless they asked for assistance from the local community via the caretaker, they would not be disturbed. Most importantly, he had told them that no one had any idea what their business was, and that if they looked under the floorboards in the built-in cupboard of the smallest room, they would find several handguns and a quantity of ammunition.

By the time Malik had first arrived at the house, Dalia had figured out the heating system and purchased a number of necessities including a radio, powerful torches, and a laptop computer with remote Internet access and new bedding. With purchased cleaning equipment, she added a much needed freshness to the house and after two nights of the gas fire burning in the living room, the smell of burnt dust had finally disappeared. Dalia had also purchased some tools and a number of new locks, and before anything else she changed every door lock and improved security by adding more. She also added a new padlock to the garage in which was parked her Audi A3.

All Dalia's purchases had come from large department stores and supermarkets some distance from her temporary home. She thought it important that no one local had an opportunity to see too much of her, or think it odd her moving into the area when everyone else was packing to leave. Her food shopping was thorough and designed to provision both herself and Malik for several weeks, help conceal the oil drum that she had removed from her Audi and placed on the floor in the larder, and, she admitted to herself, provide her with the opportunity to seduce Malik. She need not have been concerned, for eight days ago on the first night they rejoined each other since leaving Gibraltar, he had been hungry for her love both before and after they had eaten the delicious Kashmiri meal she had cooked from fresh ingredients for much of that afternoon.

The safest way to enter the house was to ring the doorbell and warn Dalia of his arrival, so that is what Malik did every day he returned from work. It was 6 p.m., and Malik had spent much of the afternoon assisting the police inspect the sunken wreck of *Dutch Master* from Temple Pier on the North Bank.

Malik entered as Dalia opened the door and immediately his senses were bombarded with the delightful smell of cooking. After a cold and wet day, this was just what he needed but only after a long and passionate kiss with his partner.

Dalia looked up at him as she held him, not wishing to let go. 'Did they find it?' she asked anxiously.

'No. Two divers spent several hours inspecting the wreck. It could be they were looking for more than just the accidental damage, but I doubt it.'

Dalia's heart raced. 'Do they suspect you?'

'No way, that is unless they are incredibly good actors. No one followed me home either. Everyone appears content that a prop shaft universal coupling failed.'

Malik had travelled on foot today, using the increasingly unused but nonetheless operational London Underground network. The Underground trains were the lifeblood of London, and the Mayor of London had decreed that a limited service would remain operational until the last possible moment.

'So what happened?' asked Dalia as they walked down the short hallway into the kitchen.

'I met the river police as agreed on Temple Pier on the North Bank directly in front of the wreck at two o'clock as planned and answered all their questions. There were some people there from the boat's Dutch insurance company accompanied by the Captain. The police divers inspected the entire boat before focusing on the engine room.' Malik grinned mischievously.

'And?' asked Dalia impatiently, as she chopped vegetables and dropped them into a wok.

'One of them opened the forward hold and two fenders burst out and jumped to the surface before floating away. I assume the diver trapped the rest in the hold. It was a tense moment.'

An unfinished smile froze on Dalia's lips. 'Perhaps the police intend to go back?'

'I don't believe so. After inspecting the engine room, they appear satisfied that the cause of the damage was equipment failure or, more precisely, the failure of a universal joint, although they could only find parts of it. Apparently it had shattered into many pieces. The loose prop shaft that was connected to an engine at full power simply smashed through the fibreglass hull in a number of places causing the boat to sink.'

'You were lucky.'

'Not really. Baba knew what he was doing. Sinking so quickly was a stroke of luck. Anyway,' said Malik with a sigh, 'the police will examine what's left of the universal joint and produce their report. Meanwhile the insurance company may choose to conduct its own investigation. I'll stay here several more days to avoid suspicion.'

'Surely they will want to conduct their own inspection as soon as possible?'

'That's what I thought. But after talking with the police the insurers feel confident that the cause of the sinking is a warranty issue and if so, liability falls on the boat's builders or the manufacturers of the defective part. The insurers may not inspect it at all but simply pass the police report on to the builder. In any event, it's doubtful another inspection will take place before May 2nd.'

'Surely any future underwater inspection would only be interested in the engine compartment anyway?' asked Dalia confidently.

'Probably. According to the Captain there is no way the wreck will be salvaged this side of May 2nd.'

'What about Karima?' Dalia whispered, changing the subject.

Malik felt his chest seize. He was ashamed how easy it was to forget his daughter's kidnapping by the Mailman. He could only think of one plan. 'Her best bet, our only bet, is to see our mission through and ensure that both bombs remain undiscovered. That means my staying in London for as long as necessary. I'm convinced the Mailman will not release Karima before the attack is over, if ever. We have no guarantee that he does not intend to double-cross us; we know too much. There is nothing stopping him killing us all, just to play safe.'

Dalia shivered. 'Someone silenced the Doctor. It's obvious they don't trust us to complete the mission, or they would have ordered us to kill him rather than involve anyone else, and they would not have seized Karima. I think they intend to kill us.'

'I agree,' replied Malik calmly. He fell silent as he considered their next move.

After thirty minutes they sat down to eat.

'We can fly direct to Cairo from Luton and stay on *Last Tango*,' suggested Malik at last. 'There we will talk to our friends and organise Karima's rescue. I only hope she's with the Mailman and has not been taken elsewhere.'

'We could use my car to get to Luton,' added Dalia eager to seek whatever help they required.

Malik reached across for Dalia's hand. 'You could. You should go now. I can find my way in several days. There's no need for us both to remain here.'

'No, Malik, I'm waiting for you.' It was clear by Dalia's expression that she would not tolerate argument.

Malik saw advantages in her staying. After all he loved Dalia, and her company would be welcome in this increasingly desolate and desperate city, and two pairs of eyes were better than one.

'Thanks. We'll leave in several days, I promise. Karima will be safe for as long as the whereabouts of the bombs are unknown, though she must be rescued before midday on May 2nd. After that her life will be worth little to them.'

'Shall I book the flights?'

Malik appreciated her eagerness to rescue Karima. 'Not yet. Booking flights at this time of year will not be a problem. If it is then I will charter a jet.'

That evening after supper Malik prised up the carpet in the closet of the third bedroom and lifted the loose floorboard. Neither he nor Dalia had felt they required the weapons in London before now, as on-the-spot searches in the streets by the police and troops looking for weapons had become commonplace, and always resulted in offenders being led away to detention.

Malik found four hand guns along with magazines and a large quantity of ammunition. Three were boxed and included a Beretta with a fourth, an FN Browning, contained in an airtight bag. It had been clear from the dusty containers that the weapons had been hidden there for some time. After stripping and rebuilding each weapon and magazine they selected the two identical Sig Sauer SP2009s complete with suppressors and returned the two older weapons to the floor space. Using whatever suitable materials they could find, including string, toothbrushes, cotton sheets cut into narrow strips, and the thinnest clock oil Dalia could find in the absence of gun oil, they patiently cleaned and lightly oiled both weapons until they were satisfied.

Unknown to Malik and Dalia, Jamali was sitting outside in the back of a stolen van listening to their every word through the electronic listening devices that he had carefully inserted into all four of the air bricks located at ground level around the outer walls of the house. Jamali was smiling to himself for he had discovered the final resting place of each of the two bombs, and now Malik and Dalia would die. He had already decided that he would take no risks, and that he would kill them separately, first Dalia in their house, then Malik as he returned home one evening. With a twelve-kiloton nuclear bomb detonating in the larder, there would be no evidence that any one of them had been there.

Chapter 102

April 15th, Z – 17 Days
London, England

Regardless of Government press releases, a great many people hoped that the nuclear threat had, in fact, been holed up in Canary Wharf Tower. After all, it's what much of the popular press had been suggesting. In effect, they wanted to believe al-Qa'eda over their own Government. After the successful recapture of the tower and the release of the 6,203 hostages by the SAS, people were desperate for the threat of London's destruction to be over.

After all the hype and expectation, the cruel blow of disappointment came when the Prime Minister delivered the official verdict of the investigation on a live television broadcast from Chequers. It left people wondering just who they could believe, and to avoid blame, the media were left with no choice but to turn on the only organisation that had delivered the truth. Although the Government was blameless, it was a massive blow for their credibility and also for the intelligence and security forces. The disappointment left the remaining four million Londoners, and those who had evacuated, terrified, devastated, frustrated and annoyed.

The public could hardly be blamed because throughout the siege they had been bombarded with media reports channelled through newspapers, radio and television about how an end to the tower siege would finally overturn the downward spiral of economic and human devastation. Ignorant politicians and other officials had publicly pronounced that the SAS were to be used as the last resort at the tower to bring an end to the ordeal. Some of them went as far as suggesting the Government knew that a nuclear bomb was holed up in the tower simply to make the front page. Crisis experts had been carefully chosen by television producers who went into graphic detail to explain why the tower was the logical choice for the terrorist, its height enabling them to detonate the nuclear bomb at the optimum distance from the ground and cause maximum destruction. Other experts had majored on the effects, terrifying many Londoners into scrambling out of the city before they had had time to pack their personal possessions and material goods, or before they had secured their homes. Many others had determined to stay, preferring to put their faith in the SAS and the force's ability to locate and disarm any weapon before it was too late. Whatever their decision prior to the assault, it was the final straw for many Londoners who felt they had been let down by their leaders.

The Prime Minister's televised address did nothing to allay fears or pacify the public. He put the blame for misinformation and exaggeration squarely on the shoulders of the media, claiming that at no time did the Government confirm that either a nuclear or radiological bomb was located in the tower. But the media were having none of it and turned on those individuals from central Government and the London authorities who had given them the false expectation, while at the same time undermining the attempts by the Government and the security forces to resolve or even contain the worsening situation. It was not long before two junior ministers who had spoken out of turn were forced to resign.

Most of those that had evacuated in haste immediately before the SAS assault returned immediately to recover the possessions they had left behind in their rush to leave. Londoners took to the streets in impromptu and unorganised protests despite the State of Emergency and laws banning meetings, protests and marches. The protests encouraged more disgruntled evacuees to return and join in. Several violent street gangs that the police had targeted with success remobilised, and professional protestors saw an opportunity to profit from organising a march the likes of which London had never seen before.

People became distressed by the inescapable disintegration of London and were increasingly frightened and annoyed by the apparent inability of the Establishment to prevent it. Most people now believed that those who were paid to provide law and order could not deliver, and that the Metropolitan Police were swamped and out of their depth. The outcome of the Canary Wharf Siege caused a breakdown in law and order, and London mob rule was to return after three hundred years.

The biggest-ever protest to take place on British soil saw a sea of people massed shoulder to shoulder between Parliament Square and Trafalgar Square. The protest was estimated by the police to consist of over four hundred thousand people, a tenth of London's remaining population. Placards and posters vividly demonstrated the issues that infuriated them. Only one issue, the apparent inability to find the nuclear bomb, united the protestors, the remaining issues jockeying for status and attention. The most vociferous group demanded more focused law and order and a stop to Government lies and the indiscriminate fire-fighting tactics of the Metropolitan Police, who they felt should be targeting those responsible for the widespread violence, looting and destruction, and not the innocent who only sought to protect themselves and their property. The race for second place was between a protest for a more effective war against terror and a protest against the financial and insurance markets, the latter of which was failing to respond to the demands of their clients after decades of huge profits for names and massive fat-cat bonuses. Other groups were protesting about racism and nuclear disarmament. A large minority waving civil-rights banners protested about the treatment they had received from the police and the shooting of innocent bystanders, and many individuals were simply appealing for information about a relative or friend who had disappeared. There were numerous petitions too, the most popular of which indicated people's intention to reject the Home Office instruction to evacuate London.

It was at 11 a.m. when the violence flared. Ironically it began among the very group that was protesting against the inadequate response to lawlessness. The Home Secretary was spotted grinning and waving at the crowd from the back of his large black Jaguar as it turned off Westminster Bridge. The car became detached from its two police motorcycle escorts as they turned into Parliament Square, with the car slowing as it drove up St Margaret Street. As the dense crowd surged forward to vent their fury at the provocation, the low barrier in front of them collapsed, rapidly folding all along the two-hundred-metre frontage of the Houses of Parliament. With the angry and suffocating crowd pressing forward, the thin line of police had no choice but to fall back to the fence line and low walls that surrounded the imposing building. An Asian businessman in a suit was holding a placard that proclaimed he had lost everything, including his wife and livelihood. Without difficulty he climbed onto the smart shiny bonnet of the Home Secretary's car that had been forced to a halt. To the delight of the mob he dropped his trousers and bared his backside, waving it at the passengers. Seconds later he jumped down to loud applause and cheers, and was swallowed up by the crowd.

The two thousand police and one thousand soldiers on duty in Westminster were outnumbered and outmatched. Spread far too thinly and with so much noise, all sense of command and control quickly evaporated, and it was each person for themselves. Security personnel detached from their colleagues were outfaced and could do nothing but watch as they were stripped of their weapons and equipment. Many of them were crushed against the walls and railings, and were so deafened by the angry clamour that they could not talk themselves out of the situation never mind access and operate any equipment they might still possess. Some dropped their weapons and equipment in fear, only to see them sucked away into the crowd, while others escaped the mob by making the six-metre drop into the dry, grassed moat to the front of House of Commons. Over a hundred police officers and soldiers were viciously assaulted in the minutes after the Home Secretary waved at the mob, most by concealed knife attacks.

Standing under the arch of the St Stephen's Entrance to the House of Commons, the arrogant and grossly overpromoted superintendent in command of policing the debacle, a man who had completely misinterpreted the mood of the crowd and only half an hour earlier confidently informed the Command and Control Centre that he could handle anything thrown at him, attempted to regain control by getting five of his officers to fire a sporadic volley into the air. The response was immediate. A large group of anarchists in the middle of the mob that had been waiting for such a moment launched a counter volley of miniature petrol bombs and small arms fire in the direction of the firing squad. The superintendent and another officer fell burning, while the other officers fled by lunging over a low wall into the deep dry moat on their right. With the entrance barred by nothing but two huge oak doors, the rioters threw more improvised petrol bombs against the doors in an attempt to burn their way into the sitting House of Commons.

Meanwhile, the Home Secretary, who was intending to arrive early for one of the last debates in the House before it evacuated to Birmingham City's county council chamber, was suffering a barrage of abuse. Alarmed that he would be hauled from the car and torn limb from limb, his security detail assured him no one could gain entry to the heavily reinforced car. He would have been more terrified if he had known that two seized weapons were just metres away behind several tight ranks of rioters and slowly getting closer. As the car received a brutal and sustained attack from the outside, the front passenger radioed the Command and Control Centre to ensure that backup was on its way. Meanwhile the driver sat back, unable to edge the car forward.

The demonstration which had by now become a full-scale riot got very ugly for the Home Secretary when someone fire bombed his car and another madman began firing into the flames with a M9 Beretta semiautomatic pistol that the Home Office had signed on loan from the US Defence Department. The mob around the car scattered, all except the charred remains of a woman who had chosen to lie on the road and was now wedged under a front wheel.

The riot spread up Whitehall, beginning with groups threatening security personnel followed by fighting between rival gangs and ethnic groups. Back in Parliament Square several people died of their wounds as paramedics could not gain access through the massed ranks of the mob. But the worst place to be right now was not in the Home Secretary's car but in the dry moat where fifty police officers and soldiers were trapped and at the mercy of the mob above.

As the paint peeled and the flames mercifully died away on the Home Secretary's car, the Army approached the mob from all directions. A Lynx helicopter hovered over the roof of the black Jaguar, and gunmen abseiled down and covered the ground either side. Others swooped down to protect the dry moat and the burning entrance to the Houses of Parliament. The businesslike, heavily armed and somehow familiar soldiers dressed in black with respirators covering their faces, and the noise and downdraft of the helicopters, dissuaded the mob from drawing close.

Slowly but confidently the Army pressed forward on the ground, ten ranks deep in every street that converged on Trafalgar Square and Parliament Square. Loudhailers encouraged people to drop any weapons they may be holding, to disperse quickly and peacefully through the military ranks and to go home. Search teams and snatch squads lay in wait behind the front ranks, beyond which anyone could receive first aid. Military and civilian film crews filmed the entire operation, however gruesome. The Army meant business and if anyone raised a lethal weapon he or she was shot dead. If they resisted they were incapacitated with stun guns. Tear gas or water cannon were not an option, as they would create additional confusion to what was a remarkably uncomplicated situation.

The military recovery operation broadcast worldwide by an ecstatic media was controlled by the Permanent Joint Headquarters from Northwood, on the direct orders of the Cabinet inside the House. The scenario had been predicted by the Defence Crisis Management Centre weeks ago and had been prepared for and practised by the Permanent Joint Headquarters, who held a brigade of troops in reserve for such an emergency. The Metropolitan Police Commissioner and his Command and Control Centre at Scotland Yard had been unceremoniously replaced until law and order was restored by the Chief of Joint Operations, who was in command of an operation against his own people and in his own country, using live pictures fed to Northwood from a fleet of Lynx ground surveillance helicopters.

The final death toll was forty-seven civilians, seventeen police officers and two soldiers. All of them had been either crushed, shot, burned, kicked or stabbed to death. Over two hundred people were arrested on the day, though nobody was ever charged with murder or manslaughter due to insufficient or conflicting evidence.

The media nicknamed the riot the Battle of Westminster. It was to mark a milestone in the annals of British history for it heralded the first time that martial law was to be imposed by the Government on the British mainland.

Chapter 103

April 15th, Z – 17 Days
London, England

Malik followed Dalia into the living room of 36 Richmond Avenue where she was preparing to watch the evening news on television. It was a few minutes before 6 p.m. and he had just returned from another long, cold day sailing up and down the River Thames. He was enjoying the distractions that the work provided and found that the activity kept him alert as he waited for further news of *Dutch Master*'s salvage. However, his wait was to end, not with any news but with his last day's work tomorrow. Taking off his coat and fleece then slinging them over an armchair, he glanced at his wristwatch and saw that there were a few minutes before the programme started. He settled beside her, and she nestled herself against him as he wrapped an arm around her. He needed to catch up with the news, but there was still time to talk.

'Thames Cruises was refused its extension to the twenty-eighth, so the Captain will wrap things up and be out by midnight next Thursday. With the loss of *Dutch Master* half his workforce including me is no longer needed. It's my last day tomorrow.'

Dalia was delighted. 'Then let's leave the day after. Let's move out of the city, perhaps to a hotel at Luton, and take the next flight to Cairo. He must leave time to rescue Karima.'

Malik's eyes welled up. He had tortured himself over Karima and his longing to organise her rescue. But she was safe as long as the bombs were secure and he still had no workable plan. '*Insh'Allah*. Without the extension we must be outside the cordon in just eight days, by midday next Friday. People seem to have lost any hope of finding the bombs and are flooding out of London now. The longer we stay the more exposed we will be.'

'I don't think we'll need to come back and check the bombs next week, not without a good reason,' said Dalia. 'Any news on *Dutch Master*?'

'Nothing. The Captain is beside himself, but no one else has had time to consider the claim. There will be no further inspections or salvage. Little Boy is safe.'

'Then why work tomorrow?'

'Because he expects me to, and there is no reason to endanger my cover. Until tomorrow evening the Captain needs two boats and crews in the water. After that, he reduces to one for the last four days. He does not want to leave a boat inside the cordon.'

'He seems very dedicated,' said Dalia quietly.

'I suspect he intends to safeguard his boats, then return to London and hide away. He was born in London. London represents his life, and without it I think he'll lose the will to live. His wife died and was buried somewhere in Putney ten years ago and I reckon he has no intention of leaving her behind.'

'A television programme estimated that up to a hundred thousand people will attempt to stay in London and the authorities will be powerless to stop them. Some want to protect their property, some to die in their own beds, especially the old, and some think the threat is a conspiracy by their own Government. There are even those that believe James Bond will neutralise the bomb with seconds to go.'

'I'm not sure even he can be in two places at once,' replied Malik with a slight smile. 'At least these people believe in something. A belief in their city is better than no belief at all, or a belief driven by fear. I'm not sure what I believe in any more, except Karima, you and our future. Just what is evil, Dalia? Once I thought it was the Americans, the Russians, the Jews, corrupt Islamic governments, the Indians. But that's because of what I was told. But now I think for myself and I'm not sure. This evening on the Underground I saw a gang of youths attack three Muslims at Islington Tube Station. The Muslims were kicked and beaten, then one of them drew a gun. He shot one, then the gun was wrenched from him and he was shot dead.'

'Attacks like that are common occurrences now,' said Dalia. 'People who believe in nothing fear those who believe in something.'

'When these bombs explode, World War III will begin, we

both know it,' Malik paused briefly to consider his next remark. 'It will generate a previously unimaginable level of fear, not of terrorists, but of Muslims. Muslims will be slaughtered everywhere, by thugs, gangs and governments, in much the same way as the man I saw killed at the station.'

Dalia nodded in agreement. 'There was a huge riot in the city this morning. Sixty-six people were killed, Malik, most of them Muslims. The Army had to stop it by shooting people. The people here are not used to living with death as we are in our daily lives. This modern city is tearing itself apart in the face of an imminent nuclear attack that is much, much worse than anything the world has faced before. The people here are really afraid. They have a fear that none of them have ever experienced before, and they don't know how to respond other than to hate it and fight back any way they can. Many choose to fight the Muslim community or the police, or their Government, because the real enemy is so distant and faceless, and unworthy of such an attack.'

'I heard of the riot and I'm not surprised by it,' replied Malik. 'People react to fear in many different ways but the most common are aggression or submission. A person with hope will always be aggressive. As hope grows from religion or wealth, I think that Islam and the West are ready to destroy each other.'

'I saw another three Arab or Asian shops broken into and looted today. No one stopped it, no one cared, not even the police,' Dahlia reflected solemnly.

'But they were armed, why not stop it?' asked Malik.

'There were about two hundred rioters and as many police. But it was more than that. The police had no desire to stop them.'

The extended television news began and dealt exclusively with the aftermath of the tower siege and the riot in Parliament Square. An underlying theme was the willingness of Muslims to kill fellow Muslims, as it had been revealed that nine Muslims had been killed during the storming of the tower and that a tenth had subsequently died, and that there had been 303 Muslim hostages in the tower. A terrorism expert was drafted in to make sense of what he termed an irony as he asserted that al-Qa'eda was a tangible force to be reckoned with, as if both sides could be drawn up against each other in line of battle. Malik sneered when the expert drew parallels with the Christian and Muslim battles of the Crusades.

'This man appears to be advocating a religious war with no boundaries. No one can hope to win a religious war unless they advocate genocide,' Malik whispered peevishly. 'They are so ignorant. The key to a better world is the elimination of fear, and the source of the world's fear is in the West.'

Dalia added tersely, 'They cannot understand the ideology of the Network because they did not invent it. Nor can they believe that it was the West who empowered the fundamentalists and put bin Laden at its head, and called it al-Qa'eda.'

'People believe what they want to believe, not what's true,' offered Malik. 'I thought it was the FBI that invented al-Qa'eda, soon after the US embassy bombings in Africa.'

Dalia frowned. 'I think that was when it happened. During the Afghan–Soviet War bin Laden was an officer in the Islamic Jihad group led by al-Zawahiri. Afterwards he created his own Islamic World Front for the Struggle against the Jews and the Crusaders.'

Malik's eyebrows creased together. 'I first met bin Laden when I was ordered to help train the Arab Mujahidin in Peshawar. I even worked alongside CIA operatives. The fact remains that al-Qa'eda is little more than a label under which all militant Islamist groups now act if they want to receive the support of bin Laden and receive the global recognition they crave. I believe Westerners would call it a franchise.'

'But after the Afghan–Soviet War, bin Laden had about ten thousand followers,' replied Dalia doubtfully.

'There were ten thousand Arab Mujahidin, but almost all of them immediately returned to their own countries, their own groups. Only his personal guard followed him to Sudan, and years later back to Afghanistan. As an organisation, al-Qa'eda has no more than twenty permanent members that I know of.'

'You've met the man, Malik, what does he believe in?' Dalia asked, ignoring the remainder of the news broadcast which was just more of the same that she had been listening to, or reading, for most of the day. Malik, too, had lost interest in the broadcast as the riot was of little strategic interest to him.

'He preaches the driving of American and Western influences out of all Islamic states and government by religious rule and Shari'a law. In doing so, he wants to destroy Israel and topple pro-Western dictatorships around the Middle East. Essentially he wants to unite all Muslims and establish, by force if necessary, Islamic nations adhering to the rule of the first Caliphs. According to bin Laden's fatwa it's the duty of Muslims around the world to wage holy war on the US, American citizens and Jews, in order to achieve his aims. Muslims who do not heed this call are declared apostates.'

'People who have forsaken their faith.'

'Yes. He likes to refer to his ideology as jihadism. It's marked by a willingness to kill apostate and Shi'ite Muslims, and has an emphasis on jihad.'

Dalia shivered despite the heat from the gas fire. 'But jihadism is at odds with nearly all Islamic religious thought.'

'That depends on your interpretation of the Qur'an. Jihadism has its roots in the work of two modern Sunni Islamic thinkers. Mohammad ibn Abd al-Wahhab claimed in the eighteenth century that Islam had been corrupted a generation or so after the death of Muhammad. He denounced any theology or customs developed after that as non-Islamic, including more than one thousand years of religious scholarship. He and his supporters took over what is now Saudi Arabia, where Wahhabism remains the dominant school of religious thought. Despite his loss of citizenship, bin Laden has many supporters in Saudi Arabia. Sayyid Qutb, a radical Egyptian scholar of the mid-twentieth century, declared Western civilisation the enemy of Islam, denounced leaders of Muslim nations for not following Islam closely enough, and taught that jihad should be undertaken not just to defend Islam but to purify it.'

'You and I are Shi'ites,' Dalia checked.

'And so is Karima.'

'Why did he recruit us?'

'The Network recruited us, though he probably suggested me. They recruited us because we are the best and we will be successful, and because we are expendable. He recruited us as mercenaries, not believers. To him we are misinformed people who may be eliminated for the jihad. No one attacks us here because we are more Western than many Westerners in a multicultural society. Those youths I saw killing a Muslim thought they were doing people like us a favour.'

'Malik, I am sorry but I must ask. Are you certain Karima is still alive?'

Malik was seconds ahead of her. Leaping up from the couch, he walked through into the adjoining dining room and sat down in front of the laptop computer. Within minutes he had composed and typed a simple electronic message to Muhammad.

Muhammad,
We are now concluding our holiday in this great city but before we depart we will buy some gifts to take home. How we miss home. We must know that everyone is well before we continue. Please ask my beloved what she would like to match the gift I gave her on my departure and send a recent photograph. PBUH.
Mohammad.

Dalia read the message over his shoulder, then leant down and hugged him from behind as they reviewed it.

Malik clicked on the 'Send' icon.

'It's very clear,' Dalia said as they stared at the 'Message Sent' window.

'If they have harmed her I'll destroy them,' Malik muttered bitterly.

Dalia did not ask how. Instead she disappeared into the kitchen and prepared a light supper, then joined Malik in the living room where they sat together in silence and ate.

After supper Malik sat waiting at the laptop, while Dalia settled down to watch a television programme called *Newsnight* that projected the events that would unfold during the last two weeks of London's existence. There were two scenarios, one involving the discovery of the nuclear bomb with seconds to go, and the other, Armageddon. A ten-minute time slot before the beginning of the programme was dedicated to a phone-in poll to determine which scenario the public thought more likely and would like to have broadcast tonight.

Dalia voted by text.

The pessimists won with eighty per cent of the six million votes cast.

The programme was terrifying and distracted Malik's attention away from the laptop. Anarchy was to ensue on the deserted streets as the security forces withdrew, with street gangs and madmen running wild and intent on spoiling themselves before making a dash for the cordon or meeting a swift death. The aftermath not only obliterated London but was to contaminate one-third of England and much of Europe for a thousand years. But none of that really mattered, as the planet was knocked off its axis by one-tenth of a degree and the hole in the ozone layer grew to the size of Antarctica. The global changes thawed the Arctic ice cap over ten years and caused sea levels across the world to rise by a metre. The associated rise in global temperature and reduction in sun protection caused a sharp rise in deaths from skin cancer and a multitude of other heat-related diseases. Millions of people were displaced, only to be swept up in a brutal and unstoppable religious war that knew neither boundaries nor rules, confined only by the limits of human imagination and religious extremism. It was known as World War III and was global anarchy of biblical proportions. By 2020 with the war still raging, food production severely limited and disease rampant, the lifespan for those that remained had plummeted to forty years.

At the end of the programme Dalia was speechless, her face sallow.

'We'll leave for Cairo on Saturday morning. Book somewhere to stay at Luton tomorrow night,' ordered Malik quietly.

Dalia simply nodded.

Chapter 104

April 16th, Z – 16 Days
London, England

Jamali listened and watched from the white van as Malik left 36 Richmond Road for Signet Quay for the last time. He checked his watch, which read 6:45 a.m. and decided that he would continue to monitor Dalia's movements throughout the day and strike when an opportunity arose. Still wearing his earpiece, he allowed himself to sink down into his chair in the back of the van and drift off into a light sleep. His dreams were filled with images of Dalia.

Jamali woke at 3:30 p.m. to the faint sound of running water in his ears. He knew that Dalia was about to take a long shower after exercise, something she did in the confines of the house most afternoons. This was his chance. Grabbing his gloves and baseball cap, he picked up several hand tools and placed them in his outer jacket pockets. He then searched his inner jacket pocket for his 9-mm pistol, released the safety catch, cocked it, released the hammer then reapplied the safety catch before replacing it back in his jacket.

Checking the street through the windscreen and rear-view mirrors, he slipped out of the back of the van and walked towards the house. He knew the bathroom was at the side of the house overlooking the garage, and that the master bedroom, the one used by Malik and Dalia, was at the front of the house. He casually approached the front door, all the while looking around for any inquisitive neighbours, but everywhere appeared deserted. Satisfied the neighbourhood was clear and that he had not been noticed, he walked quietly down the concrete path to the side of the garage, easily climbed over the six-foot gate and made his way to the back of the house. He already knew that the rear of the house was secluded from view by trees and fences.

On reaching a dining-room sash window, he took out a glass cutter from his right-hand pocket and a glass holder in the form of a rubber sucker from his left. In seconds he cut a neat hole in the glass, reached in, and opened the finger lock that allowed him to raise the lower of the two window panes. Jamali climbed in and froze for a moment. As he fought to bring his breathing under control, he listened intently. He could hear the sound of running water, and music from a radio that he thought was coming from the master bedroom. Placing his tools on the dining-room table, he removed his jacket then smoothed his hair before smiling to himself.

For days he had listened to Dalia's cries of ecstasy as Malik had made love to her, and now it was his turn to enjoy himself before completing his mission. Jamali removed his loaded pistol and a silencer from the inner pocket of his jacket, then he cautiously peered out of the dining-room door and up the stairs. He screwed on the silencer and released the pistol's safety catch then crept up the staircase. On the upstairs landing, he waited for a moment until he was satisfied that Dalia was where he thought. Tucking his pistol into his trousers at the small of his back, he gently pushed the bathroom door further open and entered.

Dalia instantly sensed a presence from behind the shower curtain but it was too late. As she grappled with the feeling of foolishness that came over her, Jamali pulled the shower curtain open and punched her on her solar plexus below her breasts, knocking her breath away. As she doubled up, he grabbed her long brown hair, pulled her head back then smacked the side of her head hard against the wall tiles behind her causing one to crack. Although she was not cut, Dalia lost consciousness for several seconds, her legs crumpled and she fell helplessly into the bath.

Dalia came around and felt herself being dragged by her arms across the landing to her bedroom. Looking up at Jamali, she locked onto his insane eyes and noticed they were the same dark brown she remembered, but this time they were full of lust. She saw him look away, down her naked body. She tried to grab a banister with her left hand but he simply chopped it away. She yelped in agonising pain and realised her wrist had snapped.

Dalia continued to struggle as he pulled her into the bedroom.

Her heart started racing as she realised what he intended and she went to scream, but he quickly smacked her hard across the face. She cried out in pain but he only slapped her again, this time harder. The pain was overwhelming and she felt herself slipping back into unconsciousness.

Jamali shoved Dalia onto the bed face down, and she knew there was nothing she could do. He was simply too strong for her as he leant with his full weight on her back. Her body froze with fear when she realised she was helpless; she could not turn around and she could not use her arms. She attempted to kick backwards with her ankles but Jamali merely laughed. She was defenceless. She thought fleetingly of her pistol on the dressing table over on the other side of the room. Hearing Jamali put something heavy like a pistol on the bedside table gave her more ideas, but the thoughts were just as useless.

Dalia started to tremble as she felt the hot breath of the heavy man on the back of her neck, then wet kisses and licking, followed by biting. She grabbed hold of the duvet with her one good hand and clenched it with her fist. Her legs shook and weakened as she felt Jamali lean on her as he grappled to open his trousers one-handed, the other on her shoulder blades forcing her down. Seconds later he was spreading her long legs apart and positioning himself between them. She tried to draw her legs together, but they would not respond. She felt his stomach and chest on her as one hand reached around and started fondling her breast, the other guiding himself into her. Dalia did not scream or attempt to speak, thinking irrationally that he might believe she did not know who he was, perhaps thinking he was a burglar, and that if she was compliant he would let her go. But in her heart and head, she knew that was not Jamali's intention, and that she must make her inevitable death as quick and painless as possible. As Jamali penetrated her, she naturally resisted him but with each thrust he went deeper inside her. She thought nice thoughts, of Malik and *Last Tango*, and the short time they had had together, and of his daughter whom she had never met. She held her eyes tight shut but the tears rolled down her cheeks.

When Jamali had finished, he lay over her for several minutes enjoying her warmth. Eventually he rose up and knelt on her back once more. Dalia prayed to Allah for vengeance. Grabbing his pistol from the bedside table he covered her head with a pillow, aimed the weapon and fired two shots in quick succession. Dalia's body went rigid, then she died. Jamali stared down at her for several seconds, then kissed the small of her back as if to say farewell. Then he got up and zipped his trousers.

Taking her Sig Sauer from the dressing table, and satisfying himself it was loaded, Jamali left the music-filled room and walked to the bathroom where he turned off the shower. Next he went to the larder to look at the oil drum, but left it alone.

As the evening drew in, Jamali did as Dalia would have done, switching on lights, closing curtains and switching on the television. He even made himself a mug of hot, sweet coffee. He found a ready-made curry and placed it in the microwave, then waited for Malik to return.

Chapter 105

April 16th, Z – 16 Days
London, England

On a bright and sunny mid-spring evening, Malik approached 36 Richmond Avenue by foot, for what he hoped to be the last time. Tonight, he and Dalia were to drive out of the city to Luton where Dalia had booked the Kents into a hotel prior to tomorrow's flight to Cairo. Turning into the avenue from Liverpool Road, he noticed another reduction in the numbers of cars.

Each day as he walked down this leafy avenue he had carefully studied the cars left parked on either verge, particularly those that were parked within sight of his home. The cars that remained were clearly vacant, though he was less sure about the white van that was obviously still in daily use as its parking slot had varied each day. Alarmingly, it was always in direct sight of his home. It could have belonged to a neighbour, someone who was using the van to evacuate their possessions, but as each house in the vicinity had a reasonably sized driveway it was odd that the van was not parked off-road to ease loading. What made him even more cautious was that the van was an ideal surveillance vehicle with no distinguishing features. It was a typical white van, one that a casual onlooker would have difficulty noticing the make and model of. Malik stopped behind a thick tree trunk about thirty metres short of the van and dug in his pockets for his cell phone.

Whenever Malik rang Dalia on her cell phone, she would always answer immediately and today should be no exception as he knew she was at home waiting for his return. If she had left the house, she would have called to tell him. But as her phone rang until voice mail was offered, his heartbeat accelerated and he broke into a cold sweat. He hung up and redialled but still there was no answer. Something was wrong. He had wanted

Dalia to observe the van from the house as he approached it, but he would have to manage himself. Switching his incoming call alert to vibrate, he still hoped that Dalia would pick up the missed call and call back, but a sixth sense told him she was unable to.

As he stood behind the tree, as if waiting for someone, he surveyed the van and considered his options. He quickly concluded that either his fears were unfounded or the security forces had found their hideaway, had captured Dalia, and were waiting for his return in order to arrest him. After considering his daughter in the clutches of the Mailman, he accepted that he could not abandon Dalia without at least an attempt at reaching her.

Two hours later darkness had fallen, and there had been no call from Dalia. Outside it was dry, and the cloudless sky was lit with a half-moon and the unnatural light that beamed up from the eerily silent city. There had been no movement from the van, no telltale misting of windows, no running of the engine. Malik had also taken time to survey each house up and down the street and, with the exception of six houses in the vicinity that had lights burning behind curtains, the remainder were dark and appeared empty.

He had decided on his route to the van, a route that was almost entirely out of sight from the house. With all the curtains at the front of the house drawn closed as usual, it was unlikely anyone would spot him from the house without him seeing. Fitting a silencer to his Sig Sauer and quietly chambering a round, Malik advanced slowly along his chosen path down the silent street to the van. Stopping occasionally to check for any other visual or audible signs of life, he was soon up against the driver's side of the van that faced away from the house.

Malik already knew that no one was sitting in the front of the van, so he manoeuvred the wing mirror and peered into the rear. Although a cloth partially obscured the view, in the semi-darkness he determined that unless they were lying down, no one was in the cargo area. He also figured that if someone had been inside, the cloth partition would have been properly fitted. Malik knew that in the poor light he would not see through the rear windows of the van that suspiciously faced the house and on which one-way privacy film had been applied, so instead he began to feel the side of the van with his hands as he knocked gently. There was no warmth and no response. With no sign of life within the van, the time had come to show his hand. After confirming his getaway up the narrow alleyway opposite that led back towards Angel Islington Underground, he aimed his pistol at the front offside tyre, looked about, and then shot it out. Despite the van's tilt and the muffled shot, Malik kept his senses focused on the van. Nothing stirred. He took time to peer directly through the driver's window. The front of the van appeared unremarkable, but without breaking into the van he had no way of knowing if the cargo-bay floor was empty. He certainly could not make out anything incriminatory. It had, of course, occurred to him that Dalia could be restrained in the van, perhaps bound or unconscious and unable to respond, but he concluded that if that were the case, he would have to come back later and release her as he could not afford any noise that might alert anyone in the house.

Scanning the front of the house and up and down the street for any sign of life, Malik was satisfied that he remained unobserved and that there were no enemy either inside the van, or stood by elsewhere in the street. This very fact made him wonder quite who he was dealing with, as he knew that security forces would have had people outside, and that they would have attempted to snatch him by now.

Malik rechecked his weapon, then ran across to the garage and down the same path that Jamali had taken earlier that afternoon. He knew that there was no point in attempting access from the front of the house and that he must look to the back or the first floor for a surprise entry. Malik also had one other problem, for he had no desire to attract any undue attention to the house and compromise Fat Man. After reaching over and opening the same side gate that Jamali had climbed earlier, Malik silently surveyed the back of the house starting with the ground level. He had intended to climb onto the garage roof and inspect the bathroom window access, but it was not long before he noticed the missing glass cut from a window to the dining room. Something tightened inside and his breathing quickened. His mind raced through his conversation with Dalia the night before, and his message to the Mailman, and how Dalia had feared they would be double-crossed and killed. Malik knew that whatever was inside was waiting for him, and that it was not the security forces.

Malik checked his weapon as he reconsidered his options. He thought that there would be one or more assassins, with at least one covering the front door, Malik's likely entrance. Crouching in a flower border, and listening through the hole in the dining-room window, Malik concluded that at least one gunman was watching television in the living room. Judging from the sweet smell of cooking spilling from the kitchen, he thought that there may be another located in there, or possibly it was Dalia, though that made little sense. Finding his way in the darkness of the overgrown garden, for the third time that evening Malik tried Dalia's cell phone but this time he waited for the voice mail.

'Hi Dalia, it's me. I'm staying with the Captain for a while. I won't be back until nine. Call me.'

Malik hoped that an assassin might check her voice-mail messages for information, especially if he was later than expected. Content, he walked back to the window and sent her a text as well. Within seconds he heard a familiar vibrating sound accompanied by a buzz from the lounge, followed by a man cursing in Spanish. Malik associated the shadow he saw move across the kitchen blind with the same man and manoeuvred himself to see as much of the kitchen as he could through a sizeable crack between the blind and the wall. On seeing the man, Malik recognised him immediately. It was Malik's turn to curse. He now doubted there was anyone else in the house apart from Dalia, Jamali being foolish enough to believe that he could dispatch them both with ease.

Malik thought of Dalia as he waited for Jamali to move back into the living room. He knew what Jamali had come to do and what the man was capable of. Malik feared for her life, and fought to control his overwhelming sense of despair. He relied on his professional training and thoughts of Karima to pull himself through.

The back door of the house had two frosted-glass upper window panels and provided limited visibility into a short passage with the larder on the left, a broom cupboard on the right and an inner opaque-glass door to the front that led directly to the kitchen. What little light illuminated the passage came through the glass door from the kitchen, and from the moon in the night sky. Malik noticed several fresh cigarette butts crushed on the concrete path outside the back door and realised their presence made sense. Sliding a long key into the keyhole in the back door, he gently turned the recently-fitted mortice lock. Feeling the lock slide open, he removed the key, then quietly rotated the door knob. To his surprise the door opened, for someone had been out and not closed the shoot bolt Dalia had fixed. He knew that Dalia always kept this bolt closed, day and night, and felt a sense of relief. His remaining option was to gain entry through the same window used by Jamali, and that would have been considerably riskier, despite the closed curtain.

Entering the passageway, Malik silently closed the back door then carefully approached the inner door expecting at any moment somebody to appear the other side. No one did and after satisfying himself that no one was in the kitchen, he cracked open the inner door before going back to the cupboard. He pulled open the cupboard door, found the master switch he was looking for beside a small, dull green light, then shielded his eyes.

As soon as Malik's night vision was satisfactory, he pulled the master switch and plunged the house into darkness. With his pistol in front of him he ran through the inner door, through the kitchen and into the hall then living room. In the pitch-darkness he clattered straight into Jamali who was advancing towards the hall with his hands held out in front of him, one grasping Dalia's Sig Sauer. Both of them pushed each other away in an attempt to get a clear shot, but each of them was swallowed up in the darkness guarded by the thick curtains.

The first wild punch from Jamali smacked Malik's jaw, and the metallic taste of blood flooded across his tongue. Whipping his arm forward in a blind thrust, Malik pounded the butt of his gun against Jamali's jaw. Spit flew out of Jamali's mouth, and for a split second Malik could have sworn he saw the small gap between Jamali's yellowing teeth. Both professionals knew that the first to fire would probably be the first to die, the muzzle flash from the speculative shot in the pitch-darkness immediately giving the shooter's position away. Each of them knew that a wounded man was equally deadly. And so the sightless fight continued, with each man feeling their way, lashing out at shadows. Eventually Jamali found a grip on Malik's clothing, and he swung Malik back towards the couch. As Jamali raised his gun towards what he thought to be Malik, Malik rose and charged like a bull, smashing Jamali back into the television which rolled back on its stand into the corner of the room. A lamp shattered, and china and glass objects went flying. Malik staggered forward and cranked his arm back and this time ploughed his fist into Jamali's ear. Crumbling to his knees, Jamali cried out and cupped the side of his head as he simultaneously fired a muffled and speculative shot that illuminated the room for a split second, dazzling Malik. Jamali had his eyes closed and reacted first as Malik hesitated for a second, fearing a searing electric shock of pain that never came. Spinning over then leaping up before Malik's eyes and brain had readjusted, Jamali let loose with a high kick that crashed into the side of Malik's head. His head snapped to the side with an audible crack. Jamali grabbed Malik and pushed him towards the dining-room table. Malik stumbled and fought to stay on his feet, but he lost his balance and fell over backwards, dropping his weapon. Malik saw a silhouette form against the pale curtains in front of him and used his legs to toss Jamali back onto the mantle above the fireplace. On impact, the edge of the shelf stabbed Jamali in the back of the neck, and as his head snapped back he, too, dropped his weapon. For a second Jamali could see nothing at all. With both men flagging, they eventually found each other. But Jamali was the stronger of the two and he wrapped his fingers around Malik's throat and pinned Malik back against a bookcase. Malik was about to pass out, and there was no let up. Gagging from the pressure, Malik felt the blood flood his face. He gritted his teeth, trying to suck in one last breath, but he couldn't breathe. As Jamali tightened his grip further, Malik fought for air. Jamali squeezed tighter and Malik floated to images of Karima and Dalia. Malik could smell Jamali's breath in front of him and imagined the insane grin that accompanied it. Before long Malik's body went limp and he fell to the floor. For Malik it was like being in the sea, being sucked down by the tide.

But Malik was alive as Jamali stood over him in the darkness with a cocky grin. In a last desperate effort, Malik reached down for his silver knife that was tied under his trouser leg against his right calf. In one practised movement he unsheathed the knife and thrust upwards under Jamali's rib cage and directly into his left lung before twisting. The lung collapsed instantly. Jamali doubled in agony, then his senses faded and he fell forwards onto Malik.

Malik pushed Jamali away, then coughed in a chestful of new-found air before hurriedly feeling the floor around the bookcase and fireplace for his weapon. He felt the familiar shape of a Sig Sauer, picked it up then fired in the direction of Jamali who lay just yards from him. The first shot hit Jamali in the shoulder but the second did not. There was a dull, sickening thud as the second bullet penetrated Jamali's skull through his left eye and flung him back onto the floor. Two more shots quickly followed, blowing away half of Jamali's skull.

Malik felt his way past the coffee table and collapsed onto the couch still gasping for breath. Tucking the Sig Sauer into his waist band, he carefully manipulated his left fingers and forearm. As soon as his breath regulated, he found his way back to the cupboard near the back door and switched on the mains electricity. Despite the fight and the shots fired, Malik knew that they had made little significant noise. With the lights on, he hastily surveyed the living room and found the second Sig Sauer he knew to be Dalia's.

Satisfying himself that Jamali was dead, Malik ran up the stairs two at a time and went first to the master bedroom, their bedroom. Any hope of finding her alive immediately evaporated as soon he saw the still greyness of her naked body lying face down on the bed and the scorched pillow over her head. Overcome with grief he ran to her side throwing the scorched pillow to one side before gently turning her over and gathering her up in his arms. Numb with disbelief and horror, he ignored his wounds and held her lifeless and bloodied body closely in his strong arms. For several minutes he rocked her back and forth mumbling incoherently to her. Not wanting to abandon her, he lay her down then stood for a moment, unsure what to do. In a trancelike state he grabbed a bath towel that was hanging over a nearby radiator and spread it neatly over her body. With tears flooding from his eyes, he closed her eyes then leant down and kissed her bloody head before he knelt and cursed al-Qa'eda. He prayed to Allah in her native Punjabi. He would mourn her death later, but now he knew what he must do to avenge her grotesque and untimely death and to give her life the meaning and purpose he knew she craved.

Trancelike, Malik ministered to his wounds in the bathroom. He found that the very bloody gunshot to his arm was little more than a deep scratch and that he still had full although very painful motion. After cleaning himself up he grabbed their hold-alls and packed their scant belongings. Although he was confident that neither DNA nor fingerprints would ever be linked to their true identities, he knew the same did not apply to Jamali. As he searched the house for anything evidential, he came across Jamali's weapon in the kitchen, a US-made M9 9-mm Beretta, the same gun used by the US military and the gun that he guessed had killed Dalia. He left it where it lay.

Malik drove the Audi out of the garage and parked it on the driveway before relocking the garage. After visiting Dalia for a final time, he swept the house again. Satisfied he had done everything he could to protect both his and Dalia's identities he loaded the bags into the Audi. Armed with his curfew pass, he wept as he sped north towards Luton.

Chapter 106

April 16th, Z - 16 Days
London, England

As Malik was fighting for his life with Jamali in Islington, the Prime Minister and his Cabinet were sitting in the Cabinet Room at Ten Downing Street debating whether martial law should be formally declared in London from midnight. The Metropolitan Police Commissioner and the Chief of Defence Staff were sitting behind their respective secretaries of state, but up until now neither man had participated in the discussion.

After an hour of debate and argument about the issues and single recommendation raised in his written report to the Cabinet Office, the Police Commissioner finally grew impatient. During a rare lull in the lively proceedings he rose to his feet behind the Home Secretary. 'Prime Minister, I wonder if now might be a good time for me to address the Cabinet on the reality of the situation?' He had no doubt that his report was perfectly clear, but he still had plenty more ammunition and he could not see an end to the debate between the hardliners and the liberals.

The Prime Minister, sitting in his customary armchair at the middle of the table, studied the Commissioner for a moment. He raised his hands to attract everyone's attention and the Cabinet Room eventually descended into silence. 'Ladies and gentlemen, we simply must reach an agreement today. A stalemate on this issue in Cabinet will only exacerbate the situation, and I would very much like to reach a unanimous agreement. Please, everyone listen to what Sir Stephen has to say then reconsider.'

The Commissioner remained standing so that he had a clear view of everyone around the oval table and so he could meet every pair of eyes. He then informed the Cabinet with brutal clarity what was happening on the streets of London and how it was escalating out of control. Although he knew that several members of the Cabinet had already suffered at the hands of 'the mob', he knew he must recapture and hold the attention of each and every person in the room. And so he was considerably more graphic when speaking than he had been in his report. Leaving nothing to the imagination, several members felt themselves being attacked.

The simple fact was that London was on its knees, and in ten shocking minutes the Commissioner got his point across. The terrorist plot to bomb London, cunningly suspended until May 2nd, was working. Fear was rising by the day among the millions of Londoners who had either already evacuated or still remained. He did not define this as a 'sudden' terrorist act like a suicide bomber on a London bus or in the Underground; this was a very lengthy, 'continuous' terrorist act, like the hijacking of an airliner, but for much, much longer and for considerably greater stakes. This was the cleverest and most damaging form of terrorism the world had ever faced. It was a 'no win' situation for the continuous act always made the world news and lingered in people's minds the world over for decades. The enemy was winning in London because fear was spiralling out of control from within, particularly as the storming of Canary Wharf by the SAS had not unearthed the nuclear bomb as many had hoped. And even if the elusive bomb was not detonated on May 2nd, a massive amount of death and destruction had already been inflicted that could not be undone. It was up to this Cabinet to minimise the degree of victory that al-Qa'eda enjoyed prior to May 2nd, as well as preventing the cataclysmic bombing itself. The Commissioner also pointed out that it was considerably more difficult to find the bomb and terrorist cell when chaos reigned. The numbers of murders, rapes, hate crimes, incidental attacks on property, arson, gang warfare, burglaries, spontaneous riots and disturbances by mixed as well as ethnic communities were all rocketing out of control. Physical attacks on the emergency services were on the increase too. Worse still, 27 policemen and other emergency services personnel had been killed since the threat began, 227 in total including civilians, and the figures were rising at an accelerating rate.

'And does that include those who died at Canary Wharf?' interrupted the Chancellor, as if making some profound point.

The Commissioner stood his ground and glared at the man,

almost as if the Chancellor, personally, was responsible for the bombings.

The Prime Minister saw the danger and intervened, fixing the Commissioner with his eyes. 'Well, does it?' he asked.

The Commissioner continued to stare at the Chancellor. He was in no mood for games. 'Actually, no, sir,' he replied. 'Another sixty-seven lost their lives at Canary Wharf, excluding ten terrorists.'

This was not the answer the Chancellor was expecting. He shrank back into his chair, and the Commissioner took it as his cue to continue. He explained that there were still three million people in London, and how he feared that a proportion of those did not intend to leave. The simple truth was that the Metropolitan Police were no longer able to uphold the law and control the public, and he feared that the anarchy his officers now faced on a daily basis was prompting an unlawful use of retaliatory force that was in turn further escalating the violence. In his opinion, it was only a matter of time before one or more of his officers, as it were, 'fired directly into a crowd'. He argued, simply, that the situation would rapidly worsen over the next two weeks and that rather than impose martial law a day or so before May 2nd or indeed after any nuclear explosion, the Government's and nation's interests were best served if the Ministry of Defence took immediate control of law and order in London, until such time as it was possible to police the streets once more. The Commissioner concluded that there was only one way forward now, the immediate introduction of martial law.

The Prime Minister turned to the CDS. 'Would you like to add anything, Sir Peter?'

The four-star general took a moment to consider the offer. 'I believe it will help, sir.'

'Then please do.'

The CDS had already met and spoken to the Defence Secretary in support of the Police Commissioner's report, and although he agreed, the Defence Secretary had warned him not to provoke the more liberal members, otherwise they would entrench themselves. He considered such reactions as childish, but that was one of the many side-shoots of democracy.

With the Defence Secretary's words in mind, he emulated the Commissioner and got to his feet. He was pleased that the Commissioner had already won over several doubters and that a detailed record was being kept of the proceedings. Nonetheless, it was vital the Cabinet voted for the right reasons and understood precisely what they were voting for. He took ten minutes to carefully remind the Cabinet that once martial law was declared in London the normal civil rights that the police and their current military support had worked so hard to uphold and protect over the last few months would be suspended and that summary military justice would be applied to the civilian population. Although statute law provided the mechanism for the Cabinet to invoke martial law, the CDS told the Cabinet that any acts by the Armed Forces 'done by necessity' under common law would be limited only by the conventions of warfare. He also informed everyone at the meeting, for the record, that the judiciary or justice system had no right later to review military decisions or actions conducted under martial law, under any other law. The CDS summarised by stating the obvious for the record – that martial law was the government of the civil population through military forces without ordinary rule of law. Essentially there were no rules other than military, and the Armed Forces would respond in any way it considered necessary to prevent anarchy and protect the nation's interests. The CDS concluded by highlighting to the Cabinet that they were effectively being asked to endorse what he loosely termed the 'conditions', before the Armed Forces could be called upon. As he sat down, a relieved Defence Secretary turned around and nodded gratefully.

The Prime Minister asked the Cabinet for any final issues from around the table. There was one, from the Secretary of State for Environment, Food and Rural Affairs.

'May I just be clear on one issue? Martial law is to apply to London alone. Is that correct?'

General Sir Peter rose to answer. It was a reasonable question, and he immediately identified where it was leading. 'That is correct, Minister, except that those resources, personnel or otherwise, that are required to enforce the law inside London, will also be subject to the law when located outside of London.'

'Thank you,' replied the Environment Secretary, who added helpfully, 'Then as I see it there really are no issues left to discuss.'

The Prime Minister thanked the Environment Secretary then

looked towards the Secretary of State for Constitutional Affairs. 'I have one last question. Sir William, is all this lawful?'

'Entirely, Prime Minister.'

'Thank you.' The Prime Minister then asked the Cabinet to support the proposal. At last there was unanimous agreement.

Thanking the Cabinet, the Prime Minister asked the senior military officer whether he was in a position to enlighten them now on how he intended to proceed. Not wishing to cause alarm, the CDS rose to his feet once again and carefully explained.

He began by stating that the Chief of Joint Operations at the Permanent Joint Headquarters at Northwood would assume command. The CDS explained that he would require the continuation of the Gold Group, and that he intended to strengthen current law-enforcement deployments with an additional ten thousand servicemen over the next week. The CJO wished to soften any fears of martial law by maintaining a police presence alongside the Armed Forces, though it was the latter who had primacy. Essentially the plan to evacuate London was to continue, but with some notable changes. From midnight tonight, anyone not cooperating with martial law was to be immediately arrested and, if they were not detained, ejected from London with their passport confiscated. There were to be no half-measures, no need for evidence. Non cooperation was all it would take, and there would be zero tolerance. Anyone foolish enough to resist questioning would be subjected to the appropriate use of force. The CDS put it simply. If a suspect attempted to evade arrest by the police or soldiers, after a single verbal warning the security forces would hunt down and shoot to kill without fear of retribution. The suspension of all civil liberties also meant that the numbers of 'on the spot' identity checks, vehicle control points and surprise property searches would escalate. The CDS reminded the Cabinet that the role of the Armed Forces was to prevent anarchy during a national emergency and was a last resort, and that failure was not an option. He ended by stating that the Media Emergency Forum would relocate to the PJHQ Media Operations branch at Northwood.

Not expecting any questions, he sat down and gave a curt nod to the Prime Minister. For twenty minutes every member of the Cabinet had been mesmerised.

'General, are we to see tanks on the streets?' asked the Secretary of State for Northern Ireland.

The General stood up again. 'The current threat does not call for tanks. I will be limiting road vehicles as far as practicable to fast, soft-skinned vehicles like Land Rovers and cars, They may well be lightly armoured, and indeed in some boroughs we may need additional protection against small arms fire. That will require armoured personnel carriers, possibly the Warrior armoured vehicle which carries a 30-mm cannon. But I have no current intention of deploying tanks.'

The Prime Minister summarised the meeting by reminding everyone present that one of the greatest freedoms everyone had a right to expect was freedom from fear, and that was what he would be telling the nation this afternoon as he declared martial law.

Chapter 107

April 18th, Z - 14 Days
Chertsey, Surrey, England

Malik had checked into the Marriott Luton Airport Hotel yesterday evening a little after 11 p.m. Such was the demand that the hotel had prepared and occupied converted storerooms and recreational rooms, but fortunately for Malik, Dalia had booked a suite for one night regardless of expense. En route to Luton, Malik had been concerned by the curious glances his facial bruising may attract from fellow guests and hotel staff, but at that hour he need not have worried.

Wrought with grief over Dalia's death and the circumstances of her suffering at the hands of such an evil man, he had found sleep hopeless, so instead watched television and surfed the Internet in the privacy of his suite. In the early hours of the morning Malik received a reassuring email from the Mailman confirming that his daughter Karima was alive and well and living with him in Peshawar. She had answered his question correctly, asking for a pair of red shoes to match the red dress he had given her on his departure for Europe. The Mailman had also given instructions for Malik to watch the al-Jazeera television news that morning which was to include the latest video message released by al-Qa'eda. On this occasion it featured bin Laden and the Mailman, accompanied by several hooded men and women in the background who each held a selection of the day's Arabic newspapers as well as their weapons. There were also three hostages, two men and a girl. Each was blindfolded but unmistakeably recognisable to anyone who knew them. Malik did not recognise the two men but the girl was Karima.

Malik's heart stopped when he had seen his daughter, but his relief was quickly replaced by intense anger, then later, surprise. Immediately satisfied that it was her he had seen in the broadcast, he watched several reruns of the recording and studied his daughter and her environment. The pang of guilt was long and painful for Malik, though she looked brave, and well. Malik had more money than he could ever have imagined, but he had lost not one but two women and three children, all of whom he had loved very much. He was not about to lose his last child, not for anything.

There were, he had decided, only three options available to him: trust al-Qa'eda and hope they would keep to their word and release Karima; attempt to rescue Karima or secure her release using his own resources that were based largely on wealth, his knowledge of the Network, and a great many contacts; or seek the help of the British and their allies to save his daughter and destroy the Network. Yet time was against him. Malik had known in his heart from the moment he saw Dalia's dead body that he would seek the help of the British and their NATO allies to destroy al-Qa'eda. This morning, after comprehensively researching his nemesis, Harry Winchester, Malik formulated a plan. He dared not imagine what would happen to his daughter if he failed but knew this was her best chance.

Despite the shortage of hotel accommodation throughout the south-east of England, after searching on the Internet and several telephone calls Malik found a convenient place to stay. Checking out of the hotel at midday, he drove until he found Mizzard Farm, off the A30 near Chertsey, a typically quaint English bed-and-breakfast establishment as well as a working dairy farm with over three hundred head of cattle. He found the owners and the only other guests, an elderly couple from London, both friendly and trustworthy, and after paying the farmer's wife in advance, he asked for directions to the old Manor House.

An hour later Malik was sitting in the Audi in a lay-by opposite the entrance to Mercury. On his way Malik had stopped at a local country store to purchase a pair of binoculars and some fresh clothes including boots, a coat and a hat. He had also bought some snacks in a grocery shop, although he found an old single-decker bus crudely painted black and yellow parked in the same lay-by advertising all-day breakfasts, burgers and beverages. He had no idea how long he would have to wait until an opportunity to talk to Winchester presented itself, but he was grateful for the distraction and cover that the bus provided.

For the next three hours Malik observed from the Audi as a number of vehicles pulled into and out of the entrance to the manor's long driveway. Eventually he spotted a Range Rover turn into the driveway, with a man driving and a woman on the man's left. Although he did not get a long look at her, Malik instantly recognised the driver from newspaper and Web photographs.

The bus served as a mobile cafeteria and was due to close at 7:30 p.m., so he decided to stretch his legs and have another coffee before it shut. Malik stepped into the bus through the central swing doors and climbed into the public area that took up the rear half. As he glanced over the menu that hung above the stainless steel counter for the second time that evening he saw the same fiercely large lady was eyeing him with suspicion from her kitchen as she rigorously dried her hands.

'It's not that I mind but what you doing hanging about in my bus then? Not got a home to go to?' the lady demanded as she placed another steaming mug of black coffee on the counter that divided the bus across its centre. 'A good looking man like you should have a home to go to.'

Malik was prepared for such an enquiry. 'Minding my own business, that's what I'm doing.'

She pulled a sour face and Malik laughed apologetically. 'If you promise not to tell a soul then I'll tell you.'

'Nobody here but me,' the lady shrugged. 'Usually my husband Stan is here to help me but he had to see the doctor today, with his bad feet and all.'

'I'm waiting for a beautiful woman.'

'Oh yes,' replied the lady, suitably scandalised.

'She's leaving her husband today and I'm meeting her here.'

'You her friend then?'

'I'm her lover.'

The lady looked unsure, unsure whether to disapprove or not so Malik continued.

'There are no kids involved and he beats her. He's been doing it for years. I've been helping her and we've grown to love each other. We plan to get married as soon as her divorce is settled.'

The lady was hooked. 'Well, good luck to you. My Stan is my second. My first was a good-for-nothing bully too though I gave him as good as I got mind. You meet all sorts in this lay-by, you do. Would you like something to eat?'

'No, not right now thanks.' Just as he shook his head and turned back to his car, Malik saw through the dirty rear windows of the bus the same Range Rover pull up to the end of the driveway, this time with one occupant, Winchester. Leaving the coffee, Malik jumped down the steps of the old bus, ran back to the Audi, fired her up and followed swiftly in the Range Rover's wake.

Malik soon caught up with the Range Rover and followed it to the outskirts of Chertsey where it pulled into a large, dimly lit and virtually deserted supermarket car park. Malik followed, and then watched from the Audi as the driver climbed out from the car and walked into the store. Opting to wait until Winchester came out Malik scanned the neighbourhood then decided he would approach from some trees as the man returned to his car.

It was ten long minutes before Winchester emerged from the supermarket carrying four bags of groceries, two in each hand. At the darkest point en route to his car, from under the blanket of two mature trees, Malik emerged from behind.

'Harry Winchester, do not turn around.' The man froze immediately, as if it were an everyday occurrence.

'My name is Malik, and I have a silenced gun aimed at the back of your head. If you move without orders, I'll kill you without hesitation, no one will find the bombs and the world will never be the same again. Do you understand?'

'You said bombs?'

'Do you understand?'

With little choice and no desire to do otherwise, Harry nodded. 'Yes.' He knew the man he was dealing with was no fool, and frankly he needed to listen to what the man had to say.

'Good. Do not drop your bags. Continue walking slowly back to your car, now.'

Harry did as he was told, sizing up the dim shadow of his attacker and the brief silhouette of a long-barrelled pistol as he went.

'What do you want?' Harry asked as they proceeded. About thirty metres away several late-night shoppers engrossed in conversation walked by, but he had no intention of evading this meeting, even if he could. Harry knew that Malik wanted something badly enough to warrant this meeting and he needed to know what it was.

'Can you make decisions? Is it true that you can act on behalf of your Government?'

'Yes, but how do I know you're the man I seek? The man I want has no need to risk a meeting.'

Malik considered this for a moment and realised it was vital to demonstrate who he was before they could continue meaningful conversation. 'You've been asking for me to meet you. Now ask me a question.'

'Are you Fox?'

'Yes.'

Both of them knew that the answer confirmed nothing. The code name had been referred to in the media for weeks.

'What nationality are you?'

Malik smiled. 'Try again.'

'Where's your partner?'

'Again.'

Unknown to Malik, Harry smiled. 'You can't blame me for trying.' Thinking of something that was unique, Harry asked, 'The factory in Buenos Aires, what was its name?'

'Iguazú, after the waterfalls in the north of the country.'

'And the colour of the walls in Doctor Baloch's living room?'

Malik thought for several seconds, considering the fact that Winchester had been there. 'That dump in San Carlos de Bariloche? It's lined with wood panelling below light-blue paint.'

Harry nodded. 'Thank you.'

Reaching the Range Rover, Malik ordered Harry to drop the grocery bags, slowly withdraw his key fob, open the car then drop the key fob where he stood.

'You armed?' asked Malik.

'Yes.'

'Make any sudden movement and I'll kill you.'

Harry didn't doubt it for a second. It occurred to Harry that that Fox was more than a common mercenary; he appeared to be a trained professional.

Malik knew that Harry was right-handed. 'Using your left hand, drop your weapon on the ground by your keys.'

Harry's Browning was loaded but not made ready with a round in the chamber. He could never have used it in time anyway, so he slowly took it out and placed it on the ground.

'Any more?' asked Malik as he studied Harry's reflection in the dim light.

'No,' was the response.

'Take your shoes, socks and sweater off.'

Harry did so, revealing an empty leather holster around his waist.

'Pull up your trouser legs as far as they will go.'

Harry did so, revealing nothing but his legs.

'What's that in your back pocket?'

'A wallet.'

'The other pocket?'

'A mobile phone.'

'Place them on the ground.'

As soon as Harry did this, Malik ordered him to step forward then halt.

Without taking his eyes off Harry, Malik stooped, picked up one item at a time and threw it into the darkness, even the jumper and socks. They both heard a clatter as the heavy items hit the ground.

Malik ordered Harry to climb into the driving seat then close the door, turn off the interior automatic lights then place both his hands on the steering wheel. Once Harry had done so, Malik opened the rear passenger door and climbed in behind Harry. With his silenced Sig Sauer aimed at the back of Harry's head, he closed the door. Eventually their eyes met in the rear view mirror.

'We can help each other,' Malik began, 'so I hope we can be sensible and not let arrogance or stupidity get in the way. Do you agree?'

Harry felt his pulse quicken. Could this finally be the breakthrough the operation had been looking for? His mouth was dry and his response sounded more like a croak. He knew now he was dealing with a professional, but someone who did not hold all the cards.

'Yes.'

'My people have successfully delivered several nuclear bombs into the heart of London, and you will never find them without my help. I'm the only one left alive who knows where the bombs have been hidden. You already know that they will detonate at midday on May 2nd, unless they are found and deactivated.'

'How many are there?' asked Harry.

'More than one.'

'What size are they?'

'Any one is capable of destroying London. Do not interrupt again. I do not have much time and neither do you. The terrorist organisation I represent is a network led by al-Qa'eda that includes a number of fanatical Islamic groups. This much you will have guessed already. I know where each bomb is, the names of the leaders and the locations of their camps, and I know how the attack was funded.' Malik paused for effect. The information he was offering had eluded the West for many years despite their overt and covert operations. 'The Network arranged for an assassin to murder my colleagues. The assassin killed Doctor Baloch and has killed my partner, the one you call Vixen. He meant to kill me, too, but died in the attempt. The Network has also kidnapped my daughter as some kind of insurance, and they will kill her as soon as they receive confirmation that I'm dead, or as soon as I return home.'

Harry sensed an opportunity. 'Your daughter, is she unharmed?'

'Yes.'

'Do you know where she is?'

'Yes.'

'How?' Harry sensed Malik hesitate. 'It's important I know. I will be asked when I go upstairs.'

Malik considered his next comment carefully. 'Did you see today's al-Qa'eda broadcast on al-Jazeera television?'

Harry nodded.

'My daughter was the youngest of the three hostages. I know the room it was filmed in.'

Harry remembered the girl in the pretty Western-style white dress, about ten years old. 'You're sure?' he asked doubtfully.

'I recognised the wall paintings. They are unique.'

Satisfied, Harry asked, 'What do you want?'

'I want you to help me rescue my daughter and destroy the Network.'

Harry studied Malik's eyes in the mirror. 'Anything else?' he replied evenly.

'My daughter and I walk free with new identities.'

'British?'

'Yes. We want our freedom. In return, I'll tell you everything I know.'

Harry relaxed, now confident that Malik was the real deal without weakness save that of his loved one. The man had been double-crossed, sold out, and his own daughter taken as insurance.

'I'll need to take this to the top floor, Malik. They'll need more information.'

'There will be no more information until we have an agreement. But I do have one more condition. We must assault with precision if my daughter is to be saved. There will be no indiscriminate attacks, no carpet bombing of hillsides or careless rescue missions. All of this must be agreed by you and your partners.'

Harry nodded. 'How do we contact you?'

'I'll contact you at Mercury by email. You will reply immediately you have an answer from your Government.'

Malik climbed out of the car, and he melted away into the night leaving Harry, who had no intention of following Malik, to retrieve his belongings.

Chapter 108

April 18th, Z - 14 Days
London, England

As Malik met with Harry the evening sitting of the Cabinet at Ten Downing Street was dominated by the effort to find the nuclear bomb and the terrorists behind it. The Prime Minister looked first to the Defence Secretary to update the Cabinet on his Department's input, followed by the Foreign Secretary then Home Secretary.

The Defence Secretary briefed the Cabinet on the military support that Operation Enduring Freedom was receiving from NATO members, NATO partners and non-NATO countries from across the world, on land, on the sea and in the air. When he had finished, he introduced the CDS who rose from his customary place behind the Defence Secretary as there was insufficient room for everyone present to sit at the oval table.

The CDS summarised life in London under martial law and how the Armed Forces had reacted to prevent a repeat of the riot outside the Houses of Parliament that had taken place several days ago, prior to focusing on the search for the bomb and terrorists. He reported that every inch of London had been searched for illicit radioactive emissions and that a map of known radiation sources had been produced. He supported MI6's belief that the hijacking of Canary Wharf Tower had been a feint and that the bomb would be found elsewhere. He then went on to explain how continuous systematic radiological sweeps of the city were taking place to locate any new emissions and hopefully the bomb. He ended this topic by speaking of the quick reaction team that was stood by to cordon any locality and deactivate and remove the bomb. The CDS also spoke of house-to-house canvassing with the photographs of two of the suspects, and the high number of call outs to false alarms. When pressed by the Prime

Minister about publishing the photographs through the media, the CDS said that until now it had been considered to be fruitless and misleading, as the terrorists were likely to be disguised, and the photographs would generate a huge number of calls that would further swamp the services. However, a dedicated call centre and response team had been established and the two photographs had been released at this evening's press conference. By the end of his short briefing it was clear that the Armed Forces were doing everything they could.

Next up was the Home Secretary, who lucidly described how the UK's police forces, Customs, Immigration and MI5 were reacting to the challenge. Although much work was being done to apprehend possible terrorist suspects, Home Office tactics were not popular in the media or among the public. Nonetheless, the hot lines were swamped with reports of suspicious activity, and every one was being followed up, but so far nothing. It was as if, on leaving Argentina, the terrorists had disappeared. He ended by reporting that the Passport Office had just completed a review of all UK passports issued within the last two years and, although six forgeries had been identified, none pointed toward their terrorists.

The Foreign Secretary felt the burden for good news on his shoulders, but began by reducing the expectation. He reviewed the NATO Secretary General's recent announcement that the attack on London was an attack against all twenty-six NATO member countries within the terms of Article Five of the North Atlantic Treaty. He also explained to murmurs of approval from around the table, how each of the member countries had approved some kind of joint military offensive against the perpetrators, that the NATO Response Force was stood by on seventy-two hours notice, and that many members had offered to augment any military action, including the US.

That, said the Foreign Secretary, led him neatly to the intelligence battle that aimed to locate the bomb, the terrorist cell and the perpetrators. He reiterated that it was MI6's view that the terrorists had delivered the bomb while all eyes were focused on Canary Wharf, and that they were now likely to be fleeing the country. He ended by stating his hope that the radiological teams, now that they had finished their survey of the city, would locate the bomb.

As the Foreign Secretary finished, Sir Michael stood. He reported that none of the painstaking intelligence work had led to anything tangible on Fox and Vixen, and that they were stumped by the complete lack of intelligence from across the world. He explained how his team were attempting to appeal subliminally to Fox and Vixen, whom his expert profilers assured him were susceptible mercenaries not fanatical terrorists, most definitely not the same breed. He ended by complimenting the media in general for their support in reaching out to the terrorist cell responsible, and reminded the Cabinet that all it took to locate the bomb was one short, anonymous telephone call.

'It appears these bastards have got us by the balls,' said the Prime Minister when it was clear there were no further contributions from around the table. 'The full evacuation of London is now our immediate priority. It seems there's nothing more we can do, than we are already doing, to prevent it. Sir Michael?'

'Yes, Prime Minister,' answered Sir Michael as he stood up again.

The Prime Minister hesitated only for a second. 'I will never negotiate with terrorists, but we must find and deal with these mercenaries in whatever way we can. Do I make myself clear?'

'Yes, sir, that's very clear.'

'You should let me know immediately contact is established, and seek my approval on any agreement as you see fit.'

'I understand, Prime Minister,' replied Sir Michael sombrely, maintaining eye contact with the Prime Minister.

'Good. Let's hope you get the chance, and if you do, for all our sakes make sure it's palatable.'

Chapter 109

April 19th, Z – 13 Days
London, England

The Foreign Secretary looked strained and tired, but like everyone else in Sir Michael's office at Vauxhall Cross, he could do little to conceal his excitement and relief. The two men were accompanied by Sir Michael's deputy, Rosalind Washington, Harry, Tess and Tim Bernazzini, all of them sitting in the dark-green leather armchairs facing the Director MI6. Like the 'Whitehall Warriors' in the Ministry of Defence, and 'Essential Staff' in the Prime Minister's Office and Cabinet Office, the Foreign Secretary and his closest advisors and the MI6 operations staff had no intention of evacuating London until the last possible moment, and that gave them several more days.

Rosalind would brief remaining key players later in the morning, just as soon as it was clear what direction they were heading. The jungle drums worked as well in Vauxhall Cross as anywhere else, and she knew perfectly well that most of their senior analysts and operatives were at this very moment gathering in the ops room down the hallway, hoping for a hint of what the excitement was about. It could mean only one thing, that there was some kind of breakthrough, and whatever the intelligence was, it might just help each of them place their own piece of the jigsaw.

'It looks like your plan may have worked, Harry. But it's essential the Government is not perceived as negotiating with terrorists. And why should we trust him?' the Foreign Secretary continued, having listened with rising excitement to Sir Michael's briefing. The public will want to know why we didn't put him in play, follow him, arrest and interrogate him, neutralise the bombs, then throw him into Belmarsh with the rest of his kind.'

Despite his own elation, Sir Michael forced himself to remain calm for he did not want the conversation to deteriorate. 'Minister, our Government and justice system regularly negotiate with this kind of individual every day. We should consider ourselves fortunate Fox is not a fanatical terrorist but hired help. There are countless precedents of when our security services have bargained with terrorists and criminals for the greater good. Harry will be negotiating with someone who can provide a vast amount of priceless intel in return for his life, and the life of his daughter, another innocent in all this. I'm certain that very few, if any, people will see it differently. It's not as if we're negotiating with bin Laden, we're bargaining in order to destroy him.'

'We can trust Fox with the life of his daughter, and there's no point in putting him back in play either,' added Harry briskly. His job in London is finished, and he's simply too smart and well resourced to be caught. Our line is the same as it was the day we met the experts at MI5. He is an agent of al-Qa'eda, and is recruited as a double-agent. Fox may prove to be the most successful double-agent in the country's history.'

The Foreign Secretary couldn't help but grin at the analogy and to everyone's relief including his own, he moved on. 'I alerted the Prime Minister at 2 a.m. and convinced him not to hold another Cabinet meeting today. He has given me this morning to appraise the situation. But he does expect me to brief him on the way ahead early this afternoon, before a full Cabinet meeting first thing tomorrow morning. By the way, are you all right, Harry?'

Harry grinned. 'Nothing more than a hurt ego, Minister.'

'I just hope for all our sakes that he gets back in contact,' the Foreign Secretary responded abruptly, not sure yet whether Harry should have taken the opportunity to seize Malik.

'Harry,' said Sir Michael calmly, 'perhaps you should brief the Minister on your get-together with Fox in your own words. Then we can address the way ahead.'

Harry outlined the events of last night. 'In sum, Minister, Fox aka Malik is prepared to reveal the locations of the bombs and provide as much intel as he can on the terrorist groups responsible, including names and whereabouts, funding details, and probably anything else he can think of, in return for the safe return of his daughter and a safe haven – that is, their immunity and UK citizenship.'

The Home Secretary stared at Harry. 'Why not US citizenship?'

Harry shrugged his shoulders, making it clear to the Foreign Secretary that he would not speculate in the presence of the CIA.

'And what is your professional assessment, Harry?' asked Sir Michael.

'He doesn't want money and is probably already wealthy as a result of some kind of advance payment. He holds a great hand of cards and he knows it. He is a very careful man and he won't trust us. Any deal will have to involve us trusting him, that is, us providing the goods first. If his daughter dies, so will London, for the next millennium. In this regard at least, he's a man who sees no difference between one death and a million. The intel he holds will not only allow us to save London and the economic health of our country, but it will enable us to deal a blow against Islamic militancy and terrorism of a vastly greater magnitude than that dealt by the US-led Coalition forces when we defeated the Taliban and their allies in Afghanistan back in 2002. With the appropriate political will of host nations, Fox may represent a lasting opportunity for Western nations to undo some of the complications that have arisen in the Arab world over the last century and support them further by physically ridding them of most, if not all, Islamic terrorist groups, certainly all of those without populist support.'

'Which is all of them apart from the PLO,' suggested Bernazzini.

'That's right,' replied Harry. 'I believe that Fox is sincere and that the intel he has and evidence he represents can change the course of mankind if handled correctly.'

'You still don't believe we can defeat terrorism by force and security alone?' the Foreign Secretary asked.

'The old wisdom no longer applies,' answered Harry, who knew from their previous discussions that the Foreign Secretary was a convert but that he was seeking reassurance. 'The traditional belief is that if you cut off the head, the body will die. This still applies to the more independent terrorist groups and if the intel is good I suspect it will apply to some of the minority groups involved in this plot. However, al-Qa'eda works to a new paradigm. Even if we destroy its head there is no standing army to die, and new leaders will quickly appear unless the world order is changed. Al-Qa'eda contracts out its attacks. It represents extreme

Islam and appeals to impressionable Muslims everywhere, inciting them to conduct their own, home-grown attacks. It seeks partnerships with any number of independent terrorist groups that have their own foot soldiers, and ideology that includes attacking the West. A scary development is that al-Qa'eda can bring together established groups from across the world, each with their own armed cells but widely differing ideology. I believe this is what we face today.'

'If al-Qa'eda is to be destroyed permanently we must not only neutralise the leaders but remove the conditions that generate support,' added Tess. 'Groups seek and receive financial support from bin Laden and in return they conduct attacks. The only way we can defeat al-Qa'eda is through a combination of political, military and financial action.'

'It's possible we could wipe out al-Qa'eda in the next few weeks,' Harry added. 'It's also possible that we could destroy many other Islamic terror groups but the world must address the conditions that foster global terror, otherwise they will simply rise again.'

'Thank you, both of you,' said the Foreign Secretary when it seemed they had finished.

Everyone hushed unnecessarily while Merissa brought in refreshments and offered them around.

'So how should we proceed?' asked the Foreign Secretary as he sipped from a teacup.

Sir Michael and Harry had discussed this. He nodded for Harry to continue.

'For now our primary goal is to save London. Our secondary goal is to destroy as many terrorist groups as possible. After that, we are into politics and that's your department Minister. I see no value in Fox regarding the political situation. He referred to more than one bomb and as an act of faith we must demand that he give them all up immediately, though we must be prepared for him to retain at least one as leverage. They will be neutralised immediately by the Army, but in absolute secrecy. Unfortunately it's vital that the Government, the public and the media play out this scenario and London's evacuation to the very end. Any suspicion within al-Qa'eda or any one of the other terrorist groups involved that Fox has struck a deal and we can kiss everything goodbye.'

The Foreign Secretary looked ashen. 'The riots, the beatings, the burnings. They will continue? No one will like that.'

'Not necessarily,' replied Harry. 'Everything must be done to maintain law and order. Meanwhile, the population of London will be rapidly decreasing. Soon there should be no one left.'

'The show must go on,' the Foreign Secretary mumbled to himself. 'Damn it, you're right. Continue, please.'

'NATO plans a secret assault on every terrorist hideout known to Fox, to take place on the first day of May. Precision assaults, nothing heavy-handed. We must limit collateral damage if we are to retain hearts and minds for the political response that we know must follow. NATO members' counterterrorist task-forces, supplemented where necessary by their Special Forces and the NATO Reaction Force, will be called upon to act. Afterwards host nation governments can take the credit as part of the political response, but NATO must command, control and conduct each op. The Brits must lead the assault on the location where the girl is held hostage for obvious reasons and that must be the first strike.'

'There are masses of complications,' the Foreign Secretary noted.

Tim Bernazzini spoke up. 'The worst is that a number of the host nations may be compromised. We have evidence of one Government that is dirty and suspicions about several other Arab states. There is a mole high in the Pakistan Government, of that we are certain.'

'So we must act first using NATO troops, and only then justify the invasion to the host nations?' asked the Foreign Secretary.

'A necessary evil, Minister,' Bernazzini answered. 'The problem is that there are no agreed rules for responding to global terrorism, particularly when stealth is required. There is now a need for a global task-force with powers to deal with this type of warfare but there simply isn't one. One thing though, it's the President's view that it's London under threat so it's up to the Brits to prove the requirement using NATO and demonstrate it in real play. We'll support you all the way.'

Sir Michael added, 'I spoke to Jim Ridge early this morning, he said the same thing.'

'What about the UN?' asked the Foreign Secretary.

Sir Michael had thought about this. 'The UN is simply too

transparent, and regrettably its Charter simply does not adequately cater for global terrorism or this kind of response. Of course it should do, but the UN will have to be tackled later. The good news is that the vast majority of UN members have voiced their strongest support for our plight already, and given the degree of provocation, justifying the invasions outside of NATO shouldn't prove too difficult. The better news is that NATO has Article Five and is prepared to act upon it, and in secret.'

The Foreign Secretary was convinced. 'Who would command such an operation?'

Bernazzini answered. 'Actually it would fall on the shoulders of an American General, General Sid Sheldon. He is NATO's Allied Commander in Naples, Italy. Conveniently, his deputy is a Brit, a General George Washington, would you believe. The Supreme Allied Commander Europe based in Brussels is American too, but of course you know him.'

Harry saw a chance to continue without going further into the political quagmire. There was, after all, a huge Government machine to deal with the political and military issues both within the Foreign Office and the Ministry of Defence. 'Minister, that brings me to the issues of funding and assets. Fox alluded to information regarding the funding of the operation. Also, you are aware that bin Laden and several other terrorist leaders are very wealthy men in their own right. Bin Laden and his Sunni followers own considerable assets in Saudi Arabia and the Sudan as well as Egypt, the United Arab Emirates and Yemen.'

Tess followed up. 'Since the dissipation of the Arab Mujahidin after the Afghan war, bin Laden's influence has extended across the entire Arab world. We also know he owns a bank in Sudan. It seems the Sudanese Government's request for him to leave their country did not apply to his assets. Bin Laden runs al-Qa'eda like a business, and we need to put a stop to all his financial operations and those charitable and other financial operations that support terrorism.'

'Thank you, Tess,' Sir Michael said gratefully. 'Minister, this is a vital part of NATO's operation. I propose that we support the leaving of this dimension to the Americans, specifically the FBI. Bill Darling, the Director FBI, is able to work with NATO, but he needs access to Fox's intel. He wants to shut down bin Laden's financial operations, and expose every possible terrorist funding operation he can find, acting with NATO's authority and seizing assets in NATO's name where possible.'

The Foreign Secretary sat up. 'NATO would be very grateful I'm sure. Even NATO is not prepared for this type of multi-dimensional warfare. Al-Qa'eda considers all three dimensions and so must we – political, military, and financial.' The room fell silent a moment. 'Can we really prepare and incept all this in less than two weeks, and in secret?' he added apprehensively.

Harry answered. 'It all depends on Fox. Minister, that brings me to my last two points.'

'Yes?' the Foreign Secretary asked, reluctant to hear more complications. He already had plenty to discuss with the Prime Minister.

'It's imperative that only Tess and I interrogate Fox prior to the op. Questions and answers must be collated and distributed through us.'

'Sir Michael?' asked the Foreign Secretary.

'Minister, the point is valid. We don't have much time. Harry and Tess need to strike up a relationship with Fox and fast. No one else can be allowed to contaminate that relationship. It's doubtful Fox will answer questions after the operation so the debriefing must be down to them.'

'Agreed.' The Foreign Secretary looked at Harry. 'You said two points.'

'Fox will want to be present when we strike on his daughter's captives. He will want to see that everything is being done to save his daughter. It must be part of the deal.'

'He could be useful on the ground too,' added Tess.

The Foreign Secretary stared at them both. 'It's not my call, but I'll support it. He will be entirely your responsibility, your joint responsibility.'

'Thank you, Minister,' Harry replied.

Chapter 110

April 20th, Z – 12 Days
London, England

'I'm sorry to keep you all waiting,' the Prime Minister began as he took his seat. 'As you know I've just been speaking with the US President. I hope your time has not been wasted.'

He glanced at the Deputy Prime Minister on his right and received confirmation that the Foreign Secretary had indeed been making the most of the time available. In fact, the Foreign Secretary had just finished briefing the Cabinet on the breakthrough.

'Good. The aim is simple, ladies and gentlemen. In the next eleven days our Special Forces will mount an operation to rescue the girl as part of a NATO-led operation to destroy the terrorists. The country's highest priority is the rescue of the girl, and I intend to do everything within my power to make that happen and so prevent more deaths and the destruction of London. Of secondary importance to the country is the destruction of the perpetrators of this attack, wherever they may be. British Forces will focus on the situation in London and the recovery of the girl, which combined will save London, and support NATO's destruction of the girl's captors.'

After his short opening address the Prime Minister asked his Deputy, who had attended the very same briefings prior to the Cabinet meeting, to continue while he revised his notes.

'No doubt you will all have realised that a great many toes are going to be trodden on as NATO strike against those involved, and we have no doubt there will be considerable recriminations afterwards. It will make the bruising that both we and the US took toppling Saddam Hussein feel like a petty neighbourhood squabble. But, we know that we can count on the full support of every member of NATO. The reality is that there are no international treaties or adequate protocols in the UN Charter that support NATO's move. NATO will be setting a precedent in desperate circumstances. But ultimately, the British public expect us to protect them, whatever the cost, and that is precisely what we are going to do, wherever it takes us. The UN is still not prepared to deal with the threat of global terrorism, and in the light of 9/11 and subsequent attacks across the world it damn well should be. The UN must address this omission in the coming months as we face the aftermath. After all, we already have most of the Security Council on board.'

The Prime Minister took up the reins. 'You all know my feelings already. If we are to defeat global terrorism, we must change the political paradigm by working towards the "what if" scenarios rather than always reacting to "what is". In future we must be truly proactive and not reactive. It seems to me that the only political party who truly know how to be proactive in British politics are the Greens. Right, let's crack on.'

Harry, sitting at the back, was impressed. The two senior Government ministers had been well briefed, and were speaking straight from the heart.

The Foreign Secretary continued. 'Prime Minister, it would be helpful if we could all reach a consensus at this point on the overall plan; that is, the "arrangement" with Fox.'

'The Cabinet's endorsement would be helpful. I would also feel more confident if I knew we were all singing off the same hymn sheet.'

'Certainly, Prime Minister. This afternoon MI6 will offer Fox the safe recovery of his daughter, their immunity and British citizenship in return for all the information he holds on terrorist operations including the attack on London, their organisational structures and their funding. Fox will also provide timely information on the locations of the nuclear bombs in London, with the possibility of all but one being neutralised before the rescue of his daughter.'

A low but positive sigh was heard across the room.

'Meanwhile, NATO will prepare to destroy the terrorists. As you all know, secrecy and surprise is vital for this operation if London is to be saved. The UN will be officially warned by NATO only as the operation begins. NATO members will collectively shoulder any "fallout", and the international community and UN will be strongly encouraged to make the most of any opportunities that arise from the operation.'

'Addressing the UN Charter is a tall order but one on which the UN must engage. So, what of the wider plan, does anybody disagree?' the Prime Minister asked confidently.

The Home Secretary drew a deep breath. 'I don't disagree with the operation, but I'm concerned with the increasing desperation among Londoners. I don't have to spell out that in the next eleven days more lives and billions of pounds will be lost. Given what we now know, is there something that can be done to prevent or at least reduce the human and economic havoc that is being caused?'

The Chief of the Defence Staff, sitting behind the Defence Secretary, stood up. 'Prime Minister, if I may?'

'Please.'

'Martial law must continue if we are not to raise suspicions. In the meantime I will ensure that the Armed Forces and supporting services acts with as much compassion and understanding as possible. Thankfully London should be largely deserted from midday this Friday and the numbers of serious incidents will rapidly reduce as the population is evacuated. But there are some evil people out there who mean harm to persons and property, and the public will expect them to be dealt with swiftly and firmly. The upshot is, I cannot stand here and make guarantees, for it's ugly out there, at times very ugly, but we will act with as much consideration and as close to English law as we can.'

The Prime Minister replied, 'Thank you, General. I know we all understand the situation. We want damage limitation but my priority is operational security, however distasteful its cost may be.'

'I entirely understand, Prime Minister,' said the CDS before sitting down.

'Good. We're all agreed on the plan,' the Prime Minister said decidedly. 'What's NATO up to?'

The Defence Secretary pulled himself up in his chair. 'Prime Minister, NATO has five surface carrier fleets at its disposal, including two American and one of our own, all within striking distance of the Middle East and Central Asia. There is also another fleet in the region, the Russian Black Sea Fleet, should we require it. Within a week each NATO fleet will be capable of projecting an air assault force of up to brigade strength. Our own 16 Air Assault Brigade is at twenty-four hours' notice to move. However, based on the intelligence so far, I expect the incursion teams to be small, perhaps within the capability of specialist counterterrorism units. So far, and in addition to the SAS, NATO has the American Delta Force, the German Kommando Spezialkräfte or KSK, and four other NATO counterterrorist units including the Italians and Spanish at their disposal. The French have also offered up their Groupement d'Intervention de la Gendarmerie Nationale, or GIGN, but they are policemen, not military Special Forces. Under NATO's banner, they are all willing to infiltrate hostile or uncooperative territories, though there remain some issues over sovereignty. Every NATO country has offered support in one form or another, particularly troops. Finding the right troops for the operation, whatever it shapes up to be, should not prove a problem. The Russians have offered their Alpha Unit, and I also received a call from the Israeli Ambassador who offered us their elite counterterrorist unit, Unit 269.'

'Does either of them know anything?' asked the Prime Minister warily.

'Only what they see on the news.'

'Well, let's see where the enemy lies and what NATO proposes before we recommend involving either of them,' replied the Prime Minister sagely. 'This will be the last time we meet here. I would like another meeting in two days at Chequers to review progress. Can everyone make that?' Without waiting for an answer, the Prime Minister continued, 'Good. Does anyone have anything else?'

'Prime Minister, I assume we mean to eliminate the enemy, and that despite NATO's involvement, this is a Black Flag op?' asked the Home Secretary.

The Prime Minister was surprised by the question and that it was the Home Secretary who asked it. Black Flag operations were those that involved the authorised killing of targets for the greater good of the nation. Without this authority, counterterrorist teams had to act within the law because they were not considered at war. Within the law teams were to try and stop the terrorist from killing the hostages though naturally, in most cases stopping the terrorist meant killing the terrorist.

Sir Michael, who was sitting beside Harry in one corner of the room and already thinking along these lines, rose to his feet. 'Excuse me, Prime Minister. Although it may be considered more appropriate to answer that question when we are in receipt of information from Fox and have analysed additional information from other sources, I believe we can answer that question satisfactorily now. We know that this enemy is small and disparate, but that it's as lethal as any army. Every counterterrorist strike force that NATO employs will act within the rules of war, not the rule of law. This means that they may legitimately destroy the enemy, not necessarily capture or neutralise or arrest them but destroy them. This is the premise on which NATO is preparing. With respect, we must stop thinking of the masterminds behind this attack as criminals. Although state terrorists can be said to be criminal, the terrorists we face are our enemy in a global war, and on this occasion they must be destroyed; that is, killed, if we are to have any chance of winning the war.'

'Thank you, Sir Michael, that was very succinct,' responded the Prime Minister gratefully. 'I'm here to make difficult decisions and sometimes I am denied the luxury of moral absolutes. But in this case it's clear. We have consistently and properly advised and supported NATO's aim to destroy the enemy. Labelling this a Black Flag op suggests we are still otherwise endeavouring to work within the rule of law. No, this operation is not a Black Flag op, this operation is a deadly counter-attack in time of war.'

'And what if the terrorists surrender?' asked the Chancellor mischievously.

'Then they are taken as prisoners of war,' responded Sir Michael. 'We must be very clear on what we are doing. In the event that any terrorist surrenders he may be recovered as a POW and, if necessary, tried for war crimes or crimes against humanity. It's only by challenging the boundaries of international law that we will ever comprehend, and be properly able to react to, global terrorism.'

'Sir Michael's personal experience speaks for itself, ladies and gentlemen. We would all do well to heed it,' the Prime Minister added.

Nobody spoke for several seconds as each person in the Cabinet Room digested the words. Establishing that everyone was in accord, the Prime Minister directed his full attention at his

Foreign and Defence secretaries and his senior military advisor for the last time that morning.

'NATO must do what it can to avoid any disasters either politically with sovereign nations or through unnecessary collateral damage. Given the utmost need for security I believe it would be prudent for NATO to inform each host nation immediately after each assault. Political leverage will need to be prepared, but we should remember, too, that almost all Islamic countries support the effort to defeat global terrorism, publicly at least.'

The Prime Minister's face looked determined. 'On another matter, I hope that we will not make the mistakes of previous counterterrorist disasters such as the slaughter of the Egyptian Special Forces by the Cypriot National Guard as they landed at Nicosia Airport to deal with a terrorist hijacking. Nobody had informed the Guard that Force 777 was coming. Then there was the poor support provided to Delta Force by the US Defence Department when the US attempted to assault the besieged US Embassy in Tehran. Apologies can be made in the aftermath, but lives cannot be recovered.

'Innocent civilians must not be targeted, and by that I mean we must have clinical precision. And we must all remember that "Arab" is not synonymous with "terrorism"; the vast majority of Muslims want to live peacefully with the West. As the US President and I agreed an hour ago, NATO must keep a tight grip on its troops if we are to receive global support in the aftermath.'

Harry saw that the Prime Minister's words, taken from a brief written by Sir Michael, had struck home.

Chapter 111

April 21st, Z – 11 Days
Chertsey, Surrey, England

At 2 a.m., Tally was still at work listening for the audible alarm that betrayed each incoming email arriving into the company's unsolicited messages folder. Usually someone else monitored the folder and she kept her own workstation's audible alarm switched off, preferring instead to glance at the incoming messages window open at the bottom right-hand corner of the flat screen. She was making the most of the time, catching up on a large number of low-priority tasks that would not have a cat in hell's chance of completion during normal office hours. The message that Mercury was waiting for finally arrived at 6:30 a.m., and within ten minutes of the alert from Tally, Harry and Tess were entering her office.

Tally had already admitted to herself that she was insanely jealous of Tess because of the close proximity the woman enjoyed with Harry both day and night, but she was not the kind of person to let it show or affect her work. Privately she had convinced herself that, although Tess was gorgeous and exciting, she was not right for Harry, who was simply too reserved and who needed to settle down. Tess thought she knew Harry well, and believed that even if there was a relationship it wouldn't last. Mercifully, she had not noticed how advanced both physically and emotionally the relationship was, as Harry and Tess were working hard to maintain a professional distance.

'Hey,' Tally said in her best American drawl as she turned to face Harry and Tess approaching her desk. 'Here it is.'

'Are you sure it's Fox?' asked Harry as Tally opened the message.

There was no need for Tally to respond as Harry and Tess were already reading the message over her shoulder.

'It's explosive,' Tally offered jokingly.

Harry and Tess both smiled, appreciating the banter.

'Flick it across, Tally,' said Harry, barely able to contain his relief. 'We'll reply to it in my office.'

'Jolly good,' added Tess in her best English accent.

'Coffee, you guys?' Tally asked as the two operatives walked toward Harry's office.

After meeting Malik the night before last, Harry had briefed Tally by telephone and asked her to arrange a roster, 24/7, to monitor the company's electronic mailbox for messages from either Fox or Malik. Soon after the Cabinet rose yesterday lunchtime, she had called and confirmed that a simple message from the man called Malik had arrived.

Winchester,
Time is running out. Do we agree?
Malik.

As Tess had driven Harry back to Chertsey from Number Ten, he had had the message traced and discovered it was forwarded from an anonymous server somewhere in India. He had carefully considered his response and what his reaction would be to his own reply if he were Malik. Confident he had interpreted Malik's intentions correctly, he had told Tally to respond on his behalf.

Malik,
We agree to your demands but require a sign of faith. We need proof you are genuine. I urge you to provide me with the type and location of the bomb. When it is recovered I will take you to a safe house near Chertsey where my partner and I will talk to you. As you say, time is running out.
HW.

The reply was sent at 4 p.m. yesterday. With no response from Malik by midnight, Tally and an assistant secretary had volunteered to maintain the vigil at her desk.

* * *

'She adores you,' Tess whispered as she closed the office door and followed Harry into his office.

Harry smiled softly in response. He switched on his computer, logged in and connected to the Web. 'I adore her, but I love you,' he whispered back. 'She's very kind, very considerate and an outstanding secretary. In truth, she runs the firm. I'd be lost without her.'

Tess wrapped her arms around him and kissed him on the forehead. 'I know. Good thing I'm not the jealous type.' Pointing at the screen, she added, 'Is this guy for real?'

'We'll soon find out.'

'And you're certain about the soft ball approach?'

'This man is trapped between the proverbial rock and hard place. If we force him in any way he will dismiss us as incompetent, the type of people that might cause his daughter's death. We must remain a far better option to him than any other he may have.'

'I hope you're right; I'd hate to have to marry an outcast from the intelligence community,' Tess chuckled.

Harry took his eyes away from the screen, a bright smile forming on his face. 'Was that a proposal?'

'No way,' answered Tess, squeezing her arms around Harry's neck. 'I expect you on your knees, Winchester. Think of it as a positive indicator.'

When the email forwarded by Tally appeared on the screen they both read it again, searching for additional clues within the message.

HW,
I will trust you for now. There are two bombs. One I will give you now, the other I will give you when my daughter is safe. A nuclear bomb is hidden in an oil drum in the larder at 36 Richmond Avenue, Islington. It is armed with a simple mechanism and no traps. You will understand its discovery must remain secret. Care for my partner's body which is to be returned home. The second body is the assassin, Jamali, who killed Baloch and my partner.
Malik.

'So what can we extract from this?' asked Harry calmly as he studied the message.

'You mean apart from *two* bombs?' Tess replied, unwilling to betray her concern.

'Yes, anything else?'

'He's happy to play soft ball. Do you think his partner is his lover?'

'I do. That may be what caused him to turn, her murder and his daughter's kidnapping. I wonder where "home" is.'

'He wants us to hang onto her until he's ready to tell us,' Tess suggested.

'So it would appear,' replied Harry. ' "No traps" probably means no anti-disturbance mechanisms.'

'There was never any need for booby traps so that makes sense. In his mind he is giving little away but the location of his dead partner. Also, he wants us to maintain a news blackout for obvious reasons. He will not care about Jamali, or the loss of one bomb.'

'OK, I'll forward it to my satcom then send it to Rosalind at Vauxhall Cross. The Chief of Joint Operations has a two-hundred strong team on stand-by waiting for this.'

The nuclear response team had been on thirty minutes' notice to move from Northwood for the last eighteen hours and included an SAS counterterrorism squad, atomic weapons experts, bomb disposal experts, medics, and a large posse of police and soldiers who would establish and maintain the necessary cordons.

The nuclear bomb and two bodies were recovered within eight hours of Harry contacting Rosalind, a fast response time considering the nature of the target. There was little media coverage as the operation was billed as another false alarm.

While the nuclear response team worked at 36 Richmond Avenue, the two operatives visited the Government's defence research agency bordering onto Harry's small estate. Here they met with several MI5 and MI6 operatives and a senior executive from the local headquarters. Harry and Tess organised the preparation and all-round defence of a safe house in the grounds that was required for three days at most.

At midday, Harry received a call from Rosalind confirming that the recovery was complete and that Malik's information was sound. Returning to his office in Mercury, Tess typed a message to Malik as Harry dictated.

Malik,
We are grateful for your information and agree to your proposal. I suggest we pick you up in person where we last met. When shall we meet?
HW.

The reply came inside twenty minutes.

HW,
In one hour.
Malik.

Harry leant over Tess's shoulder and typed in a short reply.

Malik,
If you get there early perhaps you could find my left shoe.
HW

Tess gave Harry a look.
'You can be the bad cop,' Harry grinned.

Chapter 112

April 22nd, Z – 10 Days
Chertsey, Surrey, England

The four-bedroom house owned by the Ministry of Defence was intended for use by the family of an employee who worked at the defence research base at Chertsey, though it was currently unoccupied. It was situated at the end of a cul-de-sac adjacent to other unoccupied married quarters, with its garden backing onto the vast military equipment testing ground. Importantly the house was 'behind the wire' and therefore easy for the security services to guard. On their arrival yesterday afternoon, Harry had declared the house a weapons-free zone, then he and Tess had prepared to interview Malik while others ordered food from the mess and prepared plenty of fresh coffee.

The initial interrogation had begun at 4 p.m. yesterday and continued well into the early hours. With the need for thoroughness but with so little time, Harry and Tess had kept the questioning simple; they believed that Malik was sufficiently motivated to tell them what they needed to know, accurately and quickly. By 1 a.m. that morning they had established the preliminaries, including Malik's and Dalia's identities, at least the little that Malik felt obliged provide, how and why they had been contacted by al-Qa'eda through the Muslim Kashmiri terrorist group the Harakat ul-Mujahidin, or HM, why they had agreed to support the terrorist operation, and why he was now prepared to switch allegiance.

In return, Malik had asked of the current whereabouts of Dalia's body, and that her body be released to Pakistan Embassy officials. Malik had also continued to insist that he be present when his daughter Karima was rescued. Harry had agreed without difficulty to both demands and had asked for Malik's and his daughter's vital statistics in order that British citizenship and other identification papers including passports could be produced. With no photograph of Karima available, Malik and a technician from Vauxhall Cross, aided by bin Laden's most recent video broadcast, had produced an identikit substitute photograph which Malik verified as a true likeness. Before leaving at 2 a.m., the technician had assured Harry that he would be back with the new passports and other identity papers by 4 p.m.

It was 10 a.m. on the day that London was to be evacuated by everyone except for the security forces and those authorised to remain by the City of London Corporation, when Harry, Tess and Malik resumed the interrogation. After labelling a fresh cassette, Tess primed the recording equipment and Harry introduced everyone present for the purposes of the tape before continuing.

'Malik, you'll appreciate that we have to complete our interviews today so that preparations and plans can be made for our retaliation and for Karima's rescue. You'll also appreciate that the financial support the terrorists groups receive is of importance to us and so later today several banking experts, including two FBI Special Agents, will arrive to establish what you know. However, we will begin by establishing what more you can tell us.'

Malik sighed. 'I have come to realise over the last six months that acts of terrorism and unrestrained state retaliation only multiply the problem. Whether violence is used in a terrorist action or in a Government's retaliation, it's the common people who always suffer. People die, but their deaths bring no compromise and provide no final solution. You cannot justify your actions under Western laws and simply ignore the other societies and religions that inhabit the planet. If the West wants an end to Islamic terrorism then it must undermine its ideology respecting Muslims and not by pushing them to extremism.'

Harry and Tess understood his sentiment, but there was no time for philosophical or political debate.

'How did the plan to attack London begin?' asked Harry.

'Al-Qa'eda is a group of about twelve full and active members. There are about three hundred "messengers" spread across the world on which they can rely, most of them clerics or preachers working in mosques, and, I estimate, five thousand warriors who are prepared to act and possibly die for the cause. Most warriors are members of regional Islamic terrorist groups that for a time fought for the Muslim Brotherhood in Afghanistan while some are trained for specific missions. Of course, there are millions of Muslims across the world that sympathise with their cause and make financial contributions or who are willing to assist in some way, however small. Bin Laden is a very clever man. He is appealing to disaffected extremists by heralding an ideology, and has the West chasing ghosts. All al-Qa'eda's money, of which there is billions of dollars, is spent sponsoring terrorist attacks or on encouraging support through generous donations channelled through mosques. He is not materialistic and he has no home to speak of, but lives a nomadic life with colleagues where they plan and finance attacks that may take place in months or even years. I have written down the names of the twelve and where I believe they are hiding along with the other leaders and their groups that were involved in this attack on London.'

Malik handed over the list and witnessed their delight as his interrogators began to read. Passing over a second list, he continued, 'And this list details other messengers, warriors and other terror groups known to me. I have marked the people on both lists who were at the Gathering in the Pamir Mountains.'

Harry and Tess studied both lists in amazement. After several minutes, Harry read them out loud for the tape.

After Harry finished, Malik continued. 'Groups in the Network rarely communicate with each other, but when they do, they either meet or use simple, secure electronic mail organised by a communications officer called the "Mailman". Untraceable cell phones are also commonly used. Some groups still use the ancient trade routes that connect West Africa through the Middle East to Asia and beyond, while others use the latest computer and cell phone technology. Much is still passed by word of mouth. The most effective means of communication between the groups and their followers is openly made through the media, particularly announcements and declarations on television.'

But Harry wasn't listening. He was deeply suspicious that bin Laden was listed as living in a village near Khartoum. He stared into Malik's eyes, searching for deceit. 'Malik, bin Laden was thrown out of Sudan by the Government in return for the lifting of US sanctions.'

Malik grinned mischievously. 'He went back to Afghanistan for a short while, and then returned to Sudan once the Americans were satisfied. Bin Laden's business interests in the Sudan are worth more to the Government's ministers than the lifting of the US sanctions. The Sudanese Government concocted a plan that satisfied both parties. Did you know he owns a bank?'

'I did,' replied Harry gravely.

'He doesn't use his own bank,' added Malik with an ironic smile before getting back to the point. 'You see, bin Laden did not approach these groups. Over a period of time these groups approached him for support and as they did so he realised the possibilities that there were in a single combined strike against the West, on a scale greater than 9/11. As each group approached him, he convinced them of another plan, the same plan, and why they must all work together. Once bin Laden had the necessary support from across the Islamic world he called them together at the Gathering. The Mailman contacted them all and organised the hardware, and a man known as Abu Zubaydah Saudi organised the meeting and coordinated the funds. Dalia and I were responsible for the conduct of the operation, and while we were waiting for it to begin we assisted Abu Saudi. Some groups provided equipment, others valuable information. Between them all they had everything they needed, including money and an incredible web of contacts and information.'

Tess continued to question Malik in detail about the twelve members of al-Qa'eda, who were split into two localities, one at Peshawar, Pakistan, where Malik knew Karima was held and the other near Khartoum in Sudan. Meanwhile, Harry considered the names of the other terrorist groups on the first list. He was shocked by the numbers of groups involved and the ability of such groups to join together into such a powerful entity. It included the Egyptian Islamic terror group Islamic Jihad led by al-Gama'a al-Islamiyya. Iraq was represented by the militant Shi'ite Mahdi Army and Algeria by the Groupe Islamique Armée, or GIA. The Palestinian Islamic resistance movement, Hamas, had been represented by its chief, Sheik Ahmed Yassin. Lesser known groups had also been present at the Gathering and included the Harakat ul-Mujahidin, or HM, from Muslim Kashmir, the Islamic Movement of Uzbekistan, or IMU, and the radical Islamic group Jemaah Islamiyah that had claimed responsibility for the Bali bombing in 2002. There were also a radical Chechen Islamist group led by the son of Khattab, the infamous terrorist who was killed in Chechnya by the Russians in 2002; a group from Somalia; a Palestinian Liberation Organisation splinter group based in South Yemen known as the Popular Front for the Liberation of Palestine, and groups from Iran and Saudi Arabia. Harry even considered that Special Forces across NATO would be stretched. They might need the Russians after all.

After Tess had finished questioning Malik about al-Qa'eda, including details of their locations, operating procedures, weapons and routine, Harry asked the same questions about each of the other terror groups in turn. Of the sixteen groups on the list, Harry considered that Malik had provided sufficient knowledge of ten of them to make an immediate attack a viable option. Harry and Tess found it hard to contain their rising excitement but this was quickly scotched by Malik.

'You realise that the groups were in these locations months ago,' Malik said ruefully. 'It was common practice, especially for bin Laden, to keep moving. I cannot say with any certainty that they are still at these locations.'

For the next three hours Malik told the two operatives everything he could about the terrorists, the details behind the plan to attack London, and the conduct of the operation. All the time he hoped that he was securing the release of his daughter as well as contributing to a new world order. Something about Harry and Tess, and the questions they asked, assured him that they intended to save his daughter and destroy the terrorists, but there was more to it than that. As the interrogation progressed he realised that Harry and Tess wanted to do everything they could to enable a full and sensible political response from the West, particularly from the US and UK, and not simply to achieve a short-term retaliatory strike against the perpetrators.

At 4:15 p.m. the financial experts arrived and Malik told them what he could about the funding of the groups, as well as the funding of the operation to attack London. On Harry's advice, everyone present simply sat back and listened for a further two hours to the story as it unfolded. Malik spoke of the huge amounts of funds that were generated by Islamic charities from across the world including the US, UK, Belgium, the Netherlands, Germany and France, and how money was extracted by extortion and from the opium trade, and of the monies provided by Islamic states including Iran, Saudi Arabia, and others. He explained that when Yasser Arafat had publicly supported Saddam Hussein in the 1990s, and many of the richer Arab states that had previously been giving him financial support shunned him, the states had looked for another group to fund and found bin Laden, the global strategist who was treated as some kind of a central clearing bank for the sponsoring of Islamic terrorism the world over. This show of loyalty to the Islamic militant cause bought the sponsoring states immunity from terrorist attack, thus making it easy for Malik's interrogators to guess which states were implicated and which were not. Jordan had suffered twenty al-Qa'eda related attacks in the last year alone, whereas Iran and Sudan had suffered none.

Until now Western powers had been unable to stop the flow of money, but by the end of the interrogation, the two FBI Special Agents were brimming with ideas and a new-found confidence. But Malik had saved the best until last. He handed over another sheet of paper that provided details of banks and bank accounts the world over. The list included every terrorist account of which he was aware, including his and Dalia's personal accounts, each of which resided at Global Financial Services Limited, Cayman Islands. In each account there was the sum of one and a half million US dollars waiting to be traced and seized. Although Malik knew these two accounts would be found, there were no trails to the six large deposit boxes packed with bonds and dollars that were in the vaults of the bank next door.

At 8 p.m. a team of MI6 administrators arrived with a truck loaded with office equipment, maps and stationery and by 9 p.m. the house resembled a medium-sized company's office. Tape machines, a photocopier, a facsimile machine and printers were whirring. There were two large stand-alone computer workstations, each loaded with an impressive array of off-the-shelf and highly classified software.

By 10 p.m. the interrogation was over, and in an air of excitement the interrogators quickly polarised into two groups, NATO and the FBI, and everyone began to compile briefing sheets and reports. Tomorrow afternoon both groups were to brief foreign ministers and top NATO generals at NATO's headquarters in Mons, Belgium.

Malik busied himself watching television upstairs, answering frequent questions throughout the night.

Harry telephoned Sir Michael at midnight and suggested that the three of them continue after Mons to NATO's southern command in Naples, Italy, so they could provide first-hand support to the additional surveillance and urgent military planning that must be conducted over the next seven days.

Sir Michael gave his immediate approval.

Chapter 113

April 25th, Z – 7 Days
Naples, Italy

Chequers was the private residence of the UK Prime Minister as Camp David was for the US President. It provided an environment where the Prime Minister could talk to people in private. As the Prime Minister prepared to welcome the US President on the front steps at Chequers, a thousand miles away in Naples, Malik, accompanied by Harry and Tess, was assisting the Intelligence Division of NATO's southern Joint Force Command headquarters.

The President had landed in Air Force One at Brize Norton two hours ago where he had been met by his own Secretary of State and the UK Foreign Secretary, who had themselves returned to the same military airfield only one hour earlier on a Royal Air Force flight from Brussels. The President was at the start of a four day visit to Europe, which included two morale-boosting days in England followed by a visit to NATO's southern command in Naples via its headquarters in Brussels, both in his capacity as the Supreme Commander American Forces.

The two secretaries of state were themselves returning from another top-secret meeting of the North Atlantic Council, which had been immediately preceded by a NATO–Russia Council meeting. Foreign ministers from all NATO countries, Russia and Uzbekistan, had gathered with the Secretary General of NATO, Jaap de Hoop Sheffer and NATO's senior military general, the Supreme Allied Commander Europe or SACEUR, US Marine Corps General James L. Jones. Here, after six hours of debate, they had unanimously agreed on SACEUR's offensive concept of operations against the enemy. And so Operation Lightning Strike was approved, an operation that was to be NATO's timely response to the terrorist attack on one of its member states, this time the

United Kingdom. This was to be NATO's first offensive operation outside the Euro-Atlantic area and it underlined NATO's new military concept and preparedness to act against terrorist attacks directed from abroad against its populations and territory.

NATO had been formed in 1949 from the Washington Treaty and was an alliance of North American and European countries that were committed to safeguarding the freedom and security of its member countries and the Euro-Atlantic area by political and military means. Within twenty-four hours of the terrorist stikes against the US on 9/11, NATO had declared them an act of war against all NATO member countries within the terms of Article Five of the North Atlantic Treaty. This landmark decision had been followed by a vast reorganisation of NATO that provided the Alliance with an ability to respond rapidly and effectively to any future act of war against any one member, including that which London now faced.

NATO consisted of two constituent parts, political and military. Although the political arm was plagued by instability, selfishness and bureaucracy, the military arm enjoyed a physical cohesion born from the camaraderie of military personnel. To the insider, NATO was busier now than it ever had been. With just six days to go before Zulu Day, the political challenges imposed by Operation Lightning Strike had yet to be resolved, although military preparation was advancing. It was already clear to NATO chiefs that because the time for planning such a momentous and precision operation was so critically short, the counterattack would not take place before the early hours of Zulu Day.

SACEUR commanded NATO's strategic operations from the Allied Command Operations centre near Mons in Belgium, but it was the southern of the two standing subordinate commands, the Joint Force Command Naples, that was to lead Operation Lightning Strike. JFC Naples was commanded by a US Admiral, Admiral Michael G. Mullin US Navy, otherwise known as COM JFC Naples. Its Air Component Command was located at Izmir, Turkey; its Maritime Component Command was co-located in Naples, and its Land Component Command was in Madrid, Spain. Without any specific Area of Operational Responsibility, and after NATO's reduced military role in the Balkans, Admiral Mullin considered his command well situated to conduct the offensive operation spread over Western Asia and the Middle

East. Working for the Admiral in Naples was an integrated military staff of three hundred people representing many nations across Europe and North America. And now there were liaison officers from Russia and Uzbekistan. Despite the differing nationalities, every single officer was committed to the offensive action, as were their nations.

The headquarters at JFC Naples was responsible for destroying ten of the twelve targets. The other two targets that remained under NATO's operational command had been assigned by Brussels to NATO's partners, Russia and Uzbekistan. The Chechen warlord and his immediate followers who resided in Groznyy were to be destroyed by Russia's Alpha Unit, which was currently conducting battle preparations on a Russian naval carrier group laying off the port of Sochi in the Black Sea. The Islamic Movement of Uzbekistan, the IMU, was to be destroyed by Uzbekistan's own Special Forces.

At JFC Naples every division was working hard, but none more so than the Intelligence Division's multinational and multicultural workforce for whom sleep had become a luxury. In the new era of enhanced intelligence gathering and multinational cooperation since 9/11, a vast supply of information was generated, all of which had to be carefully analysed, collated and distributed. The Planning Division was reacting to the intelligence, formulating plans for the combined assault against ten terrorist groups that they now knew were hiding in a total twelve different countries, and fine-tuning the plans each time ground surveillance, satellite imagery or other intelligence confirmed or denied assumptions. As the intelligence arrived, so confidence in the plans grew. Then there was the Operations Division which controlled NATO's Response Force during the assault, and was currently occupied reorganising and preparing troops for deployment to the carriers.

Although Malik was kept under close custody by Harry and Tess, the rumours spread through the corridors of NATO's southern command that an ex-Pakistan Special Forces officer had single-handedly uncovered accurate information that had, since 9/11, eluded every intelligence service in the West.

Although NATO had demonstrated its resolve and solidarity since 9/11, neither it nor anyone else had managed to strike at the heart of al-Qa'eda. But now, thanks to this officer's information, NATO was able to fight back. After the success of the Cold War, a new generation of soldiers would prove themselves and they were eager to do so.

The NATO Response Force was a technologically advanced and flexible 30,000-strong army that was deployable anywhere in the world inside five days to tackle the full range of military missions. This high-readiness military capability, augmented for this widespread operation, included six carrier groups that were already in position in the Arabian Sea and Eastern Mediterranean and elite soldiers from each member state, the largest single unit provided by the US Marine Corps, closely followed by the US Rangers. Each country also had Special Forces stood by, although control of these resources that were vital to this type of operation was being retained by JFC Naples until the headquarters knew precisely what each tactical commander was up against. With the exception of Special Forces units, the Combined Joint Task Force was required to complete its deployment in the next forty-eight hours.

After careful reorganisation, the NATO Response Force provided Admiral Mullin with a land component of ten subordinate task forces that within hours, would begin deployment to the six carrier groups. A formidable air component of ground attack and fighter aircraft from sixteen nations, supported by AWACS aircraft from three nations, completed the orbat. Although Admiral Mullin was to adopt his usual hands-off approach and allow each of his subordinates to plan and execute their own strikes, critical assets were to remain under his control through an intricate web of detailed plans and alternate plans. Most challenging was the necessity to control the battle space that comprised the ground, sea and air, in particular over the crowded air corridors of the Middle East. There was also the need to coordinate the military effort with the political effort at NATO's headquarters, responsible for liaising with the UN and resolving issues arising from sovereignty.

Standard procedures dictated that each attack, whether into hostile territory or not, would involve the securing of the ground by each task force before assigned Special Forces would move in to destroy the enemy. But none of the task-force commanders were constrained by standard procedures. It just helped to have models against which plans could be considered. Such was the need for security that there was to be no reliance on friendly host nations or for that matter neighbouring countries without political approval.

The task-force commanders and their senior planners spent many hours in Naples with Admiral Mullin as they awaited target verification and confirmatory orders from SACEUR. They discussed hypothetical plans and learned from each other as well as from previous operational successes and failures, such as the successful Israeli raid on Entebbe and the unsuccessful US raid on the US Embassy in Tehran.

The assaults were to remain deniable, whether it involved hundreds of soldiers or a small hit squad. Equipment markings were removed, identity tags and other identifying marks left behind. Friendly dead and wounded were to be recovered.

It was late in the evening when Admiral Mullin received SACEUR's confirmatory orders. The orders informed him of additional political constraints, particularly regarding allocation of targets. The Admiral was reminded that there was to be no contact with host nations or their neighbours without SACEUR's approval.

Thankfully, the political constraints on target allocations were few, and so the pre-prepared plan that coordinated task forces to carrier groups, Special Forces to task forces, and allocated missions and critical assets, was soon revised. An appreciation of the time required for completion of deployment to final assault positions, and for vital battle preparations, led the Admiral and his generals to agree that the attacks would be synchronised for 2100 hours Zulu, 9 p.m. GMT, on the morning of May 2nd.

The US Delta Force was tasked with four targets supported wholly by the US Marine Corps and to their chagrin, the CIA's Special Recovery Unit. They were to destroy bin Laden's headquarters near Khartoum in Sudan, Ayman al-Zawahiri's Islamic Jihad headquarters on the Sinai Peninsula, Egypt, al-Gama'a al Islamiyya's headquarters in Luxor, Egypt and the headquarters of the Shi'ite Mahdi Army in Kirkuk, Iraq. Aside from the NATO mission to destroy the enemy, the CIA had presidential authority to attempt to seize at least one leading al-Qa'eda lieutenant under their clandestine Rendition programme of arrest and interrogation.

The SAS, supported by elements of the UK's 16 Air Assault Brigade, was tasked with two targets, the al-Qa'eda base near the Pakistan city of Peshawar where Karima was known to be held, and the destruction of a four-man cell of the Harakat ul-Mujahidin at Skardu in the Muslim Kashmir province of Pakistan. The Prime Minister had ordered the capture alive of the Mailman, though not at the expense of the mission or the lives of friendly forces.

Meanwhile, the French GIGN was to destroy the headquarters of the military apparatus of Sheik Ahmed Yassins's Hamas in Remallah, Lebanon, and the Turkish Special Forces were to destroy the Jemaah Islamiyah cell hiding in Djibouti. With the Russians and Uzbekistan controlled by SACEUR in Brussels, this left the German GSG9 unit, supported by the UK's Special Boat Service, to destroy the Groupe Islamique Armée headquarters in the coastal town of Hadjadj, Algeria; the Italians, supported by US Navy Seals, to destroy the maverick Palestinian cell seeking refuge in al-Mukalla on the coast of South Yemen; a combined Dutch and Belgian force to destroy a murderous and very active terrorist group in Rabigh on the Red Sea coast of Saudi Arabia; and the Spanish with what all generals saw as the most challenging mission of all, the destruction of the terrorist training camp at Babol on the Caspian coast of Iran.

The *Madrasah* at Babol was built like a fortress. Inside it there were twelve known terrorists to be eliminated, records to be snatched and a huge cache of weapons to be destroyed. But there were also over two hundred unpredictable orphans who were to be left unharmed. The children were to be left in the care of the unsuspecting Iranian authorities, who were to be resourced and closely scrutinised by the UN. The Spanish had the huge difficulty of target identification and their response to attack from the children. Their solution was to form a special combat unit, prepared with stun guns, flexi-cuffs, tape and other immobilising equipment whose mission it was to pacify the children where they were found. The Spanish had authority to use Turkmenistan, a NATO partner and neighbour of Iran, as a forward mounting base.

Chapter 114

April 28th, Z – 72 Hours
London, England

As London's traffic-regulating signs and other signposts were no longer operational, and all non-specified electrical lighting was prohibited, the continued use of diffused municipal street lighting was considered essential to the maintenance of martial law at night. Businesses, commercial organisations and private dwellings across London were following Home Office instructions and had extinguished interior and exterior lighting, and without the heavy traffic, advertising billboards, and other light emissions associated with a modern, vibrant city, London lay in near darkness. One of eight UK scientific satellites known as Radiance Four, currently orbiting the Northern Hemisphere, recorded a ninety per cent fall in the levels of light pollution over London.

On reaching the deadline for evacuating London, the Metropolitan Police and City of London Police assumed responsibility for the security of the cordon and the control of access points to the city, leaving the Armed Forces, supported by specialised troops from other NATO members, to police inside.

With a shortage of heat-seeking devices and plethora of sources, it was the pursuit of silence or as close to it as nature and their own movement would allow, that was demanded by the military forces inside the cordon. According to the CJO, there were just two kinds of noise. One was considered friendly noise, which was produced from the constant hum of military aircraft that patrolled the city from above, or from the motorised ground troops and their support personnel. Everything else was considered hostile noise, until it was checked out, and if possible disabled.

Current estimates suggested that approximately 116,000 people remained inside the city cordon, but only 16,000 passes, which expired at the final evacuation deadline in two days, had been issued by the City of London Corporation. Everyone else should have left last Friday, six days ago. Apart from military personnel, persons authorised to remain included essential city municipal workers, several indispensable Government employees and intelligence operatives, and specialists that filled shortfalls in military trades including ambulance and fire crews, electricians, vets, and rare-breed zoologists.

Over 200,000 people had passed through the cordon since the deadline of midday last Friday, but the outflow was now reduced to a trickle. It appeared that the remaining population intended to stay, and it was the hunt for them, tracking their noise with directional sound sensors, that kept the military patrols busy. Hostile noise was emitted from a vast array of sources, ranging from occasional gunshots through to the crazed crackle of flames, but the most common source was security or fire alarms. Although Home Office instructions directed that these items were to be deactivated as buildings were abandoned, many owners had chosen to ignore this mandatory directive without realising the difficulties the incessant noise caused the security effort. Most audible alarms were deactivated simply, and by the quickest available means, often an accurate and short burst of rifle fire. As soon as a hostile person – anyone without a valid pass – was located they would be surrounded, detained, then escorted out of the city. Despite every effort by the security forces to prevent loss of life, in the six days since the public's evacuation deadline, twenty-six civilians had been shot and killed.

Under normal circumstances, over one-third of fire brigade emergency call-outs were non-fire related and eighty per cent of fires were caused by humans. With the loss in population, fire crews were expecting to respond to no more than thirty fires a day in the period leading up to final evacuation deadline of midday, the Saturday of the May bank holiday weekend. Remarkably this figure had remained constant, although most of the current fires were found to be arson. After the final evacuation deadline had passed, fires were to be left to burn unless its potential spread was life-threatening.

Of the twenty-six civilians killed, seventeen were during shoot-outs and eight during hot pursuits. Another had been a sniper who apparently believed he was a Russian soldier at Stalingrad repelling German infantry, since he was heard shouting Stalinist and Red Army slogans immediately before he shot himself through the mouth. When soldiers reached the body they had found him wearing a Russian World War II soldier's uniform complete with boots, a .303 Lee Enfield rifle, a World War II British officer's service revolver, and no identification save for a dog-eared sepia photograph of a young woman, probably taken in the early 1940s. His age was estimated as eighty but the mystery sniper was never identified.

Other than the military patrol teams there were the radiological search teams that combed London's streets every hour of every day, continually surveying the city against their newly networked wireless computer database for new sources. Soon after the initial radiological survey of London had been completed several months ago, a new and sophisticated software programme had been produced, which contained details of all known radiation sources plotted on an electronic map of London backed up by supporting information. Each of the ten search teams now possessed a new truck, also on loan from the US, in the back of which was a large radar screen that pin-pointed radiation sources. Positive readings glowed red on a computer monitor which also pinpointed the location of the truck. A simple check against the database by the operator confirmed whether the source had already been identified and investigated. Unbeknown to the operators, although the equipment was state-of-the-art, finely tuned and able to identify lower emissions over a wider range, it was still not sensitive enough to locate the remaining nuclear bomb.

The nuclear threat to London over such a long period of time had resulted in a rollercoaster ride for all Londoners. Now, feelings of resignation and hopelessness were replacing desperation and panic. None of them had any idea that one of two nuclear bombs had already been deactivated and that there was a chance that the other may be neutralised.

After the final evacuation deadline, martial law was to be maintained using air reconnaissance and teams of airborne quick-reaction forces. Although attempts were to be made to remove remaining persons, they might equally be abandoned to their own fate.

The massive media presence that hovered around each of the eight control points at the cordon gained their news from the remaining trickle of desperate evacuees, and official military press releases. They counted down the time in hours rather than days to a world increasingly gripped in an ever-escalating fever.

The terrorist leaders from the Gathering, who were now spread around the Middle East, northern Africa and Central Asia, were among the billions of eager spectators.

Chapter 115

May 2nd, Malid al-Nabi, Zulu Day
Peshawar, Pakistan

Operation Lightning Strike began with the arrival of four British civilians who flew into Islamabad with false identities on separate flights leading up to Malid al-Nabi, the Prophet's Birthday. After meeting at an international hotel on the outskirts of Islamabad with a contact from the British Consulate, who provided them with a US-made Jeep with local plates, a long-wave radio and a sizeable cache of weapons and ammunition typically used by terrorists and mobsters, the four men drove towards the earthquake-striken Karakoram Mountains of Kashmir and the town of Skardu. They bivouacked en route overnight near Srinagar as planned, where they spent several hours cleaning weapons and conducting dry weapons drills until each weapon was as familiar to them as their own, back at Hereford. The following day, May 1st, they tested the weapons in a remote valley twenty kilometres south of Skardu.

NATO's British Carrier Task Group, Task Force Enterprise was led by the carrier HMS *Illustrious* and stood by on station on the Tropic of Cancer two hundred kilometres due south of Gwadar, a small port lying on the coast of Pakistan. *Illustrious* was accompanied by four surface ships and two submarines, though only two ships, HMS *Illustrious* and HMS *Ocean*, were to launch the land operation. Two destroyers, HMS *Manchester* and HMS *Glasgow*, the frigate HMS *Northumberland*, and the attack submarine HMS *Trafalgar*, maintained air and sea control, as the secretive HMS *Vanguard*, another submarine, provided the United Kingdom's grand strategic nuclear capability and leverage should it be required.

The role of the Joint Force Commander on HMS *Illustrious* was to command and control the two British assaults against the terrorists in Pakistan. With the assistance of her supporting vessels, HMS *Illustrious* was to provide optimal access for the assaulting land forces by maintaining control of the necessary air and sea space. To assist, Task Force Enterprise was assigned a NATO AWACS aircraft currently over-flying Afghanistan and a squadron of British Tornado GR1 ground-attack aircraft at Bagram Airbase twenty kilometres north of Kabul in Afghanistan, standing by at high readiness. Apache Longbow AH64 helicopters with fully tailored payloads were also standing by at a temporary airbase west of Jalalabad in eastern Afghanistan, ready to provide close air support to either ground operation. Task Force Enterprise included her own Tailored Air Group with a fixed wing element comprising a Joint Harrier Force of Royal Navy and Royal Air Force Harrier GR7s for air defence and Sea Kings to assist with surveillance and control. Twelve versatile Merlin helicopters with their state-of-the-art navigation and fire-control systems were available to conduct troop insertions and casualty and prisoner evacuation. The Merlins were to receive close air protection from a flight of six Apache AH64s that carried a mixture of Hellfire missiles, air-to-air missiles and cannon rounds. HMS *Ocean*, an amphibious helicopter carrier, carried the land force, which comprised two Special Air Service squadrons totalling over eighty troops and a smaller cadre of twenty troops from 9 Assault Squadron Royal Marines.

The Joint Force Commander, an admiral, had spent many hours debating the assault with his sizeable Force Planning Team on board HMS *Illustrious*. The Admiral's Quarters and the Ward Room had been converted to a Planning Room, where the Joint Force Commander and his fleet captains, flight commanders and the Commanding Officer 22 Special Air Service, who was the Land Forces Commander, discussed the forthcoming operation. Even after the Task Force had received confirmation from the four-man SAS assassination squad that they were on their way to Skardu after a successful rendezvous with an MI6 operative, the plan for the assault on the challenging primary target at Peshawar was being revisited. Joint Force Command, Naples had already dictated the necessity for a naval support to land operation, low flying over Western Pakistan, Afghanistan, then back into northern Pakistan, rather than attempt a direct assault from Afghanistan and risk another of the innumerable lapses in security over the years that had caused successive failures in bids to capture leading al-Qa'eda suspects, including bin Laden himself. Afghanistan's role as a launch platform was to be restricted to airspace and reserve close air support.

Harry, Tess and Malik were accommodated on HMS *Ocean*, but whenever planning rounds took place on the flagship, they were required to accompany the ship's captain to HMS *Illustrious* so that Malik could be made immediately available for questioning. This meant that for the majority of their time they were confined to the Mess Deck.

The secondary target was a small, detached house in the more affluent quarter of Skardu occupied by two of the region's most wanted men. At H hour, 2100 hours Zulu, 2 a.m. local time, on the morning of May 2nd the four-man team was to neutralise four of the most ruthless Harakat ul-Mujahidin terrorists holed up in a townhouse, who together had conspired with al-Qa'eda to destroy London. The targets were also known to be personally responsible for the deaths of over two hundred people comprising ten nationalities, some of them British.

By comparison, the primary target was a fortress. In fact, it was a colonial mansion set in approximately two acres of walled land and guarded by about twenty armed mercenaries or terrorists hired by al-Qa'eda. It represented a much greater challenge than the assassination. The NATO mission was to neutralise the terrorist stronghold, but it was also desirable to seize bin Laden's communications expert Abu Zubaydah aka the Mailman and any associated evidence they could find. Most important, however, was the safe recovery of the hostage, Karima. The building itself, the dead terrorists, and other hostages were to be left to the Pakistan authorities. A combination of Malik's knowledge and pinpoint satellite surveillance determined that security was limited to high walls and well-armed guards. This intelligence led to a simple plan that was constrained by aircraft fuel and lift capability.

A total of eighteen aircraft, twelve Merlin helicopters and six Apaches took off in two flights from HMS *Illustrious* and HMS *Ocean* at L Hour, 1.30 a.m. local time. Contour flying below radar, the two flights encountered no difficulties as they followed the barren Iran–Pakistan border into Afghanistan. Since the aircraft were heading north and none of them were returning by the same route, there was little operational risk associated with any visual sightings by the border patrols of either country. After the raid, both flights were to land and refuel at the temporary airstrip near Jalalabad in Afghanistan before heading to Bagram, where the troops would catch a Royal Air Force flight to RAF Brize Norton, England.

As the first flight approached the Khyber Pass, with the second flight just sixty seconds behind, the flight commander gave a fifteen minute warning to target. In what felt like less than five minutes, Harry, sitting with Malik and Tess in the rearmost Merlin, was listening to the first wave going in. It was H hour.

The first flight of Merlins landed in the garden around the house as its three accompanying Apaches circled overhead. As soon as the cargo of thirty personnel disembarked, the six helicopters rose as one and the entire flight disappeared, making way for the second wave. It was not until the first wave left that Harry heard staccato firing through his headset, and as the firing increased he heard a pilot warn that they had ten seconds to touch down and that the drop zone was 'hot'.

Soon Harry, Tess and Malik were jumping off the rear ramp of their Merlin onto a damp lawn where they remained in the shadows with the assault commander and his two heavily laden communications operators. Crouching in the fierce down wash of the aircraft they waited until the Merlin flew off to be swallowed up by the dark night. As soon as the helicopter left they followed the commander in silence to a gazebo in the garden adjacent to the house, where they were joined by a squad of four troopers.

As four squads from the first wave secured the grounds, during which four X-rays and two dogs were reported killed, two teams assaulted the house from the eastern end. Seconds later two squads from the second wave of aircraft had abseiled down onto the roof of the mansion and were assaulting from above, as another two assaulted the mansion from the west.

For the next twelve minutes Harry listened to the progress of the six assault squads as they swept through the house. With the need to save Karima and seize the Mailman alive, the troops used flash-bangs to incapacitate X-rays in each room before expertly entering and clearing it with accurate and deadly fire. All the talking had been done in the days before the assault during the countless rehearsals on the flight deck of HMS *Ocean* and every trooper knew what to expect. Even so, Harry could sense Malik's nervousness as the mercenary stood nearby in the darkness listening intently to the action through his own earpiece. The X-rays were in no mood to surrender which suited the SAS and after eleven violent minutes a further ten X-rays had been reported killed with no friendly casualties.

In the twelfth minute a squad leader reported they had seized the Mailman in his bedroom at the end of the first floor corridor, with another man who appeared to be his close protection but who had also chosen to give up without a fight. In the thirteenth minute the house and gardens were reported clear by all six squads with a total of sixteen X-rays dead and two prisoners, but no one had found Karima.

For the first time, crisply and devoid of feeling, the assault force commander communicated with Delta squad leader. 'Delta, this is Zero. Find out where the girl is.' The meaning was clear to everyone listening.

Time was against them. Delta leader knew exactly what was expected. Withdrawing his pistol from his calf holster and pressing his transmit switch, in plain English he ordered the bodyguard to give up the girl's location. The guard did not answer but wet himself as he stared at the floor. Keeping his pistol aimed at the guard's head, the squad leader ordered the Mailman, whom he knew spoke excellent English, to give up the girl. The Mailman failed to answer and two shots were heard through every trooper's headset. The Mailman began to speak rapidly in Dari as the pistol was levelled at him.

'Speak English, arsehole,' barked the distinct voice of Delta leader.

The Mailman was terrified. 'The girl is alive. She's in the shed by the pool.' He stammered.

'Any guards?'

'Maybe one or two, I don't know,' the Mailman quivered. 'Two, I think.'

'Get that boss?' Delta leader asked calmly.

Without answering, the assault commander snapped, 'Alpha, she's yours. Bravo in support. All stations we're coming in. We have three minutes to be at the pick-up point. Hawk One copy that?'

'Copy, Zero,' shot back the flight commander. 'No sign of locals.'

'Out.'

Although the mansion was miles from its nearest neighbour everyone in the command squad, everyone except Malik, thought it odd there was no sign of any response from the police or even the military. The plan was to be in and out before the local authorities showed up. It was the shortest police response time that had determined the time available for the ground assault.

Protected by the reserve squad and guided by Malik, the command team began searching for useful material. Other squads provided all-round defence or helped search for evidence. Already loaded with their own weapons and equipment, there was little they could seize except papers, photographs and miscellaneous items of computer hardware.

'Zero,' reported Charlie squad leader excitedly, 'we need the Mailman in the study. There is one big, fuck off walk-in safe here.'

Just as the squad leader finished speaking, the unmistakeable sound of flash-bangs and shots were heard from the area of the pool house.

'Two X-rays down, we have the girl,' was heard over the radio net. Bravo squad leader didn't bother identifying himself.

Malik, unable to constrain his emotion, ran in the direction of the shots with Harry and Tess in pursuit.

'Delta, get down to the study now,' ordered the assault commander, leaving Harry and Tess to deal with the mercenary.

Two minutes after he arrived, the Mailman had failed to open the old combination safe. It was the assault commander's call. 'Hawk One, how long can you wait?'

'No sign of hostiles. Fuel says another three minutes, otherwise you walk,' came the instant reply.

'All stations, pick up is postponed for three minutes.' Everyone was alerted. Apparently the contents of the safe were worth whatever risk there was to lives.

As Malik ran towards the pool house he slowed as he saw eight men striding towards him. One of them held Karima effortlessly in his arms, and recognising Malik he shouted to him that she was all right, just dazed by the flash-bangs, and frightened.

It was then that their luck turned.

As the trooper handed the girl to Malik, Tess spotted an assault rifle raised towards them from behind a nearby hedge.

'Down,' Tess screamed as she raised her pistol towards the target. There was no time to identify the target with fire-control orders. Neither was there time for her to take aim as she charged to within ten feet of the source to block the fire, blasting off six rounds in rapid succession before she fell.

The terrorist saw her as the threat and targeted her mercilessly, spraying her with rounds before turning on the remainder of the group who had melted into the ground, Malik shielding Karima. But the terrorist had no time to search for targets. His unnecessarily long burst at Tess had given away his position and as he searched for a new target he was torn to shreds by a fusillade of automatic fire from assault weapons and by two fragmentation grenades.

As the command to cease fire was made, and the incident reported to cries of 'man down', Harry dashed over to Tess and fell by her side. Despite her armoured vest and Kevlar helmet, she was mortally wounded by shots to the neck and shoulder. With no chance for words, they stared into each other's eyes, Harry mouthing the words 'I love you'. Harry saw Tess smile, then felt her life extinguish. He scrambled to find a pulse, found none, and hugged her body to him fiercely.

Asserting control, Alpha leader barked several orders and troopers fanned out to ensure the lone gunman was dead and that the garden was, in fact, clear.

One trooper gently prised Tess's body from Harry and another retrieved her weapon. He fought to control his emotions as he felt a lump rise in his throat and his breathing become difficult. He began to gasp for air as grief overcame him. Soon Harry felt a hand on his shoulder; it was Malik.

'I'm sorry. Tess was a brave woman,' said Malik quietly as Karima hung on. 'We must go now.'

With effort Harry collected himself and together they made their way to the PUP.

With less than one minute to go until the first flight of six Merlin helicopters landed at the PUPs, the safe was opened. The troopers in the spacious study were clutching empty grips and were prepared to collect what they considered useful when the safe revealed its contents. Charlie squad had been speculating whether the safe was full of cash and deciding how much should go behind the bar at Hereford.

But it was empty.

'That's going to cost you a hundred fucking handbags,' laughed the Delta squad leader who was the first to react to the embarrassment and begin the hefty ribbing that would inevitably come Charlie squad leader's way in the bar back at Hereford. Each 'handbag' carried six bottles of beer, and there were lots of disappointed, thirsty troopers.

'Fuck that. Everyone, move out now,' the assault commander screamed as everyone bomb-burst from the room and house towards their PUPs.

The flight commander, who had been listening to the events as they unfolded, grinned, and then called upon the first wave of Merlins to pick up.

During the short flight to Jalalabad Harry found peace among the thunderous noise and darkness. He collapsed next to Tess, her lifeless body lying on a medivac stretcher at the rear of the helicopter. The pang of loss was huge and painful. He felt choked, sick, and could not prevent his eyes from welling up. He hoped that Tess felt the strength of his love for her as she had died. He thought of her funeral and her parents, and whether he should meet them and explain who he was.

The time was 2.27 a.m. local time, and the assault had taken just twenty-seven minutes. With one fatality, several casualties, nineteen terrorists dead, the release of Karima and the capture of the Mailman alive, Harry knew the operation would be considered a success. During the flight the assault commander reported that the assassinations in Skardu had also been successful.

Thirty minutes after take-off, they landed at the temporary refuelling point outside Jalalabad and once the din from the engines had subsided, people removed their earpieces and relaxed. Despite the loudness of the engines and vibration from the rotor blades, the uncomfortable safety harnesses, the buzz from the flight-deck and the incessant radio traffic over the loudspeakers, Karima had somehow managed to fall asleep in Malik's arms.

As he left the aircraft the assault commander, one of Harry's peers, nodded sympathetically, pausing to place a comforting hand on Harry's shoulder. It was somehow fitting that the SAS squad filed out past Tess in reverent silence into the still, warm night.

As Malik passed with Karima in his arms, he also paused and whispered, 'I owe you an explanation. I'm truly sorry about Tess. She was an exceptional woman and gave her own life for my daughter. We owe her everything.'

Harry gave a confused look, but let it pass. He too had noticed Tess had thrown herself into the line of fire. He tried hard not let his feelings overwhelm him. Right now he knew that he must complete this mission that meant so much to them all, a mission that Tess had given her life for. Locking eyes with Malik, he croaked, 'Thank you, but if her death and Karima's life are to have any purpose, I must know where the second bomb is. Where is it Malik?'

Malik answered without hesitation. 'It's fitted inside a red boat fender and is in the forward hold of a riverboat named *Dutch Master* that sank off Westminster Pier on April 13th. The device was set by Doctor Baloch to detonate at midday local time today. It's identical in design to the bomb you found in Islington.'

'Stay in here with your daughter,' Harry ordered as he rose reluctantly from Tess's side.

Jumping from the rear of the helicopter he made his way to the airstrip's operations room, conscious everyone was watching him. Within minutes he was speaking by secure telephone to Sir Michael, who was with the Cabinet at Chequers.

In England it was 11 p.m., still May 1st, with thirteen hours to go to detonation. Although the Cabinet had already heard of the success of both UK assaults, they were still anxiously waiting for news of the location of the second nuclear bomb.

As Harry returned the field handset to its cradle he thought he heard applause and cheers through the receiver.

Chapter 116

May 2nd, Malid al-Nabi, Zulu Day
FBI Headquarters, Washington DC, USA

The two-hundred-strong multinational task force of many of the world's greatest computer and finance experts remained in the FBI Headquarters' building overnight. Linked to NATO and the Pentagon, they were kept fully abreast of Operation Lightning Strike as it unfolded. Buoyed by the news that the assaults against the terror groups had been successful and that the second London bomb had been deactivated, at 0600 hours Zulu, 1 a.m. EST, it was their time to act.

The financial intelligence on the terrorists groups provided by Fox acted as the long-awaited catalyst. The FBI, long recognised as the world's leading establishment in the fight against global financial crime, wanted the coordinating role. Acting on behalf of NATO and with the approval of the President and Capitol Hill, the FBI took control of the strike against the financial heart of the world's leading terrorist groups. In just ten days a team of six personnel had rapidly expanded to two hundred, as more avenues had been uncovered from Fox's intelligence and the details of the global financial operation emerged.

Although further investigative work would inevitably uncover further accounts, assets and funding sources, there was a risk that the ground assaults would drive illegitimate funds and their fund managers deeper underground. NATO wished to strike at the financial heart of global terrorism at the optimum time across the world, and that was now, within hours of the ground assault.

Within minutes of 1 a.m. EST a bank of thirty-six operators on the first floor of the J. Edgar Hoover Building had emptied and frozen seventy-two accounts across the world into one single account, an action which NATO approved due to non-cooperation by either the banks or the host nation. It had been decided that the legalities of jurisdiction would, if necessary, be challenged later. To NATO there was no issue; their action was an act of war against each account holder and not necessarily with the bank or country in which the account resided. NATO believed that it was now time for a precedent to be set in the fight against global terrorism, leaving the perpetrators without the ability to sustain themselves.

At the same moment, the law-enforcement agencies of forty-two cooperative countries across the world used either electronic or physical means to freeze 204 bank accounts and seize vast quantities of bonds, stocks, shares, securities and safety deposit boxes.

As the FBI was unable to determine from accounts if the generation of revenue within any one business was illegal, they acted on the basis that knowingly transferring funds to a terrorist group was. Equally significant was the identification of those people responsible for the management of terrorist accounts and of those who administered the flow of money to those accounts. The FBI held a list of 212 individuals who were identified as being directly involved in managing terror funds, from board directors to bank managers and charity fund managers. NATO was resolute in arresting and bringing to justice those people involved under international law, and publicly naming and warning the public of those businesses and charities across the world that financed terrorism. Of the 212 people, it was determined that at least sixteen had been neutralised during the assaults on the terrorist groups earlier that night, leaving the remainder to be arrested by law-enforcement agencies across the world. Only in seven countries was it necessary for clandestine NATO 'recovery units' to secure the arrest and detention of suspects for themselves. As the arrests were confirmed, arrangements were made for arresting officers to escort the prisoner to a holding area outside Brussels where they would be later indicted and tried by an international court for war crimes.

At 1400 hours Zulu, 3 p.m. in Brussels, the NATO Secretary General broadcast a live statement to the world declaring Operation Lightning Strike over.

Chapter 117

May 3rd, Z + 1 Day
Kabul, Afghanistan

Before catching his flight to Brize Norton, Harry saw Malik and his daughter onto one of the few scheduled flights out of Kabul international airport. The flight to Athens was due to depart at 11:30 a.m., an hour before Harry's Royal Air Force flight to England.

They had been at the airport two hours already, and had watched alongside a small crowd of UK and US embassy officials as a brilliant white CIA Lear jet took off carrying Tess, heading for Andrews Air Force Base outside Washington. Immediately the ceremony concluded, Harry had insisted that the British Ambassador and George Galway not wait for his own departure, wishing instead to speak to Malik alone.

Sitting in one corner of the large, war-torn and ramshackle waiting area drinking black coffee with just thirty minutes to boarding, Harry was reminded of the lack of local police or military activity during the assault on the Mailman's residence. 'You had something to tell me,' Harry asked. 'Was it to do with the local police or military not responding?'

'Maybe no one saw or heard anything,' replied Malik furtively. 'Maybe people didn't want to get involved. They are very afraid of the terrorists and the hold both they and the mobsters have on our country. Murder, intimidation and torture are commonplace, and the authorities are increasingly powerless. No one is safe, Harry, not my family, not even the President. Have you been to Islamabad or Karachi recently? Millions of lives are being ruined by several thousand terrorists and mobsters.'

Harry saw the genuine anguish in Malik's eyes.

'No one responded because the authorities knew you were coming, Harry. They had orders not to obstruct your success,'

Malik answered, a look of apprehension then relief sweeping over his face.

Harry had suspected as much but had not expected such honesty. 'You told them we were coming?'

'Harry, I said on the helicopter that I owe you and Tess an explanation and I do. You, of all people, will understand when I explain that I cannot tell you everything. In any event, my President will be discreetly informing your Prime Minister of Pakistan's involvement during his state visit in two weeks' time. You see, I spoke directly to my President soon after Dalia was killed and before I met you, and I spoke again with him this morning.'

Harry knew when it was time to let someone speak and now was one of those moments.

Malik glanced over to Karima who was reading magazines provided by George Galway at the British Embassy, where they had stayed since arriving in Kabul. 'I was the commanding officer of the Pakistan Special Air Service when the previous Pakistan Government ordered the Army to halt the Mujahidin invasion of Indian Kashmir. It was discovered that contrary to wishing for a fully integrated Kashmir state with Pakistan, the Mujahidin intended to double-cross the Government and demand full independence. Worse, India threatened Pakistan with tactical nuclear weapons unless the Mujahidin were forced to withdraw. We successfully halted the invasion which the Government had initially supported, but in response my family were brutally murdered at home by a car bomb while they slept, all except Karima who was badly wounded.'

Harry listened intently. Malik sounded in agony and his voice was like ice.

'Your SAS killed the men responsible at Skardu, and for that I'm grateful. I resigned, but months later there was the coup and, as you know, General Musharraf suspended the constitution and took office as President.'

Both men waited as a group of US Green Beret soldiers filed noisily into the waiting area, before sitting down.

Malik sighed. 'I should have mentioned that our President is my uncle. He's a good man, governing in increasingly difficult circumstances. I know of no one better to lead us.'

Harry was dumbstruck.

'My country was flooded with thousands of Arab Mujahidin after the US-led invasion of Taliban Afghanistan. Most of these people are thugs released from Arab jails to fight in the jihad against the Russians, and for years now they have been undermining our country and we are powerless to stop them. Most have sworn allegiance to al-Qa'eda, the Islamic Jihad or other terrorist groups and have become mobsters. You cannot differentiate between the two in our country. They are influential and corrupt our police, army and even our Government.

'The Pakistan ISI presented many plans to our President which he passed on to the Americans and British, requests for help that would assist my country in annihilating the terrorists that threaten our very existence. All of them were rejected. Then one day, through our agents close to the HM, we heard of bin Laden's plan to attack London with nuclear bombs.'

Harry stayed silent, and watched as Karima sucked quietly on a straw stuffed into a paper cup.

'I was recruited by the Pakistan ISI for the operation, and Dalia, who was an undercover operative in the HM, introduced me to the group. I was provided with a false identity as a rogue ex-soldier, and between us we ensured that we matched perfectly the profile of the people the Network was rumoured to be recruiting. Both educated in the West and experienced gunfighters, we were readily accepted by bin Laden's lieutenants who believed we were what we appeared. They even vetted us on our own National Criminal Intelligence Computer and came up with two bad arses. All trace of our original identities had been removed from the files.'

Harry stared into Malik's intense-looking eyes. 'How did they gain access?'

'There was a traitor in our Government, a junior minister in the Ministry of the Interior who had access to such things. We used him to provide al-Qa'eda with false information. The man was responsible for many murders in Pakistan, even an assassination attempt on our President. He was arrested several months ago and will now face a high-profile trial. If guilty of treason, he will be executed. Of that there is no doubt.

'Originally, Dalia and I were to remain undercover for as long it took to locate the key components of the Network, then offer the information to the West. But as the threat was exposed and

NATO came to your aid, and there was much talk of retaliation, we saw an opportunity to increase the likelihood of lasting success by continuing with the threat until NATO were pressed into action, maybe even supported by the UN. There can be no doubt that with so many global terrorist groups destroyed, the world is a safer place. And now, the UN is likely to sanction NATO's surgical response as an acceptable use of force against global terrorists, and the precedent will have been set.'

'Where did the nuclear bombs come from?' asked Harry.

Malik considered this for a moment. 'They were seized from a munitions train in India by the HM. Somewhere near Julundur in the Punjab, last December. The weapons were destined for Indian Kashmir, where they were to be used to threaten Muslim Kashmir and Pakistan. The HM originally intended to seize the bombs for use as their own deterrent and to prevent their use by India, but the terrorists killed in Skardu had already sold them to al-Qa'eda.' Malik made no reference to Dalia and her orders to snatch them from India.

Harry looked sceptical. 'But the weapons in London were live. They could have detonated at any time.'

'No my friend they could not. It was impossible for them to detonate. The Zeon Tech timing device in each bomb was radio controlled and kept within a millisecond of local time, anywhere in the world. Using similar technology the Pakistan ISI arranged for the devices we used to be modified for remote deactivation. It was necessary for Doctor Baloch to believe each device was active if he was to be allowed to live after completion, so as not to attract suspicion. Only a few trusted people, including our President, knew that after each bomb was sealed the arming mechanism was immediately deactivated by remote control and both bombs disarmed. If your scientists examine the devices carefully, they will find this is true.'

'Why let Baloch go?' asked Harry, already suspecting the answer.

'You have a saying do you not? Better the devil you know...'

Harry gave a slight smile then interrupted. 'Does your uncle really expect NATO to sit back and accept being played like a fiddle? Do you really expect my Government to accept what has happened to London, to Londoners, and our economy?'

'We don't expect either your Government or anyone else to

find out. In Pakistan we wish for the world to be free of Islamic terrorism, and for all Muslims to be released from any association with global terror and live in peace in the world. In the knowledge the world is prepared to act, my country will now round up the Mujahidin terrorists and mobsters. Their leaders have been destroyed, their funds seized, and there's a worldwide determination not to let global terrorism survive. London and your economy will recover, and the sacrifices made were small in comparison to the global achievement. My President and I love your country. We both went to your Sandhurst Military Academy. You have just won a world war, a war that the West has been fighting and losing for many years. Are you, Harry, willing to unravel such advancement in world peace and security? The United Nations is faced with an opportunity that it must seize.'

Harry understood Malik's reasoning. 'The end justifies the means. How will you justify the attacks in your country?'

Malik grinned. 'We have suffered so many similar attacks against mobsters and Government officials alike that the public are clamouring for action. We are pleased that NATO is to keep their attacks in Pakistan secret. We'll blame terrorist infighting for the deaths in Skardu and take all the credit for the attack at Peshawar. Our President will make public promises about clamping down on terrorism, organised crime and corruption then follow it up with immediate action. He will also demilitarise the HM and publicly reject any further military offensive action over Indian Kashmir. Incidentally, we would like the Mailman back immediately, to face public trial in Pakistan.'

Harry said nothing, and both men sat in silence for a moment as they considered that thorny issue. He knew it was intended the Mailman stand trial for war crimes alongside the financiers in Europe. Both sides not only wished to interrogate the Mailman, but to make huge public statements, that in Pakistan would end with his public execution. It was not an issue Harry could resolve and he said so. Changing the subject, Harry asked, 'Did the Network hire Jamali?'

Malik's face turned bitter. 'Yes. Jamali was the worst kind of killer, rapist and thug, not an idealist. He was involved in the bombing and destruction of the Israeli Embassy in Buenos Aires back in 1992 on behalf of Hizballah. The bastard revelled in telling me his gruesome tales. He drove the van the bombers used to flee the scene. It was later found by the authorities. Who knows, maybe now DNA can support my evidence? The Argentine authorities and Mossad will rejoice. Twenty-nine were killed and 242 wounded on that day. He raped and murdered Dalia, and he murdered Baloch, but you know that.'

At the last call for boarding, Malik stood up and made his way to the gate with Karima. They carried little more than the fresh clothes that they were wearing, several papers including their new British passports and hand luggage, all provided by George.

Harry fussed over Karima for a moment, referring to her collection of Western fashion magazines.

'I'd like you to know that Dalia and I knew nothing of the attack on the tower,' Malik whispered, 'and I'm truly sorry for the death of your partner. I will never forget her sacrifice.'

'I'm sorry for Dalia too,' replied Harry sorrowfully. 'I understand your grief. Dalia and Tess were brave women, fighting for, and dying for what they believed. We can be proud of them both.' Unsure what else to say, Harry added, 'Do you have everything you need?'

'I have everything right here,' responded Malik softly, hugging Karima.

'Sean Kent, if ever you make it to England, call me,' Harry offered.

Malik grinned. 'I own a business, remember.'

Without saying farewell or shaking hands, Malik and his daughter turned and walked through the boarding gate and onto the apron.

Harry was left with plenty to think about on his flight home, beginning with Tess. A cruel twist of fate had taken her life, just as the operation neared its end and as they had fallen deeply in love.

It was only when he briefed Sir Michael in the back of the Jaguar en route to Vauxhall Cross that Harry began to wonder just how much Dalia and Malik had been paid by the terrorists and why Malik had requested through tickets to Cairo via Athens.

Chapter 118

May 4th, Zulu + 2 Days
Chertsey, Surrey, England

Harry spoke to Tally for the first time since Operation Lightning Strike from Sir Michael's car as it had sped towards London from RAF Brize Norton. He had told her that Tess had been killed, that he was OK, and that they could expect him in the office the following morning. After the short phone conversation, Sir Michael had commiserated over Tess and attributed her death to the overwhelming success of the NATO operation, the recovery of the second nuclear device, the death of bin Laden and his lieutenants, and the destruction of al-Qa'eda and other leading global terror groups. In turn, Harry had briefed Sir Michael on his conversation with Malik at Kabul airport. The Director MI6 had not appeared concerned, in fact far from it.

Sir Michael had not condoned President Musharraf but focused on his achievement. He said that many of Pakistan's problems stemmed not only from Islamic militancy, but from British rule, partition and from independence in 1949. He added that the Prime Minister was looking forward to the Pakistan President's visit and referred to him as a close ally in the global war against terror. As for the Mailman, Sir Michael had simply stated that the prisoner was to be returned to Pakistan, along with evidence taken from his house, but only after MI6 and the CIA had finished their interrogations.

Now, after a long day debriefing at Vauxhall Cross, Harry was relieved to be back in his office at Mercury. This morning had begun with a telephone call from his father, followed closely by a personal visit from his father's accountant, Veronica. Although he appreciated her sentiments, and the information she provided on the company, Harry had been grateful it was cut short by an impromptu management board meeting hastily arranged by Tally.

At the meeting it rapidly became clear to Harry that everything was under control and that he had not been missed, not in a business sense. Everyone was delighted and relieved to see him but that did not prevent them from making the most of the meeting by pressing home the need for additional personnel. It seemed to Harry that little, if anything, had changed since he had left for Afghanistan. As the last item wrapped up, everyone looked to Harry for the Chairman's final remarks.

Harry leant across to his desk and picked up the telephone. He whispered several words before hanging up then smiled mischievously at everyone. 'As soon as we can fix it, my father and I have decided to turn Mercury into a private partnership with every grade and scale of employee owning a fair proportion of the firm and its profits. The estate will remain mine, but essentially all employees will own a slice of the company and its profits.'

Stunned silence was quickly followed by excited chatter.

'Perhaps we should reconsider the need for more staff,' someone joked as the door opened and Tally's assistant walked in with a tray of glasses and several bottles of chilled champagne.

Tally frowned at the young girl who had known something she didn't.

'There is another thing,' added Harry quietly. 'We will be setting up an enabling contract with MI6 and taking on more of their work. As a partnership, you can all make decisions in my absence, and I can be more actively involved where I belong, at the grass-roots.'

'What kind of work?' asked Tally sourly.

'Oh,' replied Harry nonchalantly. 'I'm sure it will be mundane, passive ops that can be commercially and routinely outsourced. They would hardly give us anything serious.'

Everyone laughed, everyone except Tally.

EPILOGUE

The Near Future
London, England

Repopulating London had not been simple, and responsibility for a coherent plan fell to the Permanent Joint Headquarters who retained control of the capital under martial law for a fortnight after the second bomb was found.

On May 3rd, the Chief of Joint Operations incepted a plan designed to ensure a trouble-free repopulation and return to civil law enforcement. He needed to maintain public safety and avoid the chaos that could easily result from millions of people simultaneously reclaiming their lost lives.

First, with the assistance of the police from bordering counties, the Metropolitan Police Service and City of London Police extracted themselves from their duties at the cordon and returned to their posts in the city. Then a legion of engineers were sent in to survey and repair sewerage, water, electricity, gas and transport systems including the traffic control system and the London Underground. This was followed by the return of the remaining blue-light services and the Government's secret services. The fourth phase saw the reintroduction of local Government departments followed by central Government, and Phase Five, the return of public transport including flights, trains, buses and cabs. The final phase was the reintroduction of the judiciary, businesses and the general population from 8 a.m. on Monday May 9th.

At midnight on Sunday May 15th both police services resumed control from the Armed Forces and martial law ended. However, it was not for another month before London was to regain any semblance of the order it had enjoyed six months previously.

The London Stock Exchange remained suspended until Tuesday May 24th, in all for a total of five months. Nevertheless, with the notable exception of the insurance sector, stocks enjoyed a fast recovery. Experts suggested the unpredicted optimism in the financial markets was a testament to the ability of UK businesses to continue working through such a difficult circumstances, while others thought it more to do with the warm spell in the weather and the spontaneous 'feel-good' factor fuelled by widespread public celebrations that took place on the afternoon of the late May bank holiday, the likes of which had not been seen since Victory in Europe Day in 1945. National euphoria had broken out immediately after the Queen had made a moving speech to the nation live from Buckingham Palace after returning from an internationally celebrated thanksgiving service in St Paul's Cathedral.

And there was much to be thankful for in the country, particularly in London. For most people, personal savings and investments assumed lost had recovered and most insurance companies eventually made good their promises. Retail and business outlets throughout the capital restocked and were trading within days, and it was not long before the street markets of Covent Garden and Petticoat Lane reopened. Theatres, cinemas, museums, palaces and restaurants reopened, schools began their summer terms later than usual and house prices recovered sharply. Londoners of all faiths were united in their desire to prove the terrorists had won nothing but lost everything, and everyone looked forward to the predicted hot summer and tourist season. Football fans from around the country visiting London's stadiums at the end of a prolonged football season epitomised the nation's revived sense of humour as they chanted 'Nuke 'em' at their teams. Within six months shops in Oxford Street were reporting reaching pre-threat retail sales figures. Repairs to Canary Wharf and all other buildings damaged during Operation Enduring Freedom were scheduled to be completed within a year.

The Government's foreign policy was to hold the limelight for several years. Naturally there was the need to steady the economy after a long period of uncertainty, but a higher priority for the Government was the requirement to improve national and global security in repsonse to international terrorism. The Government declared that the economy was not to be enslaved by the sustained threat to its capital, and with financial support from the EU and the World Bank it successfully managed the cost of the defence of London at over two billion pounds sterling, equivalent to the entire UK defence budget for one year.

Months after Operation Lightning Strike, NATO embedded its offensive stance against global terrorists into policy. The policy was introduced without opposition from any one of its members because it carefully specified the lawless groups themselves and did not threaten the civilian populations in which terrorists so cynically hid. The nuclear threat on London had dispelled any underlying differences of opinion that had previously threatened to undermine the very existence of NATO, such as the toppling of Saddam Hussein, and provided another unifying entity that had so successfully defended Europe during the Cold War.

To underpin Operation Lightning Strike the UN Security Council quickly acknowledged the use of NATO's military force to restore global peace and security as an act of self-defence, and held her attacks on global terror groups as proportional and discriminatory.

The diplomatic struggle within the United Nations was to take several years to resolve, but with pressure from the UN Security Council and all NATO members and partners including the US, UK, France, Germany and Turkey, the UN finally passed resolutions that addressed its weaknesses in combating global terrorism.

A new Chapter was added to the UN Charter that recognised and defined global terrorism as a threat to world peace, and it enshrined principles designed to assist nations with its eradication. It defined global terrorism as premeditated religious or politically motivated violence by individuals or groups who were unwilling to accept the norms of International Law or Laws of Armed Conflict. It decreed that cross-border terrorism was an act of war against the recipient country and that sovereignty would not prevent the destruction of any global terrorist group harbouring within a state. It also decreed that provision of funds to any global terror group violated International Law.

Heralded by the UN Secretary General as the foundation for global peace, the revised UN Charter recognised the destruction of global terrorist organisations as a legitimate form of defence, but without the devastation of their host state, unless it, too, was complicit, and without harm to innocent civilians.

The issue that vexed the UN was how to promote tolerance and understanding between such differing but legitimate nations in an attempt to eradicate the conditions for terrorism. Whatever the regime, communist, democratic, religious or otherwise, the UN recognised the right of a legitimate nation – one that did not persecute or subject its people – to uphold its laws, and in the interests of humanity it required minority groups to respect the rule of law.